A TRILOGY OF DESIRES
HARRIS & KAT PARTS I-III

STEELE INTERNATIONAL, INC. - JACKSON CORPORATION A BILLIONAIRES ROMANCE SERIES CROSSOVER BOOKS 4-6

CHARMAINE LOUISE SHELTON

CONTENTS

Free Book   vii

Also By Charmaine Louise Shelton   ix

About STEELE International, Inc. - Jackson Corporation A Billionaires Romance Series Crossover   xi

INTRIGUE MY DESIRES HARRIS & KAT PART I

About Intrigue My Desires Intrigue & Kat Part I   5

1. Prologue   7
2. Harris   12
3. Harris   25
4. Kat   34
5. Kat   39
6. Kat   46
7. Harris   52
8. Kat   61
9. Harris   67
10. Kat   77
11. Harris   89
12. Harris   98
13. Kat   106
14. Kat   115
15. Harris   124
16. Harris   132
17. Kat   139
18. Harris   150
19. Kat   161
20. Harris   173
21. Kat   181

22. Kat   192
23. Harris   203
24. Kat   214
25. Harris   225
26. Harris   236
27. Kat   246
28. Harris   252

DECODE MY DESIRES HARRIS & KAT PART II

About Decode My Desires Intrigue & Kat
Part II   261
 1. Kat   263
 2. Kat   270
 3. Harris   279
 4. Kat   287
 5. Kat   295
 6. Harris   305
 7. Kat   311
 8. Harris   320
 9. Kat   325
10. Harris   333
11. Kat   342
12. Kat   351
13. Harris   358
14. Harris   368
15. Kat   376
16. Kat   387
17. Harris   396
18. Kat   401
19. Harris   410
20. Harris   419
21. Kat   429
22. Harris   438
23. Harris   447
24. Kat   456

25. Harris		465
26. Kat		475
27. Harris		486
28. Kat		496

HONOR MY DESIRES HARRIS & KAT PART III

About Honor My Desires Intrigue & Kat Part III	511
1. Harris	513
2. Harris	522
3. Harris	531
4. Kat	538
5. Kat	546
6. Harris	553
7. Harris	562
8. Kat	571
9. Kat	580
10. Harris	588
11. Kat	600
12. Kat	609
13. Harris	618
14. Kat	627
15. Kat	636
16. Harris	645
17. Kat	656
18. Kat	665
19. Harris	675
20. Kat	683
21. Harris	692
22. Harris	704
23. Kat	715
24. Harris	725
25. Harris	734
26. Kat	743
27. Harris	753

The STEELE Family 761

The Jackson Family 763

Note From Charmaine Louise 765

Preview: A Trilogy of Desires Sebastian & Lola Parts I-III 767

Welcome to CharmaineLouise — The Sensual Lifestyle 777

FREE BOOK

Get the start of the STEELE International, Inc. A Billionaires Romance Series with *Discover My Desires Sebastian & Lola Prequel* FREE!

Click Cover Below or visit **bit.ly/CLBooksNewsletter** to subscribe to my newsletter for latest news and launches, books from my author friends, and sizzling reads in book promotions. Plus, start reading the steamy billionaire romance *Series Prequel* of Sebastian Steele and Lola Lewis.

Their stories. Their discovery of unknown desires…

FREE BOOK!

EXCLUSIVE FOR SUBSCRIBERS!

ALSO BY CHARMAINE LOUISE SHELTON

**STEELE INTERNATIONAL, INC.
A BILLIONAIRES ROMANCE SERIES**

Discover My Desires Sebastian & Lola Prequel
(Available Exclusively to Subscribers)

Fulfill My Desires Sebastian & Lola Part I

Heighten My Desires Sebastian & Lola Part II

Ignite My Desires Roger & Leonie Part I

Stoke My Desires Roger & Leonie Part II

Justify My Desires Roger & Leonie Part III

Deepen My Desires Sebastian & Lola Part III

Capture My Desires Malcolm & Starr Part I

Embrace My Desires Malcolm & Starr Part II

Cherish My Desires Malcolm & Starr Part III

A Trilogy of Desires Sebastian & Lola Parts I-III

A Trilogy of Desires Roger & Leonie Parts I-III

A Trilogy of Desires Malcolm & Starr Parts I-III

Series Extras

Series Playlist

STEELE INTERNATIONAL, INC. - JACKSON CORPORATION
A BILLIONAIRES ROMANCE SERIES CROSSOVER

Tempt My Desires Lachlan & Haley Part I

Tease My Desires Lachlan & Haley Part II

Grant My Desires Lachlan & Haley Part III

Intrigue My Desires Harris & Kat Part I

Decode My Desires Harris & Kat Part II

Honor My Desires Harris & Kat Patt III

A Trilogy of Desires Lachlan & Haley Parts I-III

A Trilogy of Desires Harris & Kat Parts I-III

Series Extras

Series Playlist

ABOUT STEELE INTERNATIONAL, INC. - JACKSON CORPORATION A BILLIONAIRES ROMANCE SERIES CROSSOVER

Welcome to the titillating world of the multibillion-dollar global companies and the love affairs of the families that controls them.

STEELE International, Inc.- Jackson Corporation is a series of interconnecting Billionaire romance. Follow the Steele and Jackson families as they fly around the world chasing the women they love and their happily ever afters. Get ready for glitz, glamour, and steamy romance books. What's better than that? The Jet-set Lifestyle has never been hotter...

The Desires Series is not for the tea set; it's for the top-shelf vodka straight up in a pretty crystal glass coterie!

Don't miss any of the sizzling romance books in the STEELE International, Inc. - Jackson Corporation A Billionaires Romance Series Crossover:

Tempt My Desires Lachlan & Haley Part I

Tease My Desires Lachlan & Haley Part II

Grant My Desires Lachlan & Haley Part III

Intrigue My Desires Harris & Kat Part I

Decode My Desires Harris & Kat Part II

Honor My Desires Harris & Kat Patt III

A Trilogy of Desires Lachlan & Haley Parts I-III

A Trilogy of Desires Harris & Kat Parts I-III

Series Extras

Series Playlist

Visit CharmaineLouiseBooks.com for the complete list.

Intrigue my DESIRES

HARRIS & KAT PART I

Charmaine Louise Shelton

I dedicate this novel to those who think they'll never find their true love.
Never give up. One day you'll meet them.

Fulfill Your Desires.

xoxo
Charmaine Louise

ABOUT INTRIGUE MY DESIRES INTRIGUE & KAT PART I

Intrigue My Desires Harris & Kat Part I

Welcome to the titillating world of the multibillion-dollar global companies and the love affairs of the families that control them.

Harris

I'm the last man standing in The STEELE Quaternity—my brothers and I dubbed such by the media as the most sought-after of the world's eligible billionaires. One by one they fell. Suckers.

Me? I hold onto my playboy card like a life preserver in a tsunami, as my fraternal twin sister teases me. Until the day I don't...

Kat

Those Jacksons think they're all that. Well, they're wrong. Dead wrong. And I'll use whatever and whoever I can to get what I want. Revenge. My red hair, pretty face, and curvy body get 'em every time. Including that Steele sucker.

Will Kat claim Harris' playboy card or will her true desire destroy the Jacksons and the Steeles?

Join Harris—her mouse—as he chases his Kat from Aberdeen and the Channel Islands to Thailand and more in their steamy, playboy falls for The One billionaire romance.

Anthem: "Nasty" Janet Jackson
https://www.youtube.com/watch?v=-s1fHtIVqiQ

Playlist:
https://www.youtube.com/playlist?list=
PLXwYvn0e218CfLUoSrHt0sWHJ2Thd8TIU

Visit CharmaineLouiseBooks.com

PROLOGUE

PROLOGUE

"Tilt your chin towards the corner over there. I want the light to cross the planes of your gorgeous face... A little more... Just... Right there! Now, hold still and allow me to capture your beauty."

My muse-cum-lover preens as my brush skims across the canvas before me. Her nipples pebble as though the soft sable tip caresses her flawless, porcelain skin. Sky blue eyes twinkle when she moves them to catch a glimpse of me at work.

I tsk at her, and a small smile plays at the corners of her Cupid's bow mouth.

We continue in silence for the next hour until I notice her shoulders shake from the exertion to maintain her position for an extended period of time. With a sigh, I finish one last stroke to the curvaceous hip on the canvas before I release her.

"Relax, My Beauty. We are done for now," I tell her as I cover the canvas with a tarp. My preference to keep the unfinished work hidden mars her lovely face with a scowl. "No, you cannot see it yet."

"Oh… You're so mean to me!" She huffs and crosses her arms beneath her ample bosom. The move only serves to present them to me like a platter of tantalizing treats. "Well, I can't see. So, neither can you!"

She wraps the white silk sheet around her like a toga as she rises from the red velvet chaise gracefully. A glance over her shoulder as she sashays towards the ancient stone stairs drives me from my stool.

My long legs make short work of the distance between us.

My Beauty squeaks when I grip her hips and hoist her over my shoulder with ease. A firm smack to her rear makes her yelp and flail her arms and legs. Her tiny hands pummel my broad back, to no avail. Another round of smacks, and she drapes her torso over my shoulder in complete submission.

"Good, girl," I murmur as I carry her to the bed at the center of my studio.

She bounces on the feather mattress when I toss her to the middle. The silk sheet slips open to reveal her naked beauty in all its mesmerizing glory. The thatch of dark hair at the apex of her thighs glistens with her arousal. She notices my lust-filled stare and covers her mound as her porcelain cheeks flush a contrasting crimson hue.

Quick as lightning, I grab her wrists and pull them from her treasure trove to place them above her head. One hand pins them to the mattress while the other parts her thighs. A single thick, calloused digit breaches her slick folds.

Her back arches from the bed as a moan escapes her lips.

Rhythmic thrusts that graze the textured patch and stroke her inner walls have her writhing beneath me. A second digit has her panting. A tweak to her swollen bud, and she screams my name.

My mouth crashes over hers as I plank above her. Our tongues dance, and I swallow her moans greedily to capture every piece of her—beauty and pleasure. A shudder runs through me when her fingernails rake along my bare back.

Her dainty fingers reach between us, eager to unleash my turgid member.

Both of us groan at the carnal contact as her hand fists my erection. Her gentle tugs do not suffice to quench my lust.

With a primal growl, I take control and slam deep within her slippery core. Her warmth engulfs me from tip to base. My eyes roll to the back of my head.

My hips snap of their own accord as I drive her into the mattress. She meets each thrust with one of her own as her core flutters along my length.

The sounds of our carnal passion resound off the stone walls of my studio to soar towards the ceiling high above us. Through the open windows, the sea crashes to the shore in time with my thrusts. Her cries match the seagulls in their quest for food.

The base of my spine tingles. Three final snaps of my hips, and I roar my release. It ignites another climax for My Beauty. She keens her pleasure as she bows from the bed. I collapse atop her, and she winds her arms and legs about me.

I roll to my side, still intimately connected to my lover. She cuddles against my chest as my fingers draw circles around the two dips above her round derriere.

With the release of my creative and carnal passions, my mind returns to the request—rather demand—my father sent to me. I am to meet him along with my younger brother in the city tomorrow.

Undoubtedly, it's another of his threats. I will attend. But nothing he says will change my mind. Nothing.

I shake my head to rid it of the sense of impending doom. With a sigh, I roll My Beauty onto her back to lose myself within her welcoming embrace once again.

* * *

"Hello, Father, brother."

I nod at each of them when I enter my father's office.

My brother greets me with a sorrowful smile.

"Glad you can join us," my father responds gruffly. His dissatisfied scowl takes me in from head to toe, not at all pleased with my attire of a smock shirt, trousers., and paint-stained brogues. "You could not find an appropriate suit? Never mind. Sit."

Once I'm seated beside my brother, our father settles behind his massive wooden desk. My artist's eye takes in the ornate carvings appreciatively. A master craftsman's finest work.

"Have you come to your senses and will take your proper place as the next to run our family's company?"

My father's question draws me from my musings.

I glance over at him.

We stare at one another for a heartbeat.

I look away first.

He sighs.

"With all due respect, Father. We have had this conversation many times before. I intend to follow my passion. I do not care to follow in your footsteps," I respond as I bring my gaze back to his angry one.

My brother cringes beside me. He knows the roof is about to blow off the building. Again.

Surprisingly, our father remains silent. He studies my face for any sign of a change of heart.

I remain steadfast and hold his gaze.

He rises to tower over me.

"From this day forward, I disown you and no one will speak your name ever again. Your presence erased from this family's history completely. As I speak, your *studio* is being destroyed and your harlot removed. Leave this city with what you have at this moment. Do not let the sunset find you here. Never return. Contact none of us again. Ever. Do you understand?"

His pronouncement sends a chill through my very soul.

The sense of doom comes to fruition.

I scan his face, hoping to find a crack in his countenance. Nothing. I turn to my brother, and he glances away from my imploring gaze. My eyes shift back to my father. He stands indomitable and raises his hand to point at the door.

"Leave now, or I will have you escorted from the premises," he commands.

I never guessed my father would go so far as to banish me. To obliterate me from our family. Ruin my dreams.

I open my mouth to implore him. But as he rounds the desk with an expression of such detestation, I flinch. Then suck in a breath when he grips the back of my shirt and lifts me from the leather chair.

Forcefully, he pushes me towards the door.

I stumble before I catch myself.

One last glance over my shoulder reveals his imposing figure glaring at me and my brother's stiff back as he stares straight ahead. No remorse. No sympathy.

"Goodbye, Father, brother."

HARRIS

The past few weeks have gone a little something like this:

Me:

"Hey, bro, the Knicks play the Warriors tonight, and there's still room in our box at the Garden. Steph's been on fire scoring thirty-point games and dropping 3s left and right. Let's make a night of it."

Sebastian:

"Ah, damn. Sounds like a good time. But sorry, bro. Lola and I have date night tonight since Mom and Dad are in town and want to babysit Slade, Sabrina, and Stella."

Me:

"I scored the last tickets to ride in the supersonic stealth jet XR-T2 before they decommission it. In two days, me and you will soar through the stratosphere under the radar, bro! You know you can't resist a thrill."

Malcolm:

"Two days? Fuck me. Can you change the date? Starr and I are taking Elios, Selina, Dione, and Iris to Aspen with Peace and Sun."

Me:

"Hey, bro. I'm in town Friday through Monday. How about we meet up at Jackson Smoke&Scotch Paris? Lucien has a pairings event Saturday night with Lachlan's new Jackson Scotch blend. He says it's one of his best ever."

Roger:

"No can do. Leonie and I jet to Villa dei Fiori with Rodolphe, Gaspard, and Daphne on Thursday after work for a week of R&R with Guy and Josy."

Me:

"Remember those triplets we hooked up with at LEVELS New York? Well, they left a message for us with the concierge. They're back from Buenos Aires tomorrow and want to see us again. You game for that hot action, or what, cuz?"

Laurent:

"Shhh! Hold on a minute... Now's not a good time to talk. But no, I'm not game, anyway. Gotta go, cuz."

Yeah, I'm the last man standing in The STEELE Quaternity—my older brothers Sebastian, Malcolm, Roger, and I dubbed such by the media as the most sought-after of the world's eligible billionaires. Handsome; six plus feet; ebony hair; shades of gray eyes; powerful Alpha Doms and males. One by one, they fell. Suckers.

Me? At thirty-two, I hold on to my playboy card like a life preserver in a tsunami, as my fraternal twin sister Haley teases me.

But what strikes me as odd is my cousin and partner in playadom Laurent Jackson. What the hell was he shushing me for and blowing me off? Like me, he's the youngest male of his family and an eternal playboy. Along with Lachlan and Lucien, he makes up the Jackson Trio of more of the world's eligible billionaires. Handsome; six plus feet; sable brown hair; shades of green eyes; powerful Alpha Doms and males.

Well, excluding Lach now that he's married to Haley—he's her fairytale Earl of Aboyne teenage crush and Sebastian's best friend, talk about forbidden love. Even their oldest sibling, Lydie, isn't single anymore. Cla-clank!

The Steeles and the Jacksons. An unbreakable bond forged by our mothers—Michelle aka Shelley a native New Yorker and Lucinda aka Lucie a New Orleans transplant, respectively—being best friends since their days in Manhattan as a shopgirl in a STEELE International, Inc. retail store and a bartender at a Jackson Corporation pub.

Then they met our fathers Morgan Steele and Connor Jackson, Marquess of Huntly. Titans in their industries with the New York City based luxury real estate development and management company and the Aberdeen, Scotland-based fine dining, distilleries, and vineyards corporation, respectively. Both multigenerational, multibillion-dollar businesses with offices and properties all over the globe that attract royalty and the über-wealthy. Our closeness extends to our businesses as we partner in multiple ventures. Jackson's world-renown and award-winning eateries and products pair well within STEELE's casinos, hotels, resorts, and residential and retail properties.

Each of my siblings works at STEELE: Sebastian, CEO, president of the Retail Properties Division, and Chairman of the Board; Malcolm, president of the Entertainment Properties Division and First Vice President of the Board; Roger, president of the Residential Properties Division and Second Vice President of the Board; Haley the hacker and me the techie, co-founders of the subsidiary STEELE Technology and Cyber Security and members of the Board.

The same with our cousins working at Jackson: Lydie,

COO and Vice President of the Board; Lachlan, CEO, President of Liquor, and Chairman of the Board; Lucien, President of Jackson Corporation Restaurants/Bars/Lounges and Second Vice President of the Board; Laurent, Director of Jackson Corporation Cigars Division and member of the Board.

Both families are close even without sharing DNA. Hence our cousin relationship and Aunt Lucie and Uncle Connor. We travel together and spend the holidays as a combined clan. Besides Baz and Lach being best friends, Malcolm and Lucien and Laurent and I are best buds and hang out the most. Being the youngest in the bunch, Haley, Laurent, and I spend a lot of time together. Lydie sees Baz as a confidante, and Roger floats amongst us all. Our relationships work well.

As I reflect on the last few weeks, I'm not mad at my brothers and my cousin for ditching hanging out with me in favor of their little family activities and for who the hell knows what. I wish them all the best. Good luck with all of that!

The best part of my siblings' pairings are my adorable AF nieces and nephews. I love those little buggers madly. Not saying that I want a child of my own any time soon, though. Uh, no.

Do their happily ever afters make me lonely and depressed?

Let me think about it for a millisecond…

Hell, nah!!!

I'll keep my playboy card happily thank you very much. No need to let that bad boy go. At. All.

Especially with a sinfully sexy toffee drop headed my way. The sway of her grip-worthy hips moves to the throbbing pulse of the sensual beat playing in the dance club at

LEVELS London. The sight of the tantalizing beauty keeps any sad thoughts at bay.

Like the never ruffled lone wolf I am, I appraise her over the rim of my Waterford Crystal snifter with no outward emotion. My appreciative dove gray eyes take in every inch of her curves showcased in a gold beaded mini dress. Long, toned legs end in fuck-me stilettos.

She tosses a mane of chestnut curls over her shoulder as her obsidian eyes sparkle in the lights. A come-hither smile plays on her lush lips.

Our eyes lock.

I take a sip of my Jackson Special Blend Scotch, then twirl the amber liquid in the glass. My ten-inch cock twitches with interest in the trousers of my bespoke suit as she nears. A smirk lifts a corner of my full lips.

Yeah. Who needs to tie themselves down for eternity with one woman when you can indulge in a plethora of lovelies? Particularly since they're readily available at any of the LEVELS clubs.

I have Lucien and Malcolm to thank for my hunting grounds.

While completing his hospitality and culinary training at the prestigious Le Cordon Bleu in Paris, Lucien thought of a BDSM/dance club. He figured the club would fill the void for safe, uninhibited sexual activities amongst the world's wealthiest and most influential people. They convinced Sebastian a global, luxury, members-only entertainment venue focused on hedonism would add to STEELE's bottom line. Baz, the net-net guy, saw the potential and gave them the green light for the flagship in New York's Meatpacking District.

For consistency and members' comfort, locations share the same layout:

Main entry foyer has two sides with two greeter stations for access to Dine & Dance levels and BDSM levels, an All-Access member can choose from any of the seven levels: 7th Sky Lounge that offers a bar, restaurant by day dance club by night, coverable pool that's open for the summer, and a glass-retractable roof; 6th and 5th multilevel dance club with two bars and a lounge for food and drinks; 4th Level 4 Restaurant and bar open for breakfast, lunch, and dinner; 3rd has twelve private suites for members to continue their pleasure apart from the BDSM levels; 2nd Peepshow for BDSM with seating alcoves, main stage, performance rooms, and a bar that serves non-alcoholic mocktails; below ground the Cellar BDSM dungeon with mocktails bar. The Dine/Dance members only have access to the party levels—Sky Lounge, Dance Club, and Level 4 Restaurant.

London is the third after Paris of the exclusive clubs. Its site is a former bank set in the City of London, also known as The City and Financial District. They use the original vault for private parties. Locked behind its massive, thick steel door, who knows what all goes on inside. This LEVELS is an ode to the debauchery of money and the wealthy who wield it as power over others. How appropriate the Sky Lounge provides an unobstructed view of the Tower of London—the beast's lair.

Their venture with a high profit margin proved it's bigger than "a titty bar" as Baz originally called LEVELS. Malcolm and Lucien opened additional locations in Beverly Hills, Verbier, and Aberdeen. Even the LEVELS Laucala Island—a five-star resort in Fiji—sold out when it opened. An idea Lucien—*The Sexy Chef*—literally cooked up is worth millions and does more than add to STEELE's bottom line. It gives all of us a place to play.

And play I will tonight…

On my tantalizing toffee treat's wrist rests a green enamel bracelet signifying she's available to play. Perfect.

To avoid unwanted interactions amongst club participants, the system requires partnered subs to wear collars given to them by their Dom; partnered Doms wear gold bracelets; available subs wear red; available Doms wear white; voyeurs wear black; partnered couples wear silver; those available to play wear green.

I leave the Dom shit to Baz, Malcolm, Lachlan, and Lucien. Sure, I'm an Alpha male who enjoys giving a good spanking and bondage, even role playing. But I don't want a submissive. I want a woman who gives as good as I do. A feisty little thing, one who will challenge me. And that's more than enough to satisfy my carnal needs. Just for the night, that is.

Despite being the youngest Steele man and the jokester of our family, I fuck fast and hard but with finesse, bringing my partner to heights of exquisite pleasure. Years of honing my skills with girls around my age and with their mothers formed me into a skilled inamorato and a connoisseur of the female body and needs.

Let's see if Toffee will be the lucky one tonight.

"Hello, handsome. You seem to enjoy your drink… and the view. Might I join you?"

My smirk widens at her opening line. Her ultra-posh Queen's English accent in a raspy Demi Moore tone gives her extra points. Not bad.

I nod and lean back to ask the bartender for a glass of Champagne. Toffee appears to be the sophisticated type not partial to cutesy umbrella cocktails. The gleam in her eyes brightens at my request. Bingo. Am I playa, or what?

I stand and help her onto my vacated stool, then hand the flute to her.

She drags the tip of her tongue across her plump lower lip before she raises the glass to taste the sweet nectar. A smile blossoms on her heart-shaped face. She sighs as the essence slides over her palate.

My cock jumps at the thought of it being on her tongue and pouring my jizz down her throat. By far better than the Dom Pérignon.

"Does it meet your expectations?" I ask in a husky baritone as I bend down to murmur in her ear. Purposefully, my warm breath wafts across the delicate shell, and she trembles.

"Yes, it does, thank you," Toffee whispers throatily.

The outer curve of her ample tit brushes against my biceps. Her heat seeps beneath the wool of my suit jacket. When she rubs like a cat, I growl low in my chest. She purrs as her eyes flash.

"Do you toy with me, Toffee?" I ask as I trail the tip of my index finger along the bare skin of her inner arm. The touch to the sensitive erogenous zone makes her tremble again.

"N-N-No," she stammers, then throws her head back when I tweak her nipple poking against the front of her mini dress.

I take advantage of the exposed slender column and brush my lips from her collarbone to her ear.

"Then be very careful, or you will arouse the beast too soon. Before we properly prepared you to handle it," I growl. "Dance with me."

She agrees breathily and places the Champagne on the bar.

I hold her hips as she slides from the stool. The petite thing barely reaches my chest when I settle her on her feet. She grips my arms to steady herself.

Taking her elbow, I lead her past the others to a spot on the dance floor. The opening chords of Grace Jones' "Libertango" make Toffee lift her arms overhead with her wrists crossed and shimmy her hips in a slow, seductive swirl. She mouths the words as I watch, mesmerized.

When she pivots on those fuck-me stilettos, I press my front flush to her back. My palms rest on her hips, and I guide her movements to my sensuous beat. Her fingers twine in the long hair atop my head, then stroke the shorter sides, dragging her fingernails against my scalp.

The bite of pain makes my already achingly hard cock thump against her lower back. It demands more from this vixen.

As she drops to a squat, she undulates against me and trails her fingers down my custom dress shirt to grip the waistband of my trousers. The back of her head presses into my cock. She tilts her head back to glance at me with hooded eyes, impressed with my length and girth. When she licks and bites her lower lip, I grip under her arms and hoist her up.

"Now, you will learn your lesson, Naughty Girl," I growl in her ear.

She mewls.

Without hesitation, I take her hand and stalk off the dance floor, headed for the elevator. The private suite I reserved awaits my latest tryst.

Toffee waltzes inside of the suite. The golden beads swish with each step, drawing my hungry gaze to her round ass. My palm itches to spank it for riling the beast after my warning. But first...

"What are your limits, Naughty Girl?" I ask.

Slowly, she spins around, grips the hem of her mini dress, and pulls it over her head. Her bare mons appears, followed by her bouncing double Ds. The puckered brown nipples make my mouth water.

"None," she states as the beaded material tinkles to the hardwood floor.

I smirk.

"Safeword?" I ask.

She drops to her hands and knees and crawls towards me—ass high, head low, tits sway—as she purrs, "Sticky pudding. Nice and warm."

Fuck. Me.

A trickle of pre-cum drips from my cockhead.

"Hand signal?"

She rises to her knees before me and snaps her fingers.

In the blink of an eye, she has my pants and black silk boxer briefs at my feet and my turgid dick in her fist. Her tongue flattens along the veiny bottom as her mouth engulfs my full length down her throat.

Did I say, Fuck me?

My thighs quiver as my head lolls back, mouth slack, and eyes closed. I'm lost in the sensations of her sucking me deep, swirling her tongue, and humming in carnal delight.

I inhale through my nose for a calming breath to regain control, then grip the sides of her head. My heated gaze meets hers, and I smirk. My pelvis pulls back for only my tip in her mouth, then my hips snap forward.

She gags as I hit the back of her throat. Tears pool in her eyes as I hold her nose to my groin. My cock widens her throat. A tear slips from each eye, and I pull her off to my tip for a breath. I repeat the movements a few more times to acclimate her to my girth. When her breathing evens out, I take it as my cue and fuck her face.

Toffee catches my rhythm and places her palms on my muscular thighs for balance. Soon the suite fills with the rhythmic slapping of my balls to my thighs and slurping. The sounds mingle with my grunts and groans of pleasure.

Erotic fire licks at the base of my spine and zips to my heavy balls. With a guttural roar, I unleash the beast's full force and fuck her face ruthlessly. She gasps around my massive girth and squeezes my thighs. But she doesn't use her hand signal to stop me.

My toes curl as I rise to the balls of my feet. A torrent of cum blasts from my throbbing cock straight down her throat to land in her belly. Her swollen lips kiss my groin as my hips rock to ride out my release.

"Such a good girl," I pant.

She hums and purses her lips as she preens from pleasing me.

"Up you go," I say as I lift her to wobbly legs. Then turn her towards the red leather spanking bench and smack her ass. "Drape yourself over the bench. Do not assume I forgot your punishment, Naughty Girl."

She yelps and hurries across the room.

I toe off my Gucci loafers, step out of my trousers and briefs, then stalk after her as I shed the rest of my clothes. I take a moment to appreciate her bodacious ass before I slip her wrists and ankles into the suede-lined cuffs.

She shudders when I trail a fingertip from her inner ankle up her thigh and along her puffy, soaked seam. To reward her for a most delightful blowjob, I plunge two digits into her pussy and curl them to stroke her G-spot.

Her inner walls grip them greedily. But I withdraw before her orgasm surfaces.

She huffs in dismay and wiggles her ass.

My palm connects with her left ass cheek. I set a swift pattern of left, right, sits bones, left, right, upper thighs until she sags on the spanking bench. A smack to her pussy coats my fingers with her juices. I lick them clean and growl in satisfaction. She whimpers.

I sheath my cock with a condom from the shelf then position myself between her spread legs as I fist my erection. In one brutal thrust, I breach her slippery folds and sink into her sticky pudding. Nice and warm.

She keens as I finally allow her to cum. Her muscles grip me like a vice, and I grunt from the force. A spank to her right ass cheek has her loosening her grip. My hips piston as I pinch her engorged clit. She screams and cums again. Her arms and legs jerk at the restraints. But the cuffs hold fast. Another climax has her begging me to cum. But no safeword.

I continue to fuck her fast and hard until my balls threaten to explode.

"Cum with me," I command as I tighten my grip on her hipbone and tug at her clit.

She jerks and screams as another orgasm overtakes her wrecked pussy.

My groin slams against her red and heated ass as I throw my head back and roar my release. It reverberates around us and triggers another orgasm in her. She wails and collapses against the soft leather, replete.

Once I recover from the mind-blowing sex, I slide out of her pussy gently, pat her ass, and release her from the cuffs. I carry her limp form to the king-size bed and lay her on her belly, then stride to the en suite bathroom for a warm wet cloth and soothing gel. I toss the full condom and return to her side. Aftercare complete, I tuck her beneath the silk sheets.

I exhausted the poor thing, and she curls onto her side without opening her eyes. I wait a few minutes to ensure she's all right before I take a shower. Fully clothed, I leave a note to thank her for a spectacular time and to enjoy breakfast. I am a gentleman, after all.

One who hits it and quits it.

HARRIS

$\mathcal{A}$ LEVELS London chauffeur maneuvers the Black Badge Rolls-Royce Cullinan through the still-busy streets towards Knightsbridge. While in town for a STEELE Technology and Cyber Security summit and a tech conference at ExCel London, I'm staying with Haley. She and Lachlan have a penthouse flat in One Hyde Park—the world's most expensive apartment building and only the best for the Countess of Aboyne. I snicker at the thought, since my twin is as easygoing as I am, despite our limitless wealth.

We're super close, so she wouldn't hear of me staying at STEELE Mayfair or at any of our other hotels in London. Since pregnancy with Lilias, Leith, and Lewis, she's become motherly towards me. She fusses over what I do and how I'm still single. I indulge her new instincts and don't argue, despite not having any interest in settling down.

Her move across the Pond to Aberdeen didn't hamper our connection with me remaining in New York City. In fact, it's grown stronger. Not being a floor apart in The

STEELE Tower or sharing offices makes us stay in contact more frequently, whether via video conference, FaceTime, or text messages.

Over two years ago, we split our offices and client list based on our locations, with Haley expanding our satellite office in STEELE London with some of her existing staff and new ones. The process went smoothly and even gained us new clients abroad.

Twice a year we have summits with our teams to gather as a whole for brainstorming, updates, and a chance to bond. Usually, the summits take place at one of STEELE's resorts over four days. Some team members extend their stay to a vacation afterwards. This time, we'll host it at STEELE London, since the biggest tech convention of the year begins the day after our summit ends.

I blink from my musings as the back door of the SUV opens. So lost in thought, I didn't realize we arrived at One Hyde Park. I thank the chauffeur and slide from the buttery leather, then nod at the doorman. The concierges greet me as I stride through the opulent lobby to Haley and Lachlan's private elevator.

Once outside of the penthouse flat's double doors, I type in the passcode to unlock them—the system one of many I designed. I get a glimpse of Hyde Park through the bespoke glass fireplace that separates the entry foyer from the double-height reception room with floor-to-ceiling windows. The stunning panoramic view includes the lights of London's buildings as they glow beyond the park's expanse of trees.

I take a moment to appreciate the view before I head to the kitchen for a late-night snack. As I enter the massive chef's delight, I spy Haley standing in a spotlight at the waterfall-edge marble island. A spoonful of her favorite butter pecan ice cream halfway to her mouth and the quart on the countertop.

With a smirk, I swipe my palm over the overhead light switch. The kitchen floods with light, and Haley squeaks. Her dove gray eyes—so like mine—narrow at me.

"Harris!" She hisses as she jabs her empty spoon at me. "You almost gave me a heart attack! Ugh!"

I chuckle as I stride across the stone floor and take a spoon from the utensils drawer next to the custom, hand-made French La Cornue range. I shake my head at the sight of the impressive appliance since my twin hates to cook and, despite taking lessons, still sucks at it. Brainiac but no chef.

"Sorry, Hal," I say, dipping my spoon into the quart. "Why are you in the dark, anyway? Not to mention up so late."

She huffs and swats my spoon away to dig hers into the tasty treat.

"Blame the hormones and the demands of twins," she replies as she pats her babies bump. "Round two coming up!"

Only months after the birth of their triplets, she and Lach expect a set of twins. Virile fucker. But she's happy, so I'm ecstatic.

I grin and swipe some more of her ice cream.

Haley cocks her head at me.

"Where are you coming from, Casanova?" She smirks.

I pivot on my heel and prowl towards the refrigerator for a more substantial snack. With my head stuck inside, I mumble a response.

"Sorry, Harris, I didn't quite catch your answer," Haley snickers. "Care to repeat it?"

I turn back towards her with a platter of baked lasagna—

clearly from one of Lucien's restaurants. I set it on the island and walk around her to the dishes cabinet. Before I can lift a square of the pasta to my plate, Haley jabs me in the side.

"Hellooo, Harris… Where were you?" She persists.

I face her, and she tilts her head back to eyeball me. Not that she's petite; she's five feet, eight inches and only five inches shorter than me. Formerly shy, she's now a fierce woman. But I know how to get her good.

"Banging the back out of a nice piece of ass at LEVELS London," I deadpan.

Haley's mouth drops open as her face flushes crimson.

I knew a crass response would shock her speechless.

With a snicker, I stride to the microwave hidden in a drawer. Then yelp when an object dings me in the back of my head. She can't cook, but she has a damn good aim.

"You filthy mouthed sexist—"

"Whoa, there, Ms. Prim and Proper. You asked for it," I reply as I pick her spoon off the floor. "Anything else I can answer for you?"

She rolls her eyes and gets another spoon. Then glares at me as I wait for my pasta to heat. The ding breaks our silence.

"Sit with me while I eat," I say as I bump her with my hip on my way to the banquette. Then add with a smirk, "Spend some quality time with your older brother."

"You know what, Harris…" She says brandishing her spoon again. "You're lucky I love you!"

"You better!" I retort and point to the bench opposite me. "Now, sit your preggie butt down. I'm sure standing for long isn't good for your ankles, Mom."

Haley rolls her eyes again as she settles across from me. Her nose twitches as she catches the delicious aroma of the lasagna. She grins and scoops some off my plate, then shoves it in her mouth. She closes her eyes on a contented sigh.

"So fucking good! Give me this and you get some more," she demands as she slides my plate in front of her.

I throw my head back and laugh.

"Don't mess with a preggie lady and food, twin!" She exclaims gleefully.

After I heat some more, I rejoin her at the banquette. We eat in silence until I sense her appraising stare. Glancing up, I raise my eyebrow at her questioningly.

Haley shrugs and lowers her eyes to her plate.

"Spit it out, twin," I demand.

"Baz told me it disappointed you he couldn't go to the Knicks and Warriors basketball game with you. Then Malcolm mentioned the jet and Roger said he couldn't hang out with you either," she starts then pauses to gauge my reaction.

I blank my expression.

She bites the corner of her lower lip before she continues with a sigh.

"We're all married and have children. I don't like that you're alone, Harris," she says, then lifts her hand to stop me from speaking. "I know you'll say you're not interested in a relationship. But *I* know you, twin. You're covering up your loneliness with bravado. Don't even try to hide it from me. I love you, Harris, and want you happy like all of us," she finishes.

Her dove gray eyes shine with unshed tears. But she holds my stare, determined to make me understand.

I get it. I just don't agree.

Sure, they're all boo'd up with kids. But I'm not so sure that's for me—at least not at this very moment.

I close my eyes, take a deep breath for a count of six, hold it for six, and exhale for the same time before I respond. My yogi sister-in-law Starr taught the cleansing breath technique to me, and damn if it doesn't soothe my soul.

"Haley, I understand what you're saying. I do. But I am not at the point in my life where I want to settle down. I'm happy for you guys. Truly. But it's not in the cards for me. At least not right now. Okay?" I respond as I clasp her hand.

She swipes at her eyes with the heel of her other hand and nods.

"I don't want you to be alone with all of us paired up. I only want you happy, Harris," she says wistfully.

"I know, Hal. And I thank you," I respond quietly.

I know she'll say it's the hormones making her teary. But I know it's not. She speaks from her heart. We've always done everything together. Now she's married with kids, and I'm still single over a year later.

Well, such is life.

"Hey! What's going on here?"

We jolt at Lachlan's booming voice.

He strides over to the banquette and drops down next to Haley. He wraps an arm around her shoulders and pulls her to him before he plants a kiss on her temple. Then he turns his emerald green eyes to me.

"Well, if it isn't Little Lord Fauntleroy... How may we help you, milord?" I quip.

He chuckles as he shakes his head.

"Late night, Harris?" He asks.

I roll my eyes and take a bite of my lasagna.

"Oh, leave him be, My Lord. Not all of us are on lockdown, you know," Haley retorts cheekily, with a mischievous wink at me.

Lach growls. Clearly not amused.

I grin around my fork and return my twin's wink.

No matter what, we always have each other's backs.

* * *

"Hi, Harris. I loved your presentation. You're just so incredibly smart!"

I glance down at the unfamiliar female who caught me after my session at the tech conference. I smile and thank her, then move on. Her hand on my forearm stops me. A glance over my shoulder and cock my eyebrow.

She giggles but doesn't let go. Instead, she loops her arm around mine and steps beside me.

"I'd really love to hear more about your thoughts. Perhaps we can have a drink later, or…" she says as she squeezes my biceps with her other hand. Then she licks her lips and adds, "I'm game for whatever you have in mind."

Good grief.

I've had enough of the women who stalk after me in hopes of a night in my bed or my ring on their finger. Often they'll attend my presentations—like this one—pretending to be techies just to get access to me.

One pretended to be a journalist for *Wired* and pulled out all the stops with a call to my offices to schedule the interview, then tried to jump my bones in the press suite. Upon investigation, she was the editor's girlfriend and wanted more than he could offer her. She wanted the multi-billionaire he wrote about. Ridiculous as it seems, shit like that happens. All the time.

But not today.

"Miss, remove your hands, or I will call security to escort

you from the premises," I reply tersely as I pin her with a sharp look.

A flush creeps up from beneath her low-cut silk blouse to her hairline. She steps back, flabbergasted, stung by my curt tone.

I pivot on my heel and stride in the opposite direction without a backwards glance.

My mobile vibrates in my trousers pocket. I smile when I see it's a call from Haley.

"Hey, Hal. How'd your presentation go?" I ask.

"Awesome! Let's meet for lunch before the afternoon sessions begin," she responds. "We have three potential clients I want to tell you about!"

We end the call, and I increase my pace to reach the restaurant. Haley's excitement has me pumped. This is what drives me—accomplishments in our work. Nothing compares to the rush of success.

Well... A blinding, toe-curling, legs-give-out climax that empties my balls completely still tops my list. Naturally.

I laugh out loud. Haley would really pummel me if I told her that one!

The rest of the day goes as planned, and her driver takes us back to Knightsbridge.

I opted for babysitting duties while Haley and Lachlan have a date night. So I change into a long-sleeved t-shirt and sweats so I can romp around with my niece and nephews. They crawl around like nobody's business, and I need to keep up with them.

We spend the night in their nursery suite's lounge playing with toys, a tickle fest, and bottle feeding all on our own. Although I call Nanny Gail when it's time for diaper changes. Ain't no way this boy's dealing with stinky nappies! Nope.

By the time Haley and Lachlan return, I'm worn the fuck out and crawl to my guest suite, strip, and dive under the covers. Who knows how much later, I jolt upright with a pounding heartbeat and a sweaty face. Scanning around the bedroom, I realize it was only a nightmare. For a frightful minute there, five babies toddled with arms outstretched towards me, calling me Dada.

My entire body shudders at the thought, and I swipe my hand over my heated face.

One last peek around the room ensures all's safe before I pull the comforter over my head.

A calming breath, and I'm out like a light.

KAT

"*O*kay, lads, you can share the ball. Here, let me show you a game you can play together. It's really fun..."

I stand aside and watch them play. A wistful smile pulls at my lips as I think back to being their age. Unfortunately for my siblings and me, we didn't have a beautiful and wonderfully equipped children's center to spend our youth in Glasgow. We were too busy busting our butts selling newspapers and scraps, babysitting, running errands. Hell, we did anything to make some money so we could eat and pay the rent for our three-room flat.

Sure our parents—Ramsay and Allison—were around. Our mum cleaned for rich families. But our father, he was a dreamer. Always creating some invention or the other that would make him gobs of money. Until he died at a young age from a heart attack.

I toss my waist-length Titian hair over my shoulder as I glance up to the sky, lost in memories. Titian for one, I scoff. An ex-boyfriend said my hair reminded him of the

Renaissance artist's paintings of red-haired women. Whereas I always thought of my locks as a brownish-orange color. But I went along with him since he was more worldly than me, and the fancy description stuck.

Of course, Payton—my older brother by three years to my twenty-seven—teases me relentlessly about it along with other things. *Bah! You're a plain-old ginger, lass! Don't get it twisted with that uppity wanker you're with.* It's worse since I'm the only redhead while everyone else has brown hair.

My relationship with my other siblings—Michael, who's three years younger, and Charlotte, who's twenty-one—is better. Michael is a bit of a dreamer, like our father, and escapes our dreary lives through his sketches of Glasgow's architecture. Charlotte is the quietest of us and prefers to keep her head in the books. She looks up to me and wants to get out through a higher education, too.

I love each of them dearly and will do all in my power to make their lives easier.

After our father died, I realized the only way to escape poverty was to use my brain. My drive to succeed pushed me to study hard not just books, but the ways of the rich. I didn't want to get into a school and stick out. Rather, I wanted to blend in seamlessly. I studied French and the Classics, read the top fashion magazines and business periodicals at the library, and polished my accent. My goal: become a suitable candidate for the finest university I could gain acceptance.

Ultimately, I won a full academic scholarship to the University of Edinburgh. I strove for not only the most prestigious institution in Scotland, but one of the best in the world. I, Katrina Roberts, entered its hallowed halls and continued to excel.

Less than one hour from the dingy flat to the beauty of

the university—a whole new world awaited me. One in which I thrived. Always good with figures and strategy, I earned an MA Business Management degree and graduated with honors at the top of my class.

None of my family attended because of their obligations. But I prefer to keep my Glasgow life separate—less muddying of the waters. Besides, Payton would find a way to embarrass me. No, thank you.

"Ms. Roberts!"

"Ms. Roberts!"

Cries from the boys drag me back from the past.

I shake my head to clear it and smile at them as they come back into focus.

"Yes, lads?" I ask.

Their urgency spurred by who won since they tied makes me laugh out loud. Wow, if only my siblings and I had such simple concerns as tykes!

I offer them a solution that appeases both just as the bell rings for lunch break. They thank me, and I tousle their hair with a grin.

"Wow! What a busy morning, huh?"

I glance around to find my close friend—Isla Ritchie.

Looping my arm through hers, we turn towards the building and the cafeteria within it.

"I know, right! My highlight was refereeing the World Cup," I respond with a giggle as my emerald green eyes dance behind tortoise-shell frame glasses. "And I lived to see another day. Whew."

Isla giggles and shakes her head. Then tells me about her morning sessions.

We met at Aberdeen's Children's Center, where we volunteer on Wednesday evenings and all day on Saturdays.

Around the same age, we became fast friends. While Isla is happily married, I'm single.

Sure, I've had a few dalliances over the years. But for the most part, work and studies then work again dominate my time. And when I need to scratch an itch, I reach for my trusty BOB—Battery Operated Boyfriend. Not quite a red-blooded male, or the sensation one can give to me. But it provides relief without complications. Unless I use up the batteries as known to happen…

Once we have our trays with sandwiches and soup, Isla and I settle at a table near the expanse of windows. I glance briefly at the beautifully landscaped playground and shake my head again. So nice.

"Ugh! I'm eating like a cow. But I can't help myself. At least I get to blame the baby," Isla says as she pops a Walkers Salt & Vinegar crisp in her mouth. She closes her eyes and hums in delight.

"Your hubby will love you no matter what state you're in, Isla," I tell her with a giggle.

I'm so happy for my friend. She and Gregor have been trying for a while now to get pregnant. So I say eat whatever makes her smile after months of sadness. She deserves it.

"So, how's it going with your boss? Is he still a prat, or what?" Isla asks with a frown marring her pretty face.

I sigh and roll my eyes.

"Yeah. But it's a great opportunity. So unless something more impressive comes along, I'll stick it out," I respond with a shrug.

After graduation, I turned down offers for management trainee positions in favor of an administrative assistant position at an international company's C-suites. Since then, I've had a few. I figure the best way to learn about business is straight from the source—the higher ups who actually run it.

Many a person takes a job as an AA to a ranking officer, gets to learn the ins and outs of the entire company, and lands a prime position either at the same place or at a comparable one. That is, if one has the smarts to do so, and I most definitely have what it takes, thanks to my upbringing and my doggedness.

"Well, I'll keep my ears open for an opportunity at Jackson Corporation or somewhere else. No sense in working at a place that's unpleasant," Isla says, then winks. "Until then, *smiogaid suas, nighean!*"

I lift my chin and grin at my friend as I repeat the Scottish Gaelic phrase for *chin up, girl*—my lifelong mantra.

Our conversation turns to plans for the weekend, and soon it's time for the afternoon sessions. We part in the corridor leading to the study rooms where we'll tutor the older children.

By the end of the day, I'm ready for a soak in my tub, a glass of wine, and a round with BOB. No better way to ease stress!

KAT

"*N*ow, don't be nervous, Kat. Mr. Jackson is not like your current boss. Mr. Jackson demands the best from every employee. But he's fair and makes sure we have the guidance and training we need to achieve our goals. I've learned so much from him over the years. He counts Gladys and me as integral parts of his team and praises us for being smart and dedicated to our jobs. Plus, working directly for Mr. Jackson has major perks!"

Isla grins at me as she squeezes my arm with one hand and cradles her baby bump with the other.

She's heavily pregnant. So she and Gregor decided it's best for her to take an early leave, followed by maternity time off after she gives birth.

True to her word from a few months back, Isla recommended me to Lachlan Jackson—CEO, President of Liquor, and Chairman of the Board of Jackson Corporation—as her temporary replacement. She believes once I get my foot in the door, he'll see my potential for a permanent position by the time she returns as his administrative assistant.

Isla also thinks my chances of securing the role are high since Mr. Jackson met with quite a few potential replacements for her position. But not one reached his expectations. Prior to my interview with him, Isla had me meet with Gladys Sinclair—his personal assistant. I did my research on the company and impressed her enough that she recommended he meet with me after Human Resources did their background checks. Isla tells me he agreed, since my resume and references prove I'm worthy of an interview.

Now, my stomach churns as we leave the private lift area for his suite of offices on the executive floor of Jackson Town House. It's the landmark property on Union Street built by the company's founders of the famous Aberdeen granite. Jackson Town House is the second largest granite building in the world.

My gaze wanders as I take in my surroundings. The executive floor has offices for their legal, finance, operations, and technology departments, along with various conference rooms. Their other divisions have designated floors below. I scan the employees who move about busy at their tasks. The hum of their conversations and activities mixes with the soft classical music piped in through the surround sound system.

The decor highlights the Old World feel of Jackson Town House. A palette of caramel and Bordeaux hues with gold accents reminiscent of our Scotch and wines blend with the dark mahogany woods and leather furniture, crystal light fixtures, and original artwork. The reception area has a spacious desk. Three attractive receptionists with headsets in their ears and custom-tailored caramel-colored dress suits and skin-tone heels that serve as uniforms sit behind it. I smile and nod at them as Isla and I pass—my heels silent on the luxurious Aubusson rugs.

My emerald green eyes widen as we approach portraits of past generations who founded and helped continue the legacy of Jackson Corporation. First with who I recognize as the founder and the creator of the finest single malt Scotch Whiskey. He set Jackson Corporation on the path to the most renowned liquor company in the world. After him, successors of each generation have portraits ending with one of Lachlan Jackson.

I can't help but admire his breathtaking movie-star appearance. He resembles the classic American actor Cary Grant with his rugged masculinity and gorgeous looks. Blazing green eyes stare back at me from the canvas. Thick, sable brown hair slicked back from his chiseled cheekbones and strong jawline with a cleft chin add to his heartthrob persona.

"I know, he's a gorgeous man! And happily married," Isla whispers as she tugs my arm. "Come on, we don't want you late."

Heat suffuses my alabaster skin a crimson shade. Damn! I didn't realize I stopped and gawked at Mr. Jackson's portrait. Get it together, Katrina Roberts!

"Er… Right… Sorry… Let's go," I mumble, embarrassed by the blatant act.

We hurry our steps until we reach Mr. Jackson's outer office. I take note of a reception area, conference room, and a desk for Isla and one where Gladys sits. She lifts her gaze from her laptop screen and smiles at me. She's in her mid-forties and the type of woman I admire for her intelligence and cultured presence.

"Hello, Kat. You look lovely. Good luck. Although I'm certain you will do well!" She says with a thumbs up.

"Thank you!" I respond with a nervous smile.

I smooth down the front of my navy blue suit's A-line skirt, then swipe my palm over my hair to ensure no strands crept from the chignon. I learned the importance of investment pieces and purchased a few well-tailored, sensible suits, silk blouses, and heels. My biggest purchase—the Mulberry City Briefcase in hunter green for money—I hold tightly in my left hand.

"Isla, call through via the intercom. He's waiting for the both of you," Gladys adds with a nod towards the imposing double doors to Mr. Jackson's office.

Isla walks to her desk and presses the call button.

"Mr. Jackson? Are you ready to meet with us?" She asks.

He responds in the affirmative, and she smiles at me encouragingly before she opens the doors.

Mr. Jackson stands beside an equally gorgeous young woman not much older than me seated on a leather sofa in the seating area. Three adorable babies—a girl and two boys—sit on her lap and next to her as he helps her to settle.

He strides over to his beautifully carved mahogany wood desk as he gestures for Isla and me to sit in the guest chairs opposite.

As we take our seats, I glance at his wife and children with a smile and nod as I wave my fingers at one of the boys, who watches us intently.

"Oh, don't mind us. Do carry on with your meeting," his wife says with a genial smile.

I nod again and bring my attention back to Mr. Jackson.

"Mr. Jackson, this is Katrina Roberts, my friend who I recommend as my replacement. Katrina, this is Mr. Lachlan Jackson, CEO of Jackson Corporation," Isla says.

I reach across his desk to hold out my hand as I rise slightly from my seat.

"Thank you for the opportunity to interview with you, Mr. Jackson," I say as I grip his sizable hand firmly and look him straight in the eye.

"You're welcome Ms. Roberts—"

"Oh, please call me Kat," I interject with an amiable smile. My green eyes twinkle like emeralds behind tortoise-shell frame glasses.

He nods.

"Do you need me any further, Mr. Jackson?" Isla asks as she rests her hand on her baby bump.

He scans her face as though assessing her wellbeing before he responds.

"No, that is all for today. Call for one of the company cars to take you home. They can pick you up in the morning, so you can leave yours in the garage overnight," he tells her.

Isla expresses her thanks and turns to tell Mrs. Jackson good night before she leaves his office. He watches her with a concerned expression as she makes her way across the office and through the doors.

She wasn't joking when she told me he cares for his employees and about the major perks. A ride home and back the next morning in a chauffeur-driven company car? Wow.

He turns his emerald green gaze back to me.

"So, Kat, tell me about yourself and why you believe your skill set makes you suitable for the role of my administrative assistant," he says.

Okay, Katrina Roberts, *smiogaid suas, nighean!*

I take a deep breath and sit up straighter in the comfortable leather seat. Then I proceed to answer in detail. My goal: get the job.

An hour later, Mr. Jackson calls an end to the interview

and escorts me to the doors of his office.

Gladys looks over, and he asks her to see me to the lobby.

With a smile, I extend my hand, and he shakes it.

"Thank you, Mr. Jackson. I do hope I satisfy your requirements and hope to hear from you soon," I say with another firm grip. Then shift my emerald green gaze to his right and smiles. "Nice to see you, Mrs. Jackson. Your triplets are adorable."

"Thank you, Kat," she responds with a brilliant smile that illuminates her dove gray eyes.

Another nod to Mr. Jackson, and he shuts the door behind me.

I sag in relief and place a hand over my heart.

Gladys laughs as she rises from her chair.

"That's a good sigh or a bad one?" She asks.

I join her in laughter and respond, "Both! Good because I think I did well and bad because he didn't offer the position at the end. I couldn't get a read on him."

Gladys pats my arm and shakes her head.

"Mr. Jackson keeps things close to his chest. He wouldn't have kept you for an hour if he weren't somewhat interested. So don't worry," she assures me.

Once we're in the well-appointed lobby, I thank Gladys and wish her a good evening. Standing outside, I turn to face the magnificent Jackson Town House. Then lift my gaze to the sky and nod. I did my best. Now, let's wait and see.

* * *

"Ms. Roberts!"

I glance down at the cute little blonde-haired lass and smile.

"Yes?" I ask.

"Can you read the story again? Pretty please!!!" She responds as she clasps her tiny hands together and widens her baby blue eyes.

I can't help but to chuckle at her and to agree with her request.

It's raining this evening, so my volunteer work keeps me indoors. I'm just thankful to have a distraction from worrying about the job at Jackson Corporation. It's been a few days and no word. Isla doesn't even have an update for me.

With a sigh, I re-read the fairytale, enacting the characters the way the children enjoy. Just as I finish, my mobile vibrates. The screen reveals an unknown number, but I answer anyway—fingers crossed.

"Hello?"

"Ms. Katrina Roberts?" The woman asks. When I confirm, she continues. "This is the Human Resources department for Jackson Corporation. Mr. Lachlan Jackson would like to extend an offer to you as his temporary administrative assistant..."

I barely contain my whoop of delight as I hop to my feet and rush from the library at Aberdeen Children's Center. When she finishes, I accept the offer and agree to come in during my lunch hour the next day. We end the call, and I do a jig. Then I send a text message to Isla to thank her and to tell her I'll call once I return home.

The rest of the evening goes by in a blur, my mind on tomorrow. I'll resign after I sign the offer letter. Goodbye to the old prat! Hello to a fresh path!

KAT

"**K**at, kindly come into my office. Thank you."

My heart stutters in my chest at Mr. Jackson's unexpected request. Various scenarios race through my mind: someone detected my unauthorized access to the server; security spotted the listening devices I planted around the offices; tiny cameras found. Bloody hell.

I school my face before I rise from my desk. A surreptitious glance at Gladys doesn't reveal any hint of what I can expect. She's typing on her keyboard while she schedules Mr. Jackson's upcoming trip to South Africa's Coastal Region for visits to their wineries.

Pull yourself together, Kat Roberts! You're too good for them to catch you.

Besides, I've only set up surveillance for now. No need to rush despite Chet's demands for intel like yesterday. This is my play. I will follow my schedule—not to mention my gut that's guided me all these years successfully.

Chester Stewart, aka Chet, the forty-year-old vice president of Stewart Scotch. His family's company is Jackson

Corporation's top competitor. Add on a centuries-old bitter rivalry over some silly noble title the king gave to the Jackson family instead of to the Stewarts, and you've got the perfect partner for me. One that has the resources to supply the costly equipment and connections I need. Plus the millions to pay me.

In researching the Stewarts, I opted to approach Chet instead of Bram—his younger brother by two years and also a vice president. Their father Magnus serves as the CEO and Chairman of the Board. However, it's well known the brothers vie for the lead positions. Their father encourages the competition and will only announce his successor when one of the brothers "proves their worth." And Chet wants the role. Badly.

My thoughts wander back to my first encounter with him as he left his la-di-da men's social club—The Royal Northern & University Club Aberdeen—one evening.

"Chet Stewart, I can help you destroy the Jacksons."

He gawks at me for a moment, surprised by my forthright pronouncement, before he blanks his face. His denim blue eyes do a scan from my Titian head, pausing on my full breasts and curvy hips down to my heels. An appreciative gleam shines in his irises as he zones in on my pretty face. Tilting his head to the side, he responds.

"That's a bold statement, little lass. But I'm a busy man with no time for your game," Chet sneers as he moves past me. Purposefully, his arm brushes the side of my breast.

The arrogant prat.

I pivot and follow him to his Bentley sedan idling at the curb. As he slides in, I slip in behind him.

He starts, then scowls at me.

"Everything all right, sir?" His driver asks as he leans into the door he still holds open.

I arch my eyebrow at Chet and repeat my statement as I cross my long, toned legs.

His eyes track my movement, then lift to search my face. Satisfied with what he sees, Chet nods and tells his chauffeur to drive until instructed otherwise.

The soft thud of the door sends a shudder down my spine. However, I straighten it, determined to prove myself and to set my plan for revenge in motion.

"Yes, Mr. Jackson. I'll be right in, sir," I respond through the intercom in an unruffled tone.

Then I smooth my suit skirt and brush my hand over my hair. I straighten my shoulders and lift my chin, confident my expert hacking skills didn't fail me nor my gut mislead me.

Okay, Katrina Roberts, *smiogaid suas, nighean!*

"Have a seat, Kat," Mr. Jackson says as he nods towards the guest chairs across from his desk.

He watches me approach with an unreadable expression on his handsome face. Once I'm settled on the chair, he leans back in his seat and runs a hand through his silky brown hair.

"You have acclimated well to the company and to your tasks as my administrative assistant in the few months you have worked for me," he begins.

Then he sits forward and folds his hands on the desk's surface. His emerald green eyes seem to stare into my soul.

I have to force my gaze to remain on his face impassively and my body not to fidget under his scrutiny. Again my mind whirls, wondering if he knows something after all.

"—the position on a permanent basis."

I snap back to attention at his words. However, I missed the first part and curse myself silently for allowing my nerves to distract me. With a shake of my head to clear it, I ask Mr. Jackson to repeat himself.

A slight frown appears between his eyebrows but disappears quickly.

"Isla contacted me a short while ago. She and her husband decided she needs to remain home with their newborn and not return to Jackson Corporation after her maternity leave ends. I offer you the position on a permanent basis," he responds. He pauses to gauge my reaction before he continues.

"Also, remember I will take my paternity leave in two months, and you will report to Ms. Jackson. She will split her time between here and New York City. Her administrative assistant will help, too."

Instead of jumping up and double fist pumping in the air, I take a breath and smile.

"Thank you, Mr. Jackson. I appreciate the opportunity and promise to do my absolute best," I respond. While in my mind, I tack on *to ruin your bloody family.*

"Oh, Isla! I'm so happy for you and Gregor! Not to mention delighted to have the position permanently. But only because you're not returning, of course!"

I exclaim with a grin as I curl up on my couch with a glass of wine later that evening.

The time couldn't go by fast enough for me to get out of Jackson Town House to make my calls. The first one goes to Isla.

Oh, Isla…

Little did she know I befriended her as a means to infiltrate Jackson Corporation.

As one of the few employees in the CEO's inner circle

and with the most access, I chose her since we're closest in age and share a commonality of being from less fortunate families. The Aberdeen Children's Center served its purpose. I volunteered since she spends so much time there and would never expect I was after her job.

When she confided her difficulties in getting pregnant, I asked Chet if he had any connections with a reputable fertility doctor. He came through with an appointment with a renown OB-GYN fertility expert and paid the hefty fee. Isla only had a minimal amount to cover. I shared the details —sans payment arrangements—with her. Then poof, she's preggie. And owes me.

Isla fell for the stories about my bosses. Chet arranged my most recent job with managers who would supply recommendations, and in the case of the last one, go along with the prat scenario. The man has many who owe him favors, and he's as manipulative as me.

Now with Lachlan going on paternity leave, I'll move to the next phase of my plan. However, they call his sister *The Shark*—not that her brother is a slouch. So, I'll have to be extra careful with her. At least she'll only be in Aberdeen part time.

Sadly, Isla is right. He's a decent guy and treats his staff well.

I shake my head and admonish myself. *Smiogaid suas, nighean!*

"You deserve it, Kat! Especially after the prat. But if you need help with anything, just let me know. I'm here for you."

Isla's words add to the tiny, tiny nugget of second thoughts. But not enough to change my mind. No.

I make an excuse to end our call. I cannot allow even a modicum of emotion to influence my decision.

With a nod, I pick up one of my many burner phones.

"What have you got for me?"

I roll my eyes and bite back a groan.

This guy here…

"Isla resigned. I have the position permanently and will have something for you shortly," I respond in a clipped manner.

After Chet tried to feel up my leg in the back of the Bentley, he learned the hard way not to fuck with me. We keep things strictly business and our conversations to the minimum.

"It better be soon and worth my time."

I pull the mobile from my ear to stare at the screen.

He hung up.

The bloody prat.

HARRIS

"Hey, preggie twin. You look fantastic, Hot Mama. How're you feeling?"

I flew on Lachlan's Sikorsky S-92 Executive Helicopter to Aberdeen after a week in London at STEELE Technology & Cyber Security offices. With Haley due to give birth next month, we're in the process of reviewing projects and assigning staff to prepare for her maternity leave.

Just as before, with the birth of The Trips, we expect our work to go as planned uninterrupted by her absence. I'll split the month with two weeks at our offices in New York City, followed by two weeks in London.

Knowing Haley, she'll make herself available for video conference meetings within a couple of weeks of giving birth. Sure, she'll have a second nanny. But I'll insist she stay focused on her little family. No need to rush back to business like she did the last time.

Even with our expanding portfolio, I'm confident STCS will continue to prosper.

Haley gives me a wry smile and pats her sizable babies bump.

"Oh, just fine with two cantaloupes battling for space in my belly…" She responds with an arched eyebrow. "But thanks for the compliment."

I chuckle and shake my head.

"Five and counting, huh?" I ask.

She whacks me with the back of her hand and growls.

"No *and counting*, Harris Steele! You better cut it out!" She responds with a glare. "Do not tease your twin like that. And boy, I cannot wait until the shoe is on the other foot! You know karma is a—"

"You-know-what." I interject, nodding my head towards Lilias, Leith, and Lewis, who play on the floor in front of us with Bonnie and Bella—their Golden Retrievers.

WHACK!

"Don't tell me to watch my words! I know, Harris Steele!" She snarls as she cuffs me again.

Mouth agape, I rub my arm and stare at my twin.

The scowl falls from her face, and she opens her arms for a hug.

Warily, I lean over and pat her back.

"Sorry, Har. It's the hormones, and my back bothers me… My legs are all crampy… My ankles swelled up to cricket balls. I'm an absolute mess," she says, then hiccups.

I squeeze her to my chest and rub the back of her ebony haired head.

"It's okay, Hal. I get it. But there's no way you're *an absolute mess*. Heck, you can't be because we look alike, and I'm a handsome devil," I say.

That gets her giggling, and I smile.

I give her another squeeze, then pull back to scan her face.

"Good?" I ask.

She sniffs and nods, dove gray eyes glimmer from the tears.

"All good," Haley responds.

I reach for my laptop and nod for her to pick up hers. We spend the next couple of hours going over work. As I expect, she jumps right in and forgets about her bit of sadness. Like me, Haley loves what she does and thrives on it. We live up to the nickname our brothers gave to us—the Dynamic Duo.

After we're done, I go to my guest suite in Haley and Lachlan's Aberdeen penthouse to change for my lunch with him. As much as I tease Lach, I enjoy hanging out with my cuz-turned-brother-in-law. Not to mention he's the liquor guy!

I go back to Haley's home office and tell her and The Trips I'll see them after lunch when we'll go to the park. Bonnie and Bella yip in excitement since they recognize the word *park*. I grin and scratch them behind their ears. Their feathery tales thump on the floor.

Hey, bro, I'm sitting in the lobby.

A moment passes, then the three dots appear indicating Lachlan is typing a response appear on the screen of my mobile.

On my way down.

I scroll through my email while I wait.

"Mr. Steele? Mr. Harris Steele?"

A soft Scottish lilt says my name like I'm Bond. James Bond.

And like a Bond Girl, this one is stacked. Her prim librarian facade of low heels, stockings, a conservative suit with an A-line skirt and a waist-length jacket, pussy bow blouse, and tortoise-shell glasses fails to hide her bodacious body. Thick, glossy red hair pulled back in a no-nonsense bun. Talk about a scene at LEVELS London. Hot damn!

As my gaze takes in her long legs, grip-worthy hips, ample tits, and lush mouth, her natural beauty takes my breath away. Emerald green eyes stare back at me, unaffected—dare I say bored—by my heated gaze.

I put on my most dazzling, panty dropping smile and mimic her Scottish accent in my deep baritone timbre.

"Aye, bonnie lass. And who might ye be?"

I think I see a flash of something in the depths of those intriguing emerald orbs. But it's gone in, well, a flash.

She squares her shoulders and peers down her nose at me.

Her attempt to show confidence only serves to push her delectable tits out.

I smirk.

Her eyes narrow slightly. Then her face blanks again.

Lady Gaga's "Poker Face," anyone?

"Kat, Mr. Jackson's administrative assistant," she responds.

Oh, fuck me. Why does this one have to work for Lachlan? Damn.

The realization wipes the flirtation from my mind in an instant.

"Mr. Jackson asked me to escort you up to his offices as a call detained him," Kat continues. "Kindly follow me, Mr. Steele."

Without waiting for me to acknowledge her statement, Little Kat pivots and stalks towards the executive floor's elevator.

Okay, Little Kat may be Lachlan's admin. But the sway of

her hips and her round ass call to me like a siren's song. I follow like she's the Pied Piper.

The alluring scent of her perfume fills my nostrils as we stand side by side in the elevator. I guesstimate her height at five feet, eight inches in her two-inch heels since I tower over her by five.

Surreptitiously, I ogle her in my periphery. Wild thoughts of yanking the pins from her bun to free that red mane, hiking her skirt up, and hoisting her long leg around my hip as I drive my hungry ten-inch cock balls deep inside of her wet, willing pussy fill my head.

The ping of the elevator doors opening interrupts my sexy fantasy.

As I follow Little Kat, I adjust my burgeoning length. And avoid staring at her sexy strut.

She knocks on Lachlan's doors and opens them.

"You may enter, Mr. Steele," she says as she steps back.

"Thank you, Kat," I say with a nod. The taste of her name sweetens my mouth.

I step inside, and she closes the doors behind me.

My hand drags down my face as I blow out a long breath.

Fuck. Me.

When I open my eyes, Lachlan stares at me with his head cocked as he continues to speak on the telephone. I shake my head and point to his en suite bathroom. He nods but watches me with a furrowed brow.

Once inside, I fully adjust my cock, then stare in the mirror.

"Did that Little Kat crawl under my skin? Fuck… Am I doomed like my brothers by one glance?" I say aloud to my reflection. Then I grin. "Hell nah! Not this playa, baby!"

I chuckle as I shake my head to dislodge *that* unsavory

thought, rinse my face with cool water, and stride from the bathroom.

Lachlan lifts his gaze from his laptop when I re-renter his office. He lifts an eyebrow questioningly. Then goes back to his call when I wave him off.

I plop down on the leather sofa and grab a magazine to distract myself from the memory of Little Kat's allure. With each flip of the glossy pages, my mind falls back to her glossy red hair. I want to run my fingers through it like they slide across the pages. It's her gorgeous face with its smooth complexion and luminous green eyes that stare back at me from the photos. The scent of her floral perfume still swirls in my nose like a fresh bouquet of roses.

"Earth to Harris!"

I jolt and slam the magazine closed. A guilty flush of crimson climbs up my face as though Lachlan caught me with my nose to the centerfold in *Playboy*. I glance up to find him standing on the other side of the coffee table, frowning at me.

"You didn't hear a word I said. Did you?" He asks as he shakes his head. "And I take it you weren't really reading that magazine, either. Were you?"

I open my mouth for a retort, but glance back at the magazine's title. Oh, fuck me… It's some parenting gibberish. Cold busted like a mug.

To save face, I shrug it off and rise from the sofa.

"I do have nieces and nephews, you know. It never hurts to learn more about taking care of them," I respond, buttoning my Tom Ford suit jacket. "Do you have a problem with that, Little Lord Fauntleroy?"

He snorts and turns towards the double doors of his office.

"Whatever you say, Uncle Harris," Lachlan chuckles.

I follow him out to the reception area and smile at Gladys. But I avoid eye contact with the redhead siren. However, she doesn't get the memo…

"Good day to you, Mr. Steele," she pipes up pleasantly.

Not to be rude, I glance over my shoulder. Her eyes glitter like the gemstones they resemble, while her face remains a cool mask. I nod and mumble a response, sure that my voice would crack like a pubescent boy if I verbalized an answer.

The corners of her lush mouth quirk up briefly before she lowers her head to her laptop.

I turn back and bump into Lachlan, who smirks at me.

We walk to the elevator in silence, only broken by his staff greeting him as we pass. Once inside, he cocks his head at me. After no words from him, I shrug with both hands palms up.

He chuckles. But the doors ping open. He signals for me to go first and follows.

We enter Jackson Restaurant through its lobby entrance. Lucien turned the generations-old eatery into a three Michelin star restaurant that features his versions of traditional Scottish fare. The tantalizing aromas make my stomach growl, reminding me I haven't eaten yet.

The hostess smiles politely at Lachlan but widens it when her eyes land on me. I note she's a pretty brunette with topaz eyes and a slim figure. But no reaction whatsoever.

Well, damn.

I shake my head, confused by my lack of interest.

She leads us to a center table in the bustling dining room filled with the lunch crowd. Several people acknowledge Lachlan's presence—including some women. He ignores their hungry looks as he shakes hands with some others.

The women flick their gazes to me, and I frown. They know Lach is married. His and Haley's wedding was the talk of the UK and worldwide. Thirsty broads, I harrumph.

After we order the day's specials—Lucien's fancy versions of Cock-a-Leekie Soup and Scotch Pie. I take a sip of Jackson Cabernet Sauvignon and settle back in my chair.

"So, what's on your mind?" Lachlan asks with a smirk. "You seemed flustered when you entered my office and when we left. Oh, and before you give me some bollocks story, I would guess it has something to do with Kat."

I choke on my next sip of wine.

He grins like the Cheshire Cat and lifts his Waterford Crystal glass in salute.

"Cold busted, Harris," he chuckles.

I decide the honest route the best course to take. Besides, I have nothing to hide.

"Aren't you Sherlock Holmes, Lachlan old chap?" I smirk as I appraise him over the rim of my wineglass.

The fucker throws his head back and laughs uproariously.

"Hell, I can admit she's an attractive woman. So what? She's your administrative assistant. Therefore, she's hands off," I respond coolly.

Although in the back of my mind, I hope he's not bothered if I am interested. Not saying I'm walking down the aisle or anything like that. Nah! But a good—rather a great —shag sounds about right. Besides, Little Kat may not be interested. Yeah right!

Lachlan makes a wry face and snorts.

"Don't pull that unaffected attitude with me, Harris Steele. I've known you your whole life, bro. She has you in all sorts of ways. And no, she's not hands off. You're not a Jackson, so it's not inappropriate if you pursue her.

However, she's a good AA and I don't need your personal shit fucking up her work. And she's a grown woman who can decide on her own," Lachlan says.

At first, I roll my eyes at him using my full name. Obviously, he's picked up on Haley's habit. But when he gives the all-clear, I grin wolfishly and damn near howl.

He chuckles. Then he threatens my balls if I make Little Kat run for the hills screaming and leave him stranded without an administrative assistant. When I tell him she would scream but not for the reasons he thinks, it's his turn to choke on his wine.

I take a sip from my glass and smirk when it goes down as smooth as silk.

Just as I imagine Little Kat will soon.

KAT

"*K*at, I have a last-minute call. Kindly escort my brother-in-law Harris Steele up from the lobby. He's over six feet tall with jet black hair and gray eyes. Resembles my wife. Thank you."

I acknowledge Mr. Jackson's request and stride towards the elevator.

Harris Steele.

As per my research, he's the last single brother of their family, never pictured with the same woman twice, a brainiac. And bloody hell… More handsome and captivating in person. Even from across the lobby, he exudes the primal sex appeal of an Alpha male who's accustomed to yes and only yes. No way I'd miss that strapping lad.

I have the sudden urge to run my fingers through the longer strands of the glossy ebony hair atop his head. My other palm cups the back of his head, skimming over the shorter sides. I tug as he buries his stunningly handsome face between my quivering thighs. The slight scruff on his cheeks abrades my sensitive skin as he makes a meal of my throbbing pussy—

"Oh! Excuse me, lass! I didn't realize you were stopping so abruptly. Are you all right there?"

A bump from behind jolts me from my erotic reverie.

My hand flies to my chest as I gasp.

I glance around to ensure Harris Steele didn't notice before I nod at the older gentleman. Then smile to reassure him as his dusky blue eyes scan my face. Once he moves on, I straighten my spine and admonish myself for drooling over a relative of the enemy.

But as I near Harris Steele, my steps slow. It won't hurt to observe him while he's distracted by his mobile. Always good to know your enemy in all states. At least that's the reason I claim, not because he's a magnet, and I'm a piece of, well, steel.

His full lips curl up into a smile at something on the screen of his mobile. A laugh rumbles in his chest as he runs his fingers through that hair. And my fingers flex in jealously. My pussy clenches when he draws the corner of his lush mouth between his perfectly straight pearly teeth. I want my lower lips in that mouth. More jealousy strikes, sending a shudder down my spine.

I blink and shake my head.

Pull yourself together, Kat Roberts!

"Mr. Steele? Mr. Harris Steele?" I ask as I quicken my pace to stand before him, seated with his muscular thighs spread wide on a leather sofa. His expensive suit enhances his mouthwatering physique.

Again, I can't stop myself from admiring his masculine beauty.

Below thick eyebrows, dove gray eyes brighten to

molten platinum as his gaze glides over me from my legs to my face.

It takes a Herculean effort for me to school my expression while my thighs press together, my lower belly flutters, and my nipples pebble. But I do. I stare back at him with what I hope is a look of boredom, despite his lust-filled gaze.

My resolve falters when Harris' face lights up with a million-dollar—no, scratch that—a multibillion-dollar smile.

"Aye, bonnie lass. And who might ye be?" He asks with a flawless Scottish accent in a deep baritone timbre.

Forget molten platinum. Melted chocolate drips all over my naked, heated skin as the sensuality of his words engulfs me. A crack forms in my bored visage. Bloody hell, Harris Steele is good!

Stop it, Kat Roberts! Focus.

Once again, I square my shoulders and peer down the bridge of my nose at him. Unfortunately, the movement lifts my full breasts higher.

A smirk replaces his megawatt smile as he enjoys the new view.

I narrow my eyes, then school my face. I refuse to allow him to get to me—more than he already has…

"Kat, Mr. Jackson's administrative assistant," I respond.

Harris' eyes widen, and it's his turn to pull himself together.

My belly flutters again at the expression of disappointment in his dove gray orbs. Well, I guess I'm not the only one who senses an attraction between us. I shake my head. Enough!

"Mr. Jackson asked me to escort you up to his offices as a

call detained him," I continue, proud I pulled it off in my most professional voice. "Kindly follow me, Mr. Steele."

Without waiting for his response, I pivot and walk towards the executive floor's elevator. I dare not glance over my shoulder at him.

A delicious warmth wraps around me as I sense his gaze on my ass while he follows. An extra oomph sways my hips to give this player something to play with. Not saying I want him to play with me, per se.

I do my very best to ignore his covert glances as the lift rises. But the compellingly sensual scent of his cologne—floral, earthy, and vanilla—permeates the air to heighten my unexpected arousal. My lips part to breathe through my mouth as an avoidance. Now, I taste him on my tongue. Hmm, what must his cock taste like? My mouth waters. Bloody hell!

Harris towers over me as I risk a side glance up at him. A slight furrow forms between his eyebrows as he closes his eyes and shakes his head. It gives me a moment to take in his face unseen.

Simply gorgeous.

The lift doors open, along with his eyes.

I avert my gaze and hurry ahead of him. Not soon enough, we arrive at Mr. Jackson's doors. I take a deep breath before I knock and open them.

"You may enter, Mr. Steele," I say as I step back.

"Thank you, Kat," he says with a nod before he steps inside.

With a sigh of relief, I close the doors behind him. My body sags from the sexual tension and the loss of Harris Steele.

"Are you all right, Kat?"

Gladys' question makes me raise my head and re-open my eyes.

I plaster a smile on my face and turn.

"Oh, yes. Just catching my breath. I didn't want Mr. Jackson to wait too long, so I hurried to fetch Mr. Steele," I respond as I head to my desk. "Did I miss a call or anything?"

As Gladys assures me all is well and tells me she appreciates my enthusiasm to please Mr. Jackson, I think the best way to avoid detection is to detract. I don't need her to question my behavior in any way. Remain under the radar, Kat Roberts.

And keep your legs closed!

Moments later, Harris follows Mr. Jackson out to the reception area and smiles at Gladys. He avoids eye contact with me.

Jealousy flares within me.

"Good day to you, Mr. Steele," I say in my most bonny voice. My Scottish lilt rolls off my tongue as a reminder of his mimicry from earlier. However, I maintain a detached expression. No need for him to think I want him.

He glances over his shoulder, nods, and mutters an incoherent response.

My mouth quirks up briefly before I lower my gaze to my laptop. I note how in his haste he bumps into Mr. Jackson, who smirks.

As they walk away, my mind whirls with possibilities.

Well, perhaps I should rethink my strategy.

The single Steele and twin of Mrs. Jackson could prove a boon to assist in the ruination of the Jacksons and perhaps the Steeles too.

I'll use whatever and whoever I can to get what I want.

Revenge. My red hair, pretty face, and curvy body get 'em every time.

Including that Steele sucker.

HARRIS

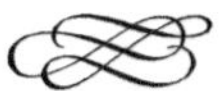

"*And* how's my Hot Mama twin and my newest nephews this bonny morn?"

Haley's smile could light the darkest corner of the most remote Scottish moor during the winter months.

A week ago, she gave birth to the Honourable Stirling Jackson—a city known as the Gateway to the Highlands—and the Honorable Struan Jackson, the Scottish word for stream. She and Lachlan named their twin boys in honor of the Steele name and Lachlan's love of the water and sailing.

We think it's because their eyes bear the Steele trait of gray hues while their ebony waves match ours. As our Mom declared, The Trips look like their Daddy, and The Twins look like their Mama. I say both sets are absolute perfection, just like my twin.

"Oh, Harris! We're fantastic. A wee bit tired, but great nonetheless," Haley says with a weary grin.

I bend down and press my lips to the top of her head. She leans into me and sighs.

"You look fantastic, too," I say as I stand and grin at her.

"I told Little Lord Fauntleroy I would escort you and the little lads to brunch. Shall we?"

I bow and raise my hand to her.

Haley giggles and takes it, then curtsies.

"Why thank you, dear brother. You are so kind," she replies.

I gather Stirling and Struan into my arms while Haley loops her hand around my biceps. As we walk to the elevator, she tells me about their latest achievements. Struan lifted his head while on his tummy. Stirling acknowledged Haley wiggling her fingers at him from a foot away. I crack they're smarter than their *Da*, then chuckle when she whacks me.

"Guess who's here!"

"Oh, sweetheart, you're flushed!"

"Bonjour, chérie!"

As always, the entire Steele and Jackson clans, along with the Beaulieus and Knights, flew in for the birth, and over the next few weeks, some will remain, and others will return. To allow Haley to bask in motherhood, I plan to work from STEELE London and stay Friday evening through Monday morning here at Aboyne Castle. My babysitting duties will kick up to the next level with the addition of The Twins. However, their two nannies will be of the utmost help, naturally. No poo and wee nappies for Uncle Harris to change!

"So, week one down. How do you and Lachlan feel with five tykes?" Baz asks with a smirk.

"Yeah, the newly crowned Big Papa. Tell us all about it," Malcolm adds with a chuckle.

Lachlan grins and runs a hand through his hand.

"Not as debonair now," I say with a chuckle at the disheveled *Da*.

He laughs, and everyone joins in.

"No, but I couldn't be happier. You should try it soon, Harris," Lachlan responds. Then adds with a smirk, "You may find yourself a bonny lass while you're here."

"Yeah, like that New York Lotto commercial. *Hey, you never know!*" Roger chimes in.

Laurent shakes his head and grumbles, "Yeah, tell me something I don't know…"

Outwardly, I roll my eyes. But I have to admit to myself since I first saw Little Kat last month, I can't get her out of my head. She stunned me then and left an impression so deep, I haven't entertained another woman. I've left LEVELS New York unfulfilled.

So, yeah, I don't mind in the least working out of London and staying in Aberdeenshire. Both give me access to the redhead siren, who taunts me in my dreams. Not to mention the fact her less than enthusiastic reaction to me poses a challenge. It's rare a woman doesn't throw herself at me, or at the very least, displays a spark of interest.

Lachlan may be on to something more than he realizes.

* * *

"Ah, hello, Ms. Roberts. What keeps you late at the office?"

She yelps and spins around. Her tortoise-shell frame glasses slip down the bridge of her nose. A flush creeps across her cheeks as she presses a palm to her ample tits.

I raise an eyebrow questioningly.

"Oh, Mr. Steele. I—I didn't hear you. Excuse me," she says breathlessly.

The rise and fall of her chest distracts me.

She angles her body to showcase her curves fully. With a

shy smile, she stares up at me from beneath her thick fringe of eyelashes.

"I was so caught up in my filing, I must have lost track of the time. What is the hour, Mr. Steele?" She responds. Her emerald green irises glint in the light.

I swallow around the sudden lump in my throat, then slide my suit jacket sleeve back to glance at my Audemars Piguet The Royal Oak Complication watch. Clearing my throat, I tell her it's half past seven.

Little Kat gasps and widens her eyes. Her breathing speeds up again and I find myself staring at the wall behind her to avoid ogling her heaving rack.

"Oh, my! Time sneaked up on me. I'll just finish up on Monday," she says, then pauses. "What brings you here, Mr. Steele? Might I help you with something?"

The inflection of her voice makes me wonder at a double meaning. I cock my head to the side and bring my eyes to hers.

"Well, since you asked so nicely, Mrs. Roberts, Mr. Jackson asked me to pick up something for him before I continue on to the castle," I respond. "I'll be sure to tell him how diligent you are in his absence."

Lachlan started his paternity leave and left Lydie in charge. Since she had a dinner meeting, I volunteered to bring files to him.

What a delightful surprise to find Little Kat.

"Thank you, but not necessary," she says with a smile as she leaves his office.

The scent of her perfume wafts through the air when she steps past me. Fascinated, I turn to watch as she struts to her desk. The loose-fitting skirt does nothing to hide the curves of her ass and hips as she bends over to retrieve her handbag and attaché from the bottom drawer.

"Mrs. Roberts," I call out.

She stands and faces me.

"Would you care to join me for a drink downstairs at Jackson Restaurant? I'll only be a moment," I ask, pinning her with an intense stare that leaves no room for argument.

Slowly, she blinks and brings her gaze back to mine. The tip of her little pink tongue pokes out to moisten her lush lips.

"Yes, that sounds lovely, Mr. Steele," Little Kat purrs.

My cock jumps. And expel the breath I didn't realize I was holding in.

"Mr. Steele is my father. Harris will do, Kat," I say thickly.

She nods and responds, "Harris, then. I just need to pop into the ladies' room to freshen up, then will meet you by the lift. Good?"

"Indeed," I say. "Although you are *lovely*, Kat."

The scarlet flush reappears on her alabaster skin.

Briefly I muse if her round derriere will appear the same shade should I spank that ass.

She must sense my colorful thought since her cheeks deepen to crimson before she scampers away.

I chuckle wickedly and readjust my burgeoning erection, ready to poke a hole in my bespoke trousers.

Minutes later, I extend my elbow to her as we exit the elevator in the lobby. At this hour, the staff closed the lobby entrance for the restaurant. I lead Little Kat into the cool summer night to the main entrance.

While she was in the restroom, I called the host to reserve one of the high tables by a window in the bar. He shows us to our seats, and I help Little Kat into a tall leather and wrought-iron chair. She graces me with a beatific smile as she thanks me.

A server appears to take our order.

I'm surprised when she orders a neat Jackson Special Reserve Scotch. Impressed, I request one.

"Good choice, Mr.... Er... Harris," she says as her emerald eyes sparkle in the light of the candles on the table. "A man after my own heart."

I smirk and nod.

"A woman after mine," I counter as I give her a heated stare. "Now, what would you like to nosh? I wouldn't want you to think I'd get you drunk and take advantage of you."

Her tinkling laughter floats around us. The sound fills my heart with joy.

"Oh Harris, I would never think such a thing of a man like you. Despite you being a notorious billionaire playboy. Oh, no!" She scoffs gleefully.

Ouch, that stung.

So that's what Little Kat thinks of me? Hmmm. Not the best. But not the worse either, I suppose. But I need to change her perception of me in my way.

"Correction: multibillionaire, little lass. Is it so horrible I have no inkling to settle down? Does that make me a play-boy? Really?" I question.

She pauses her answer as the server places our drinks in front of us and takes our food order. Once she steps away, Little Kat leans across the round table and pats my shoulder.

"Duly noted. I wouldn't say horrible. However, I would think it's unfulfilling to go from one woman to the next that never satisfies your heart and soul," she says. Then she sits back and adjusts the napkin on her lap. "But I do not judge you and your needs, Harris."

She glances up at me from beneath her thick eyelashes. Her eyes scan my face for a reaction.

It's a bit of a blow and not the response I expected. It certainly doesn't change her perception of me. At. All.

I bite my lower lip and nod.

"No worries. Perhaps I have not met the one woman who will satisfy me in every way?" I say, then pin her with an intense stare. "Or perhaps I have?"

I let the question hang in the surrounding air. A shift in the atmosphere heightens the sexual tension between us.

Little Kat likes her lips and swallows as her gaze drops to her lap again.

In a blink, she meets my stare with one of her own as she raises an elegantly arched eyebrow.

"By the end of this evening, we shall see," she rejoins.

Challenge accepted, Little Kat.

We spend the rest of our time asking about our families, favorite pastimes, and other getting to know you on a first date questions.

It strikes me in a not so unpleasant way that our time together indeed resembles a date and not a precursor to fucking. Not that I'd mind getting Little Kat writhing beneath me. The carnal sounds of her purrs and her moans amplified as I pound balls deep within her soaking wet pussy. My cock thumps in approval of the thought.

But like most first dates, tonight is not the time to shag my bonny lass.

However…

"Would you care to have dinner with me tomorrow evening, Kat?" I ask.

Once more, I stun her, and she blinks.

What seems like hours pass before she offers a shy smile and nods.

"That would be wonderful, Harris, thank you," she

responds. A frown mars her beautiful face. "But aren't you headed to the castle now?"

I shrug and take the last sip of my Scotch.

"My plan will change if you're interested," I respond as I watch her over the rim of the Waterford Crystal snifter.

The liquid goes down as nicely as her response.

"Oh, I *am* interested, Harris," she purrs, then finishes her drink with a smile.

"Well, then, it's settled. Where shall I pick you up at eight?" I ask in a deep rumble.

She recites her address and phone number as I type them into my mobile.

After my driver and I drop Little Kat at home, he takes me back to STEELE Aberdeen. The door to my suite shuts, and I strip as I hasten to the shower. My aching cock can't wait another second for relief.

Warm water sluices over my tense muscles as I press my palms against the marble wall of the Roman shower. My head hangs with eyes closed as I drum up a vision of my Little Kat kneeling naked before me.

Her flaming red hair plastered to her head and down her back. Strands kiss the top of her ass. Long eyelashes spiked from the water cast shadows on her cheeks, pinkened by the steam. The enticing fragrance of her arousal and pheromones fill my nostrils as I take a deep inhalation. The scent imprinted on my brain.

My cock thickens and lengthens to jut proudly toward her lush lips, parted to allow its entry. I fist the base and stroke the velvet-covered steel shaft. A smirk spreads across my face as she watches my movements with emerald eyes darkened to malachite with carnal lust. I tap the mushroom tip against her mouth, and a drop of pre-cum falls to her bottom lip.

Her little tongue darts out to lick my essence into her mouth.

She hums and closes her eyes in bliss.

I groan.

"Open wide for me, Little Kat," I command. My voice gruff with desire.

Her eyes open, then narrow seductively as she does my bidding.

The wet warmth of her tongue wraps around my girth. She teases the vein on the underside with the flat of her tongue and hums in delight. A delicate hand cups my heavy balls and kneads them.

My hands slip into her tresses to cup the back of her head. Shifting my stance, I hold her head as I drive to the back of her throat with one snap of my hips. Her gag spurs me on.

"Open your throat for me, Little Kat. I want my bulge outlined in it," I growl.

She moans in response.

I slip deeper down her slim throat. It's a snug fit, but she works it with ease, accustomed to my demands.

"Make me cum, Little Kat," I command. "Swallow every single drop of what I give to you. Understand?"

She nods and hums as tears slip down her flushed cheeks. The slippery sounds of her taking every one of my ten inches echo around us. The rhythmic slapping of my balls to her chin reverberates off the marble. Her drool mixes with the water.

I throw my head back and bellow.

My release damn near knocks me to my knees. I slap the shower wall with one palm while the other jerks my cock viscously. Copious jets of cum shoot out of my angry purple cockhead to smatter against the marble. It drips to the floor.

"Every fucking drop, Little Kat," I growl.

The vision of her smiling up at me as the last of my jizz flows down her throat to fill her belly dances behind my closed eyelids.

I groan and press my sweaty forehead to the cool marble.

"Soon, Little Kat, my dreams will become our reality."

KAT

"Hi, Mum, I won't be able to come home this weekend after all... I know. I'm sorry. But I have an important dinner tonight... Work related—"

"What the bloody hell, Kat?! Ever since you got that hoity-toity job, you act like you're too good to spend time with your family! Now you have Mum all upset. Again!"

My mouth drops open at my older brother's rant. His accent thickens the more he goes on and on. Nothing new there.

Payton seethes since he lost another job and still lives at home with our mother's support. If he would do something with his bloody life like I have with mine, he wouldn't hate on me. Well, then again, he'd still find something to complain about and start a fight. As usual.

I'm sure he was counting on me bringing the cash I give to my mother each month. Without a doubt she gives him some, if not all, of it every. Single. Time. When I call her out on her charity to Payton with the money I earned, Mum uses the same excuses he does for his lack of work. The boss

"

treated him poorly; his co-worker crashed the delivery van; the customer lied on him.

And here he is yelling at me for not coming home. Give me a bloody break!

But I haven't missed many of my monthly visits to Glasgow since I left home for school years ago. Do I enjoy being back in the little flat? Uh, no. I go because they're my family. The only one I have and the connection to them is important.

If only Payton would stop his madness.

"—Charlotte came home from university. You can't make it from work?! What? Your time is more valuable than any of ours?!"

"Zip it, Payton! If you'd get off *your* high horse, maybe you'd keep a *job* longer than four bloody days!" I snarl. "Now, give the phone back to Mum. Or. I. Will. Hang. Up."

Silence.

Heavy breathing.

A snarl.

"Who the bloody hell do you—"

"Enough, Payton Roberts… Kat, it's Mum. I just miss you, lass. But I understand. Come home when you can. We love you," my mother says.

I swallow around the tears that clog my throat.

"Sorry, Mum. I love you more than anything. It will be better soon. I promise. Talk to you next week," I whisper.

My fingertips swipe at the tears as they flow down my flushed cheeks. I close my eyes and visualize how our lives will improve once I get the millions from Chet Stewart.

No more cleaning after rich families for my mother. I'll move her into a gorgeous flat and hire a maid to clean for her! Michael will study architecture in a formal university program. Charlotte won't have to work as a part-time server at a pub and as a tutor while she finishes her degree. Payton, well, he'll have to work and prove he will not squander money I'd give to him.

Me? I'll have the financial security I've always wanted and travel the world for a year. Unwind and do nothing but follow the sun. No worries.

A deep breath clears my head.

I open my Swiss bank app on my mobile and smile when I see the balance in my secret account. Chet was true to his word and deposited a lump sum of six figures when I delivered my last intel.

Jackson Corporation has a new launch for a Scotch blend the master distiller has worked on for the past sixty years. It's a limited-edition run in a custom hand-blown Lalique Crystal bottle with a storage box made of the most rare and most expensive African Blackwood. The price tag? A whopping one-million pounds.

Clearly, I couldn't get the recipe. But I was able to uncover the launch plans and other details Chet agreed were worth the hefty sum he paid to me. He didn't tell me how he plans to use the intel. Undoubtedly, he will use it to Stewart Scotch's advantage and sting Jackson Corporation.

Not my concern. Only the dollars matter, along with the pleasure I derive from knowing he hurt that family makes a difference in my life.

I click the transfer confirmation button on the bank app to send the first of several deposits for the monthly money to my mother's account. To avoid a money trail, I set up increments that won't draw attention. Plus, the transactions go through quite a few channels after my account before they end up in hers. One can't be too careful.

With a sigh, I log out of the app and power off the mobile for my family and banking. I toss it onto the table.

Later I'll put it back in the lockbox beneath the floorboards in the closet.

I pick up my everyday mobile and click the phone icon to call Isla. Oddly enough, what started as a ruse turned into a genuine friendship. I don't keep many friends—better to remain aloof. But find I enjoy spending time with Isla.

"Kat! How are you?" She asks after one ring.

A broad smile stretches across my face as I sit back on the sofa and tuck my legs beneath me to settle in for our chat.

"Good! How's everything with you? Tell me all about the babe's latest developments," I respond.

Isla gushes on about her new little family and the joys of motherhood. Her happiness is contagious. By the time we end our call, my disposition brightens, and the argument with Payton fades.

I head to the Aberdeen Children's Center for my Saturday volunteer sessions. With the school year complete, fewer kids show on the weekend. But those who do still need us to spend time with them. Even more so since they must not have summer activities or time with their families to occupy them. Reminding me of myself at their ages. I love helping those kids even more.

By the time I return home, I need a shower after hours of kickball, potato sack races, hide and seek... Whatever they had in mind, we did it and then some. But it was just what I needed to keep my mind off dinner tonight with Harris Steele.

That man is a god.

Powerful, handsome, sexy AF.

But he's one with the enemy.

Yet the idea of him makes my nether region sing.

Ugh!

The steamy shower does nothing to wash that man out of my head. If anything, it makes me wonder what shower sex with him would be like. My back slams against the subway tile. Ankles crossed behind his firm ass. Screams pour from my gaping mouth as he pummels my pussy with his massive cock.

Fuck!

I slide my hand down the flat expanse of my belly. Fingers slip between my swollen lower lips. Moisture from my arousal coats them as they glide along my seam to pinch my engorged clit. The zing curls my toes. My other hand cups my heavy breast while my thumb and index finger tug the turgid nipple. A second finger joins the first as they fuck my tight, wet pussy in the way I imagine Harris Steele would with his dick.

A true wail bounces off the shower walls when my climax knocks me sideways.

I lean my shoulder against the tile. My pants puff the steam around my head as shudders wrack my limp body. I dial down the heat to cool off.

"You look lovely, Kat."

"Thank you, Harris," I respond as I glance down at my outfit.

Not sure of what to expect, I chose a wrap mini dress in lilac chiffon with tonal sequins and a plush velvet belt. The length accentuates my long, toned legs while the v-neck draws attention to my décolletage. The blouson sleeves and loose fit keep it classy. Paired with iridescent lilac slingbacks and a green clutch, the look can fit in any occasion.

I bring my eyes back to his and smile as I toss my hair over one shoulder and down my back. Not the style I wear for work. But this isn't work, is it? And if I want to hook this playboy, I need to bring it.

His heated stare confirms I did well with my selection.

"Come," he says.

We leave my flat with his hand on my lower back.

I note the possessive move and can't say it displeases me. At. All.

With a courteous dip of his head, the driver opens the back door of the Rolls-Royce sedan. I slip inside. My thighs slide along the supple leather seat. Violins from a classical music score flows from the high-quality sound system. An inhale fills my nose with the decadent scent of Harris' cologne. I close my eyes for a moment to revel in it.

"Are you all right?"

His deep baritone voice and the weight of his sizable hand on my bare thigh rouse me.

A slow smile spreads across my face.

"Yes," I respond.

"Good. I want you to enjoy yourself this evening," Harris murmurs as his dove gray eyes dilate. "I have plans for you."

A shiver makes my nipples poke against the fabric of my mini dress.

His eyes drop, and he licks his full lips.

I swallow thickly and nod.

Am I out of my depths with this one? Oh, do I hope so.

To steer the conversation to safer territory, I ask him about his choice of music. For the rest of the ride, our conversation stays away from riskier subjects. Yet the undercurrent of sexual tension hangs in the air.

The sedan pulls up in front of Moonfish Cafe on Correction Wynd—the popular one Michelin star restaurant. I've always wanted to eat here, but they have a notorious wait list for reservations. One needs to know someone to even sign on for a spot six months out. And here Harris invited me only last night. Of course, he'd get in with ease.

The valet opens the door, and Harris steps out. He reaches back inside to help me from the car.

I grin to myself when his eyes light on my thighs. With care, I keep them closed to avoid a snafu and slip from the seat. His powerful hand lifts me to my feet. I lean into him to catch another whiff of his masculine scent.

The maître d' glances up as we enter. She smiles in welcome at me. Then her dark brown eyes gleam when her gaze lands on Harris behind me.

"Mr. Steele, welcome to Moonfish Cafe, sir!" She gushes as her caramel cheeks flush. "Mr. McFarley told me to expect you. I'll show you to the sought-after table in the kitchen. You'll have the pleasure of watching the chef prepare your meal. Unless you require anything else, kindly follow me, sir."

She flutters her long eyelashes as she stares up at Harris.

I bite down on my molars to prevent a retort from escaping. Gratification comes when he squeezes my hip and tells her he's good.

As we pass through the restaurant, I notice other women ogle Harris. Some even seated with men of their own. The brazen hussies! Once again, he makes it all about me and disregards their blatant stares as he keeps his hand on my lower back. It doesn't hurt some men turn to gaze at me. Vindicated, I raise my head high and sashay behind the hostess.

"Steele! Good to see you again, mate."

A man with a full beard, wire-rimmed spectacles, and shoulder-length hair approaches us as we enter the bustling kitchen. So captivated by the tantalizing aromas, I almost missed him.

"McFarley! I didn't expect to see you tonight. How's your beautiful Edith?" Harris asks as the two men bro hug.

They exchange pleasantries before Harris introduces me as his date.

Butterflies swirl in my belly, and I barely hear the owner of Moonfish Cafe tell us he has a tasting menu the chef designed for our dinner. The fact I'm on a date with one of the world's richest bachelors excites me more than I care to admit. It makes my focus on using Harris more complicated. However, pretending to be attracted to him will be super easy.

I start to admonish myself but decide to give in to the moment and bask in the benefits of being on the arm of a man like Harris Steele. And being the focus of his attention. As I am now with him staring into my eyes intently.

"Have you been here before, Kat?" He asks as he extends his hand across the table.

I place mine within his and shake my head.

"Never. It's impossible… Well, not for you apparently," I start with a giggle. "It's been on my list for a while. Thank you for bringing me here."

Harris rubs his thumb over my inner wrist.

The sensual touch causes goosebumps to scatter across my skin. I bite my lower lip and glance up at him through my eyelashes.

His eyes flash like lightning, then narrow in on my mouth.

Purposefully, I let my lip pop out from between my teeth and flick my tongue across it.

A growl rumbles deep in his chest.

"What you do to me, Siren," Harris says gruffly.

He brings my palm to his mouth and kisses it. His eyes never leave my face.

"Tell me," I say, suddenly bold from his attraction to me.

He lowers his eyelids, and the lashes—long and thick enough to make women jealous—fan across the tops of his cheeks. When he raises his gaze back to mine, his hooded eyes reveal more than words could ever convey.

The chef appears, and Harris lets go of my hand.

The loss of contact makes me sigh.

While the chef explains the dishes and accompanying wines, Harris locks his eyes on me with a carnal stare. He's more interested in devouring me than any item the chef offers. Harris nods his head and licks his lips. Nothing and no one disrupts his stare.

The attention unsettles me in a good way. My pussy clenches, and I have to shift in my chair, concerned my thong may not provide enough coverage to prevent a damp spot. I avert my gaze to the chef.

Not to be denied, Harris uses the top of his shoe to snag my calf. He lifts my leg until his hand catches it. Deft fingers knead the muscles.

I bite back a groan of pleasure.

When he slips my slingback off and runs his knuckles along my instep, a gasp escapes my mouth. I bring my wine-glass to my lips as cover. He smirks wolfishly.

The chef leaves us.

"Ready for a delicious meal, Siren?" Harris asks in a sinfully deep timbre. "Or shall we skip to dessert?"

I choke on my sip of wine.

Real cool, Kat Roberts…

He rises in a flash and uses his napkin to dab at the liquid on my chest.

My nipples pebble to the point of pain.

"Careful, Siren. We want you at full capacity," he says as he crouches at eye level.

I swallow.

"I'm fine, thank you," I whisper.

"Indeed you are, Siren," he murmurs.

I watch as he returns to his seat.

Our server brings another linen napkin to him and offers a glass of seltzer for me to clean the wine from my mini dress.

Another server sets our first course before us.

I glance across to Harris for a clue.

If he lifts his fork, I will too. But if he wants dessert, I am all for it.

Disappointment washes over me when he places the napkin in his lap and reaches for his knife and fork.

Darn…

Throughout the meal, erotic energy pulsates between us. To heighten the attraction, I moan around a forkful of Thai Prawns with Miso Brown Rice. His nostrils flare.

"Come," Harris says as he pushes his chair back from the table.

I arch an eyebrow.

He extends his hand.

I take it and rise.

He pulls me onto his lap, uncaring of those around us as they move about the kitchen. I no longer care about them when the massive bulge of his erection presses against the curve of my hip. He purrs in my ear.

"I want to feel the vibration of your moans as I feed you, Siren," he states.

My head jerks, and my mouth gapes.

He takes advantage of my surprise and pops a morsel of his steak into my mouth. The juices dribble from his fingertips to my lip. He leans forward and licks the drops off. With a groan, he nips my lower lip.

"Even more succulent," he purrs.

Surprise turns to shock, and my mouth remains agape.

Harris chuckles wickedly. His fingertips come below my chin and press up to close my mouth. As I chew, his thumb brushes my lips while his eyes bore into mine.

"Good, girl," he says in a smokey voice.

I mewl.

Harris continues to feed me from both of our plates until I'm too full. Then he finishes what I left and brings his fingers to my mouth for me to lick them clean. All the while, I sit on his lap.

The servers clear our plates, and the chef returns to present the dessert.

Too enthralled with each other to hear the details, Harris and I listen barely. His hand rests beneath the hem of my mini dress with his fingertips grazing my inner thigh. When the chef finishes, Harris spoons some of the dessert into my mouth. The erotic feeding continues between sips of Jackson Scotch.

"Satisfied, Siren?" Harris asks when we finish.

"Yes, thank you," I reply, my voice low and throaty.

"Excellent," he says. "Let us get you home."

Once again, my mouth falls open.

Home? What the bloody hell?

He wound my body tighter than a gnat's chuff!

Harris chuckles, and I realize I spoke aloud.

I drop my head to his shoulder and groan in embarrassment.

"Thank you for a lovely evening," he murmurs with his lips pressed to my hair. "Will you have dinner with me next Friday? I promise I will make it worth your while, Siren."

Despite the disappointment of not having him pound my pussy with the monster against my hip, a thrill runs through me at his proposal. Even though a week seems so far away… I understand he works in London, so I'll deal.

I raise my head and smile.

"I had a lovely evening too and look forward to your promise, Harris Steele," I respond.

HARRIS

"*N*ow, do tell me what restaurant requires us to board a helicopter, Harris?"

I grin like the Cheshire Cat at Little Kat as she approaches me atop STEELE Aberdeen.

Her eyebrow quirks up as she cocks her head to the side. Emerald eyes glint with excitement.

"The kind that takes longer to get to than a drive in the car," I reply. Then I take her elbow to guide her to the open door of Lachlan's Sikorsky S-92 Executive Helicopter. "Hop aboard, Siren."

She returns my grin with a dazzling one of her own as she climbs the steps.

I hated ending our first date without her writhing beneath me. But I wanted to gauge her reaction to my advances. If she rebuked them, then we wouldn't go any further. Except I know for a fact I wouldn't give up so easily.

This woman intrigues me like no other.

Not only does she stay on my mind, a sense of loss when we're apart overtakes me. I shake my head as I recall Baz telling me when I fall, I'll fall hard, just like he did for Lola after one glance. At the time, I scoffed at his declaration. Now, I wonder.

The dinner last week was a good barometer. She blossomed from a demure librarian to a sexy AF Siren. That dress was a hot number. She even ditched the eyeglasses. A complete 180. Her body so responsive, she warmed beneath my touch and ate from my hand like a baby bird. By the end of our night, I struggled to leave her at the flat's doorstep.

This time—little does My Siren know it's not just for dinner, but for the entire weekend—will push it to the limits. No holds or positions barred. If we end up wanting more of each other after this tryst, we're golden.

One thing I learned from my brothers and from my twin, the heart always knows when it comes to love.

Love?

Well, maybe I won't go that far just yet. But it is one step —the first of many, many more—away from my playboy card for sure. I've never felt so inclined with any other woman. So I'll give it a chance to unfold.

To repeat Roger: *Hey, you never know…*

"The pilot is ready for lift off when you are, Mr. Steele."

The flight attendant's comment brings me back to the cabin.

I glance at Kat beside me in a leather captain's chair. She smiles, and I turn to the flight attendant with an affirmative nod. He leaves us and closes the privacy door that separates the crew from the passengers.

"Where are we headed?" Kat asks as she glances out the window at Aberdeen below.

"It's a surprise," I reply, waggling my eyebrows. "So sit back and enjoy the stunning view. I certainly intend to do so."

Her alabaster cheeks blush.

I brush my thumb over one. She has the softest silky skin.

She closes her eyes and leans into my touch with a sigh.

"Okay, you got me," My Siren whispers.

Little does she know.

"HOLY COW! Are you serious with me right now? This is much more than a car ride, Harris!"

If I thought Kat's emerald eyes bugged out when the helicopter landed beside my Gulfstream G650ER private jet at Aberdeen International Airport, they damn near fall out at Jersey Airport.

Since I couldn't reveal my intention to fly her away for the weekend, I had to opt for a destination that would not require her to present a passport. Not officially a part of the UK, the Bailiwick of Jersey is one of the Channel Islands known as a Crown Dependency. Situated in the English Channel between the UK and France, Jersey offers the perfect weekend retreat.

Plus, it has STEELE Jersey, a five-star restored manor house built in the fourteenth century. A boutique property comprising only twenty rooms and suites set on twenty pristine acres with gardens, swimming pool, tennis court, and spa. Guests can charter its luxury yacht to cruise the English Channel. STEELE Jersey provides an ideal intimate —dare I say—romantic escape.

One can never say Harris Steele doesn't know how to charm a woman.

Except this woman scowls at me.

"I assumed we were going far, but to another country?!" Kat screeches as she jabs a finger at the airport signage.

"Well, you know the old adage about when you *assume*. And what a bonny ass I see," I reply with a smirk.

She spins and shoots emerald daggers at me. Her arms fold beneath her tits, and they jiggle under her silk pussy bow blouse when she stomps her foot.

How cute.

Since she arrived straight from the office, she's back in her librarian garb.

I'll soon divest her of the suit. That is, after a bit of role play.

"Is it really so bad to spend the weekend with me, Kat?" I ask with an arched eyebrow.

A flurry of emotions blankets her face. Her eyes dart from me to the jet and back. Teeth worry her lower lip.

I wait. The decision is hers.

She nods her head.

"Words, Kat. I will have your words," I say.

Her eyes widen at my command.

"Y—Y—Yes, Sir," she stammers.

Now I nod my head.

"Not Sir, Kat. I'm an Alpha male but not a Dom. And you, lass, are no sub," I correct her. "Let's get going. I am starved…"

Her cheeks turn crimson, and she agrees, verbally. Good girl.

I take her hand and lead her to the awaiting platinum Rolls-Royce Wraith convertible with white leather interior.

She slips inside when I open the passenger door. Then grabs my hand as I step away.

"Thank you, Harris. It's a wonderful surprise," Kat says softly.

I lean over and slant my mouth over hers. My tongue flicks inside as she gasps. It sweeps around to gather her flavor—buttery and malty flavors of Scotch—before her tongue dances with mine.

We groan in unison.

My hand cups the back of her head to angle it for a deeper kiss. Electricity shoots through our connection. The pent-up passion flares hot.

"Taste so sweet," I murmur against her plump lips.

She mewls and laps at my mouth like a kitten.

Kitty Kat.

I may not be a Dom. But I wouldn't mind my diamond collar around her graceful neck.

My Kitty Kat. Mine!

I nip her lip and rise.

Blown pupils stare up at me as she sucks the bite.

A feral growl falls from my mouth.

The ride to STEELE Jersey can't end fast enough. The entire time, my erect ten inches tents my trousers. I keep Kat's hand on my thigh with her pinky finger resting against the base of my pole. She doesn't squirm.

So far, so good.

The general manager meets us in the lobby to escort us to the Lord's Suite. Situated on the manor's grounds, it's a private stone cottage with two bedrooms with en suite bathrooms and closets of new clothes for us, a lounge, and a kitchen. Panoramic views of the gardens and of the English Channel lie beyond the mullioned windows. The cottage will serve as our own little world. A hideaway within the retreat.

"Oh, Harris! So gorgeous," My Kitty Kat exclaims.

I cock an eyebrow and retort, "Why thank ye, lass. I am a bonny lad."

She giggles and swats my arm as she shakes her head.

"I mean the cottage, silly!" She says, then winks. "However, Harris Steele, I agree you are a bonny lad."

The general manager chuckles.

I forgot he was still here. A quick thank you, and he's gone.

Alone. At last.

I prowl towards My Kitty Kat. The wolf and the cat face off. I growl as I pull her into my arms and cover her mouth with mine.

She melds her soft, curvy body against my hard, muscular frame. A purr vibrates from between her kiss-swollen lips when I suck on her tongue.

"Tell me. What do you want, Kitty Kat?" I growl.

"You, Harris. Only you," she breathes.

I sweep her from her feet and carry her to the primary bedroom. My heart pounds with each step. Without a doubt, she must feel its rapid beat against her pillowy tits.

Beside the king-size bed, I let her slide down my body until she lands on her feet. My hands glide along her flanks to rest at her hips. Once again, I devour her mouth. Her hungry moans spur me on. My fingers dig into the soft flesh.

"I want you. I crave you, Kitty Kat," I utter in a hoarse whisper, barely audible.

She shudders. Her tits jiggle against my chest.

"Please," she cries.

Deftly, I disrobe her and toss the offensive garments to the side. No time for role play tonight. I want to bury myself balls deep within My Siren. Librarian be damned.

Bared before me, My Siren takes my breath away.

Luscious DD-cup tits tipped with rosy pink distended nipples make my mouth water. The flat expanse of her belly leads to a smooth mound. Pussy lips drip with her juices as her engorged clit peeks from between them. Grip-worthy hips add to her hourglass figure. Long, toned legs beg to wrap around my hips and lock at the slim ankles. Even the fire-engine red polish on her toenails calls to me.

Her siren song plays in my ears.

MINE!

I take her mouth in a savage kiss to conquer her once and for all. The searing kiss ends, and I nip, lick, and suck my way down her throat. She swallows, and the sensation sparks against my lips. My head dips to one plump nipple. I engulf it. Then suck. Hard.

She groans from the pain-tinged pleasure and bows her back. Pushing her tit deeper into my hungry mouth.

I want to fuck her until I can't walk. Until I'm blinded by my orgasm, and I pass out.

My Siren must sense my need and tears at my suit jacket. The buttons of my custom dress shirt scatter to the hardwood floor as she rends the front in two. It hangs open, only held together by the cuff links at the sleeves. Her tiny fingers tug at my belt and zipper until my rock-hard cock bounces free to thump against my eight-pack abs.

Pre-cum dribbles from its purple tip.

"Oh my God, you're huge!" She pants. "I—I don't know if you'll fit. I—I haven't had sex in a while—"

My mouth descends on hers to stop her babbling. I possess every inch of her mouth until she sighs and leans against me heavily.

I lift her up and toss her onto the bed where she bounces amongst the countless fluffy pillows. With my eyes on hers, I toe off my Oxfords, remove my cufflinks, and rip the rest of my shirt off. My trousers follow it to the floor.

One knee plants on the bed as I reach over and grasp her ankles.

"Spread your legs for me, My Siren," I demand.

They fall open to reveal her engorged clit and the glistening pink petals of her pussy. Her juices coat her inner thighs.

I descend on her bounty.

My tongue, teeth, and fingers coax three orgasms from My Siren before I deem her ready to take my length and girth. I want her sore from my fucking. But not in pain.

I kiss my way up her body until our mouths meet again. I make My Siren taste her pussy juices still fresh in my mouth as I drive my tongue between her slack lips.

She moans and sucks the musky flavor.

My hips settle between her thighs, and my forearms frame her gorgeous face flushed from her erotic pleasure. I cradle her head against my palms. Otherwise, my first thrust will send her flying towards the headboard. I. Want. Her. Bad.

My tip notches to her core.

"Open up and let me in, My Siren," I command.

She trembles but relaxes beneath me.

I surge forward with a snap of my hips.

One thrust impales her on my condom-covered dick.

She wails at the massive invasion.

My hips still to allow her pussy to adjust to my size. I cover her face and mouth with hungry kisses to urge her body to accept me.

The soft yielding of her core intoxicates me.

I shift position to lower my hands beneath her round ass. Each one grasps a butt cheek to hold her steady for the impending fucking.

"Look at me, My Siren," I growl. "I want to see your eyes as you cum all over my cock. Do not look away for a second."

She whimpers. But her hooded eyes focus on mine.

My hips draw back until only my cockhead breaches inside her pussy. Then I ram my dick forward to the very end of her core. The sensation of possessing My Siren fully makes my eyes roll back in my head.

A long. low groan falls from my slack mouth.

"Fuuuck… You feel so good. So… tight… So wet," I rasp.

"Oh God, Harris… Oooh…" she wails and stiffens.

The first flutter of her pussy along my length signals her fourth orgasm. Her inner walls clamp down on my cock in a vise-like grip.

I grunt and begin to piston my hungry cock in and out of her creamy core. Time stands still as my dick stretches and fills her tight pussy. I open my eyes to stare down at her as my fingers dig into her lush ass to hold her just so.

"I can feel how you respond to me, My Siren. So willing and so soaking wet," I grunt between thrusts.

She shudders and cries out in wild abandon as another orgasm rips through her quivering pussy.

"YEEESSS!" I roar as I pummel her again and again, chasing an epic release.

My knees dig into the mattress to gain purchase. One hand lifts to grip the back of her neck and lift her torso to my chest. Her flaming red hair falls around us like a curtain as she holds on to my shoulders. My pelvis punches up.

Deeper.

Deeper.

Deeper.

"Unh… Unh… Unh…" I grunt.

A zing races down my spine. My heavy balls draw up.

When my release is upon me, I throw my head back and roar.

"MINE!!!"

HARRIS

"**G**ood morning, Kat."

She moans as I cup her swollen mons and press my front against her back.

I know she's sore. Over the course of the night, I fucked her again, fed her, then woke her up to fuck her twice more. As expected, she barred no positions. My Kitty Kat has a well-used pussy.

My fingers play with her clit. The sensitive bud still responds to my touch as it blossoms. I stroke it gently with my thumb while my index finger caresses her puffy seam.

Despite my hard rides, My Kitty Kat arches her back and plunges her fingers into my hair. She tugs, and I groan. Her head turns to seek my mouth.

I oblige her unspoken request with a slow-burning kiss. Her moans get swallowed up as I stroke her tongue with mine. I play with her some more but won't take her again. Not yet.

"Come. Time for a nice warm soak," I say as I press a kiss to the side of her neck.

She tilts her head to give me better access, and I give her more kisses before I smack her ass and rise from the bed.

I chuckle at the sight of the tangled sheets, then at the comforter with most of the pillows on the toppled to the floor. I make a mental note to call for housekeeping for fresh linens. We need our nest ready for the next bout of mind-blowing sex.

"Mmmm... That sounds lovely. I hope they have some essential oils," Kat says as she stretches her arms overhead and arches her back.

My eyes jump to her DDs. The puckered nipples call to me. I lick my lips but shake my head. Not now.

I toss her over my shoulder and carry her into the en suite bathroom.

She giggles and slaps at my ass. Her tiny fists bounce off the firm muscles. I flex them to give her a show. She can thank their power for the multiple orgasms she screamed from all night long.

Bending my knees, I place her atop a vanity, then turn to the oversized antique copper tub. A shelf has an assortment of oils and salts. Perfect.

"What do you prefer? Lavender, ylang ylang, bergamot, lemon?" I ask.

Kat hops down and stands beside me. Her head reaches my shoulder barely.

"Let's mix lemon with bergamot. I need a pick-me-up after that sex marathon!" She exclaims with a laugh and nudges my side.

I kiss the top of her head and chuckle.

While the tub fills, we brush our teeth, and she combs her hair into a topknot. My fingers never stopped running through them. Talk about bedhead.

She purrs like a satisfied kitten as I bathe her. Then I

loosen her hair to wash and condition the long fiery tresses. Afterwards, she insists upon washing me—not that I complain.

We tear into breakfast like starved animals. Only the sounds of her moans fill the cottage. And bring my cock roaring back to life. When our platters of sausage links, bacon, and pastries sit empty alongside the carafe of freshly squeezed orange juice, I sit back and smile at Kat.

"I appreciate a woman with a hearty appetite," I say.

Her gaze turns to the window, and she slips the napkin off her lap.

Fuck! Did I embarrass her? She doesn't strike me as the type of woman who gets upset with whatever she does.

"Hey," I say as I reach across the table for her hand. "I didn't mean to offend you, Kat. You have a banging body, babe."

For a moment, my hand hangs in the air. When she glances at it and puts her hand in mine, the breath I didn't realize I was holding escapes with a sigh of relief.

"No, you didn't offend me, Harris," she says as she squeezes my hand. "From a child, I've always eaten whatever I was given. Nothing wasted..."

Kat trails off and rises from her seat.

I tug her hand to bring her attention back to me.

"You haven't told me much about your family. I'd like to know more. Do you have siblings? What about your parents?" I ask.

She's shared her school years, work, and volunteering with Isla. But nothing about her family. I didn't want to pry since I know from my Mom and Aunt Lucie family isn't always close. Now, with Kat mentioning her mother, I'd like to learn that side of her life.

She ducks her head, and her hair slides over her face, effectively blocking it from my view.

I push my chair back and pull her onto my lap. My fingertips brush her tresses behind her ears, and I cup her chin. At eye level, she can't hide from me.

She squirms but stops when I cock an eyebrow and growl.

With a sigh, Kat stares out at the English Channel.

I wait.

"I prefer not to speak about my family, Harris. A drunk killed my father and mother in a car accident. It's just me. Okay?" She says as her lower lip wobbles and tears glaze her eyes.

This is worse than the food gaffe. No wonder she doesn't talk about her life before university. My Kitty Kat is all alone.

I band my arms around her, pulling Kat flush to my chest. My lips kiss the tears away. But I can do more to ease her sorrow.

I cup her ass and rise to carry her back to the bedroom. Not for a sex marathon, rather for gentle lovemaking.

* * *

"How phenomenal, Harris!"

As the wind whips Kat's hair, she clings to the railing on the port side of the yacht as it cuts through the waves. Salty sprays fly back and sparkle like diamonds in the summer sun. The receding coastline of Guernsey forms the backdrop of Kat's elated visage.

It's our last day, and I want to make it extra special. After two days holed up in our little world, I chartered STEELE Jersey's yacht to take us island hopping in the Channel. We motored by the uninhabited islands of Jersey and head to the Bailiwick of Guernsey and its outlying islands of Herm, Jethou, and Lihou.

The chef prepared local favorites and fresh seafood, including the delicacy ormer. A selection of wines accompanied each dish for perfect pairings. Crème brûlée and an assortment of fruit for dessert rounded out the delicious meal.

"I don't want to leave. Ever!" Kat exclaims.

Her tinkling laughter makes my heart swell.

So much better than her moment of sadness when she spoke of her family.

I shudder at the thought of losing mine. It must be hard as fuck for her all alone. Holidays, birthdays, celebrations of accomplishments. They didn't even get to see her graduate university. Damn.

The situation reminds me of Lola and her parents. I make a note to tell my sister when Kat meets my family.

Meet my family? Um.

"Would you care for some tea and scones, Mr. Steele?"

The steward's question breaks through my thoughts.

I drag my gaze from Kat to the crew member.

The woman preens with her enhanced tits pushed out beneath her fitted polo shirt as she flashes me with a dazzling white smile.

"Or something else to your liking, Sir," she purrs as her fingertips skate along the hemline of her thigh-grazing skirt.

"I—"

"We are fine. You may go below deck. Now."

My head jerks to my left.

Emerald daggers shoot out at the steward. She flinches

at Kat's biting command before she scurries away without another glance at me.

Hmmm… My Kitty Kat's claws came out. Meow!

She flicks her gaze at me. Eyes narrow to gauge my reaction to the steward's advances. When I grin, Kat purses her lips and folds her arms beneath her tits—way better and natural.

"Find something amusing, Mr. Steele?" She snarls.

I tug her onto my lap and kiss her silly.

The only response necessary.

DURING OUR RETURN FLIGHT, Kat slumbers with her head against my shoulder. She didn't want to sleep in the bedroom since we're airborne for a little over an hour.

I can't blame her since we gave the cottage an explosive going away party. My cock throbs at the memory.

To prevent a full-blown—no pun intended—dick, I open my laptop to work on some code. No better way to stave off an erection than data structures, syntax, variables, blah, blah, blah. Soon I'm immersed in my second favorite pastime.

The running joke is how Haley and I speak English, French, and code. Yup, the Dynamic Duo through and through.

I chuckle to myself and get back to my business.

As the lights come up to prepare for landing, I notice in the reflection of my screen Kat's eyes open as she stares at my work. For a moment, it strikes me as odd she didn't move or speak up when she woke. Only sat in silence. I'm not sure for how long.

But I shrug it off when she lifts her head and stretches her arms. The move bares the creamy skin of her belly as the midriff top rises above the waistband of her skin-tight jeans. I run my index finger along the patch of skin, and she giggles.

Her arms drape around my shoulders as she slants her mouth over mine for a searing kiss. Soft moans stir my cock again.

Sadly, the pilot announces the time to buckle up for landing. Otherwise, My Siren and I would have made the Mile High Club.

"Oh, well, Mr. Steele," she purrs as she sits back and inserts the tongue into the buckle.

I'd like to insert my tongue into her tight sheath.

Once we step out of my jet at Aberdeen International Airport and spy the Rolls-Royce sedan with the driver beside it and STEELE London's Sikorsky waiting for us, reality sets in.

Our weekend rendezvous ends.

Kat will ride home, and I'll board the helicopter for London.

We haven't discussed when we'll see each other again.

I glance down at her, and she's biting her lower lip, eyebrows pinched. I cup her chin to bring her gaze to mine.

"Hey, I hope you had fun," I say as the pad of my thumb frees her lip. "I did. Thank you for giving me a chance."

She sucks my thumb into her mouth.

I groan from the wet warmth.

She pops it out and peeps up at me from beneath the thick fringe of her eyelashes.

"Thank you, Harris, for the best weekend of my life," she whispers. "I'd give you another chance if you let me."

Hell. Yeah.

I lean over and capture her mouth with mine. All the

passion we shared over the weekend comes out in a blistering kiss.

We groan, and she rises on her toes to grab fistfuls of my hair. The erotic pain shoots straight to my semi. In seconds, it's fully erect.

I pull her into my embrace and bend my knees to align our pelvises. Mine grinds into hers to prove just how much I'd give her another chance.

When we come up for a breath, panting heavily, I press my forehead to hers and breathe her air.

"I have to go to Thailand for business Thursday and Friday. Will you join me after work? I'll send my jet back for you," I say.

My Siren squeals and tightens her grip on my hair as she bounces on the balls of her feet.

"Ouch!" I yowl.

Kisses pepper my face as she strokes my head.

"I take that as a yes?" I chuckle between kisses.

"Absolutely!" She squeals.

I give My Siren another kiss, then walk her to the Rolls-Royce.

She hugs me tightly with her face pressed against my chest. A parting kiss, and she slips onto the back seat.

I close the door and wave as the sedan drives off.

As Baz said, the harder I'll fall.

KAT

"**K**at, I want you to know your work pleases me. Despite Mr. Jackson being out on paternity leave for a month, you maintain your duties, and accept more responsibility from me. I relayed my sentiments to him, and he agrees you've become an asset to Jackson Corporation quickly. We upped your clearance level to give you access to information I may need posthaste…"

I sit stunned before Lydie Jackson.

When she called me into her offices, I feared the worse. Especially with the Head of Security seated in the guest chair. My steps faltered as I entered. I assumed the worse.

The Shark breaches the surface for the kill.

Duuuunnnn duun… duuunnnnnnnn dun dun plays in my head.

Inwardly, I sigh in relief as I plaster a smile on my face and thank her. Then my grin spreads as I realize the intel now available at my fingertips. However, I must place my steps carefully. No way do I want blowback.

Strategies formulate in my mind. I can use the excuse of familiarizing myself with the information as I glean viable intel for Chet. Done in stages to prevent unwanted attention. Perhaps over a month or two works best.

Hell yeah, Kat Roberts!

"My administrative assistant has the day off tomorrow. I want you to sit in on my meeting with Lars Gustave, our Head of Technology. My admin added the event to your calendar," Lydie says.

This just gets better and better.

I accept the invite and my updated security pass. As I leave Lydie's offices, my buoyant step carries me back to my desk.

With Gladys in only three times a week until Mr. Jackson's return—she's still paid in full, talk about perks—our area stays quiet. Perfect for me to check out my new access without interruption or a questioning glance.

I reboot my laptop to allow the settings to change. Once loaded, my fingertips fly across the screen. This first glance serves to provide an overall view of what I can access. And it's a lot. A whole lot. Clearly, not at a super-high level. But enough to offer Chet intel in exchange for big bucks.

An alert sounds for a staff birthday party. A quick glance at my clock reveals lunchtime. I perused for over two hours! Reluctantly, I log out.

My attendance at the party and at other social gatherings —baby showers, wedding engagements—keeps my ruse strong. Who would suspect the quiet librarian-type who gives hand-knitted blankets as the culprit?

I stand and push my glasses—not a prop—up the bridge of my nose. Then pick up the bag with the knit scarf gift from my closet. A glance around confirms all is in order before I leave Mr. Jackson's offices suite for the conference room downstairs.

"How was your first day back after the weekend? Able to sit okay? Or do you still feel my cock deep inside of you, Siren? The sting of my palm on that round ass?"

Even over the line, Harris makes my face heat with his naughty words.

Sure, I've had sex before. But not one guy compares to Harris' virility. The man is definitely an unstoppable, insatiable god. The way he makes my body thrum and draws out orgasm after spine-tingling orgasm speaks to his skills. Fingers, hands, lips, tongue, and above all, his ginormous dick.

Oh, my!

My eyes flutter closed as my empty pussy clenches.

What Harris Steele does to me… Exquisite.

"—tell me you're thinking about me. Right. Now."

I missed the first part of his words, so busy reliving our weekend fuckfest. My heart races.

"Most certainly. And yes, you left quite an impression on my ravaged pussy and on my sore ass. Not to mention my throat," I respond. Another flash of heat sweeps over my body at the memories.

Harris chuckles wickedly.

"Nice to hear," he responds, then he continues in a deep baritone. "Do you want me inside of you now, Siren?"

I squirm on my sofa and nod.

"Absolutely," I purr.

My nipples pebble and heat floods my core. I squeeze my pussy walls for a modicum of relief.

"Ah, ah, ah," Harris says.

Like a misbehaved lass caught by the teacher, I sit up straight and widen my thighs.

"I want you hot and needy for me this weekend. Do not touch my pussy. Do not use the spray from a shower head. Do not seek any form of relief. And most definitely, do. Not. Cum. Understood?" He states.

And he says he's not a Dom…

Yet like a sub, I comply.

"Yes," I whisper.

"Good girl," Harris says. "Now, I have the logistics for you…"

I can barely listen to his instructions since he made me so hot for him.

All I want is to jump in bed with my trusty BOB—Battery Operated Boyfriend. Not that the toy can replace the mushroom head and the thick, long, veiny shaft of Harris' beautiful cock. Even his sac of heavy balls is a work of art. Better than Michelangelo's David for sure—and a helluva lot bigger. Again, a total god. Adonis. Apollo. A deity of pure masculine beauty.

"—the sky turned green."

I jerk my head back and frown. Whaaat???

Harris snickers.

"You are not listening to a word that comes out of my mouth, Kitty Kat," he admonishes. "What's on your mind, little lass?"

I smile at his flawless execution of a Scottish lilt. I exaggerate mine.

"You, Harris Steele. You taunt and you tease me. What's a wee lass to do?" I respond, ending in a giggle.

Silence.

I shift in my seat and stare at the mobile screen, wondering if I lost the call. No, he's still there.

"Har—"

FaceTime rings on my mobile. I accept the video call. Harris' face fills the screen.

Did I say gorgeous? Damn.

"Go to your bedroom. Strip. Lie down in the center of your bed. Legs spread wide. Prop the mobile between them," he commands.

I blink.

"Now," he adds with an arched eyebrow.

I hasten to do his bidding. My pulse quickens, and my body tingles. In position, I await his next command as I hold my breath in anticipation. His demanding tone has my pussy juices dripping to the sheets beneath my ass. The mobile rests against the bunched-up duvet.

My pussy and my puckered hole on full display for his wolfish, dove gray turned obsidian eyes. A shudder wracks my body.

"Good girl," he purrs. "So beautiful. Pink and wet. Show me what you want to do as you think about me fucking that greedy little pussy raw."

My mouth falls open.

"Do not turn shy now, Siren," he rumbles. "Show me. Or you will not cum until Friday. If at all…"

My eyes widen. But I settle back on my forearms and close my eyes.

"No. Eyes on me the entire time," Harris commands.

They fly open and stare straight into his hooded feral gaze. I moisten my lower lip with the tip of my tongue.

He groans.

I pile pillows behind me to keep my head propped up and my gaze on his. Then resettle into position. Ready to give Harris a proper show.

One hand reaches up to cup my heavy breast. Fingers

knead the mound and tug at the turgid nipple. I cry out. The other hand glides up my belly to tease the untouched nipple. The palm strokes the sensitive bud. Thumb and forefinger pinch it to bring it to a point.

My hips lift from the bed as his pussy contracts from the erotic zing.

Both hands lift to my mouth, and I suck on the fingers. Suitably moistened, they pinch and twist my peaked nipples to mimic Harris' mouth and teeth. I throw my head back and moan lustily.

He growls, and I return my hooded gaze to his.

Once again, I moisten my fingers. This time, they slide in and out to the knuckle. I twirl my tongue around them and pull the wet digits out of my mouth with a pop.

Harris groans and tucks his full bottom lip between his teeth.

I purr seductively with half-closed eyes.

The fingers slither down my flat belly to the bare mound. They cup my sex and come away dripping. I bring them to my mouth and suck. Hard.

"Fuuuuckk," Harris breathes out as he shakes his head.

The fingers slip back to his pussy and pinch the labia. I groan as they part and skim across his engorged clit. My hips buck again. The heels of my feet dig into the mattress as I widen my legs. First one, then another finger slides inside of his pussy, knuckle after knuckle. Fully seated, they stroke his inner walls and tease the sensitive G-spot.

Unable to keep my eyes open, I thrash my head from side to side and cry out in wild abandon as a climax sneaks up on me. His pussy pulsates around the buried fingers, clamping down on them like a vise.

"Do. Not. Stop!"

Harris' command comes with the sound of skin on skin

as his hand jacks off his cock. Heavy breathing and grunts sound through my mobile speakers.

"Oh, Harris!" I wail as fingers plow into his clenching pussy.

Another climax rips through me when the other fingers pinch his clit. My back bows from the bed. Sweat dampens my flushed skin. I keen.

My thighs quiver, and my feet slide against the sheets, unable to hold my limp form. My chest heaves with each pant from my agape mouth.

"KAAAT!!!"

Harris' roar breaks through my orgasm-induced coma.

With hazy vision, I lift my head from the pillows and glance at the mobile. Not in sight. I drag myself up and rifle through the strewn sheets and duvet until my fingers grasp the device. Harris' half-mast eyes stare back at me from his flushed face. We gaze at one another, unable to use our motor skills just yet. Still caught in the erotic rapture.

He's the first to speak.

"No more orgasms for you until Friday. Good night, Kitty Kat," Harris murmurs.

An incoherent mumble falls from my mouth as I roll over into a fetal position. Exhausted, sleep takes me as soon as my eyelids close. The pleasant thought of seeing Harris wraps me in a blissful cocoon.

My only wish to reawaken aboard his jet on Friday and not face any of my life's concerns. Like my meeting with Chet.

* * *

"I do not have loads of bloody time. You called this in-person meeting. Get on with what you have for me. And it better be good."

As Chet barks, I envision his face melting. His eyes droop and slide along his cheeks while his lips drop off his face and the hole of his mouth fills with the gooey substance until he chokes.

The bloody obnoxious, self-possessed prat!

For a moment, I consider storming away. To hell with him!

But revenge simmers in my soul for the Jacksons to fall to their knees.

Then a flash of guilt passes through me since Lachlan and Lydie treat me well. And I've fallen for Harris more than I care to admit. Tomorrow can't come fast enough.

I take a deep breath to clear those thoughts. The only one that matters: take care of my family with the money Chet gives to me. That thought must remain forefront in my mind. Period.

With a sarcastic smile stamped on my face, I hand the flash drive to Chet. It contains information on Jackson Corporation's upcoming launches. The most intel I could uncover without drawing suspicion.

He cocks his eyebrow as he stares at the memory stick.

"Well, what's on it?" He asks with a sneer.

I hold back an eye roll and tell him.

His beady eyes gleam as he snatches the drive from my fingers. He mutters how he'll wire six figures to my Swiss bank account if his *people* confirm the intel worthy.

Now, I roll my eyes and respond snarkily, "It's bloody well worth it, and you know it!"

His eyes widen, then narrow.

"Fine. I will complete the transfer in the morning," Chet grouses. Then he rolls up the window of his Bentley sedan.

I watch as it pulls into traffic.

"Prat!" I whisper shout before I stick out my tongue.

I head to the bus stop for the ride home. My mind drifts to Thailand and to the Adonis who waits for me. Again guilt rears its head. I know Harris is as attracted to me as I am to him.

Well, I can have fun before I disappear for good. I deserve it.

KAT

"Nice bag, Kat. Where are you off to for the long weekend?"

"Yeah, you look like you can't contain yourself!"

Two assistants from the finance department approach as I wait for the executive floor lift.

They're friendly enough. But I'd rather not disclose my weekend getaway with Harris. Too many women fall all over him, even when he's with me. If I broadcast being with him, it's bound to reach the tabloids. I've seen plenty of photos of Harris linked to a bevy of beauties and tales of his conquests splattered across the Internet.

No, thank you.

I smile and shake my head.

"Thanks. But nowhere special. Plans to attend a friend's birthday party in Newtonhill," I say, then deflect. "What about you?"

We ride down to the lobby and head for the doors.

Harris' Rolls-Royce sits at the curb with the driver beside it. He tips his hat and opens the back door for me.

115

"Wait a minute, Kat."

"Nothing special, you say?"

I grin and waggle my fingers over my shoulder. Then slide into the back after the driver takes my bag. The door closes with a soft thud. I gaze at the pair from behind the window's darkened glass.

Their mouths hang agape as the sedan pulls off.

My grin widens bigger than the Cheshire Cat's smile as my mobile rings with a FaceTime call from Harris.

"I see you're in the car," he says.

My gaze lifts to the privacy screen. I guess the driver told him.

"No, he didn't tell me. I have my ways," he smirks.

I giggle and shake my head.

"A man of mystery. I like," I say.

We talk until I get on the elevator at STEELE Aberdeen for the ride up to the roof where Lachlan's helicopter awaits to take me to Aberdeen International Airport. My mobile rings once we're airborne with another FaceTime call from Harris. Aboard the jet, we continue to talk until well after midnight in Thailand.

Afterwards, I enjoy a delicious five-course meal on Bernardaud China and water and wine in Baccarat Crystal glasses. The white linen tablecloth and napkin with silver cutlery finish the posh dinner. I thank the flight attendant for a snifter of Jackson Reserve Scotch before I move to the living room area and stretch out on a white leather sofa to watch movies.

When my eyes droop, I head to the bedroom and change into the red silk negligee and robe laid out on the bed. I notice it's Lola's Coterie—his sister-in-law's luxury lingerie and evening wear company. They're elegant and to die for. I take a selfie, blowing a kiss and text it to

Harris. When he awakes, he'll have a reminder of what's coming.

No sooner than my head touches the down-filled pillow encased by platinum gray silk, my eyes drift closed. The soothing scent of lavender wafts through the air. Once again, dreams of a life with Harris lull me into a peaceful slumber.

* * *

THE GULF OF THAILAND'S sparkling aquamarine water tipped with white caps stretches out beneath the helicopter as we fly towards Maenam Beach on Koh Samui. Coconut trees sway in the breeze. Their abundant fronds cast shadows on the powdery white sand. The idyllic spot clear of locals and tourists.

As we near, I spy one figure with a hand shading his eyes. He stands bare chested in white board shorts. Tan skin over taut, lean muscles glistens in the sunlight. He raises a hand in a wave. A grin spreads across his handsome face.

Harris Steele.

Sex on the beach. Yum.

I'm out the door as soon as the flight attendant opens it. Harris jogs towards me, and I leap into his arms, wrapping my legs around his narrow hips. My sundress rides up my thighs.

He growls as he cups my ass and slants his mouth over mine for a toe-curling kiss.

My needy pussy clenches from the heat of his body. Sans panties, I grind my core against his washboard abs like… Well, like a cat in heat. I swallow his growls as we devour each other's mouths.

How I've missed this man. *My* man.

Leaving the butler to gather my bag, Harris turns around and strides back through the stone path between the foliage. Its density hides the helipad from the gardens of the magnificent beachfront villa. Fragrant scents of jasmine and hibiscus fill the balmy air. I'm nearly dizzy with delight.

"Missed you, Kitty Kat," Harris murmurs against my lips. "A lot."

I nip his lower lip, and he groans.

"I missed you more, Harris Steele," I purr. "How will you make up the time to me?"

He chuckles darkly as his eyes flash silver.

My Wolf prowls.

"Oh, Siren, you are not at all ready for what I am about to give to you," he responds with hooded eyes. "My tight, little pussy will need ample prep time until it gushes and begs to be fucked long and hard."

I shiver and mewl.

Carnal images dance in my head. Every single one involves a strapping Alpha male fucking me senseless in each of my willing holes.

"Keep looking at me like that, and I will fuck you against the next coconut tree, Siren. Staff be damned," he growls.

He strides up a set of stairs, and I glance over my shoulder.

My jaw drops.

Up close, the luxurious villa leaves me breathless.

In keeping with the local style, it has five thatched-roof, open-air, whitewashed pavilions. The center structure includes an oversized salon, dining room, chef's kitchen, and full bathroom. On either side, two pavilions connect to the main one via stone pathways. The four structures house enormous suites with sitting rooms and indoor/outdoor bathrooms.

Lush green grass and more flowering plants surround an infinity pool with white chaise lounges and umbrellas beside it. A stone terrace has an outdoor kitchen, a sitting area with white sofas and a firepit, and a dining area with a long elliptical wooden table and chairs. The table reminds me of a supersized surfboard.

The stunning beach spreads out before the villa. An invitation to dive into the calm aquamarine waters.

Simply paradise.

"So beautiful," I whisper in awe.

"So beautiful," Harris repeats.

I turn my gaze back to him.

He stares at me with lust-filled eyes, obsidian with his carnal need.

"I mean the villa and beach, silly," I giggle.

"I mean you, Siren," he rejoins, eyes pinned on mine.

My hands cup his face.

"Well… I'm hot and needy just like you wanted. So what will you do about it?" I purr as I lap at his full lips, hungry for his taste.

The thick shaft of his cock thumps against my pussy. I couldn't ask for a better response.

I tighten my grip on his shoulders and bounce up and down along his cock. My heels dig into his firm ass for leverage.

"I want you now, Mr. Steele," I rasp.

He smacks my ass, and I shudder to a stop.

"You get when I give, naughty lass," he growls. "Lucky for you, I am ready now."

With that, he shifts me in his arms to toss me over his shoulder. Three smacks to my exposed rear end make me screech and grab his waist. Another flurry, and I cry out as my pussy contracts. Juices make my inner thighs slippery.

Harris runs a thick finger along my seam to collect the proof of my arousal. A sucking sound follows.

My cheeks redden—as crimson as my alabaster ass—with the knowledge he's cleaning my juices from his finger. At the same time, the action turns me on even more. I whimper in need.

"Oh, I got you, naughty lass. Do not worry," he croons, stroking my ass.

He strides into a bedroom suite pavilion closest to the beach.

A gentle breeze sways the white gauzy curtains tied back with stands of fragrant yellow flowers. A king-size bed covered in white sits in the middle of the suite opposite the open fourth wall. Carved wood nightstands with white shade, blown glass lamps flank the bed. To the left of it, an arched opening leads to a bathroom with a closet. The other side serves as the sitting area with white sofas and more carved wood tables with lamps and more flowers. Sand colored tile covers the floor.

Before I can comment on the tranquil space, I fly through the air and bounce on the bed. A yelp bursts from my mouth. My arms and legs flail, then splay out.

Harris pounces.

His hands make quick work of my sundress. I lost my flip flops along the way. He puts my crooked eyeglasses on the nightstand, then kneels between my thighs as he pulls the string on his board shorts. His massive cock springs free.

Absolutely ready.

Pre-cum gathers at the bulbous tip. Veins stand out in bas-relief along the hard shaft. Heavy balls sway as he rolls a condom over his dick, then lowers to his elbows.

Arms loop under my thighs for firm hands to hold the

tops. Fingertips skim my inner thighs, enticingly close to my sopping core.

I wiggle to bring the digits closer to my most-needy place, only to yelp when Harris nips the sensitive skin of an inner thigh.

"Behave. Or you will not cum, naughty lass," he snarls. "Last warning."

I swallow and nod. Then catch myself and verbalize my understanding.

Harris smirks.

When the tip of his tongue prods my engorged clit, a low and guttural moan escapes me. At last, relief…

Just as starved for me as I am for him, Harris gorges on the bountiful fount of my pussy. He hums his appreciation as he laps up my cream. The vibrations flow through me, increasing my pleasure.

I lose count of the orgasms he wrings from my core. My mind blown.

"Now you are as ready as I am, Siren. A soft and yielding pussy ripe for fucking," he purrs, then kisses my lower lips.

Harris continues a trail of kisses to my mons, up my quivering belly with a pause to lave a beaded nipple. His suckling steady. As he passes the valley between my breasts, he sucks skin into his mouth and worries it—sure to leave a mark. He murmurs *mine* before he moves to the other nipple.

I mewl and arch my back. Fingers dive into his ebony hair to cradle him to my breast. His mouth feels so good.

Kisses pressed to the side of my neck lead to my lips. Our tongues tangle until he nips mine with a low growl of passionate dominance. I respond with a soft cry of acceptance.

Harris' hand snakes between our damp bodies to fist his

rock-hard dick and press it against my slick seam. A snap of his hips seats him fully within my core. His tip grazes my cervix.

I cry out from the burn of his massive cock as it stretches and fills my tight pussy. Greedily, it sucks him deeper, fluttering along his turgid length.

He murmurs filthy words against the delicate shell of my ear as he thrusts and circles his hips before he drags his cock out to the mushroom head. The pace constant. The rhythm as old as time.

A blinding orgasm shoots down to curl my toes and up to bow my back. I gasp and wail because of the unexpected rush.

Harris grips my hips and flips me to my forearms and knees—ass high, head low. With a feral bark, he pounds into my pussy. Hips snap my punished ass. Balls slap my swollen clit.

My fingernails shred the sheets as he impales me over and over on his long, thick cock like a rag doll. Screams and grunts echo around us as another climax rips through me and he chases his release.

More dirty words fly from Harris' mouth as his cock grows impossibly larger and harder. He stills and throws his head back with a conquering roar. His cock pulsates deep inside of my wrecked pussy. His sweat drips onto my back. Nearly replete, his thrusts switch to a languorous pace as he spills every drop into the condom.

I whimper from the loss when he withdraws.

His hands guide me flat onto the bed with my head on my folded arms. A kiss to my lower back and the mattress shifts. I hear him pad to the bathroom and return a moment later.

A damp cloth cleans the sticky cream from my thighs

and my butt cheeks. I purr in a state of sheer euphoria and wiggle my hips.

Harris chuckles. His warm breath tickles my ear.

"Be careful what you ask for, Siren," he warns with a sharp smack to my ass.

I smile as my eyes drift closed.

Yeah, a life with Harris Steele sounds and feels good.

nother missed weekend? What's going on with you? Who has you ditching your fam? Fess up to your twin, Harris Steele...

I chuckle at the text message from Haley. She's on point with her guess. Always in tune, we can never hide anything from the other. Talk about Wonder Twins powers activate.

I had meetings in Thailand and stayed for the long weekend. I'll see you when I get back. Give my niece and nephews zerbets on their tummies. Love ya, H

Three dots appear as Haley types her response.

Mmmhhhmmm... Love you, too.

Ah, Haley. She's going to give me hell when she finds out I've been seeing Kat. One woman for more than one encounter? I snort. Obviously Lachlan didn't break the Bro Code and spilled the beans to Haley. I would have heard from her by now. Good man.

Not that I want to hide Kat or our fledgling relationship. No. However, I want to give it some time. See how it goes. I'll tell Haley since we don't keep secrets from each other.

Especially since I forced her to cave in about Lachlan. And I'll tell him too, since Kat is his admin. Only fair.

As for the rest of our family?

Well, STEELE Foundation's annual fundraising gala happens in a few weeks. If all is still well between Kat and me, I'll fly her over to my family's beachfront compound—Steele Southampton Village. That'll put us at two months together. A good amount of time before I introduce her to everyone.

Satisfied with my decision, I rise from the sunbed and dive into the shimmering waves. I glide under the water until I reach Kat and put her thighs on my shoulders before I surface. She screeches as she shoots out of the water.

"Harris!" She yells as her fingers grip my hair for purchase.

I laugh and nip her inner thigh. My hands hold her legs as I dog paddle to keep us afloat.

"You nearly gave me a heart attack!" Kat continues. "Don't drop me!"

"If you haven't noticed, lass, I'm a brawny lad," I say. "But it's time for you to get… WET!"

Kat squawks as I drop back below the surface until we're submerged. Beneath the water, she wiggles from my grasp and spins around to face me.

I grin and reach for her waist.

My little mermaid lass doesn't want to be caught. She turns and swims for the shore. Topless with her round ass covered by a tiny string bikini and long, toned legs, she enthralls me. I swear I hear her Siren's call. And don't hesitate to follow it.

As we swim back, I swipe at her legs. Kat growls and carries on. When her feet touch the sandy bottom, she pivots and arcs her arm through the water to douse me as I stand.

"Take that, Harris Steele!" She shouts.

A water fight ensues until I grab and toss her over my shoulder. She squirms but settles down when I swat that ass. I lower her to the sunbed and straddle her hips.

"You proved too irresistible, Kitty Kat," I tease as I tickle her. "I can't keep my hands off of you."

She squeals and wiggles until breathless.

I lean down and suck a puckered nipple into my mouth. Warm salty water and Kitty Kit's natural taste slide across my tongue. I pinch and roll her other nipple to a peak. As I lick my way to it, my fingers slide down her belly and beneath her bikini. I finger fuck her to a quick climax then sit back on my haunches to clean my fingers.

"Better?" I ask between licks.

She stretches like her namesake and purrs in contentment.

I smirk and rub sunblock on her alabaster skin, then lie down beside her. When she rolls over and rests her head on my chest, I kiss the top of it. With the warm sun on my body and my woman in my arms, I smile and close my eyes. Bliss.

* * *

"THAT'S IT! GO, KAT, GO!"

I cup my hands around my mouth and shout more words of encouragement as she rides a wave for the first time.

Seconds later, the surfboard zips from beneath her feet, and she falls into the water with a spectacular splash. With the ease of an experienced surfer, I jump up and catch the next wave to help her. Kat surprises me and pops out of the water, laughing and wiping her face. She swims to her board and slips out of the water to straddle it.

I grin and wolf whistle at her upturned rear, clad in a black bikini bottom. Unfortunately, a long-sleeved rash-guard covers her luscious tits. But her nipples press against the shirt.

Kat laughs.

"Not bad, huh?" She asks with a wink. "Now I know why surfers love it so much. I could do this all day. Fersure, dude!"

I raise my hand with thumb and pinky up and middle fingers curled as I wave it back and forth.

"Right on, dudette!" I respond, grinning. "Let's go again."

We drop on our boards and paddle back out to the surf line. As we approach, other guys congratulate Kat on her ride. I bristle at their attention to my woman and throw glares at them. They nod their heads in understanding and resume their watch for the perfect wave.

"Caveman."

I glance back at Kat, and she rolls her eyes.

"They were only being nice, Harris," she admonishes me.

"Well then, call me Captain Caveman because I do not give a fuck," I say. Then raise my eyebrow and fold my arms across my chest. "Unless you need them to be nice, Kat."

She huffs and pouts.

I cock my head.

"Of course not, Harris! Give me a break," she responds. "And by the way… Did I get my knickers in a bunch when every woman on the beach and everywhere else, for that matter, ogle you?"

I drop my arms.

"Exactly. Now excuse me while I catch a wave," she says and paddles off.

I watch her go. She makes good on her word and rides a wave almost all the way to the shore before she falls off her board. A couple of surfers help her, and I bite back a growl.

This woman gets under my skin like no other.

I swipe my hand over my face and take the next wave. As I stride to our blankets, I ignore the women who sidle up to me. Yeah, I can see what Kat means. Not that I'm a conceited prick, but women flocking to me happens so often it doesn't faze me. It comes with the Steele name, my billions, and of course my handsome mug.

"What's so funny?"

I stop chuckling at the sound of Kat's voice.

"You're right, I'm a possessive bloke, bonny lass. So get used to it. I'll make a deal with you. We're exclusive," I say as I drop beside her. "Deal?"

She blinks, then scans my face for any sign of deceit. Finding none, a brilliant smile spreads across her gorgeous face, making her emerald green eyes glitter behind her glasses back on after surfing. She throws her arms around my neck and presses her lips to mine.

"Deal!" She says between ardent kisses.

"This is incredible. It feels like a dream."

Kat tilts her head back to gaze at the rocky cliffside as the longtail boat meanders along the channel between the natural walls. Water eroded the sandstone, leaving the cliffs with dramatic fissures and caves. Fauna covers the surfaces as plants and trees cling to the sides, growing in abundance. Their vibrant green hues reflect in the water below for a turquoise tone. The clear water glints in the dazzling sun and reveals its depths where colorful fish in every shade of the rainbow swim.

I smile at her excitement as I sit back and watch her reactions to the natural beauty of Thailand.

As I plan for every trip we take to end on a bang, I arranged the cruise and dinner on a secluded beach. I want My Kitty Kat to leave with a smile on her face and the desire to see me again makes her needy. I want to show her and give her things she's never had before me. What no other man can do for her. Make her addicted to me and not just to Harris Steele, the multibillionaire.

And so far, so good.

"Oh, Harris! I've seen nothing like this. Amazing," she whispers in reverence. "Will you take our picture?"

Mission accomplished.

I grin.

"Of course, babe," I respond as I hold my hand out to her.

She moves from the front of the longtail boat to where I sit along its side. When she settles on my lap, I take her mobile and extend my arm for the shot. I wait until a vibrant patch of the cliffside appears behind us and press the button. I kiss her cheek and take another as she giggles. Then a third with her kissing me back.

"Thank you so much for another incredible time, Harris," My Kitty Kat purrs against my lips.

I rest my forehead to hers and breathe in her air for a moment before I respond.

"You are more than welcome, Kitty Kat," I murmur. "But you have more to see."

Right on cue, the channel widens and the longtail boat glides towards the beach.

"Look," I say as I clasp her chin between my thumb and forefinger to shift her gaze.

She gasps.

The gentle breeze blows the white gauzy canopy with its four posts covered in ropes of yellow ratchaphruek Thailand's national flower and colorful hibiscus and jasmine. It floats above a table set for two with a floral bouquet at its center. Chairs have more gauzy material draped over them with a bow in the back and a wreath of flowers. The billowy topper resembles the clouds above and the table appears as one of the many islands of the country.

Bamboo torches around the perimeter and white tapers on the table will provide lighting once the sun sets below the line of the cliffs.

Phase two will be make love beneath the stars. We'll move to the sunbed covered in white, sumptuous bedding beneath a second gauzy canopy. A bonfire to the side and more bamboo torches situated nearby, ready to be lit. Next to the sunbed, Dom Pérignon Champagne and two Baccarat Crystal flutes chill in a bucket nestled in the sand.

A romantic ending to our rendezvous. If I must say so myself...

I CARRY A STILL SPEECHLESS Kat through the shallows to the beach. Her gaze darts from the table to the servers and the sunbed.

As we near the setting, the tropical scent of the flowers mingles with the aromas from the tantalizing dishes on the white linen tabletop.

I nuzzle My Kitty Kat's neck and inhale the alluring scent of her perfume. Combined with her natural musk, it surpasses any of the tropical flowers and foods that surround us.

"Oh, Harris," she breathes at last as I set her on a chair.

She cups my face and continues. "I don't know what to say. You treat me so well—"

Her words catch in her throat. She glances away with tears shimmering in her eyes as her hands drop to her lap.

I crouch beside her and lift them to my lips. I place a kiss on the tip of each finger and on her palms.

Her eyes remain averted as she shakes her head.

The situation overcomes My Kitty Kat, I muse. However, I will not allow her to sit quietly.

"Kat, you fill my heart like no other woman. I never expected to fall for you at first sight. But I did, and you please me beyond my wildest dreams. True, we have only known each other for a short period. However, time means nothing when your heart tells you otherwise. I only want to please you, too. Enjoy our time together. Each and every second, sweetheart, because I know I do," I say.

The words pour from my heart unchecked. Yet I do not regret them. The truth holds power I will no longer deny. I can't say it's love since I've never experienced love of a woman aside from my mother and my sister. But it's pretty damn close to what I imagine it to be.

The breath I didn't realize I was holding falls from my lips when My Kitty Kat returns her tear-filled eyes to gaze at me. Her chin wobbles as she sucks in a breath.

I stroke my thumb over her bottom lip before I cover it in an emotion-filled kiss. I pour my heart and soul into it. My body backs up my words as I claim Kat Roberts as mine.

She wraps her arms around my neck and sags into me. Completely giving in to our newfound commitment to one another. To us. Just as I did moments before.

"Spill it."

I chuckle at Haley's blunt demand. My twin's expression brokers no room for denial.

We're sitting on chaise lounges by the swimming pool at Aboyne Castle. Since it's a warm August day, the staff retracted the glass walls and ceiling of the pool house. It's one of several outer buildings on the castle's one hundred acres of manicured lawns and rolling lands.

Not far away, the impressive six-story castle sits. Made from Aberdeen granite, it features towers on one side of the center keep and battlements on the other. From the highest point, the Jackson heraldic flag ripples in the wind. A granite bridge spans the sparkling stream that flows before the castle.

Lachlan took Lilias, Leith, and Lewis to the stables for their daily visit. Even though they're only thirteen-months old, he wants to familiarize them with horses to prepare for riding lessons next year. As an avid polo player—along with

Uncle Connor and his siblings—the equestrian lifestyle ranks high for him.

My siblings and I ride too, so I get it.

While Stirling and Struan asleep in their nursery with the nannies, my twin and I have time to ourselves.

And it's obvious she's not wasting any of it with preamble. Straight to the point for Haley.

"As long as you promise not to crow I-told-you-so, I'll fess up," I respond.

Haley rolls her eyes and blows as she shrugs her shoulders.

"Yeah right. If it's a woman, you might as well get ready to hear it, brother!" She snorts. "So get on with it already."

Always true to her word, I have no doubt Haley will rub it in. If the roles were reversed, I'd do the same. I smirk and give in.

"Yes, a woman. Specifically Kat Roberts, Lach—"

"Lachlan's admin?!" Haley shouts. When I nod, she continues. "For real? Does even he know? Since when? She's not using you, is she? Give me a break. Not another bloody gold digger…"

Haley goes on and on.

Understandable since she's witnessed a stalker sub with Malcolm, a money-grubber kidnapper with Roger, among other unsavory encounters. Add in some friends of hers who used Haley to get to her brothers and cousins— including Lachlan. *That* did not end well. So, yeah, Haley is super protective of us. Who can blame her?

Hell, I know when I introduce Kat, Baz will have his *guy* do an extensive background check on her. Even when I tell Baz not to bother, since she passed Lachlan's Human Resources review when they employed her at Jackson Corporation. As the eldest sibling, Baz takes his Big Brother duties seriously. He's our second father and has become more paternal since he's had children.

And God help Kat if she is up to no good—not that I believe so—then Malcolm *The Enforcer* will handle her. He's the one others come to for solutions. We don't ask what he does. We just know the situation ends in our favor.

On the other hand, our mother will be ecstatic. Her last baby involved in an actual relationship? The first woman to meet the family since my high school prom date? But being a mama bear, she won't tolerate a woman with ulterior motives.

Poor Kitty Kat.

I hold up my hands palms out to halt Haley's sound off.

She sits back against her chaise lounge and folds her arms across her chest. Eyebrows furrow and lips purse to the side as her dove gray eyes narrow.

"Fine. Go on," she huffs.

I sit up with my feet on the travertine pavers to face her. Of everyone, my twin's opinion matters the most. I need her to like Kat and for them to get along.

She'll also need to do well with Lola, Leonie, and Starr. From the start, my sisters-in-law blended into our family and became loved members to the point where I consider them sisters like Haley. I'm sure they'll embrace Kat.

"Hal, I understand how you feel and appreciate your concern. Trust me. However, Kat is different. She's not some chick aiming for a phat ring. Nor just a date for an event or a one-night stand. I actually like her and enjoy being with her," I say, then smile when Haley's expression softens. "The moment I laid eyes on her... I—I felt an attraction to Kat. To be honest, her banging body hidden beneath a demure suit helped—"

"Oh, Harris! Really?!" Haley cuts in and swats my knee.

She mutters about men and which head they think with before I continue.

"But seriously, Hal. I get what Baz said about Lola. Hell, what Roger said about Leonie when he heard her laughter outside his office door. Or Malcolm when Starr bumped into him," I say. "Only you knew your true love all of your life. Now I think I may have found The One."

Haley's eyes fill with tears, and she sniffs. She sits next to me and wraps her arms around my neck.

I hold her while I say a silent prayer of thanks.

"Okay, so what did I miss?"

Lachlan's' booming voice sounds from behind us.

Haley and I turn to face him as he strides over in an open short-sleeved shirt, swim trunks, and flip flops. He grabs a colorful Missoni terrycloth towel from the pile and tosses it over his shoulder. The sun glints off his aviators as he grins.

My twin looks at me, not wanting to divulge my news— not even to her husband—without my consent.

I smile at her, grateful for the consideration.

Lachlan kisses the top of her head and claps me on the shoulder. As he drops onto another chaise lounge, he cocks his head expectantly.

"Kat and I agreed to be exclusive," I say.

Lachlan lowers his sunglasses and flicks his eyes between Haley and me.

"Don't cockblock, Lachlan Jackson!" Haley orders, as she folds her arms again and glares. "Kat may work for you. But her private life is none of your concern."

Lachlan and I guffaw at Haley's feistiness.

"Yes, ma'am," he says, then he turns to me. "I already told you I have no problem with you seeing Kat."

Haley gasps.

"Wait a minute. You knew before *I* did???" She asks wide

eyed. When Lachlan nods, she narrows them. "And you didn't tell me??? Something about *my* brother?!"

I open my mouth to save Lachlan from her wrath. But he speaks first.

"Yes. And if he wanted you to learn about it first, he would have told you. It's not my place to mouth off about his business," Lachlan responds. Then he raises his eyebrow and adds, "Besides, you and I have had plenty of secrets kept from The Big Four."

Haley rolls her eyes at her nickname for her brothers and mention of the secrets with Lachlan they kept from us as they dated. But she relents with a sigh.

"Fine," she says reluctantly.

Lachlan blows a kiss to her, and she snatches it from the air to plant it on her lips as she giggles.

Any other time I would tell them *eewww, gross*. But now I get what it's like to feel strongly about someone and to share wussy moments with them. So instead, I grin and tell the lovey-dovey pair my plan to introduce Kat to the family over Labor Day weekend.

They agree it's a good idea, and Lachlan says she can take a few days off from work to make it a full holiday. Since I have to fly back to New York City before then, they'll let Kat join them on their jet for the flight over. They're staying for a while. So, I'll send her back on my jet, or Lucien can drop her off in Aberdeen before he returns to Paris.

With my news shared and well received, we dive into the pool and romp around. Haley challenges me to ride the giant inflatable ball, and I accept. The damn thing proves harder to wrangle than I imagined. As I flounder around, she slips from the pool and starts a video with her mobile.

"No way will I let everyone miss your shenanigans!" She

laughs. "The last time Roger was here, he did it without a hitch!"

Her taunt of Roger's success gives me the gumption to ride that ball like a bronco, to Haley's delight. My twin laughs so hard she snorts and the mobile almost drops into the water. Lachlan bumps me off and takes over. She keeps recording until he falls off.

When we tell her it's her turn, she says it's time for lunch with The Trips and darts to the ladies' showers. Lachlan and I call her a chicken and climb from the pool to head for the men's changing room. Freshly changed, the three of us take the golf cart back to the castle. A far easier ride than the blasted ball…

"Malcolm texted back. He challenges you both when we get to Southampton Village," Haley tells us. "Yeah, Mr. Daredevil himself, always down for a thrill!"

I whip out my mobile and text back: *Challenge accepted. Come strong or be gone!*

Lola replies she's in, and Lydie adds she'll take bets.

Back at the castle, Lachlan calls for the nannies to bring The Trips to the terrace where the staff serves lunch. Since Stirling and Struan woke from their nap, they'll join us too.

As we settle at the table, the butler appears with Uncle Connor and Aunt Lucie.

"Surprise!" She exclaims.

"We were in the neighborhood," Uncle Connor adds.

"All the way from Jackson Castle?" Lachlan snorts. "Just admit you want to see your grands."

They laugh and nod.

Right on time, the nannies walk through the glass doors and Lilias squeals when she sees her grandparents. Leith and Lewis toddle forward, arms out. We scoop all three into our arms, and Haley and Lachlan take the twins.

Lunch waits while we catch up and play with the lass and lads. I tease Haley they sound more and more Scottish every day. Uncle Connor puffs his chest out and sharpens his emerald green eyes on me.

"Of course! They are Jacksons, you know!" He states emphatically.

We laugh at his pride in the Jackson family.

After his failed attempt at a marriage between Baz and Lydie, Uncle Connor pushed Lachlan for heirs. Now, Uncle Connor has five wee ones, and he couldn't be happier. Or more possessive…

"When are you flying to Southampton Village?" Haley asks.

"That's also why we stopped by. We want to know how long you're planning to stay," Aunt Lucie responds.

They chat on about logistics while Uncle Connor, Lachlan, and I talk sports—shinty, who realized?—and sailing.

Instead of flying back to London, I stay the night along with Uncle Connor and Aunt Lucie. I want as much time with the grands as they do.

After this month, I won't be in Scotland as much since I'll rotate back to our New York City offices. If things go well with Kat, we'll meet up for the weekends. More than likely I'll fly to Aberdeen since I can get to STEELE London for work quicker than she can get to Jackson Corporation from Manhattan. Or we'll pick a spot within a short flight time from Scotland. Either way, we'll manage for both of us. As couples do.

I chuckle at the thought. Me—the ultimate playboy—a willing part of a couple. Ha!

KAT

"$\mathcal{H}$i, Mum! I'm here! Where are you? Michael? Charlotte?"

I put the bags of groceries and Indian takeaway I picked up on my way from the bus station onto the kitchen counter. Then put the bouquet onto the table. While I wait for them to appear, I place the milk, cheeses, steaks, and other perishables in the refrigerator and freezer.

"Hey, Kat."

I glance over my shoulder to find Michael striding towards me with a grin. His emerald eyes sparkle as they meet mine before he pulls me in for a hug.

"Hey yourself!" I say, then rub his chin. "Nice beard."

His cheeks flush, and he ducks his head.

"Kat, honey?"

We turn to our Mum and Charlotte—who smiles in greeting beside her. I embrace them while Michael puts the rest of the groceries into the cupboards.

"Wine, too? Thanks, Kat!" He says, holding up two bottles of Cabernet Sauvignon.

"And flowers for you, Mum," I say as I hand them to her. "Your favorites."

She palms my cheek and smiles up at me.

"Such a good girl you are, Katrina. Thank you," she says. "Charlotte, will you hand me the vase, honey?"

While our Mum arranges the flowers in the chipped Waterford Crystal vase one of her employers planned to toss, Charlotte and I set out the food. Michael comes over with plates and forks, then goes back for glasses and a bottle of wine.

I don't bother to ask about Payton since it's Friday night.

Undoubtedly, he's at the pub around the corner getting drunk with whatever money he scraped together over the week. He'll come around soon enough when he realizes I'm here with money.

Even though I transfer funds into our Mum's bank account, I always bring some cash for her to have on hand. To avoid an argument at the start of our weekend, I'll just pretend I don't notice her giving it to him. At least not in front of her. However, I *will* tell him to his face he's a lazy louse!

I turn to Charlotte.

"How're your classes going this semester?" I ask.

She smiles and, like Michael, her eyes sparkle bright as the gem.

"Fantastic!" She says then gushes on about classes, study groups, and a guy she's seeing.

I smile happy for my younger sister. She reminds me of my excitement for a new phase in my life, away from the not-so-stellar environment we shared. I also smile at her enthusiasm for her new relationship. Also like mine.

It did not thrill Harris we wouldn't spend time face-to-face this weekend. He'd asked me to join him in London. He said he wanted to share an experience with me. But gave in when I told him I had a Girls' Getaway planned months before.

The lie didn't sit well with me. However, I have no other choice. I can't very well let him know my parents didn't die and my nonexistent siblings exist. That would ruin everything. All that I've accomplished thus far. And that I cannot allow.

So, I refocus on Charlotte.

Michael teases her about being gaga over a bloke for the first time. She retorts how he's just as into her as she is into him. They banter back and forth while our Mum smiles on.

Despite the dark circles and the sag to her shoulders, her eyes still shine with love for her children. She's done so much for us on her own. Tolerated so much from employers —some of whom treat her poorly. It's not her fault she married into a family cursed with dreamers. She deserves a long, happy life free from financial constraints and the stress they cause.

And no matter what—or who—I will give it to her.

After dinner, I wash, Michael dries, and Charlotte stores the dishes as we did since we were children and I stood on a stool at the sink. And Payton did then what he does tonight, make himself scarce. Then we take the last of the wine and join our Mum in the living room where she plays music on the record player.

Michael bows and extends his hand to me for a dance.

I giggle and place mine in his, roughened from labor.

We twirl around the room mindful of the furniture while our Mum and Charlotte dance together beside us. When Michael insists we *listen to music from this century*, he pumps up the volume on his mobile for tunes from a playlist.

Charlotte attempts to show our Mum the latest dance moves, much to her delight. Michael and I clap and urge her on with words of encouragement. Not bad for a woman who turns fifty next year!

I go back to the kitchen for the second bottle of wine. When I return with it held aloft, everyone cheers. Our dance party gets more boisterous and continues until well after one in the morning.

Our Mum tells us goodnight and goes to her bedroom at the far end of the hall. Still giddy, I bump hips with Charlotte as we head to the room we shared. Michael pulls out the bed from the sofa since he prefers to sleep in the living room instead of in the bedroom with Payton. Who could blame the lad? Not I, said the Kat!

CRASH!

"What the bloody hell?! Dammit, Payton!!"

"Oh… f-f-f-uck offff… M-M-Michael…"

Charlotte and I jump up from the bed. But I stop her from leaving the room. She protests. But I shake my head and whisper no sharply.

I rush down the hall towards the living room.

Michael stands in pajama bottoms, glaring down at Payton, who's sprawled out fully clothed on the sofa bed. The stench of cheap liquor burns my nostrils as I move closer.

"Watch out for the lamp!" Michael says as he points to the floor at my bare feet. "The dumb wanker knocked it and the table over before he fell onto my bed. And me."

He shakes his head in disgust.

"Hold on. I'll get the broom and dustpan," he adds as he spins on his heels and strides to the kitchen.

"You prat, Payton!" I whisper shout so as not to wake our

Mum who's still asleep. "When will you bloody well grow up?!"

In silence, Michael returns and sweeps the shards of pottery and glass while I angle the dustpan to collect them. Both of us tired of our eldest sibling's abhorrent behavior.

"Help me roll him. He can sleep on the floor. You sleep in your bed," I tell Michael.

His mouth drops open as he stares at me, shocked by my words and vehement tone.

"Come on," I add.

He nods, and we manage to move Payton's dead weight to the space between the chair and the sofa. Michael turns Payton's head so his cheek rests on the hardwood floor to avoid him choking should he vomit in his sleep.

I fold my arms over my chest and shake my head in disgust. I am beyond pissed right now. He's just ridiculous and needs to help our family, not make matters worse. Add to the equation, not subtract.

Michael takes the garbage bag with the remnants of the lamp, broom, and dustpan back to the kitchen. When he returns, he gives me a hug, and we part.

"What happened?" Charlotte asks as I climb back into bed with a heavy sigh.

"Your drunk brother Payton knocked over the table, broke the lamp, and passed out on Michael's bed. I'll order a new lamp as close to the other one as I can find," I respond. When she frowns and opens her mouth, I add, "Don't worry. Go to sleep. Since Mum is off tomorrow, let's go get mani/pedis. My treat. Cool?"

Charlotte shakes her head.

"I know what you're doing, Kat. It's not fair to you to make up for Payton. But... I appreciate and love you very much," she says, then hugs me before she snuggles back under the covers.

As I lie in bed, I ask for the strength to be the leader of our family. To take the burdens from our Mum's shoulders. To provide for my younger siblings. With that prayer in mind, my eyes drift close.

* * *

"Which color did you pick, Mum?" I ask as she sits between Charlotte and me at the nail salon.

Our Mum glances at the bottom of the bottle with red polish inside. She squints her eyes and hands it to me.

"Vivacious Vixen… Risqué!" I laugh and hand it to the aesthetician, who smiles. "Even for your hands?"

Mum shakes her head.

"Oh no. Don't bother with color on my hands, miss. It'll just get worn off in a few hours," she responds as she looks at the aesthetician. Then looks at them and adds, "But she can tidy the nails up. The cuticles are a bit ragged, I suppose."

I flick my gaze to Charlotte, who bites her lower lip as though holding back a comment.

I know what she's thinking.

Our Mum doesn't wear gloves when she cleans. Never have and never will, she tells us. So naturally, the polish won't last when she dips her hands into hot bleach and water solutions. Years of harsh chemicals leave her hands rough and flaky, despite the special creams I send for her to use. But she's set in her ways, and we don't want to argue with her.

We say nothing in response. No benefit to upsetting our Mum.

"What did you choose, Charlotte?" I ask to change the subject.

"Retro Pink for my hands and Vavavavoom for my toes," she responds with a small smile. "And you?"

I raise the bottles and show them a blush pink for my hands and a fire-engine red for my toes. Like our Mum, my work dictates my hands. I don't want a flashy color. The nude pink pairs well with my conservative attire. But they don't need to know all those details.

We chat while the aestheticians finish our nails. It's so nice to unwind with my Mum and sister. Michael, Charlotte, and I didn't tell her how the lamp broke specifically, only that during the night it bumped from the table.

Of course, Payton was still asleep when she came out into the living room. Not that he'd remember, anyway. Michael managed to put him back on the refolded couch.

I found a replacement lamp and ordered it to arrive in a few days. At the end of the day, that's all that matters. It's not quite a match for the other lamp. But then again, nothing in the flat meant to go together. Our Mum made the individual pieces work.

"How about we go for lunch? We can call Michael to join us," I suggest, as we leave the salon.

"Kat, you really shouldn't spend your money on us like this," our Mum says.

"I agree with Mum, Kat. The mani/pedis were enough," Charlotte says with a shake of her head. The sunlight glints off the natural highlights of her shoulder-length brown hair.

I shake my redhead and respond, "Well, we have to eat. Don't we? It's not a waste if it's a necessity in life. Right?"

"Fine!" They say in unison.

We laugh, and I call Michael.

Eagerly, he agrees to join us at a chippy near the salon in

twenty minutes. It's his day off too, and he's nearby sketching some buildings.

Our Mum, Charlotte, and I stroll towards the fish and chips restaurant. We take our time window shopping at the stores we pass along the way. It's a beautiful sunny day, and we take advantage of the August weather.

When we enter the chippy, the delicious scent of fish and chips permeates the air. I smile at the welcoming aroma as my tastebuds water. As much as I aim to blend in with the posh crowd, I still love the everyday person's meals. Fresh haddock with lots of chippy sauce will do me just right!

As we settle into a booth, Charlotte spies Michael glancing around at the entrance. She stands and waves him over to our table.

"Hey!" He greets us as he slides onto the bench next to our Mum and kisses her cheek. "Don't you lasses look refreshed? Show me the fingernails."

Our Mum giggles and holds out her hands. The fingernails gleam from the buffing in the sunlight filtering in from the window beside our booth.

Charlotte and I take turns showing our hands to him as we giggle. Michael nods his approval.

The server comes over, and we place our order. The food is as delicious as I expected. Golden brown, crisp, flaky fish and chips. The sauce adds the right amount of flavor. The pints of stout complement our meal.

"We showed our fingernails to you. Now, it's your turn," I tell Michael.

He chuckles and raises his hands.

I roll my eyes.

"Not your nails, silly. Show us your drawings," I say.

Michael picks his battered leather rucksack off the stone floor and pulls the sketchpad out. As always, his talent and attention to detail amaze us. Without him saying, we recognize the buildings he's put on paper. Amazing.

"Incredible as always, Michael," I say with a smile.

Charlotte raises her glass.

"Here's to a wonderful day of beautiful buildings and sexy mani/pedis!" She exclaims.

"Hear, hear!"

"Yes, honey!"

"Absolutely!"

* * *

Late Sunday night, I return home from Glasgow, reinvigorated and refocused.

The weekend was fun except for Payton's stunt. My only concern was Mum being short of breath and lightheadedness on Saturday night. She attributed it to the wine the night before and to Saturday's activities.

So she, Charlotte, and I spent Sunday binge watching romance movies on Netflix in our pajamas. Michael went out with a lass he's seeing then came back in time to watch the latest Chris Hemsworth movie with us.

I call Mum to let her know I made it and then crash onto my bed.

Just as my first dream forms, I hear the distant ring of my mobile. I jolt awake, fearing it's from my Mum. But realize it's my regular mobile.

"Hello?" I ask.

"Hi, Kitty Kat."

A grin spreads across my face as sleep falls away. It's Harris. His distinctive baritone voice sends a shiver through my body. And I miss him immediately.

"Hi," I purr.

He chuckles.

"How was your Girls' Getaway? Did you miss me?" He asks.

I roll over onto my side and hug the mobile to my chest. This man is just what I need after Payton's shenanigans. A reminder that someone can take care of me. Give me insurmountable pleasure. I sigh and place the mobile on the pillow next to my head.

"It was nice. But not as nice as our weekends together," I respond. "Did you miss me as much as I missed you?"

A groan slips from his mouth.

I moan in response to my lover's need for me.

"More than you can imagine, Kitty Kat," Harris rumbles.

My pussy clenches, and my nipples pebble. But I can't take my pleasure. It belongs to him. I whimper.

"Next weekend I'm sending a STEELE helicopter for you. It'll be you and me in London Friday night through Monday morning. I'll get you back in time for work," he growls. "Do not even try to say no, Siren."

I close my eyes and inhale deeply. This man knows how to make me want him more and more every. Single. Day.

"Did you hear me, Siren?" He demands in the silence.

My eyes pop open, and I sit up as though he can see me. The mobile held aloft.

"Oh, yes, Harris, I heard you and will be ready—dripping pussy and all," I respond.

He inhales sharply through his nose.

It excites me I can elicit such a lusty response from him.

Air slowly seeps from his mouth as he regains control.

"Good girl. You will need all the natural lubricant you can produce to get you through what I have in mind," he says in a voice laced with dark promises.

Another shiver drops me back to the mattress.

"I cannot wait," I respond breathlessly.

"Good. Now get some sleep and dream of me," he purrs. "Good night, Siren."

I sigh as I roll onto my side.

"Good night, Harris Steele," I whisper. "Dream of me, lover."

HARRIS

"Cheers to the perks of doing what you love for work and being able to do it anywhere in the world. Even on a superyacht in Monte Carlo on a summer evening!"

"And dressed in a tuxedo with a fine glass of Scotch in hand and a beauty on the arm!"

I chuckle and raise my Baccarat Crystal snifter at Lucien and Lauren's remarks.

We're aboard the STEELE Monte Carlo's four-hundred-foot yacht for a Jackson Hole party.

Six years ago, Lydie and Lucien approached Baz for STEELE International to partner with Jackson Corporation's new members-only, high-end, jet-set hot spots. The concept a combination of beach bar, restaurant, and dance club with the first location at our hotel and marina in Monte Carlo followed by our St. Barth's resort.

The name, as expected, is typical Lucien—Jackson Hole, a play on a watering hole for drinking liquor and accessible body areas. Their brands of liquors and cigars would be the exclusives and Lucien would create the menus and signature cocktails. The three areas would be the bar, the restaurant, and the beachfront that offers cabanas, beds, and chaise lounges. Sexy hosts, bartenders, and servers plus dancers and live bands and deejays would round out the staff and entertainment. In essence, Jackson Hole's version of LEVELS on the beach minus the BDSM.

Over the course of five years, they rolled the spots out at key STEELE properties worldwide. As with LEVELS, people sign up for the new member's list that averages a five-month wait, and that's just for the application. The business of pleasure thrives.

Laurent called to tell me about the party, and I jumped on my jet for a chance to leave the variable weather—even in the summer—of London behind. And as Lucien said, being my own boss and with my business on my laptop, I can work anywhere. Who wouldn't opt for the sunny clime of the French Riviera?

Besides, it's been a while since I hung out with my partner in playadom Laurent. Although judging by the dynamic between him and the stunning Yessenia, he's off the market like me. Now, I know why he's been missing in action…

Which reminds me of My Kitty Kat.

Almost every night we FaceTime. Not just for the amazing video sex. But we share our days and talk about normal, everyday stuff. I look forward to seeing her giggle when I crack a joke, as much as watching her break for me in ecstasy.

Next weekend she'll meet me in London, and I'll ask her to come to Southampton Village. She hasn't asked about meeting my family. But don't most women expect it and view it as the next step in a relationship? Especially since she doesn't have a family of her own.

I turn to the superyacht's railing to gaze at the onyx colored water shimmering with the silvery reflection of the full moon. The marina and the lights of Monte Carlo shine in the distance. I'll have to bring My Kitty Kat here for the weekend. She'll enjoy the glitz and glamour of the city.

I lift the snifter to my mouth for another sip.

"*Bonsoir*, Harris."

The Scotch goes up my nose as I jerk. Fingers glide along the front of my trousers and tweak the tip of my cock.

Who the *fuck*?

"Mmmm… Still so impressive. It's been far too long, *amoureux*."

As I spin around, the back of my hand wipes droplets from my lip and down my chin. Before me stands a buxom brunette in a floor-length white gown. The front dips to her navel where a thigh-bearing slit curves from her hip. Her taut nipples poke through the silk material.

Quickly, I avert my gaze to her face.

Full red lips curve into a seductive smile. Predatory hazel eyes glitter.

"Here, let me get that for you," she purrs.

She reaches up and cups the back of my head to draw my mouth down to hers. Her tongue slips out, poised to lick the Scotch remnants from my lips.

A camera flash dispels my shock.

"Stop," I growl.

She chuckles huskily and places her other hand on my chest. Her fingers skim along the silk lapel of my tuxedo. She shakes her head. Raven colored waves tumble around her heart-shaped face.

"Don't tease me, Harris. Let's have fun tonight," the

brunette says. "I'll use my tongue to make you scream again."

With a wink, she opens her mouth to show the impressive titanium barbell piercing. Her tongue wiggles from side to side like a cobra snake ready to strike.

Oh, hell no.

I extricate myself from her clutches.

"Listen, mademoiselle. I do not recall a night with you. Nor do I have any interest in one now. You are a beautiful woman who will find a willing partner with ease. *Bonsoir*," I tell her, then turn back to Laurent and Lucien.

The elder Jackson hides his laugh behind the rim of his snifter. His gemstone eyes glint with mirth as he watches the brunette saunter away. The flowy train of her backless gown shimmers as her hips sway.

"What a delightful start to the evening," Lucien chuckles. "But do tell why you passed up such an enticing creature?"

I clap him on the shoulder and grin like the Cheshire Cat.

"Other priorities, cuz. I'm a reformed player," I respond.

Lucien cocks his head and glances between Laurent with Yessenia and me. He grins and lifts his snifter in a salute.

"Well, well, well, gentleman. Here's to you," he says with a nod.

Laurent pulls Yessenia closer to his side and kisses her. When she comes up breathless, he raises his glass.

"I second that!" He smirks.

"Third!" I say.

Yessenia giggles and buries her face against Laurent's chest.

"When do we meet the woman who wrangled *your* heart, Harris?" Laurent asks. "You should have introduced us to her tonight."

I tell them I will do the honors in Southampton Village. They rib me about secrecy. But I hold firm.

Laurent takes Yessenia to dance while Lucien and I go mingle. I see a few CEOs and CTOs whose companies—and personal—I'd like to add to the client roster for STEELE Technology and Cyber Security. It's at events like this one where deals get made.

By the end of the night, I've scheduled meetings in the coming weeks. With Haley still on maternity leave, I space them out to allow enough time for travel to several countries. Being the competitive bunch we are, I bet her I'd secure more business while she lounged around Aboyne Castle as the Countess.

I had to cover my ears from her shouts at me for equating raising babies with laziness. I responded her behavior was not becoming of her noble title. She blew her lid. I chuckle as I put my mobile away and head to a bar for another drink. A well-earned one!

By the time I return to my suite at the hotel, it's too late to video call with My Kitty Kat. But I notice a missed call and a text message from her as I dump my pockets on the dresser. My foot pauses midair when I click play on the attached video.

My Siren wears a smile, and a pink ribbon tied in a bow around her neck. Nothing else.

Buck naked, she crouches on the sofa in what better be her living room. Back straight, hands on her thighs, and knees bent wide. The pink lips of her pussy glisten with her sweet cream. The bud of her clit pokes between them. She trails the middle finger to circle an areola. The nipple beads with each pass. She pinches it with a small cry before she slips the finger into her mouth.

Wide emerald green eyes stare at the camera as she sucks

on the long digit. They flutter close when she withdraws it from her mouth with a pop. Eyes closed. Mouth open in a perfect O. My Kitty Kat lets her head fall back. Glossy red hair cascades below her ass. Nipples point toward the camera.

She spreads her knees to the maximum and puts the moistened tip of her finger onto the engorged tip of her clit. A shudder wracks her body.

A zing races through mine.

We groan in unison.

With hooded eyes, My Siren gazes at the camera.

"I'll let you finish me off in London. Good night, Mr. Steele."

The video goes dark.

Fuck. Me.

On my way to the shower, I replay the video, cock hardening to the point of pain. It demands release. If not inside of My Kitty Kat, my fist will have to do.

I place the mobile on the vanity and strip. With each step to the shower, my cock thumps against my happy trail, grazing my navel. The bulbous tip an angry red and shiny with pre-cum. My palm glides over it to lubricate my shaft. As hot as My Kitty Kat made me, this will be fast and dirty.

Grunts pour from my mouth as the vision of My Kitty Kat perched on the sofa fills my mind's eye. Her alabaster skin flushed rosy from her arousal. Pupils dilated. Mouth voracious.

The muscles in my forearm flex. My balls tighten.

My vision expands to include me in the scene.

With my head thrown back, the wolf howls as he unleashes a torrent of cum over My Kitty Kat's belly and her bare mound. Hot ropes of the wolf's cum run down between her parted legs to pool beneath her ass. I reach down and rub my seed into her clit and pussy, marking her with my scent.

She stares up at me, enraptured by my feral claim.

"MINE!" I growl.

My Kitty Kat shivers.

"Yours," she purrs.

* * *

"*MERCI*, MADEMOISELLE."

"*De rien*, Monsieur Jackson."

The server flashes a seductive smile at Laurent as she passes a Mimosa to him. Her fingertips slide along his as he takes the flute's stem.

His smile turns into a scowl.

"You do know Jackson Hole discourages staff from flirtatious behavior with members?" He asks her, then continues when she confirms. "That stance applies to members of the family, too. Be sure to keep that in mind to avoid a reprimand from Human Resources. *Ça va*, mademoiselle?"

She swallows thickly and bows her head as she backs away.

"She's more thirsty than you, lover boy!" I taunt. When he rolls his eyes, I ask, "Where's Yessenia?"

Laurent smirks and tips his chin towards the hotel.

"She's recovering," he snickers and sips his Mimosa. "Later, she'll meet her friends for shopping and lunch. Which gives you and me time to catch up."

He shifts on his chaise lounge, where we sit on the beach. The sunlight glints off the lenses of his aviators as he lifts them to cock his eyebrow at me.

"I'll go first. Then you tell me what's up with you, *lover boy,*" he says, then raises his hand to stop me from speaking. "And don't give me that bullshit about Southampton Village. I share now; you share now."

He proceeds to tell me about Yessenia. He's as gone about the vivacious beauty as I am about My Kitty Kat. I bring him up to date on my fledgling relationship. Who knew Laurent and I would fall at the same time?

A paddleball lands in the sand next to my chaise lounge.

I bend over to retrieve it and glance up for its owner.

A statuesque blonde in a white string bikini jogs over. Her tits bounce each time her feet touch the sand. She smiles and waves the paddle in the air.

Ordinarily Laurent and I would jostle one another for dibs. But neither of us have an interest. Instead, I stride over to return the paddleball. She thanks me and jogs back to her friends who await her near the water's edge. They wave and offer their thanks. A bevy of beauties, and my cock remains flaccid.

The sparkling turquoise waters of the Mediterranean Sea beckon.

I turn to Laurent and tell him I'm going for a swim.

He replies he'll join me after he finishes a text message to Yessenia—who recovered, apparently. I chuckle and stride to the shoreline.

The first wave wraps me in the warmth of the Med as I dive in. The crystal clear water allows me to see all the way to the pontoon off shore. I pass snorkelers who revel in the colorful fish below the surface.

I climb onto the deck and settle on an empty spot facing the beach.

Laurent's powerful strokes cleave through the water. In moments, he's beside me. He leans back on his elbows with his face towards the sky.

"You really can't beat the Riviera during high season," he says with his eyes closed. "Who can blame Lucien for living here half of the year? Or Rog and Leonie."

I agree and stretch out on my back with my hands clasped beneath my head. The sun dries the water from my skin before we dive back into the depths.

"Race you!" Laurent shouts when we break the surface. He pushes my head underwater and kicks off.

I catch up to him before his toe touches the sandy bottom. My hand snakes out and yanks him backwards by the ankle. He thrashes and wrenches around to grab me in a headlock. We wrestle as we've done since we were kids.

Water splashes all around us, scattering the swimmers nearby. They egg on our antics with whistles and shouts.

Evenly matched—despite Laurent being two inches taller than me—we call it quits as we stride onto the sand. I give him a last shove. He retaliates with one of his fancy Scottish martial arts moves and trips me. I stumble but regain my footing as I call him an ass.

He smirks.

We throw ourselves down on our chaise lounges. Shadows block the sun.

I open my eyes to reveal three women standing over us.

"Aren't you Harris Steele and Laurent Jackson?" One asks in an American accent.

Laurent nods.

She turns to her friends, and they giggle.

"You're even more handsome in person! Do you mind if we take the chaise lounges next to yours?" Another pipes up.

I shake my head and gesture to the free seats, then cover my eyes with the crook of my elbow. No need to encourage conversation…

Refreshingly, they don't say anymore to us. They chatter

and laugh as they pose for selfies amongst themselves. Apparently, they're members of Jackson Hole Miami, and it's their first time to Monte Carlo for a birthday.

I overhear them trying to decide where to go for lunch, and what to do tonight to celebrate.

"Not to be nosy. But I recommend…" I lean up and share the best places to go, and they thank me.

After a while, Laurent and I head back to the hotel.

Freshly showered, I step out onto my suite's terrace. The azure water of the Mediterranean Sea sparkle beyond the white walls. The scent of the salty air mingles with the tantalizing aromas of lunchroom service set on the table.

I settle on a chair and lift the stainless-steel cloche. The bouillabaisse makes my mouth water. Once I've eaten and room service removed the dishes, I set up my laptop to work. An hour later, my mobile rings.

A grin spreads across my face at My Kitty Kat's name on the screen.

"Hey, babe—"

"Did you get my text message?" She cuts in.

I blink at the sharp tone of her voice, then respond no as I check the app. Links appear. I click on one, and it opens to photos from last night of me with the brunette. "Exclusive: Harris Steele and Mystery Date Cozy Up on a Superyacht in Monte Carlo!"

Other links reveal photos from this morning on the beach.

"Harris Steele and His Big Paddle!"

"Last Single of The STEELE Quaternity Frolics with Babes!"

"Harris Steele and His Triplets!"

I groan and run my hand over my face.

"Well?!" Kat demands.

I switch the call to FaceTime.

Emerald green slits glare at me from the screen. Eyebrows pinch together. Her mouth an angry slash on her reddened face.

"Kat, those images are out of context. As you can see, I'm all alone in my suite," I tell her as I pan the mobile around. "The woman from last night approached me, and I told her no. The ones on the beach sat next to my cousin Laurent and me. I gave them some advice on what to do while they're here. Okay?"

She purses her lips.

"Come on. You know how tabloids spread lies. I can understand your reaction. But trust me. Nothing happened," I continue in her silence. "Okay?"

Kat turns from the screen to speak to someone at the office. When she returns, she sighs.

"Fine. I trust you. It's just upsetting to see women throw themselves at you, and I'm all the way in bloody Aberdeen," she responds.

I waggle my eyebrows and tell her, "London's calling, Kitty Kat…"

I couldn't believe the ferocity of the possessiveness that rolled through me like wildfire through dry brush at the sight of Harris—my man—with those women. The pampered born with a silver spoon in their mouths kind. Who could have any man their hearts' desire with a flutter of their long eyelashes or the beckoning of their little fingers. Those who never had to lift said finger to work a day in their entire entitled lives.

Aargh!

Gladys was in the office. So when Harris didn't respond to my text message, I went to the break room for the call. On the way, the images burned into my mind. My anger increased. I struggled for a steady voice.

As he spoke and his honest face on the screen doused the flames. His reminder of our next rendezvous in London cleared the smoke. My mind and vision returned to normal.

Now, I glance at him as we ride to my surprise.

I can appreciate women's attraction to Harris Steele.

Tonight, he wears a vest and pants in buttery soft black

leather molded to his muscular body. His biceps and pecs flex as he maneuvers the vintage Aston Martin Vanquish. Thighs bunch as he shifts the gears. Heavy black leather boots add to his kick-ass look.

I reach over and tangle my fingers in the longer hair atop his head, then cup the back of it.

Harris angles his face to glance at me and smiles.

Heart-stoppingly gorgeous.

My man.

"Excited for your surprise, Kitty Kat?" He asks with his eyes back on the road.

I grin and respond, "Absolutely! I wish you would tell me already. Pretty please?"

He chuckles but shakes his head.

I sit back in my seat and pout.

He wouldn't tell me about our destination. But he selected my outfit.

On the bed at our sumptuous suite in STEELE Mayfair, he laid the most exquisite hand-crafted black corset with a matching thong by Lola's Coterie. The sculpting design creates an hourglass figure with lace panels across the front in a butterfly shape and nipped in at the waist with a narrow strip of velvet. Elastic trim crisscross to form the shoulder straps, center panel, and outer panels of the lace. Suspender straps attach at the front and back to silk stockings beneath my butt cheeks that lift from the silk stilettos on my feet. A bow around my neck and tiny ones between my breasts and at the top of the thong make me look like a present. Harris' present.

His mouth curved into a devilish smile when I sashayed out of the bedroom. He twirled his finger for me to spin. I kept my eyes on his, glancing over my shoulders with each rotation. His grin spread, and his dove gray eyes blackened to obsidian.

As he helped me into a duster coat, he murmured how we'd never make it to our destination if he didn't cover me pronto. We rode the private lift down to the garage and slid into the sleek sports car.

We ride on as music plays over the sound system. The erotic beat of The Art of Noise "Moments in Love" thrums through my body. I side glance Harris to determine if he's as aroused by its sensuality as me.

A smirk tugs at the corners of his lips as his eyes remain on the road. But he doesn't return my stare.

I huff and fidget on the leather seat.

We pull up to what appears to be a former bank. A queue of well-dressed people forms outside of it. I notice their attire differs drastically from Harris' and mine. No lace in sight. Only expensive dress shirts and trousers and designer mini dresses affix their bodies. They're ready to party, and we're ready for who knows what.

Before I can ask Harris about the differences, a valet opens my door. He extends his hand, and I slip from the low seat, careful to keep the duster closed. I'd hate for the others to think less than of me.

Harris strides around the bonnet and places his hand on the small of my back. He guides me to the front door of the building, where two men in black bespoke suits hold clipboards and wear earpieces. They greet him by name deferentially and avoid eye contact with me.

I frown and glance up at Harris.

He stares straight ahead as we enter the lobby. A gorgeous man bids us good evening—Harris by name—and takes my duster. Then he gestures towards a tray of colorful enamel bracelets. Harris picks up a silver one and places it around my wrist. I admire the lovely piece of jewelry while he closes one on his wrist before the man opens the doors behind him.

Once my eyes adjust to the dim lighting, my jaw hits the floor.

WTF?!?!?!

All around the massive room, men and women—clothed like Harris and me—partake in erotic acts. Some on stages while others carry on at seating alcoves clustered along the darker perimeter. Still more stand about, engrossed by the surrounding happenings.

The sounds of their moans and groans—including some cries of pain—fill my ears. My wide eyes dart about the room, unsure of where to settle for more than a second. One attraction after the other draws my attention like a carnal carnival.

I don't realize I halted a few feet beyond the door until Harris nudges me along. An eager couple behind us surges ahead. The woman holds a leash attached to another woman's neck as she crawls on all fours, naked save for the thick black leather collar. Her upturned ass hides nothing.

I gasp audibly when the woman slaps her partner's rear end with a cane.

The cracking sound blends in with the other hedonistic noises.

"Welcome to LEVELS London's Peepshow. Come, Siren."

Harris' warm breath against the delicate shell of my ear startles me. He chuckles and clasps my hand as he leads the way through the other people. He navigates around the room, pausing at one stage after the other. Never does he speak.

The further we enter the bacchanalia, the more my pussy

throbs. My nipples already poke against the lace of the corset. The images swirl around my head, increasing as the melodic pulse of sultry music accompanies the moans and groans of the revelers. While the air is heavy with the mixture of expensive cologne, alluring perfume, and immeasurable arousal. The heady aroma alights on my tongue as I gasp from the thrill of the scene.

We enter a hallway with rooms on either side where behind floor-to-ceiling windows more people engage in acts of spanking, bondage, role playing, and more. Whatever sexy fantasy one can imagine comes to life within the four walls of each room.

A robust man stands between the thighs of another who's trussed up by heavy chains attached to the ceiling. He pours wax from a red candle over the bound man's torso. He hisses and jostles the chains when the hot liquid lands on his erect cock.

I watch, enraptured by the sight of the man nibbling the wax from the hard shaft. My pulse quickens with each passionate cry of the man in chains.

Harris moves me from the window to the next where a woman flogs a man cuffed to a large standing X made of wood. His back, ass, and thighs welted by the lash. I cringe as each flick of her wrist administers another potent strike.

Yet another room reveals two men and two women. They're so intertwined it's hard to distinguish one from the other. Their moans and groans reach the viewers as though we stood beside them.

I bite my lower lip to hold back a savage moan of my own.

Behind me, Harris' erect cock presses against my lower back. He's as turned on as I am. I tilt my head back to glance at him, only to find his hooded gaze already on mine.

I shudder as my cheeks heat.

The last room contains the setup of a doctor's office. A woman lies on the table while the doctor—a man dressed in green scrubs barefoot with a stethoscope about his neck—exams her pussy. He uses what appears to be a clamp on her clit attached by a slim chain to ones on each nipple. The contraption holds her lower lips open while his fist dives into her core. With each thrust, she screams in ecstasy. Head thrown back and mouth wide open.

I shudder and moan with her. Each knuckle drags along the walls of my dripping core.

I fear if Harris were not with me, I would drop to the ground and seek my own release, eager to cum from my overloaded senses.

He must sense my need because he leads me from the exhibition hall back to the primary room.

Newcomers replace those who were on the stages previously. I watch, fascinated by a woman bound by ropes suspended from the ceiling as a man fucks her forbidden bottom hole. She writhes and screams as the ropes sway with each impressive piston of his narrow hips. His leg muscles bunch from the power.

I cringe at the sight—never an anal girl before. Although now, I wonder what it must feel like since the woman screams in rhapsody.

"I can't wait to claim *your* ass, Siren."

Harris' unexpected words make me jump and squeak.

He chuckles wickedly as we move on.

My head swivels on my head. I do my best not to ogle now that the initial shock lessens as it registers we're in the BDSM club owned by Lucien Jackson. Since Harris says he's not a Dom, I didn't expect him to be a member here.

I glance up at him.

"Good?" He leans down to ask in my ear.

"Yes," I respond.

We continue on to stairs that lead to a floor below. At the bottom, a fascinating pair flank a set of heavy wooden double doors with two large, iron circular pulls. The woman wears thin black laces that drape over her naked torso and hips. The man dressed only in a black leather loincloth so tiny it covers his massive bulge barely. Both have strips of black leather around their throats.

"Welcome to the Cellar," they speak in unison with their eyes downcast as they tug the iron pulls.

A woman's wail pierces the air.

My knees buckle.

Harris tightens his hold on my hand and grips my hip to steady me.

"Whoa there, lass. I guarantee the woman enjoys the pain," he murmurs in my ear. "Come."

Curiosity kills the cat?

Well, I need to know. So I allow Harris to guide me through the doors.

"Bloody hell…" I whisper at the even more outrageous sights before me.

An expansive, grand hall, austere in design houses this new erotic playground. A multi-beamed high ceiling; cobblestone floors; brick walls; lighting that resembles flickering torches in brackets on the walls and in metal stands scattered around the room; an assortment of what looks like Medieval torture devices placed in clusters.

My wide eyes jump from one section to another. I watch what I assume to be a voyeur watch five men well use all three holes and two hands of one woman. Before another giant wooden X, a woman in an all black leather jumpsuit flicks her wrist to snap the tip of a whip onto the quivering reddened skin of a man. His cries muffled by a ball stuck in his mouth and tied behind his head.

A long wail draws my attention to the near corner, the source of my earlier fright. A woman hangs upside down, arms bound to her torso with her knees bent by red rope. Red wax drips onto her exposed pussy.

The man administering the pain covers her seam with his mouth. The wail morphs into a guttural moan. Her body shudders. The ropes tremble. No sooner than silence comes from her O-shaped mouth does the man release her from the ropes and bundles her still shuddering body against his solid bare chest. She buries her face in his neck as he murmurs in her damp hair.

My pussy throbs at the carnal panorama. I'm so aroused my cream coats the thong and seeps past the gusset to drip along my inner thighs. Unsure whether my cheeks flush from embarrassment or from unfulfilled desire. I shift on my feet, eager for relief.

"See, Siren? She enjoys the pain."

I jump.

Lost in my hedonistic thoughts, I forgot Harris stood behind me. His palms glide up and down my arms as he nuzzles the side of my neck. Soft kisses a contrast to the erotic torture surrounding us in what I presume is the dungeon.

I mewl and tilt my neck to give him better access. My hands reach behind me to find purchase on his thighs. Giddiness weakens my knees.

Harris stoops to place a forearm beneath them and the other behind my back. My arms wrap around his neck, and I find myself burying my face as the wax woman did. Now, I understand. Her feelings were so intense she needed to hide from them, safe in her lover's powerful arms. As I am in mine.

My gaze lifts when he sets me on my feet and squeezes my hip bones to gain my attention. I glance around to find we're in an alcove with dark red velvet curtains held by metal links suspended from the ceiling. They separate us from the primary floor of the Cellar.

"How do you feel?" Harris asks as my eyes return to his.

"I thought you weren't a Dom," I reply in a rush.

He smiles and squeezes my hips again.

"I am not," he responds, then continues. "But I do enjoy giving pleasure beyond the vanilla. You *have* enjoyed the spankings and edging, correct?"

My flush deepens, and I know it's from lust. I lick my bottom lip before I nod my head.

"Words, Siren. I will have your words," Harris says.

I swallow.

"Yes, I have," I respond. "And I want more."

A predatory gleam brightens his eyes.

"What's your safeword? A word for all play to stop at once," he asks gruffly.

I think a moment before I respond, "Titian."

"Titian," he repeats as he fingers a lock of my red hair. "Come."

Harris guides me to an X and turns me with my back to it as I face him. His eyes rove down my body and back up slowly. He licks his full lower lip.

"I knew you'd look sexy as fuck in this corset"—he sighs and shrugs—"Alas, it must come off." Then he bares me naked before him.

He bows his head to lick each nipple with the flat of his tongue. The texture of it furls my nipples, and I moan. A nip to one sends a bolt of lightning to my pulsating core. His hands grip my hips as he trails open-mouthed kisses along my belly.

My butt hits the wood of the cross. I gasp, shocked we moved. A groan slips from my mouth when Harris parts the petals of my pussy with his tongue. He laps at my cream in deliberate, slow strokes.

Each time my orgasm nears the surface, he withdraws and nips my inner thighs. The pleasure followed by pain heightens my desire. My pelvis grinds against his mouth.

Two sharp smacks to my swollen pussy lips jolt through me.

I scream.

"Stay still, naughty lass," Harris commands.

I want to argue. But I want to cum more. My pelvis stills.

"Good lass," he murmurs as his lips glide along my calf.

He taps an ankle and tells me to widen my stance. Suede cocoons my ankle when he closes a cuff around it. He repeats the process with my other ankle before he rises.

My eyes lift to his as I press my hands to his firm chest. The muscles ripple beneath his warm skin as he takes one wrist and then the other to attach more cuffs. Bound, I cannot move, but a couple of inches. A sense of ease descends over me. I am no longer in control. It rests in Harris' hands. My eyes close.

"Hey, are you still with me?" Harris asks softly as he holds my chin between his thumb and forefinger. When I open my heavy-lidded eyes and respond positively, he smiles and kisses my lips. "Good lass."

I watch as he strides to a chest of drawers and returns with a peacock feather and a crop in one hand and a fist.

He tucks the implements in the back pocket of his leather pants, then kisses me as he fondles my breasts. His head lowers to suckle a nipple while his fingers dip into my pussy to collect cream he smears on the other one. He alternates between the two until my head lolls on my neck.

I hiss at the bite to my peaked nipple. Before I can question Harris, another bite closes on the other one. A glance down reveals rubber-tipped metal clamps pinch my nipples. A chain dangles between them and leads to Harris' fist.

"What—"

"Safeword?" He asks.

I blink as I consider, then shake my head.

"Then, quiet," he says.

He crouches before me and licks my pussy seam.

My head falls back against the X as the pain mingles with the pleasure. Until a third bite jerks me from bliss. This time, my brain screams *Titian*, but my body hums wait.

Harris sits on his haunches as he studies my reaction. When I don't use my safeword, he leans forward and kisses my mons.

"So beautiful, Siren," he murmurs against the heated skin.

He rises to his full height and towers over me. Then he steps back and whips a red silk blindfold from his front pocket. Deftly, he covers my eyes.

The room disappears as my hearing ramps up. Every sound intensifies, including the beating of my heart.

I tremble as the feather tickles my skin. Goosebumps rise in its wake. A whistle sounds. A snap stops all goosebumps in their tracks. The crop lands on my outer hip. I cry out and struggle against my bonds even as Harris demands I remain still. A flurry of whistles followed by snaps has my hips, thighs, and breasts afire. Cries turn into yowls.

The feather returns to tease the marks I'm sure appear on my alabaster skin.

"Safeword?"

Harris' whisper against my panting mouth jolts me.

Once again, I consider how my body feels. The feather that tickled now stresses the crop's snaps. Not enough for tears from my eyes.

But my pussy weeps.

I nip Harris' lower lip in response.

He growls and grinds his raging hard-on against my lower belly.

I whine from the loss of contact when he steps back. Then I wail when the crop snaps my dripping pussy lips. A nip for a nip, I suppose.

Harris continues to evoke pain and pleasure until my head hangs as I sag in the cuffs worn out from the unexpected orgasms he demanded from my body. The crop clatters to the floor. His mouth closes on my clit. A burst of pain radiates from it. I scream.

His mouth worries the sensitive bud until another climax blanks my mind again. He swallows my cream noisily, then trails kisses up to my breasts.

I brace myself for more erotic pain. Not disappointed, I scream again as blood rushes to my tender nipples.

Harris cossets them with his tongue while he plays with my clit. The head of his cock breaches my pussy lips in one swift thrust to the root.

I wail as another orgasm rocks through me. Fists clench. Thighs quake. Toes curl.

He pounds away until he stiffens, and his cock pulsates as he shoots his load into the condom. His roar overtakes those in the primary room as he continues to piston his hips.

My pussy milks his dick as his orgasm triggers a final one of mine.

Fully spent, my mind floats in blissful oblivion.

My Kitty Kat slumbers curled on my lap. Her face pressed into my neck. Soft snores prove the depth and peace of her sleep. She's content.

As am I.

I brush my nose over her damp hair, inhaling her alluring scent. I smile at her choice of Titian as her safeword. The gorgeous hue of her hair reminds me of the Renaissance master. I wonder what he'd think of his name as a safeword used in BDSM. I shake my head and chuckle. Hey, I'll always remember it.

She stirs and mumbles my name as she leans further into my chest.

My hand rubs her back as I rumble in my chest to soothe her into rest. It makes my heart swell that she calls for me, even in her sleep. Her need for me matches mine for her.

I know Kat cares for me, and it's a relief her care is for *me* and not for my name or money. But I worry still. It would suck big time if she did not differ from others. I shake my head to rid it of the troublesome thought and let it replay our scene.

"Harris?"

My head jerks up as I open my eyes and glance around. The rhythm of a sensual bass blends with the moans of pleasure register first. The scent of sex mingles with expensive perfume and cologne. My Siren's face tilts up to meet mine.

She kisses my lips.

"You fell asleep, too," she whispers hoarse from her screams of ecstasy. "How long were we knocked out?"

I lift my wrist. An hour passed since we finished our scene. Well, damn.

"An hour. We have a suite reserved upstairs, or would you prefer we return to the hotel?" I ask. But I hope she's ready to leave since I'd rather wake up at the hotel than here and have to go there in the morning, anyway. "I want you to have the full experience of LEVELS, so it's up to you, babe."

She stretches her arms overhead, and I slip a nipple into my mouth. She mewls and runs her fingers through my hair.

"I love it so far. But let's go back to our suite. I'm ravenous," she replies.

Her nipple pops from my mouth when I lift my head.

"For me or food?" I ask with a smirk.

She giggles and rolls her eyes.

"For… both!" She teases.

I chuckle and lift her from my lap. Steadying hands on her hips prevent her from dropping to the stone floor. She smiles when I ask if she's good, and we dress again.

During the ride back, I ask her about LEVELS.

Her eyes light up as she recounts what she saw and asks about what she doesn't understand. Based on her reaction, we agree she's into the BDSM lifestyle. We decide to explore her newfound interest to determine her limits and favorites. Her excitement is contagious. I can't wait to teach more to her. Bind My Kitty Kat to me from the pleasure I instill.

I steer the Aston Martin Vanquish into the garage beneath STEELE Mayfair and help her from the low seat. She giggles when I lift her into my arms and carry her to the private elevator. On the ride up to our suite, she kisses me until my knees wobble. The vixen returns from carnal bliss with an unquenchable passion.

But I know she needs a break. So I set her down inside the foyer of the suite and tell her to ready the shower. When she pouts, I turn her around and smack that ass. She sashays away, swaying her hips enticingly.

I watch—caught by her Siren's call—then dial room service for a banquet of edible delights. It's late, but they know a Steele is in residence at the President's Suite and hop to it. I smirk. The name does have its benefits most times…

As I head to the primary bedroom, I strip and toss my leathers onto the sofa in the sitting room before I join My Kitty Kat in the shower. Steam fills the bathroom. I can just make out her curvy form under the water's spray. My cock hardens.

I stride to the glass door and open it. My cock twitches at her bodacious body, wet and begging to be fucked. Hard. Again.

She glances over her shoulder at me and shimmies her grip-worthy hips. Her ass bounces.

Fuck. Me.

"Oh, Mr. Steele, so good of you to join me," she purrs. "If memory recalls correctly, you told me how you can't wait to claim my ass. Well…"

Her unspoken words hang in the steamy air.

I blink.

Say what now?

She wiggles her proffered treat and braces her palms against the marble wall.

Now, I know I just said she needs a break. But… I'll clarify… Her pussy needs a break, not her more than willing ass…

She winks at me.

And.

It's.

On.

"Oh, Siren, be careful of what you wish for," I warn with my lips against her ear.

She shudders but holds strong.

"*You* better be careful, Mr. Steele. You opened my sexual tastebuds to so much more…" she retorts. "Now, will you live up to your promises? Or fizzle out. Poof."

I growl and smack her ass, sits bones, and upper thighs in quick succession. She dances on her toes as her palms slap the marble wall. I yank her hips back and press my torso on her back to lower her parallel to the floor.

"You sure you want all of this in your ass, naughty lass?" I ask as I circle my hips. My erect cock settles between her ass cheeks.

She mewls.

I smack that ass.

"You forget yourself, naughty lass," I growl.

"Y-Yes!" She yelps.

I align my cock with her pussy. One thrust sends her to the balls of her feet. She moans, and I grunt. Her wet pussy grips me.

My thrusts increase in speed as I use her natural cream to lube my cock. Satisfied, I withdraw and press the mushroom head to her back entrance. The muscles of the puckered hole resist. But I pinch her clit, and she screams through another climax. I slide in.

"Push out, Siren, and let me in," I wheeze through the tight grip her ass has on my cockhead.

She mewls and shifts on her feet, unaccustomed to anal sex. And especially not to my sizable dick.

I take it inch by inch until she relaxes to let me in balls deep. My movement ceases while she adjusts. When she undulates her hips, I move.

We find our rhythm for her forbidden hole.

To ensure she finds as much pleasure as I do, my fingers work her clit. She cums again, and I howl from the pressure. Then I let loose. She matches me thrust for thrust until I cum with an explosive knee-buckling climax. My seed jettisons into her ass. Some of it escapes the tight fit to dribble down her cheeks.

I collapse over her back and band my arms around her waist. My legs give out, and we slide to the shower floor. Once I soften, I slip from her puckered hole and pull her onto my lap. The warm water sluices over our skin.

"So good, Siren. So fucking good. And all mine," I croon against the top of her head.

She mewls and leans into me heavily.

"How do you feel?" I ask.

My Kitty Kat purrs and kisses my nipple.

I purr in response.

After a while, I stand with her in my arms. She wobbles. So I set her on the bench and bathe her gently as I thank her for her gift. Then I wash off and carry her from the shower to dry our bodies. I put robes on us and carry her to the dining room.

The room service staff set our late-night meal on the table.

I settle My Kitty Kat into a chair and lift the stainless-steel cloches.

"Mmmmm. Smells delicious," she murmurs.

I fix us a plate and lift her so I can sit, and she rests on my lap. I alternate feeding her and myself, equally hungry after our scene and lovemaking at the club and in the shower. At first, she fusses. But after I growl my displeasure, she opens her mouth.

When we're full, I carry her back to the sitting room of our bedroom. I light the fire in the fireplace—even in August, London nights have a chill in the air. I sit on the sofa and pull her onto my lap.

"STEELE Foundation has its annual fundraiser next week. Will you come?" I ask.

She stiffens between my legs.

"I'd like to introduce you to my family. It's at our beach-front compound in Southampton Village, New York. Remember, I have to return on Monday to New York City for a while. It's been some time since I was in our main office…" I ramble on.

She shifts and puts a finger over my lips.

"Of course, I'd like to come. But I have work, Harris," My Kitty Kat says remorsefully. "I can't very well fly across the globe on a whim. I have responsibilities."

I grin.

"Lachlan agreed to give you a few days off so you can make it a full holiday. So what say you now, Kitty Kat?" I ask more sure of her answer.

She frowns and leans back.

"You spoke to Mr. Jackson before you spoke with me?

You mean, he knows about us?" She asks, folding her arms beneath her tits.

Oh boy…

"I mentioned it to him and to my sister, Harley. He's cool with you and I dating, and my sister wants to meet you," I respond. "No need to worry."

She flares her nostrils.

I poke her sides and grin.

"Come on. Is it all that bad for them to know and for you to meet my family?" I ask. I go for nonchalance. But my heart thunders in my chest.

She's pissed about Lachlan and Haley knowing?

She doesn't want to meet my family?

Don't women want to meet their boyfriend's loved ones? WTF?

At last, she sighs.

I release the breath I held with a gush of air.

"Fine. But you should have spoken to me first, Harris. I don't want your family to think poorly of me," she says.

I'm still trying to understand how to do a relationship. But I know she has a point. So I cup her face.

"As long as you're true to me, my family will hold you in high regard," I say, then continue. "No pressure, but you're the first woman I'll bring home to meet everyone. No one has not inclined me to do so before you, Kat Roberts. You are special to me."

As before, an indecipherable expression flashes in her eyes.

"Everything okay, Kat?" I ask, concerned.

Her gaze flicks away for a moment, then returns to mine.

It's as though she's struggling. And I don't know why.

She shakes her head, and a smile replaces the scowl.

"I am truly honored, Harris. I will not disappoint you," she says, then continues with a grin. "Thank you for getting my days off cleared, too. I've never been to the glitzy Hamptons. In fact, I've never been outside of the UK before you."

Her face brightens as she asks me about my family and what she should bring. I tell her I'll take care of her gown and anything else she wants. When she protests, I tell her it's my idea, so my responsibility. After I flip her over my thighs and spank that ass, she gives in.

Her hooded eyes tell me it's time to go to bed.

I make love to My Kitty Kat until neither of us can lift a finger.

KAT

"**M**s. Roberts."

A gentle shake of my shoulder rouses me from sleep. I lift my head from the silk pillow to face the flight attendant for Harris' private jet. She smiles at me and continues.

"We land in thirty minutes. You slept soundly. So I didn't want to disturb you for dinner service. Would you care for a beverage or a snack after you freshen up?"

I return her smile and thank her. Once she leaves, I head for the bathroom, then switch into a pink floral maxi dress and gold gladiator sandals. I leave my hair flowing down my back the way Harris likes it and apply pink lip gloss. A spritz of perfume tops it off.

Despite Harris' offer to buy some clothes for me, I splurged on a few pieces, including this maxi dress, others, and some bikinis. I want to make a good impression on his family. Not to mention hold my own against the chi-chi women in their social circle. I don't want to appear as some know-nothing lass with the accent.

With a sigh, I settle in a cushy leather chair and glance out of the window.

Incredible!

We fly below the clouds with a clear view of the Atlantic Ocean's blue palette before the coastline, where ribbons of sand separate lavish mansions from the water's edge. Sailboats and power yachts bob on the sparkling surface. People on colorful towels and frolicking in the surf dot the beaches. Not one ready to let summer go yet.

"Here you are, Ms. Roberts."

The flight attendant rouses me from my thoughts.

I nod to thank her for the cool glass of water. My nerves make my mouth dry the closer the jet noses towards the airport. The landing strips and tower come into view.

This next week will be a testament to my ability to deceive not only Harris, but his entire family. He told me we're staying in his wing at his parents' mansion in the compound. Which means I'll be under constant surveillance.

Not to mention all the Jacksons will be at their compound next door. One on one with Lachlan or Lydie differs vastly from face time with their parents and their brothers. Talk about uncomfortable.

The flight attendant collects my empty glass as she tells me to buckle up for landing. I thank the crew as I disembark.

"Hey, babe!"

Harris strides towards me. His smile even more brilliant against his olive-tone skin kissed by the sun. A lock of his ebony hair falls over the aviators as he reaches me.

I brush it away and palm his face between my hands. On tiptoe, I slant my mouth over his for a passion-laced kiss.

He slips his sunglasses off, then swings me from my feet into a circle. His powerful frame captures me effortlessly. I squeal in his mouth, but his lips lock fast. He doesn't stop until we need to come up for air.

"I missed you, Kitty Kat," Harris murmurs, with his forehead pressed to mine. Our breaths intermingle as he stares into my eyes.

"I missed you more, Mr. Steele," I whisper.

And I do. And it makes it harder every time to continue with my revenge. I wish his connection to the Jacksons didn't exist. It's just so complicated now.

I sigh heavily.

"Hey, what's wrong?" Harris asks as he leans back to check my face. "You look glum. Was the flight all right? Do you feel okay?"

I bite my lower lip to hold back a distressed cry.

Damn. This is hard.

I shake my head, hoping to clear it and to answer his questions without having to speak. My mouth dry again.

He cocks an eyebrow and studies me.

Okay, Katrina Roberts, *smiogaid suas, nighean*!

I take a deep breath and plaster on a convincing smile that reaches my eyes.

Harris scans my face, but I pull him in for an embrace.

"I just missed you a lot, Mr. Steele," I whisper in his ear. It rings true because it is.

He buries his face in my hair and inhales deeply. The rapid beat of his heart touches mine as he holds me tight.

"We better get out of her, or I'll fuck you where you stand," he says with a cocky grin. His dove gray eyes shine.

"Would it be so bad?" I taunt.

He growls and swats my ass. Then takes my hand and

leads me to a Rolls-Royce SUV. We thank the ground crew for placing my luggage in the boot as Harris opens the passenger door for me. He jogs around the bonnet and slips behind the wheel.

Our conversation turns to catching up since we last spoke and what I should expect for the coming week. Along the way, Harris points out sights and gives me a bit of history. I can appreciate the appeal the Hamptons hold on people.

He turns off the major thoroughfare to pull onto a private road. A security guard in a gatehouse triggers the oversized wooden gates set between stone pillars with wrought iron lanterns to swing open. A long driveway of pressed oil and natural stone meanders through trees like a ribbon.

Once past the impressive gates, it's like nothing I've ever seen before. The property rests on fourteen acres all beach-front. Its incredible surroundings include native trees, grassy areas, and closer to the ocean's sandy dunes. The briny scent of the ocean through the open windows fills my lungs. The calls of seagulls ring out as they search for food.

On either side of the primary driveway, secondary ones appear as we drive along. Harris points out houses for his brothers as we pass their entries. Glimpses of their gray weathered shingles and painted shutters peek from between the trees and bushes.

We continue to the end of the driveway that circles before a classic Hamptons-style mansion. The sprawling house has three stories, multiple chimneys around a widow's walk, and balconies. Sea green shutters flank the windows while below them perch flower boxes filled with white blossoms. The top half of the white Dutch door stands open to welcome us inside.

My mouth gapes at Southampton luxury living at its most extravagant.

Self-doubt rears its ugly head again.

I glance away.

"Come on, let's get you settled," Harris says, unaware of the emotions that make my stomach roil with angst. "I'll get your luggage. Head on inside."

My eyes sweep around the entry. It's a center hall with a double staircase rising along the walls. The cream, pale green, and white hues complement the stone floors. Canvas covered furniture with the accent colors fill the great room. While still elegant, the room gives a relaxed vibe.

Beyond, the view of the ocean through the wall of windows makes me gasp.

Drawn to the endless expanse of the Atlantic Ocean, I walk over to step onto the huge teak wood deck. Out on the private beach, caterers prepare for the clambake. They dug the pit and lined it with large stones and wood. The fragrant scent fills the air. Harris says they have it every year they come together for the holiday.

Clusters of adults gather around with children and dogs playing. A woman turns and shields her eyes, then waves as she grins. Others turn and wave. Shouts of hello carry over the breeze.

Harris appears at my side and waves back at who must be his family. He kisses the top of my head as he takes my hand.

"I'll introduce you after I show you our wing," he says. "They're excited to meet you."

I nod and glance over my shoulder as he leads me inside.

An older woman waves, and I return her welcoming gesture. She must be Mrs. Steele.

Oh boy…

Harris gives me a tour as we walk through the massive home on our way to his suite. He tells me he usually stays at The Bachelor's Nest with Lucien and Laurent on the grounds of their family's compound. But we'll stay here for my visit.

When Harris told me we'd stay with his parents, I envisioned being a couple of doors away from their room. But no. His wing takes up the second and third stories on the other side of the center hall. Not only a bedroom, but several rooms for his gaming, a study, guest suites, a kitchenette with dining area, and more.

He explains he shared the wing with Haley. After she and Lachlan wed, they bought a beachfront mansion on the other side of this one. The purchase extended the family's compound by even more acres. I can only nod in response.

What wealth can do.

We leave the maid to unpack my things—even though I said I could do it—and head for the beach.

My nerves peak.

Harris must sense the change this time. He stops and cups my chin and bends his knees to bring our gazes in line.

"Do not worry, Kitty Kat. They will welcome you. If you get overwhelmed, just tell me and we'll go for a walk along the beach. Okay?" He says.

I gather up my strength and take a deep breath.

"Okay," I respond, then squeeze his hand. "And thank you for understanding."

He kisses my lips softly and leads me through the open glass doors and to the beach.

"Hey!"

"Welcome, sweetheart."

"Hello, Kat."

Both clans gather around us. Harris makes the introductions. Malcolm teases him for giving in finally while Roger watches me. His intense platinum gray stare worries me until Harris whispers it's Roger's nature. I nod, relieved.

But the Jackson Patriarch garners my attention. I've studied photos of him from the Internet and read all I could find about the man. But one can't glean the power of his presence from on screen. He commands the group as does the Steele Patriarch. In fact, the amount of Alpha testosterone engulfs me.

"You look as though you're going through it. Take a slow, deep cleansing breath."

Startled, I jump and swivel my head towards the woman.

Starr Steele is beautiful. An angelic face with sorrel brown eyes filled with concern as she peers at me. Her long, curly, dark brown hair blows in the breeze around her face and down her back. An inch shorter than me, she has a sexy body to die for, fit, yet still curvy. Dimples pop from sculpted cheekbones beneath chestnut-colored skin as she smiles warmly.

"Come on, Kat. Let's sit with the girls," Starr says as she nudges shoulders with me. "Harris won't mind if we steal you away."

I follow her advice and inhale deeply. The salty ocean air fills my nostrils and lungs. I close my eyes as I exhale slowly. When I open them, Starr grins.

"Excellent! Do you do yoga?"

We walk over to where Haley, Lola, and Leonie sit with friends. They glance up at our approach and smile.

"You probably didn't catch all of our names," says a woman with chestnut brown hair and cerulean blue eyes. Her ultra-posh Queen's English accent will help me remember her. "I'm Blair Thomas. Nice to meet you, Kat."

I smile and nod as I respond, "You're right. So, thank

you. Nice to meet you, Blair. And if you ladies would be so kind as to remind me of your names and forgive my lack of memory."

They wave off my words and tell me their names: Billie a Southern Belle who resembles Tyra Banks, Adrienne a native of Los Angeles like Starr, and Márcia a Brazilian spitfire. All of them gorgeous and swish but not hoity-toity.

I sit on an oversized blanket with Blair while Starr sits beside Márcia. She works for Starr and Adrienne is her partner at Starr Light Fitness & Wellness Center. They have locations around the world, with one in Southampton Village. So Starr wasn't joking when she asked me about yoga. She's a certified fitness instructor in many disciplines.

Blair and Billie work for Lola as her CMO and COO, respectively. They've been close for years and more like family than employee. The same holds true for Márcia and Adrienne.

The tension inside of me melts as we chat and sip cocktails Billie made. Lola calls her their resident mixologist and to be careful since her drinks pack a punch. I laugh, then choke as I take my first taste.

Billie's laughter tinkles around us. It draws the attention of her Scottish beau—Patrick Rockett. Being one of the few multibillionaires in Scotland, I know of him. He strides over and lifts the petite beauty in his arms for a kiss, then sets her back before he strides away.

She giggles about him being a caveman.

I snort, thinking of Harris and his possessive behavior.

Leonie smiles at me and says, "Yes, *chérie*, all of our men are Alpha males—"

"And some even more controlling," Lola cuts in with a giggle.

Starr fans herself as she nods her head vigorously.

Blair's blush makes me wonder if her Parisian banking magnate—Luc Montaigne—counts amongst the latter.

Márcia grins behind her cup as her eyes flick to the imposing Russian Borya Alexeyev—the former MMA champion.

His Russian cousin—Anton—holds Adrienne's attention.

My comfort increases knowing the women and I share the same attraction for powerful men. More than likely, they're members of LEVELS. But it's too soon to ask such a personal question.

The caterers announce the seafood feast can begin.

We rise from the blankets and join everyone at the white-clothed tables.

Harris calls to me and I make my way to him beside one of the buffet tables.

Perfectly steamed clams, lobsters, potatoes, and corn on the cob topped with melted butter await us. Dessert options include warm blueberry and apple pies with vanilla ice cream. Harris tells me it's their traditional menu.

My stomach growls as we fill our plates, set them on a table, and go to the beverage stand. We pair our scrumptious meal with local beer and white wine.

"Where's Lydie?" I ask as we eat.

Harris swallows a mouthful and responds she's unable to make it this year.

Sebastian engages me in conversation and Lola chimes in. They're a cool couple who obviously love one another. And I guess he's of the *more controlling* category!

We enjoy the New England Clambake—another first for me—with the backdrop of a glorious sunset over the Atlantic Ocean. Afterwards, we sit on logs around the roaring bonfire to chat.

I sit between Harris' legs and lean my back against his

broad chest. An oversized blanket wraps around us to ward off the evening's chill.

"How do you like it so far, Kitty Kat?" He murmurs in my ear.

I glance around at his family and friends. A touch of sadness hits me. I wish I had the same closeness with all of my family members, or more specifically, with Payton. It also reminds me of my lack of friends besides Isla.

It's been so many years since I've done nothing but study and work hard, unable to just rest and live a normal twenty-something's life. Add on the news that struck me in the gut, and I've had a doozy of a life.

My heart rate increases as the thoughts race through my head.

Then I remember Starr's cure and take a deep cleansing breath. And allow myself to relish in the here and now.

"I don't like it, Harris," I respond.

He sits up and turns me to face him.

"I love it!" I giggle.

He rolls his eyes and leans his forehead to mine.

"You gave me a scare, naughty lass," he grumbles. "How will you make it up to me?"

My pussy clenches at his voice dripping with seduction. I lick my lips.

"I'll let you decide, Mr. Steele," I purr.

Now it's his turn to take a deep cleansing breath as he closes his eyes.

I lean forward and press my lips to his ear.

"Any way you want…"

He jumps from the log and scoops me in his arms.

"Good night!" He shouts as he carries me from the gathering.

Wolf whistles, catcalls, and choruses of good night fill the air.

Then my man fills me with delight. All. Night. Long.

KAT

"Thank you for having breakfast with me, Kat. I know yesterday was a lot for you to adjust."

Mrs. Steele—I mean Shelley since she corrected me when we spoke last night—says as we sit on the deck.

I was able to join Starr and some of the girls for beach yoga shortly after sunrise and shower before I had to meet Shelley. Lola and Starr told me not to worry about my first solo interaction with her. They adore their mother-in-law and consider her as a second mother.

Starr said the meditation portion would help calm my nerves. It did. But they ramp up again. Butterflies fill my belly more so than the fruit, French toast, and sausages on my plate. I swallow some water to clear my throat.

"Thank you for inviting me. Harris speaks highly of you all the time. It's nice to meet you at last, Shelley," I respond, proud my voice didn't waver.

She smiles.

"Eat. You don't want your food to get cold, sweetheart," she says as she pops a piece of strawberry into her mouth.

I do as she suggests, and we finish our meal in a comfortable silence, broken my occasional comment on the tastiness of the food and the beauty of the surroundings.

"Well, Kat, I feel at a bit of a disadvantage. Harris told you about me, but me little about you. Tell me about yourself and your family," Shelley says after the butler clears the table and serves tea.

I take a sip from the delicate Limoges teacup before I share the story about my parents and the car accident that resulted in me being alone. When she clasps my hand in hers and offers her condolences, a twinge of guilt hits my stomach.

Shelley is so genuine. The sadness for my pain obvious in her warm brown eyes.

"My dear, words alone cannot help with your grief. But I want you to know should you need anything or anyone, never hesitate to contact me. I will give you my direct contact information," she says. "We take care of our loved ones, sweetheart. Know you are not alone."

Tears burst from my eyes as a sob wrenches my chest. All the pent-up pressure releases as my shoulders sag. I drop my head.

Arms enfold me as Shelley pulls me close. Soothing sounds only a mother can make eases the turmoil in my heart. She rocks me as I let go and my tears flow unchecked. For the first time in so long, I feel free.

But guilt wracks my soul.

I sit back as I thank Shelley for her kindness.

She pours water from the pitcher into a glass and dips a linen napkin into it before she dabs my eyes and cheeks. Her eyes filled with concern scan my face.

"Remember, time heals all, Kat. Even insurmountable loss," Shelley says softly.

I nod.

"Now, why don't we go for a walk on the beach. I usually find beautiful sea glass around this time of day. What do you think? Up for treasure hunting?" She asks with a warm smile.

"That sounds like fun," I respond as I recall the collection of colorful bits of glass in the entry foyer.

We rise, and Shelley loops her arm through mine as we walk towards the stairs for the beach.

An hour later, we return with a mini bounty. We found oval, triangular, teardrop and even heart-shaped pieces of weathered glass broken down by time, salt, and tumbling in the water. As Shelley shows me how to clean them, Harris appears.

"Oh, now I know where you've been," he says as he enters the utility room Shelley uses. "Mom has a new recruit for her expeditions."

She laughs and nods.

"Indeed, and look at what we found," she says as she holds up a piece of red sea glass shaped like a heart. "Not bad for Kat's first haul, huh?"

Harris marvels at the piece and the others as we clean the sand from their frosty surfaces. He helps us to dry them and put them in the large bowl with the rest of the treasures collected over the years.

"Kat, you keep this one as a reminder of how what was once one way can morph into another," Shelley says, as she places the heart in my hand. "And it's red the color of life and love."

I bite my lower lip to keep the tears at bay and nod my thanks. Harris frowns, but I smile and hug Shelley.

"I believe you and the girls have a day of shopping and later our time at the spa. See you then!" She says as she turns for the staircase that leads to the wing she shares with Morgan.

Harris cups my cheek, and I lift my face to his.

"You okay, Kitty Kat?" He asks softly.

I widen my smile.

"More than okay, Mr. Steele," I respond. "Now, I ask you to help wash the sand from *me*..."

He chuckles and grabs my hand. We race up the staircase to his wing for more treasure hunting in the water.

"I'M HERE! I'M HERE!" I call out at the Rolls-Royce SUVs as they sit in the driveway before Morgana and Shelley's home. The girls wave from the open windows.

"Hurry up, slowpoke!" Lola responds. "Tell Harris to speed it up next time!"

"Dammit, Lola! How many times do I have to tell you I *do not* want to hear about my brothers' sex lives!" Haley shouts from the second SUV.

Starr, Blair, and Márcia laugh in the surrounding seats.

Lola winks at me as I hop in with her, Leonie, Billie, and Adrienne.

"Who's in the third SUV?" I ask, since I account for all the girls in the first two.

"Our security team, *chérie*," Leonie responds, then goes on when my eyebrows raise. "Long story for another time. Today let's have a fun Girls' Day Out!"

Everyone cheers, obviously accustomed to a security detail.

I let it go and join in their excited chatter.

"So what are you wearing for the gala, Billie?" Adrienne asks.

Billie's green eyes light up like jade as she claps her hands.

"Oh, honey, a custom Lola's Coterie gown, of course. Must represent, you know! Especially with all the photogs who will blast the images across the Internet. Free publicity, honey," she responds with a wink.

"Same here!" Lola and Leonie say in unison, then giggle as they high five.

We join in their laughter.

"Well, someone forgot to give the memo to me... I'm wearing a Roberto Cavalli gown," Adrienne says. "I picked it up when I was in Florence after one of our fitness retreats in Tuscany. A hot little number, I might add."

Billie turns to me and asks, "What about you, honey?"

When Harris invited me, I googled past galas to get an idea of what to wear and how to style my hair and makeup. Just as Billie said, thousands of images filled my screen. And my jaw dropped at its lavishness, even on the beach.

The guests don all white according to the fundraiser's theme. Women wear designer gowns like the girls and stunning jewels—typically diamonds in keeping with the theme. Their hair in updos or loose. Men wear just as costly dress shirts and trousers or lightweight suits sans ties. Every attendee dresses well.

Not having the budget for a high-priced gown, I went to different vintage shops for my outfit. After days of scouring, I lucked up with the ultimate find. A Versace dress with a halter top, deep v-neck leading to a large crystal starburst, and a hip-grazing slit appeared like a dream. Someone only wore the magnificent piece once, and it's missing a few crystals. I replaced them with those on a crystal-embellished clutch from the same collection. Paired with strappy sandals, it's perfect for the gala. Talk about score!

I describe the gown to the girls, and they're impressed. I didn't go into detail about it being from a vintage shop. Not necessary.

Leonie remembers the season. As a megamodel, *The Lion* opened and closed the fashion show. But she doesn't ask how I came about the gown. Instead, she congratulates me on such a marvelous choice.

"And don't forget, the glam squad will arrive to do our hair and makeup. They're scheduled to arrive at each of our residences two hours before the gala begins," she adds.

Lola shimmies and claps her hands.

"Yes! We'll be ready with our spa treatments that will wax and buff us into silky soft beauties," she says.

The girls express their thanks for the pampering sessions.

Haley reserved her favorite spa in town for us exclusively. Shelley and Lucie will arrive later in the afternoon to join us. Full-body waxes, body scrubs, massages, mani/pedis, and even aromatherapy, cupping, and reiki therapies. Every method imaginable to pamper us.

I laugh out loud at me being pampered like the princesses who rake my nerves. The girls turn to me with questioning expressions. I wave my hand in front of my face to cool down my cheeks heated from my outburst.

"Pardon me! The idea of me—a lone lass from Scotland —being pampered like a Countess and her wealthy friends tickles me," I say. "Remember, I'm just her husband's administrative assistant."

The SUV quiets.

Glances exchange amongst the girls.

Great, Kat. Talk about a major faux pas…

I start to backtrack. But Billie holds up her hand.

"Well, honey, nothing wrong with being an administrative assistant. Blair and I began as ones to Lola before she promoted us," Billie says. "However, Blair and I come from wealthy families. Yet we chose to work our way up in a field we love."

"Same with Starr and Márcia," Adrienne adds with a scowl. "What's so terrible about being an admin?"

Now, my face heats not from mirth, rather from embarrassment.

Can the roof of the SUV open up and eject me??? Oh right, the driver has the panoramic moon roof open already. Let me jump out…

My eyes dart around the girls. They wait for my response. I clear my throat.

"No offense meant. It's just that I never imagined in my younger years after a drunk killed my parents in a car accident—"

Lola gasps.

"*Mon Dieu!*" Leonie exclaims.

I'm forgotten when everyone turns to Lola.

She glances out of the window.

"*Chérie*! She couldn't have known," Leonie says as she wraps her arms around Lola, who nods.

She shifts in her seat to face me.

"I lost my parents as a teenager to a drunken driver. An only child, I was alone until Luc and Leonie—along with her parents—became my family. Then, Baz, the Steeles, the Jacksons, the Knights, our babies, and my girls expand my loved ones," Lola says softly.

She reaches her hand out for mine, then squeezes it as she continues.

"So you see, we never belittle ourselves, as we value all and love all. I understand your loss and the way it can make you doubt your worth. But don't," she smiles. "As the woman in Harris' life—my brother—you are my sister. All of ours, as an extension. We're a close-knit clan and go hard for our loved ones—including you, Kat. Understand?"

Tears fill my eyes as I blubber an affirmative response. My stomach clenches. The lies dig deeper and deeper.

Billie puts an arm around my shoulder and places a dainty handkerchief in my fist. I murmur my thanks, then thank all of them with a watery smile.

"Well then," Lola starts as she glances at each of us. "Let's make this day extra special with a Girls' Night Out! We'll go to Jackson Hole at STEELE Southampton Village and party!"

The SUV erupts in hoots and claps. Everyone's mood lifts—even Lola's—who smiles knowingly at me.

Bloody hell, Kat Roberts.

"YAAASSSS, GIRL! SHAKE THAT THANG!"

Starr's dimples pop as she laughs with her arms thrown overhead and her hips shimmy to the beat of Britney singing "Outrageous."

One can't miss Starr in her bright yellow micro mini dress with shimmering sequins and crystals. The draped cowl neckline and barely there straps accentuate her awesome figure.

I raise my arms and bump hips with her. The club's lights spark off the colorful psychedelic sequins that create the illusion of tie-dye on my mini dress. The hem rises to showcase more of my long legs, ending in sky-high strappy sandals. I throw my head back and toss my hair.

It feels so good to let loose. Even more so after hours of spa treatments.

"Whoohoo!!!" I shout. "Get it, girl! Get it, girl!"

"Hey now!"

We glance up to find Blair strutting towards us through the crowd. Also dressed to impress, the light flashes on her micro mini dress dripping in glossy pink paillettes. Her hair piled atop her head and the five-inch stilettos put the statuesque beauty over six feet. Heads turn as she approaches us.

"Uh, huh! Party over here, baby!" She says as she joins us.

The music pumps, and the crowd vibrates.

We lose ourselves in the beat.

"Hey there, sexy."

Hands reach around from behind to hold my hips. A firm body presses against my back. The rock-hard erection obvious. Warm breath blows on my ear.

I stop mid shimmy.

No, sir!

I put my hands on top of his and pry his fingers from my body as I turn my head to glare up at him.

"Take your—"

I pitch forward.

Blair catches my flailing arms.

Her mouth opens to a perfect O as her eyes widen.

I glance over my shoulder to find the guy gripped by the throat. His hands clutch frantically at the sizable hand that holds him.

Harris!

He drags the guy close to speak into his ear. The guy shakes his head and turns to me. But Harris jerks him, and he returns his gaze to Harris, who says something else. The head bobs again, and Harris lets him loose. Without a backward glance, Mr. Handsy skedaddles away, lost in the crowd seconds later.

No one blinks an eye. Not even Starr and Blair, who I

look to for a reaction. They shrug and dance on. I turn back to my caveman.

He stalks towards me. Eyes flash. Mouth a stern slash on his gorgeous face.

"Th—Thank—"

"No one touches you but me, Kat," he growls. "No. One."

My pussy throbs at his possessiveness.

"Yes, Mr. Steele," I purr in his ear as my arms wrap around his neck, and I grind my body against his solid one.

His hands tighten on my ass as he dips his knees and presses our pelvises together.

Now, *this* is an erection. Not some short, short man.

I hum in the back of my throat and leave Harris to take the lead as he moves our bodies in sync to the sensual thrumming of the bass. His masculine scent ramped up by testosterone drives me wild.

The two mojitos I drank catch up to me.

My body wants to climb Harris like a tree. Impale myself on his thick branch. Ride him until the leaves fall off.

He must sense my need for him.

"Did you enjoy his hands on you, Siren?" He purrs in my ear.

I shudder and shake my head vigorously.

He smacks my ass and growls.

"N—Nooo!" I whine. "Only your hands, Mr. Steele."

His chest rumbles.

My nipples furl.

"Good," Harris purrs. "MINE!"

We continue to move to the hedonistic beat of the music. Only dimly am I aware Malcolm has Starr pinned to his muscular body as they dance lost in each other's eyes, and Luc rocks with Blair as though no one else exists.

I lose all sense of time enraptured by my man.

After a while, he leads me from the dance floor. We join the others in the VIP section. Each man found his woman—unable to spend one night without them. I smile at the happy couples.

Lola's right. They are a tight-knit clan.

And my man includes me in it.

"Those things look dangerous... And look at the road! It's muddy... and narrow... and... You have to watch out for the trees! Promise me you'll be careful, Harris. Please."

My Kitty Kat's emerald green eyes beg me from behind her glasses as she glances from the mobile screen to my face. She holds up the website for the ATV sports company where my bros and I plan to have our Guys' Day Out.

"Don't worry, babe. I've ridden ATVs my whole life and taken those trails—not roads—hundreds of times," I say as I finish tying my boots. "It's a guy's thing. We don't do cutesy stuff like a day at the spa. We like it rough and hard."

I pull her into my arms and nibble at the side of her neck where it meets her shoulder.

She squirms, and I swat her ass.

"Whatever, Harris. I'm serious. Be careful," she says as she relents and wraps her arms around my waist. She angles her head to the side, and I plant kisses on her throat. A soft moan escapes her lips.

I rise to my full height and cup her face.

"I promise," I say as I stare into her eyes.

"Thank you," she whispers.

Mesmerized by her beauty—and still hyped from our shower sex—I don't notice my mobile vibrating in my jeans pocket.

"Um, that's your mobile," My Kitty Kat says with a smirk.

I dig it out and answer the call.

"Helloooo… We're outside waiting for Kat," Lola says.

"Right. She's coming down now," I respond.

"I'm sure she's cuming…" Lola says, then laughs as she ends the call.

I chuckle as I relay the message to Kat, who rushes to our bedroom's door. I call her back for a kiss, and she hurries to meet the girls.

"Hey, bro, ready?" I ask when Malcolm answers his mobile.

"Yeah, we're on our way to pick you up. Come on down," he responds.

Everybody's coming or cuming, I chuckle to myself.

I grab my gear bag and leave the bedroom.

Two Suburbans sit out front with my brothers, cousins, Anton, and Borya inside. I toss my gear bag in the back of one and hop in.

"It's a good day to hit the trails," Lucien says.

Along with Malcolm, Anton, and Borya, they make up the thrill seekers who travel the globe for their extreme sports. Freshwater cave diving, heli-boarding, skydiving, hell, even figher-jet flying. Although Malcolm prefers the less dangerous ones since his accident and becoming a father. But it doesn't stop him from taking it to the very edge. Wild Boys, I call them.

"Yeah, baby!" Anton says as they high five. "Time to get it on."

Borya grunts and mutters, "Not for weak little *kiskas*."

Nope, not for *pussies*. Nothing with this bunch is for the weak at heart.

The rest of the ride, they talk about a trip to the South Pole on an expedition ship. Something about glaciers, icebergs, penguins, aliens, whatever. But no thanks. I'd rather not be at the bottom of the world.

We arrive at the ATV site and change into our gear. The staff lined up our rides—black-on-black Polaris Sportsman 570 Ultimate Trail Le. It's a beast of a ride. Only the best will do.

"Ready to rock-and-roll, fellas?" Malcolm asks through the headpiece built into the helmets.

He's a total badass dressed in all black as Lil' Kim says. Although he's no Damien.

"Let's get it!"

"Hell, yeah, bro!"

"Affirmative!"

We're raring to go and rev the engines to prove it.

Malcolm circles his finger in the air, and we fall in line behind him while Anton takes the rear.

For the next hour, we ride along the trails throughout the backwoods of the Hamptons—an oxymoron if ever there was one. The sun's rays break through the canopy of trees whose branches cross over the trail. Leaves still green not quite ready to change into the stunning golds and russets of fall. A light rain from the night before muddies areas to splatter our goggles and clothes with the wet dirt. The sounds of the engines roar as we shift gears.

We climb hills and cut through pastures, then zigzag through a stream. Water splashes and washes the dirt from the twenty-six-inch tires. We pass over a wooden bridge to a glade on the other side.

Malcolm announces a break, and we dismount.

The staff setup tables with beverages and snacks. We gather around and replenish ourselves as we talk shit about each other. After a while, we jump back on the ATVs to head back.

A different route—as scenic and challenging as the first—returns us to the ATV company. The staff rush over to assist us with the vehicles and to give us bags to put our dirty gear inside. We grab some water and pile into the Suburbans.

We pull into the Jackson compound and stop in front of The Bachelor's Nest. As we walk around the side of the mansion to the beach, we strip down to our swim trunks. On the deck, we drop our clothes and race for the waves.

I dive in. The cool water envelopes me from head to toe. The stiffness from riding for over two hours over the bumpy trails washes away with the current. Refreshed, I shoot for the surface.

"Damn, bro! That was a great ride!" Baz says to Malcolm.

"Better than—"

With a growl, Baz dunks Malcolm under the water, knowing he was about to name Lola. The Alpha Doms wrestle as we urge them on.

Evenly matched—not only in physique, but in looks—they break apart laughing. Only two years separate them, and people often confuse one for the other or assume they're twins. Much to Malcolm's chagrin when he was younger—second son syndrome and all.

"Fuck you, Malcolm," Baz says.

Malcolm grins cockily.

"Oh, bro, I believe you have the wrong one," he smirks. "Your woman is shopping…"

We laugh, and Baz joins in. Nothing new with our ragging on each other.

Being a competitive crew, we race each other from the Jackson property to the edge of ours and back. Like orcas—the wolves of the sea—we swim as a pack slicing through the waves our minds on the goal. Win.

On the leg back, I jostle Laurent for the lead. He retaliates with a head butt to my flank. Sideswiped, I lose the advantage. Roger surges ahead. Anton a close second slips past Laurent and me. I use Laurent as a springboard to gain on them. But Roger hits the sand and races to chaise lounges.

"Take that, take that, take that!" He boasts as he does a victory dance shadowboxing the air.

"You win, brother," Anton says as they clasp forearms.

The others come onshore, not far behind us.

"Who won?" Patrick asks.

"There can only be one… And I take the prize," Roger responds, fingers lifted in victory signs as he smirks.

We give him shit while he grins and waves his hands.

I grab a bottle of water from the cooler before I stretch out on a chaise lounge. The others do the same or lie on towels. The warm sun dries our skin.

The house guy for The Nest brings baskets of sandwiches, chips, and fruit for our lunch. We thank him, and he goes back inside.

"So, did I or did I not say you'd get hit hard?" Lachlan asks me.

"I told him the same damn thing," Baz adds with a chuckle and a shake of his head.

"Yeah, and he kept her hidden for months. Just as his twin did…" Malcolm adds as he eyes Lachlan.

I throw up my hands as they go on and on, ribbing me about My Kitty Kat. But I take it since they don't lie. Oh, how the mighty playboy falls.

"That's all well and good. Congratulations and all. But since it's serious, we have to do a background check on Kat," Roger says. Then he raises his hand when I lean forward. "We've all experienced enough bullshit with women to know it's a necessity."

"I don't disagree. However, Jackson Corporation did one before they hired her. And well, she they hired her. So… She must be legit," I tell them as I gaze at each face.

Lachlan shrugs.

"Well, yes, and no. The checks are for work, not for a potential wife"—I roll my eyes and he continues—"Or girlfriend. I agree with Roger. Sorry, cuz."

Baz clears his throat, and we turn to him.

"This conversation is moot. I spoke with my guy during the clambake. He'll have his report to me shortly," Baz says in a voice that brooks no argument.

I sit back on my chaise lounge.

"Fine. I get it. Especially after Roger and Malcolm's experiences," I say, then nod at Baz. "Thanks for having my back."

He returns the nod and responds, "As always, brother."

The conversation moves to sports and to the upcoming holidays. I smile at the thought of sharing Thanksgiving in Capri and Christmas and New Year's in Verbier with My Kitty Kat. She won't be alone during one of the loneliest times of the year ever again.

. . .

"LISTEN, I will not sit here on my ass while my woman shakes hers at that bacchanalia Lucien created. Especially in that minuscule dress and fuck-me heels she wore. Despite my disagreement with her choice of attire, mind you. Security or not, I'm out."

Roger hangs his cue stick on the wall rack and heads for the stairs.

We're in the game room on the entertainment level of The Bachelor's Nest. Some of us shoot pool while others play video games and bowl. But Roger's proclamation stops all action.

"Right with you, bro."

"Damn right!"

"Hold up. I'm out, too."

We separate to change into club outfits, then take the Suburbans to Jackson Hole to claim our women. The air is thick as we ride. Each of us thinks of the thirsty men who want to get their hands on what's ours.

It's not that we don't trust our women. We do. It's the greedy bastards out on the prowl for a good time. And we should all know since we were those bastards not too long ago. Yeah, so take one to know one and all that…

We jump from the SUVs to leave them with the valets and stride past the line of hopefuls who wait to get into the Hole. Lucien nods at the two security men, and they lift the velvet rope for us. We fall in as our eyes scan the crowds at the bar and at the restaurant.

I don't see My Kitty Kat, so I head to the dance floor. A glance around reveals her shaking said ass with Starr and Blair. I nudge Malcolm and Luc, then tilt my chin in the direction of our women. As one, we move through the crowd.

And gotdamn if some fucker doesn't slide up behind

My Kitty Kat and put his hands on her hips. I see red. Then he pulls her against him. I charge forward with a growl.

My arm lashes out to spin him around. I grab him by the throat.

He fumbles at my fingers as his eyes pop from his head.

I drag him to speak into his ear.

"Did she ask you to put your hands on her?" I growl.

He shakes his head and has the nerve to glance at my woman.

On reflex, I jerk my arm to bring his attention back to me. When he does, I lean close.

"Did I tell you to look at her?"

He shakes his head vigorously.

I give him a hard glare, then drop my hand. I watch as he bolts through the crowd. Then I prowl towards my woman.

"Th—Thank—"

"No one touches you but me, Kat," I growl. "No. One."

"Yes, Mr. Steele," she purrs in my ear as her arms wrap around my neck. She tries for a distraction by grinding her hot little body against me. The Siren.

My hands drop to her ass and squeeze the firm, round cheeks as I bend my knees to show her what she does to me. I'm hard as fucking steel.

And get even harder when My Siren hums in the back of her throat. My hips sway and hers move with them to the rhythm of the music.

"Did you enjoy his hands on you, Siren?" I purr into her ear.

Her tremble reverberates through me as she shakes her head.

Not good enough. My hand comes down on those cheeks. Hard.

"N—Nooo!" She whines as she jolts. "Only your hands, Mr. Steele."

My chest rumbles.

"Good," I purr. "MINE!"

I continue to lead us on the dance floor. Everyone and everything fade to black. If we keep at it, no one can hold me responsible for ravaging my woman right here, right now. It's time to leave the erotic energy of the dance floor behind. For now.

The VIP section and a drink call. I grin when I note the men claimed their women. They're gathered around on banquettes—some sit on their laps—as they laugh and sip cocktails. Excellent.

I take a seat next to Patrick and guide My Siren to my lap. She settles, and I place my hand on her thigh. My thumb brushes the hem of her dress. We'll have to have a conversation about the length of her dresses for future outings.

The server appears and takes our orders.

"So, you decided to crash our Girls' Night Out, *Amoureux*?" Leonie asks Roger.

He lifts his snifter to his lips and nods. After a sip, he responds, "*Oui*. And lucky you were sitting here and not shaking that ass in that little dress."

She bites her lower lip to hold back a giggle. Her feline-shaped amber eyes sparkle with mirth as she stares back at him.

Roger can't stay upset with his wife and grins. He leans over and whispers in her ear. Crimson suffuses her golden caramel skin as her eyes widen. Roger sits back with a smirk and pats her knee. She shivers.

He winks at me when his gaze meets mine. His platinum gray eyes flick to Kat, and he smirks again.

I can't help but to grin widely.

For all the tough guys we are, we're wusses for our women.

For the rest of the Combined Night Out, we dance, drink, and have fun. The marrieds cut loose harder than those without rings. Nothing slows them down as they party the night away.

When Kat declares a Scotswoman can hold her liquor in an almost indiscernible accent, then wobbles on her feet giggling, I turn to the others and call it a night. Time to get my bonny lass showered and tucked into bed.

We have a long day and night tomorrow.

On the ride back to the Steele compound, she rests her head on my lap. Her soft snores fill the SUV. I keep my hand on her hip to hold her steady.

Back at the mansion, I carry her up the stairs and to our wing. In the shower, My Siren reemerges. Her tiny hands reach for my girth—hard, even though I have no intention of fucking her while she's intoxicated.

"Harris Steele... You're so bloody sexy... I can't believe you're mine..." she gets out.

I take her hands and bring them to my lips—my cock weeps in dismay.

"Believe it, Kitty Kat," I murmur against her fingertips as I stare into her glazed eyes—more bottle green than emerald. "And you are mine."

I finish bathing her, then leave her on the marble bench while I turn towards the spray to clean myself.

Hands slide around my waist. Fingertips trace the v-shape muscles on the lower sides of my abs. A zing runs through me as more blood pumps to my cock. Full lips kiss along my spine as the fingers grip the base of my erection. They slide to the tip and swirl the pre-cum around the swollen mushroom head.

My other head lolls back as I close my eyes to revel in her erotic touch.

My Siren continues to caress me with gentle strokes. It takes every ounce of my self-control to combat the urge to snap my hips. She picks up speed. I match her rhythm. With a carnal cry, I unleash a torrent of jizz.

"Oops…"

She giggles and plants a last kiss on my shoulder blade.

I turn off the spray, scoop her into my arms, and dry us before I carry her to our bed. Tucked beneath the silky sheets, she drifts off to sleep. I press my front to her back with her head cradled by my biceps and rest a hand on her pussy.

MINE!

KAT

"Good morning and welcome, everyone! I know after the night we had, we're in need of a more grounding session. First, Adrienne will lead you in pranayama. The practice of breath work in yoga. Prana Sanskrit for vital life force, and yama means to gain control. Next, Hatha—ha sun and tha moon for balance—with me to allow our minds to withdraw from external objects. Then end with meditation with Márcia. Namaste."

I bow my head with hands palms together at heart center as the divine light within me bows to the divine light within Starr.

When Harris awoke me this morning, he assured me I agreed to beach yoga. Fortunately, it wasn't in the wee hours of the day's start. I grumbled but dressed in leggings and a long-sleeved t-shirt to ward off the chill before the sun could warm the Earth. Then trudged after him to the sand.

However, as I sit on my yoga mat and practice the alternate nostril breathing technique Adrienne teaches to us, my mind clears. The hangover dissipates with each inhalation and exhalation. Plus, the concentration tunes everything out as I coordinate my breathing.

By the time we move on our mats for Hatha, I'm more settled—just as Starr predicted. The flow of the poses focuses on rooting us into the Earth. Then Starr adds a twist for the peak pose. She has us face our partners and move into a boat pose with the backs of our legs and the tips of our fingers or palms touching.

Naturally, some of the guys make comments about the intimate position. Starr laughs from where she's with Malcolm, demonstrating the pose. He smirks at us.

We end in savasana. After the repose, Márcia calls us to a comfortable seat for meditation. Her soothing voice guides us deeper within ourselves. The sound of the waves acts as a backdrop to her message of release. She incorporates the rhythmic flow of the Atlantic Ocean into the meditation and likens it to the ebb and flow of our thoughts. Just let go, she reminds us as the session comes to an end with the tinkling of a bell.

Once again, we bow to each other.

"Feel better, Kitty Kat?"

I glance over my shoulder at Harris. He smiles. It's as warm as the sun higher in the clear blue sky.

"Much, thanks for the reminder," I respond as I kiss his lips. "These are my first adult sessions. When a guest teacher comes to the Center for the lads and lasses, I join in."

"Well, we'll have to do something about that," he says. "I want you nice and limber."

"Last one in is a rotten egg!"

Haley shouts, then squeals when Lachlan lifts her from the sand midstride and tosses her over his shoulder as he races to the water. Her laughter trails behind them.

"Better hurry!" Harris says as he grabs my hand and hoists me to my feet.

We charge down to the waves and dive in with the others. The sun hasn't heated the water yet, so I yelp as I break the surface.

"Reminds me of home," Borya shouts. "Good for the soul!"

"Not my home! Rio is always sultry," Márcia quips as she bobs next to him. Then squeals when he ducks beneath the water and lifts her onto his powerful shoulders.

"Better now?" He asks as she laughs.

Our bodies adjust to the cool temperature as we frolic in the surf. Anton follows suit and lifts Adrienne. She and Márcia scrabble to unseat the other. The rest of us cheer them on or swim along the shoreline.

After a while, Sebastian calls for breakfast, and we clamber out of the water. We head along the beach from in front of Harris and their parents' mansion to the deck of his and Lola's equally impressive one. We step under the outdoor showers to rinse the saltwater and sand from our bodies. Up on the deck, the nannies bring the babes out along with their six dogs. The meal is buffet style prepared by their chef.

We have a delicious—albeit rowdy—breakfast. And I love every minute of it!

"I know my beautiful Billie is ready. So, you lasses all set for the evening?" Patrick asks.

"Oh, yes! And we cannot wait for the glam squad to arrive," Haley responds. "It's been a while since I last dressed up in anything fancier than joggers and a t-shirt!"

Lachlan leans over and presses his lips to her temple.

"And oh what a sexy Hot Mama you are in those clothes, babe," he says.

She grins at her husband and thanks him.

"Don't forget the diamond pieces from Harry Winston—this year's jewelry sponsor. Their reps will have a selection for you to choose from an hour before the gala begins," Sebastian says.

I gasp and turn to Harris.

"Yes, you too, babe. So, pick whatever you want," he says with a grin.

My heart pounds as I recall the fabulous jewels the women wore at the prior galas. Now, I'll get to sparkle too. I cannot believe my luck!

"Thank you!" I exclaim as I throw my arms around his neck. "This is going to be an incredible night I'll never forget."

"The first of many, Kitty Kat," Harris murmurs in my ear as he embraces me. "Choose wisely. If you're a good lass, maybe I'll let you keep them…"

My heart stops, and I gasp again.

No bloody way!

Harry Winston jewels of my very own??? They're worth a fortune. That's more than luck. It's a miracle.

"I promise to be a very, very, *very* good lass, Mr. Steele," I purr against his ear, then nip it with a slight tug.

He buries his face in my hair to muffle a groan.

I turn back to my breakfast with a grin on my face. Fantastic!

"Your hair is a pretty color."

The words and tiny fingers twirling my hair draw my attention to my side. One of Leonie's twin boys stands beside me. He's a miniature Roger and has the sparkle of a free spirit in his eyes like his mother. He smiles at me. So adorable.

"Why thank you, lad. But you have me stumped. Are you Rodolphe or Gaspard?" I respond, returning his smile.

His eyes dance.

"You have to guess," he says. "You have two chances so it's easy."

I snort at his precociousness. He's a smart little bugger!

"Hmmm, now let me think… Ropard?" I ask a blend of their names.

He pauses a moment to consider my guess, then throws his head back and laughs.

"You're funny! No one has ever called us that before," he says. "Gaspard."

I ruffle his silky ebony curls.

"Now, I won't confuse the two of you ever again," I tell him with a grin.

He nods and runs back to the other babes yelling Ropard to his twin. I watch as Rodolphe laughs, then waves at me. I return the gesture and sit back in my chair.

"You're so good with children, *chérie*," Leonie says as she beams at me.

I tell them how I volunteer at the Aberdeen Children's Center twice a week and love children. Leonie shares how she mentors girls and teens at a center in Paris and hosts a charity gala for it every year. We exchange stories and laugh or offer advice. It feels good to tell a truth for a change.

After we finish, everyone separates for their residences. Harris takes my hand, and we walk through the gardens of the property back to his home. He plucks a red flower from a bush and places it behind my left ear with a wink. I blush at the significance I'm taken.

Back in his wing, we take a shower and make love. Harris has to do some work and goes to his home office. I gaze at the big fluffy bed longingly. Well, it was a long night and an early morning. Plus, I need to be fresh for the gala… I run to the bed and dive under the covers. Nap time!

"HONEY, you have luxuriant hair. The color… it's to die for and not the bottle kind either. Let's get you glammed up for all those photos you're bound to get captured in. Between your gown and your beauty—not to mention being on Harris Steele's arm, that elusive bachelor—you're front-page news, honey! Let's not disappoint."

I grin as I sit in the leather swivel chair before a full-length mirror in Shelley's full-size salon decorated in shades of white. It has two of every station: sinks with leather chairs for washing hair, vanities with floor-length mirrors and leather swivel chair, manicure tables, leather massage chairs and sinks for pedicures, and massage and treatment rooms.

The glam squad finished her gala prep earlier since she has to see to the event. Now it's my turn, and I'm beyond excited.

The squad begins their magic as I watch, transfixed. The hairstylist sweeps my hair into an updo *to accentuate the stunning bone structure and graceful swan neck*. To frame my face, he leaves a side bang that swoops past my ear. In the back, he secures the rest of my hair in a large, loose bun with tendrils dropping to meet the tips of the side bang. He pronounces it's a masterpiece and steps aside for the makeup artist.

She tips my chin and moves it side to side as she studies *the angles*. Meanwhile, her assistant whips out an assortment of brushes, sponges, and trays of colors. Arrayed on the table beside the artist, she makes a selection, and her hands move across my face. With a satisfied smile, she spins the chair towards the mirror.

My eyes widen at my reflection. It's still me, but so much more. A glammed-up version. Sophisticated.

"You like?"

I lift my gaze to the hairstylist and grin at him and the makeup artist.

"Thank you! I absolutely love what you've done!" I exclaim. "I feel like Cinderella going to the ball."

The stylist snorts.

"Perhaps. But it won't all go away at midnight, honey! No splattered pumpkins for you," he says, shaking his head with an elegantly arched eyebrow.

"Most definitely," the artist agrees with a nod. "Now, time for your gown."

The dresser steps forward and helps me from the chair. We walk to the adjoining dressing room, where my vintage Versace gown hangs on a rack with my strappy sandals below. A barely there nude G-string rests on the table.

I swap the silk dressing gown for my gala one. The dresser slides my feet into the sandals and ties the straps around my ankles. When she finishes, I glide to the triple mirror. I glance over my shoulders and spin around to check every angle is perfect.

"Sensational."

My eyes fly to the middle mirror to find in the reflection Harris leaning on the doorjamb. He's simply divine in a white suit and dress shirt open at the collar. The hair I love to run my fingers through slicked back from his handsome face. His dove gray eyes darken to obsidian as they sweep over my body from head to toe.

The erotic energy palpable, the glam squad excuse themselves and scurries from the dressing room—if not the salon.

"Spin for me, Siren," Harris commands.

My cheeks heat as I duck my head, then I lift it to meet his gaze. With deliberate slowness, I pivot in a complete circle. As I face him again, I stick my leg through the hip-grazing slit and place a hand on my hip. I thrum my fingertips against the exposed skin.

Harris growls and stalks towards me.

My nipples tighten and my pussy clenches as his waves of erotic energy lap at me.

A long finger slides along my inner thigh, leaving goosebumps in its wake. When it grazes the side of my G-string, I shudder. It rims the silk and prods my engorged clit. I whimper and clutch his shoulders as my head bows again.

"If this were anyone's event, I would say fuck it and ravish you right now. But I cannot disappoint my mother," he says as his finger withdraws. "However, later, you. Are. Mine."

Harris takes my hand and leads me from the dressing room on wobbly legs.

"Mademoiselle, you look incredible and will honor the Harry Winston jewels with your beauty."

I peek around Harris, and my jaw drops.

Trays of glittering diamonds sit on the center island in the salon's anteroom. They dazzle beneath the lights.

"Kindly make your selection, or I can recommend pieces to compliment your look," the representative says.

Harris urges me ahead of him when I linger, ogling the jewels at a distance. I smile and thank the rep as I walk to the table, eyes still mesmerized by the glittery gems.

An array of necklaces, earrings, rings, bracelets, and even hair clips rest on navy blue velvet beds or drape from stands. The sizes of the stones range from large to humongous. The rep hands a pair of white gloves to me. I gaze at them questioningly, then notice she has on a pair, too. I slip them on.

A necklace with a cluster of diamonds at its center and two rows of diamonds leading up to and around the neck catches my eye. It reminds me of the crystal cluster on my gown. The rep senses my interest and hesitation, lifts it from the stand and holds it up to catch the light.

It sparkles as though tiny fires live within each gemstone.

She places it around my neck, and her assistant lifts the mirror.

My breath catches in my throat.

Instinctively, my fingers reach up to caress the diamonds. But I stop afraid to damage it in any way.

The rep steps around the table with matching cluster earrings in her hands. I take them from her and slip them on, then turn to the mirror. Blindingly breathtaking.

Struck dumb, I don't notice her and another assistant place bracelets on each of my wrists until they lift my arms to reflect in the mirror.

I gasp.

Hundreds of carats of diamonds grace my ears, neck, and wrists. Never in my life—and probably few of many other peoples' lives—would I ever experience being covered in Harry Winston High Jewelry. Talk about posh!

"How do you like them?"

Once again, Harris stands behind me, closer this time, reflected in the mirror. His eyes glitter like black diamonds.

"Love," I whisper.

He cocks an eyebrow.

"The diamonds or… something else?" He whispers. His eyes blaze.

I swallow.

Bloody hell, Kat Roberts. Slip of the tongue?

I open my mouth to answer. But he shakes his head. The internal fire extinguished.

"They look lovely on you. Take them all," he says with a small smile. "We need to get going."

He steps away, and the heat of his body evaporates with him.

I shiver from the loss—in more ways than one.

With a less stellar smile, I thank the representative and her assistants. She tells me a man from their security team will shadow me discreetly. I nod, numb.

The man and I turn to Harris, who's at the door typing on his mobile. He glances up when I touch his elbow. He extends his arm, and I loop my arm through it.

We walk through an outer door towards a group of photographers and television crews lined up along a platinum gray carpet. Behind it stands a white wall printed with company logos. As guests exit their cars—left with valet attendants on the driveway—they walk across the carpet and pose for the cameras. Flashbulbs spark in the night sky.

Harris quickens his pace when he spies Malcolm and Starr ahead of us. I hurry to keep up with his long strides. Roger and Leonie appear along with Haley and Lachlan. Sebastian and Lola call from behind us.

When we reach the beginning of the carpet, Harris glances down at me.

"Showtime. Smile for the cameras," he says with a smile on his face—albeit one that doesn't quite reach his eyes. He turns to speak to Roger.

I tug his arm.

Harris tilts his head to gaze at me.

"Are you okay?" I ask.

He maintains his smile, and nods before he leads me down the carpet.

Billie and the hairstylist weren't kidding when they said the photographers would go into a frenzy. They call out to Harris and his siblings by name. Haley and Lachlan they address as Countess and Earl. Megamodel Leonie gets personal shout outs too. She turns her multimillion-dollar smile to full wattage towards the cameras to strike a pose.

I let the worry over Harris' reaction to my slip of the tongue go. A smile spreads across my face as brilliant as the Harry Winston jewels. Someone asks Harris who the beauty is on his arm, and he smiles down at me. He lifts his gaze back to them and says my name, then moves on before he answers who I am to him.

A twinge hits my belly, but my smile doesn't falter.

I've had to fake my way through many a time. Tonight, will be no different. Would I have preferred this Cinderella night was unlike no other? Yes. But I've learned to mask my disappointment.

Pumpkin, anyone?

Why the fuck did my heart dip when Kat hesitated? Hell, I can't say I love her either. But damn if it didn't hurt like a mother.

I guess for one wuss moment, I got caught up with all the talk of background checks for wives, the way she blends in with my family seamlessly, hanging around all the lovey-dovey couples. Being the only Steele playboy left standing...

Fuck.

How the hell do I deal with these crazy emotions? Other than my female relatives, I've never cared about a woman loving me. And now this?

I whip out my mobile to send a text message to Haley.

Hey, where are you?

A touch to my arm, and I glance down to find Kat at my elbow. Mentally, I shake off the unsavory thoughts and extend my arm. She places her hand on my forearm, and I lead her downstairs and out the door.

We near the step and repeat highlighting the event spon-sors, including STEELE International, Inc., Jackson Corporation, Lola's Coterie, Starr Light Fitness & Wellness Center, Banque Montaigne, Harry Winston, and other notable companies. Ahead of us, I spy Malcolm and Starr. I quicken my pace.

For any STEELE event—particularly for the STEELE Foundation—we show a united front as a family. The platinum gray carpet serves as the platform for the media to capture our photos and garner interviews. And this evening is no different. So I set the glum mood aside.

Roger and Leonie. Haley and Laurent. Sebastian and Lola. We all fall in line at the beginning of the carpet.

I glance down at Kat and smile.

"Showtime. Smile for the cameras," I tell her before I turn to step behind Roger. Age order and all.

I pause when Kat tugs at my arm. She glances up at me anxiously.

"Are you okay?" She asks.

A flicker of victory ignites within my heart. She knows she did me wrong. Good.

My smile remains fixed in place since the flashbulbs already pop off in rapid succession as Baz steps to the carpet. I nod in response to her question, then start us along the line.

The media calls our names as we gather before them. We pose as a group, couples, then the men step aside for our women to get glam shots.

I watch as Kat preens and works that fuck-me slit up her thigh like nobody's business. She glows and not just from the diamonds worth millions of dollars. Her innate beauty and poise make her striking. The photogs go wild for her.

When it's time to move on to the gala, I step forward and put my hand on the small of her back.

"Who's the beauty on your arm, Harris?"

I glance from the reporter and smile down at Kat.

"Kat Roberts," I respond.

"Who is she to you?" The reporter persists.

Always leave them guessing. An air of mystery never hurt anyone. In fact, it makes them beg to know more.

I stride away with Kat on my arm, leaving the question unanswered.

We walk across the giant side lawn, aglow by thousands of fairy lights and lanterns. Parallel to the beach below, two giant white pavilions sit: one for dinner and the other for dessert and dancing. The white table settings and flower centerpieces glow warmly in the light from candles and crystal chandeliers beneath the silk pleated canopies. On the sand, several bonfires burn to light up the beach for those who wish to venture for a stroll in the moonlight.

Servers from Lucien's catering company mill about with trays of Champagne and wines or hors d'oeuvres. Two bars sit on opposite corners for those who prefer to select a drink or the signature cocktail. To one side, a band plays lively music piped through speakers, also heard out on the beach.

Guests mingle and chat in the different areas, all dressed in the theme of the annual STEELE White Party.

It's already bustling since it's the party of the season and everyone wants a ticket for a chance to see and be seen amongst the world's elite. Not to mention raising funds for STEELE Foundation.

I spot our mother and father speaking with other couples. Uncle Connor and Aunt Lucie stand beside them. I continue towards them.

"Excuse us," I say as I interrupt their conversations.

My mother smiles and tilts her head.

I kiss her cheek.

"Shelley, this is amazing. So beautiful!" Kat gushes as she double kisses my mother's cheeks.

"Thank you, sweetheart. And you look phenomenal! How you sparkle," she responds as she holds up Kat's left hand. My mother stares pointedly at Kat's bare ring finger, then up at me. Her eyes dance with mischief.

Great.

"Well, sweeties, enjoy the night. The fireworks will be spectacular later," she adds with a wink.

"Kat, you do look lovely, dear. Go have fun, you two," my father says as he draws my mother back to the guests.

We say hello to Uncle Connor and Aunt Lucie—who also eyes me with a smirk.

These two besties…

I snag two glasses of Champagne from a passing server and hand one to Kat. She takes a sip with relief. I do the same.

"Harris? That is you, darling! Where have you been all summer?"

I glance around and find a socialite I fucked a few of times over the years.

Her ice blue eyes scan my body as she licks her lower lip. With each step, her tanned, long legs peek out of the front slit in her floor-length, one-shoulder gown. Her blonde hair cascades down her back. Yeah, she's a beauty.

Kat stiffens next to me.

"Hello, Bernadette—"

She leans into me and reaches up to kiss my lips. But catches the corner of my mouth as I turn my head away. She frowns at me. Then her eyes slide to Kat, who placed her hand on my arm possessively. Bernadette's eyes widen, surprised to see a woman claim me, then narrow at the sight of the many diamonds.

"Well, no need to claw at Harris, pet. We've known each other since we were children," Bernadette says to Kat, then turns to me and places her palm on my chest. "We'll talk another time."

She sashays away.

Kat drops her hand from my arm and finishes her Champagne in one gulp. A server passes, and she replaces the empty flute with a full one. As she takes a sip, she eyes me over the rim. Emerald fire blazes.

Oh, so she's pissed? Huh.

"Kat! I love your dress, honey!"

We turn around to Billie and Patrick. The petite beauty looks stunning in a below-the-knee-length flowy gown with double straps connected to the fitted bodice by crystal coins. Her full breasts nearly spill from the low cups. Ropes of diamonds adorn her neck.

Patrick keeps a possessive hand on her side below her breast. We talk while the girls chatter.

Unknowingly, they paused the questions Kat more than likely to have for me.

Good.

I'm still working on the love situation and don't even want to get into it about a past fuck-buddy.

More people approach us during the cocktail hour. Then it's time for dinner. Kat goes to freshen up with Blair and Leonie. Luc, Roger, and I wait for them before we enter the pavilion. When they return, we make our way to our tables.

I help Kat into her chair and sit beside her. We're at a table with Haley and Lachlan and other guests. Our mother always arranges for Steeles and Jacksons to sit at different tables throughout the space, so guests feel a connection to their hosts. And as our father reminds us, business can take place anywhere.

Kat loosened up after her second flute of Champagne. She smiles and chats with her seatmate and the others at the table as though it's second nature for her to attend a high-society event. Her laughter tinkles. She charms everyone. They're captivated by her Siren's call.

As am I.

I take a swig of my Jackson Cabernet Sauvignon and shrug. So she didn't tell me she loves me. It's not a deal-breaker. Our connection hit me hard from the beginning. She feels it too. I know it.

A small hand rests on my thigh.

I turn my gaze to Kat.

"Will you dance with me?" She asks with a small smile. It widens when I rise from my seat and help her from hers.

As we dance, I pull her close, and she melds her soft body to mine. We glide across the floor. Our steps fluid.

She tilts her head back.

"Are we okay?" She asks as her eyes search my face.

I take a moment to think about it. Then lower my mouth to her ear.

"Yes, Siren," I respond.

Later that night, our fireworks best those above the Atlantic Ocean. Beneath the moonlight, her alabaster skin glows as brilliantly as the diamonds on her naked body. I prove to My Siren we are more than okay as we explode again and again.

* * *

"YEAH, I received the alert a few minutes ago… Right… I'm taking care of it now. From the looks of it, they didn't get past the first firewall… No, not sophisticated at all… Don't worry. Go cuddle up to Little Lord Fauntleroy… Ha, hilarious! A true comedian…"

I end the call with Haley and return my full attention to our client's corporate network. True, a member of our STEELE Technology and Cyber Security team could handle the task. But I prefer to do the task since it's for a longtime client.

The process doesn't take much time and gives me a chance to pull up the beta technology for a program I'm developing. A few more tweaks and I'll have it ready for market. Haley thinks it's groundbreaking, and I agree. The revenue the program should generate would please Baz immensely.

I leave my office and head for the kitchenette for a bottle of water and a banana. We have the VIP post-gala brunch soon, so I don't want to eat too much. My mobile rings, and I talk to Laurent for a while, then return to my office.

Kat sits behind my laptop. A frown pinches her eyebrows together as she scans the screen.

What the fuck???

She was asleep when I left her in our bed an hour ago. Now she's snooping through my business?

"Kat," I snap as I storm over. "What are you doing on my laptop?"

She startles and pushes her eyeglasses up her nose. She's worn contact lenses most of the days, but they dried her eyes last night when she removed them. The little librarian shouldn't get into my laptop.

"Harris! Bloody hell! You scared me," she responds.

I yank the laptop from beneath her fingers.

"I—I was only searching the Internet. Billie sent a text message about photos from last night. But my mobile died as I was scrolling through them. Sorry!" Kat babbles.

And damn if Page Six's website isn't on the screen. Loser alert…

I lower my head and peek at her.

Her flushed cheeks and wide eyes make me feel like an ass.

Great, Harris, good job.

"No, I'm sorry," I say as I close my laptop and set it on the desk. "It's my work laptop. So I don't let anyone but Haley use it."

I round the desk and crouch beside Kat as I spin the chair around with her legs on either side of me. My palms rest on her bare thighs and slide up to the hem of my dress shirt she donned. It swallows her up and calls to my possessive nature.

She folds her arms beneath her braless tits and scowls at me. I do my best to not get distracted by their pebbled nipples poking through the cotton.

"Oh, so you don't trust me?" She bites out.

I shake my head.

"It's not that I don't trust you. It's beyond me. That laptop has proprietary information on it, and I'm responsible for a lot of data. As I said, only Haley has access. Not even Sebastian," I tell Kat. "But I shouldn't have thought you were in the files and spoken to you so harshly. I apologize. Forgive me?"

She purses her lips, unimpressed by my response.

I skim my index fingers along her seam, still swollen from last night.

My Kitty Kat squirms in the chair and tries to move away from me.

I won't have it.

Leaning forward, I slant my mouth over hers. My tongue probes against her lips as my fingers stroke her pussy. Her squirming turns to writhing. As her mouth opens, she moans. Her juices gush. I swallow her cries, then dip my head to lap at her cream.

"This year's gala surpassed our expectations. We raised over thirty-five-million dollars! The sponsors, tickets, and donations accounted for seventy-five percent while the silent auction and journal ads made up thirty percent. So far, we've received favorable media coverage. Thank you all for a successful fundraiser!"

Our mother stands at the podium beneath a pavilion and beams at the VIP patrons as she claps.

Proud of his wife, our father rises from his seat at the head table and claps too. Everyone joins him for a standing ovation.

I glance around to find my siblings and cousins clapping the loudest and with whistles. Beside me, My Kitty Kat grins with her hands above her head to clap. She glances up at me, and her smile widens.

My mother yields the podium to the sponsors. One by one, they speak to the VIP patrons to thank them and to plug their companies. When it's their turn, Baz and Lachlan outdo each other to raise their donations and many in the crowd re-open their wallets to give more. My mother thanks everyone again to rousing applause.

"You must be so proud," My Kitty Kat says. "Your Mum does incredible work."

"*She's* incredible and feels strongly about affordable housing for urban, lower-income families," I respond. "Not everyone has the advantages provided by wealth or name. It's important to give back and not just monetarily. Every summer since we were thirteen, our parents made certain we worked at the construction sites and in the Foundation's offices to learn firsthand what it takes to help others. We never hung around at the beach all day. And we're thankful."

My Kitty Kat stares at me a moment. That flicker passes through her eyes, and I can't decipher its meaning again. She nods.

"You up for surfing after this?"

Laurent crouches between us.

I glance back at My Kitty Kat and raise an eyebrow questioningly. She nods enthusiastically.

"Well, I think you have your answer, cuz," I respond with a grin. "We'll meet you on the beach."

"Eager, huh?" He chuckles. "Sounds good, I'll ask the Wild Boys."

An hour later, we're at the surf line astride our boards. My Kitty Kat bobs on the surface as she glances over her shoulder, searching for the right wave. She furrows her brow in concentration. When she spies one on the horizon, she flips to her belly and paddles. The wave catches her, and she hops to her feet, wobbles a bit, then finds her balance. She rides the wave almost to shore before she slips off. She pops to the surface and whoops gleefully.

I can't believe she's picked up the technique so quickly.

"Stop gawking at your woman and catch a wave already."

Lucien chuckles as he paddles past me back from his last ride.

Yeah, wuss…

I glance over my shoulder and skip the next wave. The one after has my name written all over it. I drop to my stomach and paddle. The wave slides beneath my board, and I hop up to ride it in. Malcolm rides it too and gives me the shaka hand wave as he grins like the Cheshire Cat.

We reach the beach at the same time. He picks up his board and claps me on the back.

"A girl who surfs... You got yourself a real winner with Kat, bro!" He says.

Now I grin like the Cheshire Cat and nod enthusiastically.

"*A* girl could really get used to this celebrity lifestyle!"

My Kitty Kat giggles as the driver maneuvers the platinum Rolls-Royce Phantom Extended behind the line of cars and limos leading to STEELE Aberdeen.

After our Labor Day getaway, I stayed in New York City and Kat flew back to Scotland with Lucien, who continued on to Paris. The week went well despite my reaction to her avoidance of the l-word for me.

We had a great time, and my family *loves* My Kitty Kat. My Mom made more than one hint about the future I could have with Kat. Hell, even my Dad—who rarely involves himself in our relationships—urged me to consider long term with Kat.

She impressed my parents with her smarts, sense of humor, and her ability to blend with the rest of our family and close friends. Add in her independent streak—like my sisters-in-law and Lydie—and she came out the winner. Ding, ding, ding.

At this exact moment, I can't say I'm ready to put a ring on it à la Beyonce. But I admit the idea of a future with Kat Roberts intrigues me. As my wife, as the mother of my children, I can see it. Just not tomorrow…

However, before I return to New York City, I plan to ask her to spend the holidays with me. The girls were talking about Capri and Verbier during Labor Day. Kat listened raptly.

Lola told me My Kitty Kat shared the tragedy of her parents and subsequent orphan status. Lola impressed upon me the importance of not allowing Kat to be alone while we're all together for Thanksgiving, Christmas, and New Year's. Not to mention I'd rather not have her in Aberdeen and I'm elsewhere. So I promised Lola I'd ask Kat to join us. Pleased, Lola gave me a big hug and kiss.

Now, I shift in my seat to face My Kitty Kat.

She looks ethereal in softly pleated layers of wispy pink silk-chiffon. The elegant column gown with sweetheart neckline and train that gathers between her shoulder blades to float to the ground behind her makes My Kitty Kat resemble an angel.

Once again, she denied my offer to purchase her attire. But she does wear the suite of Harry Winston diamonds I gifted her. They glitter in the dim lighting of the sedan as she stares out the tinted window. In the reflection, her eyes dart around as a smile plays at the corners of her lips.

I chuckle.

"Get used to it, babe. The social season is upon us," I reply. "And did I tell you just how spectacular you look?"

She giggles and shifts to face me.

"Yes, you did. Many times!" She responds as her emerald green eyes twinkle like the diamonds.

"Just checking," I smirk.

The sedan stops, and the valet knocks on the window with his gloved hand to ensure we're ready to exit before he opens the door. I rap back, and the door swings open.

"Showtime. Smile for the cameras," I say to My Kitty Kat.

She holds back a giggle and nods. I wink at her and exit the car, then turn to take her hand. She rises regally.

We line up at the edge of the Scotch-colored carpet before the step and repeat. Tonight, it's Aunt Lucie's fundraising gala for Jackson Foundation. It operates alcohol treatment centers for lower-income individuals and provides support for their family members. It's Aberdeen's event of the season attended by royals, nobles, high society, and dignitaries. Both clans come out to support her.

I spot Lachlan and Haley being interviewed by a reporter with a cameraman. Roger and Leonie chat with another reporter. Lucien—*The Sexy Chef*—charms a starry-eyed guest. All along the carpet, they engage with the media and attendees.

Soon it's our turn. I glance down at My Kitty Kat, and she squeezes my arm. Again, the photographers call out to us. This time, they say Kat's name, and her smile widens. We catch up to the others for group photos and such before we head for the ballroom.

"Lucie, this is gorgeous! Thank you for inviting me," Kat says as we greet my aunt in the receiving line.

"Oh, darling, thank *you*. But you're gorgeous! Your dress is divine. Harris better be good to you!" Aunt Lucie replies as she clasps My Kitty Kat's hands between hers.

She glances up at me and smiles as she says, "He does!"

I double kiss my aunt, and she whispers how pleased she is to see Kat here tonight. Uncle Connor welcomes us, and we move down the line.

As we walk through the crowd, I pass a flute of Champagne to Kat. We find a suitable spot to stand. Guests come by drawn to a Steele like a magnet. They introduce themselves, or if I know them, I introduce them to Kat. While I speak with the men, she chats with their wives or girlfriends.

Luc and Blair join us. She knows many of the attendees since she comes from a wealthy English family whose industry is manufacturing. Luc—being a French duc—is part of the royal set. They make a striking pair. The older, distinguished Frenchman and the younger English Rose.

When Blair mentions the silent auction, we go peruse the lots.

STEELE International, Inc. offers a month-long trip to three of our properties in Southeast Asia with transportation aboard a company jet. Jackson Corporation has two lots: two weeks at their Malbec bodega in Mendoza, Argentina and a guest appearance for four on Lucien's show, along with a private cooking lesson.

"Oh, this sounds incredible!" My Kitty Kat says. "An expedition to the South Pole. Think of that! The bottom of the world!"

"Ha! You see, bro, good pick."

I snort at Malcolm's words as he comes up beside me. Of course, he gives Kat more cool points for being a thrill seeker like him.

"Yeah, well, I have no interest. The whole thing freaks me out," I say.

Malcolm shakes his head.

"Oh, little bro, you will learn to do what makes your woman happy. Or suffer the consequences..." he tells me. "And bear in mind, we're sideways on the Earth right now. Have you fallen off?"

He walks away, chuckling with his hand on Starr's lower back.

The waitstaff walks through the ballroom to announce dinner.

Kat takes my arm, and we head to the tables.

I notice Callum Graham and Fiona Ridel—now Graham—at a table. He lifts his head and nods when he sees me. I return the gesture. The fucker and his missus tried to play my twin and Lachlan.

Moving on.

Baz waves us over to the table.

"You wear the gown fabulously, Kat! Thank you!" Lola gushes as I pull My Kitty Kat's chair out for her to sit beside Baz.

She thanks Lola and winks at me.

"Lola asked me to wear a piece from her new collection. Good for publicity, you know," Kat tells me.

"Well, you look mahvahlous, dahling," I say, doing my best Billy Crystal imitation.

She giggles and turns to Lola.

The program for the evening ends on a high note with Aunt Lucie's announcement the patrons raised over £30 million the highest ever. She calls her staff to the floor and thanks them before the sponsors speak. Once again, Lachlan and Baz do their thing and encourage others to donate more on the spur of the moment. They do to a standing ovation.

I take Kat to the dance floor and pull her close.

"Having fun?" I ask as we sway to the band's rendition of "Then Suddenly Love" by Frank Sinatra—Ol' Blue Eyes himself.

"Oh, yes!" She responds.

I spin her out and pull her back in with a dip at the end.

She giggles and kicks her leg up.

We come back together as others clap. Then I really put on a performance thanks to years of ballroom dancing lessons. My Kitty Kat keeps in step with me. We end the dance with her held aloft and arms reaching for the ceiling. We wow the crowd.

I lower her back to her feet with a dip and a kiss.

More claps and laughter surround us.

I bow and she curtsies before we leave them, begging for more.

"Showoff," Baz chuckles as My Kitty Kat takes her seat.

"What can I say when I have a beautiful woman in my arms?" I smirk.

Baz shakes his head and takes Lola to dance.

"I have a surprise for you, Kitty Kat," I tell her as she takes a sip of water. She glances at me and smiles. "We're spending the weekend in Banff at Jackson Castle. Everyone's flying up tomorrow early morning. I'll have you back in time for work on Monday. Good?"

Her eyes widen in surprise.

"Oh, Harris, the Jackson family seat?" She asks.

"The one and only," I respond.

"Wonderful, thank you!" My Kitty Kat says.

"Good, because I asked Haley to help me put together a bag for you with clothes and all. It's upstairs in our suite, so you don't have to worry about going home to pack," I say. "And don't tell me you could have purchased the items for yourself…"

She giggles and kisses my cheek as she thanks me.

* * *

"This looks straight out of a fairytale! I've never been to any of the castles and great houses before."

My Kitty Kat leans close to the Sikorsky's window as it flies over the stone wall that marks the boundary of Jackson Castle's five hundred plus acres along the coast of northeast Scotland.

The landscaped grounds are dotted with carriage drives and horse trails, walking paths, and a few ornamental buildings, including the chapel where Haley and Lachlan exchanged vows and a watchtower, he restored for her as a wedding gift.

As the castle comes into view, My Kitty Kat's mouth drops open.

I tell her the history of the impressive baroque mansion since I've come here all my life. They built it in the early eighteenth century to replace the original fortified castle the Jackson family erected two hundred years earlier. At the time, King James VI titled the Jackson family as Marquess of Huntly with their seat in Aberdeenshire.

The later generations wanted a majestic status symbol. The castle has a four-story center structure with two grand curved east and west wings of three stories each. Six staircases, elaborate fireplaces, and elegant formal entertainment salons along with an extensive art collection make for a splendid interior.

My Kitty Kat takes it all in as the helicopter lands. We—along with Haley, Lachlan, their babies, nannies, and two Golden Retrievers—hop in Range Rovers and drive to the mansion. The others will land shortly as each helicopter lifts off again.

Uncle Connor and Aunt Lucie arrived last night with my parents. They meet us in the entry.

"Welcome to Jackson Castle, Kat, our family seat," Uncle Connor greets her. Pride puffs out his solid chest.

"Thank you, Connor! I don't know whether I should curtsey or shake your hand," she quips.

His laughter booms around the entry hall. We join in.

"No, darling, not necessary for family," Aunt Lucie responds with a smile. Then she turns to me. "Harris, I put Kat in the room Haley used to stay in. You have your room down the hall. The footman will bring your bags upstairs. Breakfast is in the dining room."

She raises an elegantly arched eyebrow.

"Yes, Aunt Lucie," I reply, knowing she won't relent on the room arrangements since Kat and I are unmarried.

She smiles and pats my arm.

I put my hand on Kat's lower back and guide her to the dining room. Her eyes rove around as we pass through the many rooms. I answer questions she has about the paintings, coats of arms, and portraits. I promise to give her a full tour after we eat, unless Aunt Lucie has other activities planned.

My Kitty Kat walks to the windows and stares out at the rich colors of fall that paint the picturesque landscape. I come ups behind her and slip my arms around her waist to rest my hands on her lower belly. My chin atop her head.

"It's so beautiful. More so than I expected," she whispers reverently.

"Yes, it's always been a favorite place of mine," I say.

Excited barks sound behind us. Bonny and Belle enter the dining room with the feather tails wagging. The Golden Retrievers bound towards us. I scratch their head. Rodolphe and Gaspard's Bichon Frises follow. The adorable white fluff balls' afros bounce as they scamper towards us for attention too. We oblige them with belly rubs.

"They like you, *chérie*," Leonie says as she walks in with Roger, their kids, and her parents—Guy and Josy.

"I love dogs," My Kitty Kat says with a bright smile.

I ignore the twinge in my chest at the l-word again. Not going there.

Kat doesn't notice and goes on to talk to Leonie.

Once everyone arrives, the staff serves breakfast. As I expected, Aunt Lucie has activities for us. So I tell Kat I'll show her around later.

A flash of disappointment crosses her face. But she smiles.

After we eat, I take Kat upstairs so we can change for horseback riding. I leave her at her bedroom door and continue on to mine. I don't want any trouble from Lieutenant Lucie.

The sight of Kat in tight britches makes my cock twitch. It's been far too long since I last had her beneath me. Now, she's a filly I'm ready to ride.

Instead, we go to the stables, and I choose my favorite gelding. The stablehand selects a mare with a gentle temperament for My Kitty Kat since it's her first ride—well, horseback. She pets the mare's neck and coos to her.

Soon we're out on the trials. The October air crisp. Not a cloud in the clear blue sky. Lachlan and Haley lead us along the cliffs overlooking the North Sea. The sounds of the waves as they break against the shoreline reach us up above.

Ahead, the watchtower rises. When we were young, we played amongst the ruins, despite Uncle Connor's warnings about the danger of the crumbling stones. Abandoned years ago, the rain, high winds, and salty air sped up its demise. Now the watchtower is back to its original dramatic structure set on the open field high above the North Sea. A proud sentinel once again. As Haley and Lachlan's private hide-away, they ride past it.

Ahead of me, Kat slows to a stop. She stares at the watchtower.

I pull up beside her.

Her face is expressionless.

"It's a beautiful sight. Even better up close than from the helicopter. Come on, let's keep up with the others," I tell her and rein my gelding back around.

I nudge him forward. But she's still enraptured.

"Kat, let's go," I call to her.

She shakes her head as though to clear it, then nods and turns her mare in our direction.

When she nears me, I ask her if she's okay. Distracted, she nods again then tells me we better hurry and catch up. Her mare increases their pace to a fast walk.

I follow behind, then glance over my shoulder at the watchtower once more.

KAT

"**K**at."

I whirl around at the sound of Chet's voice. He's in the back of his Bentley sedan and beckons me with his finger through the open window.

Damn!

My head swivels to scan the street, busy with the evening commute. People bustle by, unaware of my dilemma. Chet ambushed me only a couple of blocks from Jackson Town House on my way to the bus stop after work. Not good. It would never do for anyone to see me with him—Jackson Corporation's archrival.

"What the bloody hell do you think you're doing?!" I whisper shout.

"Don't just stand there out in the open! Get in the car, Kat," Chet commands. When I hesitate, he opens the door and adds, "Now."

I take another look around. No familiar faces appear in the crowd. I rush over and duck inside as Chet slides to the other end of the back seat. I shut the door as the window rises and whirl on him.

"How dare you risk me being seen with you, Chet?! We're only a couple of—"

"Well, I see you have forgotten yourself, Kat," he interjects with a sneer. His denim blue eyes flash cobalt as he glares at me with such vehemence. I push back against the door for distance between us.

"Now, you listen to me, lass. You are nobody. Only someone I can use to destroy the Jacksons. So no matter how many fancy galas you attend on the arm of Harris Steele"—my mouth drops open, and his sneer widens as his eyes narrow—"Oh yes, lass, your photos with the... Now how did they phrase it... 'The Last Single of The STEELE Quaternity Gets Hooked' appear all over the Internet. You're a sensation, lass. But do not for one moment let the celebrity go to your head with me—Chet Stewart."

My mind whirls as I slump back against the door. The air in the sedan thins. I can't catch my breath.

Chet continues.

"So what do I say to myself when I see the photos of you cozied up with Steele and gallivanting with his family and the Jacksons?" He asks, then pauses to narrow his eyes at me.

I swallow and wait.

He tilts his head to the side with his index finger beside his chin as though deep in thought.

"Chet, now you can ruin not only that Jackson clan but also their buddies, the Steeles. And guess who's going to do it for me?" He asks as he brings his gaze back to me. He stares me down until I glance away.

"Bingo! The nobody lass Kat Roberts," he answers himself.

My mouth opens to speak. But he raises his hand.

"You listen to me, and listen to me good, lass. I plan to take them all down, and you will give me the means to do so. Use that pretty face and hot little body of yours to distract Steele. Fuck him. Drug him. I don't give a damn. Just get me intel from his and that twin of his technology and cyber security subsidiary at STEELE International. I want access to their clients' company and personal data. Even better, get me some new tech program he has. And I mean something big. Now go, I have dinner plans with a lady."

He reaches across me and opens the door, then pulls out his mobile as he sits back.

When I don't move, he lifts his gaze from the screen and glares at me.

"Go," Chet says as he shoos me with one hand. "Now."

I slip from the sedan and stand on the curb.

He rolls the window down again.

"And do it sooner rather than later. I want this… *business* with you done already," he demands.

Chet calls to his driver to go, and they pull away into traffic.

"Hello, Ms. Roberts. Fancy meeting you here."

A broad chest covered by a black cashmere sweater appears before me as I walk through the lobby doors at Jackson Town House, heading for home. I glance up to find Harris grinning at me. He leans down and kisses my lips softly as he pulls me into his arms.

"What are you doing here? I thought you had business in Geneva," I ask when he steps beside me and takes my hand.

We walk towards his Rolls-Royce sedan at the curb with the driver next to the back door. He tips his hat to me in greeting.

"Good evening, Ms. Roberts," he says as he holds the door open.

"Good evening, thank you," I respond, then slip inside.

Harris gets in and pulls me onto his lap. Her massive cock rests against my hip.

"I finished earlier than expected," he responds, as he nuzzles my neck. "I didn't stop at the hotel. Do you want to go there or to your flat? I'm game either way."

I shiver as he sucks the sensitive skin at the base of my neck. His cock thumps.

"Ahhh... Let's go back to my flat. I need my things," I respond.

"What do you want for dinner? I have a taste for sweet and savory Kitty Kat," Harris growls in my ear.

I purr in delight. But my stomach growls deeper than Harris. I skipped lunch to work on my project.

"As much as tasty Harris fills me, I need to eat some food. How about some curry takeaway?" I ask.

He nods, and I give the driver the address for my favorite shop. Harris hops out to pick it up, and I watch his firm ass flex in black joggers as he strides into the hole-in-the-wall restaurant.

Even in the brief time between the sedan and the door, two women gawk at Harris as he passes them. Oblivious, he turns and winks at me before he enters. The women follow his gaze, then stare at me as I sit in the Rolls-Royce with the window down. One of them narrow their eyes filled with envy. The other smiles as if to say go, girl. I ignore one and smile at the other.

Harris appears with the takeaway bags and gets back in

the car. The tantalizing aroma of the curry wafts through the interior. What a crazy contrast between a cheap restaurant—with good food nonetheless—and the über-luxurious Rolls-Royce. Just like the man and the nobody.

"Fuck, Kitty Kat, you feel so good. So. Good."

Harris mounts me from behind. My damp forehead drops to the mattress between my arms as I keen from the thrusts deep inside of my dripping pussy. My thighs quake from the orgasms he's given me. The only thought on my mind is the carnal bliss I float in.

My pussy walls flutter along his length as his bulbous tip grazes my G-spot on each entry. Harris groans from the pressure. I clench again and push my ass back against the cradle of his pelvis. He leans over and bites my shoulder as he groans deep in his chest.

Hot streams of his cum splash into my pussy. The excess drips from our intimate connection to coat my inner thighs.

He pinches my engorged clit, and I wail as a final orgasm rips through my well-used core. His torso collapses over me as his arms bracket my head. Warm breath puffs above me. The beat of his racing heart thrums through my back. Our sweaty bodies slide against each other.

I relish the sensations of his cock buried to the root inside of me and the weight of his solid body pressing me into the mattress. We remain motionless while our breath and heartbeats return to normal.

Harris bands an arm around my waist and rolls us to our sides. My ass remains pressed to his pelvis. His hand slips down to rest on my lower belly. The possessive gesture soothes me as my eyes drift close. Full from food and from Harris, I enter a peaceful slumber.

Motion on the bed wakes me. Still caught in sleep, I notice the sun's first rays peek through the sheer white curtains. It's quiet. Harris lies on his back with his arm thrown over his eyes as though hiding from the sunlight. I watch him for a moment. He's still asleep, only shifted his position.

Up on my elbow, I study his handsome face. The strong jawline with a hint of stubble. Full lips. Sculpted cheekbones. He rests without a care in the world. And why shouldn't he?

"I love you, Harris Steele," I whisper. "No matter what."

Revenge is sweet. But love is ambrosia.

HARRIS

"I'm so glad you guys came with us. I know it's best for society's expectations and all. But I do *not* enjoy engaging with Princess Fiona the Fair…"

Haley grimaces as we stand with My Kitty Kat and Lachlan for an exhibit opening at Fiona's Ridel Art Gallery in Aberdeen.

I chuckle at her reference to Fiona. Haley compares her to a willowy mythical creature with her ash blonde waist-length hair, violet eyes, and Scottish lilt who graces the heather meadows. I glance back at Fiona, who stands before the crowd. Haley's description is spot on.

"You're more than welcome," I respond. "Hopefully Callum stays over there with his wife."

I incline my head in his direction, and Haley nods.

"Absolutely!" She says.

Since I was in town, she asked me to come tonight. I told My Kitty Kat, and she wanted to come. We'll make an appearance, then go to dinner. Have some real fun.

I glance around at the paintings on the walls. They're a

mixture of landscapes featuring the fields above the North Sea and the rolling countryside of Aberdeenshire. The ones that show the most color and passion are the portraits of women.

Well, I can appreciate an artist who revels in the beauty of the female form. My kind of guy.

I glance down at Kat.

She stares at the paintings with wide eyes.

I'm glad she's enjoying herself. It's her first gallery show, and I want to give her a pleasurable experience.

"Great, it's a full house," Lachlan snorts. "Chet Stewart is here. The wanker."

I shift inconspicuously to the left and spot the fucker. He stands next to a brunette, but he glares at us with open hostility.

"What's his problem now?" I ask.

Lachlan shrugs and sips his drink.

"Who the bloody hell knows?" He asks rhetorically.

"Looks like Princess Fiona the Fair is about to speak," Haley says as she gestures towards her. "All bow down in her presence…"

Fiona moved to stand in front of a piece covered by a white drape. The murmur of the crowd lessens as she calls for everyone's attention.

"Ladies and gentlemen, I am Fiona Graham, Duchess of Montrose. Welcome to Ridel Art Gallery this evening," she announces.

Haley giggles and whispers, "Fiona loves her new title."

I chuckle and nudge my twin.

"Now, now, Countess of Aboyne, play nice with your noble peers," I chide her.

She rolls her eyes. Very unlady like…

"It pleases us to share the paintings of an unknown

artist. The new owner of an abandoned factory in Glasgow discovered the vast set of works in a loft. My team restored the ones you see around the gallery. The others will make their appearance soon. We know no history of the artist. Only the initials IJ on the earlier paintings and IR on the later ones appear. We know from the style and the strokes, the two are the same person. More than likely a man based on the subject and the age of the paintings."

Fiona pauses for dramatic effect.

"The portrait behind me is the most extraordinary of the entire collection. The size larger than the others. Attention to detail superb. He draws you into the intimate sanctuary of the scene. The vibrancy of the colors speaks to his love of his muse. See for yourselves. May I present to you… *Siren in Repose*."

Fiona pulls the tasseled rope with a flourish, and the white drape slips to the floor.

The portrait displays a striking red-haired woman with a white silk sheet artfully arranged around her curvaceous body as she lies on a red velvet chaise. Sky blue eyes set in a face of flawless, porcelain skin stare seductively at the viewer. Her Siren's call bewitching.

Something about the woman—her hair, the shape of her eyes, something—triggers a memory. My thoughts get interrupted by My Kitty Kat's gasp.

I glance down at her.

She covers her mouth.

"Wow! If not for the eyes, Kat looks just like the woman! Crazy, huh?" Haley exclaims.

I turn to her, then back to the portrait.

Now, I see it. The shape of her face. The rich Titian color of her hair.

"Yes, they do resemble one another," Lachlan says, then chuckles. "Kat, are you reincarnated?"

The three of us laugh and turn to face My Kitty Kat.

Her alabaster skin appears even more pale than usual. Her pupils dilated. As she flicks her gaze from the portrait to us. She seems unsteady on her feet.

"Hey, are you okay, Kat?" I ask as I reach for her arm. "Babe?"

Tears fill her eyes, and she shakes her head. She glances at Lachlan, then brings her emerald green eyes to me.

"I—I'm so sorry..." She stammers, then rushes for the door.

* * *

Harris & Kat's Story Continues: *Decode My Desires*

STEELE INTERNATIONAL, INC.
JACKSON CORPORATION
A BILLIONAIRES ROMANCE
SERIES CROSSOVER

Decoding my DESIRES

HARRIS & KAT PART II

Charmaine Louise Shelton

I dedicate this novel to those who deserve a second chance and to those who give it to them.

Fulfill Your Desires.

xoxo
Charmaine Louise

ABOUT DECODE MY DESIRES INTRIGUE & KAT PART II

Decode My Desires Harris & Kat Part II

Welcome to the titillating world of the multibillion-dollar global companies and the love affairs of the families that control them.

Harris

Who's the sucker now? Me, that's who. The One really took me—not to mention my family—for a ride. I never should have given up my playboy card. Well, it's back in hand, and I have to make up for lost time.

Kat

What's that saying about best laid plans? Yeah, tell me about it. Hopefully my new goal to figure out Harris and what I feel for him works out better...

Can Kat redeem herself, or has she lost the opportunity for The One?

Travel with this playful pair as Kat makes her moves on Harris from sky-high penthouses on Fifth Avenue and the Sunset Strip to a private villa beside a lush Hawaiian lagoon and more in their sizzling, second chance billionaire romance.

Anthem: "Come Back to Me" Janet Jackson
https://www.youtube.com/watch?v=-5ecZWwO_hQ

Playlist:
https://www.youtube.com/playlist?list=
PLXwYvn0e218CGttnEJo1AjzohDVB0NGdd

Visit CharmaineLouiseBooks.com

KAT

"*I*'m so glad you guys came with us. I know it's best for society's expectations and all. But I do *not* enjoy engaging with Princess Fiona the Fair…"

Haley Jackson, the Countess of Aboyne née Steele, grimaces as we stand with her husband Lachlan Jackson, the Earl of Aboyne, and her twin brother Harris Steele. We're at Duchess of Montrose Fiona Graham's Ridel Art Gallery in Aberdeen for an exhibit opening.

Me, Katrina Roberts, the lass from the less-than-favorable upbringing who clawed her way from a dingy flat in Glasgow to the hallowed halls of the University of Edinburg on a full academic scholarship. I worked hard to escape poverty from the premature death of my father through graduation with an MA Business Management degree to administrative positions for C-suite executives. The latest Lachlan Jackson. But the position with the CEO of Jackson Corporation does more than train me for the best way to learn about business—straight from the source, the higher ups who actually run it. No, that position serves one purpose. And one purpose alone.

Revenge.

My eyes flick from a painting on the wall to Harris as he chuckles at Haley's reference to Fiona. Haley compares the woman who wanted to marry Lachlan to a willowy, mythical creature. Fiona with her ash blonde waist-length hair, violet eyes, and Scottish lilt appears as one who graces the heather meadows.

"You're more than welcome," Harris responds. "Hopefully Callum stays over there with his wife."

Harris inclines his head in the duke's direction, and Haley nods.

"Absolutely!" She says.

Ah, Harris Steele, my fledgling boyfriend, multibillionaire at thirty-two, the last single of The STEELE Quaternity. The four brothers and heirs to STEELE International, Inc. Sebastian, Malcolm, Roger, and Harris dubbed such by the media as the most sought-after of the world's eligible billionaires. Handsome; six plus feet; ebony hair; shades of gray eyes; powerful Alpha Doms and males.

And I made the last one fall for me in a few short months. I've said it once and I'll say it again. My red hair, pretty face, and curvy body get 'em every time.

Now not only am I in the prime position to ruin the Jackson's but also the Steeles. The power rests in my hands.

I flick my gaze to Chester Stewart, aka Chet, the forty-year-old vice president of Stewart Scotch. His family's company is Jackson Corporation's top competitor and has a centuries-old bitter rivalry over a title. Chet glares at me.

He hates me.

I hate him.

But we each serve the other's purpose.

Revenge against the Jacksons.

Now, he wants the Steeles, too.

But I question, do I want to take both clans down? Even after the families welcomed me like one of their own into their world of luxury, love, and loyalty?

Then again, I need to remain loyal to *my* family and the correction of the dirty deed that put us on the polar opposite of both clans.

I scowl at Chet, then turn my gaze to Harris.

Even though he lives in New York City, he has stayed in London working from his offices in STEELE London, jetting me around the globe for weekend getaways, or coming to Aberdeen. This is one such time. He returned from a business trip to Geneva to surprise me.

After our toe-curling marathon reunion, Haley asked him to come tonight—no pun intended. I agreed—whether or not pun with that walking sex on a stick. The plan to make an appearance, then go to dinner. Have some real fun, as Harris says.

I let my gaze wander. The paintings a mixture of landscapes featuring the fields above the North Sea and the rolling countryside of Aberdeenshire. Others capture women.

The hairs on the back of my neck rise.

No!

My eyes narrow on the painter's signature in the corner of the closest piece. The beam of light from the fixture above shows it clearly. IJ.

Is it possible?

I shift to get a better view of the next painting. IR.

A few more marked by either set of initials.

There's no denying it.

What the bloody hell do I do?!

"Great, it's a full house," Lachlan snorts. "Chet Stewart is here. The wanker."

"What's his problem now?" Harris asks.

"Who the bloody hell knows?" Lachlan asks rhetorically.

"Looks like Princess Fiona the Fair is about to speak," Haley says. "All bow down in her presence…"

I watch—frozen in place—as Fiona moves to stand in front of a piece covered by a white drape. The murmur of the crowd lessens as she calls for everyone's attention.

"Ladies and gentlemen, I am Fiona Graham, Duchess of Montrose. Welcome to Ridel Art Gallery this evening," she announces.

Haley giggles and whispers, "Fiona loves her new title."

Harris chuckles.

"Now, now, Countess of Aboyne, play nice with your noble peers," he chides his twin.

"It pleases us to share the paintings of an unknown artist. The new owner of an abandoned factory in Glasgow discovered the vast set of works in a loft. My team restored the ones you see around the gallery. The others will make their appearance soon. We know no history of the artist. Only the initials IJ on the earlier paintings and IR on the later ones appear. We know from the style and the strokes, the two are the same person. More than likely a man based on the subject and the age of the paintings."

Fiona pauses for dramatic effect.

My breath catches in my throat.

"The portrait behind me is the most extraordinary of the entire collection. The size larger than the others. Attention to detail superb. He draws you into the intimate sanctuary of the scene. The vibrancy of the colors speaks to his love of his muse. See for yourselves. May I present to you… *Siren in Repose*."

Fiona pulls the tasseled rope with a flourish, and the white drape slips to the floor.

The portrait displays a striking red-haired woman with a white silk sheet artfully arranged around her curvaceous body as she lies on a red velvet chaise. Sky blue eyes set in a face of flawless, porcelain skin stare seductively at the viewer.

I gasp and cover my mouth with my hand as the blood drains from my face, making the alabaster skin more pale. My pupils dilate. I have to get out of here before I faint.

"Wow! If not for the eyes, Kat looks just like the woman! Crazy, huh?" Haley exclaims.

"Yes, they do resemble one another," Lachlan says, then chuckles. "Kat, are you reincarnated?"

The three laugh and turn to face me.

My gaze flicks from the portrait to them. My knees wobble.

"Hey, are you okay, Kat?" Harris asks as he reaches for my arm. "Babe?"

Tears fill my eyes, and I shake my head. I glance at Lachlan, then bring my emerald green eyes to Harris.

"I—I'm so sorry…" I force out the words before I rush for the door, blinded by tears.

Well, I guess I have my answer.

No, I don't want to take both clans down.

The new question: is it too late to save myself from *their* revenge after all I've done?

"Kat! Wait up!"

I continue to the doors, intent on putting as much distance as possible between Harris and me.

What the bloody hell can I say or do now?

Mumbled apologies fall from my lips as I push through the crowd awed by the paintings, then burst through the gallery's front doors. Out on the street, I glance left and right for the fastest route away.

Harris' Rolls-Royce sedan sits at the curb with his driver inside. Can't go straight. I dodge around a couple staring in the gallery's front windows. Perhaps if I get around the corner before Harris sees me.

A hand grabs my elbow.

My back collides with Harris' firm chest as he bands his arms around my waist. Locked against him, I can't move. His familiar scent washes over me. A sob escapes my mouth. I struggle to free myself.

"Kat, babe. Talk to me," he says frantically as his grip tightens.

"What happened?"

"Is she all right?"

Lachlan and Haley's questions urge me to get away. I cannot face them. Not now. I renew my efforts. But Harris will have none of it. The Alpha male comes to the forefront.

"Kat! Enough! Tell me what happened," Harris says as he spins me around to face him. His dove gray eyes—obsidian in the glow of the streetlamps above us—scan my face. A frown mars his masculine beauty.

I swipe at the tears and press my teeth into my lower lip to bite back another sob. My eyes flick from his face to Haley, then to Lachlan. His emerald green eyes so like my own fill with concern.

I lower my head and mutter a curse under my breath.

"What?" Harris asks as he slips a finger beneath my chin to align our gazes. Softly he adds, "Talk to me, Kitty Kat."

My resolve breaks as a great sob crests the surface from the depths of my soul and knocks down the last vestiges of my defenses. I've held so much anger, bitterness, and pain for decades. Fought my battles and those of my mother Allison, elder brother Payton, and younger siblings Michael and Charlotte.

The only time I've ever found peace has been in the arms of my lover—Harris Steele.

And here I am on the brink of destroying not only his extended family but his too.

KAT

"*H*arris, wait a minute. Kat, honey, do you want to speak to me without these guys around? We can go to the restaurant and sit at the bar for a Girls' Chat. They can sit at the table or go home and to the hotel. Whichever you prefer. Okay?"

I glance over at Haley. Her dove gray eyes reveal the sincerity in her words and make my heart ache even more. Perhaps she's right. If I confess to her—alone—maybe it won't be as bad to see the pain I'll cause Harris and Lachlan. She's been nothing but kind to me. So maybe she'll be less upset.

She's super close with her sisters-in-law Lola, Starr, and Leonie, married to Sebastian, Malcolm, and Roger, respectively. They refer to each other as sisters and bond whenever the guys get overly protective. For a moment, I felt a part of their inner circle. But now...

As I open my mouth to respond, a movement beyond Haley catches my eye.

Chet.

Bloody *hell!*

He left the gallery and stands glaring at me with such animosity I shiver as the waves of his anger hit me full blast.

"Babe, you're shivering. Go. Go talk to Haley. She'll listen," Harris says worriedly as he presses me towards his twin. Then he nods to his driver who stepped out of the Rolls-Royce sedan when he noticed us on the sidewalk. "Ride in my car. I'll go with Lachlan."

"Yes, Kat. Harris and I will wait at the penthouse flat. Come over when you're ready. Take your time," Lachlan adds.

Neither notice Chet as he puts his index finger to his mouth in a shushing motion, then brings it down to slash at his throat as his evil glare intensifies.

My eyes widen at his threat, and I turn away.

What have I gotten myself into? Chet dares to threaten me with *death*? In public for anyone to witness?

I shudder at the thought, realizing he has the means to do so and no one would ever know.

Oh, Kat Roberts…

My mind scrambles to backtrack. No way can I admit what I've done now. Not with Chet and not knowing what he'd do to me. I need time to figure out this bloody mess. As much as I hate to do it, more lies slip from my mouth with ease.

"Haley, Harris, Lachlan," I start as I lick my dry lips and glance at them in turn. "Thank you so much. I—I was a tad bit overwhelmed. Forgive my outburst. I don't want to ruin our evening. Let's go back inside—"

"Kat."

"You ruined nothing."

"No need to apologize, Kat."

The three of them speak at once. But Haley raises her hand, and the guys go quiet.

"Kat Roberts. You will not stand here and tell us *lies*," Haley says adamantly.

My heart stops as my mouth gapes. Fuck!

Haley is a top-notch hacker. I have to admit she's far better than my self-taught skills, as good as they are for my needs—although they're unaware of my tech savvy. Harris is an expert coder. Together, they formed STEELE Technology & Cyber Security and known as the Dynamic Duo. Brainiacs, to say the least.

If my spell—or Siren's call, as Harris refers to it—didn't distract him, I'm certain he would have noticed something by now. Their subsidiary handles Jackson Corporation's technology systems. Once Lydie Jackson—the eldest of the siblings and COO—increased my security access, I delved into their files to uncover intel Chet could use to destroy them. Periodically, I fed it to him over the last few months in exchange for six-figure sums wired to my Swiss bank account.

But I'm not selfish.

The money goes towards a monthly allowance I give to my mother, who cleans the homes of rich people in Glasgow. One day soon, she won't have to get on her knees for anyone ever again. I help my younger siblings too. Michael works but loves to sketch the architecture in Glasgow. I want to enroll him in a formal program. Charlotte is at university on a full academic scholarship and works too. She needs to focus on her coursework fully without concern over money for food or textbooks. I try to make their lives a little easier, too.

I think of the reasons for my actions—including the dirty deed—take a deep breath and straighten my spine.

Okay, Katrina Roberts, *smiogaid suas, nighean!*

"Ha! Haley, you got me! It's a tad bit embarrassing. So, I'd rather not say at the moment. You're right. Why don't we go have our Girls' Chat and meet the guys at your flat afterwards," I say with a smile. I do my best to make it reach my eyes.

Haley grins and loops her arm through mine.

"Perfect!" She says to me, then turns to Lachlan and Harris and wiggles her fingers. "Tootles, fellas. We'll catch you later."

Lachlan leans over and kisses her as she waltzes past him. He whispers something in her ear, and her face flushes scarlet. He chuckles and steps back.

"Okay, babe. Take your time. I'll be there when you need me," Harris says before he bends down to kiss me.

My throat constricts as my heart stutters from his sweet words. They're all so caring it adds to my discomfit.

"Thank you, Harris," I whisper as I squeeze his forearm. I can't quite make eye contact, but I offer a wan smile.

He kisses the top of my head and motions for his driver to open the sedan's back door.

Haley and I slip into the luxurious interior. Once the door closes with a light thunk, she turns to me.

"First, I want you to know you can trust me with whatever you have to say, Kat. Harris is my twin, and I love him with every ounce of my being. But I know how my brothers can be. So if he did something, do not hesitate to tell me," she says earnestly as she squeezes my hand.

I return the gesture with a smile.

"Thank you, Haley. I truly appreciate you. I admire how close you, your sisters-in-law, and friends are to each other. How I wish we could have had the same—" I stop as I realize the tense I used. Damn!

Haley notices it too and frowns. Before she can question my choice of words, I squeeze her hand.

"What I mean to say is I hope I can be a part of your inner circle," I clarify and say a silent prayer she believes me.

Haley studies my face for a minute, then nods her head.

"Of course! Us girls have to stick together," she responds, then winks. "And I'll take any excuse to get a night out with my girls! So thank you."

We ride to the restaurant in a comfortable silence. At the bar, we settle into a corner semicircular booth with a low table. I glance around at the posh eatery. The patrons resemble Harris, his twin, and her husband—well dressed, wealthy, young, gorgeous.

A server who could be a male supermodel takes our orders and returns moments later.

"Mmmm. Delish!" Haley says after she takes a sip of her Manhattan cocktail made with Jackson Special Blend Scotch—naturally.

I can't help but to grin at her reaction as she smacks her full lips. Her dove gray eyes twinkle in the warm golden light from candles artfully arranged on the tabletop and sconces on the walls. She tosses her waist-length ebony hair over one shoulder as she leans back against the buttery soft suede banquette.

"So, spill," she says.

I take a swig of my Old Fashioned to wet my suddenly parched mouth. No point in dragging it out. I take a deep cleansing breath as Starr taught me in a yoga session. Showtime as Harris says...

"Sometimes, I get a bit overwhelmed... rather intimidated by others. Well, more specifically of those who come from affluent backgrounds," I start, then take another sip of my cocktail. "Over the years, I've done my best to blend in with those kinds of people and not let my less-than upbringing make me feel less than them—"

"Oh, Kat," Haley starts.

I raise my hand and continue with a shake of my head.

"It's hard for me to talk about. And I know you mean well. But if you'd be so kind as to allow me to finish?" I ask as I squeeze her hand and smile. When she nods, I continue. "Tonight and the last few weeks, Harris has immersed me in your world—not that I dislike it—and it's hit me harder than usual. That's all. I'll get over it."

Haley blinks and bites the corner of her lower lip. Her gaze goes beyond me as she considers my confession. Slowly, she nods and turns back to me.

"I can't say that I understand your experience, Kat, as I was born into a family with multigenerational wealth," she says. "However, my mother and my Aunt Lucie come from middle-class families. Not quite your situation, but they share with us the challenges they faced growing up and blending into this world. Hell, I had to learn from Aunt Lucie about being a Countess as I'll step into her role of Marchioness of Huntly—hopefully no time soon. So I understand and respect you, Kat."

I thank her and take another sip of my drink.

"Wait a minute," Haley says as she sits up with wide eyes.

I lower my glass to the table and shift in my seat to face her again. My heartbeat speeds up and my underarms tingle. What could she think??? Bloody hell.

Haley narrows her eyes at me.

"Did someone make you feel a certain kind of way while you were with us?" She asks.

Her ferocious expression makes me giggle. Harris said she's become a mama bear since having her babies. And now she displays it as she's protective of me too.

The scowl morphs into a grin. Then she laughs.

I shake my head.

"No. Everyone treats me very well, thank you!" I respond.

"Good! Or else someone would have to answer for unacceptable behavior," Haley says as she wags her index finger. "Now, let's order another round and some artichoke dip and sliders. What else?"

I pick up the menu and add some tater tots with their specialty sauce.

That's another thing I love about the girls. They enjoy their food and drink! Sessions with Starr and their personal trainers keep them fit. Besides, the guys really love their curves, and Harris is no exception.

Haley and I spend the rest of the evening talking about the upcoming holidays the Steeles and Jacksons spend together in Capri and in Verbier, the next Girls' Getaway, and Lola's fashion show during Paris Fashion Week.

The way Haley includes me as part of the family gatherings makes my heart hurt. I so hope Harris and Lachlan will forgive me.

A few hours pass, and we leave for her penthouse flat off Union Street—a ritzy area in Aberdeen.

Harris rushes over to pull me into his embrace. I rest my head on his firm chest as I wrap my arms around his waist. Lost in the compellingly sensual scent of his cologne— floral, earthy, and vanilla—my body melts against him with a sigh.

"Feel better?" He murmurs as he strokes my back.

I nod and tighten my grip on him. I never want to let Harris go. Ever.

"Words, Kat. I will have your words," he says as his warm breath skitters across my cheek.

"Yes, Harris, I feel a whole lot better thanks to Haley," I respond to the Alpha male's command.

He rumbles soothingly, then leans back to gaze down at me.

"Do you want to share with me? If not, as long as you're okay, we can leave it alone," he asks.

I assure him all is well and best to move on. Put it behind us.

We bid Haley and Lachlan goodnight and leave for STEELE Aberdeen. Once in the President's suite, Harris scoops me into his arms and carries me through the palatial rooms to the primary bedroom. He strides past the double doors and deposits me on my feet beside the king-size bed.

Without hesitation, he strips my silk wrap dress and lingerie from my body and drops them to pool at my feet. I step out of my slingbacks just as he tosses me onto the bed. I squeal as I land amidst the sumptuous linens and plentiful pillows. My legs splay open to give Harris a full view of needy pussy.

He growls as he shrugs out of his suit jacket.

I snap my knees together, embarrassed he'll spy the moisture gathering along my lower lips.

A growl of displeasure has me shuddering and my legs falling apart.

"Open!" He commands. "Do not hide yourself from me, naughty lass."

I mewl in response as I lean back on my elbows. My hooded gaze rakes over his body that puts Adonis to shame as he sheds his clothes and toes off his shoes and socks. As he stands to his full six-feet-one-inch height, his massive cock thumps against the happy trail along his eight-pack abs.

My pussy softens in anticipation of Harris' girth

breaching my folds. Another mewl slips from my slack mouth.

He rumbles deep in his chest as he planks over me.

"I always want to see you bare to me, Kitty Kat and comfortable telling me anything on your mind. I'll let it go tonight. But know we will keep no secrets from each other," Harris says as his dove gray eyes bore into my emerald green gaze.

My eyes widen at his words, and my heart bangs against my chest.

Bloody—

Harris' mouth crashes over mine. As he takes complete possession of my mind, body, and soul, I give into his passionate lovemaking one last time.

Go to Haley's now. We're having a meeting in thirty minutes.

I frown at my mobile screen with the cryptic text message from Baz.

What the hell is that all about?

I scrub my hand over my face and roll onto my back amidst the rumpled bedding. I glance to the right at the cold, empty space beside me. Only an indentation in the pillow and the faint scent of her perfume give any sign My Kitty Kat was here.

She left before I woke up. Without a word.

Presumably she didn't want to wake me. Not that I would mind, especially with my morning wood. I groan at the thought of her writhing beneath me just hours before. My cock tents the sheet as my erection grows. My Siren drives me crazy.

I sit up on an elbow and type a quick text message to her, then wait for a response. Nothing. Well, no worries since we have plans for dinner tonight. I toss the mobile onto the bed and head to the shower. Might as well get ready for the *meeting*.

On the ride over, I shoot a text message to Haley for any insight she can give to me. While I wait for her to answer, I scroll through my work emails. Since I'm in the UK, I'll spend some time in our STEELE London offices. Haley returns full time next week. So, I'll make sure all is ready for her.

As I ride up in their private elevator, I send another text to My Kitty Kat. The doors ping open onto their entry foyer. Without glancing up, I step off.

"Hey."

I lift my gaze from the mobile screen to find Haley at the open double doors to their penthouse flat. A frown knits her eyebrows together as her eyes scan my face. Her hair piled atop her head in a messy bun sags to the side.

"Hey. What's up, Hal? You look like you've been through it," I say as I lean over to kiss her cheek.

She shakes her head and glances up at me. Her dove gray eyes full of concern.

"It's not good, Harris," she whispers.

"Haley? Is that Harris?" Lachlan calls out.

"Yeah," she shouts back, then pulls my arm. "Come on."

I draw back and frown at her. But she shakes her head and tugs at me. I give in and follow her inside their flat.

Lachlan stands, arms folded, with Lydie beside him. Both stare at me the same way Haley did a moment ago as though judging my reaction—to what I do not know.

"Okay. What the fuck's going on?" I ask as I fold my arms across my chest and plant my feet. "Somebody better tell me why I'm getting a silent third degree."

"Har—"

Lachlan's mobile rings. He pulls it from his jeans pocket and glances at the screen before he accepts the call.

"He's here now," Lachlan says, as he brings his indecipherable gaze back to my face. "Okay, we're headed to my office."

He ends the call and motions for us to follow him. Lydie keeps pace with her brother. Haley remains by my side as we walk down the corridor to Lachlan's home office. Inside, he settles on a leather chair at the seating area. Lydie takes the other chair, leaving the sofa for Haley and me.

The oversized flat-screen television splits into three views. Baz sits at his desk in his home office at The STEELE Tower on Fifth Avenue in New York City. Malcolm appears to be at Steele Southampton Village in his mansion's office. Roger sits on a sofa in the home office of his Paris triplex penthouse. Each one stares at me.

What the fuck?!

"Spill it," I say, addressing Baz.

"My guy thought his research on Kat was too clean. Not so much as a traffic ticket or a late library book. Her social media imprint nonexistent as were searches of her on the Internet. Nothing appeared prior to the accident with her parents. No school grades, nothing on her parents' jobs. Nothing. A complete enigma. So he dug deeper, and he followed her—"

"Hold the fuck up, Baz!" I shout as I leap to my feet and stalk towards the television. "You mean to tell me you found this out and didn't even bother to tell me *anything*? Then you have *your guy* follow *my woman*?! Without fucking telling me?! Not cool, Baz!"

He cocks an eyebrow and watches me in silence. When I finish, he leans forward and pins me with an intense gaze more powerful than Roger's signature stare.

"First off, back down, Harris," Baz responds coolly. His platinum gray eyes brook no room for argument.

I growl and pivot on my heel. Once I'm seated again, Baz continues.

"Harris, as your eldest brother and the CEO of STEELE International, my responsibility is to you, our family, and to our company. I chose not to tell you right away because I wanted to have full details and irrefutable proof of any wrongdoing before I drew any conclusions. Do you understand?" He asks.

He's right. Baz takes on the mantle of our third parent and cares for us beyond measure. After family, STEELE ranks as his next priority. When our father named him as his successor six years ago, my siblings and I accepted and respect his leadership role too. So I know without a doubt he has my best interest at heart.

"Yes," I respond.

Baz nods and goes on.

"My guy followed Kat for a period of time. He saw her with Chet Stewart"—my head swivels to Lachlan who watches me intently, then to Lydie who purses her lips—"They spent time in the back of his Bentley before she got out and he drove away. That incidence made me call Lach and Lydie. Also, my guy uncovered Kat's real background."

Baz lifts a manila file folder from his desk, and Lachlan slides a similar one across the coffee table towards me.

"This contains his complete report, photographs, and documents. You can read the summary on the first page. We will wait," Baz says.

I glance at the manila file folder like it's a cobra weaving back and forth, set to strike a devastating blow. Haley nudges me with her knee, and I pick up the folder warily.

In all honesty, I wish this shit wasn't true. For one brief

moment, I had a taste of what my twin and our siblings enjoy every day—the love of the soul mate. I thought Kat was The One for me. The One I would spend the rest of my life, have children, a little family of my own. Fuck.

I open the file and stare at the summary sheet held by a paper clip to the top of a sizable pile of what I presume to be damning evidence. My stomach knots.

Haley—as though sensing my distress—rubs my back. The calming touch of my twin allows me to refocus. I detach the sheet and read the summary.

Fuck. Me.

Katrina Roberts, 27, of Glasgow, Scotland

Father: Ramsay Roberts, deceased at 37 of a heart attack, unemployed

Mother: Allison Roberts, 49, domestic maid

Siblings: Payton Roberts, 30, unemployed; Michael Roberts, 24, kitchen porter; Charlotte Roberts, 21, university student

Prior Residence: Glasgow, Scotland; shared with parents and siblings

Current Residence: Aberdeen, Scotland

Known Associates: Chester Stewart, Vice President, Stewart Scotch; Isla Ritchie, former administrative assistant to Lachlan Jackson, CEO, Jackson Corporation

As I scan the rest of the page, the roaring of a train grows in my ears.

I flip through the photos.

Sure as shooting, the four-color images capture Kat with Chet. She stands on a sidewalk beside a Bentley sedan. In another, she scans the street surreptitiously before she slips inside. She steps out. Chet sticks his head through the window to speak to her. He pulls off. She stares after him.

Last night at the gallery, Chet watching Kat; her looking at him.

All the fuck while on my arm.

Damn!

I toss the photos onto the coffee table and run my fingers through my hair, then yank.

Harris Steele, you dumb ass! How the hell did I fall for this trick? Siren's call my ass. And Chet Stewart? My family's competitor and rival? Hell no!

Once again, I leap to my feet. This time I pace the floor. My mind reels. Thoughts run wild.

"Let me guess, she colluded with Chet to fuck with Jackson Corporation. Why? What did she give him? I didn't get an alert about invalid access. Haley, did you?" I think aloud as I try to make it make sense.

Haley shakes her head and glances at Lachlan, then at Lydie.

"Lydie can give you more details," Lachlan says, as he nods at his sister.

"We don't know why. But we intend to find out tomorrow when we confront her at the office," Lydie says as her emerald green eyes blaze. *The Shark* is out for blood. "You didn't receive an alert because I upped her clearance to access fake information. I noticed Stewart Scotch was getting the jump on some of our launches and news. Plus, I overheard Chet bragging about us getting our comeuppance. It took a bit of time to figure it was coming from Lachlan's office. Our heads of technology and security ruled out his personal assistant—Gladys. Then we turned to Kat."

Lydie hands another manila file folder to me before she continues.

"We wanted to get her on enough shared information to ensure any action we take sticks. Her mining activity lessened, then stopped. At first, we thought she realized we knew about her activities. Then I saw how serious the two of you became with her attending the foundation galas with you. I wanted to tell you but didn't want to risk her finding out. Not that I don't trust you, Harris. Kat is the questionable one."

"So this chick faked us out the entire time?" Malcolm asks incredulously.

"Hung out with us in our homes. Embraced by our families. Not good," Roger adds.

"How the *fuck* did I miss it?" I yell at the ceiling with my fists raised.

Everyone turns to me.

"Listen, Harris. It's not your fault, and no one blames you in any way," Haley says as she stands in front of me to stop my pacing. "None of us detected any hint of deceit from Kat. Okay?"

I scan my twin's face and those of the others to confirm her words. They agree with her wholeheartedly. With a ragged sigh, I plop onto the sofa and throw my head back against the cushion.

"So now what?" I ask, staring at the ceiling.

"Lydie and I will meet with Kat tomorrow when she arrives at my offices. She better tell us everything we ask. Then we'll determine the extent of the damage before we decide her fate. Not to mention dealing with that fucking wanker Stewart once and for all," Lachlan says, eyes flashing like his sister's fiery orbs. With a shake of his head he adds, "A great first day for my return from paternity leave."

"If you find she did anything to harm Harris or STEELE, I will handle her," Baz states.

"No, *I* will handle Kat Roberts *and* Chet Stewart," Malcolm *The Enforcer* corrects with a steely expression.

Roger nods.

"Fine," Baz and Lachlan say at the same time as Lydie voices her agreement.

I shake my head as I think back over the last three months. What a fucking mess I've gotten our companies, family, and myself into. Never again will I allow a woman to use me. Ever. I groan.

"And you have jokes when I say I hold on to my playboy card like a life preserver in a tsunami…" I grouse as I scrub my hand over my weary face.

Well, back to the basics for this playa.

KAT

orning, Kitty Kat. Where did you run off to? The bed's too cold without you... H.

As I read Harris' text message, my heart clenches. I miss him so much already. Last night was a whirlwind of emotions. Too many for me to process. I need space and time to figure out this bloody mess. What the *hell* am I going to do?

As much as I want to come completely clean with Harris and Lachlan, I'm scared to death of the repercussions. I don't want to lose Harris or the respect of Lachlan—not to mention both families hating me. I've grown attached to Haley, too. And once again, she comforted me as though I were already a part of their family and her inner circle of girls.

Bloody hell!

Think, Kat Roberts, dammit!

Once I arrived at my flat, I showered. But too keyed up to eat breakfast. As I sip my morning tea, my mind races to find a way to avoid the wrath of not only the Jacksons and Steeles, but the death threat of Chet.

I shiver at the memory. How adamant he was as he slashed at his throat. Would he really go that far? I suppose so since what we did was highly illegal, and he stands to lose a hell of a lot more than I do. He and his brother Bram vie for the coveted positions of CEO and Chairman of the Board of Stewart Scotch. Magnus—their father—encourages the competition and will only announce his successor when one of the brothers "proves their worth." Naturally, Chet wants the role so much he was ripe to get intel to ruin Jackson Corporation and the family. So, yeah, I'm sure he'd find a way to hurt me greatly—or worse.

And if Chet ever found out about my family, I'm certain he would exact revenge on them, too. It's bad enough for my mother, Michael, and Charlotte, as it is without one more problem. Payton, well, he's another story. Not that I wish any harm to befall him. No. He just doesn't want to do anything more with his life than hang out at the corner pub and talk about his latest idea guaranteed to make him loads of money. Just like our father did before he died. Dreamers through and through. I need to protect all of them.

But how, Kat Roberts, when you can't protect yourself from Chet???

I circle back to the initial question: what the hell am I going to do?

With a sigh, I rise from the couch to pace the floor.

The fake life I created is solid. All documentation of the car accident and the deaths of my parents in proper order. The details of my youth afterwards match up to public records, too. The guy I dated from the records office helped me to cover all angles since I told him I had a stalker. Again, the power of my red hair, pretty face, and curvy body never fails me.

So even if Chet goes digging to get info on me, he won't stumble upon my family or any connection between them to me. They're safe.

Comforted by that realization, I think about my initial desire for revenge. The dirty deed won't ever go away. The enormity of it proves too extreme. It would be hard to forget it and move on with my life. But I'm torn now.

Aargh!

I rack my brain for how I can hold on to the fledgling relationship I have with Harris.

Is it so bad for me to want it all?

Don't I deserve some happiness at last?

Think, Kat Roberts, dammit!

One thing I know for sure. I'm tired of the lies.

My mobile dings a text message alert. My heart skips a beat. It's Harris' ringtone. I scramble back to the couch and lift my mobile from the cushion and drop onto the seat. My hands shake as I type in the unlock passcode, then tap the message app.

Guess you're busy. I'm at Haley's for a bit. I'll call you later. We're still on for dinner, Kitty Kat. H.

I close my eyes as I throw myself back against the couch. My heart thuds. Tears well up behind my eyelids and trickle into my ears. I swipe at them with one hand while the other clutches the mobile to my chest. A sob bursts past my lips.

Dammit, Kat Roberts!

* * *

As I walk through the lobby of Jackson Town House, my gaze slides to the seating area where I first met Harris.

Lachlan asked me to bring Harris up to his offices since he had a last-minute phone call that delayed him meeting Harris downstairs. The corners of my mouth curl into a woeful smile.

Harris never called me yesterday, and we didn't have dinner.

I left voicemails and sent text messages to him. At first, I assumed he was still with Haley. He loves his niece and nephews and spends as much time as he can with them.

But as time passed with no response, worry haunted the fringes of my mind. It's not at all like Harris to ghost me. He'd sent two text messages about missing me and dinner. So what happened?

Later in the evening, I went to STEELE Aberdeen. The front desk informed me they could not provide details on Mr. Steele and asked me to leave the premises—escorted or on my own. I blinked at their rebuke and backed away to hurry out of the hotel. I felt their eyes like daggers on my back as I rushed to the doors.

Outside, I stood on the sidewalk as tears slipped down my cheeks. I sent a text message to Harris asking him to please tell me what's wrong. No response.

And nothing this morning. Not a word from Harris.

With a sigh, I turn away from the seating area and head for the private lift to the executive floor.

Jackson Town House is the landmark property on Union Street built by the company's founders of the famous Aberdeen granite. It's the second largest granite building in the world.

As I step off the lift, my gaze wanders anew. The executive floor has offices for their legal, finance, operations, and technology departments, along with various conference rooms. Their other divisions have designated floors below.

Employees move about busy with their tasks. The buzz of their conversations and activities mixes with the soft classical music piped in through the surround sound system.

The decor highlights the Old World feel of Jackson Town House. A palette of caramel and Bordeaux hues with gold accents reminiscent of our Scotch and wines blend with the dark mahogany woods and leather furniture, crystal light fixtures, original artwork, and Aubusson rugs. The reception area has a spacious desk. Three attractive receptionists with headsets in their ears and custom-tailored caramel-colored dress suits and skin-tone heels that serve as uniforms sit behind it. I smile and nod at them as they greet me.

Portraits of past generations who founded and helped continue the legacy of Jackson Corporation line the walls as I make my way to Lachlan's suite of offices. The first portrait of the founder and the creator of the finest single malt Scotch Whiskey. He set Jackson Corporation on the path to the most renowned liquor company in the world. After him, successors of each generation have portraits ending with one of Lachlan.

As I approach his private reception area, I notice the desk for Gladys sits empty across from mine. That's odd since she usually arrives before me, and it's Lachlan's first day back from paternity leave. I glance at the closed double doors leading to his office. It's soundproof, so I can't hear if he's inside.

I place my coat in the closet behind my desk and my handbag in the bottom drawer. After I boot up my computer, I rise to get a fresh cup of tea from the break room. Then I stop when the doors to Lachlan's office open. He stands just inside.

"Ms. Roberts, kindly come in," he says.

The formality of his request gives me pause. Then I relax since he probably wants to keep the personal separate from the business.

I smile and walk around my desk.

"Good morning, Mr. Jackson," I say, maintaining the professional demeanor. "Welcome back to the office."

He merely nods as he steps back to let me pass him.

My smile falters when I see Lydie, their General Counsel Ryan Dixon, Lars Gustave Head of Technology, and Sam Fisher Head of Security seated at the elliptical-shaped conference table.

"Have a seat," Lachlan says behind me.

My heart races, and my armpits tingle.

Oh, no!

I do my best to blank my face, but heat rises in my cheeks. With deliberate steps, I walk to the only empty seat at the conference table—between Technology and Security. Lachlan takes his seat across from me between Lydie and Ryan.

I am fucked.

So much for trying to figure out what to do or say.

I swallow and await the first move.

"Ms. Katrina Roberts, this meeting is being videotaped and audio recorded. Do you object?" The General Counsel states.

I shake my head, my throat too dry to form words.

"Ms. Roberts, kindly respond verbally," the General Counsel says.

"Yes, sir. I mean no, sir, I do not object," I answer as I lick my lips nervously.

Come on, Kat Roberts. Get yourself together! I chide.

The General Counsel presses a button, then turns to Lachlan.

He stares at me from across the table. Unable to hold his unblinking assessment of me, my gaze flicks to Lydie. She, too, stares at me in silence. I avert my eyes to the center of the table. Another minute passes before Lachlan speaks.

"Ms. Roberts, we have irrefutable proof you met with Chester Stewart of Stewart Scotch and provided him with confidential information about Jackson Corporation," Lachlan pauses to gauge my reaction.

I school my face in an effort to avoid giving even the slightest sign of guilt. Then I wait for him to continue. Meanwhile, I fear my heart will burst right out of my chest.

"Disclose all you shared with him," Lachlan demands.

I shift in my seat.

What the hell am I going to do?

My gaze lifts to Lachlan. He's immovable. A glance at Lydie reveals the same stoic expression. Last, I peek at the General Counsel. Another controlled stare.

Bloody hell!

Well, as they say, the cat's out of the bag. All of my hard work to seek revenge ends now. The concern for Chet's death threat looms large. If I confess, they will know and destroy Chet and me. Fuck! The revenge seemed good in theory, but now...

"Ms. Roberts, kindly answer the question."

The General Counsel's words snap me back to the office. The magnitude of the situation nearly breaks me.

I nod, then correct myself and respond affirmatively.

Kat Roberts, you have no other choice.

Words spill from my mouth as I recount each bit of intel I stole and gave to Chet. The Head of Technology taps on his tablet. The General Counsel jots down notes on a yellow legal pad. Lachlan and Lydie continue to stare at me.

By the end, I sit back, exhausted. However, relief washes

over me like a soothing balm. I take a deep cleansing breath à la Starr and await my fate.

"Ms. Roberts, that covers the extent of your activities?" The General Counsel asks.

I blink and swallow.

Bloody hell. The cameras and audio equipment I installed in Lachlan's office suit.

I clear my throat and add to my list of confessions.

The Head of Technology nods at Lachlan.

"Our team found the devices. Any others anywhere?" He asks.

I confirm no others.

"One final question. Why?" Lachlan asks.

"*One final question. Why?*"

The question reverberates in my head. It increases in volume until all I hear is a roar.

My eyes close as I try to push the sound from my head. I need to clear my mind. Focus, Kat Roberts!

I swallow and shake my head. One last attempt to shake myself free of the guilt, remorse, pain. My eyes open. They settle on Lachlan with a plea for understanding.

His gaze is cool, assessing.

A deep cleansing breath and my lips part.

"Lachlan, what I'm about to say is extremely personal to the Jackson family. It would be best to limit those who hear to you, Lydie, and the General Counsel, as he cannot disclose your affairs," I respond. And wait.

Lydie glances at Lachlan, who continues to stare at me. His eyes narrow slightly at the mention of affairs. Despite his poker face, I sense his mind working to figure out what the bloody hell I mean by my cryptic response. Lydie returns her equally cool gaze to me. She waits for her brother's lead.

"Give us the room," Lachlan commands. Once only the four of us remain, he continues. "Answer the question, Ms. Roberts."

Okay, Katrina Roberts, *smiogaid suas, nighean!*

"Iain Jackson," I state with my chin held high.

Lachlan cocks his head.

Lydie frowns.

They glance at one another. Silently, the siblings ask if the other knows the name. Lydie arches an elegant eyebrow. Lachlan looks at me. And waits for me to explain myself.

"I assume neither of you knows the name," I say as my eyes flick from one to the other. Then I try a different name—perhaps more familiar. "Angus Jackson?"

Lachlan and Lydie glance at one another again. This time, recognition blooms in their emerald green eyes. As one, they turn their gazes to me.

"Not that we're here to entertain you with our family's history. However, Angus Jackson is our father, Connor's great-great-grandfather, and a former head of Jackson Corporation," Lachlan responds. "Get on with it, Ms. Roberts."

I nod, sensing I better wrap it up, or risk Lachlan losing his patience. But he'll want to hear what I have to say. So I don't let his demeanor deter me. This isn't my fault in any way.

"You do not know Iain Jackson because his father disowned him and decreed his name would never be mentioned by the family or anyone else ever again. Angus obliterated Iain from the Jackson family record," I say. Then pause to allow them to process that bit of information, as the rest is sure to shock them.

"His father is Angus Jackson. His brother is Errol Jackson—the second son—who took his place after Angus banned Iain from the family," I add, for further clarification.

Lachlan focuses on me even more intently. Lydie scans my face.

"Iain—as the heir apparent—was expected to step into his father's shoes as the head of Jackson Corporation and as the Marquess of Huntly. Iain chose to follow his dream of being a painter. In fact, his studio was the watchtower at Jackson Castle. Angus destroyed it when Iain forsook his hereditary place. You restored it beautifully, Mr. Jackson," I say.

Lachlan's mouth opens, then he closes it as his eyes narrow to slits. His brain begins to process my words and my recent actions.

But I'm not finished. Yet.

"Iain left the family seat with his lover and muse without a pence from the Jackson fortune. They moved to Glasgow —the culture capital of Scotland—to pursue his dream. Angus forbid Iain to use the Jackson name," I say.

Further dawning appears on Lachlan's face. He sits forward and appraises mine.

"Iain changed his last name to his mother's maiden name," I say, then pause as my eyes move from Lachlan to Lydie and back.

Lydie starts to speak. But I raise my hand to stop her.

"Iain changed his last name from Jackson to Roberts. Iain Jackson cum Roberts is my great-great-grandfather and your great great granduncle," I finish with my chin raised higher.

Let them challenge me. I'm ready.

And just like that...

"What is the meaning of this, Ms. Roberts?" The General

Counsel bellows as he sits forward in his chair. "What proof do you have of these claims?"

"Where do you get such information?" Lydie asks at the same time.

I ignore them and lock eyes with Lachlan.

Further recognition fills his emerald green eyes so like mine. Where his hair is sable brown—like my siblings and father—my Titian hair comes from Iain's muse and lover. The woman in the portrait that hangs prominently in Ridel Gallery. The portrait of the woman Lachlan mused resembled me. How rightly so.

My entire life, I wondered why my red hair differed from my family. Later, I discovered the reason.

"The unknown painter with initials IJ and IR at Ridel Gallery. You want us to believe the painter is Iain Jackson, then Iain Roberts, the woman his lover, and you their descendant? Thus a distant cousin of ours?" Lachlan asks with an unreadable expression on his face.

Come on, Katrina Roberts. Don't allow his cool demeanor to ruffle you. You have the proof.

I sit straighter in my chair and maintain eye contact as I respond.

"Yes, Lachlan."

Lydie snorts.

The General Counsel blusters more outrage.

Lachlan returns my stare.

"What proof do you have of these claims?" He repeats the Counsel's question.

"Iain's journals, his signet ring, and his sketchbooks," I respond.

"Where did you get Iain's items?" Lachlan asks.

I close my eyes for a moment to collect myself. Emotions wash over me.

"My father—Ramsey Roberts—died of a heart attack. When I went through his personal effects, I found a key to a safe deposit box at the Bank of Scotland in Glasgow. The bank manager told me someone paid for it in perpetuity, and no one visited the box for decades according to their records. I was the first to open it in some time," I answer, then take a breath.

Lachlan waits for me to continue.

"What I found shocked me. The bank manager assured me the contents were untouched," I say.

"Who else is aware of the safe deposit box's contents?" Lachlan asks.

I shake my head, then correct myself and respond verbally when the General Counsel taps the recorder.

"No one," I respond.

Lydie frowns.

"You mean to tell us you did not share the information with your family or with Chet Stewart?" She asks.

I shift my gaze to hers and respond, "Yes. I did not tell anyone."

"Why not?" Lachlan asks.

I sit back and close my eyes. These past few days, my emotions run like a rollercoaster. One minute I'm high on—dare I say—love. The next I plummet with the fear of being found out. A reprieve, now this low of lows.

Bloody hell.

I open my eyes and pin my gaze on Lachlan's face. The pain and anger of being stuck on the poor side while he and his siblings grew up in the lap of luxury, pampered, catered to by the world. The fact darkens the light of happiness I experienced with Harris. A brief pleasurable moment in their world. Betrayal by my great great-great-grandfather for disowning his blood simply because his son wanted to follow his dream.

Dreams...

All the Jackson cum Roberts men had their *dreams*. Never solid and responsible. Quick schemes, flighty. My father and Payton included on the list. The women in their lives left to suffer for falling in love with dreamers.

"When I read Iain's journals... The pain he felt from being tossed aside by his family. No one contacted him. Not one letter he wrote returned with a response. He lost contact with the rest of the Jackson *family*. The only person he had was his muse and lover. But he never recovered from the loss of his loved ones. One of his entries broke my heart..." I trail off as tears fill my eyes.

I swipe at my cheeks and glance out of the window.

"It was this very office in which his father told him to go," I say. Then for Lachlan and Lydie's sakes, I recall from memory Iain's viewpoint of the last time he saw his father and brother.

"Hello, Father, brother."

I nod at each of them when I enter my father's office.

My brother greets me with a sorrowful smile.

"Glad you can join us," my father responds gruffly. His dissatisfied scowl takes me in from head to toe, not at all pleased with my attire of a smock shirt, trousers., and paint-stained brogues. "You could not find an appropriate suit? Never mind. Sit."

Once I'm seated beside my brother, our father settles behind his massive wooden desk. My artist's eye takes in the ornate carvings appreciatively. A master craftsman's finest work.

"Have you come to your senses and will take your proper place as the next to run our family's company?"

My father's question draws me from my musings.

I glance over at him.

We stare at one another for a heartbeat.

I look away first.

He sighs.

"With all due respect, Father. We have had this conversation many times before. I intend to follow my passion. I do not care to follow in your footsteps," I respond as I bring my gaze back to his angry one.

My brother cringes beside me. He knows the roof is about to blow off the building. Again.

Surprisingly, our father remains silent. He studies my face for any sign of a change of heart.

I remain steadfast and hold his gaze.

He rises to tower over me.

"From this day forward, I disown you and no one will speak your name ever again. Your presence erased from this family's history completely. As I speak, your studio is being destroyed and your harlot removed. Leave this city with what you have at this moment. Do not let the sunset find you here. Never return. Contact none of us again. Ever. Do you understand?"

His pronouncement sends a chill through my very soul.

The sense of doom comes to fruition.

I scan his face, hoping to find a crack in his countenance. Nothing. I turn to my brother, and he glances away from my imploring gaze. My eyes shift back to my father. He stands indomitable and raises his hand to point at the door.

"Leave now, or I will have you escorted from the premises," he commands.

I never guessed my father would go so far as to banish me. To obliterate me from our family. Ruin my dreams.

I open my mouth to implore him. But as he rounds the desk with an expression of such detestation, I flinch. Then suck in a breath when he grips the back of my shirt and lifts me from the leather chair.

Forcefully, he pushes me towards the door.

I stumble before I catch myself.

One last glance over my shoulder reveals his imposing figure glaring at me and my brother's stiff back as he stares straight ahead. No remorse. No sympathy.

"*Goodbye, Father, brother.*"

I turn my gaze back to Lachlan, then to Lydie.

Emotions swirl on their faces.

"I hated the Jacksons and sought revenge for Iain's sake. I wanted you to pay for the pain and hardship Angus Jackson caused not only his son, but also his descendants through the years. The last with my father, who died a dreamer at a young age, leaving my mother to take care of their four young children on the salary of a cleaner for rich people. Countless lives impacted because Angus was angry his son didn't want to follow in his footsteps as head of Jackson Corporation. To disown him? Obliterate him from history? A travesty," I say with a shake of my head.

I lean forward and continue.

"I decided to use Chet Stewart to help destroy your family and to get paid millions by him for the intel I provided. I had no remorse whatsoever. Perhaps it's the cold blood in my veins inherited from Angus. But then I got to know you and the current Jacksons. You treated me well as you do your employees. I saw a different side of the Jacksons than what history proved. I grew to admire you—particularly you, Lydie. A strong, intelligent, polished woman who can go toe to toe with men, run a business, and maintain her femininity. In fact, all the Jackson and Steele women I admire. Women I dreamed of being like when I was a child working odd jobs to help my Mum take care of my siblings."

Lydie tilts her head as she watches me.

"Then there's Harris. At first, I saw him as a means to get closer to the Jacksons and to avoid detection. But he took me by surprise, and I fell for him. Now… Who knows? He'll hate me, I'm sure…" I add with a sad shake of my head.

"Towards the end, I realized revenge was wrong. It wouldn't take away the pain. Only cause more of it for others who also don't deserve heartache. I was going to tell Chet no more, especially after he demanded I give him intel about STEELE Technology and Cyber Security. To use Harris or to access files on his computer. I decided no way would I go that far and no more on Jackson Corporation," I say, then swallow as the memory of Chet's threat looms large. Particularly since I confessed it all.

"The other night at the gallery, Chet indicated he would kill me if I told—"

"He what?!"

"That's absurd!"

"No!"

I bite the corner of my lower lip and nod.

Even after all I told them, Lachlan and Lydie have concern for me. Oh, Katrina Roberts, what have you done?

"Kat, we will handle Chet Stewart," Lachlan's statement draws my attention back to him. "However, we need to examine Iain's items, and you and your siblings will need to provide DNA for familial proof along with whatever our General Counsel requests. What you did is inexcusable despite the circumstances. We will decide next steps and let you know the outcome of our decision shortly. A security detail will escort you from the premises and follow you around the clock. So do not try to flee. Do you understand?"

I nod since tears clog my throat.

Lachlan repeats the question for a verbal response.

"Yes, I understand," I answer shakily as the enormity of the situation hits me in the chest.

He rises from his seat and strides toward the doors of his office. Moment later, the Head of Security and two guards dressed in dark suits with ear communication devices escort me from Jackson Town House.

I take a moment to stare up at the beginning and the end of my family's involvement. My dawdling spurs the guards to take me by the elbow and lead me to a Range Rover for the ride to my flat.

Once at home, I give Iain's items and my hairbrush in a plastic baggie to them. They'll collect the rest from my family. The General Counsel forbid me to speak with them. He'll use a ruse to get their DNA samples. One guard leaves to take the package to Lachlan while the other remains outside of my flat's front door. Completely drained, I collapse on my bed and cry.

"**W**hat do you mean Kat's a *Jackson*???" I shout as I jump to my feet.

Lachlan called me to his and Haley's Aberdeen penthouse after he and Lydie met with Kat. Once again, we gather with my siblings along with their spouses, our parents, Lucien, and Laurent on the oversized flat-screen television. Uncle Connor, Aunt Lucie, and Lydie join us in Lachlan's' home office.

He told us about the confession and unexpected revelation Kat made. Then showed Iain Jackson's journals, signet ring, and sketchbooks to us. I stare at them on the coffee table in utter disbelief.

"Well, we *cannot* accept what Kat said without the DNA proof. I have no recollection of an Iain Jackson. Angus and Errol, yes. We were always told the watchtower crumbled from lack of upkeep and the harsh elements. We need more than what the duplicitous lass says since she lied to us all this time," Uncle Connor states adamantly.

"Exactly. She even lied about her parents' death in a car

accident caused by a drunk driver, just like mine. I bet she only said that to gain sympathy from me. Terrible," Lola says sadly.

Baz puts his arm around her to pull her close to his side. She leans her forehead against his shoulder, but not before I catch a glimpse of tears in her hazel eyes.

I clench my fists.

Dammit!

Kat hurt not only me but also my family. Lola doesn't deserve to relive the anguish of her parents' death at a young age. This is beyond fucked up.

"What have you decided to do about Kat?" Baz asks. "And it's a damn good thing she didn't give that fucker Stewart any information on STEELE, or I'd have her ass. What's worse, she upset my wife with her bullshit, and she used my brother for her own gain. Not cool, Lach. At. All."

Lachlan shakes his head in disgust.

"Yeah, Kat fucked up big time. Aside from an initial launch plan and some other fixable information, she gave Stewart fake intel, thanks to Lydie. The Head of Technology is already working with Haley's team to shore up our cyber security," Lachlan responds.

"This is all my fault for thinking with the wrong head," I grumble as I pace the floor. You big dummy.

My mind works overtime to make sense of what we learned and line it up with Kat's behavior towards me. No wonder we connected so quickly. She saw me as a dolt she could charm with her Siren's call to gain access to our family and our tryst as a smokescreen for her illicit activities.

I thought she was a Bond Girl. Turns out she's 007 himself with her expert subterfuge…

On top of it all, she's a Jackson??? A long-lost, disowned,

and forgotten relative??? Who sought revenge??? For real? Give me a break.

I cannot believe I fell for the okey-doke…

The last forty-eight hours have been torture. I ignored Kat's calls and text messages. Even when she progressed to desperate pleas. The front desk staff at STEELE Aberdeen followed my directive and turned her away from the property. I awoke from a wet dream with jizz all over my abs and my pecs. What am I? A horny teenager? It's been surreal to say the least.

And Kat's a *Jackson*!

That's why she lingered in front of the watchtower at Jackson Castle when we rode past it. She knew it was Iain's studio. Even then, she held her feelings in check with a blank expression on her face. I thought it odd when I took her on a tour of the Castle, and she had so many questions. She claimed it was the history buff in her, and her love for the great houses and castles of Scotland.

I scrub my hand over my face and stop pacing.

Un-fucking-believable.

"Harris, sit. You're making me dizzy," Haley says as she pats the spot on the sofa next to her. When I throw myself down, she continues. "No need to beat yourself up about it. Kat is the one who's in the wrong. Hell, she had us all fooled. But being a Jackson is definitely wild."

"I agree with Haley, Harris. You did nothing wrong. I'm truly disappointed because Kat fits in so well with you and the rest of the family," our mother says. She shakes her head and smiles at me with motherly affection.

"As they say, Karma is not kind to those who do wrong," Starr—forever the yogi—adds. "Wish her the best and let the Universe handle her fate."

Malcolm snorts.

"My Angel, then call me Mr. Universe because *I* will handle Katrina *Roberts*," he retorts. "Lachlan, just say the word, bro."

Lachlan nods at *The Enforcer*.

"Thanks, bro. We expect to have the DNA samples by the end of day today and results rushed. With that in hand, we'll know the veracity of her claim to the Jackson name—"

"Not that she or her family will get a bloody thing from us!" Uncle Connor interjects vehemently, then continues as his Scottish accent thickens with his anger. "Had she come forward with her findings like a civilized lass, we could have had a proper discussion. Blood is blood. I may not agree with banishing a child for their decision to not carry out their familial duty—or attempt, Lachlan. But those were different times."

Lachlan's face heats at the mention of his initial reluctance to take on the mantle of CEO and Chairman of the Board at Jackson Corporation upon Uncle Connor's retirement. It wasn't until he and Haley began to date did Lachlan use his title Earl of Aboyne. Undoubtedly, he can relate to Iain's desire to follow his passion. Albeit, Lachlan had a different reason.

"I agree with you Da. And as you say, *blood is blood*. So I'm less inclined to press charges—"

"What?!"

"Are you kidding me right now?!"

"Say what?!"

The room erupts into an uproar as everyone speaks at once. Those on the television screen voice their opinions just as vociferously as those in person. I too can't believe Lachlan's proclamation. Then I think of Kat in jail. She'd never survive it. I shudder at the thought of her in a cell.

Haley whistles, and silence descends.

"I'd like to hear Lachlan's reason," she says once she has everyone's attention.

We turn to him and wait.

He kisses the side of her head and murmurs in her ear. She grins.

Lachlan faces us and goes on.

"The initial assessment of the information she stole shows no major impact on Jackson Corporation. The surveillance videos and audio prove I'm a hard-ass worker" —we chuckle along with him—"I empathize with her and her line of descendants' plight."

Lachlan pauses to glance at each of us before he continues, "I propose Kat leaves Scotland in one week and she never returns without our advance knowledge. Her family —if truly uninvolved—can remain. She can keep the money Stewart paid her since she used it to support her family. However, we will monitor her activities. Should she hack anyone else, we will press charges. Thoughts?"

Again, everyone speaks at once. But Lachlan calls for Leonie first.

"Kat's comments about the *posh life* and how impressed she was by the things we do make sense now," she says. The girls nod and murmur their agreement. "I noticed she became less guarded the more time she spent with us. She was wistful when we last spoke about the upcoming holidays in Capri and Verbier during Labor Day. Kat listened raptly. Perhaps she saw her error but didn't know what to do to fix the situation. And for Chet to threaten to kill Kat so publicly, well... *Mon Dieu!*"

Aunt Lucie speaks next and agrees with Leonie's assessment. But adds she doesn't trust Kat, and she would have to prove herself before she could gain it back. Our mother expresses a similar sentiment.

Lachlan hears everyone out, then turns to me.

"Your thoughts, Harris?" He asks.

I nod and respond.

"On a personal level, Kat fooled me once and will not have the opportunity to do it again. From a business perspective, I take responsibility for not paying attention to Jackson Corporation's tech activity. So, as much as I want to blame Kat, I have to share some with her. Fortunately, she didn't access pertinent information. To press charges makes it public, and you don't want Jackson Corporation to appear vulnerable. That would give hackers ideas. At the same time, it reflects poorly on STEELE Technology and Cyber Security's ability to protect our clients. So, from a selfish standpoint, you should not press charges. Banish her. I did already."

Haley rubs my arm. Our mother and Aunt Lucie tsk in sympathy.

I shrug and put a cocky smile on my face.

"So don't blame me if I don't get married any time soon, Mom. It's playadom for this old chap," I declare. "I hear LEVELS London Calling."

KAT

"Oh, Kat, honey! Why did we have to come here? Is this where you work? Why did those men bring us here?"

My Mum whispers rapid-fire questions to me as she sits on the couch in Lachlan's private reception area. Her eyes scan the room as she twists her fingers in her lap.

Charlotte leans across me to whisper her concerns, too.

Michael sits in a chair. His eyes bright with awe as he scans the room, but for a different reason. He loves architecture and design. Jackson Town House must strike him as a masterpiece inside and out.

Payton scowls at me from the other chair. As usual, he's put out. Not that he's missing work or anything important. Once again, he's between jobs.

I haven't been able to speak with them since Lachlan forbid any contact. As much trouble as I'm in, I didn't want to provoke him by disobeying. I did not know they would be here today.

Lachlan had the security guards escort me to his offices

an hour ago. He told me his decision to ban me from Scotland without returning unless with his advance knowledge. Thankfully, my family can stay. Relief washed over me twice. When he said he wouldn't press charges, and when he told me I could keep the money from Chet. The caveat of no more hack jobs or face prosecution from Jackson Corporation and whomever I was to infiltrate.

I thanked him and asked about Chet. Lachlan told me not to concern myself with him. So I relaxed. But I'll make sure Chet can't find me wherever I go. I have one week to figure out just where that will be…

"Listen, I don't have time to sit in this hoity-toity office all day. I demand to know what's going on."

Payton's irate voice pulls me from my musings. He stands before Gladys as she sits at her desk.

One of the security guards steps to him, and Payton glares back. As he opens his mouth to speak, the double doors to Lachlan's inner office open. His eyes flick amongst us before they settle on Payton. A nod and the security guard moves away from Payton to resume his stance by the wall beside the other guard.

"Payton, kindly come in," Lachlan says, then turns to us sitting on the sofa and chair. He gestures towards the office. "Mrs. Roberts, Kat, Michael, and Charlotte."

We follow Payton—who grumbles under his breath into the office. The elliptical conference table extends to accommodate my family, Lachlan, Lydie, the General Counsel, and me. We take our seats.

"Before we begin, this meeting is being videotaped and audio recorded. Do you object?" The General Counsel states.

My Mum and siblings glance at me, and I nod. We give our consent.

"Mrs. Roberts, allow me to introduce ourselves. I am Lachlan Jackson, CEO and Chairman of the Board of Jackson Corporation and the Earl of Aboyne. This is my sister Lady Lydie Jackson, COO and First Vice President of the Board. And Jackson Corporation General Counsel Ryan Dixon," Lachlan states.

My Mum glances at me nervously. I smile to reassure her, and she turns to each of them and murmurs a greeting.

"My, my, my, what impressive titles you have. Congratulations. Now, what is the purpose of this meeting?" Payton cuts in as he glares at Lachlan.

Lachlan flicks his gaze at my obnoxious brother and assesses him coolly. Unruffled, Lachlan takes a moment before he continues. Payton squirms under the intense stare. Satisfied, Lachlan shifts his gaze back to my Mum.

"M—My Lord, I'm so sorry. Please excuse my son's behavior—"

Lachlan shakes his head.

"Mrs. Roberts, no need to apologize. He's a grown man who's free to speak his mind and face whatever consequences come of his actions," Lachlan says.

Payton snorts.

I close my eyes and sigh. Bloody hell. For once, can he just not embarrass us?

When I reopen them, Lydie stares at me. What seems to be a sympathetic look appears briefly in her emerald green eyes. Then her face blanks again, and she glances away. She studies my Mum and siblings while Lachlan speaks.

"We brought you to Jackson Town House to inform you of news we received recently. We were aware Angus Jackson —our paternal great-great-great-grandfather and the former Marquess of Huntly—had one son named Errol. What we learned is Angus had a first-born son named Iain.

Angus disowned Iain since he declined to follow in his father's footsteps. Iain chose his art—painting. Errol became the heir. Our line branches from Errol.

"Iain changed his surname from Jackson to Roberts and moved from Aberdeenshire to Glasgow with his muse and lover. Your husband—Ramsay Roberts—is his descendant, as are your offspring. The DNA results confirm the lineage. Were you aware of this information?"

My Mum swallows and shakes her head.

"Mrs. Roberts, kindly respond verbally," Ryan says.

"S—Sorry. No, I was not aware," she responds as her eyes flick from Lachlan to me.

"You mean to tell me we're actually Jacksons, as in the name of this building and company? We should be filthy rich with fancy titles like you lot? What do you do here, anyway?" Payton leans forward and peppers Lachlan with questions.

Please let the floor open, and I fall through the hole.

Better yet, shut Payton up.

My silent prayers go unanswered as he continues to drill Lachlan. The dollar signs practically bulge from my brother's greedy eyes.

I offer a prayer of thanks I—not Payton—found Iain's items. Payton would have sold everything to the local pawnshop for a few pounds. Fortunately, the paintings are safe at Ridel Gallery. Although I wish we could keep Iain's works in our family.

The General Counsel answers Payton's questions succinctly, and Lachlan continues.

"We cannot make up for the past. However, we can offer all of you the opportunity to have stability and growth in your lives. If you so choose to do so," Lachlan says and looks at Payton for the last bit. With only knowing my brother for a few minutes, Lachlan can already tell Payton is shiftless. How bloody embarrassing.

Charlotte clears her throat, and Lachlan moves his gaze to her.

"So we're cousins?" She asks, then continues when Lachlan confirms. "Do we change our names back to Jackson, or do we remain Roberts?"

"Or do we have a choice?" Michael asks.

"What's the offer?" Payton cuts in. "And it better be worth it."

Lydie snorts and pins Payton with a withering glare.

"Your track record proves you fail to maintain any job, and you limited your level of education by dropping out in your sixth year. And not to help your family. No. Then and now, you spend more time in the pub around the corner from your mother's flat than you do helping to support her. So whatever the *offer*, it corresponds to what you deserve," Lydie scoffs as her eyes flash green fire.

Payton shrivels beneath her scathing remarks. *The Shark* took the bite out of him. Finally.

"The eldest Jackson alive—our father Connor Jackson, Marquess of Huntly—acknowledges you as Jacksons, despite his great-great-grandfather's disownment of Iain. Therefore, the choice is yours for your last name," Lachlan responds to Charlotte and to Michael, while ignoring Payton.

"Mrs. Roberts, STEELE Glasgow has an opening for a housekeeping supervisor. With your years of experience, you qualify for the position. The salary is over three times your current pay plus superb benefits with paid time off. If that interests you, the hiring manager will meet with you this week. My personal assistant, Gladys, will schedule the appointment," Lachlan says.

My Mum gasps as she brings her calloused fingertips to her mouth that hangs open in shock. The skin on her hands leathery and wrinkled from the harsh cleaning solutions she uses every single day despite the lotions I give to her. Wide eyes flick to me, then to Lachlan.

A slight smile plays at his lips. He nods in encouragement.

"Why, thank you Mr. Jack—"

"Lachlan," he interjects.

My Mum nods and clears her throat before she accepts the offer.

"Charlotte, since your university covers your fees, we will pay for your expenses until you graduate. You may continue to work. But I advise you to focus on your studies to maintain your impressive grade point average. After this meeting, you will sit with Gladys to review your expenses and to determine a monthly allowance," Lachlan says.

Charlotte gasps.

He continues, "If you wish to work within a Jackson Corporation or a STEELE International, Inc. division after you graduate, let us know. We will arrange a meeting between you and the appropriate parties to determine the best fit. Take time to consider your goals and to research both companies."

"Thank you so very much!" Charlotte exclaims. Her emerald green eyes shine with unshed tears of gratitude.

Mine fill it too, and I swipe at the corners.

"Michael, you've helped your Mum and sister through your jobs and time. But you should hone your innate talent in architectural renderings and your passion for the field through coursework. The University of Strathclyde in Glasgow ranks amongst the highest in the UK for the study of architecture. If you wish to attend, we will arrange for a tutor who will prepare you for the application process. Should you gain acceptance—which we believe will happen—we will pay for your studies and expenses. STEELE International has divisions that require designs for residential and commercial projects. They handle Jackson Corporation's projects. Internships and a permanent position could be available to you should you wish to pursue a career at STEELE. Again, take time to decide, then get in touch with Gladys," Lachlan says.

"No need for time, Lachlan. I thank you and accept your offer!" Michael says as he stands and extends his hand across the table. His emerald green eyes spark with joy. At last, he'll have the opportunity to focus on his love of buildings without hinderance.

My heart clenches at my younger brother's happiness. Like me, Michael spends most of his life helping our mother and Charlotte. Never a complaint, only a smile. As he does now with a grin bigger than the Cheshire Cat's smile.

Lachlan rises and takes Michael's hand in a firm grip as he nods at him.

"Very well. After Charlotte meets with Gladys, you may speak with her," Lachlan responds with a smile.

They sit. The room grows silent. Our eyes turn toward Payton, who leans forward. Expectation makes his emerald green eyes glow.

Instead of addressing Payton, Lachlan brings his gaze to my Mum.

"Mrs. Roberts—"

"Allison, please," she cuts in with a more confident smile.

Lachlan returns her smile and nods.

"Allison, since Charlotte lives on campus and Michael will soon, we arranged for you to choose from three one-bedroom flats in Glasgow. We will purchase one in your name and cover your moving expenses and the cost of furnishings," he says.

My Mum shakes her head.

"Lachlan, you've offered so much already. No need for you to burden yourself any further," she says. Pride straightens her spine.

Then it's his turn to shake his head.

"No burden whatsoever. You should live in comfort," he insists.

My Mum glances at me, and I smile in encouragement. She turns back to Lachlan and thanks him.

"Last, we purchased Iain's paintings—those displayed at Ridel Gallery and the others they found. We will investigate any further works of his and acquire them should they exist. All reside in the Jackson family archives along with his journals, signet ring, and sketchbooks," Lachlan states.

Surprised by his decision, I jerk in my chair. My eyes widen as I stare at him in disbelief.

How could he just take everything? They're *our* family's heirlooms!

Lachlan cocks an eyebrow.

I meet his stare, then lower my eyes in defeat. Can I really blame him? No.

"Well then. Any questions?" Lachlan asks.

"Yeah! What's in it for me? What's my offer, *Lachlan*?" Payton demands. Fire replaces the glow of expectation in his eyes as they flash.

Lachlan hardens his expression.

"Nothing," he responds. "Should you take from your mother or move in with her, you will answer to me. The time is now for you to assume responsibility for yourself."

Lachlan passes his business card to my Mum, Charlotte, and to Michael.

"You may reach me via the number and email here and my mobile number on the reverse side," he says. "Any questions?"

His gaze flicks from one to the other as he repeats his question and ignores Payton.

"Where the bloody hell am I to live?" He asks.

"Your current flat," Lachlan responds. Then he stands. "Gladys will meet with you now."

Everyone except for Payton rises and thanks Lachlan and Lydie.

"Fuck you, Lachlan Jackson! Bloody wanker!" Payton shouts. "You won't get away with this—"

The two security guards enter the office and take Payton by the arms. They drag him from the room as he continues to hurl insults.

Again, my face reddens as I plead for the floor to engulf me.

"Why, hello there, Harris Steele. It's been a while, darling. Care to play?"

A statuesque blonde with a killer, lithe figure stands before me. Her cerulean blue eyes skim over my body, from my face to my crotch and back. A heavenly gleam fills her orbs. She's more than satisfied with my package. I must say even flaccid, it's magnificent. A sight to behold.

I smirk.

She takes my look as permission to engage. The pointy tip of her red-polished fingernail trails over my pec down the ridges of my eight-pack abs to rim my navel before continuing her pursuit of perfection.

My cock thumps at her erotic touch.

But my mind leaps back to the conversation with Haley yesterday afternoon.

"Harris, I know guys process breakups differently from women. We sit around with the shades drawn and eat pints of butter pecan ice cream as we vent about the pain to our girl-friends. For days. Hell, even for months. No interest in another

relationship for a while. But guys? You jump right back into the dating or fucking scene within a blink of the eye. Whiplash," my twin tells me as we talk on the phone.

She pauses when I grumble but goes on. Unstoppable when she gets on her soapbox...

"Don't try to deny it. I'm quite confident you've spent nights at LEVELS London. And no, I did not hack into their systems to check your attendance. I. Know. You. Harris Steele. Don't go overboard. You fell hard for she who shall not be named in a short period. Give yourself some time to recover. And I don't mean by jumping into bed with any of the more than willing members of LEVELS. Especially those who want to get their claws into the last bachelor of The STEELE Quaternity.

I'm telling you this because I love you and your pain is my pain. Also cut the crap about not marrying. You almost gave Mom a coronary. Okay?"

I hate to admit it. But Haley called it. Naturally.

Still, I'd rather partake of the fruit I gave up for months in favor of a tantalizing Siren. Besides, what I felt for Kat *Jackson* wasn't love.

On to the next one and all that.

I slip my hand around the blonde's slim hip and cup her firm ass, then give it a squeeze.

For a brief second, my mind registers her hip is more narrow and ass less round than the Siren's ample curves.

Ah well.

"Play or fuck?" I respond in a deep baritone as I pin the sexy blonde with my most panty-melting smile.

Her pupils dilate to dark pools, leaving only the edges tinged blue. The tip of her tongue darts out to moisten her glossy lips.

"Is your pussy as wet as your mouth?" I ask with another squeeze.

The sexy blonde nods and her silky mane bobs.

I cock an eyebrow.

"Words. I will have your words," I correct her.

"Whatever you wish, Sir," she responds breathily.

I shake my head.

"Not Sir. Harris will do," I say as I rise from the barstool. With a hand on her lower back, I lead her past other members as we cross the floor of LEVELS London Peepshow.

One of the global, high-end BDSM/dance clubs created by Malcolm and Lucien. Built over several levels for dining, dancing, and to satisfy sexual desires open to members and their guests. Occasionally, non-members frequent the restaurant and party at the dance clubs. Some hoping to obtain an exclusive membership. It's a rigorous process. But oh so worth it.

I direct the blonde to a hallway with rooms on either side where behind floor-to-ceiling windows members engage in acts of role playing, Shibari, threesomes, and more. Whatever sexy fantasy one can imagine comes to life within the four walls of each room. Other members— mainly the voyeurs or those seeking foreplay inspiration— gather to watch, or peep.

I open the door to an empty room. The blonde sashays in ahead of me. With a smirk, I close the door.

No butter pecan ice cream for me.

I intend to fuck the pain away.

* * *

"HEY, cuz. When do you return to New York City? Haley went back to work, so no need for you to stay in London.

I'm planning a Guys' Getaway to Puerto Rico in a couple of weeks. You game or what?"

I grin at the thought of hanging out with Laurent. It's been a while since he's busy with Yessenia, and I was with the Siren. A trip to Puerto Rico with my boys sounds like just what I need to keep that troublesome redhead out of *my* head.

"Oh, I am so game, cuz. Count me in," I respond.

"Finally, you'll get your head back on straight and let that girl go already," Laurent adds. "I don't give a damn she's my newfound cousin…"

He grumbles some more about the Siren. I don't blame him. She got to all of us.

When he stops, I cut in and tell him to send the details over. After we hang up. I get back to work at my office at STEELE London.

Haley returned full time. But she splits her days between here and Aberdeen. So it's true I do not need to remain in the UK. It's been almost a week. Time to get da steppin', as Martin says.

"Hey, Hal. Before I ask my pilot to set the flight plan for my return to the City, I want to check in with you. Do you still need me here or no?" I ask when my twin answers her mobile.

"Hey! No, I'm all good. Tomorrow I fly in for the weekly status meetings with my team. You don't need to attend. Lachlan mentioned Laurent's Guys' Getaway. Are you going? Please say yes, Harris!" She responds.

I can picture her holding her breath as she waits for my answer. She hasn't been on me about my post-relationship activities since our conversation earlier this week. But I know she still thinks about it. The mother in her makes

Haley worry even more about me, aside from our twin connection.

I'll ease her stress. With a grin, I confirm I'm going to Puerto Rico and look forward to hanging with my boys. Her relief is palpable as she exhales and claps her hands.

Now I can see her shimmying in delight. Silly girl.

"Excellent! Well, safe travels. Call me when you land," Haley adds before we end our call.

I ask my personal assistant to arrange for a maid to pack my things at STEELE Mayfair and contact my pilot for the flight plan, then get back to work.

As long as I remain busy, my mind doesn't have a chance to fall back on the loss of that redhead. At least that's what I keep telling myself.

Good luck with that, Harris…

All the fucking in the world just doesn't compare to the lovemaking my Kitty Kat and I shared.

KAT

"Thank you for your more than generous gift, Kat! I mean, your volunteerism at Aberdeen Children's Center has been marvelous, and we're grateful. But your donation… Well, it's so unexpected…"

I smile at the director as she gushes on about the money I gave to the center.

It's my parting gift before I leave Aberdeen. I made it in the Jackson name with Lachlan's approval. Using the money I received from Chet Stewart pleased Lachlan. And it just felt right to me. I'd rather have a clean slate to start my new life.

My new life as Katrina Jackson.

I chose to take the name not only for the fact it is our true name. But because Katrina Roberts is finished. No more scheming. No more lies. Plus, Chet knows me by my former name, and I'd rather he not pursue me once Lachlan gets at him.

I shake my head to clear the thoughts so I can focus on the director. I tell her I'll spend another day with the kids to have a chance to say goodbye to them, the staff, and to the other volunteers. The rest of the day goes well. The lads and lasses give me big hugs, and the staff surprises me with a cake. I leave the center to a round of applause and best wishes.

Afterwards, I take the bus to Glasgow.

As I glance out the window, the realization Iain left Aberdeen for Glasgow at the direction of another Jackson as I do now saddens me. However, I deserve it. Iain wanted to follow his passion, and I sought revenge. One for a good reason. The other bad. History repeats itself in strange ways.

I awake to the bus driver shaking my shoulder. The past week took its toll on me. Worry led to no sleep. The rhythmic motions of the bus lulled me to a dreamless slumber until we arrived in Glasgow. I thank the driver and take a taxi to my Mum's new flat.

True to his word, Lachlan arranged for her to select one in a posh neighborhood and for her new job at STEELE Glasgow. The same for Charlotte and Michael. We're spending the rest of the weekend together before I fly to London.

I swallow back tears and watch the streets of my youth pass beyond the window of the taxi. Memories flood my brain. Even thoughts of my father fill my mind. I sigh and lean back in the seat. Tears spill from beneath my closed eyelids.

New beginnings, Katrina Jackson. Embrace the new and let go of the past.

"GOOD EVENING, MISS."

"Good evening, ma'am. How may I help you?"

The first smile since I left the center spreads across my face as the doorman then the concierge for my Mum's new flat greets me. The photos she sent only hint at the fabulous building. Crystal chandeliers hang from the triple-height coffered ceiling with matching wall sconces. My shoes sink into the plush wool rugs scattered over the travertine floors as I walk to the desk. Seating areas cluster about the lobby. A family of four sit by the window overlooking the court-yard garden.

"Good evening, I'm here to visit Mrs. Roberts, her daughter Katrina," I respond to the concierge.

My Mum kept the last name since my father isn't alive to change his or not. She wants to maintain their connection in any way she can.

The concierge rings the flat and announces me. He directs me to the private lift, and I take it to the penthouse.

"Kat, honey! You made it!" My Mum greets me when I step into the foyer. She gives me a hug and tugs my hand to lead me past the double doors into the flat.

My mouth drops open at the impressive view before me. Glasgow lit up in the night glows beyond the windows. The unobstructed panorama of the city captivates me.

"Incredible, isn't it?" My Mum asks with a broad smile. It lights up her face as much as the stars in the inky blue sky. It's the happiest she's looked since before my father passed. And I'm happy for her.

"Absolutely," I breathe, then put my arms around her.

We stand for a moment, lost in our thoughts as we stare out the wall of windows.

"There you are, Kat!"

I glance over my shoulder to find Michael with Char-lotte beside him walk into the massive living room. Char-lotte dances over and bumps her hip against mine.

"Awesome, huh?" She says with a giggle.

"I say more than awesome! This is the high life!" I exclaim as I loop my arm around her waist.

Michael drapes his arms around us and rests his head on my shoulder.

"What a world of difference from our other flat," he says with a grin. Then he whispers in my ear so our Mum can't hear. "Too bad for Payton. He tried to sneak in. But Mum told him no."

"About time," Charlotte huffs.

I nod in agreement while our Mum tells me she wants to give me the grand tour.

The one bedroom, two bath flat spans half the top floor split with another penthouse accessible from a separate private lift. A terrace off the flat's front rooms extends the living space to the outdoors with chaise lounges, tables, and shrubbery. Each room decorated tastefully in classic furnishings and warm colors. The kitchen is a chef's dream. We settle in the room next to it by a roaring fire.

"So, where did you decide to go, Kat?" Michael asks. "I really wish you would stay here in Glasgow with us."

I didn't tell my family the reason for my abrupt departure, only about my desire to travel for a while. Which I will for a couple of months before I move to New York City. The director of Aberdeen Children's Center told me the nonprofit her friend works for has a position available in their offices on Fifth Avenue. With her referral, the hiring manager scheduled an interview in a few weeks. With hope, I'll get the job. If not, another opportunity will come up. New York has thousands of companies.

Most of all, it has Harris. And the chance to win his heart again.

My heart flutters at the thought. I smile at Michael and tell him it's time for each of us to follow our dreams.

* * *

How the scene flips.

I first laid eyes on Harris in the lobby of Jackson Town House as he sat on a leather chair waiting for Lachlan. The sight of Harris took my breath away. But I played it cool and professional. He was my boss' brother-in-law. Then he became my smoke screen and later my unpredicted lover.

Now, I glance around the well-appointed lobby of STEELE London as I sit on a tufted leather couch in one of the seating areas. Workers and visitors buzz about chatting amongst themselves or focused on their mobiles as they stride to and from the banks of elevators. It's just after one in the afternoon.

I expect the meeting Harris had ended, and I can catch him before he leaves for the airport. One tiny deception—and the last, I swear—garnered the information for me. There's no way I can leave the UK without apologizing to him in person. To plead for his forgiveness. And perhaps his love again?

Before I left Glasgow, I wrote letters to each of his family members—Steele and Jackson. I opened my heart to them in hopes they would understand and forgive me for my erroneous ways. Their easy acceptance of me will forever remain in my heart. I never knew people like them would care for someone like me. Carriers delivered each letter to arrive at the same time so no one would get theirs before another family member.

I tried to write the one for Harris again and again. But failed to express the depth of my feelings for him and my sorrow for hurting him so much. Words are simply not enough.

I rub my chest to ease the ache as I blink back unbidden tears.

The sound of a woman's melodious giggle followed by a man's robust laugh draws me from my musings. A glance to my left reveals a beautiful woman dressed in a navy and cream-colored Chanel suit with matching handbag and crocodile pumps. Her ruby red lips curl in a flirtatious smile as she stares up at the handsome man beside her. Her eyes dance as he grins.

Harris!

My stomach and heart clench at the same time. A gasp escapes my mouth. The hand rubbing my chest fists against my sternum.

Frozen in place, I watch as the happy couple strolls from the elevators towards the doors. Her laughter sounds brittle to my ears. Despair fills me.

Harris moved on already.

I slump back on the couch and close my eyes to erase the hurtful image of the pair. Yet it remains etched on my corneas. Burned into my brain.

Then I shake my head and admonish myself. *Smiogaid suas, nighean!*

Get it together, Katrina Jackson! Enough with the self-pity. You brought this on yourself, you liar!

A deep breath propels me from the couch. I hurry after Harris and the woman. As they walk to the door, I grasp Harris' arm.

He glances at the hand, surprised by the forcefulness of the out-of-the-blue gesture. When his eyes lift to mine, they widen, and his firm jaw falls slack.

My body comes to life in the presence of my former

lover. I fight the urge to stroke his clean-shaven cheek and kiss his full lips. My nipples pebble against the silk blouse as my pussy moistens the gusset of the lace thong. I bite back a moan—whether sadness or desire, I'm unsure.

An indeterminable flare sparks in his dove gray eyes. His lips form a perfect O. So kissable, I lift to my toes. His nostrils flare.

"Harris?"

The moment's bubble bursts at the sound of the woman's voice.

Harris pulls away as a scowl mars his handsome face. His lips pull into a sneer. Anger emanates from his body and hits me in the heart.

But I persist.

"Oh, Harris! I'm so glad I caught you. Please—"

My words end abruptly when he grabs my elbow and propels me to a corner away from the woman and the flow of others as they walk through the doors.

"You cannot be serious, Katrina *Jackson*! Why did you come here?" Harris snarls as he glares down his nose at me. When I open my mouth to respond, he raises his hand and continues. "You fucking *used* me. I will not believe a damn thing you say to me. Not. A. Damn. Word. In case it's not obvious to you, let me be very clear. That little farce of you and me? Done. Do not contact me or come near me and my family ever again. Count yourself lucky for Lachlan's leniency. I would have canceled your ass."

Without a backward glance, he pivots and stalks away from me. His long, muscular legs make quick work of the distance between me and the woman who waits for him. She flicks her curious gaze from me to Harris as he nears her. Her hand on his chest, then his hand on her waist breaks me.

I watch with tears streaming down my crimson cheeks as he guides her out the door to his Rolls Royce sedan at the curb. His driver opens the rear door for them.

The woman's glance of pity before she slips onto the seat followed by Harris' back as he joins her pierces my heart. It cleaves in two.

I cover my mouth and sob uncontrollably.

HARRIS

"*A*ll right, boys, get ready for loads of fun in the sun. No sob stories. No drama. No business. It's time to let loose and kick it up Laurent style!"

He emphasizes his declaration by lighting a Jackson Cigar and blowing smoke up towards the endless sky full of twinkling stars and a full moon.

It's the first night of our Guys' Getaway. Laurent selected to host the four-day gathering at STEELE Dorado —a luxurious enclave for royalty, international jet setters, and celebrities on Puerto Rico's northern coast. Along with our brothers, cousins Borya Alexeyev and Anton Alexeyev, and Patrick Rockett, we took over the largest private villa with twelve bedrooms and fifteen bathrooms on the beach-front property.

To start the fun with a bang, we came to Jackson Hole— the members-only, high-end hot spot for the über-wealthy in select STEELE resorts around the globe. The thumping bass of the music from the outdoor dance club vibrates in the tropical air around us. Bodies grind to the beat while

Jackson Hole dancers gyrate on elevated Lucite platforms lit from within. The atmosphere proves as hedonistic as any LEVELS club. Sex on the beach, for real.

And I'm all for it.

"Hear, hear!" I respond as I strike a match and lift it to my cigar. The strength and flavor—spicy, woody, and earthy tones—of the tobacco fills me. A hint of the rich taste of Jackson Reserve Scotch I drink adds to the pleasure. A decadent sigh escapes my parted lips as the smoke curls around my face.

No sob stories. No drama. No business.

No thoughts of that redheaded Siren.

Exactly.

"Perfect time for a quick break with the guys before the rush of the holidays starts," Roger says.

"Yeah, Dad!" Lucien teases. "Gotta play Santa for the little lads and lasses. No more ho, ho, hoes for you!"

"Don't hate on the greatness of family life, Lucien. You're not immune, you know, brother," Malcolm says with a knowing smile.

Lucien narrows his eyes and hides a smirk with a sip of Scotch from his snifter.

Obviously, something is up in his love life. But... drama-free rule.

Some guys stay in our VIP area for a rum tasting—a more mellow way to enjoy the evening. Others head for the dance floor or bar. Before I make my move, I take another sip of Scotch as I survey the rest of the club.

Borya sandwiched between two brunette beauties—twins?—on the dance floor. The former MMA world champion turned personal trainer for Baz and running buddy of Malcolm impresses the women with his massive frame. He's a killer in the cage and on the floor. His partners toss their hair and wiggle their round asses in carnal delight.

The DJ plays a good mix, perfect to entice sweet little things to let loose. I could go for a little bump and grind with one—or maybe three of them as per the norm. A snicker emerges from my mouth as I swirl the Jackson Reserve Scotch over my palate. The flavor bursts across my tastebuds then warms my chest and belly, much like the delectable essence of an aroused woman.

Well...

One woman in particular...

"Fuck!" I mutter under my breath as an unbidden image of the Siren writhing from the ministrations of my mouth, tongue, and teeth on her pussy pops into my mind. Her cries of carnal bliss fill my ears as much as her sweet nectar coats my throat. Round ass cheeks clench in my hands as she cums undone for me again and again. And again. "Fuck me..."

I shift in my seat as my cock twitches uncomfortably in the confines of my leather pants. It threatens to jab a hole straight through the crotch.

Damn that Siren!

Three weeks passed, and I still can't get her—or fuck her —out of my head. No matter how hard or how much I try. I groan and shake my head to clear it.

Then I think of Haley's description of how women and men process a breakup.

I haven't banged loads of women—a few here and there. And certainly, much less than during my original playboy days. Despite my initial reaction to make up for lost time, not much has happened. My cock misses a certain redheaded Siren. Even if my bigger head wants to ignore the ache in my heart.

Didn't Baz say I'd fall hard?

Yeah… Well…

I puff on my cigar and close my eyes as the smoke floats from my mouth. Unknowingly, my hand rubs soothing circles on my chest.

"What's eating you, mate?"

As though a kid caught with their hand in the cookie jar —pun intended—I snatch mine from my chest and clench a frustrated fist. My eyes pop open to find Patrick's questioning green-eyed gaze on me.

Another Scotsman whose family's multibillion-dollar Rockett Construction Company he leads as CEO was for decades STEELE International, Inc.'s top competitor and sought to needle us at every turn. In recent years since he met Billie, who at the time was Lola's administrative assistant, he's not out to destroy us. Although we still go head-to-head on bids aggressively. These days it's business and not personal. Not to mention he and his brothers went to Saïd Business School with Lachlan and Lydie.

Before I answer the burly Scotsman, I take another sip of my Jackson Reserve Scotch.

Like an experienced negotiator, he waits patiently for my response. He blows cigar smoke as he watches me intently.

"It's not what's eating me. Rather, who *I'm* not eating," I respond as his eyebrows knit together.

Patrick's seen me with the Siren only recently. So, I'm sure he's confused.

I shrug and continue.

"Things weren't what they seemed with the bonny lass I was dating," I clarify. "I've tried my best to forget her between the thighs of other women. Although they prove distractions, she still invades too many of my thoughts. This trip should help. Well, I hope."

He nods and lifts his snifter.

"Failing means yer playin, mate!" Patrick proclaims with a grin and a wink.

Bloody Scots' sayings. I frown and shake my head.

His grin widens as his green eyes sparkle.

"Trying and failing, but at least you are trying," he explains. "Don't let the little lass get you down, Harris. However, if she's meant to be yours again and forever, nothing will keep you apart. Trust me, mate."

He nods sagely.

I tip my snifter to his glass.

We'll see.

Meanwhile, I pat him on the shoulder as I stand and head for the dance floor. Borya could use some help with the now four beauties surrounding him.

Nothing wrong with *failing*, eh?

* * *

"CLEAR A PATH ON YOUR LEFT, slowpoke! Coming through!"

Malcolm's shout fills my earpiece as I maneuver my glider high above the lush greenery surrounding Laguna Mata Redonda.

The brilliant sun glitters like diamonds off the lake's crystal blue surface. Ripples spread across the water from the wind blowing in from Punta Mameyes. People fishing on the lake glance up as the shadows from our hang gliders skim over their boats. A few of the fishing enthusiasts wave up at us.

I change my angle of attack and tip the nose of my glider down to increase my speed. There's enough space between my brother and me to avoid a collision. So I refuse to just give way to the ardent thrill seeker. I want to experience the adrenaline rush as much as Malcolm does.

His chuckles come through the earpiece in reaction to my defiance.

A glance over my shoulder as I shift in my harness shows he's further behind me than before. I smirk.

"Get in line behind the greatest, Malcolm, my boy!" I chortle.

"Quit your shenanigans and pay attention to what you're doing," Lucien cuts in. "Safety before bravado, lads!"

We continue until we lose the ridge lift and float towards the beach. As our boots touch the ground, we run along the sand to slow our landing. Each of us make it in unharmed, naturally. The ground crew assists us with the equipment, leaving us to head for the water after we strip out of our suits and footwear.

"Race to the pontoon!" Anton yells as he runs to the shoreline.

We whoop and holler as we follow him to the waves. Upon entering the warm water of the Caribbean Sea, it eases the tension from my body. Then increases as I propel forward through the current using powerful strokes. At the pontoon, I hoist myself from the sea and high five Anton who arrived first.

"Well done, bro!" He says with barely a hint of his Russian accent. After years of being in the United States and attending Harvard University undergrad and Business School with Malcolm, Anton's native accent only sounds when he's drinking vodka or excited.

The others join us to lie out beneath the sun's rays. We shoot the shit and talk about plans for the evening. It's our last day, so Laurent wants to go out with a bang. He won't give details, only saying we'll more than enjoy ourselves.

We return to the beach for lunch at the local shacks known for savory dishes of Puerto Rican favorites—the monster sandwich tripleta, bacalaitos fried salt cod fritters, and arroz con gandules with sofrito sauce.

Lachlan sits beside me at one of the tables we choose beneath the bountiful fronds of coconut palm trees. After we place our orders with a cute server, my brother-in-law turns to me.

"I know Laurent decreed our Guys' Getaway as *no sob stories, no drama, no business*. But I want to let you know the latest," Lachlan says.

I cock an eyebrow, curious about what he has to say and nod to encourage him to speak.

"Lydie came up with a brilliant plan. She forced the Stewarts' hands to sell 51% of Stewart Scotch to Jackson Corporation, so we have a majority stake in their family's business. On top of that, she folded Stewart Scotch within Jackson Corporation as the coup de grâce."

My mouth drops open.

The Shark took a massive bite out of their historic enemy. She crippled any chance of the Stewarts destroying the Jackson family and company for good.

"Hell yeah! Lydie dealt them a death blow, bro!" I exclaim. "Damn, she's no bloody joke."

"You can say that again, brother!" Lachlan says, as he chuckles and shakes his head. "*The Shark* had a more than satisfying meal.

"You should have seen their father Magnus' face when Lydie told him about that sodding wanker Chet's illicit deeds. Magnus railed on him while Bram sat triumphant. Undoubtedly, he assumed their father would select him as the heir. When Lydie told Magnus the terms of the deal, his face turned beet red, and his nostrils flared. He sputtered in Scottish Gaelic, unable to form words in English. He even clocked Chet upside the head.

Lydie proceeded to tell Magnus—since she ignored the brothers completely—the deal was nonnegotiable. Or we would ruin their company and family name for good. He signed the contracts post haste."

I raise my glass of water in honor of Lydie. Attagirl!

Lachlan's smile changes to a more serious expression.

Once again, I cock my eyebrow at him.

"I also let Chet know under no circumstances can he go after Kat or her family. Or we would strike back," Lachlan says, then pauses to gauge my reaction.

I sit in silence.

He continues with a nod.

"She damn sure fucked up, no doubt. But I will allow no one to harm a member of my family—including Kat, her mother, and her siblings. I read the apology letters Kat sent to everyone. She's pretty sincere and obviously in pain."

He pauses then goes on.

"I didn't see a letter for you, though. Care to share?" He asks.

My eyes drift back to the sea. The waves lap at the golden sand. A toddler squeals as the water kisses her chubby legs. A smile curls the corners of my mouth. Then I glance back at Lachlan and frown.

"She didn't send me an apology," I respond.

His eyes widen as his head jerks back in shock. He mutters a Scottish Gaelic curse under his breath.

"Instead, she showed up at the lobby of STEELE London as I was leaving. I guess she wanted to apologize. But I wasn't interested in a word she said. I told her not to contact me or come near me and my family ever again," I say.

"Well, bloody hell," Lachlan mutters.

I grouse some more, and Lachlan shakes his head.

"I don't blame you for being pissed. Hell, I still am. But I believe her words. Let's see what actions she takes to back them up, Harris," he ends with a clap to my shoulder. "Now, Laurent's rule takes effect again. That is unless you have something to say."

Now it's his turn to cock an eyebrow as he scans my face.

I glance past him at the water as my thoughts drift. He gives me a moment to decide in silence. When I return my gaze to Lachlan, he raises his eyebrows questioningly.

I shrug.

"Who knows what tomorrow bring," I respond.

Lachlan nods, completely nonjudgmental.

"As for today, brother, let's end our Guys' Getaway with a rip-roaring time," I add, then call to the cute server for a pitcher—not a single glass—of mojitos.

I sure as hell need more than one drink.

KAT

"*B*abe... Babe... Kat, wake up... I miss you so much."

Can I be dreaming? Or do I really hear Harris' voice? The deep rumble of his baritone rolls over me. It ignites a fire to lick across my skin, straight to my needy core. Oh, God, please let it be true...

Slowly, I open my eyes and roll over onto my back. Leaning on my elbow, I stare in the direction of his voice. Even in the darkened room, I can distinguish Harris' sizable frame.

He stands at the foot of the bed. A swath of light from the moon crosses his face as the gauzy curtains flutter in the wind. His handsome face brightens as our eyes meet. Full, kissable lips part as he licks the bottom one with the tip of his tongue.

I close my eyes and envision that tongue and mouth on my suddenly engorged clit. A moan slips past the lips on my face even as the lower ones swell with a desperate, aching need.

It's been way too long.

Eight excruciating weeks without the man I now realize I love. And want. Forever.

Thank God he's really here.

Harris' wicked chuckle rouses me from my pitiful musings. He glances down at my bare leg resting atop the sheets, then places one finger on the inside of my ankle. As he trails the tip along my instep, I moan aloud.

"You've been a naughty girl, Kitty Kat," he murmurs.

I gasp at the pressure he applies with his knuckle to the sole of my foot.

His dove gray eyes flick to my hooded emerald green orbs. He smirks.

"You tricked me. Naughty. Naughty. Girl."

He punctuates each word with a stroke of his knuckle.

The sensation on my erogenous zone morphs from pain to pleasure. My leg jerks as I mewl.

Harris grips both ankles and pulls me to the foot of the bed. I end up between his parted thighs.

My ass cheeks hang off the edge. The white silk sheets bunch about my waist. My exposed lower half draws his attention like a magnet. My hips shimmy of their own accord. His feral growl makes my pussy clench and flood with my juices. The musky scent of my arousal fills the space between us.

A predatory smile spreads across his face as his nostrils flare.

I swallow.

He grips my ankles in one sizable hand and hoists my hips from the mattress. I hang suspended with my shoulders pressed into the bed.

"Your attempt at an apology does not suffice in the least, Naughty. Naughty. Girl."

With his other hand, Harris swats my exposed pussy lips and clit.

WHAP. WHAP. WHAP.

I howl.

The sting radiates from my core to the tips of my toes and the top of my head. An electric current of erotic punishment zaps me.

"Do you understand how much trouble you are in, Naughty. Naughty. Girl?"

When I hesitate to answer, he spanks the sensitive juncture where my thighs meet my ass.

WHAP. WHAP. WHAP. WHAP.

My legs flail as I press my hands into the mattress to drag myself away from the punishing onslaught of spanks. To no avail. Trapped.

"You can dish the pain. But not take it, Naughty. Naughty. Girl? Too bad."

Harris sets a brutal pace for my punishment. Spanks land on my clit, pussy, sits bones, and thighs. Never landing on the same spot in a row. But not in a distinguishable pattern I can expect. No matter which way I flounder, I can't avoid the blows.

My howls increase as each second passes. The time uncountable. The pain memorable.

His silence as he punishes me allows my thoughts to drift back to the many ways I hurt him, Lachlan, and the rest of their family. I even recall the hurt on Lola's face as I told her about my parents' death in a car accident, just like hers.

Each lie I told accumulates to form a mountain of unstable rocks that threaten to landslide onto me as the spanking continues unabated.

Tears stream from my eyes to pool in my ears and drip

onto the bed below. Chest-racking sobs pour from my mouth. So ashamed of my actions, I cover my heated face with my hands.

My pussy, ass, and thighs on fire, I submit.

Between howls and sobs, I beg Harris for his forgiveness.

He continues to spank me.

All tension drains from my body. Still held aloft, I sag. Spent completely. Tears continue to fall but in silence.

More time passes before the spanks change to caresses.

Soft rumblings glide over my skin as Harris soothes me. His murmurs draw more pleas of forgiveness from me. He settles on the bed and cradles me on his lap. I burrow my face into his neck as my entire body trembles. Sweat sheens on my skin, and my reddened ass ablaze.

The punishment a cathartic release.

"I forgive you, My Kitty Kat."

My heart skips a beat.

I raise my head to scan Harris' face. Can it be true?

His dove gray eyes glitter in the moonlight. They're filled with what I dare hope is love. Love for me. Even after all I did. Thank God.

His thumb brushes a tear from the corner of my eye. He slips the digit into my mouth.

"No more tears of sadness, My Kitty Kat," he murmurs before he slants his mouth over mine.

The kiss starts as a slow burn. Tendrils of warmth overtake the coldness that settled in my heart and soul. Our tongues dance an erotic tango. Flames lick through me. My toes curl as I meld my body to his muscular frame, crawling to surround him. The fire between us burns bright again.

"Need to be inside you..." Harris pants against my lips. He nips at me as he shifts position.

I lie on my back as he hovers above me. His mouth drops

to my heavy breasts. He laves at the pebbled peaks. I yelp as his teeth sink into the sensitive flesh. His tongue flicks out to lap the pain away before he suckles first one, then the other distended nipple.

My head lolls. Cries of passion fall from my parted lips. I cup the nape of his neck to encourage his ministrations. Pressed flush, he hums in pleasure. The vibrations travel through me. I mewl.

Harris stands to yank his shirt over his head. He tosses it to the floor and grips the placket of his low-slung jeans. The metal buttons pop open to reveal the swollen, purple tip of his massive cock. Commando, his erection springs free.

My mouth waters at the sight of the pearly drop of pre-cum as it glints in the moonlight. I shudder at the memory of how his turgid girth and length burns my little pussy as he stretches me.

He pushes the jeans past his narrow hips. The muscles in his arms and thighs flex as he wrestles the unwanted material from his body. Standing tall, he fists his cock. The veins stand out in bas-relief. His heavy sac hangs below.

My tongue darts out to lick my lower lip.

Harris smirks and jerks his cock.

My pussy gushes.

His eyes lower to the apex of my thighs. A carnal smile tips the corners of his lush mouth at the sight of my glistening pussy lips. The juices slicken my legs. He growls.

In an instant, my hips lift in the air, and my shoulders press into the bed once again. I yelp in surprise and grasp the sheets to ground myself.

Harris holds me by both ankles. Legs spread wide in a vee. My core aligned with his cock. A snap of his hips, and he impales me on his dick.

I scream from the thick invasion. His tremendous girth fills me. The burn oh so good.

"FUCK!!!" He roars. Head back, muscles in his neck and arms corded. Harris stills but for a moment. Then…

"Take. Every. Inch. All of it!"

He pistons balls deep within me, punctuated by each word. My only reprieve when he pulls out to his bulbous tip. Held aloft, I have no choice but to take what he gives to me. And I do with absolute pleasure.

I writhe beneath him screeching like the cat in heat I am.

Fuck, he feels so damn good…

The slapping of skin on skin with the squelch of my pussy juices mixes with his grunts and groans and my cries. The erotic sounds arouse me like no other. They spur Harris on to fuck me into the bed. It groans in protest.

"Oh! Oh! Yeeessss… HARRIS!!!" I shout as a powerful orgasm rips through me.

A flash of white light sparks behind my eyelids, squeezed shut as ecstasy rolls over me. My inner walls tighten around his pulsating cock. He growls and pummels harder. Unstoppable. Relentless.

Booms blast and bright lights explode with each of the countless orgasms Harris forces from my ravaged core.

Sweat drips from his forehead to trail between my bouncing breasts as he leans over my torso. His dominant hands wrap under me to grasp my thighs as he changes the angle of his savage thrusts. His firm pecs drag over my taut nipples. Guttural groans and growls fill my ear as Harris chases his release.

As his cock swells impossibly larger, his body judders. Hot breath puffs across my sweat-drenched neck into my damp hair.

"Kaaat…"

His carnal cry and the copious amounts of his cum bathing my pussy trigger another epic climax.

I scream in pleasure as my eyes roll back and my back bows.

Harris collapses on top of me. The last vestiges of his release drip from my core, down my ass cheeks to the drenched sheets below.

"Happy now?" He murmurs in a raspy voice.

"So happy," I respond breathily as I squeeze him tight.

A streak of red shoots past the stars high in the sky.

A boom, then an explosion of red, orange, and yellow bursts.

"Happy… Happy… HAPPY NEW YEAR!!!"

I bolt upright in the bed sweating, breathing heavily, wildly looking around.

"HAPPY NEW YEAR!!!"

"HAPPY NEW YEAR!!!"

"HAPPY NEW YEAR!!!"

My hand swipes wet tendrils of my hair plastered to my face. My eyes dart from the chaise lounge on which I lay to the sky above where colorful fireworks explode. The oversized pillow misshaped from me clutching it falls from on top of me to the tiled floor.

What the—???

I jerk to the left, seeking Harris. He's not here. I find myself alone.

Alone on the terrace of my hotel suite overlooking Sydney Harbor. I must have fallen asleep as I awaited the end of the old year. One I am more than happy to leave behind. I wanted to begin the New Year in the first big city to celebrate. A fresh start before my job in New York City.

There's no Harris here. No words of forgiveness and eternal love. And definitely no mind-blowing makeup sex.

With a frustrated yowl, I fall back against the chaise lounge. My hands cover my face as tears cascade down my flushed cheeks. Instead of my lover, cool air wraps around my sweat dampened skin. I shudder.

It was only a dream, after all.

The celebration below me only makes my misery more stark. Shouts of joy filter up from the crowds gathered to ring in the New Year. I envision couples kissing fervently. Their need to be with their loved one is strong. Promises for the future shared. Love declared.

My disappointing dream fades. Scattered on the breeze. The fiery passion a dull ache in my heart and deep in my core.

"Oh, Harris!" I cry in dismay.

The ringing of my mobile causes me to jump. With a dash of hope, I lunge for it. As I swipe it from the table, my gaze takes in the name on the screen.

Mum

Damn.

I mean, I'm glad to hear from her. But for a moment, I thought it would be Harris. Oh, well…

"Hi, Mum. Happy New Year!" I exclaim as I feign happiness. No need to upset her with my misery.

"Kat! Happy New Year! I set my alarm to call you. I wanted to be the first to wish you the best for the upcoming months. You deserve it, honey," my Mum says.

In the background, I hear Michael and Charlotte calling out their best wishes to me. Our Mum's light-hearted laughter eases some of the sadness.

With a smile, I wish them Happy New Year, too. We chat some more before we hang up with my promise to call when it's their turn to celebrate. I set my alarm for just over ten hours.

As I hold the mobile, I consider calling Harris. Would he answer? What would he say? That is if he didn't change his number or block mine.

One last glance at the festivities and I head inside to the shower. As the water sluices over my body, I visualize a cleansing. The old me and ways swirl down the drain. I step out of the glass-enclosed marble shower revitalized. A New Year Promise ready to be declared.

"*Smiogaid suas, nighean*, Katrina Jackson! You will get your man back," I vow.

KAT

"Thank you for meeting with me, Haley. I truly appreciate it. I'm so sorry for all I've done and for how my actions impacted everyone. I hope that one day you will forgive me. I know it's a lot to ask. So I'll understand if you don't."

I remembered Lachlan's calendar noted he would be in New York City for January. He scheduled meetings with Jackson Corporation's executive team and important clients to kick off the year. His calendar also included references to time reserved for Haley and their family.

As soon as I arrived in the City, I contacted her. Surprisingly, on my first try, she agreed to have lunch with me.

Now her dove gray eyes—so like her brother's—pierce my soul. Her cool stare assesses me as I speak. No telltale expression gives away her thoughts.

I do my best not to squirm. As each second ticks by, I remind myself of my goal: get your man back.

The first step, convince his twin of my sincerity. They're super close. If I can get back in Haley's good graces, she may put me in contact with Harris. A positive word from Haley would make all the difference.

I pause to see if she will respond in some way to my subtle request.

She doesn't.

Holding back a dismayed sigh, I continue.

"I also want to let you know I accepted a job offer as the Development Director for a children's nonprofit organization on Fifth Avenue. So I'm living here permanently," I say, then offer a small smile with a shrug. "I've always wanted to live in New York City. Plus, it'll give me the chance to combine my MA Business Management degree with my love of volunteerism and the skills I learned during my administrative assistant positions."

Haley snorts.

A reaction at last, even if it's regarding the use of my skills and thus my past behavior. I can't really blame her, though.

I smile humbly.

The server places our dishes on the table and pours more wine. With a nod, he leaves us.

Haley leans forward. Her dove gray eyes darken to obsidian as they narrow on me.

"Listen, Kat, I did not accept your lunch invitation to learn about your new job or life. I couldn't care less. What the fuck do you really want?" She asks pointedly.

Did I say she and Harris are close? Well, she's also a mama bear when it comes to her twin. And I just poked her. Bloody hell...

I take a gulp of wine and close my eyes for a silent prayer. When I glance at her again, she glares at me.

"Haley, I understand your anger with me. I deserve it. What I did was shitty. It would have been much better had I simply shared the knowledge about Iain with the Jacksons. However, years of struggles and self-hate blinded me to the right thing to do. I regret it. Not just because I was caught. But because as I got to know you and both of your families, I realized you're good people and don't judge me for my background. Not to mention what I initially thought was a smokescreen turned into true love."

She growls.

Quickly I go on.

"I never should have used Harris as I did. It was horrible and selfish," I say to calm Haley. I raise my hand and continue. "But I swear on my Mum's life I love Harris with all of my heart and soul. If I could erase the past, I would start with what I did to hurt him above all else."

I pause to drain my wineglass.

Haley takes a sip from hers and watches me over the rim intently. Once again, her face turns into an indecipherable mask. A cool veneer covers the simmering volcano just below the surface.

I tread carefully with my next words.

"What I want? I ask for your help to reconnect with Harris—"

"Are you *mad?!?!*" Haley erupts.

Wine sloshes from her glass as she slams it down on the table. I watch as the red liquid splatters onto the white linen cloth. The droplets remind me of bloody tears. Tears that soak my alabaster skin every night as I lie alone in bed. My thoughts on the man I love and how much I miss him.

Smiogaid suas, nighean, Katrina Jackson! You will get your man back. I recall my vow and raise my eyes to Haley.

"Yes. Madly in love with Harris," I respond unwaveringly.

Haley pushes back from the table. I rise and catch her

arm. She drops her gaze to my hand and slowly lifts her eyes to mine. Her lip curls.

Before she can speak, I interrupt her.

"Haley, please! All I ask is for one chance to speak with Harris. If he tells me to bugger off, I will never bother him again. I promise! I tried to speak with him before I left the UK. But he was too angry to listen. I hope after two and a half months he'll hear me out. I cry every single day for him. Please, Haley," I beg as tears shimmer in my eyes.

She scans my face to determine my sincerity. The platinum daggers shooting from her eyes soften into glittery diamonds. She mutters to herself, then sits back down.

With a sigh of relief, I drop into my chair. My hand covers my face as tears fall.

"Here."

I peek through my fingers to find a white handkerchief before me. A sign of peace? I pray so as I take the proffered cloth. After I dab my eyes and cheeks, I glance at Haley.

She sighs and signals the server. She asks him for a napkin to cover the spilled wine and for another bottle. Hurriedly, he and another server replace the tablecloth entirely and fill our glasses from a fresh bottle. They leave us with bows.

"Thank you—"

"Eat. You look like you could use a good meal. You've lost fifteen pounds easily, Kat," Haley cuts in. She shakes her head and mutters about women's reactions to breakups. "Afterwards, we'll talk," she adds aloud.

She's not kidding.

I haven't been able to eat much more than a few pieces of fruit or soup. The idea of food turned my stomach. I figured I lost weight since my clothes hang loosely. But for Haley to notice, I must have lost more than I thought.

I glance down at the Classic Cobb Salad before me. Knowing I may have a chance of seeing Harris, I dive in. The grilled chicken tastes divine. In moments, my bowl sits empty, and my belly is full.

"Hungry much?" Haley snickers.

My cheeks flush crimson as I shake my head. With a giggle, I swipe the last bit of tomato through the tasty vinaigrette and pop it into my mouth. Then I grin at Haley.

She laughs and nods.

"That good, huh?" She asks.

We order tea as the server clears the table. He returns with a pot and an assortment of fresh-baked cookies. The scent of brown sugar and chocolate makes my belly rumble. We indulge before Haley sits back and crosses her arms over her breasts.

"You do realize you fucked over my twin brother *and* my husband, don't you? Tried to ruin Jackson Corporation and Chet Stewart wanted STEELE International, Inc., too, right?" She asks, one elegantly arched eyebrow raised.

I blink at the 180-degree flip, then swallow.

"Yes, and I'm oh so sorry," I whisper as my head hangs in shame.

"Then you have balls to assume I would help you snag my twin," she says with a snort.

Bloody hell...

I squirm in my chair. I thought things were going in my favor. Obviously, I was way wrong.

A full minute passes.

"Gutsy. Okay, Kat. What's your plan?" She asks.

The breath I was holding burst forth in a rush. Lightheaded, I clutch the table's edge in a white-knuckled grip.

"Yeah, I can make you or break you. Never, ever forget that feeling. Because if you fuck with my family again, I promise you by all things I hold dear, I will end you for good, Kat *Jackson*," Haley says. "Do you understand?"

I nod, then remember to answer verbally when she cocks her head.

"Y—Yes, Haley. I understand," I stammer, red-faced.

She eyes me for another minute before she reminds me to answer her question.

I tell her I just need an opportunity to sit and talk with Harris. He hasn't answered my calls, text messages, or emails. If I could arrange for him to meet me, that would be great. But I'm fearful he may leave as soon as he sees me. With tears in my eyes, I ask if she can help me.

Haley glances away as she considers my emotional entreaty. Her mobile vibrates. She flips it over and glances at the screen. Her eyes flick to me.

"Uh, excuse me a moment," she says as she slides her chair back.

I reach out to stay her and shake my head.

"I'm going to the ladies' room," I say.

She nods and answers the call as I walk away.

It's either Lachlan or Harris. Otherwise, she wouldn't have reacted that way. My heart skips a beat at the thought of the caller being Harris.

Will she tell him I'm with her? Will she disclose my plan to him? What will he say?

Questions swirl in my mind as I make my way past the other diners. I wonder what Haley will do to get Harris to agree to meet with me. Or if she even does. I so hope he will hear me out.

As angry as he was, he must feel some kind of way for me. He certainly made me think so when we were together. All the passionate lovemaking we shared. The romantic trips around the world. The comfortable cuddles as we watched movies on Netflix.

I pray Harris and I can tap back into the good times and leave the past behind us.

As I return from the ladies' room, I make certain Haley finished her phone call. I'd hate to interrupt. She smiles as I settle into my chair.

"I have to go now. But dinner tomorrow night at my penthouse duplex. I'll text the address to you," she says as she rises from her chair.

I jump up and hug her as I whisper words of thanks. She accepts my embrace, then steps back and leaves. I signal the server. Once I pay for lunch, I leave the restaurant with a giant smile on my face.

It was a close one. But step one is complete!

HARRIS

"You appear rested, son. I take it Puerto Rico proved a trip full of relaxation?"

I return my father's embrace as he greets me.

We're having lunch at his request. My hope is for a catch up on life's happenings and not about the Kat *Jackson* fiasco. I scan his face as we settle into our chairs for a clue.

Morgan Steele, Alpha Dom billionaire who increased his family's fortune twice over while he reigned at STEELE International, Inc. for decades. Even post-retirement, the former CEO and Chairman of the Board remains active as Chairman Emeritus of the Board.

Most important of all roles as Patriarch of the Steele clan, he's extremely protective of his family. No one messes with a Steele or a Jackson and gets away with it. He has said little to me about the Kat *Jackson* fiasco. So, I'm certain he will reveal his perspective today.

Looking at my father mimics my reflection in a mirror thirty-seven years from now. A six-foot-four frame—he's

358

three inches taller—still muscular from regular personal training sessions. Wavy salt and pepper hair kept short and neat. Clear platinum gray eyes. Well-dressed in a bespoke Brioni suit, custom dress shirt, silk tie with matching pocket square, and A. Testoni Oxfords. Morgan Steele is a distinguished older man who emanates power and wealth.

I strive to follow in his footsteps. Each of my siblings feel the same about our father. He's an excellent role model, and we value his opinion. So I wait anxiously for his words.

"Thanks, Dad. The Guys' Getaway gave me the opportunity to hang out with my boys and on the beach. You should join us for the next one," I respond with my signature cocky grin.

He chuckles and shakes his head.

"I do not believe you and the guys can keep up with me," he says. "However, I'll keep your invitation under consideration."

The server appears. Despite being younger than me—not to mention the platinum wedding band sitting prominently on his left ring finger—she gives my father an appreciative once over.

He ignores her sultry stare and places his order without glancing in her direction.

She gets the hint and turns to me.

I pin her with a reproachful look, and she drops the coy smile instantly. Orders placed, she slinks away. I roll my eyes. My father smirks knowingly.

While we eat, we do the catch up on life's happenings. My parents plan to spend next week through the end of February on their megayacht *Serendipity* cruising the Mediterranean. After almost forty years of marriage, their love remains strong and unchallenged. Again, a feat my siblings and I wish to accomplish. Well, me, not right now.

"Tell me how you fare after the situation with Kat," my father commands as we drink coffee. His platinum gray eyes pin me with a gaze more intense than Roger's signature stare.

I swallow another sip as I form words to respond. With a shake of my head, I meet his gaze.

"Not so great, Dad," I say with a shrug honestly. "I feel guilty as fu—I mean—hell for being the one to bring Kat into our family's inner circle. To top it off, I harbored a hacker. Me, the co-head of STEELE Technology and Cyber Security, tech wiz, part of the Dynamic Duo."

I run my fingers through my hair and tug the longer strands. The thought of it all re-invokes anger and embarrassment. Damn Kat *Jackson*!

My father assesses me a moment. The server returns to refill our coffee. He waves her away like an annoying gnat as it buzzes around your head. She departs hastily.

"Harris, know not one of us faults you. Kat fooled everyone. Leave the blame at her feet, not at yours in any way," he says earnestly. "Your mother and I spoke. She wants you to know not to let this set you back. Remain open to love. It can surprise you whence it comes. Do you understand?"

I ponder his and my mother's words of advice. The weight on my heart lightens with the knowledge no one blames me truly. Not just blowing smoke up my ass to make me feel less of an idiot. Thank fuck!

"That makes me feel much better, Dad, thank you. I can't say when I'll be ready for love again. But I'll heed Mom's advice," I respond with a nod.

"Excellent. Now you get back to work. I have to pick up your mother from her spa day," my father says with a twinkle in his platinum gray eyes.

He rises from his chair, and I follow suit. I walk with him

to his Rolls-Royce Corniche. The driver taps his hat while he opens the back door. My father embraces me before he slides inside.

With a wave, I watch the sedan pull away from the curb and merge with traffic on Fifth Avenue. As I walk back to The STEELE Tower, I contemplate my next move. Being with my father reminds me of the importance of family. It's time for Uncle Harris Babysitting.

"Oh, hi, *Harris*. What's up, brother of mine?"

I chuckle at Haley's greeting when she answers her mobile. I can picture her grinning with a mischievous glint in her eyes. My twin sense tingles.

"What are *you* up to, Hal?" I rejoin with a smirk.

"You called me, remember?" She asks instead of answering my question. "I presume you must have something to share. So you tell me, *Har*."

I shake my head and chuckle. Fine.

"I haven't seen my niece and nephews in a few days. I need some *Tea Party and Transformers* time," I answer, using my name for playtime with the wee lass and lads. "Why don't you and Little Lord Fauntleroy go on a date night tomorrow? It is Saturday after all. A little LEVELS New York, perhaps? I'll babysit for you."

Haley's response comes after a moment of silence. Just as I'm about to ask her what's wrong, she speaks up.

"Why, that's perfect timing! Things always fall into place as they should when they should," she answers.

It's a bit of a mysterious comment. The tingling increases. But I opt to ignore it. Starr probably has Haley reading some New Age book, again.

"See you at seven," my twin says. "Gotta fly."

And she's gone.

What a weirdo…

I stare at the mobile screen, then out the floor-to-ceiling windows of my offices in The STEELE Tower high above Fifth Avenue and Fifty-seventh Street in the heart of Billionaires' Row. The striking, gray-tinted glass skyscraper for our headquarters and commercial, retail, and residential properties.

New York City stretches out before me with unobstructed views. Central Park to the north, the Hudson River to the west, the East River opposite, and the rest of Manhattan to the south from Midtown to Battery Park. On a beautiful, cloudless day like this afternoon, the panoramas can take one's breath away. I can spend hours watching the happenings of the bustling city. But not now.

My gaze returns to my laptop to prepare for a meeting with a recently gained client. I attained their corporate and the CEO's personal accounts while I was with that redheaded Siren. I told her she brought me luck since she kissed me before I had the initial meeting.

"Huh… Some luck she turned out to be. Get a grip, Harris Steele. You have work to focus on. Not that scammer," I chide myself aloud.

I pull up the analysis and presentation.

At the end of the day, I leave my suite of offices with a wave to my administrative assistant, who's wrapping up a phone call. I stride across the floor designated for STEELE Technology and Cyber Security's New York City headquarters. The layout and decor—as sleek as the Tower's exterior —features glass-enclosed offices on the perimeter with workstations clustered in the center, ebony wood floors, dove gray and white leather furniture, track light fixtures, Lucite tables, steel accents, and original artwork.

I make a point to chat with my staff as I make my way to the elevator. Our father taught my siblings and me to appreciate and to treat well those who work for us since they're our most-valuable asset. One reason STEELE International maintains a high employee retention rate.

As I near the reception area, I greet the two receptionists by name. They wish me a good weekend as they pack away their headsets. Like the three on the executive floor, the receptionists wear custom-tailored light gray dress suits and skin-tone heels that serve as uniforms and sit behind a spacious desk.

A member of the security team stands from his station as I approach. We talk about the latest Knicks' basketball game at Madison Square Garden while I wait for the family's private elevator. My palm to the plate by the doors calls it to the floor. The elevator links our residences on the fiftieth through fifty-seventh floors to our global headquarters on the nineteenth through twenty-ninth floors. Bonus? A less than five-minute commute to my office. Talk about a score!

I bid them a good night as I step onto the elevator.

I ride up to my full-floor penthouse on the fifty-first floor. It's above Haley and Lachlan's penthouse duplex on the forty-ninth and fiftieth floors. My other siblings' residences are above mine in age order up to our parents' duplex on the top floors. They gave each of us penthouses as graduation presents. Baz has a duplex. Haley created hers when she and Lachlan combined their residences after they married.

The elevator doors open to my entry foyer.

My mother decorated for me. She has extraordinary taste. So I trusted she'd make my bachelor's pad five-star. My only requirements were a home office with an adjacent secure room for my tech gadgets, a tricked-out game room, and an oversized sunken tub. A guy needs to relax after a long day at the office.

That thought stays with me as I make my way to my primary bedroom suite. Before I left my office, I activated the water and the essential oils to fill the tub and set piano music to play. One of my home tech systems I make great use of on a daily basis.

I walk into my dressing room to strip out of my bespoke Saville Row double-breasted suit and custom dress shirt. The silk Hermès tie and platinum cuff links drop onto the center island. I toe off my A. Testoni Oxfords and Charvet dress socks. Fortunately, my house manager keeps things tidy for me.

The combined scent of lavender, chamomile, and sandalwood evokes an immediate sense of calm as I enter my all white marble bathroom. The warmth of the room heightens the relaxing scent. A deep inhalation and slow exhalation calm me. I give a nod to Starr, who hooked a brother up with the best essential oils available.

Slowly, I lower myself into the sunken tub large enough for four people. Not that I've had three women here. Nah. I leave my trysts at LEVELS. The only woman who's ever shared my bed outside of the clubs was that redheaded Siren.

Again, she pops into my mind unbidden.

I close my eyes and lean against the side of the tub with my head on a scented pillow. More thoughts of she who shall not be named fill my mind. I try to dodge them, to no avail.

"Oh, fuck it," I groan.

Instantly, her tempting image appears behind my closed eyelids. Her lustrous Titian hair cascades down her back. The tips curl around her seashell pink pebbled nipples.

They peek through her curtain of hair as she moves towards me from the opposite side of the tub. Voluptuous curves on full display. For my eyes only.

Each graceful step causes her mouth-watering tits to jiggle and her grip-worthy hips to sway. Her bare mons calls to me as though her glistening pussy lips hum a beguiling tune. Long, toned legs ease her into the water. She dips under, then resurfaces between my thighs.

Rivulets of water trail down her flawless skin, flush from the warm temperature. Droplets bead on the tips of her nipples.

I lean forward to lick a bead off.

She shivers despite the heat.

I want to make her entire body convulse with climaxes I cause.

My hands reach through the water to grasp her hips. I pull her closer to me as my head lowers to the other nipple. My tongue darts out to circle around the delectable bud. I draw it into my hot mouth and suckle. Hard.

The Siren throws her head back as a throaty moan slips past her parted lips. She gasps when I nip, then lave her nipple. I engulf as much of her luscious DD-cup tit in my mouth as possible. She writhes. Her fingers dive into my hair. She cradles my head. Her soft cries fill my ears as she lowers her cheek to rest atop my head.

"Oh, Harris," she mewls.

My ten-inch cock thumps against my abs. Like a water snake, it winds beneath the surface in search of its prey. In this case, it seeks the tight, wet snatch of the Siren. As though sensing its need, her soft hand wraps around its base and squeezes.

Her breast pops from my mouth on a groan.

She pumps my cock and swirls her thumb around the mushroom head.

"Fuuuck…" I breathe.

The Siren straddles me. Her knees on either side of my hips as she hovers her pussy over my cock, still fisted in her hand. When the tip breaches her lower lips, she slams her ass down. She cries out in wild abandon as my girth stretches her pussy.

She digs her nails into my shoulders to anchor herself as she circles her hips, then lifts to the tip and impales herself onto my cock again and again.

"You like how my big dick claims every inch of your little pussy. Don't you, Siren?" I growl.

She bobs her head as she pants. The movement makes her beautiful tits bounce even more.

I lean forward and suckle again.

The action sets her off for another round of riding me like a champion equestrian. I buck beneath her like a bronco. Each of her slams meets one of my upward thrusts. We find our erotic rhythm with ease accustomed to one another's bodies.

Water sloshes from the bathtub onto the marble floor. Our mutual cries of carnal delight overtake the soothing sounds of the piano. Sweat beads above the Siren's top lip. I lick it off.

We fuck like feral animals—a cat and a wolf—until we pass out nearly. Countless orgasms make her limp as I chase my release. I rise to my knees and flip her over to mount her from behind. The new angle hits her G-spot just right, and she howls as her body convulses with a final climax.

It triggers my balls to draw up and shoot my load deep into her well-used pussy. The energy drains from me with the last spurt of my jizz. I collapse atop her, then roll to sit with her held in my arms. I lower my face into the back of her neck and purr in contentment.

My eyes open leisurely.

I grunt and give my cock one more stroke to empty it fully.

"Damn that redheaded Siren for making me want her..." I groan wistfully.

HARRIS

"Good morning, Mr. Steele, Mr. Jackson. Welcome back to Goodman's Men's Store, sirs. I will let Dara and Cindy know you arrived. Would you care for a Mimosa or sparkling water?"

Laurent and I thank the greeter at the men's counterpart to Bergdorf Goodman—the centuries-old retailer for women's fashion. It's the global pinnacle of style, service, and modern luxury. We're in the specialty store across the street from its location on Fifth Avenue between Fifty-Seventh and Fifty-eighth Streets.

I walked over from The STEELE Tower. Laurent rode up in his Bentley Bentayga from his loft in TriBeCa. Some items we ordered arrived, along with new pieces from the latest collections.

Part of our playboy appeal is our sharp dressing. We look good for the ladies we charm.

Laurent and I stride through the store, heading to our reserved rooms. Other shoppers and staff glance in our direction as we approach. The magnetism of two Alpha males who exude power and wealth attracts them. Whether it's our swagger or pheromones, women and some men stop and stare.

Laurent—who typically flashes a brilliant smile at his gawkers—doesn't notice them. His beauty, Yessenia, captured his heart. Oblivious, he goes on about a new tobacco leaf he's using for a special collection of Jackson Cigars.

I, too, disregard the others—even a cute little thing with tons of ebony curls around her golden caramel face that glows as she smiles at me. After last night's fantasy, it still set my mind on a certain redheaded Siren. A brown-eyed beauty fails to distract me.

With a sigh, I tune back in to Laurent as I sip my Mimosa.

We take the elevator to the second floor, where Dara and Cindy wait for us. After double air kisses, they chatter on about the latest fashion news as they lead us to the Personal Styling Services area.

Each woman is a good ten years older than us and married to successful businessmen. Neither woman has any interest in getting a ring from Laurent and me. Their professionalism and keen sense of style helped us to develop a decade-long relationship. Aside from a soaking tub, a man needs a good stylist.

We separate to individual rooms off a common area with a few raised platforms in front of full-length mirrors. My room has two racks of clothes and accessories on the console. End tables with crystal lamps flank a gray velvet sofa with a matching ottoman. A tray with pastries and fruit and a pitcher of freshly squeezed orange juice with a glass rests on top of the ottoman.

I pop a grape in my mouth as I head to the curtained dressing room. I emerge in a gray silk robe and slippers.

"Shall we begin with the suits?" Dara asks with a smile. She inclines her head towards one rack. The crown of braids gives her a regal appearance. She claps her delicate hands as her toffee eyes sparkle when I agree.

"You will adore the fit of this Tom Ford number, especially with your muscular thighs," she says with a wink.

I chuckle and duck my head as my cheeks heat. Dara knows how to charm better than I do. No wonder her husband—who manages a super profitable hedge fund—showers her with lavish gifts, like the diamond cuffs on her slim wrists.

"Oh, don't be shy, sugar. You've known me far too long for that nonsense," she says with an airy laugh. "Here, take it with this shirt back to the dressing room. We'll add the accessories after you have it on."

"Yes, ma'am," I reply with a grin.

My grin widens when I stare at my reflection in the mirror. Dara sure knows how to pick 'em. And Mr. Tom Ford damn sure knows how to make a man look like a man. The cut and material are superb.

Dara claps when I step out of the dressing room. She twirls her finger for me to show each angle. When I face her again, she gives me the thumbs up in approval.

"Now for the tie, pocket square, and socks," Dara says as she goes to the console. "Your tiger's eye and yellow gold cuff links will pair well with the suit."

When we first worked together, she came to my penthouse and had her assistant take photos of each accessory and piece of clothing I owned. As we add more to my wardrobe, she puts those images in the database app Haley created for her.

If the occasion calls for it, Dara puts together the list of items I need to pack. My house manager puts my luggage together. Then I reference my side of the app to coordinate the outfits. Looking fly on the fly. Bam!

Dara and I spend the next ninety minutes going through the collection she prepared for me. Laurent finishes with Cindy shortly after. They'll arrange to deliver the items to our residences. We bid them farewell with more kisses.

I send a text message to my administrative assistant to send a box of macarons from Ladurée Paris and a bottle of Dom Pérignon Rosé Vintage 2005 to Dara. They're her favorites. I'll send a handwritten thank you note to her by messenger later this afternoon.

"Ready to get your ass handed to you?" Laurent asks as we ride in the back of his Bentley Bentayga.

I snort.

"Yeah, right. I believe you meant to say the reverse," I retort. "It is *I* who will hand *you* your ass, dear cousin."

We're on our way to play squash, then have lunch at The Union Club of the City of New York on Park Avenue. The Steele men have been members of the one hundred-eighty plus year old, exclusive social club since its founding as the first of its kind in the City. Despite being notorious for denying membership to sons, they have always accepted us. A Steele as a founding member makes the decision an easy one.

When we pull up to the club, the doorman opens the SUV's door. Laurent grabs his leather duffle bag from the trunk, and we stride into the lobby. I salute the concierge, then continue to the main elevator for access to the men's locker room. We change into the required all-white clothing of a collared shirt, shorts, socks, and sneakers for our match.

With our racquets and goggles in hand, we head for the

courts. Laurent continues to talk shit until I cream him by winning three out of the five games. He throws his towel at me as I crow. Deftly I catch it and toss it back at him. He rolls his eyes and exits the court as he mutters Scottish Gaelic curses under his breath.

In front of the viewing area, I stop and talk with other members. Laurent speaks with a man who owns a chain of high-end brasseries in New York, Chicago, and LA—a perfect match for Jackson Corporation's brands. The club offers many opportunities to network for both business and for pleasure. Many a deal gets made in these walls.

We return to the men's locker room. A quick shower to rinse off the sweat before we sit in the sauna to soothe our muscles. After a cleansing shower, we dress in our suits and ties—the de rigueur for The Union Club, even on a Saturday.

As I pass Laurent, I can't resist tousling his collar length sable brown hair after he fixed it just so. Loser. He retaliates by throwing an elbow into my flank. If we weren't at the Club, we'd wrestle until one of us gave in. Instead, he picks up his duffle bag, and we take the stairs up to the dining room.

The host greets me by name and Laurent since he frequents the Club with me regularly. We sit at the table reserved for the Steele men. From our prime spot in the center, we can observe the entire dining room.

A few members nod in greeting and others stop by the table. The server takes our order. I go for the French Onion Soup, a green salad, and Steak Frites. Laurent opts for the lentil soup, a salad, and Chicken Française. Plenty to replenish the stores used up by the intense squash match.

"So, what's the deal with your girl?" Laurent asks once we're alone.

I cock an eyebrow and give him the side-eye.

He chuckles as he raises his glass of San Pellegrino for a drink. His bottle green eyes dance with mirth.

"Don't play dumb with me, ol' chap. I hear she's on this side of the Pond," he says.

What the fuck???

My shock amuses him, and he throws his head back for a hearty laugh.

Surreptitiously, I kick his leg under the table. Fucker.

"Ow! Damn! Was that really necessary?" He grumbles as he rubs his shin. "Loosen up, cuz. Don't shoot the messenger."

I glare at him before I ask how he knows.

"Lachlan and Baz aren't the only ones with *guys*. I put a tail on the lass the moment we found out about her shenanigans. She's been pretty busy…" Laurent responds.

Okay. Do I want to know what that redheaded Siren has been up to for the last ten weeks? And by *busy* does Laurent mean with other men? Why the fuck do I care???

I go for the safe route.

"Did you tell Lachlan?" I ask.

Laurent cocks his head and returns my side-eye.

"Of course, I told the big boss. My last report placed her at a nonprofit organization for children. She's the new Development Director. Hopefully, she won't swindle them instead of raising funds," he says with a snort.

His comment rankles me. Then I chide myself for getting defensive. She deserves it.

I shrug, feigning nonchalance.

"Bully for her. Now tell me the latest with Yessenia since you're all in my business," I say.

His eyes light up at the mention of her name. Then he

spends the next few minutes bringing me up to date. Ah, young love. It's wonderful for some.

Just not for me.

ON MY WAY DOWN!

I shoot the text message to Haley as I wait for our private elevator. The bags from FAO Schwarz sit at my feet. After lunch, I stopped by the toy store to pick up some surprises for my niece and nephew. Sure, Christmas just happened, and I gave them loads of goodies. But one can never have too many Barbies and puzzles.

I don't bother to wait for Haley's response. The elevator doors open, and I get in. My nostrils flare.

The faint scent of perfume floats in the air. Not just any perfume. Her perfume.

Can't be!

The elevator doors ping open. The scent follows me into the entry foyer outside of Haley and Lachlan's penthouse duplex.

I swear I better be mistaken. But Laurent's words come back to haunt me. She who shall not be named is in New York City. Lachlan knows. This is his residence. She's his distant cousin.

Before I can decide my next move, the double doors open. Haley peeks her head out.

"What are you waiting for?" She asks, then spies the bags in my hands. "Oh, Harris! You'll spoil them! Come on in."

Okay, perhaps I'm mistaken.

I breathe a sigh of relief. Or is it disappointment? Do not even go there, Harris Steele. I shake my head and follow Haley inside.

"Uncle Harris!" A chorus shouts my name.

Lilias, Leith, and Lewis rush towards me as fast as their little legs can carry them. At eighteen months, they've got walking down pat. They raise their arms for me to pick them up.

I put the bags down and scoop all three into a bear hug.

Sloppy kisses cover my face as chubby hands wave around. Laughter bubbles up, and my day just got better.

When I put them down, I crouch amongst them and show them their new toys. While they clamber about, dropping to all fours to get at their gifts, I rise and glance around for the five-month-old twins—Stirling and Struan.

Lachlan stands with them cradled in the crook of each arm.

I grin and make my way towards them. But I hesitate at the weird expression on his face. He flicks his gaze between me and Haley, who's still behind me. I look over my shoulder, and she plasters on a wide smile. When I turn back to Lachlan, he averts his gaze.

"Okay, clue me in. What's got you all awkward, Little Lord Fauntleroy?" I ask as I cross my arms over my chest.

That twin tingling peaks again.

I narrow my eyes at Haley as she steps around me to stand next to her husband. She drags her finger along the bridge of her nose as though pushing her glasses up. A tell she has when she's nervous. Although now she wears contacts, so it's even more obvious she's hiding something.

Then it comes together.

She's here.

Fuck. *Me.*

KAT

"*O*kay, Lachlan, what happened to *bros before h—*"

"You better not dare to finish that sentence, Harris Steele!!!"

"Oh, isn't this rich coming from Haley *Benedict Arnold* Jackson!!!"

"Harris, that's enough, bro!"

I stand just on the other side of the wall as Harris, Haley, and Lachlan argue. Over me being here. This is not how I imagined us reconnecting. The last thing I want is to cause strife amongst them. They're too close. It's just not right.

I bloody fucked up. Again.

Taking a deep breath and saying a silent prayer for peace, I round the corner. And come face to face with Harris.

My heart skips a beat. The breath leaves me in a rush. A yearning so mighty tugs at my core, it cramps. I have to close my eyes to steady myself.

When I open them, he still stands with his arms folded across his chest. The biceps bulge beneath the long-sleeved t-shirt. Sweatpants can't hide his thick thighs as they flex from his wide-legged stance. Nor can I miss his impressive bulge even flaccid—in more ways than one.

But what really sets my heart and pussy aflutter is his handsome face. He's still so gorgeous—even angry. Maybe because he's so pissed it reminds me of my fantasy. Would he spank me?

I swallow thickly.

Harris must sense the lust swirling within me. A flash of equal carnal desire darkens his dove gray eyes to obsidian. They narrow as his nostrils flare and his jaw tightens. A vein raises at his temple. He's reining in his emotions, too.

In my periphery, I notice Haley with bags in her hands ushering The Trips out the front doors. Lachlan follows with their twins. They shut Harris and me in their flat. Alone.

"Listen, *Kat*—"

"Harris, I—"

We speak at the same time. Harris outraged and me plaintive. The sound of my voice softens his features. He closes his eyes and inhales deeply. As he exhales, his eyes focus on me. He gives a decisive nod.

"I presume you spoke with my twin and somehow persuaded her to set me up. If you passed her stronghold, then I might as well give you a chance to have your say," he tells me. He gestures behind me towards the lounge.

"Thank you," I whisper, then about-face on wobbly knees.

I get the distinct feeling Harris' eyes zoom in on my ass. A peek over my shoulder confirms my suspicions. I flick my gaze forward as a satisfied smile plays at the corners of my mouth.

More confident, I exaggerate the natural roll of my ass.

The silk of my Diane von Furstenberg wrap dress swishes with the movement. The belt emphasizes my narrow waist and the flare of my hips. I chose a pair of Giuseppe Zanotti stilettos since Harris loves my long legs. Especially wrapped around his hips while my heels dig into his ass as he fucks me against a wall.

The visual hardens my nipples. A glance down reveals them pressed against the soft fabric. An obvious invitation for him to suckle the sensitive buds. Oh, please.

Gracefully, I lower on a sofa, cross my legs, and gaze up at him through the fringe of my eyelashes. My heart thuds in my chest. Will he sit beside me or opt for a chair?

Harris chooses the same sofa—albeit the opposite end. He folds his hands over his lap. But not before I notice his erection running along his inner thigh. The bulbous tip is blatant against the soft material of his sweatpants.

A vision of it breaching my wet folds floats into my mind. I bite back a moan as I shift position. I wore a black lace thong. Hopefully, I won't leave a wet spot on the back of my dress…

"Well?"

Harris' voice breaks through my reverie.

I blink and stare at him.

Here we go.

"Harris, you have every right to be angry with me. I was absolutely wrong. If I had a do-over, I would speak with the Jackson family about finding Iain's journals, his signet ring, and his sketchbooks. Ask them how we should proceed as a family. Then go from there," I say.

My gaze never waivers from his. I want him to see my sincerity. Know what I say comes from my heart. I want to atone.

The next part gives me pause. I worry the belt of my

wrap dress between my fingers as I gaze down at my lap. After a deep breath, I continue.

"Part of that do-over would include meeting you organically. Allowing our connection to grow from a place of normal attraction," I say, then go on quickly. "Not that my attraction to you was—I mean *is*—not normal. The moment I saw you in the lobby of Jackson Town House, I experienced the most visceral reaction to any man I've ever met."

I pause and tilt my head to the side. Did I just hear a low growl? A possessive rumble from Harris' broad chest? Because I mentioned other men?

Oh, please let it be true!

He crosses his ankle over the opposite knee. He uses the action to avert his eyes from mine.

I scan his face anyway. But I can't decipher his sentiment. So I go on.

"My mind told me to use you as a way to enter the inner circle of your families"—his head jerks up, and he glares at me—"But my heart holds the truth. I want more from you. I need what only you give me. The security of a man who cares deeply for me, treats me as an equal, and makes me feel worthy. I want to be all things you want and need too."

I rise from my end of the sofa and sit beside him. As I take his hand between both of mine, I stare into his eyes.

"I apologize, Harris, with all my heart and soul. I pray you will forgive me. Even if you cannot give me another chance, know I love you truly," I say.

On a whim, I lean forward and slant my mouth over his full lips. One last kiss.

He stiffens at the contact.

But I refuse to miss the chance to taste him. The tip of my tongue sweeps across the seam of his lips—a sensual caress. They part. Without hesitation, I slip inside. My tongue finds his and teases it until it tangles with mine. I lean further into him.

He groans.

When he pulls me onto his lap, my hands seek his shoulders for balance. As he deepens our kiss, the fingertips of one hand dig into my butt cheek while the other clasps the back of my neck. He angles my head just so as he takes control.

The air whooshes from my lungs. The passion he shows leaves me breathless. But I don't stop kissing him.

My moans mingle with his groans as we seek to slake the hunger built over weeks of being without the other. The scent of his cologne mixed with the pheromones of this virile Alpha male drive me wild. My fingers dive into the longer strands of his hair. I grind my pussy lips on his thick cock as it tents his sweatpants.

Oh my God, Harris feels so bloody good!

I hump him like a teenager in the back of her boyfriend's car. Without a doubt, he'll have a wet spot on the front of his sweats. Do I care? Hell no!

A strangled cry pours from my mouth when the tip of his finger skims my pussy lips while the heel of his hand presses against my clit. I jerk in his arms. Head thrown back, eyes squeezed shut, the first non-self-induced orgasm in weeks rips through my aching core. My body convulses.

"My turn."

Harris' gruff voice filters through the haze of my carnal bliss. He slides me to my knees on the floor.

I stare up at him from between his thighs. His hooded gaze demands I give him his release, too. With pleasure.

Eagerly, my hands reach for the drawstring of his sweatpants. I skim my fingertips up and over his massive erection, still pushing into the soft cotton. His dick jumps at my touch. The control I have over him makes me smirk.

I tug at the bow to reveal my present. His length makes it necessary for him to lift his hips so I can lower the sweatpants past his erection. The material bunches at his knees. I duck beneath it to get closer to my prize.

Our eyes lock.

Without breaking the connection, both of my hands fist around his dick from the base to mid shaft. He's so large even stacked my hands don't reach his mushroom head. I save my mouth for that tasty morsel. I lap the bead of pre-cum, then swirl the tip of my tongue around the head. The flat of my tongue meets the top of my hand and licks up to the slit. I squeeze first one hand, then the other in an alternating rhythm.

"Fuuuck…" Harris groans. His hips circle and pump up. The control I thought I had ends with his hands buried in my hair. He guides my movements to the pace he prefers. "Take it. Take it all…"

My palms land on his muscular thighs. I open my throat and hum.

"FUUUCK!!!" Harris roars as he pulls my head down until my nose rests on his groin. My gag makes him groan.

His quads flex beneath my fingers as he gears up to fuck my throat. Deep and rough.

I take breaths through my nose when he allows me, as his tip rests just inside my mouth. Repeatedly, his hips snap, and I take his massive cock down my throat. My jaw hurts from the stretch. But I take it, all of it, as he commands. Happily.

"Just like that…" Harris grunts as his pace increases.

His thick girth swells and pulsates. An explosion of hot,

creamy semen pours down my throat, straight into my belly. I hum in satisfaction. He roars in release.

When his grip loosens in my hair, I sit back on my haunches. His dick pops from my mouth. I marvel at how it's still hard. It's the most beautiful dick I've ever seen. And the only one I want to know for the rest of my life. At least that's my hope.

I dab at the corners of my mouth and lick the remnants of his cum off my finger. I remember he told me *no drop wasted of your cream, Kitty Kat.* Will we share more passionate moments? Or was this a last hurrah?

Shyly, I gaze at Harris through my eyelashes.

He stares at me. Then he scoops me from the floor and places me on the sofa next to him. Not his lap, but not the door either. Quickly, he fixes his clothes. He swipes his palm over his face as he blows out a breath. His head falls back against the pillow.

Confidence gone, my nerves return. I adjust the belt on my dress and smooth the material. Anything to distract me from his silence.

Harris' mobile rings. He reaches into his pocket and smirks when he reads the screen.

"Yes, Haley?" He asks dryly. Instead of words, he answers with mmhmms, nothing I can use to figure out what they speak about. He flicks his gaze at me, then ends the call.

"Listen, Kat," he starts. My heart sinks. "I need some time to think things through. I don't want to rush into anything like before."

He stands up and glances at the door.

Oh, so here it comes.

I want to shout: You didn't need time to think before you shoved your dick down my throat. Didn't hesitate then! Did you, Harris Steele?!

But I don't.

I got mine. He got his. We're even.

Besides, if I open my mouth, the tears will fall. Instead, I square my shoulders and lift my chin high. I give him a nod and move to the front doors.

Once again, he walks behind me. This time, I ignore the sensation of his eyes on my ass. A lass has to maintain a level of pride, you know.

He opens the double doors and steps back for me to exit ahead of him. His hand reaches around me to land on the plate to call for the elevator.

My eyes close as I inhale his scent one last time. It stays with me as I step onto the elevator. Our eyes meet until the doors close. I sag against the wall. My shaking hand covers my swollen lips. I will not allow one tear to fall until I'm safely hidden in the back seat of a cab.

I hold back tears as I hold my head high, walking through the posh lobby of The STEELE Tower. Not a glance left or right. I maintain direct focus on the front doors. A nod in response to the doorman's query to confirm I need a taxi almost causes a single droplet to slip from my eye. I tilt my head back and suck in a breath through my nose.

To avoid risking another slip, I dive into the back of a yellow cab with as much dignity as I can muster, given the level of hurt and embarrassment. The professional doorman utters not a word as he closes the door behind me. A rap on the roof signals the driver to pull away from the curb. And for the tears to fall freely.

By the time I arrive at my flat, tears drench my puffy face. I cry, not just for Harris' reaction—or lack thereof. But for all my pent-up frustration and the pain I caused others. When could I just catch a bloody break already???

The doorman helps me from the taxi. The greeting on his lips falters when he notices my distress. He asks if I need any assistance. Then quickly reaches for the front door when I shake my head a little too vigorously. He nods as I pass to enter the magnificent two-story lobby.

Another fabulous New York City property—One Fifth Avenue. The landmark prewar co-op a block north of Washington Square Park on the Gold Coast of Greenwich Village. With towers and multi-tiers as it reaches for the sky, the twenty-seven-story building rises above the nearby brownstones. Michael would appreciate its Art Deco design with bricks of varying colors to create depth. The thought brings a brief smile to my lips. I swipe an errant tear and avert my gaze from the concierge.

Once in an elevator, I press the button for the private tower floor on twenty-four. I refuse to glance in the mirror, certain my makeup has me resembling a raccoon. Not to mention my smeared lipstick…

I step out into the entry and unlock the double doors.

As always, the sight before me catches my breath. The incredible 360-degree views captivate me, especially at night. The lights of the Freedom Tower to the south, the ever-changing colors of the Empire State building to the south, New Jersey west of the Hudson River, and beyond the East River. All beckon to me on the other side of large picture windows.

Whenever I walk in, I also thank my lucky stars for my new friend, Vivian Murphy. Because of her largesse, I get to live in her luxury five-bedroom full-floor penthouse. We met my first day at work, and we hit it off immediately. She's the Marketing Director and was the last executive I met with before lunch. She took me to a cute cafe around the corner from the offices.

After I told Vivian I was staying in an Airbnb until I decided which neighborhood to live in—not to mention which I could afford—she offered to let me room with her. The spacious penthouse is where she grew up. Her parents moved to a villa in Tuscany when her father retired. Her older brothers moved out years before. As the baby of the family and the only girl, her parents gave the multimillion-dollar residence to her. Talk about lucky…

I peek to my right to check if Vivian is in her suite. She had a date earlier. The closed doors make me glad I won't have to face her. But bummed I don't have anyone to talk to about the night's fiasco or anything. With a sigh, I turn the other way to head for my bedroom on the other end of the flat.

As I round the kitchen, Vivian sits at the island with a glass of red wine and popcorn. She glances up. Her expression is as mournful as mine. No smile on her gorgeous ebony face. Only sadness in the pools of her toffee brown eyes.

"Awful night for you, too, huh?" Vivian asks. When I nod, she rises from the chair and fills another glass with wine. "Here, let's finish the bottle while we commiserate."

I take a healthy gulp of the wine. Its delicious flavor washes over my palate as its potency loosens my tongue. I confess everything.

Vivian sits silently until I finish with Harris escorting me to the elevator. As she watches me, I fear I made a mistake. Big mouth!

Then she nods thoughtfully and gulps the last of her wine. Without a word, she leaves the kitchen. I sit, nibbling my lower lip. Curses fill my head. She's going to kick me out. Damn!

"Time for the stronger stuff."

I jolt and spin around to find her holding a bottle of tequila.

"Margaritas and nachos coming up!" She says with a wink. "My lousy date doesn't compare to your story, Kat. So let's just skip it and get drunk. Deal?"

Tears of joy pour from my eyes. Vivian doesn't hate me or judge me.

"Deal!" I exclaim as I jump from the chair and embrace my friend.

Later in bed, I remind myself of my vow.

Smiogaid suas, nighean, Kat Jackson! You *will* get your man back. Like the most complicated piece of script in technology, I'll decode Harris Steele. All while I give him time.

KAT

"*Listen, Kat, I need some time to think things through. I don't want to rush into anything like before.*"

Harris' words haunt me despite a full month's passing. My heart still aches as though he only just gave me the brush-off after he gave me the most incredible orgasm. And I paid him back in kind. At least I thought so. Enough to make him want me, not toss me aside. Or rather, out the door unceremoniously.

I stuck to my guns and didn't contact him in any way. Vivian reassured me it's best for him to have time to think of what happened between us and to want more. It's tough, but I keep busy.

Today, Viv and I have our Pilates duet session. Twice a week we come to the airy, sun-filled studio off Union Square. Viv swears by Mr. Pilates—as she refers to him. She's been a devotee since her teens when her mother introduced the fitness practice to her.

As Viv quoted Joseph Pilates, "Change happens through movement and movement heals."

After a few sessions, I must admit I feel much better. And the resulting strength to my core and uplift to my butt makes me better exponentially. So even though I'd rather have soreness from a bout in the bed with Harris, I thank you, Mr. Pilates!

I snicker to myself.

Viv shifts on her reformer to look at me questioningly.

I shake my head and grin like the Cheshire Cat. But the rosy blush on my alabaster cheeks gives me away. She snorts, knowing my thoughts focus on Harris. What else is new?

"Hi, Vivian and Kat! How are your bodies feeling this morning? Anything happened since your last session?"

I smile at Gina, our Pilates teacher. She's a bubbly twentysomething like us who's been teaching classical Pilates for ten years. She moves with the fluidity and strength of a dancer as she walks towards the reformers where our class will take place. Gina's long and lithe body speaks to her years of training and encourages me through The Hundred —or The Tortuous, as I call the exercise!

"Hi, Gina! Feeling great! We ran here, so I'm ready to go," Vivian responds with a thumbs-up. Ever the fitness enthusiast, she lives for heart-pumping activities. "What's the plan for today?"

Even though Viv is at the advance level, she does our duets at my beginner's order. She tells me it's just as vigorous since it makes her refocus on the basics. She uses her third weekly session as a private during which she works at her higher level.

I'm thankful for her companionship.

Gina grins and puts us through our paces from the sequence on the reformer to exercises on the chair. If The Hundred gets me, Going Up Front on the chair freaks me out. It takes total concentration and the use of the entire core to maintain balance. Add in the height changes, and it's a killer exercise. But I love it!

It spares me no time to think of Harris Steele.

Once our session ends, Vivian and I take showers and head out for our favorite post-Pilates brunch spot. It's a cute cafe known for its power smoothies located between Union Square East and Irving Place. We give our orders of smoothie shots and açaí bowls to the server who's as buff as the diners. Under other circumstances, his hazel eyes and square chin would make me swoon. But no one compares to Harris Steele.

And just like that, he's back in my mind…

I shake my head to clear it and tune in to Vivian.

"So, this guy I have a date with has a friend," she starts, then raises her hands when my eyebrows furrow. "Hear me out, Kat. I know you're still into Harris. But there's no harm in a bit of a distraction. Keep your flirtation skills sharp."

I tilt my head to the side and purse my lips.

Viv giggles.

"*Anyway*. My date asked if I knew someone who would like to make it a double. What do you think?" She asks with pleading brown eyes.

I try to keep the stern look but soon relent.

"Okay, fine! I'll go. When is it?" I respond.

She whoops and shimmies in the booth.

"Excellent! I'll shoot him a text now," she says, then continues as her fingers fly across the screen of her mobile. "It's tomorrow night. Dinner at this new restaurant. For the opening. Should be fun! Let's go shopping after we eat. No sense in wearing something old for someone new."

She glances up and winks.

I giggle and drink the smoothie shot the server placed before me.

Why the bloody hell not?

* * *

"That color looks great on you. It's a striking combination with your lovely hair."

I stare up into the handsome face of my blind date. And even a blind person could see his masculine beauty. Well over six feet tall, chin length coal black hair, aquamarine blue eyes, muscular physique, Solomon is beyond swoon worthy. Even I can't ignore his magnetism.

Dammit to hell, Viv!

She and I just arrived at the bar of the new snazzy eatery in the Meatpacking District. The line was so dense, I didn't have time to read the name. The event organizers ushered us in after they checked our names off the list on their clipboards.

As we walked through the glass-plate doors, we made our way through other guests to the gleaming mahogany bar. A wall of glass with colorful bottles glittering beneath the strategically placed pot lights rises behind it. Bartenders shake and serve drinks to the well-heeled crowd gathered.

Vivian nudged me towards two just as impeccably dressed men.

"That's Brent with the blond hair," she whispered and giggled. "His friend is pretty good looking, too. Worth it now, huh?"

Now, as Solomon pins me with his electric gaze, I gape awestruck. I have to agree with Viv.

He smiles at my speechlessness. Not arrogant. Confident.

"Thank you," I squeak, then cough to hide my nerves.

"We have time for a drink before we sit. What would you like?" Solomon asks, as he signals the bartender.

I ask for a Manhattan. Why not go with the classic cocktail in the City it's named after?

He graces me with a devastating smile before he tells the bartender.

I try not to melt. Okay, I do. Just a tiny bit.

"Here you go," Solomon says as he hands the drink to me. His fingertips brush mine, and I jerk. He tightens his grip on the glass. "Whoa there."

"Must have been a shock. You know the ones you get from sliding around on carpet in socks. It happened to me all the time as a lass," I babble.

He smirks as he stares pointedly at the hardwood floor bare of carpet and raises his glass to mine.

"Here's to more electrical currents between us," he toasts.

Busted, I can't help but to giggle and shake my head before I take a sip.

"Tell me, what else did you get up to as a wee lass, Kat?" he says.

"Only if you promise to tell me some of your childhood hijinks," I respond with a grin.

Solomon holds up his pinky finger, and we swear on it as laughter flows between us easily.

As we trade stories, Brent leans over to let us know it's time to move to our table. Solomon helps me from the high chair. Again, a zing courses through me as his palm settles on my lower back. The possessive move reminds me of Harris.

I close my eyes as we wait for the hostess.

Get it together, Kat Jackson. Harris is undoubtedly not pining over you.

Pressure on my back returns me to the restaurant. I push the thought of Harris aside. This night I want to relax and enjoy myself with my friend and our dates. Besides, I haven't heard from Harris Steele in a month.

From beneath my eyelashes, I glance up at Solomon and smile. His face lights up as his fingers stroke my lower back.

I'm glad Viv convinced me to buy the red crepe midi dress. The high neckline and pleated flared sleeves give it a chic look. While the v-cut back with a gold zipper to the split at the hem adds a touch of sexy. Paired with flesh-tone stilettos, my legs appear to go on for miles.

Solomon's touch skims along the zipper enticingly.

Hmmm.

We follow Viv and Brent to a table in the center of the room. Other diners watch as we pass. The women assess us. They take in my dress and Viv's black stretch-jersey mini dress she wears with Azzedine Alaia laser-cut knee-length boots. Then their gazes shift to our dates. Some stare openly while others peer discreetly. Admiration gleams in their eyes.

I straighten my spine. One thing I learned over the past few months, I'm just as worthy as these hoity-toity women. A description Payton loves to label me. With a grimace, I push my contentious brother from my mind, too.

"This place is fantastic!" Vivian exclaims with wide eyes. "How did you score an invitation, Brent?"

He sits taller in his chair and smooths his suit jacket, pleased by her comment.

I hide my smirk behind my glass of water. Vivian excels at the art of flirting.

"The chef is a buddy of mine. We met during a parachuting excursion in the Himalayas years ago," Brent responds, as he adjusts his tie.

"Ooh! Parachuting? In the Himalayas? Do tell us more, Brent!" Vivian says as she places her hand on his biceps.

From the sparkle in her eyes, I know she's truly interested in his action-adventure side. In fact, it sounds incredible. I listen equally fascinated.

Not to be outdone, Solomon shares tales of his cycling on challenging terrains including mountain ranges around the world.

Throughout the meal, Viv and I listen to the two men. Our comments encourage them to reveal more about themselves. I don't mind since I prefer to keep private about my life until I get to know a guy better, anyway.

As the busser clears the table, Brent grins and stands with his hand outstretched to someone behind me.

"Hey, man! Dinner was superb. Congratulations on another fantastic restaurant. Not to mention scoring an invitation gave me cool points with our dates," he says. "Let me introduce you to Vivian Murphy and her friend Kat—"

"*Jackson*. Well, well, well. Nice to see you out and about in your new city… cousin."

Half turned in my chair to thank the chef, the smile on my face falls as my mouth drops open. Heat blasts my cheeks as I turn around completely.

Lucien Jackson owns this restaurant?!

"No kidding! Your cousin? And I thought I had the in," Brent chuckles as he claps Lucien on the shoulder.

Vivian connects the name to my sorry story. She recovers quicker than I do and jumps into the conversation.

"Lucien Jackson, so nice to meet *The Sexy Chef* at last. I'm a huge fan of your creations and of your show. Congratulations and here's to much more success for you!" She says as she tilts her wineglass at him. "And Brent, darling, you made it all happen. Cheers!"

"Absolutely!"

"Cin-cin!"

With ease, she defuses the situation and gives me time to pick my jaw off my lap. But unsure of how I should greet Lucien since I haven't seen him in months, I raise my wine glass and offer a slight a smile.

"*Slàinte Mhath*, Lucien" I offer to his *good health*.

He cocks an eyebrow as he stares at me just shy of a beat too long. Solomon and Brent don't notice as they sip their wine. As Vivian chats the guys up, she flicks her gaze between Lucien and me discreetly. But his chilly expression hits me directly to my chest like a fist. I wince and glance away.

Lucien leans down and double kisses my cheeks.

"Thank you," he says, then gazes at the others. "Everyone. Now, if you will excuse me."

He throws another meaningful stare at me before he pivots on his heels and strides away.

The breath I didn't realize I was holding slips from my mouth on a long sigh of relief. I gulp the rest of my wine and set the empty glass on the table.

My mind reels. Will he tell Harris? And mention me being on a *date*? What does Lucien think of me? Should I reach out to him? Try to explain?

Bloody hell…

The appearance of the server interrupts my brooding. He places the decadent Millionaire's Shortbread before each of us. The dessert made legendary by Mary Queen of Scots. Even its decadent layers of chewy caramel and thick chocolate on a buttery shortbread crust can't drag me from the depths of my funk.

"Mmm, as delicious as this seems, I must beg off. Kat and I have an early morning. Do you mind if we say good night?" Vivian comes to my rescue again.

The guys cave to her charming smile. Her beauty has Brent kissing her hand as he nods and asks her to do him the honor of dinner again.

She giggles and agrees.

Solomon smiles at me.

"I'd love to see you again too, Kat. Perhaps drinks and dinner tomorrow?" he says. "May I have your phone number?"

"Of course, that would be splendid, Solomon. Tomorrow it is," I respond, then recite my number as he enters it into his mobile.

As we make our way to the restaurant's entrance, the hairs on the back of my neck rise. I glance over my shoulder. Despite being surrounded by adoring women and some men at the bar, Lucien watches me intently.

I smile awkwardly.

He tilts his chin down with a brief smile in acknowledgement.

Well, at least he didn't throw me out or see me to the door. It's a start.

Yet I give a silent prayer Lucien doesn't ruin any chance I have with Harris.

HARRIS

The image of that redheaded Siren's luscious ass rolling and her hips swaying in that sinful dress remains forefront in my mind. Even after a month.

Her tight, greedy pussy squeezed my fingers like a vise. When she went off like a rocket, I swear I wanted to bury my aching cock balls deep in her wet heat.

But I wasn't that far gone. Hell nah! I didn't have a condom. No way would I fuck her bareback. I won't risk getting her pregnant for damn sure. Not just that Siren, but any woman.

I have a gazillion nieces and nephews. No need for me to jump on board the Daddy Train any time soon. I just got screwed with my first actual relationship—albeit a brief one. So, count me out. Not this player!

But I digress…

Four weeks, and that redheaded Siren emblazoned herself right back in my mind. I had to suppress the urge to hold her close to my heaving chest after she blew me—a damn satisfying job, I must say. She opened up to me, and I fucked her throat like I would have her pussy. Hot, wet, tight. Deep. Fuuuck!

Nothing and no one can distract my thoughts. I can't keep her out of my mind or my fantasies. I must've increased the muscles in my left forearm from the daily strenuous workouts I put it through. If I beat my cock one more time to the vision of her in the enthralling throes of ecstasy, it'll fall right the fuck off! Then I'd be dickless. Maybe that's not such a bad idea where she's concerned. Can't fuck her if I no longer have my jackhammer.

I spent plenty of time with my twin and brothers since they were all in the City for January. The time all of us work from STEELE International's global headquarters to set the new year's agendas. But now Haley flew to Aberdeen, Roger left for Paris, and Malcolm moved back to Southampton Village. I'll still get a chance to hang out with him and Baz since they work here.

However, Valentine's Day happens just over a week from now. All of them have plans with their boos, so I'm ass out. Again. Even Laurent ditched me. Not that I blame them one bit. I wouldn't say *hoes*, rather their loves take precedence over this brother.

Which brings me back to she who shall not be named.

Did that redheaded Siren really dig her claws under my skin enough for a trip back down that relationship road? Or do I just fuck her out of my system for good?

I ponder those questions as I sit in my kitchen eating an omelet and home fries from Sarabeth's on Central Park South for breakfast. The gourmet chef's dream kitchen Lucien designed serves the purpose of heating up my takeout meals. The only appliance besides the microwave— or the oven if I'm feeling adventurous—that gets use is the Vitamix. I blend my protein smoothies with it every day.

Just like the rest of my full-floor penthouse, the kitchen is spacious, the size of a New York City two-bedroom apartment easily. With enough room for the six-seater banquette I sit at to eat. The sheer size of my residence reminds me of how very alone I am. No woman other than my female relatives has been here.

For a moment, I envision that redheaded Siren puttering about the kitchen…

The delicious aroma of a full Scottish breakfast wafts through the air as I return from my personal training session with Borya. I walk through the penthouse I share with My Kitty Kat drawn by the scent to the kitchen.

She stands at the stove butt naked except for a frilly apron tied around her narrow waist and sky-high stilettos. Her glorious Titian hair piled atop her head in a messy bun. One silky tendril snakes down her back to curl around her butt cheek.

I sneak up behind her and twirl the wayward strand around my finger, then tug it. She yelps in surprise, then moans as my mouth descends on her parted lips. She tastes like the bacon she's nibbling on. I eat her up.

She grinds her bare ass against my cock tenting my shorts. Her soft cries spur me on.

I lift her onto the oversized island. She gasps into my mouth as the cool marble touches her warm pussy lips. I still her squirming with a quick succession of spanks. She moans for more.

Naughty Girl.

My hands grip her hips to pull her to the edge of the island. Fingers flex to secure the hold. The thought of my marks on her alabaster skin hardens my cock to steel. Mine!

"Lose the apron," I command.

Hurriedly, she pulls the strings and tosses the hindrance

to the floor. Her emerald green eyes glitter as she faces me again.

I press my lips to hers, then trail open-mouthed kisses along her jaw and down her neck to the mounds of her DDs. I suck as much of one into my mouth as possible. More than a mouthful, I stuff my face. My tongue swirls around until it reaches her rosy pink pebbled nipple. I suck it until she climaxes. A repeat to the other tit, and she begs me to fuck her.

But first, I need my fill of her cream.

I devour her pussy like a starved man. Legs thrown over my shoulders, ass cupped in my hands. She gushes, and I swallow all she gives to me. I wipe from my chin to my nose along her trembling inner thighs. A soft kiss to her swollen clit makes her wail.

With a snap of my hips, I bury my rod within the soaked depths of her core.

A strangled cry pours from her slack mouth.

I cover it with mine as I piston in and out of her tight pussy. Hungrily, it sucks me in each time I thrust forward. When she tightens her inner walls, a blinding light flashes before my eyes. I grunt.

"So good, Kitty Kat," I groan. "Cum for me one more time."

She digs her fingernails into my back and squeezes her ass cheeks. Her hips raise and match each of my brutal thrusts. Her pussy quivers along my length. She bites my shoulder as she screams my name.

I'm a goner.

Fire licks down my spine and up my legs. It meets at my lower back and shoots into my heavy balls as they swing like a pendulum. The force makes them draw up.

I band one arm around her waist and grip the edge of the

island with my other hand to keep from crashing to the floor. I widen my stance and use my thighs and ass to propel up and forward. Rocking on my toes, I drill into her pussy.

The breath gets sucked from me when I blow a torrent of seed deep into her womb.

I fall across her torso, pushing her flat onto the island's surface as my legs give out. Our sweat-slick skin slides on the smooth marble. Its coolness does nothing to lessen the heat between us.

The frenetic beat of her heart matches mine. I bury my face in her neck as I try to catch my breath. She whispers words of love as her hands stroke my back. She soothes me.

Once I can stand, I lift her from the island and carry her to our bedroom as I call for the home tech system to fill the sunken tub. I set her on the white terrycloth pouf and strip out of my workout gear. Our eyes remain locked. Emerald fire lights in hers at the sight of my nakedness. I smirk.

"Behave, naughty lass," I admonish as I lift her and step down into the tub.

"But you like me naughty. Don't you, my love?" She purrs as she licks my cheek.

I chuckle and nod.

"That I do, Kitty Kat. That I do," I respond.

With a shake of my head, I glance down at the cold omelet and home fries. They're defiantly not as appealing as my fantasy breakfast. I roll my eyes and dump the food in the trash.

Mind made up, I snatch my mobile from the empty island and place the call.

KAT

"Good evening, Ms. Jackson. Mr. Solomon Givens arrived for you. Shall I send him to your floor?"

"Good evening. Kindly let him know I will meet him in the lobby in five minutes. Thank you," I respond to the concierge.

My breathing speeds up as I replace the intercom handset.

As promised, Solomon and I have plans for our second date tonight. This time without Viv and Brent. It's not the idea of being alone with Solomon that has my pulse skittering. Rather, the fact I'm attracted to him.

The way he listened intently to my more pleasant childhood stories and laughed with me eased into light touches and promise-filled aquamarine blue eyes makes him almost impossible to resist. Not only ridiculously handsome, but intelligent and funny, too. Solomon Givens is the total package who makes any woman want him. And I'm no exception.

Except…

401

The comparison to Harris happened all during the blind date.

Soulful dove gray eyes light up when he laughs.

His quick wit and easy banter.

The possessive and sensual touches of his sizable hands on my ass or as he strokes my cheek.

How he slipped past my defenses and made me love him.

Alas, that was then, and this is now. As much as I want to give him time, I'm not foolish enough to believe he's gone without the company of other women. He's virile—oh, so virile—and any woman wants him, too.

Does the thought of Harris with another twist my gut? Absolutely.

Do I blame him? Sadly, no.

I brought the loss of my lover on myself by being deceitful.

The only upside is our last interaction. He couldn't resist me no more than I could him. His body responded to mine just as fiercely as mine did to his carnal demands. The proof of his desire was apparent. Just the memory sets me ablaze again.

However, I will no longer hide in my room and cry myself to sleep. I'll go on another date with Solomon. But despite my attraction to him, I can't give more since Harris has my heart and my soul. I'll make it clear to Solomon tonight I'm not ready for a relationship.

With a wistful sigh, I check my reflection in the mirror. Satisfied my LBD, hair in a chignon, and natural makeup give off classic chic and not sexy kitten, I grab my coat and my purse. During the ride down on the lift, I think of how I'll let Solomon know my intentions. My hope is he'll understand. It's not as though he won't have trouble finding a woman who can give him more.

The doors ping open, and I step out into the lobby. As I approach a sitting area, my prediction proves true. A statuesque blonde in yoga pants that make her legs go on forever stands a bit too close to Solomon. She stares up at him, laughing about something. The shrill sound grates my nerves. But like I said, no loss for him if we don't date...

"Hi, Solomon," I say from behind him.

The woman flicks her gaze at me. Her hazel eyes rake over me from the crown of my head to the tip of my slingbacks. She all but snarls at the interruption.

I grin.

"Oh hi, Kat! You look lovely," Solomon says, then leans down to kiss my cheek.

The blonde purses her lips. But she doesn't move.

"Thank you. And you're as dashing as ever," I respond, smoothing the lapel of his cashmere overcoat and turn to the woman. "Hello."

She blinks in surprise I would address her. A spluttered response is all she can manage.

Solomon, however, doesn't hesitate.

"Kat, this is your neighbor," he starts, then turns to her. "I'm so sorry. Your name again?"

A flash of irritation skims across her pretty face. Recovering quickly, she extends her hand to me.

"Blanche Reeves," she says.

My grin broadens as I shake her hand and respond, "Kat Jackson. How nice to meet you."

Solomon glances between us, then nods.

"Right. Well, it was nice to meet you, Blanche. If you will excuse us," he says as he places a hand on my lower back.

She nods in return as her eyes shift to his possessive move.

"Yes, well, enjoy your evening," Blanche Reeves says,

then slips around us to head for the elevators. She glances over her shoulder. A wistful expression replaces the irritation.

"Shall we?"

Solomon's words draw me back to him. I nod, and he guides me to the front doors, even as I hold back a giggle. Poor Blanche. If Solomon wants, I'll leave his number for her with the concierge.

A sleek navy blue Mercedes-Benz sits at the curb. The driver opens the back door when Solomon gestures towards the sedan.

"I hope you like Italian. I was able to—as Brent says— score a reservation at Carbone on Thompson Street. It's one of the hardest restaurants to get into. Not that I'm trying to one up my buddy," Solomon says with an easy laugh.

His eyes twinkle in the low light of the backseat. The glow of a streetlamp filters through the tinted window to illuminate his face. Laugh lines crinkle about his eyes as the corners of his full lips curl up.

Damn, he's gorgeous!

Good luck to you, Blanche Reeves, and to all the other women who'll have a chance with Solomon.

"Sounds delicious and well done! No pun intended," I respond with a grin.

He chuckles.

At the restaurant, we pass under the neon lights to enter a cozy dining area. A wooden ceiling, brick walls, and colorful tiled floor bring warmth from the cold of February. The host sits us amongst recognizable celebrities and models. We have more than a delicious meal of Dover Piccata and Lobster Fra Diavolo. During dessert and coffee, I recite the no relationship speech.

Solomon listens with an expression I can't decipher.

I tug the corner of my lip between my teeth as I wait for his response.

He reaches over and places his thumb beside my lip. Gently, he frees it with his thumb, then rubs the pad across my lower lip. His eyes study my face.

With a sigh, he sits back.

"Whomever stole your heart is one lucky son of a bitch. I hope he realizes how special you are. Even in the short time we've known each other, I can tell you're a gem, Kat Jackson. I'll bow out. But know if he fucks up again, I'm here for you," Solomon says.

I lower my eyes from his intense gaze as my cheeks heat. Little does he know it's all *my* fault.

"Huh! Look who's here."

My head snaps up.

Laurent stands above me. He cocks his eyebrow as his head tilts. Bottle green eyes bore into the depths of my soul. He flicks his gaze at Solomon.

"Laurent Jackson. And you are, chap?" He asks with his hand extended.

Solomon glances at me, then stands. He grips Laurent's hand and responds, "Solomon Givens. I take it you're a relative of Kat's?"

Laurent gives a mirthless chuckle. His eyes dart back to me.

My face flushes crimson. My hands twist in my lap.

Not again! Bloody hell…

"You can say that, Solomon Givens. Kat and I are *cousins*," Laurent responds. He turns back to me. "You're doing well. New city. New man. Not bad—"

"Laurent, *Mi Amor*, I'm hungry."

So taken aback by Laurent's unexpected presence and stinging words, I didn't notice Yessenia behind him.

However, her light brown eyes avoid mine. But she slides her hand around Laurent's biceps. The gesture encourages him to move away. After he throws a final scowl at me.

Thankfully, the server appears.

Solomon takes one look at my distraught face and asks for the check as he gives her his Black American Express credit card. We wait in silence for her to return.

Inside the car, I press myself against the door to put as much space as possible between Solomon and me. I'm beyond embarrassed. He must regret the kind words he told me. Evidently so since he makes zero effort to speak with me. We sit in a tense silence as I watch the streets of Manhattan slip past us.

When we arrive at my building, I hasten from the Mercedes-Benz sedan as soon as my doorman opens it. Solomon follows. At the lift, I take a deep breath and turn to him.

"Thank you for a wonderful evening, Solomon. I'm so sorry it ended on a low note. I hope you'll forgive—"

He shakes his head. Coal black hair brushes his sculpted cheekbones.

"Everyone makes mistakes, Kat. Big or small. It's not what you *did* that matters as much as what you *do* to fix it," Solomon says. He cocks his head to the side at the sound of my whimper. Once again, he rubs his thumb over my lips. "Don't fret, little lass. You can still count on me."

He leans down and replaces his thumb with his lush lips. Surprised, I open my mouth. He slips his tongue inside and sweeps around to engage mine. I lean into his muscular body and let his tender kiss clear away my misery. If only for a moment.

Solomon steps back first. He pulls his lips into his mouth as though still tasting me. His hooded aquamarine blue eyes bore into my emerald green orbs, widened by surprise.

"Do not forget what I told you. I'm here for you, Kat," he says, then pivots and strides away.

The tears I held at bay fall silently down my cheeks.

* * *

"WHY, good morning, lovey-dovey! How was your date last night with Solomon? Wait. Why the grim face? Did he do something wrong?"

Viv's joking tone changes to one of concern. She rises from the couch in the family room as I pass it on my way to the kitchen.

I got little sleep. Hopefully, a shot of caffeine will give me much-needed energy. Or is it too early for a pitcher of Viv's margaritas?

I shake my head as much to answer her questions as to answer my own. Get it together, Kat…

"No. But I could use a shoulder to cry on and the ear of a good friend to listen," I respond as I nod towards the kitchen. "A cup of coffee first."

Viv bounces to her feet.

"You know I'm here for you, Kat," she says as she loops her arm through mine.

A sob escapes my lips at her choice of words. They echo those of Solomon's from last night. Do I even deserve their friendship and consideration? I sigh as Viv squeezes my arm.

"We'll have a Russian coffee," she says. When I frown, she winks and adds, "A shot of vodka will do the trick."

I can't help but to giggle as she waggles her eyebrows.

"Sounds like just what I need," I say.

While Viv gets the bottle of Beluga, I start up the Breville. She had to show me how to operate the complicated espresso machine. All of its controls daunted me. Now, she calls me the resident barista.

We sit at the island. The scent of fresh coffee floats around us. I take a bite of the danish ring—Viv insisted we splurge. And I agree. What hips? Besides, Harris likes to grip them as he thrusts—AARGH!!!

"All righty then, Kat," Vivian says with an elegantly arched eyebrow raised.

My mouth opens and closes.

"I said that out loud? Didn't I?" I ask as my cheeks pinken.

She giggles and nods.

"Yeah, well, see, that's the problem!" I exclaim as I clutch my hair in both hands. "I can't stop thinking about you know who! As mouthwatering as Solomon is, I cannot get that other one out of my bloody head!"

Viv tsks and sips her coffee, ready for the tea.

I spill.

The entire evening from Blanche to Laurent, ending with Solomon's parting kiss and words tumble from my mouth. When I finish, I sit back and take a slug of my coffee. Still hot—since I brewed it to perfection—it burns my throat. As I choke, Viv pats me on the back and hands a napkin to me.

"Perhaps we should've gone straight with the vodka?" Viv queries. A grimace forms on her stunning face.

Once I recover, she goes on.

"Here's the thing, Kat. A breakup is never easy," she starts. "And when you add in family—especially as tight a bunch as the Steeles and Jacksons, from what you told me—plus the whole scandal… Well, you might as well forget it."

When I gasp and stare at her, Viv holds her hand up.

"Listen, I'm not saying forget it, forget it. Rather, it's a serious shitshow. Many people's feelings are involved. Not just yours and Harris'," she clarifies.

I stare bleakly at the island's white marble surface. The veining reminds me of those on Harris' long, thick dick. I shudder and shake my head.

"It's not insurmountable."

I hear Vivian continue.

"Just don't expect everyone to jump up and give you hugs and kisses right away. Maybe some will. Who's to say? But the most important thing to do. That is, if you truly want another go with Harris. You have to make amends with him. When his family sees he's accepted you back in his life. They will come around out of their love for him. Get it?"

She sits back and pops a piece of danish in her mouth.

I mull over her words.

What she says is absolutely on point. I can't expect to breeze back into their lives no more than I can into Harris'. At least not yet. I know I said I'd give him time. But maybe if I reach out to him—even just to say hi and ask how he's doing—he'll be receptive. A way to make amends.

I face Viv and smile.

"You're right. I'll call him and—"

My mobile rings. The vibrations make it skitter along the smooth marble.

I glance at the screen. My eyes nearly fall out of my head as I stare in shock.

"OMG!!! Harris!" Viv exclaims as she peers around me. "Kat! Answer it already! It's a sign!"

HARRIS

"*H*ello, I can't see your wrist. Would you like to play later?"

I glance up at the redhead before me as I sit at the long, reclaimed-wood-covered bar for LEVEL 4 Restaurant. Although she has a banging body, she's not *that* redheaded Siren.

Yesterday, I gave in and called her. It was either keep fantasizing about her or fucking her. I choose to fuck her out of my system.

One week.

She doesn't know my intentions. Yet.

I invited her to dinner at LEVELS New York. If she's down for it—which judging by her response to our impromptu tease and please, I'd bet a resounding yes—we'll start tonight. No point in delaying.

Intent on the upper hand, I arrived early. Now this beauty wants my attention.

"Nothing on my wrist," I respond as I lift my arm and push my suit jacket and cuff up as far as the links allow.

LEVELS New York's top priority is the safety of its members, their guests, and applicants. Management enforces strict protocols everyone must follow. From nondisclosure agreements to names not given unless provided by the person to super tight ongoing background checks and other security measures.

Another measure to avoid unwanted interactions amongst club participants is the requirement for partnered subs to wear collars given to them by their Dom; partnered Doms wear gold enamel bracelets; available subs wear red; available Doms wear white; voyeurs wear black. Those not seeking another wear nothing.

That redheaded Siren is on her way. Hence no bracelet for me tonight.

This one pouts as her eyes linger on my mouth.

"Could I entice you to choose a white bracelet to top me or black so you can watch me cum for you?" She purrs as she licks her berry-stained lips with the tip of her tongue.

I wait for my cock to stir in appreciation for her wanton behavior. But no dice.

"No," I answer, then offer her a winning smile when the corners of her mouth droop. "I'm more than positive you'll find a worthy partner tonight. Have a drink on me while you wait."

Her beautiful face glows as she names her cocktail —no pun.

After the bartender hands the glass to her, she pats me on the chest and leans in to whisper thank you. She tells me I'm a keeper before she sashays to the other end of the bar.

I watch the sway of her hips beneath the silk of her mini dress. With a sigh, I turn to face the elevators.

Past the bustling crowd of the crème de la crème of society who mingle as they sip their top-shelf drinks, I spy *that* redheaded Siren. Her Titian hair makes it easy to spot her amongst the blondes and brunettes.

When our eyes connect, emerald greens scorch my dove grays. Her alabaster cheeks deepen to crimson as her nostrils flare. With narrowed eyes, she spins on her heels and stomps towards the elevators.

Hmmm… Not quite the start to the evening I planned for us.

I hop off the leather and black metal stool and weave past the clusters of matching high-top tables. Despite the open-plan layout of the room, I get caught up by members who want the chance to speak to or play with a Steele. I smile and incline my head as a brief greeting, but rush towards the entry. I'm not here to chit chat or seduce tonight—at least not with them.

"Kat," I call out as she steps onto an elevator. I lunge forward to place my hand between the doors. "Come out of there."

They open, and I take her by the elbow. Without a word, I guide her along the path between the two areas of the bar towards the LEVEL 4 Restaurant's maître d' station.

She huffs and jerks. But I ignore her feistiness. While my cock responds as though I rolled a 7 in craps. It's a win-win situation.

The hostess welcomes me by name and sits us in a corner booth. As she leaves, she loosens the ties on the curtains. Immediately, the sounds and the view of the dining room disappear. The redheaded Siren and I cocooned in our own world. I prefer the privacy the booth provides. No one will overhear our conversation.

Her eyes dart around as she realizes we're in a close space. She sits less than an arm's distance from me on the u-shaped banquette. The scent of her alluring perfume fills the air surrounding us.

I fight to stop myself from closing my eyes and inhaling deeply. Instead, I watch her.

Eventually, her emerald green eyes reach my face. The blaze returns at my smug expression. She places her palms on the table and rises.

"Sit. Down. Kat."

She jerks in response to my sharp tone. But lowers her luscious ass back to the leather seat. She folds her arms across her chest in an attempt at defiance.

The move only serves to push her DDs higher. Their nipples poke the silk of her cream blouse. She paired it with a leather pencil skirt, fishnet stockings, and fuck-me stilettos.

The sex kitten came prepared to taunt me.

Well, let's play, Kitty Kat.

"Why did you come if you planned to run away?" I ask with a cocked eyebrow.

Her mouth gapes.

The memory of my dick widening her throat jumps to the forefront of my thoughts. It twitches in my pants. Down, big boy.

I wait for her response. Who speaks first loses and all.

"I did not plan to run away. Nor did I plan to see you eye fucking another woman after you bought her a drink, Harris!" She all but yells. Eyes flash. Cheeks heat.

Jealous? Oh, shit! The Siren doesn't want competition. Hmmm… Interesting. Point for Harris Steele.

"So your response is to rub it in by smirking?" She snarls. "Well, then I made a huge mistake coming here and will *leave*—not run away."

As before, I catch her elbow.

"Ah, ah, ah, Kat," I say as I shake my head. "You do not get to be pissed at me. After the shit you pulled, you're mistaken about who should be angry."

She flinches and her cheeks burn as though my words physically slapped her. The steam dissipates, and she sags against the back of the banquette. Her teeth tug at her bottom lip as her gaze lowers to the table in front of her.

I'm surprised by a pang of remorse. Then I clear my throat.

"Listen, Kat. I didn't invite you here to rehash the past. What you did was beyond fucked up. You've owned it. Time to move on," I say.

She gasps and raises her eyes shiny from unshed tears to me. The hopeful expression on her face makes my gut twist.

For a second, I'm tempted to not tell her my plan. Just have dinner and end it all forever. But then…

"Oh, Harris, thank you! I want so badly for us to have a positive relationship. Even if it's not a sexual one. I just want to know you don't hate me," she says. The last of her words trail off as her gaze drops back to the table.

Whoa there, little lass! Who said anything about no sex??? We're at LEVELS New York—a den for fucking, for fuck's sake.

"One, I do not hate you, Kat," I say. Her softened eyes rise to peer at me from beneath the thick fringe of her eyelashes. My gut twists again, but I plow ahead.

"Two, the relationship part of your statement directly ties to the point of me bringing you to LEVELS New York," I add, and pause to ensure I have her full attention.

She blinks as she considers the meaning of my words.

"Okay, what about it?" She asks, a tinge of pink returns to her cheeks.

I sit back and pour her then myself a glass of Jackson

Cabernet Sauvignon. Ahead of our arrival, I ordered our dinner and wine. Of course, we'll dine on exquisite meals prepared by chefs trained by Lucien. The staff left the bottle open to allow the wine time to breathe. When I hang the green tassel from the curtain tie-back hook, the server will bring the food.

Did I say privacy or what?

I lift my wineglass to my lips. My eyes never leave hers. I incline my head at her glass. The shakiness of her hand gets noted. She's nervous. Good.

After I take a healthy sip, I set the wineglass back on the table. I twirl the stem between my fingers as I watch the legs drip along the bowl of the glass. As the tension mounts, I wait for her to place her glass down.

Then I lift my gaze. Pinned, her eyes widen and her cheeks flush from pink to berry like her succulent lips.

My cock stirs.

I sit back against the banquette and adjust my dick, no longer content to remain confined. Soon, I think as I stroke its turgid length.

What this redheaded Siren does to me. She has no clue.

But I digress.

"Time has done nothing to ease my hunger for you. True to your nickname, you are a Siren. That night's brief encounter did not slake my need. I remain unsatisfied," I say.

The crimson color now infuses her chest and neck. Nipples peaked. Lips parted. Eyes blown. She watches me as she holds her breath.

Just as I thought.

I pinch the tip of my swollen cock to stop the pre-cum from dampening the leg of my trousers. Then swallow a moan when the tip of her little pink tongue flicks out as though tasting the air ripe with the scent of her arousal and my pheromones.

With my other hand, I reach into the inner pocket of my suit jacket.

"Here is a one-week guest pass to LEVELS New York. For you," I say as I slide it along the tabletop. I stop it smack dab in the middle between us.

Her hooded eyes drop to stare at the envelope. Katrina Jackson handwritten in swirly calligraphy dances across the cream parchment. She bites the corner of her lower lip.

Damn! My cock jumps beneath my palm.

Again, I wait for her to make the next move. The winner of negotiations often emerges triumphantly because they don't give away too much before the other party rejoins.

A minute passes.

Her chest rises and falls with ragged breaths.

"What does that mean for me?" She asks with her eyes glued to the invitation. Her shoulders rigid, as though bracing her hands from picking it up.

I wait until she looks at me before I respond.

"It means you and I have one week to fuck each other out of our systems."

She gasps as her eyes pop from their sockets like Roger Rabbit seeing Jessica for the first time. If I weren't so horny, I'd laugh out loud.

"Wh—What?" The redheaded Siren stammers.

I lean forward. Our noses mere inches apart. She swallows but doesn't pull away.

"You and me fucking until neither of us can sit, stand, or walk. Every. Single. Night. Starting tonight. Should you agree, that is," I respond.

Our warm breath mingles. The dark fruity and spicy essence of the wine wafts between us. Her arousal even more obvious than before my salacious explanation. I ache to savor more.

Say yes, Siren. Say yes, Siren. I chant like a mantra in my mind.

The sound of her swallow makes my lips quirk.

Almost there, little lass.

"After the week ends? Then what?" She asks breathlessly. Her eyes never leave mine. The pupils so dilated only a rim of emerald green remains.

I inch closer.

"I cannot predict the future. Can you, Kat?" I parry.

Her golden-tinged red eyelashes flutter as her eyes roll back in her head. A puff of air slips from between her lips. She inhales through her nose deeply.

Does she want a taste, too? I wonder.

Neither of us moves. Locked in position. Not daring to be the first to answer.

But I have the advantage. She owes me. And I'm rascal enough to take advantage.

Beads of sweat break out above her top lip. Just as pre-cum collects at my engorged tip.

Make the move, Siren, I command in my mind.

One minute.

Two minutes.

Three—

Her eyes fly open. She nods.

My breath rushes from me. But it's not enough.

"Words, Kat. I will have your words," I murmur, too lightheaded from holding air in my lungs.

"Y—Y—Yes, Harris," she stammers.

"Good, little lass," I say before my mouth crashes over hers.

We come together. Teeth and tongues collide. Hot breath

stokes the smoldering embers into a roaring inferno. No longer denied, it rages unabated. The flames lick along my shaft to the point of pain.

I groan into her mouth. She responds with a throaty moan of her own as her body trembles against me.

Kaaaaat, I think to myself. Fuck, I've missed this woman. She satisfies me like no other. Before or after.

But she can never know how much I need her.

I pull back and wipe my mouth with the back of my hand. I watch her face. Eyes closed, body leaning towards mine like a magnet to steel. Her eyes open languorously. Unfocused, they land on my face.

Seeing me adjust my clothes, she sits up straight and brings her fingertips to her kiss-swollen mouth. The gesture makes me want to kiss her all over again. She's fucking delectable. Better than anything Lucien can create.

Speaking of which…

I part the curtains and slip the green tassel on the tie-back hook.

The redheaded Siren needs to eat before I fuck her senseless.

"So, what do we do now?"

Oh, yeah, just what I want to hear. Belly full. Balls fuller. Ready to empty both of them with rounds of backbreaking sex. Expend calories and seed.

I reach over and take her chin between my thumb and forefinger. As I stare into her eyes, her lip trembles.

"Relax, Kat. This is not the first time we've been intimate with one another. Nothing has changed. Well, as far as what you can expect—toe-curling, mind-blowing orgasms by the dozens," I say with a smirk.

The corners of her mouth quirk up and the heaviness in her shoulders releases. Her hand reaches up to cover mine on her face.

I notice it's steadier this time. Her nerves passed.

Good.

"Okay," she whispers.

Her reaction tugs at my heart. But I remove my hand and slide from the booth. With my eyes on hers, I extend my hand to her. She doesn't hesitate. Her hand slips into mine, and I help her from the banquette.

Once she's standing wedged between me and the table, I lean down and place my lips on hers. Our bodies align. I don't hold back the press of my erection against her lower belly. Instead, I grind against her. She moans and sways against me, matching my rhythm as she rises to her toes. My cock notches at her pussy seam.

My arm bands around her waist to pull us flush. My other hand dives into her hair to tilt her head just so as I deepen our kiss. She whimpers against my mouth when I tug at the silky strands.

"Harris," she whispers as her breath catches.

"Let's go," I respond thickly.

The temptation to carry her over my shoulder through the restaurant and down in the elevator to my private suite flares within me. But I don't want her embarrassed by my caveman conduct. I'll save it for the bedroom.

I part the curtain and usher her ahead of me. Not just being a gentleman, but because I want to watch her ass roll beneath the supple leather of her skirt. Lifted by those heels, it sways with each of her steps. Long legs stressed by the black seam up the backs of each one.

A low growl pours from deep within my chest.

Captain Caveman alert!

I look neither left nor right as I follow the redheaded Siren past the other tables and out to the bar. I barely respond to the hostess as she bids us a good evening. Little does she realize just how *good* of an evening I plan to have with the Siren.

We make it to the elevators with no interruptions. Once inside, I place my keycard against the panel to select the second floor. It features twelve private suites for members to continue their pleasure apart from the BDSM levels of Peepshow and the Cellar.

I watch the Siren out the corner of my eye.

She stares up at the dial showing the floor. We've played at LEVELS London, so she's familiar with the layout. Each club mimics the other except for the point of interest or landmark visible from the Sky Lounge on Level 7.

Where London has the Tower of London, New York—located in the Meatpacking District—offers a stunning, 360-degree view of Manhattan and across the Hudson River to New Jersey's shoreline. The Siren and I won't have time to revel in the scenery. We'll be too busy fucking in my suite, on Level 2 or below ground.

Who needs panoramic views when I have the best view in the house of a naked Siren spread before me?

I chuckle as I hold the door open for her to walk into the hallway.

The foyer—sparsely decorated and dimly lit—sets the mood for carnality. The hypnotic thrumming of sensuous music piped in through hidden speakers add to the intensity and expectation of the sexual activities that happen behind the twelve closed doors. On this level, plush silk wool carpet covers the floor to mask the sounds of eager footsteps.

I place my palm at the base of the Siren's spine to guide her down the quiet, equally dim hallway to my corner suite. At the door, I place my palm on the plaque to disengage the lock. No need to fumble for keys. Lucien and Malcolm thought of every convenience. Haley and I implemented the best technology for security.

I usher the Siren to enter the suite ahead of me. Although she's seen the inside of one in London, her hooded eyes glance around at my decked-out suite compared to others. Since New York's club serves as my home base, I maintain a suite here for my personal use only.

With a fresh perspective, I study my suite through her eyes: set in the middle of the room is a massive, custom rose wood, king-size bed with four posters and a rose gold lattice canopy rings hang; ruby red silk sheets, duvet, and various sized pillows with a white cashmere blanket draped over the foot; from the rose wood tray ceiling, along with the Swarovski crystal chandelier and recessed lights, hang hooks; the walls and ceiling panels covered in red silk damask; the floor carpeted in deep ruby silk on silk; drawers of an antique armoire filled with anal plugs, clamps, cords, cuffs, vibrators, and more; a spanking bench and a Sybian saddle stand on the wall opposite the armoire; below windows treated to not allow visibility from the outside sits a chaise with rose gold rings; one door next to the armoire leads to the all white, Carrara marble bathroom that has a walk-in shower for four, an oversized soaking tub, double vanities, and a separate water closet for the bidet and toilet; behind the other door lies my dressing room filled with suits, casual wear, and footwear.

It pleases me to see the Siren awed by the suite's majesty —especially the toys. I smirk when her lust-filled gaze lingers on the Sybian saddle. Her breath quickens at the sight of the dildo standing tall in the middle of it. If I had the remote in hand, I would start it just to hear her gasp.

We'll add a ride on it to the list of erotic activities. Not tonight, though. Tonight, I have to have her fast and rough. It's been way too long since I indulged in her carnal delights.

I walk up behind her and lower my head to her ear. A warm breath makes her silky strands skim the side of her face and neck.

She shudders as her fists clench.

"Strip," I command in a throaty growl.

The gasp I ached to hear slips past her parted lips. Her entire body convulses. Hands unclench and fist again.

"Now," I add.

She mewls.

I step back and stand with my feet planted apart. My fingers pinch and stroke my hungry cock beneath my trousers.

Her eyes widen when she spins and sees my erotic actions. She swallows audibly. But her hands lift to the buttons on her blouse. At first distracted by my pulsating cock, she fumbles with the tiny buttons. She growls in frustration and nearly rips the placket apart.

I bite my lower lip to hold back a chuckle.

The Siren proves eager.

A growl of my own rumbles in my chest when the sheer mesh of her cream-colored bra reveals the curve of her DDs tipped by pebbled nipples. So hard they threaten to poke holes through the skimpy material. A delicate bow rests between the mounds. Sinful and sweet. Yum.

The vision combined with the friction caused by my fingers and the heel of my hand damn near unleashes a torrent of jizz. I close my eyes and squeeze the mushroom head to seal the slit momentarily. Once I regroup, I open my eyes narrowly. Just a peek reveals the Siren shimmying out of the tight leather pencil skirt. The blouse discarded to the floor in a heap.

Her tits bounce as the fullness of the tops spills from the demi-cup bra. They flash in and out from behind the curtain of her lustrous Titian hair. The color even more glorious amidst the ruby reds of my suite. How perfect.

She steps from the skirt pooled at her feet. One long leg

after the other frees her. She stands. A matching G-string conceals nothing of her bare mons. The slit of her pussy in plain view. Above the scrap of sheer material, a matching garter belt wraps around her narrow waist. The straps skim along her thighs to hold the tops of the black fishnet stockings in place. My mouth waters as my gaze follows the lines to the black fuck-me stilettos.

Her hands hesitate at the garter belt clips.

"Shall I continue?" She asks in a raspy voice.

"Yes. Remove everything," I respond. "I want you completely naked."

The clips in the front open, followed by those in the back. Fishnets slide down her toned thighs. Bent over, she rolls them down her legs before she slips her shoes off. Five inches shorter, she barely reaches my shoulder.

With a gleam in her emerald green eyes, she unfastens the garter belt. It dangles from her index finger, drawing my eyes to it. I watch as it drops to the floor atop her blouse. My gaze returns to her flushed face.

She pursers her lips as she cups her tits—too large for her hands, just right for mine. Her head lolls to the side when she tweaks the rosy buds of her nipples. She licks her lower lip.

I mimic the act.

The supposed sweet bow pops apart. Her ample tits bob freely, heavy from her arousal. Another tweak to her nipples and she loops her fingers into the G-string. They drop to the floor. She kicks them aside.

The Siren emerges in all of her magnificence.

I swallow thickly, then command her in a gruff voice to strip me.

She sashays forward. Eyes locked with mine. Confidence

returned, she makes quick work of divesting me of the unnecessary encumbrances to our fucking.

Her tongue skims her lips in a complete circle as she holds my turgid length in her palms. The moisture gathered reminds me it's time to bury my cock deep in her wet pussy.

I grip her hips and toss her onto the bed.

Arms and legs windmill as she flies through the air. Tits jounce on impact. Eyes widen, then narrow as she watches me stalk towards her. Mesmerized, her mouth hangs ajar. Ready to be filled.

My cock thumps against my eight pack with each step. Heavy balls swing like a pendulum.

I climb onto the bed, straight between her thighs, open in welcome. The slick of her arousal coats them. Her scent musky. She bleats when I lower my head, part the engorged, glistening lips, and blow a stream of warm air over her sensitive flesh.

The insides of her knees bind my head as her hips buck from the swipe of my tongue along her seam. She may be wet. But I need her drenched and pliant for my massive return.

My hands shift position to cup her ass from beneath her thighs to lock her in place. I sate my hunger for her cream. Licks, nips, and plunges draw multiple orgasms from her before I rise to plank above her.

The Siren lies limp. A sheen of sweat covers her skin dotted by goosebumps. The crimson flush reaches from her hairline to the tips of her darkened rosy nipples. Pupils dilated, she stares up at me in a daze. Pure carnal bliss.

I drop my mouth to a peaked nipple and suckle. Hard.

She gasps as her eyes refocus.

Exactly. Stay with me until I'm just as satisfied.

I lower to my forearms. Wedged between our bodies, my

cock presses into her soft belly. I groan against her tit when she spreads her thighs and hooks her ankles beneath my ass. She bends her knees and lifts her hips.

"Harris, please…" The Siren pants.

"Please what?" I ask. Our eyes meet over her pillowy mounds. I cock an eyebrow.

Her blush deepens.

"Please fuck me!" She cries out as she writhes in agony.

I grab a condom from the secret drawer in the headboard. Then I fist my covered cock, align it with her soaking pussy, and snap my hips. The forward surge sheaths me to the root within her core in one motion.

"Fuuuck, Harris!!!" She wails.

"Ask and you shall receive," I grit out as her pussy walls clamp around my cock.

She's so tight, there's no doubt. No other man has laid with the Siren. MINE!

The thought jars me.

What the hell, Harris?!

I push that unwanted line of thinking right out of my mind. This is for one thing and one thing only. Fuck this redheaded Siren out of my system in one week. Period. End of discussion.

Her sigh and the shift of her hips bring me back to reality.

I focus on my mission: mind-blowing sex again and again. All night long until neither of us can move a muscle.

My body responds in kind.

I withdraw to my tip, then slam back in. She slides up the bed from the force of my thrust. Her arms reach above her to grapple at the headboard with her hands.

Good idea, Siren…

Rising to my knees with her legs still hooked under my

ass, I collect her wrists, then bind them in suede-lined restraints. A total of four connect to each corner of the bed. The bit allows turning in every direction.

She tugs to determine the length. Realization not enough to wrap her arms around me, The Siren drops her head back with a huff.

I smirk, then slip from her sweet pussy and jump from the bed. I stride to the armoire and remove just what I need.

Back at the bed, I attach her ankles to the spreader bar. As I gaze down at her, I stroke my weeping cock. It's as keen as I am to plow back inside of her creamy pussy. She's ripe and oh so ready.

"Harris," the Siren whines as she tugs at her restraints and wiggles her hips. "Please, please fuck me."

I grip the backs of her thighs and flip her to lie on her belly. She squeals when I pull her up onto her knees. My hand presses between her shoulder blades and slides along her spine. Head down, ass up, and spread wide, I take a moment to appreciate the bounty before me.

Both holes clench when I spank one ass cheek, followed by the other. She moans, and I groan at the sight of my handprints blooming pink on her milky skin. A few more spanks, and I grip her hips to mount her from behind like a stallion.

She bucks and lets loose a string of curses in Scottish Gaelic.

I alternate brutal thrusts in with long, slow strokes out. Shifting angles to hit every inch of her pussy. She feels so good my head falls backwards as my eyes roll towards the heavens. Divine indeed.

Her pussy flutters along my length, coaxing my release. I hold out. Not ready to give in yet. I rise to crouch behind her and drill down while I play with her engorged clit. After

I demand three more orgasms from her quivering core, I brace myself for an epic climax.

It grabs a hold of me and doesn't let go until I blow my load in the condom with a feral roar. My legs give out, and I collapse on top of the Siren with one arm banded around her waist and the other on the mattress beside her tousled head.

Once I catch my breath—and my vision returns—I release her from the restraints and the spreader bar. I massage her limbs to soothe the sore muscles. When she curls into a ball on her side, I head to the en suite bathroom. There, I remove the condom and toss it in the basket before I clean myself.

Back in the bedroom, I take care of the Siren. She protests halfheartedly at being roused from her sex-induced slumber. But I persist. She'll thank me later for not being sticky with her juices and our sweat.

That is, until I get her dirty all over again. And I cannot wait.

KAT

"*O*MG!!! Harris! Kat! Answer it already! It's a sign!"

My mind processes Vivian's words like a hippo trudging through a vat of mud. The sight of Harris' name on the mobile screen slows every brain cell in my head. Only my eyes function.

"Hey! Snap out of it!" Vivian cries out as she snatches the mobile up and waves it inches from my face. "Don't miss his call or your chance, Kat."

That gets the synapses firing.

My muscles flex as I swipe the mobile from Viv and punch the green accept button. The mobile rises to my ear.

Heart pounding against my ribs I answer, "Hello."

A slight pause, then a gush of air followed by silence.

I pull the mobile away to glance at the screen. The call is still active. With a frown I raise it to my ear.

"Hello, Harris?" I ask.

This time, I hear him clear his throat. Relieved, I give Vivian the thumbs-up. She bobs her head, toffee eyes wide with excitement.

Her infectious grin makes me smile.

"Hello, Kat," Harris says in a gruff voice.

Did he just wake up, or is he nervous like me? I don't have much time to ponder when his next words rock my core—literally.

"Let us meet at LEVELS New York tonight at eight," he states.

I jolt as memories of us at LEVELS London jump to the forefront of my mind. The erotic images of us and of others in the throes of passion at the hedonistic sex club will be forever burned into my brain. And I loved every minute of it.

If Harris wants us to meet at the New York flagship, he must want to… play?

My nipples harden beneath my tank top as my empty pussy clenches with need. Heat spreads across my cheeks. I all but moan aloud.

"Kat?"

Harris calling my name—not in the way I want at the moment—awakens me from my daydream.

I shake my head to dislodge the sensual imagery and clear my throat.

"Aah, yes. Yes, Harris, I'll be there," I respond breathlessly.

Bloody hell, Kat, could you be any more obvious? Huge eye roll.

After he tells me he'll be at the bar of the restaurant, he ends the call.

I stare at the mobile's screen. Did that really just happen? I pinch myself to make sure I'm actually awake. The bite of pain confirms Harris did call me.

"Well? What did he say?" Vivian asks sitting on the edge of her chair.

Slowly, I bring my gaze to hers. I bite the corner of my lower lip and widen my eyes as my eyebrows raise to my hairline and my shoulders lift.

She laughs at my silly face of shock and nudges me.

"Spill it, Kat!" She demands.

"We're meeting tonight at LEVELS New York!" I shout as I leap from my chair and spin in a circle. I clutch my mobile to my chest as I giggle giddily.

Harris and I are going to have sex! Less than twelve hours from now. HOORAY!!!

I do a Scottish jig.

"Fantastic!" Viv shouts as she fist pumps the air.

I grab her hands and pull her to her feet so she can join me in my happy dance. We jump about and shimmy our hips until we collapse on the floor. Our giggles fill the air.

"Now what's LEVELS New York? Is it a new restaurant?" Viv asks.

In my excitement, I blurted out the club's name. I never told her about *that* side of my love affair with Harris. My cheeks heat again. I won't lie to my friend.

"Um… It's an exclusive members only BDSM/dance club founded by his brother Malcolm and Lucien," I answer.

Her jaw drops.

I nod and shrug.

"Holy shit, girl! Look at you! I never would have guessed Kat Jackson is into bondage and all that kinky stuff," Vivian says. She stares at me through squinty eyes. "Can your boy hook a sister up?"

We double over in laughter once again.

I CHECK the seams of my fishnet stockings in the reflective doors of the lift at LEVELS New York. Vivian helped me to pick out an outfit she says doesn't scream fuck me. Just whispers it seductively. I giggle at her description for my silk blouse, leather pencil skirt, and stilettos.

Getting in and out of the taxi didn't mess up the straight line of the seams, so I turn around just as the doors ping open.

Stepping out my gaze wanders around the space. They converted a warehouse in the Meatpacking District for the club. I admire the way they incorporated the old brick and ductwork with expensive pieces made of leather, metal, and wood. It makes the space warm, dark, and erotic.

I smile at the thought of the night ahead as I make my way towards the bar.

Then the smile melts from my face like hot wax on a sub's tit.

A woman stands between Harris' legs. Heads bent together they talk. I stare in shock as he orders a drink for her and watches as she struts away.

Rage boils in my gut and races outward to fuel my anger.

How dare Harris invite me here under false pretenses?!

He must feel the fire shooting towards him as he turns from the woman to face me. I *level him* with a glare and march to the lifts.

Damn if I just missed one. I slap the call button as hard as I would his face. Another set of doors open, and I hurry inside.

"Kat."

I jab the close button repeatedly.

Just before the doors come together completely his hand reaches in. Blasted!

"Come out of there."

I swat at his hand as he reaches for my elbow. He ignores the blows and removes me from my escape route. I don't go easy and pull away only for him to tighten his grip. He marches me to a booth in the restaurant where the hostess releases the curtains sealing Harris and me inside.

He sits there smug.

To hell with this, I think as I rise. The dominance of his command to sit makes me shiver. But I hide my reaction to him by crossing my arms with a glare.

I almost laugh when he accuses me of running away. Ha! I chose to remove myself from a vile situation. Namely him flirting with another woman knowing I would see them.

After I tell him just that, he thwarts another of my escapes.

His next accusation of me being the one out of line since I wronged him guts me. He's got me there. I slump in my seat defeated. When he says we can move on, I perk right back up and thank him profusely.

Then more than my spirit perks up. My entire body stands at full attention, more than ready for what Harris has to offer.

"Here is a one-week guest pass to LEVELS New York. For you," he says.

I stare at the fancy envelope and nibble the corner of my lower lip. I can't get enough air into my lungs and damn near pant. My fingers ache to grab the invitation and rip it open to find out more.

"What does that mean for me?" I whisper still engrossed by the offer on the table.

Harris doesn't respond. I glance up at him.

"It means you and I have one week to fuck each other out of our systems."

And boy is Harris a man of his word. After hours of *fucking,* my sore body, wrecked pussy, and blown mind—not to mention back—need time to recuperate. A groan escapes my lips swollen from his kisses and dick as I roll to my back at the sound of the shower.

I awoke as the sun's rays peek through the curtains. The light falls on the chaise to remind me we're in his play suite at LEVELS. He even blanked my memory...

Closing my eyes again, I mentally scan my body from head to toe. The delicious sensation of Harris' giant dick plundering my pussy lingers as does his wicked tongue on my nipples. The faint red marks on my wrists and ankles make my pulse quicken. Being bound and helpless puts a blush on my face and my cream gush.

Reflexively, my knees squeeze together. I whimper as a tremor runs through my core. Fingers dance across my belly and lower. Only a thought and I'm keyed up for more.

Moisture eases the glide of my finger past puffy lips. The tip of my finger brushes my clit. I cry out and arc from the tangled sheets.

"Harris..." I croak.

"Yes?"

My eyes fly open as I whip my head towards the sound of his voice. So engrossed in my fantasies, I didn't notice the water stopped in the shower or his re-entry into the bedroom.

A towel slung low on his narrow hips can't hide his ginormous dick. It grows right before my eyes. Like a puppet on a string, it lifts the white terrycloth inch by ten inches until it sticks straight out. And points towards me.

I lick my lips.

"What do you need from me, Siren?" He rumbles deep in his powerful chest.

Another groan slips from my mouth as a second finger joins the first to penetrate my slick pussy. Words prove impossible as my eyes squeeze shut in ecstasy. I yelp.

"Ah, ah, ah, naughty lass," Harris says as he yanks my wrist leaving my pussy bereft. "Only I will give you pleasure this week."

His reminder he only gave us a week should sting. But I'm too far gone to notice its harsh bite. Instead, I whimper and beg him to fuck me.

He swipes his fingertip along my seam to collect natural lube, then slips the digit inside of my needy core. Its thickness as it dips in and out of my channel makes me hiss.

"You're too sore for my finger. My cock will make it worse," Harris says as he withdraws completely.

He brings his finger to his full lips as his tongue darts out to lick it clean of my cream. Dove gray eyes darken to obsidian as lust takes over his vision. A satisfied masculine moan pours from his mouth.

"Breakfast time. First you, then me," he says with a smirk as his towel falls from his hips and he lowers his head between my straining thighs.

I agree wholeheartedly.

"What are you doing?"

I glance over my shoulder at Harris as he rises up onto his elbow.

We haven't left his suite all day. Hours of fucking interspersed with nourishment from meals brought to us by restaurant staff occupied our time. Not that I have a complaint. No, ma'am.

He's so bloody sexy. Even more so with his hair tousled from my fingers, lips made swollen from our fervent kisses, and ripped as fuck physique put to the test by our vigorous carnal bouts. I could drown in the pools of his dove gray eyes. Lose myself in Harris Steele forever.

Then I remember it's fleeting. Only seven stupid days. Well, six now. I agreed to Harris' suggestion because of Vivian's words. *If you truly want another go with Harris. You have to make amends with him.* And damn if I don't want to just make amends. I want to have him in my life as my lover and my friend. Maybe even more if he'll let us get that far. But then I only have six more days to persuade him…

I avert my gaze from his questioning one as tears well up in my eyes. I can't help the flush on my pale skin. But he doesn't have to see my sadness.

With my mobile in hand, I stand from the bed and walk to the bathroom.

"Responding to a text message from a friend," I answer. Thankfully, my voice doesn't waiver.

I shut the door before he can say anymore and lean against it. Head tipped back to staunch the flow of tears, I pray for strength and for Harris to relent.

He's been free with his emotions. Well, as far as making his carnal needs known. So at least he's not closed off from me completely. I think it surprised him when I was jealous of that woman from the bar. But would it upset him if another man angled for my attention?

I may never know since six days is all I have at the moment. And no, I can't predict the bloody future, Harris Steele.

With a shake of my head, I opt to take a shower. Cleanse my body and soul of all signs of negativity. Only positive hopes and dreams for me.

The warm water cascades from a rain shower head and massages me from six others positioned in the walls. I lather up in a gel scented with lavender, chamomile, and sandalwood. It reminds me of the essential oils Harris uses when we soak in the bathtub. Duh… This is his suite so this must be his special blend.

I inhale deeply to imprint the scent of Harris on my mind. Eyes closed, I hold the sponge beneath my nose and sigh.

"Miss me so soon?"

I gasp and spin around. The quick movement on the wet marble floor causes me to stumble.

Harris grasps my waist. He stares down at me. A flicker of longing passes over his features. As quickly as it came, it disappears as though the steam from the shower's warmth cloaked it in its mist. He clears his throat.

"Be careful, Siren," he admonishes. "We're only just getting started for the day with the time we have left."

My eyes drop to his chest as I nod unable to form words without sobbing.

HARRIS

Three days of endless fucking, and I still want more from that redheaded Siren. Just the thought of her luscious curves, breathless moans, and tight, wet snatch hardens my cock painfully. No matter what I ask of her, she does it without hesitation.

I've had her on her knees deep throating her mouth.

Strapped and spanked on the bench.

Buried to the hilt in her ass in the tub.

Like the other Ms. Jackson sings, "Any Time, Any Place." I make *Kat Jackson* hit high notes every. Single. Time. Plucking her keys ruthlessly.

The bummer being tomorrow—Monday looms. The countless hours of the weekend will give way to work. Maybe it'll be good to have some space from her sexual thrall.

NAH!!!

"What's so funny?"

I chuckle some more and cock an eyebrow at the Siren.

"Do you really want to know?" I question.

She tugs that plump lower lip between her teeth as she considers her answer. I want to bite it. Better yet have my cock balanced on it.

"From the expression on your face, I guess it has something to do with another round?" She responds with a smirk of her own.

I pounce and flip her onto her back beneath me. Her giggles make my heart sing.

Dammit, Harris! Enough with the sappiness already. Remain focused.

But the intoxicating aroma of her arousal mixed with my scent on her skin calls to my inner caveman. I want to mark, claim, and fill her with my seed. Mine!

This time, I don't push the errant thought away. Instead, I bury my face in the side of her neck and inhale deeply. The warmth of my exhalation causes goosebumps to erupt on her flushed skin. I suck it into my mouth, worrying it to leave a mark.

She mewls and wraps her arms around my shoulders. Fingertips trail along my back and flanks in a lazy pattern. A hum in the back of her throat emerges as a contented purr.

"Oh, Harris," she breathes.

Pebbled nipples poke against my chest as she arches into me. She parts her thighs to cradle my pelvis. I shift to widen them further as I nestle against her wet warmth.

It's moments such as this one that take me back to the months we were a couple. No drama. Just My Kitty Kat and me.

Why, Kat? You should have been honest! I yell in my head.

I nip her sensitive flesh harder than I meant to, and she cries out. Not in erotic bliss. Dammit! Way to let your emotions mess you up. Again. I admonish myself.

Crooning to her, I lick the spot while I rock my dick against her pussy to soothe her. She settles. But my heart races.

"Um, Harris?"

"Yes?" I respond with my eyes still closed.

The room is dark. So I hear more than see the Siren shift to a seated position beside me on the bed. The lamp on the nightstand by her bursts to life. I throw my arm over my eyes and groan.

"Oh, sorry," she says but doesn't turn the lamp off.

I squint up at her.

She pulled the sheet over her tits. But it can't hide her erect buds. Titian hair tangled about her head. Cheeks and lips stained like raspberries. Absolutely fuckable.

My cock twitches.

I stifle a groan.

"It's late, and I need to get home. You know work tomorrow and everything," the Siren says, eyes skittering around the suite. "I, uh, need to go. Now."

That lights a fire under my sexually sated ass—well, for this minute. I sit up and study her face. She meets my gaze, then averts her eyes.

"What?" She asks. Fingers twist in the sheet draped over her lap. "Why are you looking at me like that, Harris? Do I have something on my face or something?"

She reaches up and swipes at her mouth and chin.

I smirk at the memory of my jizz dribbling from her lips as she struggled to swallow.

She blushes and rolls her eyes, knowing where my carnal thoughts went. Then huffs and slides to the edge of the bed, taking the sheet with her.

"Hold on, Kat," I tell her as I catch her forearm. She continues to stand and my hand slips to hers. Our fingers intertwine. Out of habit, I rub the pad of my thumb across the back of her hand.

She looks down at the intimate contact. Her lips part.

I yank my hand away. But cover the move by running my fingers through my hair. Fuck! That was close. Not at all on the plan. I already chided myself for kissing her. She proves impossible to resist, ever still.

"Well, uh, about that," I grapple for words. Then blurt it out. "It may be a work week. But you owe me four more days."

Her head snaps back as though I slapped her. Even her cheeks flush crimson from the pseudo-contact.

I rush on.

"Obviously we can't stay in my suite every hour as we did this weekend. You will meet me here at 6 each night. Pack a bag and bring it with you tomorrow because you will spend the night. Every night. Do you understand?"

Now emerald fire punches me in the face. I wince inwardly. She glares at me and stands akimbo—no longer concerned with her nakedness as the sheet slips to the floor.

"How bloody dare you, Harris Steele?! I am not some tart you can make demands of! Be here at 6… Spend the night… Warm my bloody bed!" She roars.

Kitty Kat morphed into a lion.

Hot damn!

My cock responds by taking this moment of all moments to stand tall. Her blazing eyes scathe over me.

"Oh, and now you're hard, Harris?! What would you like me to do, huh? Get on my knees and suck you off. Oh, I know… Bend over the footboard while you barrel into my from behind until the wood leaves marks on my hip bones!" She shouts as her arms flail about.

I sit stupefied.

She pins me with another glare. Ample tits heave as she breathes through flared nostrils and out of her mouth.

Completely speechless.

"Oh, nothing to say? Well, then fine… And fuck you!" She shouts and spins on her heels to race towards the bathroom.

The slamming door and rattling of the crystal chandelier rouse me.

I jump from the bed and march after her. My forward motion halts when the door doesn't open. She locked it! Dammit!

"Open the door, Kat," I say as calmly as I can muster. No sense in poking the bear or, in this case the enraged lion.

"Sod off, you prat!" She yells through the still closed door.

"No!" I shout back. "Listen here, Kat! You agreed to this week! I didn't force you to fuck me, did I? And you damn sure enjoyed each second of it based on your moans and screams of my name!"

The door opens, and she jabs me in the chest with each word, pushing me back towards the center of the room.

"You. Bloody. Prat! I *agreed* to it. But that does not give you the right to speak to me like I'm. A. TART!" She screams up at me, then spins and runs back to the bathroom.

The door slams again and the lock clicks loudly in the now silent room.

I race after her. But it's too late.

"Open this gotdamn door, Kat!!!" I yell as I bang on it with my fist. I curse the fact it's made of hardwood. Especially when my shoulder screams in protest when I use it to ram the door. It doesn't budge.

"KAT!!!" I scream.

Soundproofed suites—another standard design. So no one will hear our argument. Thank fuck.

I slam both palms on the door in frustration.

How the hell did this go so left so damn fast?!

One minute we're wrapped around each other. The next we're at each other's throats—and not in a good way.

I throw my head back and roar.

Minutes pass while the sound of the shower is the only thing I hear on the other side of the door. Oh, so she thinks she's getting cleaned up and will waltz her ass out of here? I. Don't. Think. So.

I snatch her blouse and leather skirt from the closet and stuff them under the bed. Then I drop onto the mattress and watch the bathroom door.

The water stops.

Five minutes go by. The door cracks open. Then wider when Kat pokes her head out and peeks around the silent room. She narrows her eyes when she spies me. Undoubtedly, she assumed I left. Wrong!

The door shuts again, then reopens fully. She struts out wrapped in a bath sheet that reaches her shapely calves. Back ramrod straight. Head held high. She ignores me and waltzes into the walk-in closet.

Hangers clang along the rod.

Not in there, sweetheart. I chuckle to myself.

She storms out and points her finger at me.

"Where did you put my clothes, Harris?" She demands. Her head explodes when I cross my arms over my chest and lean against the footboard. Yeah, that footboard. "Give me my clothes back, damn you!!!"

She runs across the room and collides with me. I fall onto my back with an oomph. Her fists pummel my chest as tears fall from her eyes. I can't understand what the hell she's saying, but her tears undo me.

I grab her wrists and flip us over. She screams bloody murder. I have to press my weight into her to keep her from bucking me off. My palms slide up to cover hers. I intertwine our fingers again and squeeze.

The action stops her flailing.

She stares up at me. Red eyed and red faced.

My mouth crashes down on hers. She whimpers.

My tongue breaches between her parted lips, seeking her tongue to dance with mine. She moans, and all tension dissipates. She lies limp beneath me—except for the circling of her hips.

"Kat, baby," I groan against her mouth.

"Harris…" she sighs amorously.

No more words needed.

This time we don't fuck. We make love, again and again.

I ROSE before Kat and watched as she slept. Swollen lips parted, soft snores whistled past her teeth. One hand rested beneath her cheek while the other reached for the spot where I laid. When I left the bed, I slipped her head from my chest and tucked the blankets back around her. The vision of her contentment plays before my eyes as I sit at my desk in The STEELE Tower.

Before I left, I put a note on my pillow.

The choice is hers.

Throughout the day, I refuse to check for a missed call, text message, or email from Kat. Nor do I reach out to her. The note said it all.

Thankfully, I have a full day of project status meetings, one-on-ones with my leadership team, a client lunch, and several conference calls. No time to mope about Kat. Or how we ended things.

The way she went ballistic shook me. So many pent-up emotions it overloaded her system. And made me rethink things. She may have fucked up. But I can't continue to let it eat at me. Each of us deserves more in life than so much anger and resentment.

It's not healthy.

My alarm goes off at five-thirty. I have half an hour to get from midtown to LEVELS New York. Alonzo Masa—my driver—knows to meet me out front of The Tower promptly. It's the rush hour traffic that may hamper my arrival by six.

I shut down my laptop and pack it in my Loewe messenger bag. I resist the urge to check my mobile and head for the private elevator. As I pass through the floor of STEELE Technology and Cyber Security, I bid my administrative assistant and other staff members good night.

Downstairs, I slide onto the backseat of my Black Badge Rolls-Royce Cullinan with a nod at my driver, who holds the door open. He knows where to go, so I sit back and watch the bustling streets during the evening commute.

I check my watch when we get stuck behind a delivery truck in Chelsea. Damn 5:55. I don't bother to bug my driver for a faster route. He knows the ins and the outs of the City. He'll find the way. I shoot a text message to Kat without looking for one from her.

Finally, the SUV pulls up to LEVELS. It's ten past six. Great. I don't wait for my driver to get out and open the door. I grab my messenger bag and hop out. Nods to the security team at the entrance and I rush inside. The greeters smile and welcome me as I head to the elevators.

I open the message app on my mobile. Nothing from Kat. Dammit!

But I go up to the bar for LEVELS 4 Restaurant, anyway. I'm a man of my word, after all. It's too early for a large crowd. So it's easy to see Kat isn't in the bar or in the restaurant when I glance around the dining room.

Fuck. Me.

Feeling more disappointed than I care to admit, I trudge back to the bar and order a Jackson Blend Scotch. I nurse my drink while I plot my next move.

"Rough day?" The bartender asks while he cuts lemon slices. Then raises one. "Time to make lemonade?"

I chuckle despite my tight chest.

"Yeah, you could say that, man," I respond.

"May I have one, too?"

HARRIS

"*M*ay I have one, too?"

My heart thumps in my chest.

Kat!

I swing around.

She stands there with a wry smile on her gorgeous face. Emerald eyes sparkle with mirth as she stares back at me.

"Well, what does a girl have to do to get her drink around here?" She asks with an arched eyebrow. Her gaze never leaves mine. But the bartender rushes to place a Waterford Crystal snifter of the Scotch next to mine on the bar.

"Here you are, miss," he says.

She flicks her gaze at the glass, then back to me.

"I meant a glass of lemonade because I had a shitty day that needs turning around. Starting with waking up in an empty bed," she says straight-faced.

The bartender sputters, but I throw my head back and laugh.

She can't hold the serious expression and giggles.

447

"But… We can start with this fine Scotch," Kat quips as she tosses back a healthy swig.

My girl can hold her liquor, I chuckle. Then blink at my reference to Kat as my girl. That's still to be determined.

She sits in the chair next to mine. Her head dips.

I follow her gaze to the floor, where a duffle bag rests by her feet. My face nearly splits in two. Slow down there, fella, I reprimand myself. We still need to talk.

"Good to see you came prepared, Kat," I say with a nod as I sip my Scotch.

"Yes, I did," she says. The tip of her finger skims around the rim of the glass as she stares into its golden brown depths, then she brings her gaze to mine. "Did you, Harris?"

I nod.

"Of course. Let's finish our drinks, then go to the table," I tell her, then reconsider the phrasing. "Sounds good?"

The corner of her lip quirks up and she nods.

"Sounds good," Kat responds.

We make small talk about our days.

The development work she does at the children's nonprofit organization seems to suit her. It's a great way to combine her education and passion for less-fortunate kids as she was when she grew up. When she speaks about it and the children, her emerald green gaze glows, and her words tumble from her mouth. It's apparent she revels in it.

Kat tells me about her colleague and friend she rooms with. As a native New Yorker and an heir to a company with a real estate development division, I'm familiar with One Fifth Avenue. Her friend Vivian must come from a wealthy family. Especially with a full-floor penthouse in the tower. Those residences are far from inexpensive in the eight-figure range and highly sought after. A safe and respectable place for Kat to live.

I must admit, she's doing well with a new life in New York City. It makes me wonder if she's dated anyone. I know she hasn't been with a man sexually since me. A stroke to my ego. But that doesn't mean she doesn't have any suitors. Not that I believe she would pursue a relationship with me again and have someone on the side.

The questions make me realize I still have trust issues with Kat. Perhaps after our talk tonight, we can ease my concerns. With that thought in mind, I ask her if she's ready for dinner. She nods and stands. When she reaches for her bag, I take it from her and hand it to the bartender, asking him to call a staff member to put it in my suite. He nods and picks up the house phone.

I place my hand on the small of Kat's back and guide her to the host.

It's like déjà vu. She must sense it too since she glances over at me as the host releases the curtains. I smile at her. She returns my smile with a confident one of her own.

"Harris, I want to—"

"Kat, I hope you can—"

We cut each other off. She giggles, and I chuckle. I gesture for her to speak first. She sits taller on the banquette.

"Harris, I want to apologize for my outburst. You're right. I did agree to seven days with you as a means to fuck each other out of our systems. I will hold true to my commitment. That is if you want to continue," Kat says.

"I do. But first, I hope you can forgive me for the phrasing I used. In hindsight, I realize it was wrong. I was wrong. Even though you agreed to the week doesn't equate to you being a tart in any sense of the word. You are far from it, Kat. Do you forgive me?" I respond.

She nods.

I cock an eyebrow.

She smiles and answers verbally.

Thank fuck that's out of the way, I think as I drink some water.

"Shall we wait until after we eat or now? Your letter mentioned us having a conversation to clear the air," Kat asks.

"Let's talk now so we can enjoy our dinner. If things go as I hope, we'll need the nourishment for what I have planned afterwards…" I reply with a smirk.

She laughs and agrees.

When I said we'd talk, I meant for me to tell her my thoughts on what she did and how it impacted me, not just my family. She's apologized to everyone—including me— multiple times. Now it's a matter of what happens next.

I can't promise a ring for a walk down the aisle. However, I do know these last three and a half months have not been the same as the three months we spent together. I actually felt the loss of Kat.

All of it could have been a ruse. But she didn't fake our intimate interactions and not just the sexual ones. The times I sensed her watching me, unaware I saw her expressions of longing and of tenderness. Now that I think about it, even remorse saddened her face on some of those occasions.

There's no excuse for what she did. Period.

But who am I to not forgive?

"Kat, I know you apologized and attempt to make up for your... actions. The donation to Aberdeen Children's Center further proves you strive to redeem yourself," I say aloud after my internal musings.

"I really am so sorry and want to make amends," she interjects as she leans forward.

"Good," I respond, then continue. "However, I want you

to understand the depth of the pain you caused to me personally and professionally. Not to mention the embarrassment of being the one to bring you into my family's personal world."

Kat sucks in a breath. Her gaze lowers to her lap as she sits back.

"I'm so sorry, Harris," she whispers. "I wish I could take it all back. Even the part of meeting you if it would erase your pain… So stupid of me… Bloody hell…"

Her hands cover her face as a sob slips from her mouth.

My heart wants to comfort her. But my mind says no. I hold back. She needs to understand truly. Feel a bit of what I went through. I give it time to sink in.

"Personally, I opened up to you unlike I ever have with other women"—I continue as Kat winces—"I remained exclusive to you. The closest to a relationship ever. Dalliances, yes. Commitment, no."

I take a sip of water and study her reaction over the rim of the glass.

She sits with her shoulders slumped and a forlorn expression on her crimson face. She holds my stare.

"Professionally, Jackson Corporation is a client of STEELE Technology and Cyber Security. I was unaware of your… activity despite the systems in place. Lydie told me she allowed you a higher level of clearance, so no alerts occurred. But still. I was in bed with the enemy. Had it been a different company, they would have viewed me as an accomplice. Considerable damage to my reputation and to my name—my family's name. Not. Good."

Kat's eyes widen as she inhales sharply.

Yeah, cupcake, you didn't think of that, did you? I muse to myself.

"As for my family—both Steele and Jackson—they don't

blame me," I say, then incline my head towards her. "They blame you—"

"Harris! I—"

"No, no," I cut her off. "Whether they forgive you is a different story. They do. As do I. But your actions are not forgotten easily—if at all—by any of us.

"So you see, Kat, I'm in a bind. Yes, I still want to finish our week. But I can make no promises of the future. One day at a time. And I will not tolerate any more deception from you. Or it's game over. Forever."

I sit back, finished with my speech. Now, it's up to her. The ball is in her court.

Kat gives me a pleading look. Wide eyes filled with unshed tears. Mouth agape. She opens it further to speak. But dry mouthed, she can't utter a sound. A sip of water clears her throat, and she tries again.

"Harris, I understand. What I did was terrible. I regret the pain and damage it caused. Thank you and your family for your forgiveness. I will do my very best to make up for my erroneous actions," she says.

Her hand lifts to touch the top of mine resting on the table between us. She watches as she intertwines our fingers. I watch her. She swallows, then brings her eyes to mine.

"I still want to finish our week, too. Even though you can't make promises of the future, I hope you are open to giving me—us—a second chance," she says and squeezes my fingers. "I, too, have never let a man into my life the way I have with you. And I know you feel as strongly about me as I do for you."

Impressed with her return shot, I nod.

"Well then, let's see how this goes," I respond.

Kat's gorgeous face lights up as a serene smile spreads

from her lips to her eyes. When she leans over, I accept her kiss. She licks the seam of my lip until I open for her. Our tongues touch, and she moans.

I cup the back of her head, threading my fingers in the silky strands. Deepening the kiss, I plunder her mouth with a fervent passion. Her whimpers drive me to the breaking point.

"I want you now, Siren," I growl.

Quickly, she scampers onto my lap, hitching up her skirt to the waist. I push the table back and cup her ass. My palms hold the bare globes as my fingers dig into the softness of her ass. Meanwhile, her fingers free my cock, growing harder by the millisecond.

She doesn't hesitate to impale herself on my girth. She hisses from the burn and stretch as I bottom out deep within her pussy. We groan in unison.

I tighten my grip to lift her to my tip. She slides her hands beneath my suit jacket to dig her fingernails into my shoulders through my dress shirt. I flex the muscles of my thighs and ass to thrust up as I yank her down. Each pistoning thrust entices her juices to flow. I muffle her screams of passion with another toe-curling kiss.

Time has no meaning as we lose ourselves in each other. The only things that matter are Kat's ragged breaths and moans as she climaxes around my cock. She's never felt better. So tight, slippery, and warm it's not long before my release hits me like a freight train at maximum speed.

My heavy balls draw up to unleash a geyser. Her pussy walls milk my cock of every drop to the point of pain. But I don't stop my lazy thrusts.

Kat trembles in my arms. I rub her back soothingly as I nuzzle the side of her neck. Sated, she sighs. My ego gets a boost.

As my mind returns from nirvana, I notice an unusual amount of stickiness in my lap. I know Kat climaxed multiple times. But it feels like more.

I shift her to the side of my lap. My semi-hard dick slips from her pussy.

Fuck. Me.

No condom.

"Fuuuck…" I groan as my head slams back against the banquette. My eyes squeeze shut. Never have I gone without a condom. Damn!

Kat moves from me completely. The rustling of her clothes follows. A damp napkin strokes my cum-slicked cock.

"It's okay, Harris. I get a birth control shot regularly and can give you my bloodwork from three months ago. Um, after we broke up, I got tested. Not that I expected anything. No need to worry. If you want proof, I can have my gynecologist send a note to you," she says as she gives me aftercare.

Role reversal or what?

I open my eyes.

Her head bowed over her task, she doesn't notice me watching her. The glow of erotic bliss flushes her face and neck. Bee-stung lips still swollen from our ardent kisses. Her nipples poke into her silk dress. The scent of sex surrounds us, trapped behind the curtain.

My dick pulses in her hand as she holds it up to bathe my balls and my groin. Her tongue pokes out to lick her bottom lip. Then she tugs it between her teeth. She squirms on the seat. Her arousal returns.

As does mine.

But first…

I cup her cheek to raise her gaze.

"Kat, I apologize for my irresponsible behavior. I should have had better control and stopped to put on a condom. Do you forgive me?" I ask.

She closes her eyes and presses her cheek into my hand. When she looks at me again, it's with such a tender expression, my breath escapes in a rush.

What this redheaded Siren does to me. She has no clue.

"Of course, I forgive you Harris. I was just as caught up and forgot," she says, then lowers her eyelashes. The long, golden red tips sweep the tops of her cheeks. "We could go without a condom. If you want."

My dick thumps.

She bites back a giggle.

"Well, I guess you have your answer," I say with a chuckle. "But in all seriousness, I will have my doctor send my last test results to you. I'd appreciate yours from your doctor, too, along with the confirmation of current birth control."

Nodding, her face flushes a deeper red, knowing she has to regain my trust. But if she wants a second chance at us, that's one of the necessary steps. And the basis of any genuine relationship.

I thank her for taking care of me and tuck my junk away before I hang the green tassel on the curtain tie-back. Time for that nourishment. The night's still young.

"I go out of town for a few days, and you shack up with your ex-boyfriend in a sex club? Gurrrl! New York, where dreams really do come true!"

Vivian throws her head back and laughs uproariously.

Some diners in our favorite sandwich and soup shop near the office turn in our direction. They smile at Viv, who dabs her eyes with a napkin. I can't help but to join in.

"So a call turns into an invitation, then a pledge for a week of nonstop *shagging,* as you Brits call it?" She asks as her toffee brown eyes twinkle.

I nod, giggling.

"And was it good? All you wanted and more?" She continues with a smile.

"Incredible *shagging*!" I respond with a wink.

"Well, way to go, Kat! You're on the path to a second chance with your lover boy," she chortles but raises an eyebrow at my shrug. "Okay, what happened?"

I tell her about Harris and the future. She assures me his reaction is only normal, especially given the circumstances.

The reminder hurts. But she tells me to get over it. If Harris can let it go, I can't be the one to play the victim. Viv's candor is what I need. I tell her so and ask about her trip.

We spend the rest of our lunch catching up and her plans for a Girls' Valentine's Day Extravaganza. She and some of her other single friends plan to go to dinner with dancing afterwards. It sounds like fun.

Since the week with Harris ends right before Valentine's Day and he doesn't do the future, I tell Viv to count me in for the Extravaganza. A girl can't sit at home alone and mope all night. Plus, I really like her friends. They've embraced me into their circle. So Valentine's Day is something to look forward to and not ignore.

As ever, the clotheshorse, Viv suggests we go shopping for new outfits. I remind her it'll have to be during lunch tomorrow since Harris occupies my evenings. My response starts her to giggling again.

We leave the restaurant with our arms linked, laughing all the way back to the office. On our floor, we part ways.

I filled my afternoon with proposals and grant writing. Not the sexiest part of my responsibilities. But necessary to get funding to get the children what they need and to keep the organization's programming and back office going. As the head of development, I take my job seriously. And I love it!

"Hi, Foster, anything happened since I left?" I ask my administrative assistant as I walk up to my office.

"Oh, nothing special. Unless, of course, one considers a gigantic bouquet of long-stemmed red roses average..." he responds with a straight face. He laughs and points to my closed office door. "I put them on your desk, and I didn't peek at the card. Handwritten, though. Lovely script."

Harris!

My heart skips a beat. I thank him and hurry inside my office. The bouquet sits in the middle of the desk. The heady aroma of the fragrant roses fills my nostrils. I inhale and smile. Some of the flower petals stand tall with open buds while others closed tight in the stunning bouquet.

I lift the card with my name written in an elegant calligraphy—exactly like the invitation. A grin wider than the Cheshire Cat's covers my face. How romantic!

Then it drops as I frown at the signature.

xoxo Solomon

Crap! It's not Harris at all… Solomon sent the bouquet.

I scan the message: he wishes me a happy Valentine's Day and an invitation for dinner.

With a disappointed sigh, I drop to my desk chair. The sight of the beautiful red roses makes my stomach hurt. The scent makes me queasy. Instead, I swivel to face the windows overlooking Fifth Avenue behind me.

I analyze my feelings of distress.

I assumed Harris sent them as an apology or as a thank you for continuing the week.

The fact it wasn't him hurts since he didn't think to send the flowers for the assumptions I made.

I wonder if he'll ever see me as more than a *shag*, especially since I want more from him.

Is it worth going through at all?

Then I remember another point Vivian made at lunch: cut out the victim role.

Spot on.

I shake my head to dislodge the ridiculous thoughts in my mind and refocus. Spinning around, I remove my mobile from my handbag.

"Hi, Kat!"

I smile—not as big as the Cheshire Cat, but warmly—when Solomon answers my phone call.

"Why hi, to you, Solomon. The roses are simply amazing. So thoughtful. Thank you," I say, meaning it sincerely.

He doesn't deserve to partake in my pity party. What he should have is a woman who can go to dinner with him on Valentine's Day. And that woman isn't me.

"You're welcome. Glad you like them. And dinner?" He asks. "I don't mean to be presumptuous. But I guess you may not have plans with the tosser who broke your heart?"

I flinch. Ouch!

"Thank you for the dinner invitation. However, I have plans and regrettably must pass," I respond, bypassing the *tosser* part. I hope he does, too.

A beat goes by before Solomon responds.

"I understand. Perhaps another time, Kat," he says.

"Solomon, I don't want to mislead you—"

"Nonsense. I'm an adult and can handle a rebuff," he says with a chuckle. "You can't blame a guy for pursuing a beautiful woman. Can you?"

I smile. He's good.

"You flatter me, Solomon," I respond.

"Should things change, you know how to reach me, Kat," he says.

"Thank you for understanding, Solomon. Take care," I reply.

"You, too, Kat," he says and ends the call.

I turn back to my desk and the lovely bouquet. He'll make another woman thrilled.

Smiling, I call Foster and ask him to have the roses delivered to the shelter. Their beauty will brighten Valentine's Day for someone less fortunate than me.

The reminder alert for writing my first proposal chimes.

Time to get to work. All thoughts of exes turned sort of lover and amorous interests clear out.

"Hey, Kat."

Hours later, I glance up to find Vivian standing in the door of my office. She has on her coat and carries her Chanel handbag and matching laptop case. Exaggeratedly, she looks at her gold Cartier Panthère watch, then up at me.

"Don't you have someplace to be in... oh say... twenty minutes?" She asks.

Shit!

I look at the time on my laptop screen. 5:40. The alarm didn't go off. Why? I check but I set it for 5 a.m. not for 5 p.m. *Bloody hell!*

Vivian giggles as I save my work, shut down my system, and run around my office frantically. If I'm late, Harris will punish me like he did the other night.

I stop mid stride as a thought occurs to me. A smile blooms on my face like the heat on my ass did when he spanked me bound to the bench for my transgression. I shudder at the memory as my nipples bead and my pussy clenches.

"I do *not* want to know what you're thinking right now, Kat Jackson," Viv says as she covers her ears and sings tra-la-la.

"I never kiss and tell. Or rather, spank and speak!" I quip and strut past her.

She bumps my hip with hers and laughs.

"You're a total mess, Kat," she replies merrily.

When we step outside, the back door to a Rolls-Royce SUV opens. A long trouser-clad leg comes out, followed by the top of an ebony-haired head. Standing at his full height, Harris grins at me. Dove gray eyes shine like molten platinum.

"I was in the area and figured we could ride together," he says as he meets me halfway, then leans down to kiss my lips softly.

His eyes flick to Vivian, and he blasts her with the full wattage of his sexy as sin smile.

"You must be Vivian. I'm Harris. Nice to meet you," he says as he extends his hand.

She's momentarily stunned by his masculine beauty and stares bug-eyed at him. I nudge her side, and she blinks, then closes her mouth. She gives her head a shake and giggles as she offers him her hand.

"Yes, I am and it's nice to meet you too, Harris," Vivian says with a broad smile. She turns to me. "Well, my car is over there. I'll see you in the morning."

She hugs me and whispers, "Damn, girl! Even better looking in person."

When she steps back, she eyes Harris again and grins as her shoulders shake with glee. She nods at him and heads to her chauffeur-driven Mercedes-Maybach sedan. We watch as he opens the back door, and she slips inside with a wave over her shoulder.

"Nice friend and car," Harris says as he takes my laptop case from me in one hand and my elbow in the other. "If she's single, I have plenty of buddies who'd love to date her. If Laurent wasn't with Yessenia, he'd be the first I told."

I grin at his compliments and tell him I'll let her know. Viv will be so excited!

Settling into the back of his SUV, I think how Harris may not have given me a beautiful bouquet of long-stemmed red roses. But he did surprise me with a ride. And he wants to match my friend with one of his buddies. His gestures are a more meaningful gift to me than the roses. I smile happily at him as he sits beside me.

"What?" He asks.

I touch his cheek.

"Thanks for picking me up. I lost track of time with grant writing, and by mistake, I set my alarm for 5:30 in the morning. So this is perfect," I respond.

Harris stares at me for a moment. His eyes scan my face.

My smile falters a bit at the intensity of his gaze.

Then he nods and says, "You're welcome."

The awkward moment passes when he asks me about the grants I'm reaching out to for our latest programing. As we ride down to LEVELS New York, we talk about our days. The conversation resembles those we had during our prior relationship. It makes my heart swell with hope.

By the time we get out, I'm giddy with happiness.

We make our usual stop at the restaurant for dinner, then go to his private suite for dessert. But this time, a black lace corset with a black sheer G-string and black sky-high marabou mules lie on the bed. Two black enamel bracelets rest on a white silk cloth beside the lingerie.

I stop right inside the doorway of the suite as my eyes snap to Harris. He smirks and walks past me further into the room. Without a backward glance, he saunters into his walk-in closet. I stare back at the sexy lingerie on the bed—Lola's Coterie, I'm sure.

I skim my fingertips over the intricate pattern of the lace and the boning on the corset. I lift it up to admire the detailing. On the back, double-face silk ribbons lace up in front of a black silk panel. I set the corset aside. The G-string leaves nothing to the imagination. Good thing I maintain Brazilians.

"Ready to play or what?"

I jolt at Harris' question.

He stands behind me dressed in head to toe black. A

sheer shirt with loose sleeves unbuttoned to reveal his sculpted chest and the top six of his impressive eight-pack abs. Buttery soft leather pants mold to his ample package, thick, muscular thighs, and firm ass. Heavy boots round out his bad boy air.

Who wants a good boy? Not me.

"Most definitely. Thank you for the lingerie," I purr. "Just give me a few minutes, and I'll need your help with the laces."

I scoop up the pieces in one hand and the shoes in the other. Then I sashay to the en suite bathroom. Once inside, I pin my hair in a sexy bedhead updo, take a three-minute shower, apply lotion, and don the lingerie. More mascara, bold red lipstick, and a walk through a spritz of my perfume, and I slip into the marabou mules.

Harris' eyes bulge when I step into the bedroom. His hooded gaze wraps me in a sensual caress from the top of my head to the tips of my red-polished toenails. A rumbled growl rises from his chest as he stands and prowls towards me. The wolf is out tonight.

Slowly, I pivot to ensure he catches every angle of my body.

"Will you tighten my laces? Then I'll be ready," I purr as I wiggle my shoulders and shift my hips. Then I yelp when his sizable hand connects with one bare ass cheek.

"That's for being late, Siren," Harris growls.

"H—How? You picked me up," I stammer.

He chuckles wickedly.

"And we arrived at Six. Fifteen. Naughty. Lass."

He emphasizes each word with spanks that make me rise to the balls of my fee and gasp.

Wobbly, I grip both sides of the bathroom's doorframe and cry out. But secretly, I trill from the erotic punishment.

Using my hold as leverage, Harris pulls on the corset's laces and ties them. I hate he does it so well. Briefly I wonder who else he helped into the seductive lingerie. The question flies from my mind when another spank catches the bottom curve of my ass. It jiggles from the contact.

Again, Harris chuckles wickedly, then puts his hands on my hips and spins me around to face him. I peek at him from beneath the fringe of my eyelashes and bit the corner of my bottom lip. I know it'll make him wild with lust.

He drops his head to the top of one breast and sucks the soft flesh into his mouth. He worries it until satisfied he leaves a mark on my alabaster skin.

I glance down and see it for myself.

"Now, you're ready, Siren," Harris says smugly as he inclines his head at his handi—rather mouth work. "Off to Peepshow we go. Tonight, we watch. And if you're good, I'll let you cum…"

Goosebumps break out on my heated skin as I shudder in erotic delight.

HARRIS

"Good afternoon, Mr. Steele. Mr. Lucien and Mr. Laurent Jackson have not arrived yet. Would you prefer to wait for them at the bar or at your table?"

I opt for the table and thank the host. He leads me down the ramp to Jackson Pub's primary seating area. He stops at the Jackson's reserved table in the center of the room. In clear view of the entrance and by the other guests.

I nod at or shake hands with some of them as I pass their tables. The restaurant bustles with the lunchtime eaters. Every table full and the bar busy despite reservations being scarce. The din of conversations and silverware on plates fills the air along with the aroma of tantalizing dishes.

Lucien, Laurent, and I are having lunch at one of the two restaurants. Both run by Lucien and his team in Jackson Building—their New York City headquarters on Park Avenue between Fifty-second and Fifty-third Streets. Jackson Pub is a mecca for closing big business deals or for

465

killing them since many of the world's most powerful lunch here daily.

I take a seat at our table and the menu from the host. As I scan today's specials, the server appears. Like the food, the service is impeccable. Lucien would have it in no other way.

"Would you care for a drink, sir?"

"Only bottled water for now. I'll wait for the Jacksons to arrive," I respond.

"If you have any questions regarding the menu, kindly let me know," he says as he fills my glass. He bows his head and walks to the server's waiting area where others stand.

Lucien likes for them to be visible in one spot where the guests can signal to them. He hates for guests to search for them or not have their glasses refilled or plates cleared promptly. *The Sexy Chef* is a hardass—albeit a talented, multiple Michelin starred one.

After I decide on a green salad and the Wagyu Beef with Matsutake Mushrooms, I scroll through my emails. But my mind drifts back to last night. Particularly to moment Kat stroked my cheek and thanked me for picking her up from work.

The tenderness in her eyes so full of joy struck me straight in the chest. Dazed, I could only stare at her. I scanned her face for any sign of a ruse. But she wasn't pretending, as her radiant smile stalled until I spoke.

I covered the awkwardness by asking her about her day.

Once again, her eyes lit up. This time for the happiness her job brings her. She rattled on about the grants and proposals and how they'll help support the children and the nonprofit. I thought how useful she could be at STEELE Foundation.

If things were different, I'm sure my Mom would love to have Kat work with her at our family's foundation that builds and manages attractive, affordable housing for urban, lower-income families. The name plays on the house foundation being strong and supportive like steel. Even though each of us and our cousins support it with our personal funds, Kat could help to manage external contributions.

Then she'd be like Lola, Leonie, and Starr, who partner with STEELE International. For their businesses, as in Lola and Starr's cases, and with a division Leonie runs. Kat could join on our philanthropic arm.

Okay, Harris, you're jumping the gun here, man, I chide myself. Instead, I reflect on the mouthwatering vision of Kat in the Lola's Coterie corset and G-string set I gave her. Totally fuckable. And I did.

My cock stirs in my trousers at the memory of Kat squirming on my lap as she became more and more aroused. We watched an edging demonstration on the primary stage at Peepshow. The woman naked except for the Shibari rope that twined around her body, immobilizing her completely. Leaving her unable to avoid the erotic torture of her Domme.

Over and over, the Domme played her sub's pussy like a fine instrument, only to disallow her orgasms. The poor girl had tears in her eyes by the end of the demonstration. But climaxed so hard her entire body shook as she hung suspended from the ceiling. The chains clanged from the force. Her high-pitched wails bounced around the entire room as her pussy gushed repeatedly.

Her Domme was more than happy to lap up her honey.

My leather pants bore witness to Kat's orgasm as I finally allowed her to cum with the sub. My fingers fucked her spasming pussy until she begged me to stop. Suddenly, she licked my fingers clean. Like a good little Kitty Kat.

My head jerks at the reference. I haven't called her by that nickname in months. Damn, Harris, going soft, playa?

"What's got you frowning?"

"Yeah, you look like you lost your best friend. Oh, no, can't be because I'm still here!"

Chuckles break out as I get clapped on the back.

Lucien and Laurent take their seats, laughing. Fuckers.

I give them a wry look.

"Whatever, some people do have important shit on their minds, you know, unlike you two clowns," I grumble. I shift in my seat to signal the waiter. I'll take that drink now.

"Oooh… Touchy. Yikes!" Laurent digs in.

Lucien smirks before he glances around his kingdom with an assessing eye.

"Good afternoon, Chef Lucien, sir," the server says reverently.

I hide the roll of my eyes behind the raised menu. Laurent snickers and kicks my shin under the table. I angle my menu to show him another eye roll.

Lucien ignores us and speaks with the server. After he takes our drink orders, Lucien glares at us.

"Listen, you little brats, you may be here for lunch. But this is still business for me. So cut off your antics around my staff," he snarls. *The Sexy Chef* is not pleased with our behavior.

Laurent and I exchange glances. Next, we burst out in laughter.

Lucien growls.

"Okay. Okay, cuz! Sorry. All right?" I say with my palms raised. "We're wrong, and you're right."

"Hear, hear!" Laurent concurs with his water glass held aloft in a mock salute.

The server returns with our glasses of Jackson Reserve Scotch. He leaves after we give our food selections.

It's been a while since we last saw one another in person. So, we have a lot to catch up on. Our conversation turns to work highlights—Lucien's up for a prestigious award as per the norm—and sports. We have dates set aside at the STEELE International luxury suite high above the basketball court at Madison Square Garden. The first after everyone gets back from their Valentine's Day getaways.

Which reminds me my week with Kat ends tomorrow, right before the holiday. I'm not ready to stop our time together. We won't stay at LEVELS New York every night. But I'm not opposed to us making a go at a second chance.

I consider my options—

"Earth to Harris!"

"Seriously, cuz, you're out of it today. What the bloody hell is going on in that head of yours?"

Laurent and Lucien's comments draw me from my musings. They frown at me as they await my response.

I'm not quite ready to disclose Kat and I have spent the last week together and especially not at LEVELS New York. Although Lucien may have an idea since he co-owns it. But then, strict confidentiality rules take precedence over ownership unless it involves an issue with members. So my tryst should be safe. For now.

"Sorry about that. I have some stuff going on, so I'm a bit distracted. What did you say?" I respond earnestly.

Lucien studies me for a moment.

Fuck! Does he know, after all? I wonder.

He shrugs.

"Okay, we'll quit riding you. But I do have a question," he responds. He pauses until I nod for him to continue. "What's up with you and Kat?"

Definitely a fuck…

"What do you mean?" I hedge. I won't lie. But I won't show my hand either.

Lucien narrows his eyes at me. The emerald green so like Kat's I feel a tad guilty for not being forthright.

"The other night I saw her. The night of my new restaurant opening. You know, the one you missed…" he says pointedly.

He piques my interest. So I ignore everything but him seeing Kat. Was she alone? Or was she with someone? Maybe only with her friend, Vivian.

"She was there with her friend, a stunningly beautiful woman with skin that reminds me of a decadent ganache…" Lucien waxes on poetically about Vivian.

I nod in agreement. Then he mentions they were on a double date. Damn!

Laurent sits forward.

"Hold on. Yessenia and I saw Kat the other night, too. She was at Carbone with some guy," he says, then goes on. "What did he look like? This guy has black hair and blue eyes. Muscular build around our heights."

Lucien responds it must be the same guy and how they appeared cozy. He remarks how it went from a double date to a single over night.

While they go on and on playing the Hardy Boys solving a great mystery, I fist my hands in my lap to prevent myself from punching something. Jealousy rips through every cell in my body. Who is this fucker? Did she lie to me about not having been with anyone since me? Those dates had to have happened right before we reconnected. Damn!

The server comes over to ask if we want dessert or a digestif.

I tell the guys I need to go—which I do. Like right now.

They stare at me quizzically. But before Laurent can speak, his mobile vibrates. He checks the screen, then says he has to take the call while he rises from the table. A brunette saunters over and places a hand on Lucien's shoulder.

I use their distractions to make haste. I have a stop to make before I head back to The STEELE Tower.

My driver pulls the Cullinan in front of the building for the children's nonprofit office. I jump from the back seat and stride through the doors. Security calls up to Kat, then directs me to the elevator to access her floor.

Her surprised face morphs into one of concern when she greets me in the vestibule.

"What's the matter? Are you all right? Your family?" She asks in rapid succession.

I shake my head and tell her let's go to her office. She nods and leads the way. As we walk, she casts worried sidelong glances at me. But I stare straight ahead. She instructs her administrative assistant to hold all of her calls, then steps into her office. I close the door behind us.

"Harris, tell me," she says as her eyes scan my face.

"Are you seeing someone else?" I ask without preamble. It takes effort to keep my voice level.

Her head snaps back as though slapped. She frowns, then opens her mouth to speak. Shakes her head, then tries again.

I cut her off, grasping her chin between my thumb and forefinger. Holding her head in place so she can't avoid my eyes, I lean close. Her warm breath fans across my face.

"Do not lie to me, Kat Jackson," I warn gruffly.

She attempts to shake her head. But I hold her firm. Her hands lift to my forearm. Fingers wrap around my coat sleeve, slipping along the soft cashmere.

"No, Harris. I'm not seeing someone else. Only you!" She

says, staring straight in the eye. "And I promised not to lie to you again."

We stare at one another. I gauge the veracity of her words. She assesses my reaction. I break first.

"Then who did Lucien and Laurent see you with on back-to-back dates?" I growl.

My inner caveman pushed to his limits can barely contain himself.

Realization dawns in her eyes as they brighten to a jade green. She snatches her chin from my fingers.

"Oh, so that's what this is all about? They ran and told you what they saw?" She lashes out as her eyes blaze.

The answer is obvious, so I remain silent.

Wrong move.

Kat narrows her eyes at me and pokes me in the chest. Even through the layers of my coat and suit, the tip jabs me.

"You cannot possibly be pissed because I went on *two* dates with someone when it took you weeks to contact me after we… after we made out at Lachlan and Haley's flat!" Kat snarls.

When I don't answer, she flares her nostrils and continues—jabs and all.

"Can you honestly tell me you didn't fuck other women while we were apart?" She throws out.

Now, I avert my eyes, and she growls.

She stalks away from me to the door. Pausing with her hand on the knob, she glares at me over her shoulder.

"That's not fair of you, Harris. I don't hold it against you, you were with others. So you don't get to be pissed with me for going on *two* dates. Now, I have work to do," Kat says and opens the door.

In three strides, I'm in front of her and push the door closed. I crowd her personal space, boxing her in with my hands on either side of her head and her back against the door.

Her hands come up to push at my chest. But her pupils dilate as her cheeks flush with her instant arousal.

I bend my knees so we're on eye level. Her breath comes out in pants. I slam my mouth over her parted lips. She nips my bottom one, and I respond in kind. The kiss is brutal and demanding as we battle for dominance.

I win.

Then I damn near rip the placket of my trousers as I use one hand to release my cock while the other squeezes her hip bone. She squeals into my mouth. I swallow it down and lift her up. She yanks her dress, then the skimpy lace of her panties gets pushed aside.

I grunt when she fists my cock and lines it up with her pussy. I raise her higher to give clearance, then thrust up as I pull her down. Her back slams against the door. She hisses as much from the forceful invasion as from her collision with the solid wood.

Fortunately, it holds as I pound into her again and again. Sweat beads down my back from the heat our bodies create and the clothes I wear. Kat cries out into our kiss as she clenches her pussy around my cock. Mini orgasms build to a major one. When it hits her, she cums like a tidal wave. It triggers my release, and I roar into her mouth.

"MINE!"

I mark her pussy with my seed, satisfying the caveman in me.

She twitches from the aftermath as I carry her to the desk chair. I disengage our intimate connection to set her down on it. Our combined essence drips to the floor. I stare at it, pleased, then pull my handkerchief from my suit jacket pocket. I moisten it with water from the bottle on her desk and clean first her, then myself.

Less dazed, Kat rearranges her dress. When she babbles about cleaning up in the bathroom, I put her panties back in place, securing my seed and scent inside of her. She arches her eyebrow but doesn't argue.

I rise from a crouch and kiss her breathless.

"I'll pick you up at five-thirty," I say, then leave her stunned and slouched in the chair.

KAT

"*H*arris! What are we doing at an *airport*? Wait a minute. Is that your private jet??? It's only Friday. I have to get to work!"

My mouth hangs open as I gape out the window of his SUV at the Gulfstream G650ER gleaming in the morning sun. The jet waits on the tarmac with its door open and the boarding stairs lead from it to the ground invitingly.

But this is one invitation I cannot accept.

When Harris stepped out of his Rolls-Royce as I walked through the doors of my flat's building, He happily surprised me. Picked up from work two nights in a row, then the next morning? Awesome!

He sauntered over to me and brushed his lips over mine as he murmured a good morning.

I melted.

Inside the SUV, I prattled on, really about nothing in particular. I was just so hyped by Harris' boyfriend-like behavior. He indulged me with a smile on his handsome face. I talked so much I didn't notice we weren't in front of my office building when the SUV stopped. Alonzo—his driver—opened the door.

I stood beside the Hudson River. A helicopter waited with a crew member by the open door. My head swiveled to Harris, who rounded the back of the SUV. He strode with confidence and took my elbow. But I held back and asked why we were there instead of on Fifth Avenue.

He wanted to take me on a morning flight around Manhattan to experience it from the air…

Ha!

Now, he hits me with a lopsided grin. I would swoon at the absolute sexiness of this man if I wasn't ready to strangle him!

I throw my hands up in the air and yowl in frustration at his silence. Then I knock on the partition separating us from his driver. He rolls it down and glances over his shoulder, first at Harris, then at me.

"Yes, Ms. Jackson?" Alonzo asks.

"Would you be so kind as to drive me to my office on Fifth Avenue?" I respond.

His chocolate brown gaze shifts to Harris.

"You know, never mind. I'll call an Uber," I say, then reach for my attaché and handbag on the floor.

The partition rolls up, and Harris places his hand on mine to stop me.

"Kat, it's okay. I spoke with the organization's director, and she gave you time off until the Monday after this one. She'll handle any pertinent meetings you have with the help of your team," he says.

I close my eyes and shake my head in disbelief.

"Seriously?! You took control of *my* work? To what end? And she just agreed with no incentive?" I ask, keeping my eyes squeezed shut. Maybe I can push this whole thing out of my mind.

Harris sighs.

"That's a bit of an extreme description of the situation, Kat. I wanted to surprise you with a memorable trip… for Valentine's Day. That's all," he responds.

I soften at his words. How romantic!

"Oh, Harris—"

"The director was more than pleased with the million-dollar donation I made," he continues as I speak.

My head jerks back, and I snatch my hand away from his hold. What the bloody hell?! He *paid* for me?! Like a tart. Again?!?!?!

"W—What's the matter? Why do you look like you want to kill me?" He asks, taken aback by my dagger-like glare.

He's so oblivious to the way one could interpret his actions. I can't get mad. He's also trying, and I appreciate it a lot.

So, I close my eyes and inhale deeply through my nose and exhale out my mouth for a count of ten to avoid a massive explosion. A mantra for peace and tranquility Starr taught to me whispers from my lips.

"Kat?" Harris calls.

I reopen my eyes to his concerned face.

"I apologize for my outburst," I start and wait for his acceptance before I continue. "Thank you for doing so much to take me away for Valentine's Day. How thoughtful of you.

It's the donation part that really gets to me. I know you don't see it as anything wrong and more than likely consider it charitable—extremely so, in my opinion, under different circumstances.

But to me it seems as though you bought me. And it

invoked the memory of the other night. I hope you can see it from my perspective."

Harris opens his mouth, then closes it. His eyes scan my face. He gives a shake of his head and groans as he slaps his forehead with his palm. He returns his remorseful gaze to me.

"Damn, Kat, I see it now. But as I said that night, there's not a chance I think of you in that way. At. All. Yes, I'm an Alpha male who needs control. But not outside of the bedroom. We're not in an M/s or a D/s relationship with total power exchange. Even then, the sub has the final say. However, that's not my thing, and I don't believe it's yours either.

But if you want to go to work, I'll understand. We'll go now. What do *you* want to do?"

I glance down at our hands laced together. He rubs his thumb over mine in a soothing manner. I smile.

How can I be a bitchy grump with a sexy AF man who went through all of this to surprise me with a trip for Valentine's Day? I can't.

I weigh my options… So I guess I'll miss the Girls' Valentine's Day Extravaganza!

Giggling, I clamber onto Harris' lap and hold his face in my hands. I cover it with kisses, whispering naughty words of all the ways I plan to thank him from now until we return to New York City.

He squeezes my ass and growls.

His dick thumps beneath me, and I grind down on it wantonly as I nip his plump lower lip. Circling my hips, I lower my mouth to his neck. Now, I leave my mark on his flesh. He groans and flexes his fingers to dig deeper into my butt cheeks.

"If you keep this up, we won't make it to the jet," he says as he lifts me from his lap onto the seat. "Once we're in the air, you best finish what you started, Siren."

Harris waggles his eyebrows at me.

I bite my lower lip and nod with hooded eyes.

"Yes, Harris," I purr.

He smirks and opens his door. I do the same and hop out of the SUV. He takes my hand to lead me to the awaiting jet.

He won't tell me our destination, only that we have eleven hours to add points to our Mile High Club travel bank. By the time we land, we could take a nonstop trip around the world…

"KEEP your eyes shut until I say open them. Or else."

I giggle as Harris unties the red silk blindfold from behind my head. But I heed his warning, even though I wouldn't mind his form of punishment. He put the blindfold on before we stepped off his private jet.

The clues I gathered tropical heat, the scent of hibiscus and gardenias, and waves lapping at the shoreline as my toes dig into sand lead me to believe we're on an island. The distance of eleven hours from New York City can put us anywhere.

"Okay, open your eyes!" Harris says enthusiastically.

I blink against the bright sunlight. It takes a beat for my eyes to adjust. Then I gasp.

Ahead of me a stretch of crystal-clear, shallow water separated by a low sandbank from the vast turquoise blue ocean takes my breath away. The contrast of the black sand to the white-tipped aqua hues of the water is majestic.

I clap my hand over my mouth in awe.

"Beautiful, isn't it?" Harris murmurs in my ear as he wraps his arms around me from behind. "Do you like?"

"Oh, yes, Harris," I breathe.

"Hmmm… I like how you say my name, Siren," he says, nipping my earlobe. "Come, there's much more to see."

He squeezes my hip bones, and I moan. He turns us around to bring me face-to-face with a magnificent private villa that sprawls beside the lagoon. The lush foliage reminds me of pictures I've seen of Hawaii.

"Where are we? Hawaii, right?" I ask excitedly. I've always wanted to go to the volcanic islands. The black sand beach gives it away.

Harris chuckles and nods.

"You guessed correctly—Maui specifically. Now, what should your prize be?" He responds, tapping his chin with the tip of his index finger, eyes skyward. "Skinny dipping in the lagoon? A late naked lunch of local delights? Couples massages beneath a gauzy canopy on the beach? You choose."

I turn and wrap my arms around his neck as I rise to my tippy toes.

"Each one while I'm naked?" I giggle, kissing his lips.

"This is a no-clothes-allowed week," he answers, lapping at my throat. "You didn't see any luggage, did you?"

I tilt my head to give him better access for his seductive kisses. Can this get any better?

"You choose, Harris," I purr as I grind my belly against his rigid dick. "Whatever you desire."

His warm breath skitters across my skin as he responds, "Hmmm, be careful what you offer to a cad like me, Siren."

"Don't tease me…" I moan.

Harris steps back. Immediately, I feel his loss and ache for him. I pout. He chuckles, a sound as dark and promising as the sand beneath our feet. A promise I beg for him to keep.

He takes my hand and leads me to the Balinese-inspired masterpiece for a tour. The luxury ten-thousand-square-foot compound sits on twenty secluded acres. Its four pavilions nestle amongst lush gardens, fruit trees, and serene ponds. An infinity edge pool with spa stretches to the horizon in the center. Each pavilion connects to the other by breezeways and footbridges.

We enter the main two-story pavilion with an expansive gourmet kitchen, dining area, living room, office, state-of-the-art media room, wet bar, full bathroom, plus one king-size bedroom with en suite bathroom. Harris comments we won't need the fancy fitness studio.

We bypass two sumptuous guest suite pavilions, each with a king suite and an en suite bathroom, private indoor/outdoor showers, wet bars, and lanais.

Instead, Harris takes me to the massive primary pavilion with a king suite, lounge area, wet bar, and a spa bathroom with an indoor/outdoor shower, dressing room, and a walk-in closet. Three lanais, each with distinctive views of the lagoon and the Pacific Ocean beyond.

"First course of action, we strip," Harris says as we stand on the lanai facing the sparkling water. "They train the staff in the utmost discretion. They only come on the property when summoned."

When I pull a face, Harris stops taking off his dress shirt and walks barefoot towards me. His pecs and abs flex as the material blows in the soft breeze. His happy trail draws my gaze to his unbuttoned fly. The trousers slung low on his narrow hips.

Piping hot sex on a stick.

And I want a bite.

But the idea of strangers seeing me nude. Uh… no.

He rubs my arms and stares into my eyes.

"I promise you the staff is offsite in a caretaker's house. This is a STEELE BLACK property—one of our über-luxury villas that caters to the top echelons of society. People who protect their privacy fiercely. But if you don't want to, I won't pressure you," he says, then winks. "I, however, will be in the buff all week long."

He swivels his hips exaggeratedly until I giggle and push him away. Why not live a little?

Harris whoops when I do an impromptu striptease. Fully undressed, I stand before him. He tugs his lower lip between perfect teeth. His heated gaze rolls over me like a lava flow. Hot enough to turn my body into a pile of ash.

I shiver despite the warm breeze.

"More beautiful than the view," he rasps. "It's time to get you wet."

He slips his hand in mine and walks along a path. Petals from the flagrant flowers I smelled earlier collect on the stones. Each step coaxes more of their aroma into the air to float around us. They create a heady sensation, and I close my eyes for a deep whiff.

The path leads us back to the black sand beach.

I glance around to absorb its grandeur. Then squeal when Harris scoops me from my feet and runs into the waves. I hold to his neck tightly when he dunks beneath the surface. We rise laughing.

With a twist of my slippery body, I break free of his grasp and cast a seductive eye over my shoulder at him. He catches it and reaches out for me. Like a mermaid, I undulate my legs and swim for the sandbank.

I reach the black sand before Harris—undoubtedly, he let me out swim him. Then open my arms wide, throw my head back to the sky, and spin in a slow circle. The sun licks my skin, and I know I won't have long before its pale hue reddens. But for now, I enjoy myself. Sunblock later.

Harris spins with me and shouts to the cerulean heavens.

It's so freeing to just be. Not a care in the world. And with the man I love.

Oh, so happy and grateful, I join in his shouts.

* * *

"I WISH the week didn't have to end. It went way too fast..." I pout as Harris and I stretch out on a sunbed, watching the fiery sunset.

He rolls onto his elbow and traces circles radiating from my belly button to my breasts.

My nipples pucker, and he leans over to suckle one while he tweaks the other. It's a gentle touch, like he's been for the last few days. He's still passionate. But not as feral in his need.

I worry he's finished *fucking me out of his system.* A shudder runs through me at the horrible thought of this being the end.

"Cold or aroused?" Harris asks with his chin resting below my breasts.

His dove gray eyes peer into my emerald green ones.

I shake my head.

His gaze dips to my jiggling tits, and a lazy smile spreads across his face. He turns his head and nips at the bottom curve of one. I cry out softly.

"Not cold," I purr as I push the lingering thought to the side.

"Mmmm..." Harris murmurs. "Let me see what I can do to satisfy you, Siren."

He slips between my thighs. When his mouth engulfs my sex, I mewl and arch my back. He's relentless in his ministrations. By the time he sits back on his haunches, I'm boneless. Mind blank.

Harris chuckles.

"Well, actually, I planned for us to spend the weekend in Beverly Hills. We'll leave early in the morning. So we'll have Friday through Monday. Returning to New York in time to have you at the office by eight-thirty," he says.

I jump up and throw my arms around his neck. He falls back on his butt, laughing.

"This is the BEST Valentine's Day I've ever had! Thank you, my love!" I exclaim.

Harris's laughter stops as he stiffens.

Bloody hell! I did not just call him *my love* out loud!

But I refuse to let my oopsie ruin the marvelous time we've had and will have over the weekend. So I pretend as though I don't notice the change in his body language. Instead, I distract him with a trail of open-mouthed kisses from his stubbled jaw, over the planes of his muscular chest and abs, and to his erect dick.

This time when he stiffens, it's from me swallowing his length down my throat in one go. I work his cock like my favorite sucker. The tip of my tongue swirls around the mushroom tip, flicking a bead of pre-cum from its slit. Tilting my head, I use the flat of my tongue to lick from root to tip. Then I take all of him back down my throat. It expands to accommodate his sizable girth and length.

I repeat until his thighs quiver and his hands fist my hair. Then I sit back and let him fuck my face through the explosion of his orgasm. I hollow out my cheeks to suck every drop of his cum, not spilling one bit.

Harris collapses to his side, then back, chest heaving, eyes squeezed shut.

A satisfied smirk plays on my lips as I think of what Vivian told me: use what you got to get what you want.

And make no mistake, I want Harris Steele. Now and forever.

HARRIS

It freaked me out when Kat called me *my love*. I use a lot of four-letter words every damn day. But I wasn't ready to say *that* one, not out loud. At least, just not yet.

Where I thought last week was for fucking Kat out of my system. This week confirmed it's not quite over for us. Aside from the incredible sexual chemistry and mutual satisfaction, the out of the bedroom time is great too.

Kat's natural wit and her care for children add to her appeal. Not to mention how she's trying really hard to prove to me she deserves a second chance. We deserve another go.

The weekend in Beverly Hills was a last-minute add-on. The Maui villa had another party arriving on Saturday. I couldn't very well cancel it even if I wanted to. Not a good look for STEELE International to boot out a Crown Prince and his family for their two-month-long holiday.

So ever the brainiac, I thought quick on my feet and

extended our trip to my penthouse in West Hollywood on the Sunset Strip.

It's a sleek bachelor's pad with a private full rooftop terrace that once belonged to Malcolm. Then Starr came around, and bam! The end of his Alpha Dom playboy days. Fortunately for me, I benefitted from his—well, not a loss per se—new status.

He had it so well decked out, I didn't need to change a thing. I come out at least once a month for a week and work out of STEELE Los Angeles. Then party at LEVELS Beverly Hills, Jackson's Couch, or some other hot spot. Except it's been a while since I was in Aberdeen and London, then the Holidays followed by time in New York City.

I figure it'll be an excellent test to go out with Kat like we used to for a night of fun. See if being outside of the bubbles we lived in at LEVELS New York and in Maui feels the same. I hate to admit it, but I want to see if Kat was genuine for real.

We've spent enough time in a LEVELS. So we'll skip the club here, although it's one of my favorites. Instead, have dinner at the exclusive and exquisite Urasawa—my go-to sushi restaurant—then dance at a new spot a buddy told me about. It's in West Hollywood, fifteen minutes from my penthouse. We won't have far to go to get back. Not that it matters since I have a STEELE Los Angeles driver to take Kat and me around for the weekend.

After we arrived, I took her shopping on Rodeo Drive since, no shit, she really didn't have any clothes in Maui. Save for two floral-printed silk kimonos and the dress she wore for work. A maid had it dry cleaned for Kat to wear for the flight over.

She was psyched to hit all the stores. Naturally, we went to the STEELE Galleria Rodeo Drive. Kat picked out a few lingerie pieces from the Lola's Coterie boutique there. I persuaded her to get a sexy negligee-inspired mini dress to wear tonight.

The scene in *Pretty Woman* of Julia Roberts' character shopping here flashed through my head. But I didn't want to get knocked out by Kat, so I kept my mouth shut.

We had lunch at Maude, then returned to the penthouse.

Tuckered out from a busy day of travel, shopping, and fine dining, Kat opted to take a nap before we go out tonight. I left her to rest in my bed and came up to the terrace. It gave me space to think over things and figure next steps.

Once again, I decide to take it a day at a time. Next week I travel for business and won't have a chance to see Kat until I return. Time apart may put a different perspective on the development of a relationship between us. I hate to use a cliché, but I'll see if absence makes the heart grow fonder and all that wussy jazz.

Then I'll tell my family—starting with Haley—what's going on. I won't keep them in the dark, especially my twin. It's not like I'm being deceitful now. They're all still away for Valentine's Day and won't get back until next week. Meanwhile, I'll be in South America.

I give my brain a rest and close my eyes for a catnap—no pun intended…

Wet warmth surrounds my cock. Its fat head brushes the palate as my length slides towards My Kitty Kat's throat. I stroke the top of her cheek where a tear slips from her eyes as she stares up at me from where she kneels.

"Open your throat for me, Kitty Kat," I murmur. "Relax and let me in."

She squeezes my thigh three times—her hand signal of understanding when her mouth is otherwise occupied or gagged.

I nod in recognition and ease another inch into her mouth.

She hums in the back of her throat. The vibrations dance along my length to tease me. I stare down at her with hooded eyes. She feels incredible.

Halfway there, I pull back to my tip to give her jaw a rest. She takes a breath through her mouth, then licks the slit. I shudder and slide back in, deeper still.

Soon we pick up a pattern she can handle and gives me pleasure. I put my hands behind my back and only use my hips to fuck her mouth slowly. My head lolls back. A groan slips through my slack mouth. I swivel my hips.

My Kitty Kat moans.

I can tell her fingers play with her clit when her right shoulder bumps against my thigh. My hooded gaze drops to watch My Kitty Kat pleasure herself while she deep throats me. The sight of her naked on her knees, pussy juices slick on her spread thighs, hand moving rapidly, all while she stares back at me with my cock stretching her mouth finishes me.

I grip her long, silky Titian strands in both hands to hold her head in place. My ass clenches, ready to surge ahead. I pulse on her tongue as I push as far down her throat as she can handle. A gag and I go off like a rocket. My eyes roll back in my head as a primal roar punches the air.

My Kitty Kat moans and convulses. She joins me with a climax of her own, belly full of my seed.

Hands still in her hair, I drop to my knees in front of her and cover her swollen mouth with mine. She clings to me and mewls.

Breathless, I have to leave her mouth and bury my face in her neck as the aftershocks continue to roll through me. I pull her onto my lap, unable to remain on my knees. She curls into me like a contented Kitty Kat.

"I love you, Harris," she whispers.

"I love you, Kat," I respond.

She gasps.

"You do?"

"H—Harris? Did you hear me?"

My eyes open slowly. Kat comes into focus. Her wide eyes move rapidly over my face. I frown.

Was I dreaming? Damn, I must've been because she's wearing the Lola's Coterie mini dress, not naked on her knees.

I swipe my hand over my face and sit up from the double chaise.

"What time is it?" I ask, voice hoarse with sleep.

Kat doesn't answer, so I glance back at her. I cock an eyebrow questioningly. She shakes her head and sighs.

"It's a quarter past seven," she responds quietly.

Then she rises from sitting beside me. She smooths the front of her mini dress and turns for the interior door leading to the stairs and the penthouse below.

"You should take a shower," she says over her shoulder and wipes the corner of her mouth with her pinky finger.

A cool breeze skims across my crotch. I glance down and my eyes bug out.

My semi-flaccid cock glistens with saliva as it rests against my open jeans. I jerk my head towards Kat. But she's already closing the door behind her. I look back at my dick.

"Was I fucking dreaming or what?" I ask aloud, baffled.

Then it hits me.

Kat must have given me a blow job while I slept. Okay, nice. I feel bad since I didn't get her off, too. I tuck my cock inside and re-button my jeans.

Wait a minute. Did Kat tell me she loves me? Did I tell her *I love her???*

Fuck. Me.

No wonder she looked so shocked and bolted.

I fall back on the double chaise lounge. A string of four-letter words pours from my mouth.

So a sleeping man getting his dick sucked tells no lies…

Damn.

What do I do now???

I could pretend as though I don't know what happened. Or be a man—as The Godfather says—and talk to Kat.

Well, since I'm a grown ass man…

I find Kat sitting in a chair by the window in the darkened living room. The panoramic view of the Sunset Strip lights up the nighttime sky behind her. It bathes Kat with an ethereal glow.

Even though she faces the window, I can tell by her slumped posture she's thinking of what happened.

And she's defeated.

Way to go, Harris Steele, I chide myself.

My goal is to break a woman. But that's when we're in bed and I want her to come undone for me. Climax to ecstasy.

Kat is not floating in carnal bliss. She's drowning in a sea of sadness. And it's my fault.

So deep in thought. She doesn't notice my approach until I crouch before her. She jolts.

I take her hand and watch as I intertwine our fingers, then squeeze.

"Hey," I say after I bring my gaze up to her face.

Kat stares at our hands, then averts her eyes. She lifts a corner of her mouth and whispers, "Hey."

Wanting her eyes on me so I can read her expression, I cup her cheek to turn her head around. But she keeps her eyes downcast.

"Look at me, Kat," I say, then wait until she raises her gaze to meet mine. "I thought I was dreaming. It didn't hit me until after you left the terrace, what happened—what we said—was real."

She blinks to hold back tears. But keeps her focus on me.

"I won't deny what I said. I can't. What holds me back from saying it while awake is fear of what you say and do aren't genuine. Call it PTSD. But I need to be one-hundred and ten percent certain you're not pretending," I admit.

"Harris, I—"

I put a fingertip on her lips.

"My heart feels. But my mind needs to know. We're a lot further along now than before. So there's a plus in our win column. Let's leave it at that and take each day as it comes. Okay?" I say.

Her eyes scan my face, and I remain open to her. I won't lie and I won't hide. Satisfied with what she sees, Kat squeezes my hand and smiles softly.

"Okay," she says with more confidence than a minute ago.

I nod as I rise.

"Give me fifteen minutes. A certain redheaded Siren enchanted me while I slept. So I need to shower and get dressed," I say wryly.

"Oh, is that what you call a blow job, Harris?" Kat asks as she giggles. Her emerald green eyes glow brighter than the Sunset Strip.

My Kitty Kat makes my heart soar.

Damn, I'm fucked. For real.

"HELLO, Harris. Good to see you. It's been a while."

I return Hiro Urasawa's smile as he greets me in his eponymous Beverly Hills restaurant. He's right since I dine in the ten-person shrine to sushi each time I'm in town. I will never get enough of his masterful creations. They're the best in the world.

"Good to see you, too, Hiro. I'm happy to be back," I tell him, then turn to Kat. "Allow me to introduce you to Kat Jackson. Kat, this is Hiro Urasawa the Great."

He chuckles at my introduction and bows deeply to Kat. She smiles and returns his gesture of respect. I help her into a seat while Hiro returns to his next masterpiece.

"He's incredible. I feel privileged to be here," Kat says as we watch Hiro, his movements as precise as a neurosurgeon.

I agree, and we sit in a comfortable silence as he prepares the dishes for this evening's meal. The other eight guests also watch on in reverence.

A server places an assortment of appetizers before us. Kat selects edamame, and I bite into a tantalizing beef dumpling. The flavor bursts over my tongue. I groan, it's so good. Kat hums in harmony.

I selected a cold-matured sake to accompany our appetizers. Kat tells me it's the best she's ever had and licks the corner of her lip to catch a stray drop. Even though she's not being a siren, my cock still twitches, envisioning her tongue on my slit, lapping a bead of pre-cum.

Not now. No sexual thoughts. This is a date night.

I shift my gaze back to Hiro in the center or the rectangular wooden bar around which the patrons sit on two sides. The light from above shines on the various ingredients he uses. My mouth waters, then curves into a grin when dinner is served.

THE MUSIC PUMPS from the speakers as My Kitty Kat and I grind on the dance floor. My hands grip her ass to mold her to my body. Her arms drape over my shoulders as she shimmies. Our foreheads touch with our eyes locked on the other.

Even though people moving similarly crowd the dance floor, it's as though they don't exist. Only the rhythm of the music penetrates our bubble.

When the song changes, My Kitty Kat spins around and throws her arms in the air. She bends her knees to glide up and down the front of my body. Her sensual moves make my already painfully hard cock weep and beg to enter her enticing body—mouth, pussy, or ass.

I grip her hips, bend my knees to align her ass with my cock, and sway us back and forth. She bends over and grabs her ankles, shaking her sweet thing. I damn near cum in my leather pants.

Instead, I step back and smack that ass.

She rises onto her toes but doesn't stop her gyrations. Her body begs me for more. And I oblige.

I alternate a pump of my hips with a spank to a different ass cheek. When the next song blends into the last, I tug her up by her throat with one hand and slip the other around her hip. Her back pressed to my front and held in place, my finger slides beneath the hem of her mini dress. It finds her juices coating the tops of her inner thighs.

She moans, and I groan into her ear.

"So wet for me, Siren?" I ask thickly.

"Only for you, Harris," she says against my cheek.

I growl and plunge my finger into her dripping pussy. My finger flexes and curls as the heel of my hand grinds against her engorged clit. It pulsates as her inner walls flutter. I add another finger.

She arcs her back on a moan. My mouth covers hers. No

need for others to get even a hint of what I do to My Kitty Kat. For my eyes and my ears only.

She cums with a muffled scream. Her whole body trembles. I band my arm around her waist to keep her from collapsing to the floor. She rides out her orgasm on my fingers as they slide in and out gently.

"Time to go," I croon in her ear.

She nods.

Back at my penthouse, we shower, then fall into bed. In moments, she's asleep curled into my side with her head resting on my chest and one leg thrown over mine. Staring at the ceiling, I trace a fingertip along the curve of her hip.

The night replays in my mind. I must say we had a really good date. As my eyes close, I wonder what it would be like to fall asleep with My Kitty Kat in my arms not just for a few days. But always.

KAT

"So... How was your surprise Valentine's Day trip to Maui with that sexy man of yours, Kat?"

Vivian grins at me as we leave the conference room after the Monday morning executive status meeting.

As Harris promised, he dropped me off at my office building at a half-past eight. He flies out later this morning for Buenos Aires on business. He's there for the entire week.

I pouted, and he kissed me senseless at the revolving doors. He cared little people were flowing around our passionate embrace. With a wink, he was gone. And my heart leaped out of my chest to follow him like a kitten with separation anxiety.

Words cannot describe our time away together. Maui was a spectacular paradise. Harris fulfilled an absolute dream of mine. After I got over myself with the initial anger at his actions, I couldn't be more grateful. But the brilliant beauty of Hawaii pales in the light of the' natural glow emanating from Harris' eyes as he watches me.

I know he isn't ready to give in to his love for me fully.

But the spark is there. It's grown from the embers left in his heart. Soon, it will ignite to engulf us in a fireball of undeniable love.

"That good, huh?"

Vivian's words and giggles bring me back from thoughts of Harris to the office. As the images of the black sand beach and the bright lights of the Sunset Strip fade away, I glance around the corridor. Not a palm tree in sight. I sigh.

"Viv, you have no idea. Once my anger dissipated… Wait a minute, you knew, too?!" I ask taken aback.

Her toffee eyes gleam like amber as she bites her lower lip to stifle her laughter.

"Of course! Who do you think gave him the idea to donate to make up for taking you away for so long as you've only been here for a short while? You raise funds, so you being away still brought in money. A win-win situation," Vivian says with a wink.

I throw my head back and laugh. All of my craziness and Harris hadn't thought about making a donation to pay for my time. Now, it's confirmed I overreacted. Duh. Duh. Duh.

Viv quirks an eyebrow at me.

I loop my arm through hers and tell her all about it as we walk back to our respective offices. Then I promise to fill her in on the rest over lunch—my treat. I'll make it up to Harris when I see him again. My heart lurches. He's not back for DAYS…

The rest of the morning went by quickly. The director and I met to discuss the happenings while I was away. She was more than pleased with Harris' donation. She joked he could take me away each month if he'd contribute each time, and we'd more than make our yearly goal.

I had to laugh along with her. Viv put a whole new spin

on his donation. It makes me feel so much better and erases any lingering negativity.

Vivian calls to let me know she'll meet me at the lifts. I'm shocked to find it's already half past noon. Jet lag has me at breakfast still. I wrap up an email and grab my coat and handbag. As I slip my mobile into the outer pocket, it chimes with a text message.

I grin like the Cheshire Cat.

Harris!

Hi, Kitty Kat. Getting ready to take off. I'll call you tonight. H.

My fingers fly across the mobile screen as I type back.

Safe travels. TTYL KK ;)

I wait a moment to check for a response before I drop my mobile back in the outer pocket. But no three dots appear by the time I make it to the lifts. Bummer.

It's a chilly day, so Viv and I head to our favorite sandwich and soup shop a few blocks from the office. We join the throngs of people on Fifth Avenue. Tourists mingle with workers and residents on the bustling sidewalk. The scent of roasted chestnuts beckons from a vendor on the corner. Store windows changed from the red roses, bows, and ribbons for Valentine's Day to the latest summer fashions.

I tighten the belt of my warm wool coat as I shake my head. Only days ago, I was swimming in the lagoon naked. Harris' sleek muscular frame beside me. Now, the blasted cold of New York City in February. And here retailers display mannequins in colorful bikinis and sarongs in the windows!

If only I could roll back time...

During lunch, Vivian can't stop oohing and aahing over all things Harris Steele. Especially when I tell her he offered to tell his buddies who'd love to take her on a date. Then she claps her hands and shimmies in her seat. She's been so good to me, I'm happy to return the many favors.

The following five days blend into each other. Throughout the busy workdays and long, lonely nights, my mind wanders to the lazy days and passionate nights with Harris. He calls, and we've pleasured ourselves via Face-Time. But nothing beats the real thing, including the BOB—Battery Operated Boyfriend—Harris sent for me to use while he watched hungrily.

By the time Friday rolls around, I'm keyed up and can't wait to see him tonight. He surprised me again with an invitation for dinner at his penthouse in The STEELE Tower. I greedily accepted wanting the food he ordered from one of Lucien's restaurants and for the taste of my man on my tongue.

After work, I rush home to shower and to change into a slinky black dress with a sheer mesh bra and matching thong. To complete my sex kitten look, I pile my hair into a messy bun, tie a black silk ribbon into a bow around my neck, and slip into sky-high black stilettos. Before I leave, I add shell pink lip gloss and walk through a spritz of my perfume.

"Whoohoo! Sexy Bae Alert!" Vivian says as she wolf whistles upon seeing me emerge from my room. "Somebody's getting her freak on tonight! *Rawr*, as Missy Elliot says."

She falls back on the sofa, cracking up about her own joke.

I laugh and wave.

"Have fun for me, Kat!" She calls out as I round the corner, headed for the coat closet and lift.

My mobile rings as the doors open in the lobby. I grin at Harris' name on the screen.

"Hi, Harris," I say breathlessly, in keeping with my sex kitten persona. "I'm walking towards the lobby door now."

"Hey, Kitty Kat, I'm stuck in traffic. So I won't be able to pick you up. I sent a STEELE driver with a silver Mercedes-Benz S 580 for you. He's out front. Do you see him?" Harris tells me.

I pull back a disappointed sigh and nod at the doorman as I pass. The STEELE driver stands beside the sedan and opens the back door when he sees me. I smile and tell Harris I'm getting inside.

"Okay, a member of security at The STEELE Tower will give you access to my penthouse. He'll meet you at the concierge desk. I'll be there as soon as I can. Oh, wait, hold on… I have to take this call. I'll see you soon," Harris says, then ends the call.

I glance at the mobile and shake my head as I slip it into my purse. The text alert dings.

Sorry I had to rush. Can't wait to see you. H.

I sit back against the sumptuous leather seat and grin.

"Thank you," I tell the security guard as I step into Harris' penthouse. The guard bids me a good evening and returns to the private lift.

I still can't believe Harris allowed me into his personal space, unattended by him. However, I will not snoop. Instead, I drape my coat on the bench in the entry and place my purse on top. Mobile in hand, I walk to the living room. The delicious aroma of food fills the air.

Someone beautifully decorated his home with masculine touches of leather, rich colors, and a well-stocked bar. I make a beeline for it. Naturally, the selection includes the Jackson Corporation labels. My fingers graze an impressive storage box made of the most rare and most expensive African Blackwood. I know it all too well…

It contains Jackson Corporation's Scotch blend the master distiller worked on for the past sixty years. It's a limited-edition run for an astronomical one-million pounds.

Over six months ago, bent on my revenge goal, I uncovered the launch plans and other details. Even though I couldn't get the recipe, Chet Stewart agreed the intel I stole was worth the hefty sum he paid to me. He didn't make me privy to how he plans to use the information to Stewart Scotch's advantage and sting Jackson Corporation.

With a shudder at the thought of Chet, I move on to another bottle. I pour Jackson Special Blend Scotch into a Waterford Crystal snifter and stand in front of the floor-to-ceiling windows. Hopefully, the amazing view of New York City lit up at night from the fifty-first floor will chase away the terrible memories.

I take a healthy sip of the Scotch. The burn is just what I need.

"I'm more impressed by the view of you, Kitty Kat, than you can ever be of the Manhattan skyline at night."

Lost in thought, time passed. Harris' warm breath on the side of my neck as he whispers in my ear causes me to shudder—this time in a good way.

"I missed you, Kitty Kat," he rumbles, nuzzling my neck. "Did you miss me?"

Without missing a beat, I place the snifter next to my mobile on a table and turn around to face him. My arms go around his neck as I stand on tiptoe to bring his face closer to mine.

"More than you can even imagine, Harris Steele," I murmur against his full lips, then nip the bottom one.

He growls, bends his knees, and tosses me over his shoulder. A swat to my ass only covered by a wisp of silk from my dress makes me yelp and flail my legs. He bands his arm around my thighs and strides from the room.

"You will show me just how much, naughty lass," he rumbles. "First, I feed you, then you feed me. After, we eat what Lucien has for us."

"Yes, Harris," I purr.

* * *

"Good morning, sleepyhead."

A lazy smile spreads across my face at the sight of a sexy, rumble-haired Harris staring down at me. I reach up and cup his stubbled cheek. He leans into my hand as his eyes close. He sighs contentedly.

"Good morning to you, early bird," I whisper as my fingertip drags across his lips.

He kisses the tip of it and smiles.

"Move in with me."

My eyes pop as my mouth forms an O.

Harris chuckles.

"Is that a yes or a no?" He asks as his thumb lifts my chin to close my slack mouth.

I blink.

He ducks his head and murmurs, "Don't leave a guy hanging, Kitty Kat."

Then he lifts his eyes to gaze at me from beneath his thick, ebony eyelashes. The absolute sexiness of his vulnerability seals the deal. I squeal and push him to his back as I straddle his hips and plant kisses all over his handsome face.

"Yes. Yes. YES!!!" I shout.

Harris beams at me with a beatific smile that makes his dove gray eyes shine. He sits up and kisses the tip of my nose.

"Good Kitty Kat," he says. "Let's do this now. Then you can thank me properly later."

I giggle and slide off his lap.

After we shower, he arranges for movers from STEELE International's operations department to meet us at the flat I share with Vivian. The team will pack my things up and bring them to Harris'—*our*—flat in just a few hours.

I tease Harris about how spoiled rotten he is to get this done last minute on a Saturday morning. He just shrugs. I call Vivian, and she squeals louder than I did at Harris' proclamation. She promises to help instead of going to her Pilates session.

The movers make quick work of boxing my clothes and the items I decorated my room with while there. Harris and Viv sit in the family room chatting it up like old friends. Some help they prove to be I laugh to myself as a mover carries the last box from my room.

"Okay, my little helpers, time to go," I tell Harris and Vivian.

"Oh, my, done so soon?" She asks with her hand to heart and wide-eyed, feigning surprise.

Harris grins and stands from the sofa.

"Well done," he says and wraps his arm around my waist.

I roll my eyes and nudge his side with my elbow.

We ride a lift down to the lobby while the movers finish on the service lift and at the service entrance.

"You're sure you have everything?" Viv asks before she gets into Harris' Rolls-Royce SUV.

He turns to me questioningly.

I run through my mind's eye of the room. Then I remember the last gift my father ever gave to me. A hand-crafted music box. He received it as payment for one of the rare inventions he created that actually worked. I cherished it from first sight.

"Hold on, I forgot my music box. I'll be right back," I say, spinning on my heel.

"I'll come with you," Harris offers.

"Not to worry. It'll just take me a minute," I say as I wave him off over my shoulder and rush inside.

As I pass the utility closet, I grab the step ladder and head for my former room. I left the music box on the top shelf of the walk-in closet. It hurts to look at it sometimes since it reminds me of my Da and how he passed at such a young age from a heart attack. But I keep it close.

A smile plays at the corners of my mouth as I open it to listen to the playful tune. I close my eyes and remember the day he gave it to me.

"You really think you're special now? Don't you? Well, we have unfinished business, lass."

My blood runs cold in my veins as goosebumps break out over my entire body. My precious music box crashes to the floor. The tune dies out on impact.

Chet Stewart!

How the bloody hell did he find me and get in here?!

I spin around to find him dressed as one of the movers, even down to the gray coveralls and matching cap. The hat set low on his head to cover half of his face.

He snatches it off. His eyes shoot icy daggers at me, and I freeze when he pulls a handgun with a silencer from his pocket.

My heart stops as I stare open-mouthed at the jet black metal aimed straight at my chest. I realize the dark stain on the neck of the coveralls must be blood from the mover who wore them.

Oh. My. God. Chet has gone mad.

He glares at me with such animosity, the air gets sucked from my lungs.

"You ruined me, my family, our company. You will pay, Kat *Jackson*!"

505

* * *

Harris & Kat's Story Continues: *Honor My Desires*

STEELE INTERNATIONAL, INC.
JACKSON CORPORATION
A BILLIONAIRES ROMANCE
SERIES CROSSOVER

Honor my DESIRES

HARRIS & KAT PART III

Charmaine Louise Shelton

I dedicate this novel to those who never give up no matter the challenges they face in life and in love.

Fulfill Your Desires.

xoxo
Charmaine Louise

ABOUT HONOR MY DESIRES INTRIGUE & KAT PART III

Honor My Desires Harris & Kat Part III

Welcome to the titillating world of the multibillion-dollar global companies and the love affairs of the families that control them.

Harris

Well... I finally gave in to the feminine wiles of my Kitty Kat marking the end of my old playboy ways. However, fate can be funnier than me and has other plans for our new relationship...

Kat

I vow to honor Harris. But sometimes the past has bad timing. Sure they say cats have nine lives. So how many until I get my happily ever after with the man I love?

Come along for their sizzling, soul mate billionaire romance as Harris and Kat's travels take them around the globe. New

York City, Glasgow, London, and the Maldives will never be the same.

Anthem: "Escapade" Janet Jackson
https://www.youtube.com/watch?v=UFX3gQHIroU

Playlist:
https://www.youtube.com/playlist?list=
PLXwYvn0e218A90Sz6_dDu0IECce6Pr6GS

Visit CharmaineLouiseBooks.com

HARRIS

"*H*ey, Kitty Kat. Have dinner with me tonight at my penthouse. I'll get one of Lucien's restaurants to send over food. But you'll be dessert. Hmmm… Maybe some fresh whipped cream and a couple of sweet maraschino cherries on top. Licked clean, naturally. Sounds tantalizing enough for you?"

I smirk when Kat's gasp comes through the mobile. I can picture her alabaster cheeks flushing rosy red. Not as vibrant as her Titian hair, but just as silky to the touch. The pupils of her eyes more than likely dilate with lust, leaving only their rims a dazzling emerald green. Her little pink tongue darts out to moisten her lush lips as the air rushes past them.

My cock twitches in the trousers of my bespoke Saville Row suit at the vision of my sexy Siren aroused.

Katrina Roberts cum Katrina Jackson. Yeah… *Jackson.*

The woman who nearly toppled both the Jackson and the Steele clans with her scheme of vengeance in alignment with Chester *Chet* Stewart. Kat—an unknown cousin of the

Jacksons—partnered with Stewart Scotch, Jackson Corporation's top competitor and historical clan rival amongst the world of Scottish nobility.

And I—Harris Steele, tech wiz extraordinaire—didn't see it coming. At. All.

Too busy enthralled by that redheaded Siren to see the signs of her betrayal until it was almost too late. Three months of the closest to a committed relationship I've ever had in my thirty-two years, and it ends with her admittance of misdeeds.

Lachlan Jackson—my cousin via our mothers being best friends and my brother-in-law—as CEO and Chairman of the Board of Jackson Corporation may have chosen not to press charges. He only banned Kat from Scotland.

But I banished her from my life. For fourteen weeks, that is. Unable to resist her Siren's call, I initiated a week to fuck her out of my system. All it did was make me crave her more and realize more is just what I want from Kat Jackson. My Kitty Kat.

She redeemed herself with letters of apology to each member of my family and conducted herself in the manner of one who wants to make amends. She even donated the money she garnered from giving Stewart intel on Jackson Corporation to the Aberdeen Children's Center, where she volunteered.

I'm far from a weak man and gave her hell. But there's no point in wallowing in the fiery pits when I can luxuriate deep in her warm, welcoming core. Especially when we both acknowledge what we shared over those three months was real. Despite her initial reason to use me as a smoke-screen to access the Jacksons as part of her attempt at their downfall.

Ah well...

So here we are post the Seven-day Fuckfest, a surprise trip to Maui for Valentine's Day—don't think I'm not a romantic—and a week of me in Buenos Aires for business. And I want to have My Kitty Kat cum for dinner. Yup, pun intended. And in my penthouse at The STEELE Tower on Fifty-seventh and Fifth Avenue in the midst of Billionaires' Row in New York City. My sanctuary where no women besides those of my family have crossed the threshold.

Harris Steele—Alpha male billionaire playboy—falls for The One. Hard.

The last man standing of The STEELE Quaternity—dubbed such by the media as the most sought-after of the world's eligible billionaires and heirs to STEELE International, Inc. Handsome; six plus feet; ebony hair; shades of gray eyes; powerful Alpha Doms and males. I've followed in the footsteps of my three older brothers Sebastian, Malcolm, and Roger. They succumbed and married the women who captured their hearts—Lola, Starr, and Leonie, respectively.

I once laughed and called my brothers suckers. Now, they'll laugh at me. Again. This time for good. If My Kitty Kat behaves like a good little kitten.

"Oh, Harris," she starts breathlessly. "That sounds more than tantalizing. I'd love to have dinner with you... And be your dessert."

I growl as her response ends in a sultry purr. My cock throbs in approval.

"Excellent, Kitty Kat. I'll meet you in front of your apartment building at seven tonight," I say, ignoring the twinge in my gut from her use of the four-letter word even regarding food. I'm not all the way there yet. We end the call, and I sit back in the leather chair of my Gulfstream G650ER.

"The pilot is ready for takeoff, Mr. Steele."

I turn my gaze from the window to the flight attendant and smile as I give my consent to leave Buenos Aires behind.

As much as I enjoy being the co-head of STEELE Technology and Cyber Security with my fraternal twin Haley, I can't wait to head home. Home where My Kitty Kat will be soon.

"I APOLOGIZE, Mr. Steele. There's no getting around this accident. Shall I have a STEELE driver collect Ms. Jackson?"

A glance at my Audemars Piguet The Royal Oak Complication watch confirms we'll be late picking up My Kitty Kat. I agree with my driver, Alonso Masa's recommendation. Once the STEELE driver is outside of her apartment building, I call to let her know.

"Hi, Harris," she says breathlessly. "I'm walking towards the lobby door now."

"Hey, Kitty Kat, I'm stuck in traffic. So I won't be able to pick you up. I sent a STEELE driver with a silver Mercedes-Benz S 580 for you. He's out front. Do you see him?" I tell her.

"Yes, and I'm getting inside now," she responds, in an attempt to hide her disappointment.

Join the club. I'd rather have met her, too.

"Okay, a member of security at The STEELE Tower will give you access to my penthouse. He'll meet you at the concierge desk. I'll be there as soon as I can. Oh, wait, hold on… I have to take this call. I'll see you soon," I say, then end the call.

It's from a potential client another client referred to me while in Argentina. I can't ignore it. While I answer, I pull up the message app and shoot a text to Kat. Hopefully, it'll lessen the bluntness of my hang up.

Sorry I had to rush. Can't wait to see you. H.

By the end of the call, I've secured a new client for his company and his personal accounts. I send a quick text message to Haley as a heads-up. She sends back a grinning emoji. Then follows it with a reminder I'm behind her in our monthly new business quota by two.

We're the youngest of the Steele siblings and a surprise to our parents being three years younger than Roger. As the Dynamic Duo, Haley and I have made it our mission to make our mark on STEELE International and to contribute to our family's multigenerational, multibillion-dollar company.

Consequently, our division generates a sizable amount to STEELE's bottom line and brings in clients for the other divisions—Retail Properties, Entertainment Properties, and Residential Properties. Each of our brothers runs a division, with Baz also being the CEO and Chairman of the Board. STCS has become an indispensable part of STEELE International.

I snicker and shoot back an eye roll emoji, knowing it'll get Haley riled up.

We're hella close and love each other to death. She's as protective of me as I am of her. I'm sure she'll be okay with Kat and me getting back together since Haley instigated Kat and me talking weeks ago. Based on my conversation with my Dad Morgan and my mother Shelley's message, I'm sure they'll be open to it, even if warily. *Remain open to love. It can surprise you whence it comes.*

I keep my parents' words of wisdom in mind as I walk through the living room of my penthouse to where My Kitty Kat stands staring out the floor-to-ceiling windows.

"I'm more impressed by the view of you, Kitty Kat, than you can ever be of the Manhattan skyline at night," I say. My warm breath tickles the side of her neck as I whisper in her ear.

She shudders.

"I missed you, Kitty Kat," I rumble, nuzzling her neck. "Did you miss me?"

She places a snifter next to her mobile on a table and turns around to face me. Her slender arms go around my neck as she stands on tiptoe to bring my face closer to hers.

"More than you can even imagine, Harris Steele," she murmurs against my lips, then nips the bottom one. The scent of Jackson Scotch wafts across my face.

I growl deep in my chest as I bend my knees and toss My Kitty Kat over my shoulder. A swat to her ass only covered by a wisp of silk from her dress makes her yelp and flail her legs. I band one arm around her thighs and stride from the living room.

"You will show me just how much, naughty lass," I rumble. "First, I feed you, then you feed me. After, we eat what Lucien has for us."

"Yes, Harris," she purrs like a good little kitten.

Off to a great start.

Once inside my bedroom suite, I carry her to the bed and place her on her feet. My hands skim the sides of her body from her shoulders to her thighs. With a flick of my wrists, I divest her of the skimpy, silky number she wore to tease me.

My Siren gasps and covers her DDs with her hands. More than her palms can cover, the luscious tits spill around them.

"Do not cover yourself from me, naughty lass," I admonish as I grasp her wrists and bring them over her head. I dip mine to envelop a puckered rosy nipple into my hungry mouth.

She groans and undulates her body.

My other hand drops to cup her round ass to still her movements. I want her to focus on the pleasurable sensations without distraction.

I continue to lave, nip, and to suckle her delectable tits until they're heavy with her need. Another flick of my wrist and I snap the thin material of her G-string to bare her pussy to me. My fingers skim its wet seam collecting her cream.

Her pupils dilate as she watches me slip the glistening digits into my mouth and swirl my tongue around them. My groan of appreciation makes her tremble and close her eyes as she sways.

I scoop her up and toss her into the middle of my king-size bed. Her eyes pop open, then half-mast as I kick off my shoes and strip out of my suit. My muscles ripple as I stalk towards her and lower onto the bed between her spread thighs.

My Siren widens them for my broad shoulders as I bow before her dripping fount. Her cries of carnal ecstasy as I devour her sweet pussy heighten my desire to fuck her raw.

But first she must be ready to take my ten inches. My fingers join my lips and tongue to drive her over the edge again and again. Not until her cream pools beneath her ass do I plank over her sated body.

She can only move her eyes languorously as she watches me take her legs and wrap them around my hips. She gathers the strength to tighten the hold as I align the purple, swollen head of my cock to her warm, welcoming core.

A single thrust seats me deep within her pussy. She

screams as her body adjusts to my girth and length. Her inner walls clench to draw me further inside.

I throw my head back and howl.

"So fucking good, Kitty Kat…" I groan. But remain still until she's ready for the ride.

"Harris… Please…" she begs as her hips squirm for much-needed friction.

Who am I to deny her?

My hips meet hers as I flex my ass and withdraw before pounding back into her quivering sheath.

Her head lolls as her mouth forms a perfect O. No sound slips past her lips. Only from her lower ones, as her wetness squelches from the driving force of my thrusts.

My grunts add harmony to the erotic symphony we create. Her high-pitched wails as she cums undone for me build to a crescendo. I erupt with an almighty roar.

My climax triggers another for My Siren. She keens as her pussy clamps down on my cock to milk it of every single drop. Her fingernails dig into my biceps to anchor her from flying into the stratosphere.

But I'm gone. Lost in the throes of passion.

I return to My Kitty Kat's soothing caresses and her whispered words. My face nestled between her pillowy mounds, my heartbeat slows. I wrap my arms around her waist and roll onto my back.

She cuddles into me as her head rests on my chest over my heart. She slides her hands around my flanks to hold me close. With a sigh, she settles.

"I missed you, too, Harris Steele," she whispers.

A satisfied smile curves across my lips.

"I missed you, too, Kat Jackson," I respond.

Her stomach growls louder than I did moments ago. She giggles and turns her face into my chest, embarrassed.

"Not very sexy, huh?" She asks as her shoulders shake with mirth.

I smack her ass and sit up.

"No. And not good for my ego," I respond wryly. "Guess it's time to feed you, Kitty Kat."

She bites the corner of her lower lip and nods. Then she lowers her gold-tinged eyelashes.

"We can always return for that dessert you promised," she purrs.

My cock twitches, ready for more.

"Abso-fucking-lutely, Siren," I swear.

Yeah, it's good to be home. With My Kitty Kat.

HARRIS

The early morning sun shines through the floor-to-ceiling windows to bathe My Kitty Kat's gorgeous face in an ethereal glow as she slumbers. Shadows form on the tops of her cheeks from the long fringe of eyelashes. Their golden tips catch the sun's rays. Cheeks still rosy from our fucking a couple of hours ago. Kiss-swollen lips part as soft snores slip from between them.

I wore her out. All. Night. Long.

Yet despite my morning wood, I only want to watch her sleep, not ravish her again. The last time we laid in bed, I wondered what it would be like to fall asleep with My Kitty Kat in my arms, not just for a few days. But always.

These past five days—with me waking alone—gave me time to reassess the situation. I was already partial to a second chance. Now, I want her not just in my bed, but in my home.

I feel like Baz when he moved Lola into his duplex penthouse upstairs after they met. New to the City, she didn't have a permanent residence of her own just like Kat.

Sharing an apartment—albeit a massive full-floor penthouse with her friend and colleague, Vivian Murphy—isn't like Kat having her own place. No lease to worry about, not that it would make a bit of difference. She would break the lease, and I would pay for the penalty fee.

Decision made, I continue to watch My Kitty Kat until her eyes open slowly and adjust to the sunlit bedroom.

"Good morning, sleepyhead," I say with a grin as I stare down at her.

A lazy smile spreads across her face. She lifts her hand to cup my cheek. The stubble bristles against her smooth palm as I lean into it with my eyes closed. A contented sigh escapes from my mouth.

"Good morning to you, early bird," My Kitty Kat whispers as she drags her finger across my lips.

I kiss the tip of it and smile again.

"Move in with me," I tell her, then chuckle as her eyes pop while her mouth forms a perfect O. "Is that a yes or a no?" I ask as my thumb lifts her chin to close her slack mouth.

She blinks.

Well damn, not quite the response I expected…

I duck my head at her delay and murmur, "Don't leave a guy hanging, Kitty Kat."

Then I lift questioning eyes to gaze at her from beneath my thick, ebony eyelashes.

She squeals and pushes me to my back as she straddles my hips and covers my face with kisses. Her exuberance returns a confident smile to my face.

"Yes. Yes. YES!!!" My Kitty Kat shouts with glee.

I grin like the Cheshire Cat, adding a sparkle to my dove gray eyes. I sit up and kiss the tip of her nose.

"Good Kitty Kat," I say, then smirk. "Let's do this now. Then you can thank me properly later."

She giggles and slides off my lap.

I can't resist a spank to her round ass and chuckle wickedly as it jiggles and she yelps.

During our shower, I thwart her attempts at sucking my at-attention cock—what am I nuts?—to speed things up. I shake my head at the change in priorities. But like I said, later, not never.

While I dress, I arrange for movers from STEELE International's operations department to meet us at the One Fifth Avenue penthouse. The team will pack Kat's things up and bring them to my—I mean to *our*—penthouse. Even though it's last minute and on a Saturday, the Vice President guarantees the move will take his team only a few hours to complete. Perfect.

Naturally, My Kitty Kat teases me about being spoiled rotten. I shrug. It is what it is.

Alonso drives us down to the landmark prewar co-op a block north of Washington Square Park on the Gold Coast of Greenwich Village.

My Kitty Kat rambles on about how happy she is to move in. Then she peppers me with questions about access, travel to the children's nonprofit where she works as Development Director, and what she should do with her items that won't fit.

I'll have to add her palm print to the systems when we get back. Alonso can drive her to and from her office since my five-minute commute consists of taking the family's private elevator from our residences to the floor for STCS. I also tell her we'll figure out adding her items once the movers bring everything to the penthouse. They'll organize what stays and where and what goes to storage.

She kisses my face and shimmies on the seat beside me.

Once we arrive, the doorman helps her from my Black Badge Rolls-Royce Cullinan while Alonso opens my door. My Kitty Kat and I pass through the magnificent two-story lobby headed to the elevator. She presses the button for the private tower floor on twenty-four.

The doors ping open to reveal Vivian, who throws her arms around Kat and pulls her from the elevator. Their squeals pierce the air. I chuckle and shake my head.

When they part, Vivian grins at me. She's a stunningly beautiful woman with skin that as Lucien—ever *The Sexy Chef*—says reminds him of a decadent ganache. Her toffee brown eyes gleam with excitement for her friend as she pushes a stray ebony curl behind her ear.

"Well, Harris Steele, look at you!" Vivian says as she loops her arm through mine. "Now, you and I will have a talk while Kat directs the movers. Come. We'll sit in the family room outside of Kat's bedroom."

I can't help but to grin back at Vivian and allow her to lead me through the palatial, multimillion-dollar residence. We pass windows with incredible 360-degree views. The Freedom Tower to the south, the Empire State building to the south, New Jersey west of the Hudson River, and beyond the East River.

"Mr. Steele, we're ready to begin, sir."

I pull my gaze from the captivating panorama.

Six movers wait outside of what I presume is Kat's bedroom. Already prepared with wardrobe and regular boxes to gather her things.

"Thank you," I respond to the one in charge as I shake his hand. With a nod towards Kat, I continue. "This is Ms. Jackson. She will let you know what needs to be done."

They disappear into the bedroom while Vivian and I

settle on a leather sofa. She tucks her long, toned legs encased in yoga pants beneath her. A collarless cashmere sweater falls off her shoulder to reveal a matching tank top.

Kat tells me how they do twice-weekly Pilates sessions together and how Vivian eats healthily. It's clear she takes excellent care of herself. I remind myself to introduce her to some of my buddies.

"So, this idea of Kat moving in with you just popped into your head this morning, Harris?" Vivian asks with an elegant eyebrow arched.

We've met twice only, so I still need to prove myself to My Kitty Kat's best friend.

"It's been on my mind for the last week or so. The time we spent together made me realize we might as well take it another step," I respond honestly.

Vivian studies me a moment, then nods as though satisfied with my answer.

"Okay. But just so you know, Kat is my good friend. She made bad choices. But she's remorseful and wants to make things right between you and your family—the Steeles and the Jacksons. Especially since the latter is her family, too. So do not hurt her," Vivian states.

It's my turn to nod. I can respect their friendship and protectiveness of each other.

"Wonderful! Now, tell me about these buddies of yours Kat mentioned…" Vivian says with a wink.

I chuckle at the whiplash from the change in topic and go through my list of bachelors. Viv and I continue to talk while the movers hustle in and out with Kat's things.

"Okay, my little helpers, time to go."

I stop mid-sentence at Kat's words. Vivian raises her gaze to her friend.

"Oh, my, done so soon?" Viv asks with her hand to heart and wide-eyed, feigning surprise.

I grin and stand from the sofa.

"Well done," I say and wrap my arm around My Kitty Kat's waist.

She rolls her eyes and nudges my side with her elbow.

I pretend she inflicted a mortal wound, and the girls giggle.

We follow a mover who carries the last box from the bedroom. He heads for the penthouse's service entrance, where the movers finish on the service elevator and at the building's service entrance. The girls and I go to the residents' elevators for the ride down to the lobby.

Alonso waits at the curb and opens the SUV's door.

Vivian pauses before she gets in and turns to Kat.

"You're sure you have everything?" Viv asks.

I turn to My Kitty Kat questioningly.

She tugs on a corner of her lower lip as she considers her answer. Her emerald green eyes widen.

"Hold on, I forgot my music box. I'll be right back," she says, spinning on her heel.

"I'll come with you," I say as I follow her to the doors.

"Not to worry. It'll just take me a minute," she says as she waves me off over her shoulder and rushes inside.

I watch her go as Viv slips inside the SUV.

"Are you getting inside, Mr. Steele?"

Alonso's question draws my attention. I nod and stride to the other side of the SUV. When Kat returns, she'll sit in the middle.

Vivian's fingers fly across the screen of her mobile. I retrieve mine from the pocket of my Brunello Cucinelli cashmere down parka. Even though it's Saturday, my business email account has plenty to occupy the time it'll take for Kat to return.

Caught up in the influx of messages, I lose track of time until my mobile rings with a call from The STEELE Tower.

"Mr. Steele, the movers arrived with Ms. Jackson's items. Shall I give them access to your penthouse, sir?" The concierge asks.

I frown and glance at the clock. Twenty minutes passed. My gaze goes to the apartment building's front doors. Vivian peers at them, too.

"Yes, give the movers access with two security team members to watch over them and have my house manager oversee their activities," I respond, then end the call.

"What's taking Kat so long?" Viv asks. "I sent a text message to her, but she hasn't responded."

My frown deepens as I jump from the SUV. Viv joins me as we head towards the doors and through the lobby. The ride upstairs is tense. She unlocks the front doors to the penthouse and calls out to Kat.

No answer. Only silence.

The hairs on the back of my neck rise.

"Kat!" I yell as I race towards her former bedroom. "Where are you?!"

I round the corner. The bedroom door stands open, but no sound comes from within.

Did she fall and can't respond?

Vivian catches up to me as I burst into the bedroom.

"She's not in the rest of the penthouse," she says anxiously.

My eyes scan the empty bedroom. No sign of Kat.

Scattered pieces of what appears to be a music box litters the floor by the closest.

What the fuck???

A scream from Vivian makes me pivot. Hands fisted, ready to fight.

In front of her staggers one mover.

An unclothed mover.

An unclothed mover with dried blood plastered to the side of his head. He grips the doorframe and moans.

"What the fuck happened to you?!" I shout as I rush over and grab him by the arms before he collapses to the floor. "And where the hell is Kat?!?!?!"

His head hangs and fresh blood oozes from the gash.

In the background, Vivian speaks rapidly into her mobile. The words police and ambulance filter through the red haze that descends around me.

"Come on, man! Speak up!" I shout as I shake the mover.

He sputters incoherently.

"Harris, give him a moment," Vivian says softly as she rests her hand on my shoulder.

I nod and lead him to a chair in the family room.

"Are you sure Kat isn't anywhere else in here?" I ask Vivian.

She shakes her head solemnly as tears well in her eyes.

I turn back to the mover. I refuse to give up hope Kat is okay. Who the fuck could have gotten in here, anyway? It's a secure building and penthouse. No one knew she was moving.

"S—S—Someone hit me... while... while I was in the service hallway," the mover says. "Didn't see who—"

His sentence ends with a grunt of pain from the shake he gives to his head. He clasps it. But Vivian holds his wrist to keep him from touching the bloody wound.

Shouts ring out as thunderous footfalls approach us.

"Over here!" Vivian calls as she rushes towards them.

"Where's the service hallway?!" I yell at her retreating back.

She gestures for me to follow her along with two building security men. We run through the penthouse to the other side. As we near, the door stands ajar with a bloody palm print on it.

A small palm.

A small palm print from a woman's hand.

"Step back! This is a crime scene. Everyone stand down. Now!"

The police officer's command stops all movement.

I face her and scowl.

"My girlfriend may still be in the building! Through that door! Someone needs to check. *Now!*" I issue my own command. We can't waste any time. Especially since she's bleeding. The asshole most likely hurt her. Or worse.

My gut flips at the thought someone harmed Kat.

What did they do? And why the hell did they do it?

The penthouse is full of expensive artwork from Picasso to Edmonia Lewis, antiques, state-of-the-art electronics. Undoubtedly cash, jewelry, and designer clothes.

Why would they want to take Kat???

My fingers run through my hair and tug the strands to make me focus. No point in yelling at the cop. We need their help, after all.

"Listen, this just happened. Only twenty minutes ago,

she was here. They can't be but so far," I say to the officer as another joins her.

She nods and turns to her partner. They radio in for backup and direct the security team to lock down the building. No one in and no one out, with guards stationed at each entry point. A flurry of activity ensues.

Vivian clutches my arm as the officers ask us to take a seat in the living room. I squeeze her hand as I glance down at her. She turns her face up to me. Fearful eyes stare back.

"We'll get this under control, Viv. Don't worry. Okay?" I tell her. She nods. But I worry as much—if not more—than she does.

This shit is real.

"Tell us your names and your reason for being here," the female officer demands.

Vivian straightens her spine and clears her throat.

"I am Vivian Murphy, and this is my penthouse," she responds.

The male officer scribbles on his notepad while the female flicks her analytical gaze from Vivian to me.

"Harris Steele. I accompanied my girlfriend—Kat Jackson, who's missing—here for her to move her things to my penthouse," I respond.

The male officer pauses his methodical writing at the mention of my last name. He raises his gaze to me, then arches his eyebrow at his partner. They exchange a knowing look.

"Steele. As in STEELE International, Inc.?" He asks.

"Yes," I answer.

Another look passes between his partner and him.

My patience shreds.

"Listen, we do not have time to play twenty-one questions with you. Someone clobbered one mover and abducted my girlfriend. A bloody handprint—I presume is hers—proves someone harmed her. While we're sitting here chitchatting, she could bleed to death! Get on with it, man!" My voice increases in volume as the sentence ends.

I glare at each of the police officers until they squirm in their seats. Disgusted, I whip out my mobile to place a call I never thought I'd need to make. I rise to pace the floor.

"Commissioner Flagg, it's Harris Steele," I say when the call connects me to the highest ranking police officer in New York City. I ignore the shocked gasp from the female officer and the groan from the male as I continue. "I hoped to never have to contact you for more than a social call. But someone abducted my girlfriend, and we presume injured her. We need your help."

With the commissioner on his way to the penthouse, I place the next important phone call.

"Sebastian, I need you," I say when my eldest brother answers his mobile. He knows it's serious when I use his full name and not Baz. I fill him in, and he jumps into action.

Moments later, I hang up from the second eldest, Malcolm *The Enforcer*—as we call him for his methods of handling situations for our family. He's taking his Sikorsky S-92 Executive Helicopter in from his and Starr's residence at our family beachfront compound—Steele Southampton Village. He assures me we'll get to the bottom of the situation.

I place another call to Haley who's in Aberdeenshire, Scotland at her and Lachlan's Aboyne Castle. She puts me on speaker so he can hear too.

"Harris! Oh my God! We'll fly over now," she says, and Lachlan agrees.

"No one fucks with a Jackson! Keep us posted on all details. I'm texting our flight crew now. We'll be there in a few hours. I'll tell her mother, brother, and sister. They'll probably join us," he says, pissed as fuck.

"I'll call The STEELE Tower concierge to arrange one of the guest apartments for them," Haley adds.

An incoming call chimes. I glance at the screen—Roger.

I disconnect from Haley and Lach to answer.

"Are you okay?" Roger *The Responsible* asks. Naturally, his first concern is to his family, for which I'm grateful.

I tell him I'm trying not to lose my shit, and he counsels me to keep it together. He, Leonie, and their kids, with nannies and dogs in tow, head to the private airport outside of Paris. In the background, Leonie chimes in to tell me not to worry too much, *chéri*. I can picture the megamodel's amber eyes flash with ferocity like *The Lion* she's known as the world over.

The last call I make is to my parents. They're on their megayacht *Serendipity* cruising the Mediterranean Sea through the end of February. I hate to disturb their alone time after being with the family over the holidays. But I know they'd rather be aware than not.

"Hi, Dad, I have some bad news," I say when he answers.

As fate would have it, Uncle Connor and Aunt Lucie are aboard the luxury vessel. After he swears in Scottish Gaelic, they confirm they're on their way.

As the eldest Jackson alive and the Marquess of Huntly, Uncle Connor acknowledged Kat and her family as Jacksons, despite his great-great-grandfather's disownment of Iain. He's Kat's connection to the Jacksons since Iain is her great-great-grandfather. Like his son Lachlan, Uncle Connor is very much a clan man and protects his own.

When I hang up, I send a text message to Alonso and to Edwin Nims, my house manager. As I put my mobile in my jeans pocket, I turn to the police officers. They stare at me, unsure how to react since I went way above their heads.

As if I give a fuck. Ignoring them, I shift my gaze to Vivian. She stares back at me, then rises.

"Let's wait for everyone in the kitchen. I'll make pots of coffee and tea," she says ever the refined lady of the house.

I nod and retrieve my mobile again. This time, I place a call to one of Lucien's restaurants to cater food for everyone. Baz, Lola, Malcolm, and Starr will arrive soon.

My mobile rings just as I set it on the kitchen island—Laurent, the youngest Jackson, and my best friend.

"Har! What the everlasting bloody fuck, cuz?! I'm on my way over. Do you need anything?" He asks. When I tell him his support will do, he tells me Lydie and Lucien—the rest of the Jackson siblings—will call.

Vivian puts a mug of coffee in front of me on the marble island and sits next to me as she cradles her mug. She sighs as she blows to cool the brew down.

"I'm scared for Kat, Harris," Viv whispers.

I say a silent prayer for My Kitty Kat's safety and swift return. It still perplexes me what the hell happened. My guess is someone saw activity at the service entrance and entered the building seeking to steal from the apartment being vacated. But to take Kat when valuables remain untouched makes absolutely zero sense.

"We need to see the security footage. I need my laptop," I ramble on as my brain kicks back in from the initial shock shutdown. A text message to Edwin will have Alonso bring my laptop to me. It's a start.

Vivian places her mobile back on the island.

"The head of security will grant you access to all building cameras. He'll bring his laptop here now," she says. "At least we can see what happened."

It doesn't take him long to arrive and set up on the island. But what appears on the screen reveals nothing unusual. At least on first inspection. I ask him to re-run the feed from the alley camera.

A stray cat walks from one side to the other in front of the moving truck. Okay. Then the same cat jumps back to repeat its movement.

"Fuck. Me. It's on a loop!" I exclaim.

The head of security peers closer.

"Well, I'll be damned," he mutters.

The police officers who joined us murmur amongst themselves.

"Harris, we're here!"

Everyone falls silent at the booming baritone of Baz. A natural leader, he enters the kitchen with the air of an Alpha Dom in full control. Those gathered part to allow him and Lola to reach me.

"Baz," I say as he embraces me. Then I turn to Lola and give her a hug.

"Malcolm is twenty minutes out," he says as he turns to the laptop. "What's this?"

I fill him in, and he mutters a string of curses.

"And no word from the person who took Kat?" Lola asks as she squeezes my hand. Her hazel eyes full of concern scan my face.

I shake my head.

"Commissioner, sir."

The male officer's acknowledgment draws our attention to the kitchen's entry.

Commissioner Flagg—flanked by the First Commissioner and a Deputy Commissioner I recognize as the head of Information Technology—strides towards us with his hand outstretched. We shake, and I make the introduction of Vivian to them. Baz and Lola greet them. Eager to keep busy, Vivian and Lola pour coffee and tea for everyone.

"Tell me the latest," Commissioner Flagg commands.

We replay the camera footage, and the Deputy Commissioner pulls out her laptop. She works with the head of security to play more footage. Afterwards, she taps into the City's network of cameras to expand the coverage.

New York City is one of the busiest places in the world. It'll take time to navigate so much video.

Time, I'm afraid we do not have.

KAT

"You really think you're special now? Don't you? Well, we have unfinished business, lass."

My blood runs cold in my veins as goosebumps break out over my entire body. My precious music box crashes to the floor. The tune dies out on impact.

Chet Stewart!

How the *bloody hell* did he find me and get in here to boot?!

I spin around to find him dressed as one of the movers, even down to the STEELE International gray coveralls and matching cap. The hat set low on his head to cover half of his face.

He snatches it off. His eyes shoot icy daggers at me, and I freeze when he pulls a handgun with a silencer from a pocket.

My heart stops as I stare open-mouthed at the jet black metal aimed straight at my chest. I realize the dark stain on the neck of the coveralls must be blood from the mover who wore them.

Oh. My. God. Chet has gone mad.

He glares at me with such animosity, the air gets sucked from my lungs.

"You ruined me, my family, our company. You will pay, Kat *Jackson!*"

My breath hitches in my throat as I close my eyes and raise my hands to ward off what must be a fatal shot. God help me. Chet plans to follow through on his death threat. Time stands still. My last thought goes to Harris and what we'll lose. A tear slips past my eyelashes and slides down my cheek.

Chet's evil laughter fills the space between us.

"Not so easy of a death for you, lass! Oh, no. I plan to play with this cat before I destroy you," he sneers.

My eyes fly open. His reddened face contorts as he glares at me. Teeth bared, nostrils flared. I suck in a breath to scream for help. But Chet lunges forward. He backhands my open mouth. My teeth cut into soft tissue.

The coppery taste of blood makes me gag. I bring my fingers to my lips, already swelling from the brutal blow. Then stare in horror at blood on my fingertips.

"Do not even think about calling for help," Chet growls, brandishing the weapon before my face. "Toss your mobile into the closet. Now, move!"

I leave my mobile as instructed. But hesitate to move further.

A small cry slips past my swollen lips when he pushes me with enough force, I trip over the remnants of my precious music box. The shattered pieces crush under my feet as much as my heart breaks.

Oh, Harris. The plaintive wail reverberates in my mind.

Chet pushes me through the penthouse flat until we reach its service entrance on the other side. When I pause to glance over my shoulder, Chet presses the gun against my lower back. I picture a bullet severing my spine…

"Move it or else," he threatens in a menacing growl.

I stumble and reach for the doorframe to steady myself. In the hallway, stairs lead up and down to the other floors while the lift takes up a wall. Slumped next to it lies a man naked except for his undershirt and boxers. Blood pours from a nasty gash on the side of his head. He's motionless.

"Oh, my God! Is he dea—"

"I said, *shut* your trap!" Chet snarls as he knocks me upside the head with his fist.

Stars flash before the inky blackness behind my closed eyes. Pain radiates from my temple down to my neck that snaps sideways from the impact. I cry out and earn another slap and threat.

Chet grips my upper arm and bustles me down the stairs.

My head swims as I swallow back bile. But he's relentless and forces me down the entire way from the twenty-fourth floor to the basement. He drags me towards the storage units and forces me against the wall while he divests himself of the mover's coveralls. He places them with the cap inside of a duffle bag he left on the floor, then puts on an overcoat before he swings the bag onto his shoulder.

"Now, listen very carefully," Chet starts as he grabs my throat and squeezes it until I claw at his hand. "We're going to walk out of here, down the alley, and to the street. I will hail a taxi. You will remain by my side without a word. If you so much as breathe too loud, I will put a bullet in your head. If you think to make contact with anyone, I will put a bullet in them too. Do. You. Understand?"

I cringe at the sour smell of his hot breath on my face. Then gurgle when he tightens his grip at my delayed response. Instinctively, my fingers claw at his hand. Tears spill down my cheeks. But I nod as much as possible. I cannot allow anyone else to come to harm because of Chet's madness.

"Good. Let's go," he snarls. One hand binds me to his side while the other holds the handgun hidden within the sleeve of the overcoat against my side.

I flinch at pressure on my flank from the weapon and bite back a cry. My heart batters against my ribs. Sweat trickles down my spine. A silent prayer for deliverance plays on repeat in my mind as we enter the alley.

Empty. The mantra skips with no sign of the moving truck or the other movers. No one to help me. *Blast!*

Chet quickens his pace and digs his fingers into me. He growls another warning.

I nod meekly and keep my eyes down for fear of engaging with an innocent bystander. No more shed blood on my conscious. I shudder at the reminder of the dead mover. Damn Chet Stewart!

We reach the curb around the corner from the building doorman's line of sight. No one notices us as they rush along the busy New York City sidewalk. Most people keep their heads down or have their mobiles to their ears. I envy their freedom from a deranged maniac.

A cold wind whips hair across my face. I shiver, not sure if it's from the February chill or the *bloody* gun jammed into my side.

The streetlight changes. Traffic surges ahead. Yellow taxicabs dart in and out of the flow. One stops for Chet, and he hustles me inside, careful to not draw unwanted attention from the unsuspecting driver. He gives the address to a location unknown to me. But then, I've only been here for a few weeks.

He glares at me and jabs my side again. Along with a sharp shake of his head, relays his message. *Shut. Up.*

I glance from him to the back of the driver's head, only separated from us by a transparent partition. Not enough protection from a bullet. I nod, then shift to stare out the window.

The streets blur as the taxi races down the avenue. Horns blare and mingle with snatches of conversations heard from pedestrians as we wait for red lights to change to green. Then we're off again, headed south to who knows where.

The gray sky hints at the snow flurries expected later this afternoon. It reflects the whirlwind brewing in my chaotic mind.

How will I get out of this terrifying situation?

Where the bloody hell is Chet taking me?

Can Harris find me in time? And in time to prevent what?

What will Chet do to me? When I first approached him, I thwarted his attempt at fucking me. God help me if he forces himself on me while he holds a gun in his hand. Please, God, no!

Caught up in a daymare, I don't notice the taxi stopped until Chet passes cash to the driver through the sliding screen of the partition and opens the taxi door. Chet reaches in to take my arm. I offer no resistance, especially when he cocks his head at the handgun hidden in his sleeve.

He doesn't give me time to take in my surroundings. A few long strides, and we're inside of what appears to be an abandoned warehouse. The grimy windows—some covered by wooden boards—block the little sun hidden behind thick, gray clouds. Our footsteps echo on the concrete floors in the immense space. Debris litters the floor and accumulates along the walls covered in graffiti. The stench of urine, rotten food, and decaying wood—at least I pray it's not from a dead body or bodies—fills my nostrils. Again, I fight back the urge to gag.

Chet propels us through the abysmal space quickly. The path he takes leads us to a set of rickety metal stairs. I hesitate at the first step, and he pushes me forward. Another wave of dizziness overtakes me, and I grapple for the railing. It creaks but holds firm. Not wanting to provoke another attack to my head, I do my best to climb the stairs in a hurry.

They give way to a dimly lit landing where we have to skirt around a giant hole in the floor. My heart hammers in my chest even after we pass what would surely be a fall to my death. On the other side, a heavy wooden door with a dirt-encrusted plastic window greets us.

My heart sinks at the sight of a shiny new brass lock on it. Once more, I hesitate at the threshold to my new prison. A push between my shoulder blades, and with a cry arms flail as I stumble into the room.

"Stop fucking around, Kat *Jackson*, and get your ass inside!" Chet barks.

Unable to stop the room from spinning, I land in a heap on my hands and knees. My forehead scrapes the dirty concrete floor. I close my eyes and throw up.

"*Argh*! You filthy sow!"

Chet's yell precedes the slam of the heavy door and the tumble of the lock as it clicks into place. The sound jars my already sore skull. I whimper and clutch at my head. Then it jerks back.

Chet glares down at me with a fistful of my hair. I yelp as he drags me across the floor. The rending of fabric as the knees of my jeans rip from the hard concrete surface and the scrape of my skin make me stand on wobbly legs. I scratch at his hand to stop the pain from my scalp.

"Cut. It. Out!" He snarls with a vicious shake to my head.

Another wave of nausea hits me. My hands cover my mouth. But some of the vomit seeps past my fingers. Chet grunts and pushes me towards the ground. I land face first on a lumpy surface.

A mattress!

A gasp falls from my mouth as I struggle to right myself. No way do I want to stay in this position with a crazy Chet behind me.

"Trust me, you're too filthy to touch," he sneers as he towers over me. "For now."

The last half of his statement sends a chill colder than the February chill through my body. Every cell freezes at the thought of Chet touching me. Please, God, no…

I bend my knees to my chest with my arms wrapped around them and lower my aching head. As my stomach continues to roil, I try to make myself as small as possible. With every breath of my being, I pray for a miracle.

Chet stomps around the room, grumbling to himself. Metal clangs, then water sloshes. His steps bring him to stand above me.

"Here. Clean yourself up. Can't have you stinking up the place when I have plans for you," he says as he shoves a metal bucket against my shins.

I lift my head slightly. The racking pain makes it difficult to focus my vision.

"Go on. Or do you want me to do it?" He says jeeringly.

God no!

Quicker than I believe possible, I grab the edge of the bucket and sit up straight. I tremble as Chet chuckles wickedly.

"Don't worry. You won't be able to stop me, lass," he says, then pivots and strides to the other side of the room.

I take my first actual glimpse of my confines.

Concrete floors—at least bare of garbage.

No windows except for the grimy one in the heavy door.

Two bare lightbulbs dangle from exposed wires overhead.

An interior ceiling for the room only, not the one I saw for the entire building.

A metal desk and one metal chair in the corner.

Chet lowers his frame onto the chair and watches me.

I swallow fear down and set to cleaning the vomit from my hands, then switch to my coat. Not wanting to finish soon and face what Chet has planned, I take my time.

"Forget the coat. Take it off. It's your hands and face I want clean," he commands as he leans forward with a lusty glint in his eyes.

Bloody hell...

How will you get out of this soiled mess, Kat Jackson???

KAT

"*D*on't just sit there with your mouth agape, lass. Unless you're ready for something to fill it."

My hand stops mid-stroke. A gasp falls from my mouth. Fresh tears fill my eyes as I lower my gaze hurriedly. More thoughts of escape flood my brain. I must get the hell out of here.

Chet chuckles.

"Aw, come now. Don't be bashful, lass. I guarantee you I'm a better fuck than that oaf Steele," Chet purrs in an attempt at seduction.

Yuck! My skin crawls. Bile churns in my stomach as it threatens to spew forth again. This time in pure disgust, not in fear or pain.

Between the handgun and my head wounds, I'm uncertain I can thwart Chet's sick plan of revenge. But I'll be damned if I make it easy for him.

With my eyes still downcast, I scan the room for a possible weapon. Anything.

Nothing.

As my hands wipe the front of my coat, a jingle in a pocket catches my attention. Blessed be my keys! Wedged between my fingers, they'll serve as tiny daggers. I'll slice the wanker's face and gouge out his eyes. Thoughts of victory replace doubt. I'm ready for you Chet Stewart!

"Who the bloody hell can this be?"

His question draws me from my newfound plan of attack. He whips his mobile from a pocket and stares at the screen. His lip curls as his eyes narrow.

"Great… Just what I need at this moment," Chet mumbles, then rises to turn his back to me. "Father."

Chet paces the floor as he listens to Magnus Stewart— CEO and Chairman of the Board of Stewart Scotch. Well, the former head of their family's company.

As retribution, Lydie forced the Stewarts' hands to sell 51% of Stewart Scotch to Jackson Corporation for controlling interest. Then folded Stewart Scotch within Jackson Corporation. She effectively eliminated them as competitors and tied their fate to the Jacksons forever.

No wonder Chet is reluctant to speak to his *da*. I can only imagine how livid Magnus must be with his son.

Another thought hits me square in the face. Is Magnus involved in Chet's kidnapping of me? Could he stoop as low as his wayward son?

I focus in on his side of the conversation to determine his father's knowledge. But Chet keeps his voice low and remains on the opposite side of the room. Every few steps, he throws a glare my way. I try not to shudder from the vehemence in his eyes. Despite feeling weak, I cannot allow Chet to sense how low I am.

My eyes close for a brief prayer for strength and a swift rescue.

"Fuck!"

I jolt from Chet's exclamation. Eyes wide, I stare as he slams his fist against the wall. Curses stream from his mouth. Another slap and he pivots to face me. This time, I can't help the shudder that racks my body as he stalks in my direction.

Without a word, he yanks open a desk drawer. Metal clangs against metal. A length of thick chain rises from within. Chet's narrowed glare never leaves my face.

He drags the chain behind him like a Ghost of Christmas Past as he approaches me. The metal scrapes along the concrete. The jarring sound and his malicious intent make me crab walk backwards until the wall stops my retreat. My sins return to haunt me.

Too taken aback, I forget about my keys as Chet grabs my wrist and coils an end of the chain around it. He repeats the move with my other wrist. Then moves down my body to trap my ankles. He secures the ends to metal loops attached to the floor at the four corners of the mattress. Spread-eagle on my back, I turn my head to watch him stand.

He surveys his work. A twisted gleam replaces the anger in his eyes. He nods.

"I have to step out," Chet says, then sneers. "Obviously, you will remain here. Don't bother to scream. No one will hear you."

He turns for the door where he pauses to cast another depraved look my way.

"Save your cries for later," he says with a dark chuckle.

"You. Sick. Bastard. You won't get away with this," I snarl as I yank the chains.

In a blink of an eye, he looms over me. My chin gripped between his thumb and index finger painfully. Our eyes lock.

"I already have, Kat *Jackson*," Chet sneers.

His mouth crashes onto mine. He takes advantage of my shock to shove his tongue inside. I gag as he snakes it around, lapping at my tongue. Just as abruptly, he stands.

"Sweet," he purrs, then strides from the room. The light from the bare bulbs disappears with a flick of the switch.

I turn my head to retch in complete darkness.

Nothing left in my stomach. The sound of dry heaves joins the click of the lock's tumbler as it engages.

Misery and helplessness, unlike any I've ever known before—despite years of living below the poverty line— engulf me. The pervading sense of dread heavier than the dank air of the pitch-black room. With nothing to see and belief in rescue diminishing, I close my tear-filled eyes.

* * *

My bladder wins the battle.

I cringe as a warm puddle forms beneath my ass, still fully clothed. The liquid seeps through to the lumpy mattress below. A cry of despair mixed with relief escapes my mouth. Added to the dried vomit remnants, I know I must be a sight.

The muscles in my arms and legs ache from being chained. Tingles long since dissipated. Only a dull throb remains. A reminder of my awful predicament.

Unable to differentiate time, I can only guess it's been hours since Chet left. I ignored his suggestion to save my cries and screamed for help until only hoarse whimpers passed my chapped lips. My parched throat ragged from the unsuccessful attempts.

Even my futile efforts to dislodge the chains from my

wrists resulted in bracelets of fire. Time has done little to lessen the pain. Rubbed raw my flesh burns.

More accustomed to the lack of light, my eyes make out the desk and chair along with the door in the gloom. I lower my head and stare wistfully at the bucket filled with rusty water beside the mattress. Within arm's reach. If only. What I'd give to have a sip.

My stomach growls, insistent upon not being left out of some form of satisfaction. Its emptiness further exacerbated by my earlier actions. It clenches on air.

I whimper and close my eyes.

Rest. A bit of a rest to rebuild my strength.

* * *

"Oh, for fuck's sake! It smells like a barnyard in here! Have you no self-respect, Kat *Jackson*?!"

At the same time, Chet's bellow jolts me awake, light blinds me.

I whimper and turn my head aside, squeezing my eyelids together tightly. Pain shoots up my spine. My legs jerk of their own accord. It's as though a bolt of lightning zinged through my body. Another garbled cry slips past my chapped lips. My thick tongue darts out to lick cracks that form. No moisture available to soothe them.

"I've been gone for a few days and return to you lying in your own filth. What? You couldn't hold yourself? It's not as though you had any food or drink. Damn!" Chet rants.

A few days… It's been that long??? God, help me.

"You don't even deserve the dinner I brought for you, filthy sow! And certainly not the bottle of wine…" Chet continues his tirade while I try to regain consciousness.

My muddled mind refuses to process until pain rips

through me. Chet releases the chains.

"I'm giving you exactly ten minutes to clean yourself. And don't think I have any clothes for you. You better make do with what you have…"

Slow by the lack of food and water—not to mention the pain as blood flows back into my extremities—my body won't obey my mind. Instead, I curl into a fetal position. The shift brings the stench to my nose. I gag. But nothing comes up.

"Nine minutes and counting," Chet sneers.

I pull on the last of my reserves to force my limbs to cooperate. Stiff fingers fumble with the zipper of my down coat. Flakes of vomit flutter to the mattress. I shrug the coat off, peeling the lower half from my body. The bottom of my turtleneck tunic clings to my leggings. Both bear the proof of multiple accidents.

I hesitate to remove them. Only a lace bra and soiled thong would cover me from Chet's eyes. I risk a peek at him.

He watches me with a look of contempt and lust.

"Six," he sneers, then wrinkles his nose. "Hurry up. The smell turns my stomach."

Choosing the lesser of the two, I remove my tunic. Then curse myself for the demi-cup bra I wore to entice Harris. The tops of my breasts jiggle with each movement. My nipples pebble against the black lace in the chilly air.

I don't have to peek at Chet to know he's clocking my every move. His sharp intake of air gives him away.

Hurriedly, I dip the bottom of the tunic into the bucket of water and wring it out. I'll put the damn thing back on. Better to freeze than to have Chet leering at my near nakedness.

"Oh, no you won't. It's still filthy," he admonishes as I dip my head to slip the tunic back on. "Put it aside, along with those pants."

"Y—You… s—said I could make do—"

"Y—Y—You. Stop your stuttering and hurry up. Four," he cuts me off. With a wink, he continues, "After the show, I plan to eat, then have you as my dessert. So make it quick, lass. I. Am. Starved."

I bite the inside of my cheek to hold back a flippant response. No need to provoke Chet with his mind in the gutter. I shudder in revulsion.

While still seated, I remove my sneakers before I drag the leggings down. I repeat the process of dipping the top half into the bucket of water and wringing them out. With care, I avoid water on the lower half. I plan to put them on as soon as possible.

All clothing but my thong and bra spread out on the concrete floor to dry.

"Oh, so you want me to believe you didn't soil your panties, lass?" Chet's question rankles me. "I think not. Take them off. But leave the fancy bra on. I'll unwrap those juicy tits as part of my dessert. Don't you think I deserve a treat after all you did to me?"

Damn Chet Stewart!

As much as I want to defy him, I want to survive more.

Okay, Katrina Roberts, *smiogaid suas, nighean!*

I take a deep breath and sit up straight. My hips lift from the mattress for enough space to slip out of my thong. I angle my body to hide my bare mons from Chet's leer as I clean the bit of black lace. Once done, I lay them on the floor beside the other pieces of clothing. My gaze remains on them. Then my brain short circuits at Chet's next words.

"Now step aside so I can flip this sodden mattress. We'll need it later, sweet lass."

"What do you mean you didn't implant a tracker in Kat?! It's your invention, Harris!"

"Especially after all the drama we've had from The Twins' kidnapping to my motorcycle accident. If it wasn't for your gizmos and app, we would have been fucked."

Haley and Malcolm's shocked responses to my negative answer doesn't help my pissy mood.

It's been hours since Kat disappeared. Her mobile found in the closet of her former bedroom provided no clues. Not a word for ransom money. No chatter on the dark web. Eyes strained from staring at the computer, hoping to spot any sign of her in the video footage. It's bleak as all fuck.

"Listen, give Harris a break already. They just re-connected. Who would expect something to happen in such a short period of time?" Roger's sensible response soothes some of my self-imposed guilt.

I should have placed the tracker as I have for all our family members, including the Jacksons. As Malcolm stated, we can't be too careful with our history brought on by crazies. The technology saved us a lot of unnecessary headaches. What I could have avoided with a simple injection.

Fuck!

I slam my palms against the mahogany surface of my desk and rise to pace my home office.

We set it up as the central location for all activity. I gave the cops and the equipment their head of Information Technology delivered access to my den a few doors down from my office. Lucien took over the kitchen for his staff to prepare meals around the clock. The living room serves as the gathering area for everyone else. Edwin buzzes about keeping order. This is the most activity he's ever had to manage for me.

"Exactly. Besides, that's the past. We have to focus on the present," Baz adds. He turns to me. "Harris, you need to take a break. Let's get something to eat."

I open my mouth to protest. But he gives me his don't-fuck-with-me look. Ordinarily, I'd have a wry response. But I can't summon enough energy for a good quip. Besides, he's right. I nod and pivot toward the door.

A slap on my shoulder makes me glance over.

"We'll get answers soon, Harris. We equipped everyone with the best tools we need to find Kat. You have lots of support," Lachlan says.

Once again, I nod.

My moment of respite comes to an abrupt end as we round the corner near the living room. A thick Scottish accent sounds off.

"—don't give a bloody damn! It's his fault! Why didn't he go upstairs with her? Huh?!"

Lachlan mutters Scottish Gaelic curses under his breath.

"Payton, please! That's not true. Please don't start, son—"

"Mum, you're too—"

"Enough, Payton. You will not hurl unfounded accusations around. Either help or get out," Lachlan snarls.

Of course. Payton Roberts-cum-Jackson, Kat's older brother, and the pain in the ass of their family. After hearing about him from Lach, I should have known Payton would show his ass. But guess what? I'm ready to give an ass whipping.

I pin him with a withering glare as I stalk over to him.

"You better heed your Mum and your *cousin*. I am not in the mood for your bullshit," I warn, inches from his face.

He has the sense to lower his gaze before he spins on his heels and storms for my penthouse's entry hall.

Good fucking riddance!

I turn my gaze to Allison Roberts. She decided to keep her name as it was her husband's. I hear she's a lovely woman and deserves respect.

"Mrs. Roberts, I want you to know that I will do all in my power and more to bring Kat home to us," I say.

Her mother nods as fresh tears slip down her reddened cheeks.

"Allison, come join Lucie and me."

I shift my gaze beyond Mrs. Roberts to find my mother Shelley with my Aunt Lucie. They beckon for her to join them. I nod in gratitude when she goes to our families' matriarchs. They loop their arms through hers as they usher her down the hallway to another room for privacy.

"Come on, Har. It's time for me to mother you."

I glance down at my twin's smiling face. Her dove gray eyes—so like mine—full of love. I nod and let her lead me to the kitchen.

Laurent and Lucien greet us boisterously—one with an

unopened bottle of Jackson Reserve Scotch and the other with a platter of my favorite Steak Frites.

"Load up, cuz. It's gonna be a long night!" Laurent says as he pops the top and hands the bottle to me.

I can't help but to grin before I guzzle some of the peat-flavored liquid down. The warm burn settles in my belly like a favorite blanket around one's shoulders on a brisk night. It's comforting and sustaining at once.

And from the way things are slow in progressing, I'm going to need it.

* * *

"Unfortunately, we have nothing new to report at this time. We will continue to monitor the video feed. A fourth team will surveil a broader range. The First Commissioner added more detectives to canvass the area for potential witnesses and to speak with staff at the children's nonprofit. I will check in again soon."

We thank the Deputy Commissioner, and she leaves us to rejoin her teams in the den.

Two days with nothing to show for our actions. Not a damn peep.

Vivian moved into a guest apartment a few floors below my penthouse. We have two STEELE security members as her detail. For now, she'll work from home. As I promised her family, I will not allow another woman to go missing randomly on my watch.

I run my fingers through my hair and tug at the longer strands. It would be a lot messier if Haley didn't live up to her mothering role and demand I shower, shave, and change my clothes. She catches my eye as I rise from my desk.

"Har, I'm going to take the next shift of viewing the

videos. Why don't you take Bella and Bonnie for a walk? I'm sure the Trips would love to go with you, too," Haley suggests.

Lachlan stands and stretches his six-foot-four-inch frame.

"I'll join you," he adds.

"Yeah. Let's make it an outing with the rest of the kids and the dogs. A walk in Central Park will do us all good," Roger says as he calls Leonie on his mobile.

Malcolm and Baz decline. But they let Starr and Lola know the plan. They decide to go, too. A parting glance reveals my oldest brothers deep in conversation. I can only imagine what they're up to. Best to leave them to it.

We're a rowdy bunch as we spill through the front doors of The STEELE Tower onto Fifth Avenue. Six dogs; thirteen kids; four nannies; nine adults. Laurent and Vivian come along too. Michael and Charlotte—Kat's younger brother and sister—join us for a chance to see Central Park. It's their first visit to New York City, even it is under dire circumstances. Six bodyguards surround our group as we move along. Again, no chance for shenanigans.

The crisp air of February clears my head as I take a deep inhale à la Starr's pranayama breathing teachings. Peace in. Tension out. Five times and I'm ready for our stroll through the park.

"*Allez, Oncle* Harris! Too slow!"

A tiny hand tugs mine as I glance down at my nephew Rodolphe. The eldest of the Steele grandchildren and the twin of Gaspard—two of Roger and Leonie's three children —grins up at me.

I return his smile and say a prayer of thanks he and Gaspard had their trackers implanted when the nutcase who wanted Roger kidnapped them. My heart clenches at the thought of losing my nephews and the reminder of Kat missing.

But Rodolphe's delight makes me push the negative thoughts aside.

"You're right. Let's get going!" I respond and swing him up onto my shoulders.

"Hey! Me, too! Me, too!" Slade—Baz and Lola's oldest son—calls out to me.

Roger swoops him up from behind, and Slade squeals.

Everyone laughs, and we continue to cross Fifty-Seventh Street. It's the start of lunch. Throngs of people from office workers to tourists bustle along on their way to restaurants or shopping in any of the luxury shops on the avenue.

We leave them behind as we pass between the stone walls to enter Central Park. Blanketed in white from snow-fall the night before, it's a sight to behold. Tree branches laced with diamonds of ice. Cobblestones peek from beneath snow-covered walkways. The Pond frozen over dazzles in the sun.

New York City activity doesn't cease, even here. Joggers run the trails bundled up with jackets, hats, and gloves over their gear. Mothers and nannies chat as they push babies in carriages. Teachers lead children on a walk. Dogs chase balls and catch frisbees thrown by their owners on the fields covered in snow.

Our dogs bark in excitement. Baz's pair of Siberian Huskies bury themselves in a snow pile as they yip. Laurent tosses a ball, and all six dogs give chase. He and Michael hustle after them while Charlotte claps spinning in a circle face to the sky.

I put Rodolphe down, and he takes off with the others to play in the snow.

"I'm glad to see you smiling, brother."

I glance down to find Lola staring up at me. Her hazel eyes dance.

"Remember, we walk by faith and not by sight. Kat will return to us," Lola adds. "That is unless she's too scared to face Leonie, Starr, and me…"

Lola ends with a smirk. Her way of letting me know she'll accept Kat back into our lives. But she will have to make up for her actions. If the girls take her within their fold again, we'll be golden.

I grin at Lola and kiss her cheek.

"Thanks, sis. I appreciate you guys a whole lot," I say.

"You better, big guy!" She retorts with a nudge to my side.

Leonie and Starr saunter over and pull me into a group hug. They offer more words of encouragement and take up Haley's mothering in her absence. I bask in their attention, grateful for their love. From one sister to four, well, five counting Lydie, who flew in last night. It couldn't get better!

We spend the next hour or so tromping through the park. Lola suggests going to an early dinner at her favorite restaurant growing up in the City—Serendipity. She makes the call and books the entire second floor for us. We head back to The STEELE Tower to drop off the dogs and to meet up with the others. STEELE Mercedes-Benz Sprinters take us to the restaurant on Sixtieth Street.

My parents, Uncle Connor, and Aunt Lucie sit with Allison and Payton—who has assumed the role of his mother's chaperone since our incident. Perhaps there's hope for him yet. The rest of us take seats along the banquette and on chairs across the long row of tables pushed together. Charlotte ohs and ahs over the eclectic mix of decorations on the walls and hanging from the ceiling. On the other side of the room, the children gather at tables with the nannies.

Their laughter and antics make the atmosphere buzz with joy.

I feel like a kid myself as I sip from red and white striped straws in the giant glass of Frozen Hot Chocolate. Fresh whipped cream lands on my lip, and I lick it off happily. Haley winks at me from across the table as she sips her decadent concoction. I grin back. My heart lightens for the first time in days.

* * *

"Oh, my God!"

The hairs on the back of my neck rise at Haley's cry. I drop my mobile and rush to her side just as Lachlan races over. She's on her laptop reviewing video footage as she has for the past few hours of day three.

"What is it?!" Baz demands.

"What did you find, Haley?" Malcolm asks at the same time.

She turns the computer around and points at a figure in a crowd of people on a sidewalk.

I lean closer. The image tweaks a vague memory.

"Fuck. Me." Lachlan breathes.

"Tell us!!" Roger yells.

"Chet fucking Stewart. What the bloody *hell* is he doing in New York?" Lachlan responds, then continues with a sneer. "My last report placed him in Rome at some dingy pensione."

That fucker took my woman?! I'll rip his face off!

Haley snickers.

"And I'll help you, twin," she says.

I raise an eyebrow.

"Um, you spoke out loud, Har," she responds with a smirk.

"Right. Now, what's the timestamp of that video?" I ask as my fingers itch to get ahold of Stewart.

Haley gives more details. Lachlan rises to tell the cops still in the den.

"No."

We turn to Malcolm. He stands beside Baz. They shake their heads simultaneously. So much alike physically, people confuse them for twins. Their striking resemblance even more apparent now as they stand as one.

"You figure out where Stewart is without outside help. I will take care of the fucker," Malcolm *The Enforcer* says with the eerie calm of a man not to be messed with. Trained in MMA and one who thinks nothing of cave diving in some of the most remote places on Earth is fun, Malcolm fears nothing and no one.

"Right," I repeat.

Haley and I get to work on our laptops. Time to track that fucker and get my woman back where she belongs. With our family. And in my arms.

HARRIS

"The larger heat signatures on the second floor indicate two adults. Ignore the smaller ones as rodents or other vermin. In teams of three, we'll enter at these points. The schematic for the warehouse indicates stairs here lead to the room where the perp and Kat are here."

"Our surveillance indicates the perp returned moments ago. All signs point to him working alone."

"As far as boots on the ground. Communication with others has only been to his father. Nothing marks his involvement. However, we'll glean more info from the perp once we have him."

I listen intently to the two men who lead the rescue operation. They're a part of an elite team of former Navy SEALs and Army Green Berets Malcolm works with when necessary. That's the extent of what he tells us about them, other than he trusts them with the lives of his most cherished Starr and their children. And that's all I need to know.

A crackle over the radios, and they pause the report.

While they speak to other team members, I watch the monitor. The smaller of the two heat signatures moves around on the floor. The other stays stationary. What the fuck is going on in there???

"I do not agree with you going in, Harris."

I turn from the monitor to face Baz. He sits in the van with me. Malcolm sits in another near the warehouse with more of the team. Neither will enter the warehouse. But fuck me if I don't get my woman.

"Baz, I already swore not to go beyond the two guys who will enter the room ahead of me. But there's no way in hell I will not be there for Kat. You know you would do the same for Lola. Hell, Starr fought a mountain lion for Malcolm. I appreciate your concern, but I got this, bro," I respond.

My eldest brother scans my face, then nods, satisfied.

"Let's move!"

The command snaps us to attention. Baz grips my shoulder and nods once more. I nod in return, then jump from the van.

It's after eleven at night. The streets empty in this desolate part of lower Manhattan. Dressed in all black with bulletproof vests beneath our shirts and ear comms, we make our way to a side entrance for the warehouse. The team leader clips the padlock with ease. Stewart—the dumb fuck—didn't bother to install a security system. Our win.

The streetlamps don't extend into this alley, so no light disturbs the dark interior of the warehouse to give away our entry. Night vision goggles clear the way for us to see despite the lack of light. As soon as I step over the threshold, my nose wrinkles in disgust at the foul odor of decay. I ignore it and lift my gaze towards the upper levels.

From this angle, I can't see the staircase. I glance around as I follow my team deeper into the property. I spot others as they head for various areas. Only two sets will go to the second floor. Two others guard the roof. All access points covered in case Stewart gets past us. Not happening.

Our boots make no sound as we approach the staircase. It's ramshackle but will hold. Looking up, I notice a large hole above. We skirt around it as we arrive on the landing. Across from us, a faint glow of light appears through a dirt-encrusted plastic window set in a heavy wooden door. A new lock keeps it secure. Not for long.

The leader of my team holds up his fist, and we stop on command. He points to positions we're to take on either side of the door. A finger to his lips and sharp shake of his head reminds us not to utter a word—no matter what we see beyond that door. Best Stewart won't be able to recall our voices.

My heart thuds in my chest as adrenaline pumps through my veins. So close to My Kitty Kat. I'll have you safe and sound soon, my love. And that fucker—Stewart—torn to shreds.

* * *

Kat

"Now that you're passably clean, we will eat. Come sit."

I continue to stand beside the flipped mattress with my hands covering my bare mons as I stare at Chet's smirking face. Despite my will to survive, I can't help my mouth twisting in disgust.

He sits on the metal chair with his legs spread wide as he pats his lap. His beady eyes rake over my body, pausing at my breasts and covered pussy. The tip of his tongue slips out to lick a slow circle around his lips.

My flesh crawls.

"Come sit," Chet repeats.

I shake my head as I take a step backwards. My heel bumps against the mattress. Caught between a rock and a hard place, my mind reels.

God, please let someone save me!

"Get your ass over here, Kat *Jackson*. I doubt you want me to drag you across the concrete floor. Or do you prefer it rough, lass? I hear you're a regular at those sex clubs," Chet says. Lust fills his eyes as he ogles my body again. He beckons me with one hand and palms his crotch with the other suggestively. "I've got something you'll enjoy even more… Get over here. Now!"

My terror-filled eyes flick towards the door. *Can I escape???*

In that moment, Chet lunges for me. He grabs my arm and jerks me behind him as he strides toward the table. My wobbly legs threaten to collapse. Lack of food and water weakens me. With a mournful sob, I follow him.

He sits and yanks me onto his lap. The bulge in his pants pokes my hip. He laughs lasciviously as I wiggle to break free of his vise-like hold.

"Oh, that feels good, lass. It'll be even better when I fuck you. Especially here," he says as he squeezes my ass.

"Fuck you," I attempt to tell him defiantly. But my sore and parched throat makes my voice rough and low. It's more of a barely audible murmur than a menacing retort.

"Oh, but you will. Again. And again. Before *I'm* through with you. Who knows what else I have in store for you?" He sneers in my face. "But first you need to eat. I can't have you lying there like a limp rag doll. I want your active participation. Willing or not. Open wide, la—"

The two lightbulbs flicker, then go out. We're cloaked in pitch black. Unable to see, but the sound of the wooden door splintering and the rustle of movement fills our ears. Chet's shouts turn garbled as I'm ripped from his lap by powerful hands.

As though I weigh nothing, those hands lift me against a massive chest. I cry out as I struggle feebly to free myself. Fear spikes as horrific visions of being assaulted by multiple men run through my delirious mind. I doubted I could fight off Chet. Now more?

"No… Please," I whimper as the man strides at a quick pace. I sense others as we move. No one makes a sound. Even Chet remains silent.

We descend the rickety stairs. The rusted metal groans from the combined weight. Heavy boots pound on the steps as the others follow.

I sneak a peek up at the man who carries me. Perhaps he's my hero and not a monster. Unfortunately, a dark knit cap covers his head and googles partially obstruct his face. Only glimpses of his full lips set in a stern line appear in the gloom.

He dips his head to peer at me briefly. His arms squeeze me tighter to his chest. The comforting display lessens my fear.

This man is rescuing me!

* * *

Harris

I'll kill that motherfucker!

My mind explodes at the sight of My Kitty Kat bared-assed on that bastard's lap. Only a bra keeps her from being naked fully.

The fucker has the nerve to hold a fork in his hand as though he was feeding my woman. The louse gapes and shouts as his head swivels in the darkness that engulfs them. His expression changes from surprise to anger, then to fear as the syringe jabs his neck. Thankfully, a black hood descends over his face, hiding his mug from me.

I need to focus on getting My Kitty Kat out of this miserable prison. With ease, I pull her into my arms and carry her bride-like through the broken door and down the stairs. My heart clenches when she begs for me not to hurt her.

What the hell did Stewart do to her during these three days???

I can't speak to her. Instead, I gaze down and hug her closer to me. I'll let her know it's me once we're in the van safely.

Stewart has the pleasure of riding in the van with Malcolm.

The side door slides open, and Baz leans out with a blanket. I pass My Kitty Kat to him. He bundles her up as I hop in and whip off the googles. Immediately, I pull her onto my lap. She slaps at my chest with a cry as she shakes her head, eyes squeezed shut. More pleas tear at my heart.

"Kat, it's me, Harris. Look at me," I say as I hold her face between my palms. "Baby, you're safe. You're safe."

She stills. Her eyes open wide and scan my face. Relief fills them as she recognizes me.

"H—Harris," she sighs. Tears spill down her cheeks. Cheeks bruised along with her swollen mouth.

I bite back a growl and press the back of her head to cradle My Kitty Kat to my chest. My eyes close as I rock her gently. Soothing words pour from my mouth against her matted hair. I ignore the smell of body waste and stale sweat that clings to her skin despite the barrier of the thick wool blanket.

We remain locked together until the van stops on another empty side street. Baz and I—with Kat in my arms —switch to a waiting nondescript sedan. Roger nods as he starts the engine. I sense he watches me from the rearview mirror. But I keep my gaze on My Kitty Kat who sleeps. Baz fills him in as we ride uptown to The STEELE Tower.

Both of my brothers watch me intently during the ride up from the underground garage. I offer them a nod. Words will wait until after our private doctor checks My Kitty Kat. Right now, I can't formulate any with the wild thoughts of what that fucker may have done to her running rampant in my mind.

The elevator stops on my floor. Baz uses his palm to unlock the front doors to my penthouse—each of us has access to the others' residences. The doctor waits for us on the other side.

Our parents invited everyone up to their duplex pent-house for dinner and movie night. We kept the rescue mission between us. Not even Kat's family knows. Best to keep the details of the situation amongst us.

I lead the way to my bedroom suite. Inside, the doctor instructs me to place a now awake Kat on the examination table he set up beside my bed. Baz and Roger wait in the sitting room. When the doctor asks me to join them, I cock my head to the side and raise an eyebrow. He nods and gets on with the exam.

Kat answers his questions while darting her gaze between him and me. She recounts the multiple blows Stewart inflicted. The more she speaks, the more it proves difficult for me to maintain control. I want to rip him to pieces with my bare hands. My hands fist at my sides.

When the doctor asks her about sexual assault, she stares at me and shakes her head vehemently.

The breath I didn't realize I held breaks free. My knees buckle in relief. It's bad enough he physically assaulted My Kitty Kat. But if he had dared to touch her—

"Harris, I'm fine."

My Kitty Kat's softly spoken words resonate in the bedroom. I take her proffered hand and wrap my arms around her. She cries against my shoulder. Her entire body shakes.

The doctor's cough reminds me to let him complete the exam. He determines she is indeed fine. She promises to heed his recommendation she takes a warm bath, pain meds as needed, and eats a good meal with plenty of water. I walk the doctor to the doors. I tell Baz and Roger, Kat is good and thank all three. They leave.

I rush to the en suite bathroom to prepare her bath. To the water, I add essential oils—eucalyptus and lavender to ease her sore muscles and to relax her mind. I return to the bedroom and carry My Kitty Kat to the sunken tub. She takes off the exam gown before I ease her into the water.

"Thank you, Harris," she whispers as she takes the bottle of water from me.

Greedily, she gulps half of it, then leans back with a sigh. Her face scrunches, and she shudders.

"You're safe, Kitty Kat. No need to worry anymore," I reassure her as I rub a sponge across her stiff shoulders. "Your mother and siblings came over with Haley and Lachlan. In fact, everyone came as soon as Baz and I called them. You're not alone."

My Kitty Kat opens her eyes and stares at me. I smile, and she strokes my cheek as tears cascade down hers.

I lower my forehead to press against hers. Our breaths sync as we relax—the stress of the last few days finally subsiding. A moment later, I finish bathing My Kitty Kat.

Dried and wrapped in a warm, fluffy robe, I carry her to the bedroom.

A table laden with dishes beneath cloches and bottles of water sits beside the floor-to-ceiling windows. I send a silent prayer of thanks for my brothers asking Lucien to provide food for My Kitty Kat. When I glance down at her, she eyes the table hungrily.

"Let's see what Lucien prepared, shall we?" I ask with a broad smile.

"Please!" My Kitty Kat responds eagerly.

Now, that's a plea to warm my heart.

"So, Kat, now that a week has passed since your rescue, tell me your thoughts."

I take a deep breath and shift my gaze from the psychologist to the window of her brownstone where she practices on the Upper Eastside. We've met every day. But this morning is the first time we held our session outside of Harris'—I mean *our*, as he reminds me—penthouse. I haven't had the courage to go beyond the entry hall and that's only to greet family and Vivian.

The comfort of being in the safety of the penthouse high above the streets of Manhattan and far from the gloomy warehouse helped me to get through those first days. Anytime I closed my eyes to sleep, memories of Chet hitting me and his promise to assault me woke me in fits of terror. My screams pierced the quiet of the bedroom. Sweat soaked my body, drenching my nightgown and the sheets. Only Harris' protective arms wrapped around me, cradling me to his chest, caused the nightmares to fade.

He—along with my mother and siblings, the Jacksons,

and his family—provided the support I needed daily. I'll never forget the expression of sheer happiness on Payton's face when everyone walked into the living room to find me on the sofa. He raced over and pulled me into a tight embrace. His tears mingled with mine as he held me close. Never in our lives did my older brother exhibit warmth for me. Hell, for any of us. Now, he's a completely different person—loving and attentive, not mean and self-absorbed.

Michael and Charlotte told me Payton assumed the role of chaperone for our Mum and treats them a lot better, too. I had to promise I'd go with them to the Statue of Liberty and to the Empire State Building to continue their tour of New York City. It's their sweet way of keeping me from thinking about the awful kidnapping.

Instead of only my Mum hovering over me, Shelley and Lucie make it their mission to visit every afternoon for tea. Apparently, it became a ritual for them as a means to distract my Mum. At least their bonding is one positive outcome of my kidnapping. And I do enjoy spending time with The Mums as I've nicknamed the trio.

While I was gone, Starr transformed a room into a yoga studio. She insists the morning routine of mediation and breathing exercises followed by a flow class will help ease the stress. Every morning, the girls come over for our prac-tice, followed by breakfast. It amazes me how easily they've added me back into their circle and connected with Vivian. Another plus.

Even the guys offer their support without hesitation. Malcolm spends thirty minutes a day teaching me self-defense moves. *Don't let anyone catch you off guard, Kat!* It feels good to have a bit of badass in me. Lucien makes my favorite dishes and surprises me with a different decadent dessert. *Keep your strength up, Kat!*

Just as I now have more big brothers and cousins, the Jackson and Steele Patriarchs have adopted me fully. As a member of the family, Connor insisted Harris placed a tracker beneath my skin. They explained how each family member has one, including my Mum and siblings now. The Patriarchs take on the responsibility of us all seriously. *No messing about, Kat Jackson!*

A smile lifts the corners of my mouth as I shift my gaze from the window back to the psychologist. She smiles and nods encouragingly. I take a deep breath and share my thoughts on the abundance of love and support everyone has for me. But just as important, the need for Harris to not treat me like a fragile flower.

Although he holds me, he has yet to make love to me. I've initiated intimacy, but he stops my advances and spoons me. Every. Single. Time. I need more. I want to banish the horrific memories of Chet's filthy touches and crass words. Forever.

And only Harris can do it. But he won't. *You need your rest, Kitty Kat.*

AARGH!

The psychologist tries to cover her giggle with a cough. But I cock my head and smirk.

"Go ahead. You can skip the professionalism. I'd laugh if I wasn't desperate for Harris," I say.

She grins and gives me the absolute best advice.

After our session ends, I walk into the waiting area and smile at the sight of my man. He insisted on accompanying me since it was my first foray outside of our penthouse. I don't mind his hovering either. I just wish he would hover *over* me as he pounds me into the mattress…

As though sensing my presence—or need—he glances up

from his mobile. He searches my face, then sighs in relief when my smile broadens.

"Good session?" He asks as he strides over to me and kisses my forehead chastely.

I slip my arms around his neck to pull him down to me. My mouth crushes his. My tongue demands entry. It sweeps into his mouth as it hangs agape, stunned by my forthrightness. I tease his tongue with mine until they tangle. My pelvis grinds against him, hungry for friction. As his cock grows, I undulate my hips and moan in the back of my throat.

My teeth nip his lips, along his jaw, and up to the shell of his ear. I tug the lobe. It slips from my teeth, and I lap the erotic pain away.

"Fuck me, Harris Steele. Take me home now and Fuck. Me."

He groans and places his hands on my waist. His eager fingers dig into my skin even as he pushes me away gently.

"Oh, no you will not. What you *will* do is rid me of the horrible images of Chet plaguing my mind. With each brutal thrust, you will erase that scoundrel from my memory. Now, Harris Steele, let's go home," I demand.

He blinks down at me. Dove gray eyes blown obsidian by lust. His swallow audible. He bites a corner of his full mouth as he considers my words.

I pivot on my heel and head for the front doors. An exaggerated sway to my hips. Over my shoulder, I call to him.

"Now, Harris Steele."

His deep, seductive chuckle makes me shiver.

"As you wish, Ms. Jackson."

I yelp as pain blossoms on my ass.

Harris presses close behind me as we stand in the vestibule between the inner glass and outer wooden doors of the brownstone. The air thickens with our mutual desire. The hand that didn't spank me slides around my side to my lower belly and presses me closer to his hard body. Feeling his impressive bulge, I'm thankful we didn't wear coats. The soft silk of my shift dress proves a limited barrier from his wool trousers.

"Are you being a naughty lass, Kitty Kat?" he murmurs. His warm breath skitters across my cheek. Open-mouthed kisses trail along my jaw. "Or a recommendation from the psychologist?"

I wiggle my ass as my fingers dive into his hair to pull him to my mouth. I let a toe-curling kiss answer for me.

Harris groans and tightens his grip while bending his knees to align his hard cock with the crack of my ass. He grinds up against me, and I just about spread my legs for him to take me right here. Right. Now.

He chuckles wickedly and pushes the wooden door open.

"After you, Ms. Jackson," he purrs.

I almost skip down the stairs, delighted to have Harris on the same mind frame as me.

We're going to fuck! At last!

I thank Edwin as he holds the door open of the Cullinan, then silently urge him to drive faster. Harris laughs at me bouncing on the seat. With a shake of his head, he pulls me onto his lap and kisses me breathless.

"Patience, Ms. Jackson. I've got you, babe," he murmurs against my swollen lips.

I sigh contentedly and lean against him.

On the ride up in the private lift, I blow kisses and wink at Harris' reflection in the doors. He smirks at my flirtatious antics and squeezes my hand. When he opens the entry doors, he leans in and whispers in my ear.

"Straight to the bedroom. Stand in front of the window with your back to the doors. Do not move," he commands.

A shiver races down my spine as my breath hitches. A smack to my ass drives me forward with a squeal.

I make haste to do as Harris commanded. Time passes. I try not to fidget or glance over my shoulder. Instead, my mind drifts. The memory of seeing Harris for the first time in the lobby of Jackson Town House replaces the images of the Manhattan skyline. A tremor runs through me as I recall every sensual touch and each electrifying kiss from him. I smile at his insistence I lay claim to this posh penthouse.

In those moments, my desire to build a life with the man I love increases exponentially. No one and most of all not Chet will take the happiness Harris and I have together away from us. We will move past this more than a bump in the road stronger than before. His family and my Jackson family accept me once again. Nothing can stop us.

"You're right, Ms. Jackson. *Nothing can stop us.*"

I gasp and spin around to find Harris mere feet away from me. His smoldering eyes rake over me from head to toe. He sucks his plump lower lip into his mouth with his teeth as he advances. I shiver in anticipation as waves of his carnal lust roll over me.

"I did not expect you to talk to yourself when I left you to think through what you want from me. However, I agree with you completely," Harris says.

He slips his hands onto my hips and leans down. His lips centimeters from mine. I rise to my toes. But he tsks.

"And I did not tell you to turn around. I said, *do not move,* naughty girl," he adds as he spins me to face the window again.

His fingers glide along the outside of my thighs to the hem of my dress. They bunch the soft material and slide it up slowly, sensuously. It skims along the stretchy, buttery leather of my mid-thigh boots to tease my skin. His knuckles leave goosebumps in their wake. Up and over my head, the dress goes. Harris drops it to the floor and cups my breasts.

They grow heavy in his hands as he kneads them and tugs on my nipples through the lace. They pucker from his touch. I moan wantonly as my head lolls back against his chest.

Harris takes advantage of the space to drag his lips along the column of my throat. Little nips send thrills rocketing through me. He sucks the sensitive skin at the juncture of my neck and shoulder into his mouth. His teeth worry my flesh, sure to leave a mark.

"Mine," he growls.

"Yours," I purr.

He chuckles wickedly.

The front closure of my bra pops open. He moves the cups aside to massage my aching breasts. I arch my back, pushing them further into his magic touch. My fingers dig into his muscular thighs. I need something, anything, to ground me. Or I'll float away in sheer bliss.

The musky scent of my arousal wafts in the surrounding air. It mixes with the compelling Dionysiac aroma of his cologne—floral, earthy, and vanilla—heightened by the heat of his body temperature. We're on fire for one another.

I shrug out of the bra as Harris hooks his thumbs in the sides of my G-string.

He crouches and lifts one of my feet, then the other, before he drops the lace on top of my dress.

"These boots weren't made for walking. They're made

for fucking," he growls as he slides his hands up the backs of my legs.

His left hand clutches my thigh to encourage me to bend my knee up against the window. Fully open to him, he burrows his nose into my pussy, past the slick lips. He nudges my engorged clit with the tip of his nose as he hums in appreciation.

"So wet for me already, Kitty Kat," he murmurs between bites of my lower lips and clit. "I want you to cum for me again. And. Again. Until you beg for me to fuck you."

A stream of Scottish Gaelic curses pours from my mouth as I sag against the glass. My palms and forehead press against its coolness. Condensation from my pants forms on it, receding and extending with each breath.

True to his word, Harris eats me like a starved man. Lapping at my cream as it gushes after each mind-blowing orgasm. I lose count. His guttural groans of pleasure drive me over the edge repeatedly. My body quivers. But for his grip on my hips, I would crumble to the floor completely boneless.

"P—P—Please fuck me..." I wail as my pussy clenches around his dangerous tongue.

He growls and rises so quickly, I wobble. His arm bands around me, locking me against his firm body. The sound of his zipper and his sigh of relief draws a moan from deep in my throat. He kicks my feet apart, bends his knees, and rocks forward onto his toes as he impales me on his massive cock.

My pussy struggles to accept his girth and length. But Harris has none of it. He grips me tighter and thrusts deeper until he's fully seated deep within me.

"Fffuuuck..." he groans. "So tight. So wet. So warm."

My palms slap the window, then slide up the slippery

surface as Harris pounds into me. The stretch burns oh so good. In ecstasy, I rise onto the balls of my feet still encased in the sexy boots. I throw my head back and keen.

"Still with me, My Kitty Kat?" Concern gives Harris pause.

In response, I drop hard onto my heels and grind onto his throbbing cock.

He growls.

A slow drag out to his tip precedes a sharp snap of his hips to impale me once again. He continues the deliberate pace until I beg for it faster and harder. With a fierce chuckle, he obliges me.

I explode anew.

Stars on a white shimmery backdrop dance before my eyes. My mouth hangs slack. The muscles of my core clench so intensely, my stomach cramps. Cream gushes like a fountain to coat his cock. The natural lubricant eases his passage.

He hisses in satisfaction.

Carnally connected as one, we avow *nothing can stop us*.

KAT

"**Y**ou slept well last night. Feel better, babe?"

I snicker at Harris' words as I roll over in our bed to face him. A glint of mischief dances in his dove gray eyes as he stares down at me. Leaning on an elbow with tousled hair and stubble around his luscious mouth, he smirks.

"Oh, do you mean the few moments you allowed me to close my eyes? And not in ecstasy?" I respond with a wry grin of my own.

He chuffs and planks on both elbows to hover over me. His warm breath mingles with mine as I gasp at the pressure of his heavy balls and ramrod cock on my lower belly. A knowing grin spreads across his handsome face.

"As I recall, you begged for it *faster and harder*, more and more. Not to mention the fact you screamed my name as you broke for me over and over," Harris says. His hips swivel with each word to further remind me of my pleas.

I groan and lift my hips to meet his teasing thrusts. My hands fling over my head to brace against the headboard.

"Take me again, lover!" I demand.

Harris bows his head to my breasts. His lips and teeth add to his teasing hips as he tugs at my puckered nipples. Not quite enough to make me cum. But the right combination to increase my carnal desire.

I buck beneath him. My head tosses from one side to the other as I bow my back. My movements force him to grip my hip to still me. I growl in frustration as he continues to taunt me. He merely chuckles.

"Harris, don't tease me. Please!" I beseech him.

He rewards me with two thick fingers breaching my sopping seam. They scissor within me, then flip to stroke the sensitive tissue of my G-spot. One. Two. Three times. I gush into the palm of his hand.

Toes curled, back arched on a soundless wail, my body convulses. His fingers never stop their carnal caress until I sink into the bed, mouth parted, eyelids drooped.

A musky scent fills my nostrils. My eyelids flutter open as Harris slips his fingers coated with my cream between my lips. Automatically, the tip of my tongue darts out to lap at them greedily.

He presses the digits further inside my mouth, then groans as I suck them clean. He drags them from my mouth, down my chin, and to my nipple. A pinch and I writhe.

"Good girl," he croons.

I preen.

"Come. Let's get you showered before your yoga session," Harris says. He rolls from the bed and extends his hand to me. "Up and at 'em, Kitty Kat."

I take it and rise to my knees. My other hand cups his heavy sac. I lick my lips seductively as I massage his balls between my fingers.

His eyes close as he draws in a sharp breath. The

bobbing of his veiny, velvet-covered shaft encourages my ministrations. A tortured groan slips past his lips.

"Fuck my mouth, Mr. Steele," I purr in his ear with a decisive squeeze to his sac.

I lie down on the bed with my head hanging over the edge. His thick thighs bracket me as I stare up into his face. The feral desire in his wolfish eyes makes me mewl. My mouth opens wide. The flat of my tongue reaching past my lower lip beckons to him.

With a growl, he fists the base of his engorged dick. He pumps his fist along its length and squeezes the angry purple tip. A large bead of pre-cum dangles from it.

I tip my head back further to catch it, then hum as I swallow it down. It undoes him.

"Open!" Harris commands as he grips my chin between his thumb and index finger.

Happily, I oblige.

He groans and I moan as his ample girth widens my mouth. The tip of his cock bumps the back of my throat.

Tears fill my eyes as my gag reflex kicks in. Wanting to pleasure him, I breathe through my nose and relax my throat.

Harris' eyes narrow at the outline of his cock as it stretches my throat. All ten inches.

The tears spill from the corners of my eyes to pool in my ears. Again, I ignore my body's natural reaction to dispel his erotic invasion. It's a conquering I'll gladly take. His dominance sets me off as much as my willingness does him.

My hands cup my achy breasts while my fingers tweak my nipples. I squeeze my thighs together and buck my hips. I want to cum.

Harris reaches out. His fingertips trail along my throat. The sensation of him stroking his cock through the thin layer of my skin makes me hum. He groans as his fingers continue between my breasts, over my belly, and between my folds. He pinches my swollen clit.

The moan as I climax triggers his need to release.

His hands grip the sides of my head. He pistons his hips, dragging his dick in and out of my mouth from root to tip. The controlled, measured thrusts turn uneven and feral. Now he wants to cum.

I hallow out my cheeks and suckle.

With a primal roar, Harris crushes my face to his crotch and spews ropes of hot semen down my throat, straight to my hungry belly. My fingernails dig into his quivering thighs as he pulses on my tongue.

His dick pops from my mouth as he drops to his knees. He hunkers down with his back against the bed and his head on the mattress beside mine. Our pants match as we struggle to catch our breath.

"You'll be the death of me yet, Siren," Harris rasps.

"You look radiant, Kat. That man of yours come through? No pun intended…"

I join in Vivian's giggles.

Another recommendation the psychologist gave was to get back into my routine. So after yoga and breakfast, Vivian and I ride to the office. She waggles her eyebrows as she grins.

"Nothing like some good loving to make you happy!" Viv adds with a wink of a toffee brown eye, then pouts. "Now if I could just get some."

I shift on the backseat of the Cullinan to face her.

"What happened during your date with one of Harris' buddies?" I ask.

She shrugs and shakes her head.

"I postponed it. I couldn't go out with my girl gone, you know," she responds as she peeks at me from beneath her thick eyelashes.

Yeah, that...

Viv nudges me, and I glance back at her.

"But you're back!! You can help me pick out a fabulous outfit to wear. He invited me to a Chelsea art gallery opening with dinner afterwards next week," she enthuses. "Maybe we could make it a double date?"

I laugh out loud and shake my head vigorously. The last time I went to an art gallery with Harris, my entire world flipped.

Viv's frown changes to a wide-eyed stare as she recollects my story. She sputters to respond. Words of blunders and rotten friend pour from her mouth. But I grab her hand between mine.

"Not to worry, Viv! You're by far the best friend I've ever had. Truly! And don't you go walking on eggshells around me too," I say with a laugh. "But I'll pass on the double date. Not because it's at an art gallery, per se. Rather, you need to have your first date with this guy alone. If you like him, Harris and I will join you for dinner or something. Okay?"

She bites her lower lip as she studies my face.

I tug her hand and grin wider until she nods and wraps her arms around me.

"Kat, you do not know how scared I was for you. I blamed myself. I should've gone upstairs with you or noticed sooner—"

"No, Vivian! No one is to blame except for that crazy prat. Let's forget about him anyway," I say adamantly.

She nods, then peeks at me again. Her mouth opens, then snaps shut as she glances away.

"Out with it," I tell her.

"Whatever happened to him? Has Harris said anything?" Viv asks quietly.

Good question. In all of this time, it never occurred to me. I guess my mind is more determined to forget that prat than I realized. I glance back at Viv and shrug.

She nods, then brightens and claps her hands.

"Okay, so back to my outfit. I was thinking we could go to Versace…"

"I KNOW it's not the most suitable after-dinner talk, but I forgot to ask before. Whatever happened to Chet? Do I need to give a statement or something to the authorities? Have a trial? I'd like to finish with all of it. Move forward from the whole mess completely."

The jovial chatter in the living room stops by the end of my request.

I shift my gaze from Harris. I glance around to Roger with Leonie in his lap beside us, Sebastian and Lola next to Lachlan and Haley on the sofa opposite, then to Malcolm and Starr on chairs. All heads turn to the second oldest Steele.

"Oh, that fucker? Well, he's on a slow boat to Antarctica with some eager playmates. I assure you the boys will keep him company," *The Enforcer* responds, then sits back and sips his Jackson Scotch. "But whether he makes landfall will prove impossible."

Sebastian chuckles darkly and murmurs in Russian, to which a predatory smile spreads across Malcolm's face.

"No need for you to speak to anyone, Kat. Just forget he ever existed," Sebastian adds.

Well, fuck.

Now I sit back and gulp half the contents of my snifter. The rich amber liquid rolls down my throat and settles in my stomach. With closed eyes, I cradle the crystal to my chest.

Holy crap. I picture the prat begging *the boys* as I did him to not sexually assault me. Now it's his turn to fear, except there's no rescue for him. Does it bother me? Do I care?

A sinister smile spreads across my face. I open my eyes and pin a steady stare on *The Enforcer*.

"Tell me more. I want to hear everything. From the moment you left here to the moment Harris carried me through the front doors to that prat setting sail. Leave no sordid detail out," I say.

The tension in the room vanishes.

Malcolm throws his head back and roars with laughter. Sebastian leans forward and high fives his brother. Lachlan blows out a round of curses in Scottish Gaelic before he lifts his snifter to his lips, curled in a smirk. Roger slaps Harris on the back, then grins at me.

"So, you're not upset, babe? You won't tell anyone?" Harris asks as his eyes scan my face for any sign of distress or disloyalty.

I snort and raise my snifter in the air as I stand.

"Ah pinnae, ken," I respond.

Lachlan laughs and rises with his snifter held high. He glances around the room and winks as he translates: *"I'm dreadfully sorry, sir. But I have no idea what you might be talking about."*

The others jump to their feet and join our toast. We cheer and wish the prat a much-deserved journey.

"Well, now that's cleared the air, I say it's time for a Couples' Getaway! I have a special fitness retreat scheduled for next month at LEVELS Laucala Island. I'll hear no excuse not to attend," Starr says once everyone returns to their seats. She flicks her gaze at each of us, then continues. "I'll email the itinerary to you and the others tomorrow. A week in Fiji will do us all some good."

We toast to her announcement and pledge our attendance.

The rest of the evening passes comfortably. Our guys talk about sports. The girls fill me in on the fun retreats they've had in the past. My excitement grows when they share what I can expect at the first exclusive members-only BDSM resort, or BDSM on the Beach as Starr dubbed it. We'll have the fitness session at her Starr Light Fitness & Wellness Laucala Island. She opened it to keep LEVELS LI members limber. And I cannot wait!

HARRIS

"Kat adjusted well over the past month. A lightness replaced that haunted look in her eyes."

"Or could it be the good lovin' my boy's *adjusted* her to?"

I nod at Baz and throw a smug smirk at Laurent, who chuckles. Then I glance over my shoulder towards the middle of the STEELE Gulfstream G700.

We're headed to Laucala Island for Starr's Couples' Getaway as promised. The $75-million-dollar private jet can accommodate up to eighteen passengers with sleeping space for nine. Its powerful Rolls-Royce engines and technological advancements allow it to fly internationally with ease. The spacious, luxurious interior affords five living areas with a forward galley for the flight crew.

Malcolm and his thrill-seeking buddies—cousins Anton Alexeyev and Borya Alexeyev—shift in their oversized white leather chairs to get in on the conversation. To rib me more specifically.

"Ah, the youngest of The STEELE Quaternity has fallen

for The One, has he?" Anton asks as he bats his glacial blue eyes and clutches his hands to his chest.

Borya guffaws and responds in Russian, to which Baz, Malcolm, and Anton throw their heads back and laugh heartily. The former MMA world champion known as *The War Defender* continues to smirk at his own joke as he nods at me.

I turn back and roll my eyes, clueless as to what he said, but know it's at my expense.

"Whatever, Borya. I notice Márcia occupies your time. Or perhaps not enough of it since my business ranks high for you?" I retort. Sure, it's a death wish to fuck with Borya. But I am the jokester of the family.

His glacial blues pin me as a rumble brews in his massive chest.

Bad idea, Harris? Ya think?

Then Borya guffaws and slaps me on the shoulder.

"Good one, *umnik!*" He responds.

"Yeah, Harris is a *smart ass!*" Malcolm translates. "The best we have."

Patrick Rockett—once a bitter rival of STEELE International with his family's multibillion-dollar construction firm—roars with laughter. The Scotsman adds his commentary gleefully.

My gaze returns to Kat.

She sits on the white leather sofa between Vivian and Márcia Souza. The Brazilian spitfire and Starr's assistant has the giant Russian wrapped around her pinky finger. Just as much as Kat has me.

Sure, I've given her my *good lovin'*. But it's also the release of the burden she has to worry about Stewart, compounded with making up to everyone for her erroneous actions. He's gone for good, and we've forgiven her.

Watching her laugh easily with Lola makes me smile. I feared Kat's lies about her parents' death in a car accident would ruin any chance she had to regain Lola's affection. My sister-in-law truly lost her parents to a drunk driver. This past month my sister and my girlfriend grew closer than before.

The kidnapping changed a lot for all of us. Life is too short to hold on to the past. Time for the future. And a beautiful one, I muse as I grin at gorgeous My Kitty Kat.

Even from this distance, her emerald green eyes shine with joy. Warmth floods her alabaster cheeks with a rosy hue. The sunlight sparks on her Titian hair as it swirls around her face with each bob of her head. Her tinkling laughter at something Vivian said makes my heart swell.

My Kitty Kat high fives Yessenia Rodriguez—who captured Laurent's heart. The Southern Belle twang of Billie Chandler—Lola's Coterie's Chief Operating Officer and Patrick's love—rings out. Adrienne Anthony—Anton's girl and SLFW's Co-CEO—reaches over and nudges Starr, who giggles as she flicks her sorrel brown eyes towards Malcolm. She catches my stare and whispers to My Kitty Kat.

She glances at me and blows a kiss, at which the girls fall out in laughter. With a wink, she returns her attention to her friends.

Yup. Life is definitely moving forward in the best possible way.

"I THOUGHT MAUI PHENOMENAL... But, Harris, this... Oh my... Absolutely breathtaking!"

Kat whispers in awe, eyes glued to the scene outside the window as we prepare to land on Laucala Island.

The luxury private island surrounded by varied depths

of turquoise waters Malcolm purchased for Starr still makes me ogle like a newcomer. The tropical paradise's pristine white sand beaches and lush landscape in an explosion of vibrant colors dazzle the eyes and temper any stressed mind.

Not only does Laucala Island serve as the location for a LEVELS resort and SLFW center, but our family also has twelve villas secluded on the other side. Each residence sits directly on the pristine beach or perched on the cliffside with jaw-dropping views of the expansive Pacific Ocean.

"Wait until we go on a hike through the interior. There's a spectacular waterfall under which we swim in the refreshing water. You'll love it!" Starr says, delighted by My Kitty Kat's reaction.

I watch their interaction with a smile. A movement by Malcolm draws my gaze to him.

He flutters his eyelashes à la Anton then smirks when I roll my eyes skyward. Like he did not lose himself in his *Angel* from the moment they met…

The jet lands, and we disembark to a row of silver Range Rover SVAutobiographys. The drivers take our luggage as we wait around the SUVs. We watch as the jet carrying those based in Europe lands moments later.

My Kitty Kat waves as Haley and Leonie walk down the steps. Blair Thomas—Lola's Coterie's Chief Marketing Officer—walks out next. They wave back as Lachlan, Roger, and Luc Montaigne—the French multibillionaire bank scion and Blair's love—follow them off Luc's Gulfstream G700.

Squeals erupt as the girls run to each other. Heads bob, arms clutch, feet dance as they greet one another. Their excited chatter fills the air.

I laugh along with the guys at their excitement for our Couples' Getaway. We exchange bro hugs and claps on the shoulder. Then wait for our women to glance our way before we round them up into the SUVs. With a promise to meet at Malcolm and Starr's beachfront villa for breakfast, we head to the residences.

On the ride to the other side of the island, I point out the roads leading to LEVELS Laucala Island and to Starr Light Fitness and Wellness Laucala Island. Signs handcrafted by local artisans announce what's ahead for guests. Palm trees and flowery bushes line the roads to welcome them to a sinful paradise. The buildings surrounded by the foliage sit tucked back from the primary thoroughfare.

My Kitty Kat cranes her neck for a better view as we drive by, then turns in her seat to face me.

"I can't wait to see this LEVELS! Haley told me how incredible it is. Perhaps we can go tonight?" The redheaded Siren asks with a seductive smile on her gorgeous face. Emerald green eyes glow full of carnal lust.

I lean over and grip the back of her neck. Drawing her to me, I lower my mouth within centimeters from her full lips. Our breath mingles as I stare deep into her eyes. The pupils dilate as her breath comes out in puffs. The sweet scent entices me closer.

My mouth captures hers in a searing kiss. Teeth nip until her lips part. The tip of my tongue rims just inside her wet warmth. On a needy moan, the Siren opens wider and laps at my tongue like a naughty kitten. I angle her head to retake control of the kiss and plunder her mouth. My tongue replicates the thrusts of my cock in her lower, wet warmth.

Breathy moans make my cock twitch. Delicate fingers skim along the outline of my burgeoning erection as it lengthens between my joggers and thigh. A naughty pinch to the tip makes me groan in need.

Hell yeah, we can go to LEVELS tonight!

We arrive at my villa. My Kitty Kat's jaw drops at the sight of four sprawling bures—traditional Fijian men's houses nestled against the cliff amongst tropical flowers and trees. Between the two main bures, the glistening turquoise waters of the Pacific Ocean spreads out as far as the eye can see.

"This must be what an eagle's aerie feels like high above the ground with the gentle breeze of the wind," My Kitty Kat says when we step out of the SUV. She spins in a circle, arms spread wide like an eagle's wings. "Incredible, Harris. It's only yours?"

I grin and pull her into my arms, nuzzling her neck as I nod.

"Welcome to my love nest in the clouds, Kitty Kat," I murmur against her soft skin. Her fragrance proves more alluring than the seductive scent of the surrounding frangipani. "Ready to play hide and seek?"

She melds her body against mine as she palms my ass, my erection thick between us.

"You promised breakfast," she breathes.

I chuckle wickedly and nip the sensitive juncture at her neck and shoulder. She whimpers.

"Oh, I promise you a full meal," I respond as I grind my cock against her lower belly.

She squeals as I toss her over my shoulder and carry her to the bure for my bedroom suite. Her squeals turn into cries of passion as I fill her belly, then her pussy, with my seed.

"Well, well, well, look who decided to join us."

"Um, you almost missed breakfast, slowpokes."

I help My Kitty Kat into a chair at the table and smirk at Laurent and Haley.

"Oh, I guarantee you I ate, and Kat had more than her fill," I say.

Haley scowls and covers her ears.

"Harris, please! Spare me the details of your sex life. Ugh!" She says as she rolls her eyes.

Laurent snickers and Yessenia nudges him.

"Don't encourage him, *Mi Amor*," the Latina beauty chides, then turns her tawny brown eyes to My Kitty Kat. "What are we going to do with these two cavemen?"

Laurent slides the curtain of waist-length curly black hair aside and leans over to kiss her slim neck. He murmurs indecipherable words in Spanish to his love. Her golden brown cheeks blush crimson. She takes a sip of water. He sits back and drapes his arm over her shoulders, then throws a smug look at me.

I chuckle and shake my head. The rascal. That's my boy!

"And so anyway… I believe Starr was in the middle of sharing plans for today," Haley says to Laurent and to me pointedly. Then she shifts her gaze and smiles saccharine sweetly. "Starr, kindly continue despite the nature of that unnecessary interruption."

Starr hides her smile behind a sip of pomegranate juice before she tells us we have a free day with a sunset dinner at Lucien's villa. After which those who wish to play can head to LEVELS LI for Masquerade Night, as she and Malcolm plan to enjoy, Starr adds with a wanton grin. He pulls her in for a possessive kiss.

"Not you, too!" Haley groans. She throws her white linen napkin onto the table and plops back against her chair, arms folded over her chest.

Lachlan holds her chin between his thumb and index finger and kisses her silly. When they part, she swoons.

"Now you were saying, Haley, dear twin?" I ask.

Her cheeks flush a darker shade of red before she tucks her face into Lachlan's neck.

"Exactly!" Laurent and I say at the same time.

Everyone laughs.

Once we finish breakfast, Laurent and I take Yessenia and My Kitty Kat for a tour. We stop by our villas to add bathing suits under our clothes and to grab towels and bottled waters, then take the scenic route around the perimeter of the island.

As we ride along in a Range Rover, we point out different spots. The girls can't get enough of the island's natural beauty. Even Yessenia—who was born and raised on Puerto Rico—appreciates this island's allure.

Laurent and I lead the girls blindfolded along a narrow sandy path cut through palm trees. They giggle and cling to our arms to keep their balance. When the path ends, we pause to remove the red silk from around their heads. The girls gasp at the sight of the empty white sand beach set in a secluded cove.

"*Mi Amor!* This is unbelievable," Yessenia exclaims.

My Kitty Kat claps her hands and darts ahead. She pulls her cotton dress over her head and tosses it to the sand. She spins around, kicking her sandals off and beckons to us.

"Last one in is a rotten egg!" She yells, then pivots back towards the waves.

"Not me!" Yessenia shouts as she dashes after My Kitty Kat.

Laurent and I exchange glances. I shove him aside and race after the girls.

"Guess it'll be Laurent!" I laugh as I grab the back of my

t-shirt and yank it off. Then grunt when something hits me between the shoulder blades. Laurent's flip flop falls to the sand. My hesitation gives him the advantage, and he charges ahead with a war cry.

Our Alpha male competition surges through us.

Not to be outdone, I catch up to him before he reaches the water's edge. A well-aimed foot makes him stumble. I dive into the first wave and reemerge next to My Kitty Kat triumphantly.

"Take that, take that, take that!" I chortle at Laurent as he lopes into the water.

"Fucker," he mutters.

Yessenia glides over to him and wraps her arms around his neck. She kisses his lips, then jumps back. Water splashes around them.

"Peeyoo! You stink, Rotten Egg!" She giggles as she fans a delicate hand across her face.

Laurent growls and lunges towards her. With ease, he grabs Yessenia's waist and tosses her backwards through the air.

She yowls as her arms and legs windmill far above the water's surface. She drops below, then pops back up, spluttering a string of curses in Spanish.

Laurent sloshes over and swoops her into his arms. He covers her face with kisses until giggling, she pushes him away. He doesn't let go. Instead, he floats her onto her back with her head against his shoulder.

"I hear you can put even the mighty Great White Shark into a catatonic state if you flip one upside-down. Perhaps it'll work on my fiery Yessenia," Laurent says with a laugh.

She huffs but lets him float her around.

I stand with a goofy grin on my face as I watch my partner in playadom so in love. We've come a long way from our nights—and days—of fucking around. He and Yessenia make a great couple whose love is unbreakable. But that's for another story…

"This is truly spectacular, Harris."

My Kitty Kat draws me from my lovestruck musings.

I turn to her and cup her cheeks. The pad of my thumb brushes across her mouth. She parts her lips and sucks the digit into her warm wetness. She hums. I groan.

The zing shoots from my thumb to my cock like a lightning bolt.

"The way you tempt me, Siren," I murmur in her ear. "If we were alone, I'd put your mouth to good use…"

She laughs huskily and pulls harder on my thumb. My cock throbs. It wants in on the action.

With a shake of my head, I pop the moist digit from her mouth. She pouts.

"Later at LEVELS," I promise.

"FUCK, Siren… Take me deeper… Uunnhhh, yes…"

Less than an hour passed since the redheaded Siren and I arrived at the club for LEVELS Laucala Island—the five-star beachfront resort spans across several buildings around the club. After an eye-opening tour of the seven levels for her, we settled in a private alcove.

Instead of being like the other clubs in one building, each level exists in different Fijian bures. Or rather Malcolm and Lucien's luxurious versions of the traditional Fijian men's houses. As always, they play on the local area when they design a club. Beverly Hills is within a famous Hollywood costume designer's atelier and storefront with a view of the iconic Hollywood Sign.

Here, the Sky Lounge in the 7th bure sits on the beach

with stunning views of the sunset over the Pacific Ocean and a bar, restaurant by day, dance club by night, with a coverable pool to extend the dance floor. The bure for the 6th and 5th levels that comprise the multilevel dance club with two bars and a lounge for food and drinks sits to one side of the Sky Lounge. On the other side, the 4th level bure has the Level 4 Restaurant and bar open for breakfast, lunch, and dinner. Rising above the dance club and built into the cliffside is the 3rd level with a two-story bure for twelve private bedrooms where members can continue their pleasure apart from the BDSM levels. Next to it above the Sky Lounge is the bure for the 2nd Level Peepshow for BDSM with seating alcoves, main stage, performance rooms, and a bar that serves non-alcoholic mocktails. A bure serves as the entrance where the 1st level Cellar BDSM dungeon with mocktails bar built directly into the cliff as a giant cave as opposed to being below ground. Covered paths lead from one bure to the other for an interconnecting city of consensual sin.

Overall, my boys did an amazing job recreating LEVELS to match the tropical island vibe while maintaining its core purpose. As Starr says, it's BDSM on the Beach at its finest.

And the way my sexy Siren deep throats my cock is on par with our surroundings.

My head hangs back as the cords in my neck tighten. The first tingling of my climax swirls in my belly. My ass tightens as my hands lock her head in place. The anticipation builds. An epic release promised.

Her enthusiastic hum vibrates over my engorged shaft. She swallows, and the motion ripples along my length.

My hips pump as I rise to the balls of my feet. The angle changes. My heavy balls draw up, ready for the release rolling down my spine.

With a feral roar, my seed spews down her throat straight into her hungry belly. Shockwaves roll through me. I sway on my feet. White light flashes before my eyes squeezed shut in pure ecstasy.

"Fuuuck..."

My grip of her hair lessens. The silky tresses slip from my fingers as she leans back on her heels. My cock pops from her mouth, leaving a trail of saliva from the tip.

The sexy Siren winks up at me as the tip of her little pink tongue darts out. She licks my cock clean from root to tip. She watches with a smug expression on her beautiful face as I stuff my junk back into my leather pants.

I hoist her up from a cushion on the floor into my arms and carry her to the oversized vamp red leather bench. She curls up on my lap like a good little Kitty Kat. My head rests against the wall as I stroke her back, breaths evening out. She purrs contentedly.

My mind drifts to earlier. We may be at a LEVELS club. But I'm with *my* woman. The only one I want. Forever.

Yeah, the players have come a long way from fucking around. No doubt.

KAT

"It's just a little further to go. Come on. You got this!"

My body groans in protest, despite Starr's encouragement. We were up late last night with dinner and a bonfire on the beach in front of Lachlan and Haley's villa. When Harris and I returned to ours, he worshipped my body like I was the goddess of love. For hours.

Now, he squeezes my hand and smiles down at me as we trudge behind the others. We're headed to the waterfall as the grand finale for our Couples' Getaway. Besides the amazing sight, Starr promises a refreshing swim in the cool waters and a delicious lunch courtesy of Lucien. Once we return to the villas, everyone will have the rest of the day and evening to themselves. The perfect ending for an incredible trip.

So, sure I can go along with this hike.

I grin up at Harris and return the squeeze.

We continue for another twenty minutes. The beauty of the island's interior makes the time less of a hassle and more of a walk through paradise. Harris points out colorful birds and butterflies as they flit amongst the lush vegetation surrounding us. He plucks a white flower from a bush and places it behind my ear.

"Add to your beauty, Kitty Kat," Harris murmurs.

My heart swells. This man has me good. And I couldn't be happier!

"All right! Here we are!"

Starr's words make me glance in her direction. She stands with her arms outstretched. Behind her, the path widens to reveal the dazzling waters of the waterfall. The sun sparkles on them as they rush from the cliff down to the lake. The burble of the water fills the air as it splashes. A mist hovers above the surface.

It's a majestic sight to behold.

Starr beckons us forward.

It only gets better.

The area opens up to include a carpet of green grass around the lake circled by palm trees and flowering bushes. To one side stands a white gauzy canopy with its four posts covered in ropes of frangipani. It floats above tables with floral bouquets at their center. Chairs have more gauzy material draped over them with bows in the back and wreaths of flowers. The billowy topper blows in the gentle breeze. Another canopy floats above a table laden with platters covered by silver domes and buckets of Champagne. Servers stand at the ready.

"Time for the swim I promised you!" Starr calls out.

I grin at Harris.

He nods and leads me to the area where blankets spread out over the grass. He stops beside one and kneels. His hand takes mine.

"Oh, I can get my boots off, Harris!" I giggle as I tug my hand. "No need for you to do it, silly."

He bites his lower lip and shakes his head. His mouth opens, then closes. He gives his head another shake before he peeks up at me. A cough clears his throat.

"Kat… You make me feel what no one ever has. Or ever will. I never want to spend a day of my life without you by my side. Each day I awake, it's your face I want to see first. And every night the last. I love you more than you can ever know."

He pulls a little navy blue box from his shirt pocket.

My mouth gapes.

His eyes return to mine.

"Kat Jackson, will you become Kat Steele? Will you marry me?"

The top of the box opens at the press of the sapphire cabochon. Nestled in navy silk rests the biggest diamond I've ever seen in my life. The massive stone shoots sparks of fire as it glitters in the sunlight.

Tears fill my eyes as my mouth opens and closes. Words prove impossible to form.

I fall to my knees before Harris and throw my arms around his neck as I nod fervently. My entire body shakes.

He bands his arms around me, holding me close to his powerful chest. The beat of his heart as fast in tempo as mine pounding against my ribs. He presses his lips to the shell of my ear.

"Words. I will have your words," Harris commands.

"Yes! Absolutely, positively, yes!" I respond.

Harris leans back and places the engagement ring on my finger. My hand trembles slightly, and he brings it to his lips. As he kisses the diamond, his eyes bore into mine.

In that moment, I know just how much Harris loves me.

Clapping and whoops rise around us.

I startle, having forgotten everything and everyone but Harris. He grins bigger than the Cheshire Cat as he stands and pulls me off my feet. He swings me around as his shout joins the others' hollers. I throw my head back and scream yes for all the world to hear.

Harris' mouth finds mine. He kisses me breathless. I cling to him to remain anchored to this world while my heart soars to the heavens. The words I love you run on repeat in my mind.

Once he settles me on my feet, hands grab me. My girls pull me in for hugs and kisses. They admire my ring—as big as the diamonds on their left hands. Vivian most of all, even though she's yet to find her Prince Charming. Their words of best wishes and welcome to the Steele family fill me with immense joy. My face aches from the huge smile.

I catch glimpses of Harris being bro hugged and getting slaps on the back by his boys. The happiness on his face adds to my joy. He catches my eye and winks.

Servers walk amongst us with trays of Champagne in crystal flutes. Harris grabs two and saunters over to me. I bite the corner of my mouth as I watch him approach. He holds out a flute, then wraps his arm around my waist. Melded to his side, I raise my flute with his.

"To my gorgeous fiancée. May her love for me never end!" Harris exclaims.

"Hear! Hear!"

"Salud!"

"Salutations!"

Boisterous cheers ring out louder than the waterfall cascading behind us.

I rise onto my toes and offer my mouth to my fiancé.

Harris captures it for another toe-curling kiss. He bends

me over his arm as our tongues tangle. Wolf whistles and calls for get a room make us laugh. He sets me right and bows for the crowd.

I cover my kiss-swollen mouth with my hand and giggle.

The glint of my princess-cut diamond catches my eye—twenty-three carats, Lola assures me. I give a shriek and wiggle my hand in the air. My girls stomp their feet and clap.

"Ah, yes, our Laucala Island brings out the most romance in everyone—including Harris, the last man standing of The STEELE Quaternity!" Malcolm announces with a tilt of his head. "Right, My Angel?" He pulls Starr into his side and nuzzles her neck.

Harris agrees and tugs me closer, then plants a kiss on my temple.

"Let's take a dip in the lake to cleanse the old and prepare for the new," Starr—ever the yogi—suggests.

Everyone agrees, and we strip down to our swimsuits.

Harris swoops me from my feet and carries bride-like into the sparkling azure water. He keeps me close as he dips below the surface. I squeal and cling to his neck, then gasp as he rises. He slings his wet hair and chuckles as I duck from the deluge.

"Are you happy, Kitty Kat?" Harris asks with a grin wider than the Cheshire Cat's.

I cup his face between my palms. My lips slant over his. I let the passion of my kiss answer for me. Words can never be enough to express my absolute happiness. The man I love asked me to be his wife, to live our lives together forever. How can joy not fill me?

Loud catcalls and wolf whistles break out around my fiancé and me. Laurent tells us to get a bure; Haley groans.

I press my forehead to Harris' and smile.

"I love you, Harris Steele," I whisper.

His dove gray eyes gleam.

"I love you, Kat Jackson, soon-to-be Kat Steele," he murmurs.

After our swim, we gather at the buffet table to select our lunch. The servers fill fresh glasses of Champagne.

I stand at my seat. My gaze goes from one to the other before it settles on Harris. I raise my flute.

"Harris, I promise to love you for all time and to give you all the joy you give to me and more," I say, then glance around the table again. "To my family, I thank you for allowing me back into your lives—permanently!"

More boisterous cheers fill the air.

Once we're settled, Leonie turns to me.

"So, *chérie*, I'm sure I speak for all the girls. We'd love to help you plan your wedding!" She says as her feline amber eyes glitter.

Lola claps.

"Most definitely, Kat! Not to mention the Sergeant and Lieutenant," she says gleefully.

Starr snorts and shakes her head. Her long, dark brown curls bounce around her face. Dimples deepen as she giggles.

"I'd love for you to help me. But I'm sort of in the dark. Who are the sergeant and lieutenant?" I ask.

"Oh, Sergeant Shelley and Lieutenant Lucie. Being you're a Jackson marrying a Steele, they're bound to handle your wedding planning as they did with me. Lola, Leonie, and Starr had the Sergeant for their nuptials," Haley responds with a grin. "But of course, your Mum will have as much say as they have—well, and you, too!"

"Maybe!" Starr says with a hearty laugh. "At least you can hope. But they know their stuff, and my mom helped, too."

I agree to their help wholeheartedly.

I do not know how to handle a society wedding to a multibillionaire. The closest I've come to one are the photographs in magazines and newspapers of socialites smiling up into the faces of their equally handsome husbands at their posh weddings. Their gowns masterpieces in couture. Engagement rings and wedding bands glitter. Incredible backdrops for their nuptials: cathedrals, castles, ballrooms. Incredible. Or rather incredibly intimidating…

"So, Harris, how much time will you give your soon-to-be wife time to plan?"

Roger's question draws me from my thoughts.

I shift my gaze to Harris.

"None," He smirks.

The girls and I gasp. The guys chuckle.

"That sounds about right to me," Sebastian adds.

Harris uses his index finger beneath my chin to close my mouth. He leans over and kisses me softly.

"Only kidding, Kitty Kat," he says. "If it were up to me, we'd get married right now, right here. But I want you to have the wedding of your dreams. Well, as long as it's within this year. I won't wait but so long to make you my wife, Kat Jackson, soon-to-be Kat Steele."

Tears fill my eyes, and I nod. I say a silent prayer of thanks for this man who's so good to me. I close my eyes as he swipes the tears with the pad of his thumb. He murmurs words of love, and I bury my face in his chest. Strong arms hold me close. The rhythmic beat of his heart soothes me.

"Aaawww… It's too much! My little girl grows up." Vivian exclaims.

Everyone laughs, including me through my tears of happiness.

The rest of lunch goes by with more talk of wedding

ideas. I'll need time to think of where to have it. New York City makes sense with Harris having a bigger family and most based there. But I wouldn't mind a destination wedding. So many choices. For now, I want to revel in our engagement.

My gaze slides to my left hand. The princess-cut diamond winks at me as the sunlight sparks on its massive surface. Who would have thought a girl like me would have such an opulent ring?

"It's a family heirloom. Do you like it, Kitty Kat?"

Harris' softly spoken words filter through my admiration of my engagement ring.

I wrap my arms around his neck and hug him close as I tell him just how much I love it. Nothing could be better or make me happier. It's simply stunning. Just as incredible as the rings my future sisters-in-law have on their left hands.

We take another swim in the lake and pose for photos beneath the waterfall. I float on the hike back to the main road where SUVs await us. If Harris weren't holding my hand, I'd float up above the fronds of the tallest palm trees.

We pile into the vehicles and head back to our villas. Once inside Harris', he leads me onto the terrace overlooking the Pacific Ocean. We sit on a sunbed, and he pulls his mobile from his pocket.

"When it's later in the day in Scotland, we can call your Mum. I'm sure she'll want to know you said yes—"

"She knows?" I cut in.

He lowers his gaze as his cheeks flush.

"I asked Allison for your hand in marriage, Kitty Kat," he responds sheepishly.

My heart leaps. My fiancé—the undisputed playboy—went traditional and asked my Mum if he could marry me? Holy mackerel! This man loves me truly.

I crawl onto his lap and kiss him silly.

"Well, I wanted to call my parents and let them know. But I guess that can wait until later, too," Harris says huskily as he squeezes my ass with his sizable hands.

"Mmmhhhmm…" I purr as I nip his full lower lip.

Hours later, Sergeant Shelley and Lieutenant Lucie eagerly agree to report for wedding duty as soon as I return to New York City. After dinner, my Mum recalls how Harris called her. She wishes us the best and reminds us how love conquers all.

Later that night, as I rest my head on Harris' chest in bed, I say another silent prayer of thanks. We have the support and love of our family. I cannot wait to become Mrs. Harris Steele!

KAT

"Sydney? As in Sydney in Australia? Well, that's different. Are you sure? Not here or Glasgow?" Harris' befuddled face makes me giggle.

I finally decided where I'd like us to have our wedding. Sure, people would expect New York City or Glasgow as the location. But it was in Sydney—Australia!—I started fresh and on my quest to get my man back. It's the perfect place for us to start our new life together as husband and wife.

"Yes, Sydney in Australia," I respond, suppressing another giggle. I continue when Harris cocks an eyebrow questioningly. "Last New Year's Eve, I wanted to start the New Year in the first big city to celebrate. So I flew to Sydney, Australia. It represented a fresh start before I started my new job in New York City. And where I vowed to get my man back—you!"

A smile spreads across Harris' handsome face as he absorbs my words.

"So, you began your Siren's mission in Sydney, Kitty Kat?" He asks.

I bite the corner of my lower lip and nod.

"Okay, sounds good. I'll go along with it," he says. "Now, when?"

"New Year's Eve?" I say cautiously since he wanted to get married before the year ends and that's the last day of the year.

As I guessed, Harris groans and falls back against the sofa.

"Kat, you are killing me, babe! That's eight months away! I know I said before the year ends. But did you really have to choose the absolute last minute?!" He bemoans, eyes squeezed shut and brows knit.

I cup his cheek and rub it as I purr.

He pulls away with a huff.

"Seriously?" He asks.

I nod, "Seriously. But look on the bright side. I won't make you wait to have sex until after we're married, like Haley did Lachlan."

Harris pales.

"No… way…" he asks in astonishment.

If his eyes weren't open, I'd assume he would need smelling salts to revive him. The thought of having no sex for eight months finishes him off.

"Yup. So it's not so bad after all, huh?" I respond with a giggle, then yelp when I land on my back with Harris looming above me.

His dove gray eyes flash.

"*Not so bad after all, huh?* Not *so* bad?! I'll show you bad, Siren," he growls.

The tank top I wear gets yanked above my head and wind around my wrists. Harris stretches my arms and presses them against the armrest. My boobs bounce as he wrenches my yoga pants and G-string down my legs. He tosses the garments over his shoulder.

His eyes narrow as they sear a path from my face to my heaving breasts, pausing at my pulsing pussy, then down to my parted thighs. He mutters *bad* under his breath as he grabs the back of his t-shirt and rips it over his head.

Biceps bulge. Pecs and eight-pack abs flex.

I dare a peek at his crotch. The outline of his burgeoning erection clear beneath his gray joggers makes my mouth water. I wiggle my hips to entice him. Then yowl when he spanks my exposed pussy.

"Do. Not. Move. Naughty lass," he commands.

I can't help but to shudder at his dominance. Another spank gets me to focus. *Stay still, Kat Jackson!*

Harris grips the backs of my thighs and lifts them to his shoulders as he lowers his torso to the sofa cushion. My gaze travels down the planes of my body to watch him. His flattened tongue darts out to lave my seam from start to clit.

A low moan escapes my mouth as I try my best to hold position. My fists clench above my head. Arms press deeper into the armrest to ground me.

Harris repeats the erotic taste of my pussy. The juices of my arousal coat his tongue. I lie there, mesmerized by the sight of him feasting on my cream.

One thick finger joins his tongue. It curls inside my pussy to stroke my G-spot.

My pussy clenches. My back bows. The sensation in my lower belly intensifies. I cry out.

WHAP. WHAP. WHAP.

The orgasm that barreled towards me dissipates with each spank of my pussy. I yowl in pain instead of scream in pleasure. My eyes snap open to glare at Harris.

"Hey! What the *bloody hell* was that for?" I snarl.

He wipes my cream from his mouth and chin onto my inner thighs, then gives me a smug look.

"You will not cum until I say you can, naughty lass," he answers.

Now it's my turn to throw my head back against the sofa. Eyes squeezed shut and brows knit in frustration. I growl.

Harris returns to his torture.

Each time an orgasm is within reach, he stops and smirks at me. My body shakes. No coherent thought possible. I'm wound tight with no relief in sight.

"Eight!" Harris pronounces.

I can't even begin to ask what the bloody hell eight means. But I don't have long to wonder.

"One lost orgasm for each month I lose having you as my wife, naughty lass," he continues triumphantly. He sits back on his haunches and smirks at me. "Now, should I allow you the pleasure to cum?"

Unable to formulate words, I nod.

Harris takes pity on me and lets my non-verbal response slide. He stands and strips out of his joggers. Once again, my thighs go over his shoulders. He aligns the mushroom head of his cock to my swollen pussy lips. One hand bands around my waist while the fingers of the other entwine with my fingers above my head.

With one thrust, he seats himself within my core fully. Hip bones grind into mine. His heavy balls slap my ass. I scream his name.

Harris jackhammers into me. My pussy walls clamp on his thick, ten-inch dick, never wanting it to leave. I writhe beneath him and beg to cum.

"Cum for me, naughty lass. Cum all over my cock. Coat it with your cream," he growls between grunts.

White light blinds me. Stars dance behind my closed eyes. My body stiffens. Toes curl. Tears of carnal bliss stick on my eyelashes. A wail from the depths of my soul pours from my slack mouth. I convulse from the strength of my climax.

Harris grunts as my pussy holds his cock in a vise-like grip. His fingers dig into my hip as he fuses our groins together. His cock swells deep inside of my core.

"MINE!!!" He roars as he bathes my pussy with his hot seed.

The world ceases to exist as I float free. A moment later, the weight of Harris as he collapses on top of me brings me back to Earth. I wrap my arms around him and stroke his back to soothe him as tremors run through his body.

"Sydney as in Australia in eight months, huh?" He murmurs against my sweat-slicked neck.

A smile blooms on my face as I respond, "Sydney—as in Australia—in eight months."

* * *

"Oh Harris, sweetheart, you won't have to sit through all our planning. But you do need to pay attention for this first one!"

"Exactly, Harris, honey!"

I giggle at Sergeant Shelley and Lieutenant Lucie's attempts to keep Harris from his mobile.

We're in Shelley's home office in her STEELE Tower duplex penthouse on the fifty-seventh and fifty-sixth floors where she and Morgan live on the top two floors. If one considers three generously sized rooms an office. An anteroom for two assistants' desks, a sitting area, and a bathroom, a conference room, and her inner sanctum with an en suite bathroom comprise Shelley's version of a home office. She runs her private activities from here and her foundation work from that office on the executive floor of the corporate office.

Vivian, Lola, Starr, and two wedding planners sit with us at the table. Along with Lucie, my Mum, Charlotte, Haley, and Leonie join us via video conference. The girls giggle at Harris' disinterest, too.

"Mom, Aunt Lucie, I love you with all my heart. But this is just not my thing. I will honor whatever Kat wants; Kat can have. Okay?" He tells them.

They glance at one another, then shrug.

"Fine. Go along and make some other techie gadget then," Shelley says.

"Leave the actual work to us!" Lucie chimes in.

Harris leaps from the chair, kisses me, then his Mum and aunt and blows a kiss to my Mum. He waves at the girls as he rushes from the office without a backwards glance.

We laugh, then get back to business.

"So first things first. Location and date," Sergeant Shelley says. Her Montblanc champagne gold rollerball pen hovers over her Smythson of Bond Street leather-bond notebook. She gave each of us a matching pen and notebook to track our responsibilities for the wedding planning.

I take a breath and hope she doesn't have the same reaction her son did to Sydney. Just the thought of him edging me eight times makes my pussy moisten and soften. I feel my cheeks heat. Prayerfully, no one can guess my thoughts…

"Sydney and December 31," I respond.

Lucie coughs. I shift my gaze to her on the television monitor. She arches an elegant brow.

"As in Australia?" She asks.

My shoulders shake as I laugh out loud. Everyone stares at me, but I can't stop. They give me a moment to get it together.

"So sorry! It's funny because Harris said the exact same thing!" I say as I fan my reddened face.

I go on to explain my choices, and they agree it's a good idea. Besides, as they tell me, they've had their fair share of exotic destination weddings. So why not Sydney as in Australia!

"We have the STEELE Sydney we can use for the ceremony and the reception. It has a superior view to the Park Hyatt Sydney," Haley says with the same smug expression as her twin.

Shelly and Lucie nod. We update our notebooks.

"Well, other than Starr, Monsieur Valentino created couture gowns for us. Even though it's become a tradition, do you have another designer in mind, *chérie?*" Leonie asks. "I can get any of them to make your gown and other dresses. Just say the word."

"And of course, Lola's Coterie will create your signature lingerie trousseau! We know Harris' favorites for you," Lola says with a wink.

My mind races at the thought of a Valentino original wedding gown. Few have the opportunity to wear his custom creations. It goes beyond my wildest fantasies. I nod vigorously.

"I would love for Monsieur Valentino to design my dresses," I respond as I clap gleefully. "*C'est incroyable, merci beaucoup!*"

Shelley agrees she and I will call his atelier after the meeting.

Lucie speaks up next.

"Now, Allison and Kat, you have to come up with your

list of guests. We'll need names and addresses. I will handle the nobility and royalty, along with Scottish and European society. Shelley will handle the Western Hemisphere. But we need to know what size wedding you prefer—intimate or all out."

Butterflies swirl in my belly. Not nobility and royalty! I hadn't considered the Jackson side of my family and them being nobles and all that comes along with it.

I glance at my Mum, and she's just as awestruck. But she smiles at me and nods encouragingly.

"Other than Kat's siblings and a few friends, I'll leave the list to you ladies. You'll know best," she says. "And Kat, love, you shine as bright as any noble, royal, or society lady."

"That's right!" Charlotte pipes up with a grin.

Their remarks ease the butterflies. I grin back at my Mum and my sister.

"Yes!" I whoop. "As far as my list, Vivian and Isla. I'll leave the rest to you and Mum Shelley, including the wedding size. You'll know best."

They nod and tell me I have no reason to feel less than anyone. They assure me I'm noble since I'm a descendant of the Marquess of Huntly and I can use the title Lady. Combined with me as Jackson becoming a Steele, I rank higher than the majority. Their words dispel the remaining butterflies.

I sit back and beam at everyone.

"Well, we settled the most important items on our agenda. Kat and I will call Mr. Valentino. Then we'll have lunch at La Goulue," Shelley says with a smile.

"Oh, I'm so jealous! I love La Goulue! You must get the *Moules sauce "Poulette!" Non, non, le Pavé de saumon aux lentils!*" Leonie exclaims.

Lola laughs.

"We know you and your favorite restaurant, Leonie! I'll savor each bite just for you!" She tells her best friend, who sticks her tongue out at her teasing.

Sergeant Shelley and I go to her interior office to make the call. Monsieur Valentino himself comes to the phone and tells us how very pleased he is to continue the Steele tradition. I share my thoughts on the wedding dress, and he promises to have sketches ready in a few days. We plan to meet in Paris for me to select one and my first fitting.

While we eat delicious dishes at La Goulue, Shelley turns to me.

"Kat, sweetheart, Harris tells me you're the Development Director for a children's nonprofit and your university background," she says, then continues when I nod. "Well, we believe in keeping things within the family. I'd like to show STEELE Foundation to you. You would be a great addition to us."

I'm surprised by her request. But the idea of working at the family's foundation intrigues me. I would still do what I love and it would go towards our family's endeavors. Children would still benefit from the affordable housing the foundation builds. So, it's a win-win situation.

I smile broadly at Shelley.

"I would love to see STEELE Foundation. Your work is incredible, and it would thrill me to be a part of it," I respond.

Shelley's smile matches mine.

"Excellent, Kat. You'll be a part of our family through and through!" She says, then arches an elegant eyebrow while the smile plays on her lips. "And speaking of children, when can I expect another grandchild?"

HARRIS

"How's the wedding planning going, bro? Leonie tells me Kat's been pretty busy."

Roger's question with a smirk makes me chuckle.

We're having lunch at one of Lucien's restaurants in Paris while My Kitty Kat has a fitting for her wedding dress. My Mom, Aunt Lucie, and Mum Allison are the privileged few who can see Kat's dresses. She wanted to keep her attire a surprise for everyone. Obviously, I want to see her in them during the parties and at our ceremony.

Over the past few weeks, she's blossomed under the attention my mother and my aunt have given her. Every day, My Kitty Kat tells me more of what she's learned about proper decorum for a *Lady* of her standing engaged to a man of mine. Her emerald eyes shine with happiness as she recalls guidance from Aunt Lucie.

I try not to laugh since I know My Kitty Kat takes it seriously. I understand her desire to make the right impression on people since her Mum raised her in a not so fortunate household. However, I couldn't care less about her upbringing. She's what matters. And I adore her. Tremendously.

She's also made herself at home in our penthouse. A great place before. Now, it's comfortable with her touch. She's blended her style with mine for a home we call our own. We added paintings of Iain's to the walls—after I told Little Lord Fauntleroy Kat can have some of her great great grandfather's artwork. If not for her, the Jacksons wouldn't have known anything about him or his creations.

The expression of pure joy on her face when she opened the crates made my heart swell. Giddily, she pointed out which walls she wanted to hang the four paintings— including the one of Iain's muse and her great great grand- mother in repose. I want nothing but happiness for My Kitty Kat.

When we parted in front of STEELE Place Vendôme, she hugged me fiercely and whispered, *I love you* before she slid into the back of the Rolls-Royce Phantom.

So, yeah, wedding planning is going well. Very well indeed.

"Pretty good, bro. No complaints from me," I respond with a cocky grin.

Roger chuckles.

Our father clears his throat. We shift our gazes to him.

"Harris, you make your mother and I proud of you, son. You followed your heart and made a tough decision. Seeing you and Kat together proves you belong with each other. No matter what. Well done," he says.

His words fill me with contentedness. He and my mother encouraged me to follow my heart, and it paid off. Kat will be my wife—in seven months, that is. We'll have the rest of our lives together as a couple. What could be better?

"Thank you, Dad. That means a lot to me," I reply.

"Yeah, Harris, we're all happy for you," Roger adds.

I nod. It's good to have my family's support. That's what makes us Steeles. We always have each other's backs. Loyalty and love reign supreme.

"And I understand she accepted your mother's offer to work at STEELE Foundation. Another good move," my Dad says. "We can benefit from Kat's experience with development. Especially with the Annual Gala in a few months. Your mother says Kat is a natural."

I grin from ear to ear, proud of my fiancée. She'll definitely make a positive impact on our family's foundation. It makes sense for her to move into the role.

The rest of lunch we discuss business, my recent tech program, and summer plans. Since Kat and I will be married, we'll have to find a property near the family's beachfront compound in Southampton Village. I'm sure I can convince a neighbor to part with their home…

"Hey, babe. I didn't know you were back already. Why didn't you call me?"

I enter the Presidential Suite to find My Kitty Kat stretched out on one of the silk-upholstered sofas in the main salon. Her Titian hair piled atop her head in a sexy bun makes me want to fist it as I pin her beneath me. I shake my head to clear it of the lascivious thoughts.

She opens her arms to me with a big smile.

"Hey, yourself, fiancé," she responds. "I didn't want to interrupt your time with your father and Roger. You know, bro time and all."

I drop onto the sofa and pull her onto my lap. My mouth finds hers for a passionate kiss. I swallow her moans, hungry for more. My cock presses against the zipper of my trousers as it responds to her luscious curves.

I let her come up for air, and she cuddles against my chest.

"Wow. You really missed me, huh?" She says breathlessly.

I pat her hip and nod.

"Always, Kitty Kat," I murmur as I inhale her alluring perfume.

"Ditto, Harris Steele," she says with a contented sigh as she burrows further into me.

We recall our time apart. Her enthusiasm for her dresses makes me eager to see her walk down the aisle to me—in seven months…

"Oh, have you decided on our honeymoon yet?" She asks coyly.

I chuckle at yet another attempt to wrangle that info from me. My Kitty Kat is like a kitten with a ball of string—she won't let it go for a minute. But as I told her the first dozen times she's asked me, it's a surprise.

"I think a stay at the hotel should suffice. What do you think?" I ask to mess with her.

She recoils as she gasps. Wide emerald green eyes stare at me. Her mouth opens and closes like a fish gaping.

I try my best not to laugh. But I fail.

She slaps my shoulder as I throw my head back and guffaw. She mutters how terrible I am under her breath and makes to rise from my lap.

I bind my arms around her while I continue to laugh.

"Harris! You're so mean!" My Kitty Kat wails. "You can't possibly mean that? Can you?"

Catching my breath, I decide not to keep her in suspense.

"No, I don't mean it," I respond, then go on when she

sags in relief. "But if you don't stop asking me, I may change my mind, naughty lass."

She bows her head and sighs.

"Fine. Be a meanie, Harris Steele," she says glumly.

I cup her chin and turn her to face me. I kiss her lips softly.

"Do you trust me?" I ask. She nods, and I continue, "Well, leave it to me. I won't disappoint you, Kat Jackson, soon-to-be Kat Steele."

She settles back against me. I hold her for a bit more before we have to get ready for dinner with the fam downstairs in the restaurant run by Lucien.

While she's slipping black strappy sandals on her feet in the dressing room, I come up behind her. My hands rest on her hips. She startles, but I hold her in place.

My red-headed Siren enthralls me in a white mini dress that hits mid-thigh. Capped sleeves and a scoop neckline make it sweet. But the laser cut-outs at the upper thigh and the hem make it sexy. Her Titian hair cascades down her back to brush the top curve of her ass like an arrow. And my bow is ready for its mark.

"Hey there, babe," I murmur against the side of her neck. "You look good enough to eat. We can skip dinner, you know."

She gives a throaty laugh as her head falls back against my shoulder.

"Now, who's naughty, Harris Steele? I think not. But we always have later…"

I chuckle and turn her to face me.

"I have something for you. Check my pockets," I instruct.

She bites her lower lip as her eyes gleam. Her hands reach into my trouser pockets, and I tell her to keep going when she pulls out one jewelry box. Diligently she dips into each pocket of my trousers and suit jacket. Six boxes sit atop the console when she's finished.

"Okay, open them," I tell her with a grin.

Her gasps grow as each box unveils platinum bangles encrusted with pavé diamonds. I place three on each of her wrists. Her smile widens with the click of the closures. She crosses her forearms in front of her breasts.

"Wonder Woman has nothing on these babies! Thank you, my love!" She exclaims, then wraps her arms around my neck and kisses me.

"Am I still naughty?" I quip.

She purrs and rubs against me like a content kitten.

"No. But off to dinner we go!"

* * *

"Thank you for letting us inside the Tower even though it's now your private space. It means a lot to my family to see where Iain painted."

My Kitty Kat has tears in her eyes as we stand in the lower level of the Tower at Jackson Castle. Once Iain's studio, then demolished by his father, and now lovingly restored by Lachlan for his and Haley's retreat, the Tower holds much history.

When we left Paris, we made a stop to Banff in Aberdeenshire, Scotland to visit them, Uncle Connor, and Aunt Lucie. Lachlan's offer to show My Kitty Kat and her family the Tower was as unexpected as it was kind.

Payton, Michael, and Charlotte flew in on Lachlan's helicopter from Glasgow to join us. Along with My Kitty Kat and Mum Allison, they stand in awe.

"Yes, thank you, Lachlan. This is special for us," Payton says. Again, surprising us with his maturity.

Lachlan acknowledges their words with a nod.

"You should see where it all began for you. My father will take you on a tour of Jackson Castle. It's his favorite pastime," Lachlan says, then takes Haley's hand. "Let's head back."

We climb into the Range Rovers for the ride back to the baroque mansion built in the early eighteenth century. I tell Allison and Kat's siblings how it replaced the original fortified castle the Jackson family erected two hundred years earlier. The giant status symbol has a four-story center structure with two grand curved east and west wings of three stories each. Six staircases, elaborate fireplaces, and elegant formal entertainment salons along with an extensive art collection make for a splendid interior.

I point out areas of the landscaped grounds that are just as spectacular as the castle with carriage drives and horse trails, walking paths, and a few ornamental buildings, including a chapel. Over five hundred acres along the coast of northeast Scotland comprise the Jackson family seat.

"The architecture is incredible. I can't wait to hear Connor's history on it all," Michael says from the third row.

I ask him about his studies, and his zeal makes me smile. He's most excited about his summer internship at STEELE Paris directly with Roger. Michael's updates carry us to the front door of the castle. He's so into it, he doesn't notice we stopped until Kat opens her door and hops out.

We laugh and head inside. Uncle Connor greets us exuberantly.

"There you are! Well, let's get started! Gather around here in the Great Hall," he booms. His love for Jackson Castle as strong as Michael's zest for architecture.

Although I've heard it countless times, I follow along holding My Kitty Kat's hand. As we pass through the myriad rooms, I whisper how I'll take her behind a tapestry and have my way with her. She tries to hide her giggles but fails.

Uncle Connor raises an eyebrow mid-sentence but doesn't stop his recounting of a battle as depicted in a large painting in the arms room.

I bow my head, and My Kitty Kat pokes me in the side. Her emerald eyes dance with mirth.

"Busted," she mouths.

We finish our tour on the stone terrace off the back of the castle. My niece and nephews nearly topple me as they jump into my arms.

"Whoa there, Leith!" I call out as I catch the second oldest of Haley's triplets. Lilias—the eldest and only girl—wraps her arms around my leg while Lewis jumps on my back. "You trying to knock your uncle out or what, Wildlings?"

Haley tells them to leave me be while she plays with the younger twins Stirling and Struan on a blanket in the grass. I remind her I'm the uncle and can tell them if they're bothering me, and they are not. She throws out how it's time I get my own.

My gut clenches.

"Aye, Harris, lad. Even though they'll bear the Steele name, they'll have strong Jackson blood in their veins!" Uncle Connor chimes in.

My heart skips a beat.

I chance a sideways glance at Kat.

She stares at some point in the distance, detached from the surrounding conversation.

My gaze flicks back to Uncle Connor.

"Er, at this time, let's get through the wedding before we have talk of babies," I respond and add a chuckle to lighten the mood. I reach for Kat's hand. "Right, babe?"

She blinks and turns her head towards me. I can't read the emotions in the depths of her eyes. But she smiles, and I breathe again.

"Right, babe," she repeats.

I know I'm not ready for kids yet. I have enough nieces and nephews to last a lifetime! Thankfully, My Kitty Kat feels the same. At least I hope that's the case.

"Fine," Uncle Connor says, then walks to Kat. "My dear, I know I can never replace your *Da*, and I do not know if your brothers would mind. But it would be my honor as the head of the Jackson clan to walk you down the aisle."

Kat sucks in a breath. A crimson hue blooms on her porcelain cheeks as tears shimmer in her emerald green eyes so like Uncle Connor's eyes. She nods her head vigorously.

"Excellent! Let's have some Jackson Scotch to celebrate," he says as he embraces her.

Later that night, I make slow, passionate love to My Kitty Kat. I try to use all my skills combined with my love to show her she means everything to me, even if I'm not ready for her to have my baby. Some day. Just not soon.

KAT

"**K**at, sweetheart, that's amazing news! The Wright Corporation has been elusive for a while now. Kudos for your procurement of their pledge for one million dollars in the short time you've been here. Well done!"

Shelley's high praise during our weekly executive team meeting at STEELE Foundation fills me with pride. To make such a major contribution proves I didn't just get the position because I'm Harris Steele's fiancée. Rather, my skills and experience make me a valuable asset to the team.

Not that everyone treats me differently. No. All but one member of the staff has welcomed me.

Beatrice Montgomery.

A Park Avenue socialite from an old New York family. Twenty-five; gorgeous; long, raven hair; ice blue eyes; tall, lithe figure. The type found in the society pages at functions throughout the season or vacationing during holidays.

Beatrice made it clear from the moment of our introduction she was far superior to me and was none too pleased to learn Harris was my fiancé. Oh, not so obvious. Rather subtle comments.

Scotland? My family traces its lineage to England. But my ancestors established us in New York centuries ago. What town are you from?

Interesting, Harris went all the way to Scotland to find his future wife. You must be special, Kat!

I chance a glance at Beatrice where she sits to Shelley's right across from me at her left. Despite the slight smile on Beatrice's face, her icy blue eyes hold no warmth. They pierce me like a shard of glass.

Instead of cowering, I roll my shoulders back and straighten my spine. *Smiogaid suas, nighean!*

My girls prepped me for the haters since they experienced similar outcomes once the world learned of their engagements to the Steele men. Suddenly pushed into the spotlight the minute the press releases reached the media. Instagrammers created profiles to follow their activities and clothing choices. Bloggers dedicated entire posts to their supposed beauty routines, exercise habits, meals. Hashtags and the couples' combined names became the norm.

The very same happened for Harris and me. #HarKat anyone? Bah!

As Independent Women, my girls and I don't take kindly to people assuming we're gold diggers. We weren't out to score a billionaire or lay claim to a Steele bachelor. No. We fell in love, and they claimed us. Like the cavemen they are, as Lola calls them.

The thought makes me giggle. But I hold it back as now is not the appropriate time. Especially with Ms. PAS—Park Avenue Socialite—shooting ice daggers at me.

"Thank you, Shelley. I want to contribute to the team in every possible way," I say with a gracious bow of my head.

"And how did you accomplish such a huge ask, Kat? I've known Ash Wright since we were babes, and he's definitely a charmer."

Another one of Beatrice's subtle hater comments. As if I fucked the man to get the million dollars! When will she let it go already???

I take a deep breath and shift my gaze to Ms. PAS.

"Is he? I wouldn't know since I met with his father. The senior Mr. Wright—as you probably know—still has ties to Aberdeen and contributes to the children's center there. I met him when I was a volunteer. Last week I reached out to him, and we had lunch. He understands the importance of a solid home for children to reach their fullest potential. STEELE Foundation provides such. Mr. Wright agreed to donate."

"Ah, I see…" Beatrice says with a smirk, icy blue eyes glint.

"Let's move on to the next item on the agenda," Shelley says, to change the subject deftly.

The other executives murmur their agreement and hasten to proceed as though sensing the underlying current of tension in the room. I choose to rise above it. I don't need to prove my superiority.

As the conference room clears out after the meeting, Shelley asks me to stay. I settle back in my chair and wait for the others to leave. Beatrice casts a quizzical glance over her shoulder at us as she walks towards the door.

"Beatrice, sweetheart, kindly close the doors behind you. Thank you," Shelley calls out, then waits to speak until the click of the doors sound in the room. She turns to me. "You do realize I know what's happening with Beatrice, right?"

I blink since Shelley has mentioned nothing before now. And I certainly don't mention Beatrice's behavior to her or to Harris. Why bother? But it's interesting, Shelley noticed. It makes me wonder if others are aware too.

"Shelley, I don't want to cause any trouble. Beatrice is of no consequence. Truly," I add when my future mother-in-law arches an elegant eyebrow.

"Yes, but her attitude over the past few weeks has not gone unnoticed by the Associate Director and COO. The receptionist told me she overheard Beatrice in the bathroom making disparaging remarks about you. Fortunately, the other woman did not engage with her," Shelley says.

She gives me a moment to absorb the news. Before she continues.

"Your friend Vivian would make an excellent addition to STEELE Foundation. You mentioned you're having lunch with her today. Why don't you invite her back here and meet in my office? I'd love to speak with her."

I grin and agree wholeheartedly. It would be great to work with my best friend again!

Finally, lunch rolls around, and I head to a restaurant near The STEELE Tower. Viv and I decided to eat closer to my office since we'll stop by afterwards. I enter the bustling eatery and thank the hostess for a table by the window.

People-watching entertains me while I wait for Viv. It amazes me the variety of people and their attire who walk along Manhattan streets in the summer. One man rollerblades by with the skimpiest shorts and a tank top, avoiding pedestrians effortlessly. Two teenaged girls stroll arm in arm in colorful printed maxis dresses that flow above their gladiator sandals, free hands clutch multiple shopping bags. A tourist pauses for a selfie in front of the sign for Fifth Avenue. I smile and take a sip of water. My eyes never leave the view.

"Hey, you!"

I shift in my seat just in time to catch Viv's hug. The familiar, soft floral scent of her Jo Malone perfume wafts around me. I grin. It's good to see my bestie.

"Hey, yourself! And look at you in your glamour girl shades!" I respond when she settles in the seat across from me.

She shimmies her shoulders and grins.

"Oh, I just bought these the other day. You like?" She asks as she takes them off and angles them back and forth. "Bulgari Flora, darling!"

That's what I love about Viv. She's as much, if not more of, a wealthy socialite as Ms. PAS, but my friend doesn't make me feel like dirt trampled beneath her Manolo Blahniks. In fact, she's taught me so much about the most luxurious clothing and accessories, the It places to go, and where —and not to mention who—to avoid. My very own Fairy God Sister!

"Fabu, daahling!" I say with a wink.

The server appears to pour iced tea and takes our order. When she leaves, I lean forward to share my news with Viv.

"I didn't bother to tell you about this woman at the foundation who treats me like a less-than. But now—"

"Hold on, Kat," Vivian interrupts with her hand raised to stop me. Her toffee brown eyes darken. "Who?"

I grin at my bestie's protective growl. I've been the same for her. When I tell her Beatrice Montgomery, Viv tells me she knows all about the snooty socialite. Of course, they travel in the same circles.

"Oh, please. And so anyway... Pass me the pepper mill, girl," Viv says with a toss of her curly ebony hair over her shoulder.

I giggle and hand it over.

"Well, Mum Shelley is eager to speak with you. I hope

you'll consider her offer seriously. It would be great to work together again," I say.

Vivian nods as she finishes her bite of Maine Lobster Roll. After she takes a sip of iced tea, she responds, "I will absolutely! The offices are not the same without you, Kat. You and I came up with some great and beneficial ideas together."

The rest of lunch we catch up on her dating life and my wedding planning. I asked Viv to be my maid of honor. Monsieur Valentino will create her gown too, with her first fitting next week. We made it a Girls' Getaway for the weekend, with Leonie and Haley joining us. Harris grumbled about me going to the City of Love without him but gave in after I showed him just how much I love his cock!

Now Vivian and I stroll arm in arm to The STEELE Tower. A member of the security team behind their station greets me by name and buzzes us through the turnstile. Viv nudges me and giggles. She gives a low whistle as we ride up on the private lift to the floor for the Foundation. I guide her to Shelley's offices, and her administrative assistant waves us towards the inner office.

I knock on one of the open double doors and wave when Shelley lifts her gaze.

"Kat, Vivian, sweethearts! Come in," she says as she rises from behind her Lucite desk gracefully. "Have a seat over here. Would you care for tea or coffee?"

We opt for tea as we sit on the white silk sofa. After she asks her assistant for tea and biscuits, Shelley joins us. She double kisses us before she sits on a chair.

"Did you have a pleasant lunch?" She asks. Following our responses, she continues. "Vivian, how are your parents? I haven't seen your mother since they moved to their villa in

Tuscany when her father retired. Perhaps they'll join Morgan and me on *Serendipity* this summer."

Vivian's eyes widen in surprise.

"I didn't know you and my mother knew each other," she replies.

Shelley smiles and adds, "Oh, yes! Years ago, Crystal would frequent the boutique I worked in—a STEELE property no less and how I met Morgan. Ever fashionable, your mother would select the best pieces. I used to think how a young woman like myself could have such an innate style. The difference being she was wealthy, and I was middle-class. However, we became friendly. Then, after I married Morgan, Crystal and I would see each other at social functions. She loved how I went from shopgirl to a billionaire's wife!"

My mouth drops and I exchange glances with Viv, who's equally stunned. I knew Shelley's story, but not the part about Vivian's Mum. Aunt Lucie—a bartender in a Jackson pub—and Mum Shelley's love stories make me swoon each time I think about them.

Her laughter tinkles in the air. Eyes full of merriment, she goes on.

"Darlings, don't look so surprised! I was a hardworking girl, nowhere near a socialite, before I met Morgan. I was a personal shopper for Crystal. And enjoyed it, might I add!"

"My Mom never told me! I guess she hasn't put it together with Kat being a Jackson when I speak with her about our fun. Next time I talk to my Mom, I'll tell her! And I'm sure they'd love to spend time with you aboard your megayacht," Viv says between giggles.

Shelley smiles and leans forward.

"Now, I say all of that to let you know our connection in hopes it will entice you to join Kat and me here at STEELE

Foundation. We would benefit greatly from your experience as the Marketing Director. I've admired your work for some time, Vivian," Shelley says.

I sit back, surprised since Ms. PAS holds the role currently. No wonder Mum Shelley prefaced her conversation with me about Viv with Beatrice's poor behavior. She's axing the sow!

My gaze shifts to Vivian.

"Wow, the surprises keep rolling in, huh?" She asks with a smile. "I'm flattered you think well of me, Shelley. However, I've been with the nonprofit for several years and need time to consider your offer. I do hope you understand."

Shelley's dark brown eyes scan Viv's face, then nods appreciatively.

"Absolutely, Vivian. I know money holds no concern for you. But know we offer a considerable package for a Chief Marketing Officer," she says.

Viv's eyes pop.

"Chief Marketing Officer?" She asks.

Shelley's smile broadens.

"Naturally, we would not expect you to make a lateral move with your level of expertise," she says with a triumphant gleam in her eyes.

"Wow. Well, in that case, I accept and will tender my resignation with two-week notice today. Thank you!" Vivian says as she extends her hand.

Shelley takes it and seals their deal with a handshake.

We finish our tea with more talk about Vivian's dress and our upcoming Girls' Getaway. As Vivian and I walk to the private lift for her return to the nonprofit, we bump into Ms. PAS.

She makes a show of double kissing Vivian's cheeks.

Ever the proper lady, Viv greets Beatrice. However, my bestie uses her subtle comment about not seeing Beatrice at some to-do function as a way to prove she's not included in all of their circle's gatherings. We part from a stupefied Ms. PAS with our heads held high. Once on the lift, we burst into laughter.

And so anyway...

KAT

"You love to carry me off. Don't you, Harris Steele?"

"You know I do, Kat Jackson, soon-to-be Kat Steele. And you love it more. Especially this wee trick I have up my sleeve..."

My grin widens as Harris' dove gray eyes gleam with mischief. We're flying to who knows where on his Gulfstream private jet. The unknown-to-me destination will have to top all the phenomenal others he's taken me to since he first carried me off to the Channel Island of Jersey.

I still can't believe that trip was a year ago. Thirteen months since we first met in the lobby of Jackson Town House. Together, apart, together. Now, engaged with only five months until our wedding. Incredible.

With a contented sigh, I climb onto his lap from my seat on the sofa. Forehead pressed to his and arms wrapped around his broad shoulders, I close my eyes and just breathe. The warm and sensual scent of his Tom Ford *Noir de Noir* cologne fills my nostrils. A deep inhalation sends me into the compelling world of Harris Steele. I will never get enough of my man.

His strong fingers knead my thighs. The thumbs massage the tops of each leg in circles. Closer and closer they sweep to the juncture of my core. His warm breath mingles with mine as his excitement mounts.

Oh, how I ache for him to mount me.

"Do you tempt me with more miles added to our Mile High Club, Siren?"

I mewl in response as I grind my ass atop his muscular thighs. They flex beneath me. But it's the reaction of his gigantic cock that earns a moan. It twitches. I whimper for more.

"I take that as a positive response," Harris murmurs before he blazes a trail of nips and kisses from my jaw down the column of my throat. He presses his lips against the indentation between my clavicles, then noses his way beneath the thin strap of my maxi dress.

The material gives way to slide down my arm. A wet warmth engulfs my bare nipple. It pebbles further as Harris suckles. Hard.

My head lolls back with eyes closed in carnal bliss. A hum in the back of my throat slips through my slack mouth. Heat rises from my belly over my heaving breasts, covered by Harris' pleasurable mouth. I shudder when he clamps a tender bud between his teeth and growls. My pussy softens as it weeps for him.

"Oh, Harris… I need you…"

He rewards my plea with his hand skating beneath my maxi dress. It bunches up around my waist. Clear to plunder my aching core, Harris thrusts a thick finger past my soaked pussy lips. He groans when he finds me wet and ready for him. And only him.

"Yessss!" I cry when he pulls back to add another skilled finger. My hips buck as I hiss from the stretch. "Unnhhh!"

"Always so tight for my cock, Siren. So. Fucking. Tight."

Harris punctuates each word with a thrust of his finger. They fuck me as I beg for his dick. Once again, he obliges me. The sound of the zipper on his jeans makes me shiver with anticipation.

Too eager to wait, I reach between us and free his massive cock. It lands heavily in the palm of my hand. He groans and shifts his hips upward, seeking more of my attention. It's my turn to answer his silent plea.

Too large for my fingers to wrap around his girth, I do my best to circle his shaft in my fist. From root to tip, I stroke. A bead of pre-cum serves as a natural lubricant to swirl over the bulbous head.

I pinch, and he bites.

We sound our carnal delight.

I extricate my breast from his mouth and slide down to kneel between his thighs. The plush platinum gray carpet cushions my knees. I grip the sides of his jeans with the black silk boxer briefs and tug.

With a smirk, Harris lifts his hips to allow me to yank the offensive garments from his delectable body.

"Eager much, Siren?" He quips with a wicked chuckle.

I growl and reach for the hem of his v-neck sweater. Then rip it off when he bends at the waist and raises his arms. I chuff at his laughter.

Completely bared to me, I sit back on my haunches to revel in the splendor of Harris Steele's magnificent body. Corded calves lead to sculpted thighs. His cock stands proud, like a thing of beauty Michelangelo could never capture in marble. Behind it, an Adonis belt and eight-pack abs define his midsection while pecs finished with flat male nipples flex. Sizable hands begin to stroke his fat cock. Forearms and biceps bunch to handle its girth and length. Tendons line his neck as he swallows thickly.

When my hungry gaze finally reaches his lips, he curls them.

"Do you plan on finishing what you started, Siren? Or must I find my own release?" He asks with hooded eyes beneath a cocked eyebrow. I shake my head, and he nods as though silently telling me to proceed.

I do.

I grasp his veiny cock from his grip with one hand while the other cups his heavy sac. The balls roll between my fingers as my mouth engulfs his purple head. A hum of satisfaction at his delicious, musky taste vibrates from me to him.

"Fuuuck, yes," Harris groans as I watch him watch me swallow his dick between my lips. "Take every fucking inch. I want your throat stretched by my cock."

I bob my head, eager to fulfill his desire even as my gag reflex kicks in. Tears fill my eyes. He's so *bloody* big. I pull back to collect myself, then return with gusto. Tongue swirls. Cheeks suction. Teeth drag.

Before long, Harris' hands dive into my hair. He grips the sides of my head to lock me at just the angle he wants. Long and even thrusts last but so long before his cock swells impossibly larger, and he juts his hips.

My fingernails dig into his thighs as my body wants to fight the invasion.

"Breathe! Dammit! Breathe for me."

Harris' demand snaps my focus back.

I inhale on his outward thrust, then relax my throat for his plundering return. We find our rhythm.

"Make me cum, Siren! Swallow! Every! Drop!" Harris

bellows as jets of his hot cum slide down my throat, straight to my hungry belly.

I moan around his girth as I struggle to not spill a single drop.

Harris falls back against the sofa replete. His cock pops from between my lips. A satisfied smile plays at the corners of his mouth as he leans forward to swipe a trace of cum from my swollen lip.

"Good, lass," he croons, then lifts me to swap places. His broad shoulders spread my thighs as he dives between them to lap at my slick seam. He groans rapturously. "Oh, so good, lass. You've earned your miles."

My body responds to his praise like a preening kitten. I purr and arch my back as my hands stretch up behind me. My palms slap the private jet's walls as Harris eats me like a ravenous wolf. His feral grunts and growls send shivers down my spine. My pussy creams. He laps it up in wild abandon.

By the time we land, we rack up *thousands* of points. Cha-ching!

My head may still linger in the clouds, but my eyes widen at the sight before me when Harris removes the red silk blindfold that covers them.

"Wh—what is this place?" I stutter in awe.

From the backseat of the Chevy Suburban, I glimpse Spanish moss hanging from mature trees. They form a canopy with their interwoven branches above what I can only describe as an elaborate treehouse. Not just one. Rather, several buildings nestled amongst a copse of trees. The hidden jewels float above a ground strewn with leaves. Manicured lawns surround the copse like a green lake. On one side, an oversized bed swings from ropes strung from rafters beneath one treehouse. It invites a night a decadence for two.

My gaze moves between the fantasy treehouses and their surroundings. Through the window Harris opens, humid air carries the sound of birds chirping. It fills the SUV. I lean out to take a closer look.

"Amazing…" I whisper as we near what has to be the most unusual, yet wonderful destination Harris has whisked me away to visit.

"Told ya," he says smugly. "Come on, let's go."

He opens the door and helps me from the SUV. The driver handles our luggage in the boot.

Hand in hand, Harris leads me towards the treehouses. We circle around the exterior, back to the set of stairs. I glimpse a painted replica of houses above the hanging bed. I make a note to return later.

Up the stairs on the white railing-lined landing outside of the larger treehouse, we find two ornate bathtubs. Perfectly situated to take in the incredible view of the Spanish moss-covered trees and water beyond. I thought the hanging bed would be my favorite spot. But these bathtubs? Wow!

From there we climb a short wrought-iron ladder to a deck with a cafe table and two chairs. The higher elevation is great for coffee in the morning or wine in the evening. Before we enter the primary treehouse, Harris guides me to the wrought-iron spiral staircase. Two basket chairs hang beside a dual-head outdoor shower. Can this get any better?

"Oh, but it does."

I blush when I realize I spoke aloud and giggle. Harris nods towards the primary treehouse.

We head down the spiral staircase, then round the corner of the salmon-colored wooden structure. Two walls of windows flank a set of black French doors. Wrought-iron and glass sconces hang on either side. Two of the walls have windows of varying sizes interspersed from the roofline to the slate-colored wooden deck.

I try to peek inside, but the sun reflects off the glass. The image of Harris and me greets my curiosity.

He pulls an antique iron key from a box beside the planter and opens the French doors. As he steps aside, he gestures for me to enter. His smug grin still lights his handsome face.

"Entrez s'il vous pla"t, mademoiselle," he says with a bow.

My breath catches when I step inside.

To our left, a pale blue velvet tufted settee with platinum leaf on the wood sits before the windows. A claw-foot tub with the same luxurious gilt stands on an elevated platform with an antique mirror as its backboard. Between the two, a wood-burning oven offers warmth from the corner on a chilly day.

Not only because it's July, but the lustful heat rising in my body is more than enough to dispel the cold when my gaze lands on the king-size antique French bed. It's a cloud of sumptuous white linens. The centerpiece of the spacious interior offers more than a welcome respite. It begs for couples to enact a sensual scene from Versailles. *Vive la France!*

Above it, a loft accessible by a set of stairs beckons for more seductive surprises. A glimpse of crystal chandeliers and the curved lines of furniture hint at what's more to come.

The last piece lies in the right wall staged as a kitchenette. The dark brown vintage wood of the lower cabinetry blends seamlessly with the decor. Only the three rows of shelves belie it's not another luxurious sitting area.

"You like?"

Harris' question draws me from my fantasy as a French queen playing hide and seek with her naughty king. Her long gown billowing behind her as she runs through the Hall of Mirrors. His randy reflection flicks from one to the other as he chases her with his wig askew.

I jump into his arms. He catches me effortlessly.

"I love it! But not as much as I. Love. *You!*" Each word punctuated with a kiss to his smiling lips. Then my mouth slants over his for a French kiss *extraordinaire.*

"Well, that's a rousing start to our six-months-back-together anniversary, Kitty Kat!" Harris says with a chuckle. "I can't wait to see what you'll do for our one-year wedding anniversary. That is, once we're married in *five* months…"

I giggle and kiss the tip of his nose.

"Good things come to those who wait, you know," I say as I make to stand.

But he tightens his grip and walks us to the claw-foot tub. He moves me to his hip and turns on the faucets. A scoop of lavender-scented bath salts, and he sets me on my feet. He makes quick work of my maxi dress and his clothes before he carries me into the tub with him.

We settle with me between his legs as he rests against a side. The panorama beyond the wall of windows serves as a splendid vista to unwind after our active flight. I let my head fall back against his shoulder. A contented sigh escapes both of us.

As the water loses its warmth, Harris takes a sea sponge and pours patchouli-scented body wash onto it. The spicy musky fragrance pairs well with the lavender to relax my sore muscles. I all but moan as he soothes the sponge over my skin. *Divine.*

"Your turn," I say, turning to face my man. He smiles and

leans back with his arms draped over the edge of the bath-tub. "You always make me feel so special. Thank you, my love."

I lean forward and kiss the space over his heart. Its rhythmic beat pulses beneath my lips. I lavish his body with the tender loving care he afforded mine.

When I'm done, Harris lifts us from the tub, and we dry one another. Body lotion with the same scent softens our skin. We don fluffy white robes.

While I climb amongst the pillows on the massive bed, Harris fills crystal flutes from the Champagne bottle left in an ice bath on the nightstand. He passes the plate of choco-late-covered strawberries to me and knees his way onto the bed. I accept the flute from him with a smile.

"Here's to many, many more anniversaries filled with love, Kat Jackson, soon-to-be Kat Steele," he says as he touches his flute to mine.

We take a sip, then I feed a strawberry to him.

He bites it and pins me with a smoldering stare as his lips slowly slip over my fingertips.

Heat flares immediately from the erotic point of contact. It zings up my arm to my heart and lights my core on fire. I inhale sharply, then my eyes half-mast filled with carnal lust.

Yes, there will be many, many more anniversaries filled with love… and passion.

Five months can't come fast enough.

"Are you certain you want the property on the other side of Roger and Leonie's? Or would you rather a new build on some of the land between Haley's and ours? No, it will not sit oceanfront, but your timeline will not hinge upon the existing neighbors' whims."

I consider my Dad's questions as we sit on the deck of my the Steele Southampton Village megamansion overlooking the Atlantic Ocean. Sure, Kat and I could combine a few of the acres from this residence I share with my parents and some from Haley's. But every time we're near the water, My Kitty Kat loves watching the sunrise over the ocean. I want to give it to her. We need that footage.

"Listen, let me call my go-to residential realtor—Robin Sanchez-Waghorn. Her reach extends to the Hamptons. We'll get her take on the holdup," Baz offers.

My ears prick up at his suggestion.

"Oh, yes! She helped me find my Sutton Place penthouse and did the closing for Starr's parents' penthouse in my building," Lola adds, then claps. "Robin to the rescue!"

Tension melts as I laugh along with everyone.

"But as I told Harris, I'm happy with whichever property he selects," My Kitty Kat says. She turns her face up to mine and smiles. "Home is here for me."

I melt when she touches her dainty hand to the spot over my heart.

Ohs and ahs fill the air. But I only have eyes for My Kitty Kat. I take her hand and bring it to my lips for a kiss.

"Thank you, babe. But it's *our* choice. And I want to watch your face as the sun rises with the early morning rays glowing on your beautiful face—"

"Holy shit! Listen to the *playa* now!" Laurent guffaws.

Okay, so I stepped in that one. I shake my head as I chuckle. Me, waxing poetic... Damn, but this woman changed my life. For real.

I catch more ribbing from my brothers and cousins. What can I say? Not a damn thing. So, I take it like a man, then stand for a bow.

Everyone claps jovially. Laurent gives me a standing ovation. The fucker.

"But seriously, I know you don't mind. However, settling is not an option," I say. "Plus, we can build guest houses. One for Mum Allison and Charlotte to share, and another for your brothers. You know, dudes have to have their space. Maybe Michael would like to work on the design."

He whoops and agrees. Leonie offers to create the interior design scheme.

"Son, I concur now I have the knowledge of Kat's joy of an ocean sunrise. We provide for our women, no matter the situation. I will contact some people. Between them and Robin, you will have the property," my Dad says firmly. All the guys voice their agreement.

Some may say we're a bit over-the-top. But that's

because they don't have men in their lives who love the way we do—deep and hard in and out of the bedroom.

We move on to talk about the plans for the weekend.

Everyone converges on the family compounds in Southampton Village for the month of August through the second week of September. Malcolm and Starr use their home as their primary residence. He commutes to the City for work via helicopter, and Starr is based out of SLFW Southampton Village. So, they're always here.

Aside from me, the others have personal residences. Haley and Lachlan's property bridges the gap between the Steele compound and the Jackson's to the west. They persuaded a neighbor to part with the beachfront mansion successfully, then made it their own.

Both compounds span a vast stretch of ocean frontage and land right behind. The property I have my eye on sits to the east, past Roger and Leonie's. Starr's parents—Sun and Peace—bought the oceanfront property on the farther side.

So getting that last parcel makes not only sunrise sense, but it's a solid investment. We would own all land on this much sought-after peninsula. A private enclave with a value to increase for generations of Steeles and Jacksons.

The thought of those who come behind my siblings and me reminds me of the big children's question. It dances in my mother's eyes. I overheard Mum Allison asking Kat if I want wee ones. I skipped past the living room before she could respond. Too close!

I shake my head and clear it of the unwanted-for-now thoughts. Focus on the present, as Starr says.

"I have a foursome with potential clients at the club," Roger says.

Haley sputters her orange juice. Leonie giggles as she pats her back.

"Oh, *chérie*! The golf club, not *that* club! Besides, I do *not* share!" She says between laughter.

My twin's cheeks flush crimson. She sneaks a peek at our parents. Then sags in relief when she finds them engrossed in a conversation with Uncle Connor and Aunt Lucie.

"Nice going, Hal!" I say loud enough to draw their attention to our end of the table. She glares at me, and I continue. "Where's *your* mind, missy?"

I catch the grape she throws at me and pop it into my mouth with a smirk. She mouths, *fuck you*, and I throw my head back, laughing.

Some girls decide to go to SLFW for a class with a guest teacher. The rest opt for the village.

I give My Kitty Kat a kiss and remind her to use the AMEX Centurion Card I gave her. She frowns, then yelps and glances around when I spank her ass. No one notices since they're busy getting ready to head out for the day.

"*Ours*, naughty lass," I growl in her ear, then nip it. A lick has her mewling. All thoughts of not using her Black Card dissipate. "Good, lass. Now, have fun, and I'll see you later."

I watch as she sashays away. She throws a wink over her shoulder as she follows Charlotte and Yessenia.

"She'll be back, soppy boy."

I chuckle as I shift my gaze to Lachlan. He makes goo-goo eyes and kissy noises. I throw a pillow from my chair at him. He catches it deftly and hugs it to his body, batting his eyelashes.

"Wanker," I mutter. "If you can get past fucking with me, we can decide what to do today."

He tosses the pillow back, and I put it behind me.

"My vote's on kitesurfing," Malcolm says.

"I say deep-sea fishing. We can catch tonight's dinner,"

Lucien says.

"Do both," Patrick says as he rises from the table.

We part to get ready, then head to the marina. The crew helps us get the kitesurfing gear aboard. Those who prefer to catch our dinner check the fishing tackle. No interest of mine, I go with Malcolm, Anton, Baz, and Laurent to the toy area at the stern.

"Get something good!" I shout over my shoulder at the fishermen. They give me the thumbs up.

We reach open water and anchor. Surface waves break as wind hits the deep blue water of the Atlantic Ocean. Consistent enough for kitesurfing yet won't disturb the fishing lines. A glance towards the shoreline revels fairy towns with buildings that resemble dollhouses.

"Let's get at it!" Anton exclaims as he suits up.

Soon, we're racing amongst the surface waves and flying into the air. Baz skims past me with a battle cry. Sunlight glints off his mirrored goggles. I change the angle of my kite and surge ahead. In my periphery, I glimpse Anton taking air at least seven feet above the surface. He somersaults. His victorious cries ring through the air. Wind under my kite lifts me, and I take advantage to grab the side of my board. We outdo one another as we challenge nature. Adrenaline from the stunts beats through my veins.

We catch wind-driven acrobatics while the others catch Mahi Mahi. A win-win for all.

On the trip back to the marina, we trade tales as we eat a hearty lunch. Borya has the best story with catching and releasing a marlin. The MMA champ had his hands full with the powerful fish. He chuckles as he reenacts the fight.

Once ashore, Lucien takes the Mahi Mahi to one of his restaurants to prepare for our feast. The rest of us climb into the Chevy Suburbans.

I check my mobile and grin when I open the message app. My Kitty Kat beams at me from a selfie she took with Charlotte. Shopping bags rest at their feet while they sip Champagne in a boutique. My fingers fly over the keyboard.

Well done, Kitty Kat!

The three circles appear as she types a response.

Even a surprise for you! ;)

I grin stupidly at the screen. Visions of My Kitty Kat in sexy lingerie spread-eagle on our bed play out before my eyes. My cock twitches, intrigued by the sexy fantasy.

"Hey, Har, Robin responded."

I glance over at Baz scanning his mobile screen. He summarizes her message.

"The parents still own the property. So the son can't decide to sell or hold up an offer. Robin can get it to them in Provence. Seems they retired there and don't plan to use the property anymore. They left it as a getaway for the son."

We fist pump.

Sunrises and smiles, here we come!

* * *

"This week was beyond crazy! I can't wait to unwind with a glass of wine and sit on the deck for a lovely sunset. Maybe even the entire bottle!"

I chuckle at My Kitty Kat as she makes a loony face and twirls her fingers on either side of her head.

She's adjusted well to her new role at STEELE Foundation. But the weeks leading up to the annual STEELE White Party over Labor Day weekend prove hectic. It's the culmination of the year's work and the highlight of the Hamptons season. Not to mention wanting to impress my mother since it's her baby.

I pat My Kitty Kat's thigh.

"We'll land soon enough, and you can get that bottle," I assure her.

"Starr and I can join you. She just texted me about opening a bottle before dinner," Malcolm adds across the row from us in his Sikorsky S-92 Executive Helicopter.

We're commuting with him, Roger, Leonie, Haley, and Lachlan. Blair and Billie fly with Baz and Lola on their helicopter since their schedules align.

"Sounds wonderful!" My Kitty Kat says.

"Well, count us in, too!" Haley pipes up from the rear of the helicopter. "I say we order delivery for dinner instead of going to the restaurant. I'm sure Lucien wouldn't mind having free tables for a busy Friday night."

Lachlan pulls out his mobile.

"I'll send a text message to him. He can open up the reservations since we booked the last tables," Lachlan says. As he types, he adds, "I'll tell Baz, too. He'll let the others know the change in plans."

By the time the helicopter lands, everyone confirmed, the food order set to arrive in ninety minutes, and the house staff arranged the deck for the impromptu cocktail hour followed by dinner. Our parents have plans and won't return home until late. The nannies will mind the children and dogs while the adults hang out. It comes together smoothly.

Suddenly energized, Kat bounces in the second row as I drive to the compound. The tiredness in her eyes replaced by glee. She chats with Leonie and Haley about their outfits for the gala. Then it's should Haley get a new hairstyle to debut at the event. Next, they switch to the designs Leonie has for the new beach house. The way they jump topics makes me dizzy.

I nod in response to the look Roger gives me from the passenger seat. Yeah, better to leave them uninterrupted. Happy wife, happy life and all. It's a lesson Baz taught my brothers, and now I use.

We drive past the stone wall that surrounds the compound and reach the impressive gates where the security guard waves from the gatehouse. As my Dad says, *leave it at the gate,* all tension drains from me the moment we drive through. I take a deep, cleansing breath.

The briny scent of the ocean fills my lungs from the open windows of the SUV. The calls of seagulls ring out. It's peaceful on the peninsula with over twenty acres. Its incredible surroundings include native trees, grassy areas, and closer to the ocean's sandy dunes.

On either side of the primary driveway, secondary ones appear as we drive along. I turn off to one on the left. A shorter driveway ends in a circle before a classic Hamptons-style three-story mansion. Robin egg blue shutters lean against gray weathered shingles. Beneath, the windowsill flower boxes filled with white blossoms add to the beauty of the home.

Roger hops out and helps Leonie from the SUV. They'll ride a golf cart to our parents' residence—as will Haley and Lachlan—after I drop them off at their house.

My Kitty Kat and I decide to take a shower to wash off the week. I would prefer my nightly bath soak ritual, but we don't have enough time. But I do make time to fuck her against the marble wall of the Roman shower. Always time for some good lovin'!

I set her on wobbly legs and use a fluffy towel to dry her skin. I use the excuse of applying body oil to play with her clit and nipples until she shatters for me. Combined with its scent of lavender and the toe-curling orgasms I gave her in the shower, My Kitty Kat has recovered fully from a stressful week. I carry her to the dressing room where I slip a floral maxi dress over her head.

Knowing she's bare for me beneath her dress will keep me horny until we go to bed. But the erotic torture is well worth it. Her DDs jiggle with pebbled nipples pressed against layers of silk chiffon. I imagine her curves hidden by the loose fit as the dress flows down her body to the ankles. Sexy as fuck.

I leave her putting on lip gloss to enter my dressing room. I don an untucked white linen shirt, natural linen pants, and brown leather slides. My Kitty Kat stands in the doorway as I roll the sleeves up my forearms.

"Hey, sexy," she says as her eyes blaze emerald fire from my head to my toes. "I hope your fiancée isn't home. I have plans for you this weekend."

I slip my arms around her waist and lean down to murmur in her ear.

"My fiancée is a fierce kitty who doesn't share her balls. So I'd be careful if I were you."

She gives a throaty laugh that makes my balls tingle.

"Oh, I can handle her. Don't you worry, big boy," she says as she squeezes my ass.

I chuckle and place my hand on the small of her back to guide her out of the room. Otherwise, we'll miss our impromptu evening plans.

Out on the deck, the butler and a maid stand at the ready. Even though I told them it would be a casual cocktail hour and dinner, they wait to see if we need their help. They bid us a good evening when I thank them.

Haley and Lachlan arrive first. They grab glasses of Jackson Cabernet Sauvignon and Chardonnay from the drinks table and join us at a seating area.

"Isn't that the maxi dress you bought from the new boutique the other week?" Haley asks My Kitty Kat who confirms. "I told you it would look good with your skin tone. The pinks and greens complement your alabaster skin and emerald eyes. Thanks, Haley!"

Kat stands and twirls, then kisses my twin on the cheek.

"You were right! I love it," she says as she smooths the silk chiffon along her thighs. "And the fit is comfy yet chic."

"Excellent choice!" I add with a smirk, knowing my intentions vary greatly from those of my twin.

"Hey, hey, hey!"

We turn to find Laurent bopping in with Yessenia on his arm. Behind them, Roger, Leonie, Baz, and Lola walk through the open wall of glass doors.

"*The Sexy Chef* does it again! He always remembers my favorite Prosciutto Wrapped Shrimp with Smoked Paprika." Lola exclaims as she pops one in her mouth. "Mmm mmm!"

Luc, Blair, Patrick, and Billie come around the corner of the lane that leads to the driveway. Norman Green and his wife Anita walk with them.

The former Heavyweight Champion of the World and owner of Norman Green's Elite Training Facility pretends to square off with Borya when he bumps him from behind. The two athletes and friends greet each other heartily. Márcia and Anita hug.

Malcolm, Starr, Anton, and Adrienne stop to chat with them before they converge on the drinks table. Glasses in hand, they join us at the seating area.

"Viv!" My Kitty Kat squeals when she spies her best friend.

My Mom raves how fantastic Vivian is since she accepted the position of CMO. Already she's implemented a prize-worthy marketing plan. On the personal side, Vivian has spent quite some time at the penthouse Kat and I share. We've had double dates with her and some of my buddies.

It appears as though one of my Harvard Business School friends—Perry Franck—has snagged her heart. He has a possessive hand on her lower back as he guides her towards us.

"Kat!" She squeals as they hug.

I rise and shake hands with Perry.

"Hey, man, good to see you," I say as I pull him in for a bro hug, then continue so only he hears. "You treating my girl right?"

He slaps me on the back and nods.

"Naturally. My mother raised a gentleman," he responds.

I know since she's friends with my mother. His family is one of the oldest book publishers in the world based in Paris with offices around the globe. He heads up the marketing department for their multibillion-dollar empire.

"Keep it that way," I tell him, then turn to Vivian for a hug. "Hey, Viv! A pleasure, as always. What can I get you to drink?"

"Hey, Harris!" She says, then glances around at the others' drinks. "The Chardonnay, thanks!"

I quirk an eyebrow at Perry, and he requests the Cabernet Sauvignon.

Everyone laughs and talks while we enjoy the sunset drinking good wine. We eat more of Lucien's delectable dishes, including a variety of desserts. Anton turns into the deejay and pipes his playlists through the surround sound system. The night turns into a dance party beneath an inky sky full of glittering stars.

When everyone leaves, I carry a tipsy Kat up to the balcony on our wing of the house. More than the stars glisten as I ravage the redheaded Siren. All. Night. Long.

KAT

"**Y**es, we have the gala this evening. But we must take time for self-care. Lucie, Josy, Sun, and Allison will rejuvenate with me at my favorite spa in the village. I booked it out for the day. We have the morning shift, and you, sweethearts, have the afternoon. The glam squads will arrive at your residences two hours prior to the gala. Ladies, this is our time to shine!"

We give Mum Shelley a rousing cheer for her pep talk. She beams. Then claps her hands.

"Let's go!" The Sergeant says.

We leave the breakfast room and head to the entry hall. Leonie loops arms with her Mum Joséphine Beaulieu. Although Leonie has her Parisian father Guy's height and mahogany hair, it's her Tunisian, petite mother she resembles. Her ebony hair cut in a stylish curly bob frames her fawn-colored, oval-shaped face. Pouty lips turn up in a joyful smile as she smiles at her daughter. In her early sixties, Josy could model as much as *The Lion*.

I take my Mum's hand as I reach her side. She squeezes it with a smile.

"I'm so very proud of you, honey. Shelley tells me you've done marvelous things at the Foundation. Tonight, you will definitely shine," she says. She peeks up at me and goes on. "And I'm glad you like Henry."

Ah, yes, her new man friend—Henry McGowan. He's a distinguished gentleman she met at an event Aunt Lucie hosted in Aberdeen a few months ago. His family owns a chain of popular grocery stores throughout the United Kingdom. I say, go, Mum!

And of course, Harris did a complete background check. All good.

"As long as he makes you happy, I'm happy. You deserve a special someone in your life, Mum," I respond with a squeeze to her hand.

We reach the front doors and step out onto the driveway. Rolls-Royce SUVs await us. I give my Mum a hug and wave to the other mothers, then hop into one headed to Starr Light Fitness & Wellness Southampton Village.

"What a lineup! Meditation, pranayama, ending with a flow session and yoga *nidra*. I cannot wait!" Billie says in her Southern Belle drawl. Her Granny Smith apple green eyes glow with excitement.

"Yoga *nidra*?" Charlotte asks with a frown. "I've heard of pranayama—the breathwork."

Leonie giggles and shifts in her seat to face my sister.

"It's yogic sleep. It can relieve stress by placing you in a sleep state during which the teacher guides you in meditation. The first time I tried yoga *nidra*, I didn't only 'reach a deep level of relaxation.' But fell asleep, then woke myself with my loud snoring!"

We laugh and talk about more the benefits of the eight

limbs of yoga. Perfect for the day of self-care Mum Shelley encourages.

Starr, Adrienne, and Márcia greet us when we arrive at SLFW SV. Standing in their Carbon38 Sweaty Betty, and Free People sports bras and matching leggings, they are every bit fashionable fitness enthusiasts.

"Good morning, girls! We have a fantastic day planned. Ready to get started?" Starr asks after everyone hugs, then leads the way inside.

Clients mill about the tranquil interior, sitting at tables near the café, browsing in the boutique, and on line for check in at the front desk. Everywhere women and men with amazing bodies from yoga, Pilates, Barre, and strength training sessions fill the space. The sound of piped-in music, excited chatter, and the whir of blenders for smoothies circulates in the air.

We pass studios on our way to Starr's private one. The further in we go, the more serene the environment. Cream walls with elaborate Indian woodwork surround us. Stone floors transform to warm red wood beneath our bare feet. Clients speak softly as they move to their classes. Open doors reveal some lying on mats or lined up at barres stretching before their sessions begin.

Starr's large studio accommodates us easily. We settle on mats already placed on the floor. Gracefully, Adrienne lowers to a cross-legged position on the mat beside Tibetan singing bowls. She leads us in mediation and pranayama, implementing the sounds.

Márcia takes us through a powerful dharma talk focused on self-love. She explains the asana sequence will allow us to follow our hearts, opening us up to recognize what brings us happiness. The flow expands our chests and includes heart opening poses fish, crescent moon lunge, camel, and bridge. We smile with joy when she ends with standing star pose.

The sense of jubilation continues with Starr's yoga *nidra*. Her guidance includes our recollections of joyful moments at varying stages of our lives. A sense of ease settles over me as my mind floats free to the soothing tones of her voice. At the end of the hour-long session, the calming influence of yoga *nidra* makes us feel as though we slept for hours.

"Starr, Adrienne, Márcia, thank you for wonderful sessions, as always!" Haley says once we rouse.

"*Sí*, I love the love you spread, *chicas*!" Yessenia exclaims as she re-tightens her long ponytail.

Anita—also a fitness instructor and meal prep connoisseur based in Paris—nods in agreement.

"Ladies, I always enjoy taking part in your sessions. You rank as my gurus!" She says with a bow.

We make our way to the locker room. Inside, we relax in the steam room where the scent of eucalyptus eases our sore muscles as it soothes our minds. After we shower, Adrienne reminds us about lunch at the café.

Perfect timing leads to our spa day. We walk through Southampton Village to Mum Shelley's favorite house of beauty. The manager welcomes us with frosty glasses of refreshing citrus water. Hours pass while the aestheticians buff, wax, and massage us, ending with glossy mani/pedis.

"Oh, I am *so* ready for the gala!" Vivian says as she wiggles her fingers with white nail polish. "Do you think I should blow my curls out or pile them atop my head in a sexy updo?"

I consider the Grecian gown she showed me last night, then suggest the updo like a gorgeous goddess. Viv shimmies and nods enthusiastically.

Everyone asks for similar input as we ride back to the compound. The glam squads await us.

"Well, well, well, look at this beautiful Siren before me."

My team just left, and I stand in front of the full-length mirror outside of my dressing room. As I turn to face Harris, my palms glide down the scores of white glimmering sequins covering the Italian satin column. The strapless gown would be demure except for cutouts from my flanks to midsection with a band of more sequins around the waist. A high slit in the back allows me to move sensuously as I pivot.

A seductive smile plays on my lips.

"Why thank you, my love," I purr. My gaze trails over his tuxedo-covered body. "And don't you look appetizing?"

He smirks. His eyes glitter like the diamonds in my ears and around my neck I borrowed from Bulgari—the event's jewelry sponsor. I paired the pieces with the diamond bangles Harris gave to me.

"We'll be sure to indulge in one another after the fireworks. Or make some of our own," he responds. "Come, let's go."

I take his proffered elbow.

Outside the side door of his parents' megamansion, my administrative assistant—Foster Alcott, who came with me from the children's nonprofit—approaches us.

"Hi, Kat. You look fabulous!" He exclaims with an approving nod.

Foster has become my other source for fashion advice. He and his partner rank amongst the best-dressed men I've ever seen. Including the perfectly tailored classic tuxedo he wears.

"You're a handsome devil, Foster!" I say with a wink.

He grins, then gives me an update on the gala as we walk

towards the platinum gray carpet with step and repeat. It highlights the event sponsors, including STEELE International, Inc., Jackson Corporation, Lola's Coterie, Starr Light Fitness & Wellness Center, Banque Montaigne, Bulgari, and other notable companies.

As we near, the calls of photographers from local to international media outlets and the paparazzi ring out. Guests pose for the flashing cameras or speak into microphones. Stunning evening wear and incredible jewels sparkle. The area hums with activity.

Beyond, I spy our gang at various spots on the carpet. After Foster finishes, Harris and I make our way to them.

"Showtime. Smile for the cameras," Harris tells me with a wink. He places his hand on the small of my back possessively.

We pose with his siblings and answer questions from the media. Most of it centers on our upcoming wedding. But the professional Development Director in me guides the narrative back to STEELE Foundation and our multimillion-dollar goal for the evening.

Foster catches my attention and tells me Mum Shelley and Vivian need me for an interview. I follow him, leaving Harris with Laurent and Yessenia.

When the interview ends, Viv introduces me to her parents and brothers. Mum Shelley invited them to the gala. She's determined to have everyone in the fold. Viv's parents greet me like a daughter with hugs and promises of lunch or dinner before they return to Tuscany. Her handsome brothers shake my hand warmly.

Another hand on my waist makes me turn.

Harris smiles down at me, then lifts his gaze to Vivian's brothers. Even though they introduced me to their dates, my caveman still finds the need to flex. He extends his hand to each brother and welcomes them to Steele Southampton Village.

When Perry tells Harris he and one of Vivian's brothers took classes together at Harvard, Harris smiles. They catch up while Viv and I listen on.

Aunt Lucie appears with Uncle Connor to introduce me to a princess and her husband. They RSVP'd for the wedding. Harris and I excuse ourselves and turn to them. After speaking with the couple, Aunt Lucie takes us around to other notables who confirmed their attendance.

It's been wonderful how they've taken me under their wings. Aunt Lucie even shared a notebook with details on key people for me to familiarize myself with. Each week we have a video conference not only for the wedding planning but for quizzes. I love it!

Harris and I mingle with other guests before the announcement for dinner. We join the throng of guests as they head towards the giant side lawn. Aglow by thousands of fairy lights and lanterns, it has two sumptuous pavilions, one for dinner and the other for dessert and dancing. We converge on the dinner pavilion where the scent of dishes crafted by Lucien and his team tantalizes us.

Mum Shelley rises to make her speech. Once she reaches the podium, she calls for Vivian and me to join her. We smile broadly when she introduces us and praises our efforts with the Foundation and the gala. We return to our tables to vigorous applause.

Harris stands and kisses me on the cheek. I lean into him before I take my seat.

The rest of the evening passes with the silent auction, dancing, and fireworks.

As promised, Harris and I slip away and make our own dazzling display. All. Night. Long.

* * *

"THAT'S SUCH a sweet photo of you and Harris, Kat!"

Charlotte beams as she holds her iPad up for me to see the website. We're on the deck having brunch the morning after the gala. It's recap and refuel time.

Charlotte, Vivian, and I—along with our administrative assistants—scroll through the media coverage to date. We have a press clippings agency. But I like to see what I can find, too. It also gives me a thrill to see my image on the society pages firsthand!

Viv—who's used to such exposure—does it from a business standpoint. But she nods in agreement with Charlotte's pronouncement.

"Aaaw! You guys are adorbs. The way you're leaning into him as he smiles down at you. His eyes full of pride and love," Viv says as she smiles at the photo.

Admittedly, my heart swells at the sight of it. I make a note to contact the photographer for the digital file. I'll print two and put them in matching sterling silver frames and give one to Harris. Then, I'll put mine on my desk at the office.

If the Foundation still employed Ms. PAS, she would puke her eyes out.

I giggle at the cartoonish vision and swipe to another website.

Overall, the coverage aligns with the goal—get more donations—since the initial numbers show an increase over the time of the event compared to the prior. We send our findings in a report to Mum Shelley, the CFO, and the rest of the executive team.

Work done, Foster and Viv's admin leave to enjoy the rest of the day.

We head down to the beach for a walk to the edge of the peninsula and back. Since Charlotte returns to Scotland tomorrow, I want to spend the rest of the day with her.

Tonight, we'll have dinner with Harris, our Mum, Henry, Payton, and Michael. They're staying through the end of the week. Michael will remain longer since he'll work at STEELE International for the fall semester. Roger says it will give him hands-on experience and count towards his university work. It'll be great to have my brother in the City.

As we stroll through the surf, I notice a shimmer of kelly green amidst the foam from a wave as it slides back to the ocean. Bending down, I collect it before it washes back into the Atlantic Ocean. I smile as I rinse the sand from the piece of sea glass. Shaped like an oval, its surface made smooth and frosted from the years it spent in tumbling in the saltwater.

"Here, Charlotte. I found a piece of sea glass. You admired the collection of colorful bits of glass in the entry foyer Mum Shelley collects," I say as I hand it to my sister. "Keep this as a reminder of our weekend."

She takes the piece and holds it up to the sun.

"It's beautiful, thanks Kat!" She says as she hugs me. "I'll treasure it forever."

Harris stands on the deck and raises his hand in greeting as we near the megamansion.

"There's your future hubby, Kat. Picture perfect. I'm so happy for you," Charlotte says with a smile.

I grin and nod. My heart swells the closer we get to the home. Can it get any better?

KAT

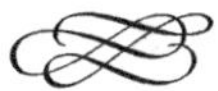

"OMG, Lola! This corset is unbelievable! However do you come up with your designs?"

Vivian asks as she admires an antique gold lace corset in the New York City flagship of Lola's Coterie in The STEELE Tower mall. She grins as she holds the matching garter belt and barely there G-string.

Lola smiles like the Cheshire Cat. Her hazel eyes twinkle with mischief.

"Well, I envision all the ways I can make Baz lose his mind with kinky lingerie. The colors and materials just speak to me," she says. "Then I wave my magic wand and the sketches appear."

We laugh at her shenanigans and continue to look through the luxury lingerie.

The boutique is breathtaking and resembles Lola's other locations—not cookie-cutter replicas, each distinct. This one gives a nod to New York City with the Manhattan skyline featured in the hand-painted wallpaper instead of Parisian street vignettes, as in her original boutique on the

Champs-Élysées. It's the largest of her boutiques with three floors and includes office space, a section for custom design requests, and private rooms like the one we're in.

"Here, I think this set would look fantastic on you, Kat," Lola says as she pulls a silk hanger from a rack.

It's a sensual and provocative vision. A corset of emerald green lace with a center panel beneath the demi-cups and a busk of silk satin. Eyelash lace and pleated tulle trim the tops of the demi-cups to make them wink. The laced gold grommet portion above the hips flare out to reveal tulle panels. Lacings trail through more gold grommets along the solid black back leading to an open and lace-trimmed backed panty. Simply stunning.

I grin and practically skip to the dressing room. An assistant helps me put on the corset. I emerge to wolf whistles from Lola and claps from Billie, Blair, and Viv—who wears the antique gold ensemble. It's as perfect against her ebony skin as my set is with my emerald green eyes.

We strut our stuff and strike poses à la *The Lion*.

"Fabulous, ladies!" Billie says. "It's going to be a Lola's Coterie night!"

"A *Lavish* Lola's Coterie night!" Blair adds. "All the girls have their lingerie selected from here and the London and Paris boutiques."

Viv hip bumps me and says, "I can*not* wait!"

I grin.

Harris came up with the idea to host an Annual Halloween Masquerade Party at LEVELS New York. He explained his parents and each of his siblings have family events: Dad Morgan and Mom Shelley Labor Day; Malcolm and Starr Memorial Day; Haley and Lachlan July 4 (even if in Aberdeen); Sebastian and Lola Thanksgiving; Roger and Leonie Christmas and New Year's. Since Harris is the trickster of the family, Halloween is the best holiday for us.

We decided to open the night up to friends, too. Each one could invite two people. Harris thought it a good way to vet prospective members. We'll close LEVELS Peepshow and the Cellar to members for the night. They can still access the upper levels for dining and dancing. And we'll still have plenty of room.

Earlier, I met Harris at the Meatpacking District flagship location. We checked the decorations on both levels matched our Rogues & Sirens theme. Oversized flat screens display movies including *9 1/2 Weeks*, *The Lover*, *Body Heat*, and *Bound*. Platters of carnal edible delights will rest on strategically placed tables, some with naked men and women covered with them.

A deejay will play sensual music on Peepshow. Male and female dancers in cages set around the room. The Rogues and Sirens can grind on the new dance floor cordoned off near the deejay.

Signature mocktails crafted by Billie—our mixologist— will flow from ice fountains sculpted in the naked form of men and women. Those not willing to imbibe the essence from a frosty penis and nipples can opt for service from the bartenders dressed only in black leather ties and black leather penis sheaths.

The Cellar—LEVELS' BDSM dungeon, an expansive, grand hall, austere in design—will have platforms where willing subs of both sexes offer themselves to Rogue Doms and Siren Dommes. Fascinating new toys available for all to play with during their scenes.

Those who don't have masks can choose from a selection of unique handmade ones commissioned from an artisan in Venice. Harris chose an ornate platinum and cream Joker's mask. I wanted to play on my name with a gold metal filigree and Swarovski Crystal cat mask.

As I carry my Lola's Coterie shopping bags to our penthouse, I envision my mask with my emerald green lingerie. It's going to look awesome. And like Viv, I can*not* wait!

"WELCOME to the inaugural evening of decadence in honor of Halloween Erotic Eve and all Rogues and Sirens who thrive on the carnal delights of this night. No rules? Oh surely, you *jest*. Rule One: only consensual play. Rule Two: all must remain shrouded in mystery behind your masks. Let the tricks and treats begin!"

Harris' proclamation earns cries of passion from our guests gathered around the primary stage of Peepshow. He raises our clasped hands in the air, then to his lips. The heat from his penetrative stare nearly melts the gold metal mask from my face.

I shudder as my nipples pebble against the molded demicups of my corset. A flush rises from the tops of the mounds up my neck to color my alabaster cheeks.

He hops down from the stage. His eyes follow the curvy shape of my body, cinched by the corset. My pussy softens and moistens as he stares at my core blatantly. His nostrils flare as though my arousal teases his senses. The tip of his tongue slips out to lick his full bottom lip. He tastes me on the air.

My Rogue continues to devour me with his molten platinum eyes as they skim down my long, toned legs ending in fuck-me gold marabou mules. He grasps me by the waist and lifts me off the stage to stand before him.

"I'll say it again. You win the Sexiest Siren Award," he murmurs in my ear. His warm breath teases the delicate shell. His hand dips from my waist to squeeze the bare cheek of my ass in emphasis. "So many curves for me to make my personal playground. Where shall I start?"

A moan escapes my slack mouth.

He growls low in his throat. The feral sound vibrates through my body.

I shudder in response.

"Wherever you wish, My Sexy Rogue," I purr. My fingers grip the front of his colorful silk shirt. Acting on instinct, my hips gyrate to grind my pelvis against the tops of his muscular thighs beneath black leather pants. I groan at the pressure against my lower belly from his thick erection. "I. Am. All. Yours."

He fists my ponytail and yanks my head back. I hiss from the unexpected sting.

"Mine!" He growls through clenched teeth before he slams his mouth over my parted lips.

The possessive kiss leaves my lips swollen and me breathless.

My Sexy Rogue pivots and stalks through the clusters of our guests as they watch demonstrations on the smaller platforms. Some of them have never been to LEVELS New York or any BDSM club. They watch in awe as Malcolm—a Dom and a Shibari master—prepares to bind Starr in white silks. I recognize them despite their masks, especially since Malcolm is bare chested. A sexy as sin, intricate tattoo wraps around his well-defined pecs to span across his back to form wings.

I only get a glimpse before My Sexy Rogue moves on.

Then do a double take when we approach another platform. A St. Andrew's Cross stands in the center. A sub in a playsuit stands bound by wrists and ankles to the cross. Her barely there lingerie has three thin black studded strips wrapped around her throat, outside the cups of her black lace demi-cup bra to crisscross over her torso to form a pattern over her lower belly, then merge with lace to cover her mons. She moans as her Dom traces one stretched arm with a peacock's feather. Lola and Sebastian!

Once again, the masks cannot hide their identity from me. While at the boutique, Lola showed us the playsuit she designed to wear for the party. I love how it resembles bondage. Perfect for the St. Andrew's Cross demonstration she takes part in with Sebastian.

"Where are you off to in such a hurry? Not sneaking away from your own party, are you?"

I bump into Harris' back as he comes to an abrupt stop. A peek around his massive frame, reveals Haley with an impish grin on her face. Only the bottom half shows beneath the elaborate red and gold mask she wears. The long red feather bobs as she giggles.

"We supplied the activity and venue. We will not play with our guests, too," Harris responds wryly. Then he counters her questions with his own. "Shouldn't you partake in all the night offers, my dear twin? Or is Little Lord Fauntleroy not enough for you?"

Lachlan growls from beneath his tiger's mask. His emerald green eyes flare.

"Surely, *you* jest. Or did your Joker's mask warp your brain?" Lachlan all but snarls at Harris.

"Oh, for fuck's sake! Enough with the pissing contest, mates."

We shift our gazes towards the Scottish accent.

A man raises his full mask and flicks his green eyes between Harris and Lachlan. Patrick!

"Put your knobs away or go find an alcove and put them

to better use," he tells them. He nods at Haley and me, then continues past us with Billie holding back giggles trailing behind him. The Alpha Dom's sizable hand clasps a diamond chain connected to a diamond collar around her neck.

Our friends hold nothing back tonight. And I am all for it!

I bring my gaze back to Harris and Lachlan.

"I agree. Use all of this testosterone for the better good of womankind—Haley and me," I tell them as I take Harris by the arm and tug him along.

Haley concurs and does the same to Lachlan as the Alpha male and Alpha Dom mutter under their breath. A fucker here, a wanker there, and they're back to loving, loyal cousins. Men...

My Sexy Rogue and I weave our way towards a darkened alcove. The erotically enamored couples, ménage à trois, and other combinations of polyamory we encounter, the higher my arousal peaks. The carnal electricity from the scenes playing out around us sparks.

It skitters across my skin, leaving a wake of tingling nerve endings. The fine hairs on my arms raise. Puckered nipples tighten to the point of pain. Juices dampen the gusset of my panty. The need for My Sexy Rogue to take me heightens. I increase my pace.

At last, we reach an empty banquette shrouded in shadows. Many others occupied by guests in various stages of sex and clothing. However, their masks remain fixed on their faces. Everyone enjoys an air of intrigue.

My Sexy Rogue sits on the vamp red leather seat. He widens his muscular thighs and settles me between them— my back to his front. His hands skim the tops of my thighs as he spreads, then drapes them over his legs. Fully exposed an additional round of carnal electricity zings through my body.

"I want you to pick a scene and describe what you see, then how it makes you feel," he says. I shudder as his lips trace from the curve of my shoulder up the side of my neck. "And do not skip one detail."

The solid rod of his massive erection as it presses against the crack of my ass proves a pleasurable distraction. But I snap to with a yelp when he plucks my engorged clit. The sopping wet gusset of my panty does nothing to limit the sting of his reprimand.

Quickly I scan the floor of Peepshow. Our guests mingle with staff subs and Doms/Dommes while voyeurs linger on the fringes, greedily absorbing bacchanalia before them. All kinds of kinky demonstrations occur. The moans, groans, and occasional scream blends with the sensual throbbing of the bass in music as the deejay spins. The air ripens with the scent of sex.

A blindfolded, naked woman astride a Sybian surrounded by four bare-chested men in tight leather pants makes my pulse race. Her full, round breasts jiggle as the vibrations from the dildo attached to the saddle jolts her pussy. A sheen of sweat glistens on her warm honey colored skin. Rainbows shimmer around her from the crystal-embellished mask she wears.

The man behind her grips her stacked forearms bound to her back by a black cord. He uses the handle to tilt her backwards. As she cries out from the dildo, rubbing her G-spot, he slams his mouth over hers. On either side, two men take advantage of the deep arc of her shuddering body to engulf her pebbled brown nipples with their hungry mouths. Her thighs quiver when the man in the front laps at her engorged clit. None pay any attention to the cluster of guests around them. The beautiful woman commands their attention during their erotic play.

My body reacts to each of their ministrations as though I wear their toy. My swollen nipples ache as they strain against the molded demi-cups of my corset. Inside my belly, excitement swirls. It reaches down into my core to set it ablaze. More cream gushes. I feel it seep beyond my panty to pool onto the leather seat.

After I share all details, I close my thighs for friction. But My Sexy Rogue widens his opening me further. The coolness of the room touches the heated flesh of lower lips as they slip from my panty. I moan in frustration.

"I did not tell you to relieve yourself. That's for me to do," he chides. A smack to my pussy lips furthers his disapproval.

However, combined with my heightened arousal, my punishment provides enough contact to elicit an orgasm. I shudder and lean limp against his powerful chest.

He growls and lifts my hips. The pinch of lace against my clit dispels the brief moment of orgasmic bliss. One-handed, My Sexy Rogue unzips his leather pants. His turgid cock bounces free heavily against my ass. He groans in relief. The rumble in his chest vibrates against me.

"I'm going to fuck you right here. Right. Now."

With one brutal thrust, he impales me on his velvet-covered steel. Its tip breaches my slippery folds and prods my cervix. I climax upon impact. He hisses in my hair.

"So fucking good, Siren. You make it hard not to cum," he grinds out through clenched teeth as my pussy walls flutter along his solid length. "Do. Not. Move."

Despite his command, I swivel my hips to encourage him to fuck me now. My disobedience earns me a quick succession of smacks to the outer lips of my pussy stretched around his impressive girth. I buck against the onslaught of spanks.

When the pain lessens, the pleasure takes its place.

My Sexy Rogue grips my hips and thrusts up repeatedly. He doesn't stop, even as two more orgasms rip through my pulsating core. His feral grunts and growls fill my ears. I bite my lower lip to prevent my carnal cries from bursting forth. He fucks me until spots dance before my eyes.

When he explodes a torrent of hot cum deep within my pussy, his release triggers another mind-blowing one of mine. He pulls my head to the side and captures my mouth. We swallow one another's cries of ecstasy with our bodies connected as one.

This is one night of Halloween Erotic Eve debauchery with My Sexy Rogue I'll never forget and look forward to many more ahead!

"Kat! Open your eyes!"

"You're missing the view of the mountains!"

"Don't be a baby! You won't have to ski back down from up there."

My Kitty Kat ignores her girls and burrows her face deeper into the partially opened front of my Moncler Grenoble parka. Her arms tighten around my waist as she tries not to tremble in fear.

I press my hand against the back of her head covered by her hood and tilt it back, so she peeks up at me with one eye closed.

"Kitty Kat, do you trust me?" I ask as my other hand bands around her waist to pull her flush to me.

She bites the corner of her mouth as she continues to peek up at me with one eye. I wait patiently for her to respond. The other eye opens. Nerves battle with trust in the emerald green depths as she flicks her eyes from my face to the window of the gondola. They widen and rush back to me. Her body quakes.

Her reaction is so cute, I want to kiss the tip of her nose —red like Rudolph. She swallows thickly and blinks.

Still, I wait.

Her inner battle ends when she nods, then catches herself and vocalizes her response.

"Y—Yes," My Kitty Kat stammers, then clears her throat. "Yes, I trust you, Harris Steele."

An intense wave of satisfaction floods my system at her trust in me, despite her fear of heights. Made even more endearing since we're riding up in a gondola with oversized windows to the highest point of the Rocky Mountains in Colorado. The majestic snow-covered peaks dominate the panorama. While below, the town spreads beyond STEELE Aspen Resort. At this distance, they appear miniature. Colorful dots in the snow.

It's Thanksgiving weekend and Baz and Lola's holiday to host for our family.

Since we're spending Christmas through New Year's in Sydney for the wedding, we'll miss being at *Chalet de la Joie* —Roger and Leonie's residence in Verbier, Switzerland. Baz and Lola decide Aspen would make up for our skiing in the Alps and chose here over their private island— Bougainvillea Cay in Exumas, Bahamas.

My Kitty Kat never skied, so I promised to teach her on the bunny trails. This gondola ride up to the top of the mountain doesn't exactly match the smaller hills. However, we won't ski down like the others after breakfast in the Peak Lodge. We'll ride back down on the gondola with her family since they're not skiers, yet.

I thought she'd enjoy the expansive view. Guess not...

My forehead presses against hers, hidden within her

hood. Our eyes lock. I slow my breathing to encourage her to follow. She does and begins to calm. Her body stills as she relaxes in my arms.

"Good, lass," I croon.

She sighs and leans against me heavily.

Lost in our own bubble of trust and love, our family and their conversations around us fade. I rock My Kitty Kat gently.

"Now, I want you to look through the front window of the gondola. Up towards the mountain peak, not down. Focus on its beauty and know I'll let nothing happen to you, Kitty Kat," I tell her.

Her eyes scan mine, then she nods and looks behind me. I move around her and hold her back to my front. My hands rest protectively beneath her breasts. A small gasp escapes her lips as the mountaintop looms ahead.

I whisper words of encouragement and smile as she settles enough to appreciate the view. Oohs and aahs warm my heart. Her level of trust in me means the world to me.

By the time we reach the gondola house, My Kitty Kat chats easily with everyone as we disembark. We make our way to the restaurant en masse. The hostess greets us by name and leads us to reserved tables beside the wall of windows facing the surrounding mountains and Aspen below.

At this super safe distance, My Kitty Kat plops onto a chair closest to the expansive view. Her smile could rival the brilliant sun in the cloudless blue sky above.

"That was beyond incredible! Well… Once you calmed me down," she says with a giggle. "Had I known we were riding in a sardine box with windows up the steepest incline in the world, I would have stayed at the base lodge!"

Her Mum laughs and pats her hand. Then, Mum Allison smiles at me.

"Harris, you really helped my wee lass. She used to be afraid of the sliding board at the park. After she got to the top of the ladder, she cried until her father scooped her off!" Allison says with a shake of her head.

"I don't regret the ride up. It feels like we're in the heavens all the way up here," My Kitty Kat exclaims.

"On the ride down, you can see what you missed," I tell her.

She faints dramatically and waves a hand over her face.

"Give a lass a minute, will ya?" She says.

Everyone at our table laughs.

The conversation turns to the day's activities. Some will continue to ski while others will sleigh ride, ice skate, or snowboard. My Kitty Kat and I will hit the bunny hill for lessons. If she picks it up quick enough, we can try an easy trail.

While we enjoy a hearty breakfast to fuel our day, the girls chat about the wedding planning. I've stayed on the periphery. Not interested in the choice of flowers or music selection, table assignments or order of speeches. Ah, no.

As long as My Kitty Kat walks down the aisle to me, I'm all good.

I took advice from my brothers for the honeymoon. They went all out for theirs and wowed their new brides. I will do the same for my Mrs. Steele. A grin spreads across my face. I cannot wait for her reaction. Priceless, I'm sure.

My parents—along with Uncle Connor, Aunt Lucie, Mum Allison and Henry, Leonie's parents, and Starr's parents—plan on dinner after an art gallery opening. The rest of us—including Payton, Michael, and Charlotte—will go to Escobar. The après-ski nightspot has a sleek vibe with popular deejays and creative drinks.

After breakfast, My Kitty Kat, her family, and I watch as the rest gear up for their trip down the mountain. They choose a double black diamond piste. All advanced skiers, they'll thrive on the challenges the extremely difficult trial offers. We bid them good luck and take the path to the gondola house.

My Kitty Kat squeezes my hand when the gondola moves beyond the opening. The expanse of the Rocky Mountains, Aspen, and beyond lies before us. She steals a peek at me. I smile and rub her back to soothe her nerves. She takes a deep cleansing breath and faces her fear head on.

To distract her, I point out key spots and talk about the fun I had spending Christmas here. They get a kick out of my mishaps on the slopes when I was younger. Particularly the time I thought I started an avalanche. Only to find out the snow from the trees above fell on me, not a horrific wave of snow down the mountain. I learned the lesson to not go off-piste alone.

When we disembark from the gondola, My Kitty Kat announces she no longer fears heights and plans to learn to ski well enough for the advance pistes. We cheer her on with claps and wolf whistles. She curtsies, then thanks me with a mind-blowing kiss.

"I do not care to see my sister in a lip lock."

Payton's grumbled remark breaks us apart. We stare at him. He grins and adds for us to get a room. Relieved he's not being an asshole, I clap him on the shoulder and laugh. The others join in, equally pleased he was joking.

Mum Allison and Henry leave us to take a sleigh ride.

I lead the rest to the base lodge where our ski butlers

await. They help us with our gear while the instructors for Payton, Michael, and Charlotte talk to them about their goals. Sure, My Kitty Kat could have an instructor. But I'll be the only one to ever pick her up when she falls, not some hotshot. Mine!

We get to the T-bar lift and the lesson begins. I explain how to lean against the upside-down T to avoid pulling it down and landing on her ass. She masters it on the third try. First victory!

At the top of the bunny hill, part two of the lesson begins. I show her how to fall to the side to avoid injury. She tries and laughs as she struggles. I demonstrate the V formation with my skis and slide down the slope, going left and right a few feet. As I sidestep up to her, she practices the V. I go down again, then call for her to try.

My Kitty Kat skis a few feet before she wobbles, flails her arms, and plonks to her ass. She laughs and falls back on the snow. Her arms move to create a snow angel before she sits up.

A little girl zips by, and My Kitty Kat laughs harder.

"Great, even a wee lass has me beat!" She says as she throws her hands up. "Help me, Harris."

I chuckle and sidestep up to her. I angle her to face parallel to the bunny hill, then grip beneath her arms and lift her. She stands on her skis and dusts the snow from her ass.

"Oh, no you don't. Part of my payment is to swipe snow from your body," I say as I replace her hands with mine.

She wiggles her hips and asks, "What's the other part?"

I rise to my full height and smirk down at her. Not wanting a single soul to hear my carnal plans, I lean down to murmur them in her ear.

She gasps and darts her eyes around to confirm no one

heard a word. Below the Dragon mirrored ski goggles, her face turns a darker shade of crimson.

I chuckle wickedly, smack her on the ass, and tell her to try again.

Two and a half hours later, we're cuddled up on the sofa beneath a cashmere blanket before a roaring fire in my family's lodge.

My Kitty Kat loves the contemporary timber and stone, twelve-bedroom mountain lodge we have within the STEELE Aspen complex of hotel, restaurants, spa, and residential properties. The gated private homes surround the hotel and have access to its amenities as a perk of being a part of the luxury resort. From our lodge, it takes only minutes to arrive in the center of Aspen or at the ski lifts. Outside the double-story wall of windows beyond the heated deck, more panoramic views of Colorado's majestic snow-covered Rocky Mountains and of the ski resort leave one breathless. It's also one of my favorite residences.

Our moment of peace ends when my nieces and nephews return from their ski lessons. They barrel into the great room after depositing their gear in the equipment room and their outerwear in the mudroom. They head straight for us with cries of *Oncle* Harris, *Tante* Kat for Roger's children and the English equivalent of uncle and aunt for the rest of the little monsters.

My Kitty Kat and I make room for their invasion after we tell the nannies we got it under control. The children regale us with tales of their exploits for the day. They remind me of myself at their ages—busy, adventurous, curious. We listen raptly and laugh along with them or offer words of support and encouragement.

Next to arrive, the skiers stride in. The parents scoop their children into their arms, and the stories begin again.

Lucien goes to the chef's kitchen and returns with mugs of hot chocolate and a tray of tasty chocolate chip and sugar cookies. It becomes an impromptu party. We spend time together before dinner, then clubbing.

Haley catches my eye and cocks her head with a smirk. I frown, confused. She purses her lips and jerks her chin to my left. I turn to find My Kitty Kat glowing as she holds Dione and Iris on her lap. Malcolm and Starr's twin daughters chatter on about the snowman they want to build in the morning.

Kat tells them she'll help since she has a wee bit of fairy dust she can sprinkle on it. Their eyes widen and ask if it's like Frosty. She tells them it's a secret and they'll see in the morning if they promise to be extra good tonight.

Mini Malcolms 2.0—as we affectionately call their second set of twins—sit stunned. Then Iris leans forward and wraps her arms around Kat's neck for a hug. Her eyes shimmer before she closes them and hugs both Iris and Dione.

My heartbeat quickens.

Does Kat want children now? Am I being selfish in not wanting them for a while? Do I want to hold off for real? Fuck!

I sit back against the sofa with my mind churning. Haley —who stared at me the whole time—starts to laugh uproariously. I throw a glare at her, which only makes my twin double over. She wipes tears from her eyes as she shakes with mirth. I groan.

Just fucking great…

KAT

armth cocoons me as I float on a cloud of bliss. Memories of Harris worshipping my body for hours cause tingles to ignite along my heated skin. His talented mouth brings me to climax again and again before his beautiful cock makes me explode. I tremble at the thought.

My hand stretches out to caress my lover.

I roll over and open my eyes to find his side of the king-size bed empty. My palm strokes cold sheets instead of his hot body. My head cocks to listen for him in the en suite bathroom since the double doors to the living room remain closed.

Not hearing any movement or water from the shower, I sit up. My eyes scan the bedroom, then land on a cream notecard set on the nightstand. A crystal vase overflowing with gorgeous blue roses stands beside it. Then I notice their delicate scent. I inhale deeply and scramble across the bed.

My True Love Kitty Kat,

As much as I love waking to your beautiful face, this morning I must wait until I see you walk down the aisle to become my wife. My heart races at the thought.

These Blue Roses symbolize trust, commitment, and relationship. All that you have given to me, and all I have given to you willingly. Blue is the rarest color of roses just as life doesn't always provide a True Love. Tonight, we become one, Mrs. Harris Steele.

Love your Husband forevermore,
Harris

Tears fill my eyes and spill to my cheeks as I finish Harris' touching love letter. Seventeen months after we first met, three months together, fourteen weeks apart, three weeks salvaging our relationship, eleven months back together, and here we are on the morning of our wedding. I fulfilled my vow to get my man back while in this very city last New Year's Eve.

Life may have been a rollercoaster with highs in love and lows in despair. But we made it this far. This day, we vow to never part from the other. Husband and wife. Forevermore.

I dab my cheeks with the handkerchief Harris had so thoughtfully left on the nightstand beside the note card. Through my tears of joy, I smile. I love my man.

Once again, I scramble across the giant bed to the nightstand on my side. I grab my mobile to call Harris.

"Good morning, Siren. Your call enthralled me to marry you and only you. How do you feel on this momentous day?" He asks as his smile shines over the airwaves.

I open my mouth to speak, but emotions overwhelm me

again. I lean back against the fluffy pillows and close my eyes. The lids help to staunch the flow of more tears.

"Babe? Are you still there?"

Harris' worried voice filters through the rising tide of my emotions. I take a deep, cleansing breath and try again to regain my ability to speak.

"Y—y—yes, my love," I start, then clear my throat thick with tears. "I feel wonderful, especially after reading your love letter. The Blue Roses are incredible. You are incredible. I—I love you, Harris Steele."

Now, his end of the call drops into silence.

I strain my ear to hear what he's doing.

A soft rustling sound, then a door closes. Harris clears his throat.

"I love you, too, My Kitty Kat," he murmurs in a raspy voice. "It's incredible you love me. Me. Not just who I am and what I have. I can't wait for you to be my wife, Kat Jackson soon-to-be Kat Steele."

"Listen, lover boy, we have to go!"

"Yeah, up and at 'em!"

Roger and Laurent call to Harris. He tells them to fuck off before more rustling.

"I presume this is Kat. So, good morning, Kat," Roger says, then continues. "I'm quite certain my mother has plans for you, and we have plans for Harris. He'll be nice and ready for you. Much love. But… Ciao!"

Roger *The Responsible* ends the call chuckling while Harris growls in the background.

As if on cue, a knock on the bedroom doors startles me. I squeak and lift the sheet over my bare breasts. The door opens.

"Rise and shine, Kat, sweetheart!"

"Yes, time to start your wedding day, honey!"

"Come along, darling. We have much to do!"

Through the now open double doors, Sergeant Shelley, Major Mum, and Lieutenant Lucie stride inside. They tsk at me still lying in bed and urge me to the bathroom for a steam shower. They allot me twenty minutes before they expect me in the living room.

I can't help my giggle but follow their command without hesitation.

Emerged from the dressing room in the flowy maxi dress and sandals they set aside for my attire, they hustle me out of the suite. One of the two wedding planners greets us when the lift opens on the lobby of STEELE Sydney.

As my future sister-in-law said, the view from their property is far superior to the one from the Park Hyatt Sydney. As we move through the lobby, I steal glimpses at Sydney Harbour. The sun shines brightly on the azure blue waters. Boats of all types float along its surface. The Sydney Opera House's distinctive series of arched white roofs shaped like the sails of boats rises above the Harbour. A magnificent day for our wedding!

My heart skips a beat knowing in only a matter of hours, I will be Mrs. Harris Steele. OMG!!!

"Don't dawdle, Kat, honey!"

Major Mum's chiding words hurry me along.

We enter the spa. Instantly, the tranquil environment slows my breaths. I close my eyes and allow the soothing scent of lavender and the calming sound of wind to wash over me. Be still my beating heart.

Arms band around me from the front, back, and sides.

My eyes fly open to find myself engulfed by Vivian, Charlotte, and all my future sisters-in-law. They swap with Blair, Billie, Adrienne, Márcia, Anita, and Isla Ritchie—my friend and the former administrative assistant to Lachlan.

They're swathed in fluffy terrycloth robes with matching slippers on their feet. Hair pulled up in topknots. Makeup-free faces beam at me.

Soon we're whisked away by aestheticians for a plethora of treatments. By the time we meet up again, we're pliant, buffed, and waxed to perfection. I'm so at ease, my feet barely touch the ground as we walk to one restaurant for my bridesmaids' luncheon. Or more like maid of honor and my girls' luncheon since only Vivian is in the wedding party opposite Laurent as Harris' best man.

As we go along, Mum Shelley and Aunt Lucie remove their military command helmets to introduce me to various wedding guests we pass.

After we went through the numbers, we found between the Steeles and the Jacksons, we had four hundred—about two hundred each. My handful put us over the four hundred number. Since the wedding is so large, our party dominates the hotel. Malcolm—as STEELE International, Inc.'s President of Entertainment Properties Division—closed the hotel for our private use during the duration of our time here.

After the hostess leads us to a table with views of Sydney Harbour and the server takes our order, I present gifts to everyone. The Mums receive sterling silver frames with a photo of Harris and me taken from our sitting with the engagement announcement photographer. Their eyes well with tears as they thank me.

Even though they're not in the wedding party, I give my sister, sisters-in-law, and friends gifts. Their contribution to the love Harris and I share makes them invaluable. Each ooh and aah over the vintage diamond brooches I collected from auctions at Sotheby's. I worked with a representative who scoured the auctions at their houses in New York City,

London, Geneva, and Paris to find unique pieces befitting each one.

As we dine on tasty food, guests stop by our table to offer words of congratulations and best wishes. Mum Shelley and Aunt Lucie make more introductions. I try my best to remember names. Lola leans over and tells me not to worry. No one expects the bride to know everyone. I smile at her gratefully.

Soon it's time to take a nap before we change for the ceremony.

My nerves amp up again. Even though I ate a light lunch of grilled balsamic vinaigrette chicken over a bed of butter lettuce, my stomach roils.

Starr must sense my distress because she takes both of my hands between hers and makes me focus on the sound of her voice.

"Slow inhalation. Pause for a beat. Slow exhalation. Slow inhalation. Pause for a beat. Slow exhalation. Continue while you listen to me only," she says, then takes me through a restorative mediation.

The sounds of the other diners' chatter and cutlery on dishes fade away. My mind latches on to Starr's soothing intonation. She tells me to open my eyes on my next exhalation.

At once, a sense of peace blankets me. With a smile, I squeeze her hands. She nods, and we rise along with the others. Once again, I float through the hotel, smiling at those I meet.

Major Mum, Sergeant Shelley, and Lieutenant Lucie escort me to my suite. They encourage me to rest in bed even if I don't sleep. My body will relax naturally.

When I step inside the bedroom, I smile. They had the maids close the drapes, turn down the bed, dim the lights, and turn on Zen music with water sounds. I step out of my sandals and strip my maxi dress over my head. The soft sheets swaddle me. Moments later, I fall fast asleep.

THE SOUND of my name rouses me.

My eyes pop open to find my Mum sitting on the edge of the bed. She smiles with tears in her eyes. I sit up and throw my arms around her. We hold one another in silence. Emotions roll over us.

"Oh, Kat, honey. I'm so proud of you. My wee lass all grown up about to marry her love—" A sob cuts her words off, and she squeezes me tighter. She takes a breath and pulls back to stare into my eyes. "Your father would be so proud of you, too, Kat. Know he is with you. Always. Although Connor will walk you down the aisle, your *Da* will be right beside you, honey."

I nod vigorously as tears stream down my cheeks. The anger I had with my father over him dying so young and leaving us with only our Mum to raise us ebbs away. In my heart, I know he did his best and loved us dearly. I send a silent prayer of love to him. It's my wedding day. I will not hold on to any negativity. Only love and light surround us.

My Mum pats me on the back and rises.

"Time to get dressed, Kat, honey," she says with a smile. "Mr. Valentino wants to make any final adjustments before you walk down the aisle."

Before we leave my suite, I freshen up in the bathroom. I check my mobile for a text message from Harris but find none. Well wishes from colleagues not invited to the wedding make me smile. I follow my Mum to the suite beside the ballroom where the ceremony will take place.

One of the wedding planners guides us through the hotel where guests won't have the chance to cross my path.

In the suite, my wedding gown hangs in the middle of the room. My breath catches in my throat. I clutch my chest. Butterflies like those embroidered amongst the flowers on my gown and my cathedral veil flutter in my belly.

The white sweetheart neckline gown floats like their gossamer wings with its layers of sheer tulle. The veil hangs beside it. Monsieur Valentino commissioned a pair of Manolo Blahnik shoes to match my gown flawlessly. They sit below the gown while my Lola's Coterie white silk panty and pale blue silk garter belt rest on a table. The entire ensemble designed to awe my future husband.

Both the videographer and photographer who followed us throughout the day capture the moment. The glam squad fixes my hair and makeup. I smile at the atelier dresser assigned to help me and step behind the screen. I re-emerge like as my fantasy bride.

Now dressed in her Valentino mother-of-the-bride dress, my Mum's eyes widen. She dabs at them with a handkerchief as she approaches me.

"Honey… Extraordinary… Oh, Kat," she says softly.

I fan my face and glance up at the ceiling to stop the tears from falling. Then often a watery smile to Monsieur Valentino when he enters the suite. His words of praise thrill me. Me. Kat Roberts—the poor Scottish lass—now dressed in her wedding gown by a master about to marry a multibillionaire. Unbelievable.

Uncle Connor walks in as Monsieur Valentino leaves with the dresser and glam squad. He greets them, then stops speechless when his gaze reaches me. He shakes his head and smiles.

"Kat, lass… You are simply stunning. As gorgeous as my

Lucie on our wedding day. It is an honor to walk you down the aisle," he says, then holds out a navy blue bag to me. "From your betrothed."

I reach inside and remove a large square blue velvet jewelry case. The click of the sapphire cabochon closer reveals a suite of diamonds nestled on silk. My jaw drops.

"Here, I will help you," Uncle Connor says as he sets the bag and case on the table.

He places the bib necklace on me. It glitters from my neck to above the swell of my breasts. Each of the drop earrings slip into my ears. I hold my wrist out for him to close the bracelet around it. My Mum slips the brooch in my hair so it shows when I remove the veil. Last, I slip the ring on my right hand. My gaze goes from the priceless jewels to Uncle Connor.

"Exquisite," he states. At the knock on the door, he raises his arm. "Shall we?"

I nod, too overcome for words.

He cocks an eyebrow.

I bite back a giggle at his Alpha Dom reaction and verbalize my response. He leads me from the room and to the man I love with all my heart, body, and soul.

No more nerves. The only butterflies that swirl about remain on my wedding gown and veil.

Mrs. Harris Steele, here I come.

HARRIS

"No turning back now, Harris!"

"You sure you've given up your player's card? For good, bro?"

"Remember what you told me when before I married Lola?"

"Yeah… Exactly!"

"You know that's right, cuz!"

I roll my eyes at my brothers and cousins as they continue to rib me.

After I left My Kitty Kat sated and passed out from hours of toe-curling orgasms, I went to the suite Malcolm reserved for me.

My Kitty Kat is traditional and didn't want to see me but didn't want to put me out of our suite. I saved her the discomfort of asking me to leave and left of my own accord. Plus, I don't want to start our new life with any chance of bad luck. We've been through enough shit to last a lifetime. The rest of this one and forevermore, I want to spend happily with My Kitty Kat—the future Mrs. Harris Steele. Thank you very much.

I showered, then went to the gym to burn off nervous energy. Not that I'd tell these clowns…

They showed up as planned, and we got in a workout before my bachelor's brunch. No, I didn't opt for the whole get drunk at a strip club and fuck some broad. Not my style, nor my boys. Hard pass.

After the wedding rehearsal last night, we hung out at the Jackson Smoke&Scotch Sydney. Lachlan did a tasting while Laurent handed out a new cigar he created. We just talked shit as usual, enjoying each other's company for a few hours. Sure, some women ventured over. But we deftly avoided their advances. They got the message and moved on. With a warmth in my belly from the Scotch, I returned to my fiancée.

Until the sun rose, I ravaged her tight, curvy body. She'll wake up sore. Hopefully, she'll be able to walk down the aisle without leaning too heavily on Uncle Connor's arm. I chuckle at the thought even as my cock threatens to swell uncomfortably in my gym shorts. Calm down, big boy. Later.

"Oh, man, leave Harris alone. He was bound to fall, eventually."

Norman's words draw me from my musings. I smile and nod my thanks to the Champ. He claps me on the back as he heads to the weight rack.

"True, I'll give him that. Besides, it's always the most vehement ones who fall the hardest," Chase Wentworth—Lydie's love—says, then continues. "Besides, I have to give him some credit for having his wedding in my hometown."

Lachlan clears his throat. We turn to face him.

"Harris, now is a good time to remind you to treat Kat

with the utmost respect. She is a Jackson. Thus, my responsibility. Don't fuck with her or answer to me," he says.

The gym erupts.

Baz grabs Lachlan into a headlock.

Malcolm throws his water bottle at him.

Roger swipes his legs from beneath him. He and Baz fall on top of him.

Lucien and Laurent jump in. To save their brother or to help take him down, I don't know.

I just throw my head back and laugh.

Eventually, we finish our workout and head for the sauna, then shower. My stomach rumbles when we enter the restaurant. With all the energy I burned off fucking and lifting, I'm famished.

Several heads turn as we follow the hostess to our table. Guests offer their well wishes as we pass them. Others stop by the table. I thank them all.

After we order our food, I signal to the server. The manager returns with bags. He sets them on the floor beside me. I grin at my boys.

"Well, brothers, I want to thank you for your words of wisdom, support, and love. Without you, who knows? Maybe I'd still be shooting my load at LEVELS with some willing female," I say with a chuckle. The very idea turns me off.

"Here's a little something to remember this momentous occasion," I add as I hand a bag to each of them.

"Hot damn!"

"Shit, man, thanks!"

I sit back and fold my arms over my chest with a smirk as they open the wooden boxes.

Inside of each rests a Patek Phillipe 6301 Grand Complications watch. The platinum case with hand-stitched, shiny platinum gray alligator strap engraved with Kat's and my names and the date of our wedding. I choose the color combination to represent STEELE. They'll always remember this day when they put on the luxurious, complicated dress watch. As fine watch collectors, they'll appreciate the gesture.

For the rest of the meal, the married ones offer advice. I take mental notes. Their trials and mistakes will help me avoid similar pitfalls. Their successes will make me a rock-star to My Kitty Kat. Without a doubt, it's a win-win situation.

Laurent calls time on our bachelor's brunch. He reminds us it's time to rest up before my big moment. His tone brokers no argument. My best man takes his duties seriously.

We part as the elevator takes us to our floors. I walk into my suite and straight to the bedroom. The workouts and food knock me out. As I head to the bed, I notice a gift box in the middle of it. I grin in anticipation of something fantastic.

I plop down on the bed and tear into the white wrapping paper of the rectangular box. Beneath the tissue paper, my finger grazes a textured surface. I move the paper aside. A dove gray leather-bound album appears. I lift it out of the box and set it on my lap.

A note from My Kitty Kat catches my eye on the first page.

My Dear Love,

You bring me such joy. Each and every day, I give thanks for you being in my life. Often, I reflect on the time we have spent

*together. No matter what, I find the good in it all. I pray you
do, too.*

*This album holds memories we will cherish for years to come.
Some moments you may recognize, while others will surprise you.
You will never know when I capture a moment we share. It is just
the start of our life together. We have many more pages to fill.*

I love you.

*Your Kitty Kat and Siren forever,
Mrs. Harris Steele*

Tears blur my vision. And no, I'm not too manly to cry. Especially when I flip through the pages to find My Kitty Kat documented so many moments in our life together. From our first getaway to the Channel Islands to me asleep at LEVELS London and most recently building a fire in Aspen.

As I close the album with several empty pages for our future moments, my heart soars. I love this woman so much it frightens me. To give my heart to someone else was not on my mind. And here I am, a few hours away from spending the rest of my life with another.

A smile of pure happiness obliterates my tears.

"I love you, Mrs. Harris Steele!" I shout.

"TIME TO WAKE UP, SLEEPING BEAUTY!"

A nudge, and I jolt awake. Laurent—dressed in his bespoke Tom Ford tuxedo—stands beside the bed, grinning at me like the Cheshire Cat.

I sit up. Yup, time to do this, like Brutus!

In no time, I'm dressed in my custom tuxedo and groomed to perfection. Can't meet my beautiful bride looking like a schmo. I walk into the living room of my suite and find Laurent and a wedding planner waiting for me. I give a nod I'm ready, and we head to the ballroom.

We take the back route and avoid wedding guests. STEELE Sydney staff offer their congratulations as we pass, and I thank them heartily. By the time we reach the ballroom, I'm euphoric. Laurent and I enter from a side door straight to the altar.

I greet the officiant. Then my eyes scan the crowd. I nod at our guests and grin at my family. When the music from the quartet changes, I face the double doors of the main entry to the ballroom. They open and Vivian walks in.

She's absolutely stunning in her gown. Her smile lights the ballroom. If she's this happy, my bride must be ecstatic. I smile at Vivian when she stands across from Laurent and me. She beams.

Once again, the music played by the quartet changes, and all guests rise. My heart pounds in anticipation. I stare at the closed doors. They open, and it's as though Heaven sent an angel.

My Kitty Kat floats down the aisle on Uncle Connor's arm. She's beyond radiant, even through her sheer veil. The diamond suite glitters in the light, adding to her brilliance. The layered skirt of her wedding gown billows around her like a cloud. I stare at her in awe.

When Uncle Connor agrees to give this woman, I force myself not to grab her and run. Instead, I shake his hand and take hers in mine.

She beams up at me. Tears shine in her emerald green eyes. Intense love flows from her to hit me in the chest at full force. I rock on my feet, then stand firm.

As we listen to the officiant, we only have eyes for each other. Laurent has to nudge me to recite my vows. My Kitty Kat follows with her vows. Laurent opens the rectangular jewelry box, and My Kitty Kat gasps.

I lift the hand harness made of a chain of diamonds connected to her eternity band on her middle finger to a princess-shaped diamond that rests atop her hand connected to a diamond double bracelet. Her engagement ring sits on her ring finger. The harness is removable. So she can wear her band and ring together.

A murmur rises from the guests, impressed by the incredible jewels and their symbolism. Kat Roberts-cum-Jackson is now Katrina Steele. My wife. MINE!

Tears shine in her eyes as she places my classic platinum band on my left ring finger. She holds my gaze as she brings my hand to her mouth to kiss my ring. She whispers, I am all yours and you are all mine.

Hell to the yes! My cock jumps to attention.

The officiant pronounces us husband and wife.

With a smirk, I lift her veil and kiss Mrs. Harris Steele until she's breathless.

The guests stand and clap. Our family whoops.

Vivian places My Kitty Kat's bouquet in her hand and rearranges her veil and gown as we turn to face our jubilant guests. Their cheers follow us as I clasp her hand and walk with her by my side down the aisle. Our future as husband and wife begins. And may it never end!

As soon as we enter the suite beside the ballroom, I pull My Kitty Kat into my arms. One kiss of my new wife will not suffice. I draw her close to me, melding our bodies together, and cover her mouth with mine. She moans into the possessive kiss as she leans against me heavily.

The weight of her body reminds me she is mine to protect, provide for, cherish, and love forevermore.

Only the knock on the door makes us come up for air. My parents, Uncle Connor, Aunt Lucie, and Mum Allison with Henry rush inside. They embrace us before we take family photos. A photographer and videographer followed my boys and me around earlier, so we have but a few more images to do.

Then it's time for the reception. As we wait for the emcee to announce our arrival, I turn to my wife.

"Are you happy with everything so far, babe?" I ask, already knowing her answer since she hasn't stopped smiling or laughing.

She doesn't disappoint. With a giggle, she rises to her toes and presses her soft mouth to mine.

"Oh, so happy, husband of mine," she murmurs against my lips.

I pull her closer to me, making sure she feels the thick erection I've had from the moment we kissed at the altar. I do a grind against her belly.

She mewls and matches my fervor with her own.

The wedding planner coughs politely, and my bride and I part with a laugh as the doors open.

"Ladies and gentlemen, presenting Mr. and Mrs. Harris Steele!" The emcee's voice carries over the throng of voices.

We stride inside, arms held high, faces lit up with dazzling smiles to rival my wife's new jewels.

Our guests cheer.

We make our way to the dance floor for our first dance. The opening chords of "Truly Madly Deeply" play as I sweep my wife into my arms. Her eyes widen and she glances over her shoulder as Darren Hayes' voice blends with the music. She squeals when he steps onto the stage to serenade us. Then she throws her arms around my neck.

Our bodies rock to the romantic song as I murmur the words in her ear. She trembles and holds back her sobs as the words evoke a wellspring of emotions in her. I bury my face in her silky Titian hair and forget all around us except for the touching words of our anthem.

When it ends, we bow to Savage Garden and make our way to the head table. I help my wife into her chair and sit on mine. My thumb brushes over the diamonds on her hand harness and eternity band before I entwine our fingers. I rest our joined hands on my thigh and lean over to kiss my wife.

"I love you, Mrs. Harris Steele," I murmur as I nuzzle the delicate shell of her ear. A lust-filled smile spreads on my face when she trembles. "Never forget. You. Are. Mine."

She nods, then catches her faux pas.

"I love you, Mr. Harris Steele. We are one for all time," she whispers.

Our attention turns from each other to Mum Allison. She makes a heartfelt speech as the parent of the bride. Her references to Kat as a child and how proud her father would be of her make my wife sob softly.

I wrap my arm around her and murmur words of love to soothe her. She cuddles against me while she listens to the rest of her Mum's speech.

The emcee announces dinner.

My wife excuses herself and disappears with Vivian. While they're gone, I enjoy the first dish of our four-course meal. My mother comes over to check on me. Her face lights up, and I follow her gaze.

My wife returns as the redheaded Siren.

She changed from her ethereal wedding gown into a

long-sleeved reception dress with a plunging, wide v-neck and fitted bodice that skims her hips and thighs to flow to the floor. The vavavavoom silhouette has a touch of demure by way of tiny pearls forming flower shapes over the subtly sheer fabric. Her flaming red hair cascades down her back in soft waves. Matte red lipstick dominates her alabaster face.

My unsatisfied cock weeps.

Enthralled, I rise from my chair and make my way to her as she crosses the room like a goddess. Those on the dance floor part. Others seated stare. My Redheaded Siren's call enchants them all.

"Hello, Mr. Steele. Will you dance with me?" She purrs as her fingertips glide up the lapels of my tuxedo jacket. Her emerald eyes smolder from an internal fire.

"It would be my pleasure, Mrs. Steele," I respond, eyes locked on hers.

After our dance, we circulate amongst the guests. Up close, My Redheaded Siren charms them with her smile, gracious words, and affectionate touches. The man all but drop at her feet. The women wish to be her.

I want to fuck her. Now.

However, the wedding planner has other plans for us. It's time for toasts. One by one, our family and friends speak stories and offer their best to us. We laugh and tear up. Especially when my father gives a deeply felt speech in recognition of his last son moving forward to add to the next generation of Steeles.

I freeze.

Children?

Everyone wants children for us like yesterday.

Me?

I'm still ambivalent. At this time, at least.

A sneak peek at my wife lets me know she may have succumbed to the enchantment of the wee ones. Her emerald eyes shine. Undoubtedly visions of little Harrises and Kats play in her mind. She lifts her head to gaze at me. But my eyes slide away. She doesn't notice and kisses my cheek.

Damn.

However, I refuse to dwell on thoughts that dim our momentous day. We move on to through the reception activities.

It's Uncle Connor's time to glide my wife across the floor. My wife tosses a replica of her bouquet to the eager single women. The bachelors prove less inclined to catch her garter. I may be a caveman, but we keep the cake cutting civilized. I place a forkful in her mouth, and she does the same for me. With a wink, she reaches up and licks icing from the corner of my mouth.

I'd rather have her ambrosial cream coat my lips than the sour cream icing. My cock aches.

Once again, Vivian links arms with my wife, and they leave the reception. I watch after them and wonder what she'll reappear in this time. I don't have long to speculate.

In My Redheaded Siren walks. She shimmers in a mini dress made of crystal strands in varying lengths. They sway and catch the light with each step she takes. Her long, toned legs end in sky-high crystal embellished sandals. Now she collected her thick tresses atop her head in a sexy bun. Fresh, matte red lipstick completes her seductive look.

Hot. Damn.

With the way she oozes sex, I don't know if we'll make it to the New Year's Eve countdown. We may just ditch it and celebrate with our own fireworks. So powerful, they'll rival those above Sydney Harbour.

But I can't deny her the night of her dreams. Instead, I rise and lead her to the rooftop dance floor where Janet Jackson steps onto the stage and sings "Escapade." It's perfect for the honeymoon I have planned for my wife. I tell her it's a clue for what's coming, and she begs me to tell her more. But I smirk and spin her out with no response.

The original Ms. Jackson performs all the way up to the countdown. The servers circulate trays with flutes of Dom Pérignon amongst the guests—all have moved to the rooftop. With Sydney Harbour as her backdrop, Ms. Jackson leads us down from ten. At one, we yell Happy New Year!

The night sky explodes with an array of fireworks. The closest to the hotel displays *Congratulations Mr. and Mrs. Harris Steele!*

My wife throws her arms around my neck as she squeals in delight. I chuckle at her exuberance and squeeze her tight. Then I press my mouth close to her ear so she can hear me over the surrounding celebration.

"Time to consummate our union, Mrs. Harris Steele."

HARRIS

$\mathcal{W}$e take nearly an hour to extricate ourselves from the reception turned nightclub. Everyone wanted a chance to congratulate us. We couldn't possibly ignore them. So I consoled myself with the knowledge we have the rest of our lives together. A few minutes won't break us.

They give me blue balls though…

We sigh in relief when the elevator doors close and separate us from the excited partiers. Suddenly shy, my wife's gaze skitters from mine in the reflection on the metal doors. I turn to face her and cup her cheek.

"Alone at last, Mrs. Harris Steele," I murmur as my thumb brushes her lips. "Your Siren's call enthralled me from the moment you walked down the aisle like a sweet angel, to now you stand before me like a seductive goddess. I can barely contain myself."

My forehead drops to hers. The floral aroma of Champagne on her breath mingles with mine. My mouth lowers to capture hers. The tip of my tongue swipes across her lips to demand entry. On a sigh, she lets me in.

Our tongues caress. The delay in our carnal satisfaction urges us on. The gentle kiss bursts into an explosive ball of passion. Lips press harder. Teeth clash and nip. Tongues tangle. We groan hungrily.

The elevator doors ding open.

I grab my wife's hand and all but drag her from the car through the lobby and onto the elevator to reach our suite. We can't keep our hands off each other on the ride up. In the hallway, I scoop her up and rush toward the suite. She throws her head back and laughs throatily.

Inside, I don't hesitate and go straight to the bedroom. The romantic sight of Blue Rose petals, lit candles, and an ice bath of Dom Pérignon only serves to make us pause briefly. With a nod, I stand my wife on her feet beside the wall of windows. My thumb and forefinger lift her face up to align our eyes.

"First, I will claim you. Then, I will make love to you until the sun rises. By morning, there will be no mistaking you are Mrs. Harris Steele. You. Are. Mine. Do you understand?"

Her eyes widen, then half shutter with lust. The tip of her little pink tongue darts out to moisten her full lips.

"Yes, Mr. Steele," she responds huskily.

My cock throbs along my inner thigh painfully hard.

I spin her around to unzip her mini dress. It drops from the weight of the crystal strands to a puddle on the floor. I offer my hand. She slips hers into mine, and I hold her while she steps from the dress.

The skimpy silk of her G-string proves no match to the flick of my wrist. The fabric flutters atop the mini dress.

Bared to me in only her wedding jewelry and fuck-me

sandals, My Redheaded Siren's song increases to a scream. I answer her call with a hungry growl of my own.

She shudders. Her DDs jounce. The rosy pink tips darken to mauve as they pebble beneath my carnal stare.

I like my lips. My hands reach out to cup her voluptuous tits. Their heaviness increases by her arousal. I pinch both nipples and tug. A guttural groan responds to her sharp cry of pain. My head bows to lavish her delicious tits.

Licks, nips, and sucks cause My Redheaded Siren to fist my hair as she writhes. Her breath comes in pants. Warmth suffuses her alabaster skin from the tips of her tits to her hairline.

"Fuck me already, Harris..." she wails.

I chuckle wickedly against her damp skin, wet from my ministrations. My tongue traces her areola, then along the lower curve of her tit. I bend my knees to continue the scorching trail over the planes of her body. Her belly, the curve of her hip, the apex of her thighs.

She yanks my hair when the tip of my tongue laps at her seam coated with her ambrosial cream.

So much better than our wedding cake.

"*Bloody*... HELL!" She screams. "Don't stop... Oooh... Right... there!" She cries before an orgasm seizes her body. It convulses with erotic pleasure.

Like a starving alley cat, I lick her cream voraciously. She rides out her orgasm on my tongue. Her pussy walls clench. She breaks again when I force another orgasm from her molten core.

I need her soft and soaked. Ready for my claiming.

One hand bands around her thigh to lock her in place. The other hand reaches up to tweak her puckered nipples. They grow more taut. She hisses from the bite of pain. My thumb brushes them to ease the sting.

She rewards me with another gush of cream.

I lap it up then rise to my full height, kissing my way up her trembling body. My mouth slams over hers for a brutal kiss. She pulls away. I smack that ass and groan when it jiggles beneath my sizable palm. She rises to her toes with a yelp.

"Mine!" I growl as I nip her lower lip. "Take what I give you, Siren."

She mewls but doesn't move again.

I finish the kiss with another smack to her ass and lift her under her with ease. Automatically, she wraps her legs around my hips. Her ankles lock under my ass. Her back slams against the window and she shudders.

My mouth drops back to her tits for a quick suck. Her nipple pops from my mouth as I slide her higher. My cock stands tall between her lower belly and my eight-pack abs. Its bulbous tip—purple from denial—leaks pre-cum. The entire ten inches disappear inside of her tight, dripping pussy with one thrust.

She cries out in wild abandon as the brutal invasion triggers another toe-curling orgasm. Eyes squeezed shut, her head thrashes from side to side.

"Fuuuck! You like how my colossal cock claims every inch of *my* tight pussy. Every part of you is mine. Tell me you belong to me!"

I pummel her pussy while she screams my name. My relentless claiming drives her wild.

"Keep cumming on my cock, Siren," I growl as the first sign of my release tingles along my spine. Electricity zings down to my cum-filled balls. They draw up. "That's it, Siren. Give it to me, and I'll give it all to you!"

Her pussy clenches hard along my dick from root to tip.

I snarl from the carnal pain. No longer able to hold back,

I throw my head back and roar my release. A torrent of jizz shoots from my cock straight into her womb. Her pussy milks every drop.

Lights brighter than the fireworks that still illuminate the inky sky outside the window blind me. My knees buckle. I lower us to the floor, twisting around to sit with My Redheaded Siren on my lap. My semi-flaccid cock glistens with her cream as it lies against her hip.

"Bloody hell, Harris. You'll kill us before we're married for a day!" My wife says between pants. Her Scottish accent is thick.

I squeeze her outer hip, and she squirms. My mouth goes to her ear. She trembles from my hot breath.

"Oh, no, Mrs. Steele. Now that you are mine forevermore, I have so much more to do to you and with you before either of us leave this Earth," I croon.

She tilts her head to the side and peers up at me through the thick fringe of her golden-tipped eyelashes.

"Well, in that case, you did say you'd make love to me until the sun rises, Mr. Steele," my wife purrs.

I growl and hop to my feet with her cradled against my chest.

"Indeed, I did, Mrs. Steele. Indeed, I did," I rumble.

* * *

"WELL, good morning, Sunshine. I wonder what has you to vibrant..."

My wife stretches her arms towards the headboard. Like a cat, she arches her back and purrs. Emerald green eyes flutter open. Lust sparks in them as she spies me naked, toweling my hair dry from the shower. She licks her lips at the sight of my cock—though flaccid—still reaches my thigh. She mewls in appreciation.

"Well, good morning to you, Adonis," she replies, then tsks. "Started your day without me? Naughty husband."

I toss the towel over my shoulder into the en bathroom. Then, like a wolf with his prey in sight, I stalk my wife. Thigh muscles flex with each stride. My cock grows.

"Naughty husband, you say?" I growl.

She nods and throws the bedding off her glorious body. Thighs part in welcome. Pussy glistens. Her hips cradle mine as I lower myself over her body. I thread our fingers as my mouth claims hers. She moans.

I rock against her seam, self-lubricating with her cream. Fully erect, I fist the base and align the tip with her pussy.

Slow two inches in, one inch out, until I fully seat myself within her wet warmth. We groan in unison. I continue with the long, languorous strokes.

My wife tugs at my fingers, still entwined with hers above her head. Her eyes narrow in frustration at my slow pace.

"Fuck me, Harris!" She demands, then lifts her head and nips my bottom lip. "Don't tease me!"

Purposefully, I slip the shaft free. Only the mushroom tip remains embedded in her greedy little pussy. I hover until she brings her eyes back to mine. I smirk.

She growls as she throws her head back onto the pillow.

"*Bloody* hell, Harris Steele!" She snarls.

My Kitty Kat turns into a fierce tiger when not fed my cock.

I snap my hips and impale her on my entire length.

She yowls.

I plunder her pussy with relentless abandon. I grunt as her inner walls clamp down on my cock. The vise-like grip sucks my cock deeper into her spasming pussy as she cums for me. I drive her into the bed repeatedly.

"Oh. Oh. OH!" She screams with each thrust. Another orgasm rockets through her core, choking my dick. "Just… like… that—OH!"

"Who exactly is naughty, Mrs. Harris Steele?" I ask as her entire body vibrates. "Your husband who just fucked you mindless?"

Lost in a state of sheer euphoria brought on by multiple mind-blowing climaxes, she can't answer verbally. However, her core clenches once again on my cock.

I chuckle wickedly.

"Yeah, thought so, Mrs. Harris Steele," I answer for her smugly.

In one swift move, I flip her onto her hands and knees. I place a palm between her shoulder blades and press down. Lowered to the bed with her arms stretched out and her forehead kissing the sheet, I grip both hips and raise her ass to my crotch. A throaty growl rips from my mouth when I sink balls deep inside of her dripping, pliant pussy.

Booted from bliss as I breach her swollen folds, my wife keens. Her palms slap the mattress. Fingers shred the rumpled sheets.

"Do you feel every ridge, every vein, every Fucking. Inch. Of my cock?" I ask in her ear as I pummel her fluttering pussy.

"Y—Y—Yeah… Unnnhhh…" She responds.

I swivel my hips and lift her ass higher in the air. The change in angle and position satisfies both of us. My dick dives deeper. It strokes her G-spot while my heavy cum-filled balls slap her engorged clit. We groan. Harris for the win.

"Now, take what I give you, wife," I bark.

She mewls in submission.

With plundering thrusts, I chase my release. My cock swells achingly bigger. My balls draw up. Three senses fade, leaving me with only sight and touch. My long, thick shaft disappearing into her glistening pink pussy makes me harder. The sensation of her tight pussy engulfing my dick, then spasming around it as she climaxes again finishes me off.

A feral growl rips from my mouth as I throw my head back. Cum explodes from my cock. It overfills her pussy and drips between her spread thighs to the sheets. I continue to thrust until my balls empty.

I collapse atop her to feel my weight. My claim of her. Her sigh signals her acceptance.

"Now, we started our day together, Mrs. Harris Steele," I say hoarsely against the side of her neck.

* * *

"GOOD MORNING, Sunshine! Don't you look radiant!"

My wife blushes as she giggles at Haley's teasing. Our tendency to think alike or finish one another's sentences is eerie.

My twin goes on to rib me. I let her have her fun. She certainly took enough shit from me when she married Little Lord Fauntleroy.

We're seated at a table for the post-wedding day brunch. It's not with all four hundred of our guests. This is for about half of them. Close friends, prominent politicians, business tycoons, and celebrities mingle with our family.

With this being the last Steele wedding of our generation, my parents went all out with the guest list. As I said from the beginning, as long as My Kitty Kat was happy, she could do as she pleased.

I glance over at her and she does glow—pat on my back. She enjoys the attention of all gathered. Not egotistically. No. She's living her dream. And I'm here for it.

I catch Payton's eye.

With a smile, he raises his Mimosa in salute. He's come a long way from the surly tosser to the loving older brother he should have been. But hey, no judgement. He's fine as long as he doesn't upset my wife.

I acknowledge his gesture.

A gasp from my wife jerks my head in her direction. I relax when she shows me a photo of us kissing on the altar from some media website. I nod and kiss her temple as she scrolls through more images.

At a nearby table, Baz holds court. He and Lola sit with some of our business partners. Whatever the event, an opportunity to benefit STEELE International, Inc. takes precedence. As CEO, Baz balances business with pleasure easily. He's a boss and Lola flows amongst the conversations like a pro. They're the power couple of the Steeles.

Malcolm sits with the entertainment crowd—including the head of a major film studio and her husband and a music mogul with his chart-topping singer. He's in his element as he converses with the owner of a Las Vegas casino he wants to acquire. Starr—her Zen to his bad boy—acts as his counterpart and charms everyone at the table. They're the rockstar couple.

My gaze lands on a table on the other side of the ballroom. I smile at the sight of Michael using his hands to speak enthusiastically with someone in Roger's group. I recognize the editor of *Architectural Digest* and the owner of a major textile company. Leonie chats with the editor of

Vogue and Monsieur Valentino. Together, they straddle the worlds of design and fashion. They're the celebrity couple.

Then I spy where my twin and Lachlan—the Countess and the Earl of Aboyne—hold court. A prince and his American actress wife chat with a king and his queen of an African nation. Haley reigns supreme and serves as the perfect partner for Little Lord Fauntleroy. They're the noble couple.

My gaze shifts back to my wife.

And what couple are we?

I'd say we're the best!

I chuckle at my declaration. But it's absolutely true.

"What's so funny? Or are you giddy from being married to my fabulous best friend?"

Vivian's question draws me from my musings.

I glance at her and smile as I respond, "Most definitely."

"Good, because she's a keeper," Vivian says.

During the rest of brunch, my wife and I walk around the restaurant. We want to speak with as many guests as possible. It's major they flew from around the world to share in our nuptials over a span of four days. We provided all attendees with luxurious gift baskets and paid for their hotel stays and activities. But a personal touch proves we appreciate them.

It's time to leave for our honeymoon, so I tell My Kitty Kat we need to say goodbye to our family. She beams and wraps her hands around my upper arm. A kiss to my cheek and we make our way to their tables.

"Oh! Have fun!" Haley squeals as she hugs Kat, then me. "And don't worry. I have you covered at the offices. Focus on your new bride!"

As my siblings before me, my Kitty Kat and I will spend two months on our honeymoon. A nice long time to just, as

Haley says, focus on each other without distractions. Sure, I'll be available if it's an emergency. But my twin can handle anything and has the support of our brothers. No worries.

We save our parents for last.

A teary Mum Allison pulls Kat in for a tight embrace. She whispers something to her daughter that makes her smile. An equally tight embrace for me and the reminder to take care of her little lass. I promise.

"Congratulations again, son. You fill your mother and I with pride. You followed your heart, and your instinct served you well. Now, you have the responsibility of another, and in the future, your children. Always do well by them," my father says.

"Thank you, Dad. I will," I respond.

He turns to Kat, who gives my mother another hug. We switch.

"Oh, Harris, sweetheart! We're so happy for you and love you so much. Start your new life with Kat knowing you have so much more ahead of you as a couple. Enjoy your honeymoon!" My Mom says as tears shine in her brown eyes.

"I love you more, Mom. Thank you for an incredible wedding celebration," I respond.

I take my wife's hand and lead her from the restaurant to the start of our new life.

KAT

"*N*o. I still won't tell you our destination. Have patience, Mrs. Steele."

I purse my lips and narrow my eyes at my husband's chiding.

Despite my best efforts, he refuses to tell me the top-secret location of our honeymoon. I didn't even pack my luggage. He asked my sisters-in-law to shop, then pack for me in my new set of Bottega Veneta Intrecciato handcrafted luggage. And I just glimpsed the bags as the crew loaded them onto Harris' private jet.

I only know there's lots of Lola's Coterie lingerie and loungewear since Lola told me she'd gift my trousseau. I attempted to pry the honeymoon details out of them since they know the type of attire I'd need. But no. They wouldn't even give me a clue. Not one. Bah!

But if no knowledge of our honeymoon is the only stroppy situation of our wedding extravaganza, I'm thrilled. Just the thought of our momentous day—as Harris calls it—

makes my heart swell with love and puts a giant grin on my face. It was extraordinary!

I glance down at my left hand. Sunlight from the jet's window makes the crazy amount of diamonds sparkle. Whether it's my ginormous engagement ring or the dainty stones of my eternity band or the varying sizes of my hand harness, no one can mistake me for a single woman. More than likely Harris' reason!

Not to mention the extravagant suite of diamonds he gave to me. Then this morning, I awoke to find the Cartier Love bracelet on my right wrist. More diamonds paved in platinum adorned my body. It's as though I won the jewelry lottery!

My Valentino gowns awed everyone. I received so many compliments. The editor of *Vogue* did a cover feature for their upcoming wedding issue. I was so nervous about the interview and the video. Harris was unfazed. Accustomed to the spotlight, he was the consummate pro.

The next morning, Viv and Charlotte showed me websites from around the world. Major media outlets to social media to blogs. Photographs and even some video footage from guests' mobiles—even though we asked them for privacy.

Leonie gave a Gallic shrug and said it's expected since people want to know about our lives. Live the fantasy and all. Said so nonchalantly by someone who's had cameras in her face since she was a teenager. Another pro—or megamodel.

The coverage reminded me of the socialites I admired. Who would have thought I'd join their ranks? Our wedding was even more fabulous than many I recall. Not that I'm being obnoxious!

Then there's getting used to being addressed as Mrs. Steele.

When the hostess at brunch greeted me as such, I almost didn't respond. It's usually Mum Shelley or one of my sisters-in-law who answers automatically. Starr giggled when I told her. She said it'll come naturally quickly. She added the special treatment we received as their girlfriends will triple with marriage.

So far, Starr isn't exaggerating.

Most notably from the flight crew. Oh, they were polite pre-wedding. But today, they all but fell over themselves for me. All immediately greeting me as Mrs. Steele. Asking if I preferred the window shades up or down. They checked the temperature was fine. Normally, questions posed to Harris they asked of me. Wow. Just wow.

Although one of the flight attendants—who was luke-warm towards me previously—has a less than cheerful face. More of a pinched, I-sucked-a-lemon face.

Now that we're airborne, the other flight attendant asks if I care for water or Dom Pérignon Champagne. I smile warmly and accept the Champagne. Then she asks Harris, who agrees. Subtle differences. But difference none the less. Meanwhile, Ms. Lemonhead prepares a snack in the galley.

I'll take all of it as Mrs. Harris Steele!

My husband shifts in his chair and raises his Waterford Crystal flute.

"You are neither a Roberts nor a Jackson. You are a Steele. Katrina Steele. My wife. Mine to protect, provide for, cherish, and love forevermore," he proclaims.

Tears of joy fill my eyes. His words, so sweet, yet so possessive, make my curiosity over our honeymoon insignificant. We matter. Nothing else. Period.

Hours later, we disembark the private jet for a helicopter. I guess the mode of transportation by the sound of rotors since my husband placed a red silk blindfold over my eyes. Of course.

The short flight ends with my husband removing the blindfold. I blink at the sudden brightness. Once my vision clears, he points out the window.

I peek around him and my breath catches.

Ahead of us floats a five-hundred-foot megayacht in sparkling azure waters. Beyond it, the water crests on golden sandy beaches of a large tropical island. As we circle around the megayacht, the glossy, jet black, sleek hull gleam in the sunlight. Four white tiers with walls of windows sit on the topmost tier. An impressive row of three-deck-tall windows command the megayacht's center. Cutouts on both sides provide several spots to soak up the sun. Bold white letters emblazon the name *Temptation* on its rear. Yeah, well, I can see why.

Moments later, the helicopter descends on a circular pad at the rear of the third deck. My husband helps me to the deck. He pauses and stretches his hands out wide.

"Our wedding song inspired our honeymoon theme to stand on a mountain, bathe in the sea, and lay like this forever with you. Prepare to enjoy two months cruising the South China Sea, Celebes Sea, and Sulu Sea. Behind us is the Malaysian island of Borneo. Sabah is our first destination to visit its highest peak—Mount Kinabalu. Let us begin with a sunset dinner, Mrs. Steele."

My husband grins like the Cheshire Cat while my eyes widen, and my mouth gapes as he speaks. He scoops me up in a bridal carry.

I wrap my arms around his neck and pepper his face with kisses.

"You always amaze me, Mr. Steele! But you've outdone

yourself this time. Unbelievable!" I squeal as he strides along the deck.

We pass the crew dressed in immaculate white formal uniforms lined up to greet us. One holds a tray with Champagne. I smile and snag two crystal flutes.

"We'll have time for an official tour of *Temptation* tomorrow. In brief, it belongs to Haley, has ten oversized staterooms, sun decks, pool, spa, salons, game room, and more. Totally tricked out for pleasure. All kinds of pleasure," my husband says as he waggles his eyebrows.

I giggle at his innuendo.

He steps onto an elevator. I hold a flute to his lips. He finishes it off in one gulp.

"Caveman!" I tease, before I take a sip of mine.

He nuzzles my neck and murmurs, "And you love every bit of me."

"Without a doubt, oh caveman of mine," I respond as the elevator doors dings open.

My husband carries me down the modern decorated hallway and stops at the last stateroom towards the bow. I open the door and gasp.

Across from the door, floor-to-ceiling windows in a horseshoe shape account for three walls of the stateroom. Based on an open-concept design, a bedroom area marked by a thick white carpet where a king-size platform bed dressed in opulent white with black piping linens and loads of pillows dominates the space close to the windows facing the front of the megayacht. A platinum vase of Blue Roses. The rest of the space has a sitting area in the middle on more carpet and a glass-enclosed white marble bathroom with a dressing room. Various types of lighting placed throughout. Ritzy, to say the least.

"This is my stateroom. It's a mini version of Haley and

Lach's full floor suite upstairs. As her favorite brother, I get the best digs. I've spent many a great night in this bed," my husband says as he toes off his Berluti sneakers.

I stiffen in his arms.

Who did he fuck in this bed? Why would he tell me about his sexcapades?

While my mind reels from jealousy, a nudge to the side of my neck refocuses my attention. I sigh, disheartened.

"Mrs. Steele... What's going on in that pretty head of yours? Hmmm?" He murmurs against my skin.

Get it together, Kat Jack—Steele! I tell myself.

"Nothing," I respond aloud. I squirm in his arms to get down. Without looking at him, I tell him I need to use the bathroom.

He hesitates and dips his head to see my face. But I let the curtain of my hair block his view. He sets me on my feet. With bent knees, he lowers to my eye level. His thumb and forefinger grasp my chin to force my gaze on him.

"We vowed honesty, Kat," he says, no sign of the jokester in his dove gray eyes. "Now, answer truthfully."

My eyes skitter away. But he's not having it. He shifts my chin until my eyes meet his serious gaze. I swallow to moisten my dry throat. Honesty. Fine.

"I hate to sound like a jealous shrew. But I do not want to know about your past lovers. Especially on the second day of our marriage. And I do not want to sleep in a bed where you fucked someone other than me and rave about it during our honeymoon."

My voice catches on the last word. Embarrassed by my lack of self-esteem, I jerk my heated face from his hold.

Surprised, he releases me.

I rush towards the bathroom. Head bowed and tears

blurring my vision, I make my escape. Only to squeal when my feet lift from the floor.

"No running from me… from us, Kat! You can't say shit like that and run off. Talk to me, woman!" Harris growls as his front crashes into my back. His arms band around my hips and he carries me to the bed. Where he sits and positions me on his lap.

"You know, now I get why Doms spank their wayward subs," he continues with a shake of his head.

I squirm, not wanting to be on his lap and definitely not on the fuck bed.

Suddenly, I'm hoisted into the air. A succession of three resounding smacks lands on my upturned ass. The pain reverberates through my entire being as it jiggles beneath Harris' sizable palm. I yowl as much in frustration as in pain.

"I've never fucked a woman in this bed. Nor would I discuss the sexual activities of my past with you," he says. Then he adds with a snarl, "And unless you want me to go on a hunting spree, do not tell me a damn thing about your past."

The ferocity of his words gives me pause. Perhaps I'm overreacting. But I have one question.

"What about your flight attendant?"

Harris' face scrunches in confusion.

"Which one, and what about her?"

I clear my throat before I bring my gaze to meet his stormy gray eyes.

"The blonde. Have you had sex with her?"

Harris' head snaps back and his eyes bulge, then narrow.

"What the everlasting fuck, Kat?! No! I never had sex with her or any other STEELE employee. Hell, you're the first and only Jackson Corporation employee I've said more than hello to as I passed them by. Where do you get that ludicrous idea?"

Chagrined, my eyes dart away. But again, Harris won't tolerate my avoidance.

"Eyes on me, Kat," he growls.

I return my gaze to him. Then shrug before I respond.

"She was always a bit standoffish towards me. Never rude, just cool. When we boarded your jet, she greeted me as Mrs. Steele, like the others. But she wore a sour expression. I assumed she was mad I went from girlfriend to wife, and she lost her chance."

Gobsmacked, he scans my face for a moment.

"You mean to tell me you were uncomfortable because of my employee in my presence and didn't tell me?" He asks incredulously.

I nod, and his nostrils flare. He answers in a none-too-pleased tone of voice.

"In the future, tell me any issue that concerns you when it happens, not months later. I'll have her spoken to by Human Resources and placed as a crew member for the corporate fleet immediately. They will monitor her behavior."

Now, my eyes widen. Even though I like his solution, I didn't want to cause trouble for her. I tell him so, but he reassures me it won't impact her career and my happiness tops all. I sigh in relief and apologize for ruining the start of our honeymoon with nonsense.

"Oh, you will make it up to me, Mrs. Steele. Every single day," my husband rumbles deep in his chest. "Starting. Now."

I squeal when he flips me over his muscular thighs. My hands fling out to brush the white carpet with my fingertips. Behind me, my legs flail. Cool air kisses my ass exposed with two flicks of my husband's wrist—one to raise my maxi dress and the other to shred my G-string.

Without hesitation, he peppers my bare ass with a round of smacks. He never hits the same spot in a row. When my ass burns from the sting, his palm connects with the delicate area of my sits bones.

I buck. My hands fly behind me to block the painful blows. Then scream in frustration when he grips my wrists in one hand at my lower back. A second later, air leaves my lungs in a burst. Pain radiates to pleasure as my mind, then body reacts to three smacks to my pussy lips and clit. My hips jerk away even as my thighs spread.

My husband chuckles wickedly.

"You like a good spanking, naughty lass. Your cream drips from your pussy. It soaks my joggers and sticks to my fingers."

His hand leaves my throbbing pussy and swollen clit. Slurping and a groan fill my ears. The cheeks on my face heat and turn as crimson as I imagine my ass.

"Ambrosia, Siren," he sighs, enraptured.

My pussy clenches as it begs for his giant cock, now fully erect against my hip. I wiggle for attention. Even the burn of his palm would trigger the orgasm hovering on the edges.

"Hungry for satisfaction, Siren?" He asks as he leans over to press his lips against my ear. The warmth of his breath makes me shiver. "I'll take your response as a yes."

I explode with a primal scream when his thick fingers plunge into my pussy unexpectedly. My toes curl as my legs jerk. I writhe on his lap, shamelessly riding out the vestiges of an epic climax. Before my body can dwell in the aftermath, I'm flipped up.

My jellied thighs straddle his muscular ones. He grips

my hips, then slams me down onto his turgid dick. His hips ratchet up to slam his velvet-covered steel into me.

I throw my head back and keen.

"So fucking snug... So soaking wet... This cock is yours, Mrs. Steele... Only. You..."

Harris' declaration—punctuated by powerful thrusts—trigger another orgasm. He doesn't stop until I beg him for no more. Then he whips us around.

My back slams onto the mattress. Hands fly to his forearms. He drags me up his body. The backs of my thighs press against his chest. Still carnally connected, he leans down. Unable to move with my legs trapped between us, Harris drills me into the bed.

"Do... You... Understand..."

I nod, delirious from the onslaught of carnal pleasure.

He lets my wordless answer go unchecked as he chases his release.

We rock more powerfully than the waves against the megayacht. I swear the bed shifts on the plush carpet. Our combined grunts and strangled cries bounce off the wall of windows.

Head thrown back, my husband's roar punches the air. His massive cock swells impossibly larger and fills my pussy with his cum. He growls when my inner walls clamp on his dick to milk him dry.

"FUUUCK, KAT!!!" He bellows as I take him deeper into core.

With a satisfied groan, he collapses to his side and pulls me with him. Our sweaty bodies slide against each other as I drop against his heaving chest. I place a kiss over his pounding heart.

"Only you and only me, Mr. Steele," I whisper.

HARRIS

"Our results for the first quarter please me. Each division and subsidiary performed at or above expectations. Keep this pace up for the rest of the year and we'll blow through projections. Well done!"

Baz claps as his platinum gray gaze meets our varying shades.

We're in his conference room for our quarterly team meeting. Malcolm, Starr, and I sit around the table with him. Roger, Leonie, and Haley join us via video conference on the giant center screen. Each of us gave our reports, followed by questions. Haley gave ours since I missed the first two months of the year on my honeymoon.

I grin as memories of adventurous days hiking, surfing, and lovemaking followed by incredible nights of delicious dinners, gorgeous sunsets, and lovemaking. Oh, did I mention passionate lovemaking? Uh, yeah, baby!

After the initial hiccup and I settled my wayward wife down, we had a perfect time. So many moments captured on camera—still and video. My favorites of us on the mountain peaks with any of the seas below. While my wife slept in *our* bed, I took photos of her beautiful face—and that hot as fuck body when the sheets didn't cover her tits or legs.

Most importantly, she loved every minute of it. When we returned, she went to dinner with her sisters to tell them all about it. I'm sure they compared notes. And without a doubt, our honeymoon was the best!

Now that we've been home for a month, the honeymoon seems so far gone. Last night we watched our wedding video while we ate dinner from Wayan—the Malaysian restaurant in Nolita. Our emotions ran high again, and we ended up making love on the sofa.

The only downside is My Kitty Kat awoke puking her brains out. One minute I had her curled in front of me and the next she ran to the en suite bathroom. I raced after her and held her hair back while her head hovered over the toilet bowl. My poor baby came up paler than usual. Emerald green eyes dim.

I only left her when she promised she'd have our family doctor come over if she wasn't better by noon. It must have been the Lobster Noodles since I ate the Crescent Duck and didn't get sick. Then again, I have a cast-iron stomach as my Mom says.

While the meeting wraps up, I check my mobile. No text message or voicemail.

"What's got you frowning?"

I glance up to find my twin leaning over to see the screen of my mobile. Nosy bird.

"Kat was sick this morning after we ate Malaysian food last night. I want to see if she went to the doctor or—"

My mobile vibrates—I had the ringer off for the meeting—and cuts off my answer. I smile when My Kitty Kat's photo pops up.

"Hey, bab—"

Muffled sobs carry over the line.

I jump to my feet. Crazy thoughts of her being kidnapped again or of her hurt somewhere fill my head. The chair rolls back so hard, it hits the console against the wall.

All heads turn to me.

"Kat! What's wrong?!" I yell in a complete panic as I stride to the double doors of the conference room. I put her on speaker while I pull up the tracking device app.

She mumbles something indecipherable.

She's not at home, and I don't recognize the address. Where the hell is she?!

I ask just that as my pace increases.

"I'm pregnant!"

The mobile falls from my hand.

"I'm so s—s—sorry!" Kat's wail continues from the floor. "It's been s—s—so bus—s—y. I forgot my shot—"

Haley grabs my mobile while I stand frozen. She shoves it in my face and hisses my name at me with a glare. She mouths, *don't you dare upset her further!*

Kat's still babbling as I take the call off speaker and raise the mobile to my ear.

My head spins. But Haley is right.

"K—" I start, then clear my dry throat. "Kat, don't cry. Are you at the doctor's office now? I'll come to you."

She hiccups and thanks someone, then blows her nose.

Oh, great. They're going to think I'm an ogre making my pregnant wife cry. Scared I'll be pissed.

Although technically… Well, pissed isn't quite the right word. It's more disappointed… shocked… upset? Or plain old, fucked. No pun intended.

"Y—yes. The address—"

"I have it on the app. I'm on my way now," I interject, then end the call.

My shoulders slump. A sudden pain shoots behind my left eye like someone jabbed me with an ice pick. I scrub my hand over my face.

"Damn, bro! Get a fucking grip! Be a man!"

Roger's blunt chastisement breaks through my pity party.

He, too, is right.

Gah!

"Listen, Harris, Kat is upset enough. Obviously, you expressed not wanting children—I guess for now. But the situation has arisen. On your way to get her, think of what you will say and how you will behave. The last thing you want is a fight over children with your pregnant wife," Baz says as both brother and a father.

"Exactly! You do not know what it's like to be pregnant. Do not make her feel worse than morning sickness!" Haley says heatedly.

Leonie and Starr agree wholeheartedly with my twin. The girls band together. A reminder not to get on their collective bad side.

Malcolm strides toward me.

"I'll walk you to the elevator," he says as he opens the conference room doors.

I nod mutely.

The others stream out behind us. I can feel Haley's glare on my back.

"I can understand your point of view. When Starr told me she was pregnant, I wasn't in the right place to show joy. And I almost fucked up our relationship, letting my ego get in the way," Malcolm starts, then glances at me. "Things have a way of happening when they should and being the appropriate outcome despite what we think. A lesson I learned from My Angel. Heed her words of wisdom and learn from my mistake."

We reach the private elevator for our family's residences that leads from them to the STEELE International, Inc. offices and the lobby of The STEELE Tower. Malcolm presses the call button and puts his hands in his suit trouser pockets.

I look at my older brother. He works hard, plays harder, and loves the hardest. I recall the stress between him and Starr. He pretended it didn't impact him. But he hurt badly. Now they're happy as all fuck with two sets of adorable twins.

He's right, too. I appreciate my siblings' concern and input.

The elevator doors open. I step inside, turning to face Malcolm before they close.

"It all works out, Harris," he says, then continues with a nod. "Make sure you don't lose her before your great adventure gains traction."

I return his nod as the doors shut.

I pull out my mobile to send a text message to my driver for him to bring my Black Badge Rolls-Royce Cullinan around the front. He replies Roger already contacted him. I smile as I put my mobile in my pocket. Roger *The Responsible*.

The ride across town takes some time with Manhattan's never-ending gridlock of traffic. Enough for me to come out of shock. The fog lifts. I consider my family's words of advice. Sure, they're right. But I'm not ready for children yet. And I've said it thousands of times—to them and to Kat, most importantly.

Does it make me a monster? Selfish?

Some may say most definitely.

Others may understand.

But here we are at this moment I wasn't expecting for at least three or four years. I wanted time to spend with Kat. Travel every chance we get. Go to LEVELS clubs. Just be us. Not happening now.

Damn.

Kat seems pretty noncommittal one way or the other. At only twenty-eight, she's still young. However, she enjoys my —well, now, our—nieces and nephews. Giving my siblings date nights as sitters. No need for the many nannies. Uncle Harris and Aunt Kat step in happily.

But one of our own. So soon? How happy will we be then?

The chaos in my mind doesn't stop even when Alonso stops the SUV in front of the address on my app. I follow the tracker up the steps of an impressive townhouse, then through the front door. A second door leads to the foyer where a receptionist sits behind an ornate wooden desk.

"Good afternoon. How may I help you?" She asks.

I clear my suddenly parched throat and reply, "Yes, my wife Mrs. Harris Steele is here. Kindly take me to her."

As I follow the receptionist, we pass the waiting room. A man with an affectionate smile has his hand on the significant baby bump of the woman he sits beside. She beams at him. He glances at me and gives a nod of one father-to-be to another. I blink.

The walls display multiple photos of newborn babies. Some posed on photography sets as pumpkins and such. Others asleep or awake in their cribs or close ups in their parents' arms—parents like the couple in the waiting room. All oh so sweet.

The receptionist knocks on a door, then gestures for me to enter after the doctor acknowledges her knock.

I scan the room for Kat. She sits on the examination table in a gown. Her eyes seek mine. Unable to determine my frame of mind from my blank expression, her chin wobbles. She averts her gaze and pulls the open-front gown closer around her body in a protective motion.

The doctor must sense the tension in the room and addresses me.

"Mr. Steele, I am Dr. Oscar Rice and Lola's OB-GYN. Your family doctor suggested your wife see me. Obviously, food poisoning does not ail her. She is fourteen weeks pregnant based on my calculations. She wanted to wait for you before we proceed with the ultrasound. Would you care for a moment alone before we begin?"

Damn. So this is happening.

I shake my head mutely and approach the examination table when he waves me over. I stand beside Kat.

Without looking at me, she lowers her back to the table.

Dr. Rice prepares to take the scan and places jelly on Kat's belly. A belly I now notice isn't as flat as normal. Come to think of it, her tits seem fuller. I thought it was all the good food we dine on each night. Duh.

He fiddles with the dials on the machine, then slides the wand through the jelly. Pulsating sounds fill the room.

My gaze shifts from Kat's belly to the monitor. The screen shows what I presume is the inside of her womb. A womb filled with a baby. My baby. Holy shit.

Dr. Rice clicks the machine as he peers at the screen. He shakes his head and chuckles. He shifts on the stool to face both of us.

"Your family is very fertile, Mr. Steele. I've never seen so many children per couple in quite some time. Most lean towards one, perhaps two..."

He drones on. But I tune him out. Mesmerized by the sudden appearance of a tiny face with a clenched fist to its mouth followed by a tiny foot that's in an impossible position. The image changes and another face without a fist pops on screen.

No damn way—

"Congratulations, you're having twins!"

"Are you all right?"

My eyes open to find Dr. Rice's concerned face hovering above me. I look beyond him to Kat sitting on the edge of the exam table. Emerald eyes wide and the corner of her bottom lip tucked between her teeth. Worry etched on her face.

I sit up and winch.

"You landed pretty darn hard on your rear when you fainted," Dr. Rice says. "Do you feel anything besides discomfort?"

Fainted?

Well, damn.

I shake my head and get to my feet. Other than a sore ass —and ego—I'm fine.

Actually, more than fine. The fall must have knocked sense into me.

I let out a whoop and wrap my arms around my wife. The soon-to-be mother of my children. Twins, to be exact.

Hot damn!

My wife trembles in my arms. Her soft sobs stab my heart. I croon words of love for her and the two gifts she's given to me. I tsk her apologies and apologize to her. She covers my mouth with her finger and tells me she understands. I respond with a kiss to her finger, and she smiles. In fact, she glows with pure happiness.

After our lovefest, Dr. Rice prints images of our twins. He gives us the option to learn about their sex in four weeks. I turn to Kat in question, and she nods eagerly. He leaves us with a reminder to book her monthly, then biweekly prenatal appointments and to call with any questions. He already greenlit sex. So I'm good. With all the pregnancies and subsequent births I've sat in hospital for, I could do his job!

Once Dr. Rice leaves, my wife calls my name softly to get my attention. I return to her side from where I walked him to the door. She fidgets with the gown. I take her hands in mine. She peeks up at me. I smile.

"Are you happy truly, Harris? I don't want you to pretend. A vow of honesty, remember?" She says as her eyes search my face for any sign of falsehood.

I bring her hands to my mouth and kiss each piece of her wedding jewelry, ending with the eternity band.

"It disappointed me when you told me," I start and hold her hands tighter when she pulls away. "But seeing you so radiant and our twins on the monitor made me realize I was a fool. How could I not be happy? A beautiful wife who loves me. And a baby—well, babies—of our own. I'm ridiculously happy. Thank you, Mrs. Steele."

She sighs in relief and sags against me.

I brush my lips against the top of her head as I slip her into my embrace and rock. I give a silent prayer of thanks for not losing my wife. Our adventure continues unfazed, just with the addition of two bundles to be.

Well, damn. Harris Steele playboy turned husband soon father. Talk about an adventure…

HARRIS

"Don't worry, babe. There was nothing wrong the last time. Some babies hide their stuff. Guess they're not exhibitionists, you know?"

My Hot Mama giggles at my attempt to ease her concern. We're waiting in the examination room at Dr. Rice's office for the gender reveal. The first scan we tried at eighteen weeks didn't go as planned. He assured her all was well with our Wee Twins.

Now, I rub her babies bump and kiss her soft lips. A knock on the door makes us turn. Dr. Rice enters and sets up the ultrasound as he asks My Hot Mama how she feels. She knows the drill and lies back on the examination table, gown loose, as she answers his questions.

I squeeze her hand as her anxious eyes stare at the monitor. The strong pulsating sound of their heartbeats fill the room. A leg appears on the screen, then an arm, again not in the position to belong to one baby. Out Wee Twins float about with limbs askew. Hopefully this time, they shifted for us to see a clear view.

"Here we go!" Dr. Rice says as he comes across a little tummy. He adjusts the wand on My Hot Mama's belly, then points at the screen. "There! This one is a boy!"

My heart skips a beat. A boy? A little Harris for the win!

I cup My Hot Mama's face. Tears glisten in her emerald orbs as she smiles up at me. I press my forehead to hers and thank her for my son.

"Hold on, now. We have eyes on baby number two," Dr. Rice says.

Our eyes fly to the monitor. Will it be another boy for identical twins or fraternal like Haley and me? The answer presents itself…

"A girl!" My Hot Mama exclaims as her finger points to our second twin front and center of the monitor. "Oh, Harris! Like you and Haley!"

"A Dynamic Duo 2.0!" I say with a goofy grin on my face. "Mrs. Steele, thank you for our gifts."

She shakes her head and corrects me, "Thank you, too, *Da*! Without your… ah, input… we wouldn't be here."

And *Da* it is!

After Dr. Rice leaves, I help My Hot Mama from the exam table. In anticipation of our gender reveal dinner with our family, she chose a white, one-shoulder dress ruched to cling to her curves and babies bump. White sky-high mules make her toned legs go on for miles. With her Titian hair in a high ponytail and minimal makeup, her gorgeous face glows. Did I say Hot Mama or what?

She must sense my sudden interest and winks at me over her shoulder as she saunters towards the exam room door.

"I see your bulge growing, Mr. Steele. And here I thought I was the only horny one," she says with a smirk. "Let's get going DILF. Everyone waits for us."

She leads, and I follow, happy for the view of her round

ass pushed up in those fuck-me heels. If I can't get some of her lovin' now, I can at least fantasize…

"Bro, don't leave us hanging!"

"Out with it, guys!"

"Oh, honey, do tell!"

My Hot Mama stands radiant at the table beside me. Her eyes sweep the room to take in some of our family seated with us and others on the giant screen Lucien put in the private room of his restaurant for the momentous occasion.

I shift my gaze from my mesmerizing wife to the others gathered around us. The expectant faces of my parents, Baz, Lola, Malcolm, Starr, Roger, and Leonie turn to us at the table. A glance at the giant screen shows similar expressions for Lachlan, Haley, Uncle Connor, Aunt Lucie, Mum Allison, Henry, and Kat's siblings.

A tug to my hand draws my attention back to My Hot Mama. She beams up at me.

"You tell them, *Da.*"

I shake my head and bring her hand to my lips. I brush mine against her eternity band.

"We tell everyone together, Mummy," I respond. "Three. Two. One. A boy and a girl!"

The room goes silent, then into an uproar as questions and cheers erupt.

We decided not to tell them about the Wee Twins, only we're pregnant. Now to spring on them twins and a boy and a girl… Well, they lose their shit.

"OMG! Just like us and Elio and Selina!" Haley exclaims as she claps her hands, bouncing on the sofa next to Lachlan, who grins. "You brought it, twin! Oh, yeah!"

"Oh, I'm sure Dr. Rice had something to say. He cracks me up!" Lola says as she hugs me. "Congratulation, brother!"

Leonie wraps her arms around My Hot Mama and says, "Well, I better get my sketch pad ready. We have nurseries to design and reconfigure! Let's start tomorrow before Roger and I return to Paris. So much fun!"

My father claps me on the back with a smile.

"Congratulations, son! You've had plenty of experience with your nieces and nephews. Now the actual work begins," he says with a chuckle.

My mother laughs and adds, "No returning them to their parents. *You* are the parents!"

After more words of wisdom, we settle at the table. The servers pour Champagne while one brings a glass of iced lemon ginger tea for the Mom-to-be. Toasts ring throughout the room from the table and the giant screen.

We don't order since Lucien had the chef prepare all My Hot Mama's favorite dishes. The others not present eat light snacks since it's after eleven in Scotland. They stay on the video conference for another thirty minutes. Before she signs off, Mum Allison tells us she'll check with her manager at STEELE Glasgow for some time off to visit us, perhaps in a month or so.

My wife's shoulders slump.

I kiss her cheek and whisper, "I got you, babe."

"Mum Allison, no need to worry about coming here. We're flying to Glasgow tomorrow. We can't only have an announcement for you and not hug your daughter in person!" I add with a grin.

They gasp, then start to talk in unison.

I hold up my hand to stop them and confirm the details of the surprise visit. I also had a realtor Lachlan suggested schedule appointments for penthouse flats. Being Glasgow is my wife's hometown, we'll need a place of our own when we travel there, especially with the Wee Twins. But I'll save that surprise for our arrival.

My wife throws her arms around my neck and kisses my face again and again. In between, she tells me she loves me and I'm the absolute best husband a lass could ever want.

Later at home, I prove I'm the only absolute best husband she'll ever have, period. Again and again.

* * *

"THIS IS a fantastic choice for your Glasgow residence. A duplex penthouse offers plenty of space for a growing family."

My Kitty Kat giggles at Uncle Connor's remarks. I shake my head with a chuckle. She hasn't even given birth before he's expanding our little family.

We flew to Glasgow yesterday morning and met with the realtor after we checked in at STEELE Glasgow. She kept this property for last, knowing it would be the one for us.

The West End duplex penthouse has six bedrooms with en suite bathrooms, lounges, an office, chef's kitchen, and more. We'll make it our own with the help of Michael. Already he makes suggestions. It would be the perfect project for him to prove himself.

"The perfect location for you! I know people who live in the area. I'll make the introductions. They'll make excellent connections," Aunt Lucie—ever the Marchioness of Huntly —says.

Mum Lucie turns from the windows overlooking a park and smiles.

738

"How lovely it'll be to walk through the park with the Wee Twins. It's always best for babes to have fresh air. It makes them sleep through the night," she says with a nod of her head.

My Hot Mama hugs her Mum. My wife is so excited about our new residence. She asked Leonie to fly over from Paris to review options for the nursery next week while we're still in Glasgow. She and Haley will be Kat's on-the-ground helpers once we're in New York City.

"It's good to see my sister so happy. She deserves to have the best."

I glance over at Payton—his eyes on his sisters and mother across the lounge. He continues to watch them as he goes on.

"I've been a prat to Kat for so long, I doubt she'll give me much of a chance to reconcile truly. But they say a mother is more willing to forgive. So maybe she'll forgive me. I'd like to be a part of the Wee Twins' lives."

He brings his gaze to mine.

"That is, if you will allow me the chance," he finishes.

I scan his face for any sign of deceit and find none. From what my wife tells me about her relationship with Payton and his with the rest of their family, my first inclination is a definite no. But then everyone deserves a second chance. Had I not given one to Kat, we wouldn't be married with the Wee Twins on the way.

"Kat shared with me her experiences with you and how you treated your family. I'm not impressed and find it fucked up, especially since you were the eldest after your father passed away," I respond, then flick my gaze from him to my wife.

She wants a fresh start. If she didn't want Payton in her

life, she wouldn't have invited him to spend time with us. So, I'll allow him to be a part of our family. But...

"As long as you do not hurt my wife in any way, we welcome you to rekindle the familial bond," I tell him.

He holds out his hand, and I grip it in a firm shake.

"The dinner reservations start in half an hour. Let's head over to the restaurant."

Lachlan's announcement gets us out the door and to our cars for the ride to the restaurant.

"Payton asked if he could be a part of the Wee Twins' life after he expressed reconciliation with you," I tell my wife while we're alone except for our driver. "I told him he could, as long as he didn't hurt you in any way."

She gazes out the window. We pass several streets. But I give her the time she needs to process his request and my approval of it. So instead of pressing her, I wait. Eventually, she turns her head to me.

"I love my brother and wish we could have had a less strained relationship. But I do forgive him. So as long as he agrees to your terms, I'm fine with him being in our lives," she says, then thickens her Scottish accent. "Aye, the Wee Twins can't sound all American. They'll need as many authentic Scottish accents around them."

I throw my head back and laugh. My wife thinks she's got jokes as good as mine. But hers—delivered in her sultry Scottish accent—takes the win.

We arrive at the restaurant and find some of the others at the bar. My Hot Mama excuses herself and goes to the ladies' room. Haley and Charlotte go with her. Woman and going to the bathroom in groups. Go figure.

As I turn from watching them go, a small hand presses against my biceps. The smile on my face fades when I realize it's not Mum Allison.

Some random woman stares up at me. She licks her glossy bottom lip suggestively. The gold flecks in her hazel eyes sparkle.

"Hello, Harris Steele, correct? I've seen your photos online. But you're even more handsome in person. Care to have a drink… Or eat?" She says. Her husky Scottish accent deepens as she finishes with a squeeze to my arm.

I stare at her in utter disbelief.

Didn't this bird just see me talking to my wife?

Did she not notice the platinum wedding band on the hand of the arm she clings to?

Saw my photos, did she? Well…

"Miss, if you've seen my photos, then you've seen my wife. You know, the gorgeous woman I was just speaking with a second before you approached me?" I respond as I extricate my arm from her clutches. "So, no, and most definitely, no."

The woman's face flames. She opens her mouth to speak. But I hold up my hand and walk over to the real Mum Allison, who now stands beside Aunt Lucie. They flick their eyes between the woman and me. The woman huffs behind me.

"Do you know her, Harris?" Mum Allison asks. Her normally calm tone of voice is now sharp as she glares at the woman.

"No, just some random woman. You know, the kind who hang out at bars hoping to snag a husband," I answer with a shrug, then grin. "But I let her know I am not the one, not with My Hot Mama wearing my rings."

Mum Allison relaxes and pats my arm.

Another hand touches my lower back. I turn, already knowing it's my wife from the alluring scent of her perfume. My arm slips around her back, and I pull her into my side snugly. As I brush my lips over the top of her head, my gaze finds the woman on the other side of the bar glaring at us. I smirk and shake my head.

Not this bloke, miss.

KAT

"This area here would work well for the pram room and whatever other outdoor equipment you'll need for the Wee Twins—"

"Oh, Michael, you are such a guy! 'Equipment?' Really?" Leonie's laughter rings out in the entry hall for the Glasgow duplex penthouse.

The rest of us girls join her while Roger—who's used to baby stuff—grins, and Harris pats my brother on the back.

He's so enthusiastic to have the chance to work his architectural magic on the residence's remodeling. Roger agreed to assign the job to him as Project Lead with Leonie as his manager. Michael's University of Strathclyde in Glasgow dean confirmed credits will apply towards his program. I'm glad he's pursuing his passion and I get to help him achieve his dream.

"Uh… right," Michael says with a grin. "Architecture, yes. Wee ones, um, no."

We laugh along with him as he continues his recommendation.

Harris and I have been in Glasgow for the last week. It's so wonderful to spend time with my Mum and siblings. And Payton has truly stepped up. We had lunch and talked things out. It was a long time coming, but so worth it. We have a better understanding. Plus, we promise to treat each other with respect and to work things out, not let them fester. He even bought teddy bears for the Wee Twins. Uncle Payton, ready for duty!

After Michael takes us through the residence, Harris and I share our feedback. We're in sync with my brother's recommendations. Leonie beams like a proud Mum. To make it all official, we sit down and sign off on the plan. Michael looks fit to burst from excitement.

"Sweethearts, you can go through the Steele storage facility to select pieces. You may find some items to incorporate into your decor," my mother offers while my father agrees.

"And of course, you have access to the Jackson archives. Perhaps you'd like to put paintings from Iain here. It would be so appropriate. A gracious nod to our relative," Aunt Lucie adds.

Uncle Connor nods and says, "That's a great idea, *mo ghràdh*. When you return, I will take you through the facility. You will find a wide selection over centuries. A bit of family history is important to include in your home."

"And you'll love the most incredible selections from both! Lachlan and I furnished our Aberdeen penthouse flat with loads of furniture from the Jackson collection," Haley adds.

"If you want to supplement those collections, you're welcome to the Beaulieu Enterprises SAS's warehouses. My family's company travels the world for antiques, antiquities, and fabrics," Leonie says.

I clap my hands and thank them all with a promise to do so on our next trip back to Glasgow. We can spend the weekend in Paris to explore Leonie's treasure trove. All sound unbelievable and I cannot wait!

"Now tell us more about the nurseries. The rooms here you selected to combine into one are in the perfect spot from the primary bedroom," I say.

Leonie pulls out her iPad and taps on the screen. She sits next to me on the window seat. She shows me her initial design ideas for not only Glasgow and New York City. But she also includes remodels for Morgan and Shelley's New York City and Southampton Village residences and a new one for their Aberdeen flat.

Shelley's enthusiastic response makes me laugh. Then I gasp.

"What's wrong, Kat?" Harris asks, crouching before me, eyes wide in panic.

I catch my breath as I grab his hand and place it on my babies bump.

"A kick, or maybe a punch! I don't know which," I exclaim, then gasp again. "Did you feel it?"

Harris' mouth drops open. His dove gray eyes were wider than two silvery flying saucers. He jumps as though punched by Norman when another movement from our Wee Twins happens.

It's the first time they made their presences known aside from their images on the monitor and heartbeats. Well, I guess my rounder belly proves their existence!

"Babe… I—I can't believe it…" Harris' words trail off as his voice catches in his throat. His eyes glisten with unshed tears. He blinks and continues. "How does it feel to you?"

I take a moment to consider, then tell him the Wee Twins' movement makes me think of butterflies' wings brushing against my womb. He nods, absorbing my response.

"Well, butterflies would make a lovely motif for the nurseries," my Mum says with a smile as she strokes my hair. "They symbolize transformation, hope, and bravery—all excellent qualities for your Wee Twins. And remember, butterflies adorned your wedding gown and veil."

I take her hand and kiss it. My Mum is the smartest woman I know!

"Brilliant, Mum! I love it!" I respond, then turn to their father. "Harris, my love, what do you think?"

He caresses my babies bump and places two kisses on it.

"I love it, and I love all three of you," he responds before he kisses my lips softly. "And I can't wait to hold them in my arms."

The gestures and his words are so sweet. I sniff and dab the tears in my eyes, despite the yawn I try to swallow. He kisses them away, then stands.

"Well, everyone, thank you for your love and support. But My Hot Mama needs her rest. We'll say our goodbyes now since we fly out in the morning," he says.

Our family wishes us farewell and safe travels with hugs and kisses. Promises of updates follow. We leave the duplex penthouse and take turns on the private lift to the lobby. More hugs before Harris and I slip inside of the awaiting Rolls-Royce sedan. I wave as the car joins traffic and the driver whisks us back to STEELE Glasgow.

* * *

"You and these blindfolds, Harris Steele! I think they're your kink."

I say as he slides one off my face. It's as though he carries one around in the pocket of every bloody pair of trousers he owns—ready for any occasion.

This time, he placed it on my face before we boarded our private jet for what I thought was New York City. But based on the salty air, vibrant sun, and the sound of French accents, this can't be the City.

I shade my eyes, trying to find a clue. My breath catches.

We're standing at the top of a gated driveway. The brilliant sun shines above in a clear blue sky. Sea birds soar on the air currents. Before us, the expanse of sparking azure waters stretches out unobstructed to the horizon. My gaze follows the white-capped waves to the shore. They meet a private sandy beach between two-story stone sea walls that surround a peninsula.

The jewel above it all sits a magnificent white villa. Its five stories set atop one another like a tiered cake decreasing in size from top to bottom. Balconies overlook the panoramic view. Around it manicured lawns with mature trees lead to an infinity edge pool that juts out above the azure water. Making it impossible to tell where one ends and the other begins. Two smaller buildings occupy the secluded acres of property. It's a lavish seaside estate in its own world.

"Unimaginable…" I whisper in awe. "Wherever are we?"

Harris slips his arm around my body and leans down to place his cheek against mine. He murmurs his response, *"Bienvenue à Villa Ciel et Terre."*

Both of us are fluent in French. I translate the meaning aloud with a contented sigh.

"Welcome to Villa Heaven and Earth. How appropriate."

"We're in the South of France town of Èze off the Mediterranean Sea—also known as the Côte d'Azur for obvious reasons. Come, I'll tell you more about it on the ride down," he says as he leads me to the white-on-white convertible Aston Martin. When I hesitate to glance over my shoulder at the stunning property, he chuckles. "Oh, you'll love it even more up close. Trust me."

He helps me into the car and secures the seat belt. Even for the short ride, my protective husband wants to ensure I'm safe, especially with his babies. He hops in the driver's side.

"One day from my parents' megayacht—*Serendipity*—I saw this property and took a tender for a closer look since it didn't appear maintained or occupied. Well, I fell in love with it and bought it. Now, it's back to its original splendor and more," he tells me with pride in his voice.

I hold my hand out for him. The diamonds on my wedding jewelry sparkles in the sun beaming down on us as we pass the second gate at the bottom of the driveway. I squeeze his hand as *Villa Ciel et Terre* stands in all its glory before us.

"I love it too," I whisper. "What made you decide to surprise me with a trip here?"

Harris grins like the Cheshire Cat and slides out of the car. He opens my door and pulls me into his arms with my back to his front. His hands rest on my babies bump as he nuzzles the side of my neck.

"Welcome to our babymoon, My Hot Mama," he says huskily. "Our time before our Wee Twins arrive. Time to give me some of your good lovin.'"

The warmth of his breath skitters across my skin. I tilt my head to the side to give him better access for the open-mouthed kisses he places on my neck. Heat floods my body. Immediately, my pussy softens and cream gathers. My fuller breasts grow heavy as the nipples tighten with desire. I lean back against his powerful chest and moan when he nudges his already massive erection against the crack of my ass.

Oh, bloody hell, the things this man makes me feel!

"But first a tour," he says, then chuckles wickedly when I growl in frustration. "Simmer down, naughty kitten. I know what you need… and when."

He takes me by the hand and leads me through the blue double doors. Inside, the villa's staff stand in a row to greet us. The butler steps forward and introduces them to me. The chef confirms lunch on the terrace in two hours. They take our luggage upstairs while Harris walks me through the interior of the posh villa. We end on the large balcony of the primary suite overlooking the lush greenery and colorful flowering bushes, the infinity pool, and the Mediterranean Sea.

"We have forty minutes until lunch. I guarantee I give you four orgasms before we eat."

Harris' huskily spoken words bring my attention back from the incredible view.

"Oh… Only four…" I tease.

He growls and stalks towards where I stand beside the wrought-iron railing. When he reaches me, his arm snakes around my waist to pull me as flush to his body as my babies bump allows. He bends down to rumble his displeasure at my comment in my ear.

I gasp when he spins me around. My balance rests in his firm grip. Facing the Med, Harris pulls the bow on my Diane von Furstenberg wrap dress. Like a gift, he reveals me.

"Harris! What if someone sees us?" I squeak as my eyes dart around the grounds below for any sign of the staff.

"And if they do?" He responds as his fingers unclasp the

front closure of my bra. He kneads my heavy breasts and groans against my neck.

I wiggle to free myself. But he steps to the side and gives my ass four quick spanks in succession. Through the silk of my dress, my bare cheeks sting. The black lace thong does nothing to protect my ass from my husband's ire. He continues to spank me in an erotic rhythm.

"B—but the staff," I cry out, rising to the balls of my Chanel ballet flats covered feet.

"I thought you said you trusted me, naughty kitten?" He responds, then continues when I say I do. "Well, then, why would I expose what is mine to another's eyes?"

One hand leaves my breasts to skim down the side of my belly, over my hip, and across to the apex of my thighs. Thighs pressed together to ease the ache building in my soaking core. He tugs my nipple and pinches my clit.

"Ohhh, Harris… please!" I wail, gyrating my hips.

The ripping of my thong from my body precipitates a spank to my swollen clit. I keen as the first of four orgasms hits me. My head lolls back against his shoulder. My mouth sags open on the last of my carnal cry.

"One."

The twitch of Harris' lips against my neck as he smirks makes me shiver.

Two thick digits dive into my pussy. So wet they glide in with no resistance. He curls them and strokes the sensitive tissue on the inside wall of my pussy. His thumb strokes my clit.

I grab the wrought-iron railing for support as my knees threaten to give out. My head bows forward. The red of my hair blacks out the turquoise blue of the sea.

Harris' fingers plunge in and out of my pussy as it clenches in hopes it locks them in place to ride them to pleasure. My body craves the orgasm just on the edge. Just out of reach.

His fingers withdraw.

I screech in frustration. My head swivels to glare at him.

He chuckles and nips my shoulder.

The wrap dress slips from my body before he tosses it inside of the suite.

"Eyes forward, legs spread," Harris commands as he collects my hair and wraps it around his fist. He tugs and my head bows back. "Wider."

I hasten to spread my legs as wide as they can go. Then brace myself as my grip tightens on the railing for support.

With no warning, Harris slams his massive dick inside of my quivering pussy. I explode.

"Two."

As I revel in carnal bliss, he tugs my clit while pistoning his hips. His thick girth drags along my inner walls. A wail and shudder define my next orgasm.

"Three."

I pant as residual wave after wave of three orgasms ignite a fever pitch in my body. Legs twitch to hold my position.

Harris switches to long, slow strokes. His hands reach up to cup my breasts and to tweak the puckered nipples. When he feels the flutters of my pussy, he withdraws to his tip.

I growl and push back against him, seeking my own release.

Resounding smacks to my ass punish my attempt at self-pleasure.

"Aha, naughty kitten. I say when," Harris chastises me. "And I say it's now!"

He impales me on his rigid cock, and I wail as the orgasm takes me.

"Four."

Boneless, I can only depend upon Harris to hold me up as he chases his release. With a bellow, his hot cum coats my pussy. It triggers a fifth orgasm, and we ride our pleasure out together. I sag against Harris.

When we return from a shared state of sheer euphoria, he carries me to the shower and bathes me. He sets me on the marble bench and cleans himself. Dried and re-dressed, we settle on the terrace for a delicious lunch with the beauty of *Villa Ciel et Terre* surrounding us.

What better way to strengthen our bond before the birth of our Wee Twins?

HARRIS

"*H*arris, I think it's time!"

The mobile falls from my hand.

Haley grabs it while I stand frozen.

"Kat, honey, where are you?" Haley asks as she jabs me with her elbow. Silently she mouths, *Get it together, Har!*

"Oooh... By the lift," my thirty-six weeks pregnant wife cries.

Her distress rouses me. I snatch my mobile from Haley as I bark at Roger to call my driver for the Mercedes-Benz Sprinter. Baz says he'll call our parents. Malcolm waves for me to follow him, as Starr calls Dr. Rice. We rush from Baz's conference room at STEELE International. Behind us, I hear Lachlan call Mum Allison.

It's like déjà vu. But even more intense. Not news of Kat's pregnancy, but of her in labor.

Fuck. Me.

"Kat, babe, focus on me. I'm on my way to get you. Do not move," I say into the phone. I remember the prenatal training Starr taught us and work with her on her breath. As always, Starr helps her sisters as their doula.

I keep my wife calm as the private elevator rises to our floor. Starr helps her to count time between contractions. She nods at me in confirmation. Our Wee Twins are on their way. Well damn!

The elevator door opens and my wife—with her hands cradling her babies bump—leans against the console. Her hospital bag sits at her feet. She raises her head and grimaces as another contraction hits. Malcolm and I carry her onto the elevator while Starr grabs the bag.

"Ooooooohhhhh!!! *Bloody hell!*" My wife screams, then turns her head to me. "Damn you, Harris Steele!"

I swallow. Oh boy. I heard about this reaction from my brothers…

We stop at the underground parking garage and hurry to the awaiting Sprinter. Alonso barely gives us time to close the doors before he's off. During the ride, Starr does her doula magic. At least enough my wife doesn't curse me in English *and* in Scottish Gaelic. I blush, and I don't even know what the bloody hell she says.

She's got me so bollixed up I use British expressions!

"How long have you been experiencing pre-labor, Kat?" Starr asks as she braids her Titian hair down her back.

My wife groans and rubs her babies bump before she answers. The pain on her face hits me straight in the chest like a sledgehammer. A combination of pain and fear fill her emerald green eyes. I stroke her hand—to hell with holding it. So she can crush it like Leonie did to Roger? That'll be a hard pass.

"I—I thought it was just back pain sine early morning," my wife gets out before another contraction takes her breath.

Starr nods and massages her shoulders.

We make it to the hospital where Dr. Rice's in-hospital team meets us with a gurney. They bundle my wife onto it while Starr gives them her status. I rush along with the caravan to her private birthing room, leaving my siblings to find her private waiting room.

Dr. Rice enters after the nurse adjusts my wife's sheet. He greets us and sits on the stool between her spread legs. He raises the sheet to exam her.

"Mrs. Steele, however, did you manage pre-labor on your own? Your cervix is fully dilated at ten centimeters. Let's get ready to deliver your twins," he says with a warm smile. "Now to set your expectations, on average it can take up to two hours for you to birth your first twin and seventeen minutes for the second twin."

A growl fills the room.

I shudder when I realize it's directed at me. I swallow before I face my wife.

Titian hair like flames licking down her back. Emerald eyes blaze like green fire. Nostrils flare,

"Sixteen hours, Harris Steele?!?!?!" She screeches like a banshee, not my alluring Siren. "This is your fau—"

A contraction cuts off her scathing words.

I take a breath as though I'm in labor.

Despite my wife's threats, I stay at her side, cool cloth in one hand and a cup of ice chips in the other. Words of encouragement between her cries and grunts. Until at last, she gives birth to our first child. Above its cries, Dr. Rice's voice rings clear.

"Mr. and Mrs. Steele, your son."

Dr. Rice dries him off and places him in a hat and blanket on my wife's heaving chest. The skin-to-skin contact soothes both. My wife smiles through her tears as my son's cries lessen to whimpers.

I stare in awe at the start of my little family. My wife's beauty shines through all the curses, sweat, and tears. She holds our son like the most precious thing he is to both of us. I melt when she turns her radiance on me and raises her hand.

The tears shimmering in my eyes spill over when I take her hand and wrap my arm around her shoulders. She places our entwined fingers on our son's rosy cheek and strokes it together.

"Thank you, my love," I murmur.

Once again, she graces me with her smile and says, "Your son and I thank you for making this all possible, *mo ghràdh.*"

Starr tells us the pediatrician would like to check on our son. We nod and I step back to give him access but follow to watch his every move. The protective caveman rises.

Just as Dr. Rice predicted, my wife goes into labor to birth our baby girl. It's a repeat of our son's arrival in the world with Scottish Gaelic ringing out. No need to worry they won't have a Scottish accent. Their first audible words provide enough of a connection to their mother's homeland.

When Dr. Rice announces the birth of our daughter and places her on my wife's chest, my world feels complete. I catch her little fist flailing in the air while she hollers louder than her brother. However, she too settles at the contact with her Mum. I embrace them and kiss the top of my wife's damp head.

The pediatrician takes our daughter, and I follow behind closely. I watch until he places her in a bassinet beside her brother. Only when Starr comes over, I leave. I smile at her and return to my wife's side.

The nurses clean her up and help her into a lace-front nightgown—one of the Lola's Coterie maternity pieces she's collected. Refreshed she's ready to breastfeed our babies. The nurse shows her how to manage twins with my help. After they have their fill, they sleep peacefully. My wife's eyes flutter closed.

It's only then I remember to take photos. I whip out my mobile and snap away.

"Congratulations, Proud Papa! I took some photos and videotaped their births for you," Starr whispers as she approaches the bed and hugs me. "I'll let everyone know the Wee Twins and Mum are well. Take your time and let her rest before we come in."

I nod, and she massages my shoulders. I groan as the tension I didn't realize existed eases from my body.

"Thanks, sis," I say when she stops and pats my arm. She winks and leaves me with my little family.

I sit beside the bed and watch over them. After a while, my wife stirs.

"Harris? Where are you?" She asks as she turns her head to scan the suite.

I rise and kiss her forehead.

"Always here, my love. Why don't you rest some more," I respond as my knuckles brush her cheek.

She leans into the caress and smiles. But she shakes her head.

"Let's introduce our family to our Wee Twins. It's time for their debut," she says with a joyful smile.

I scan her face to be sure she's ready, and she nods, knowing my protective instincts kicked into gear.

Returning her nod, I call my father. He answers on the first ring and says they'll be right in.

The door opens immediately, and they pile into the suite.

One by one they approach the bed—my mother and Mum Allison first, followed by Uncle Connor and Aunt Lucie.

Everyone exclaims how adorable they are with their ebony hair and dove gray eyes. Yup, my genes are super strong!

"So, what are their names, *Da*?" Haley asks with a grin.

I look at My Kitty Kat and her emerald green eyes twinkle. She's bursting to tell them. I take a deep breath and announce the next generation of Steeles.

"My wife and I present Felix Steele and Felicity Steele! Felix the Cat in honor of his mother Kat, and Felicity for the Ancient Roman goddess Fortuna, symbolizing happiness, luck, and good fortune."

Everyone exclaims their love of the unique names and their meaning.

When My Kitty Kat yawns, I tell our family we'll see them in the morning. Rounds of congratulations and sweet dreams follow before they depart.

Alone with my little family, I place Felix and Felicity in their bassinets, change into a t-shirt and joggers, then settle in the bed to hold my wife. Her soft snores let me know she's knocked out. I kiss the side of her head and let my mind drift. I give thanks for their health and the love of our family before I allow my eyes to close.

THE MORNING DAWNS, and I slip from the bed so as not to awaken My Kitty Kat. I stride to the bassinets and smile at my beautiful babies. Unable to resist, I gather them in my arms and stand in front of the window. The sunrise promises a new day, a fresh start.

I may not have been ready for children. But as I hold my

Wee Twins close to my heart, I know they were meant to be mine forever, just like their Mum.

***

Harris & Kat's Story Concludes For Now...

**Turn the page for the Steele and Jackson Families,
Author's Note,
and Preview of STEELE World:** *A Trilogy of Desires
Sebastian & Lola Parts I-III*

**Join my newsletter bit.ly/CLBooksNewsletter to learn
about the next STEELE World couples to have their
romances told.**

THE STEELE FAMILY

STEELE INTERNATIONAL, INC

Multigenerational, multibillion-dollar business luxury real estate development and management corporation

Headquarters & Family's Primary Residences:

The STEELE Tower, New York City

A modern, gray-tinted glass fifty-seven story mixed-use skyscraper on southwest corner of Fifty-Seventh Street and Fifth Avenue within Billionaires' Row

Global Offices:

- The United States of America (New York City, New Jersey, Chicago, California, Miami, Las

Vegas)
- The Caribbean (St. Maarten, St. Barth's, St. Lucia)
- The French & Italian Rivieras (Nice, Cannes, Positano, Capri)
- Monaco (Monte Carlo)
- The United Arab Emirates (Abu Dhabi, Dubai)

STEELE FOUNDATION: A STRONG AND SUPPORTIVE HOUSE

Builds and manages attractive, affordable housing for urban, lower-income families

Available for download at **bit.ly/STEELEFamily**

THE JACKSON FAMILY

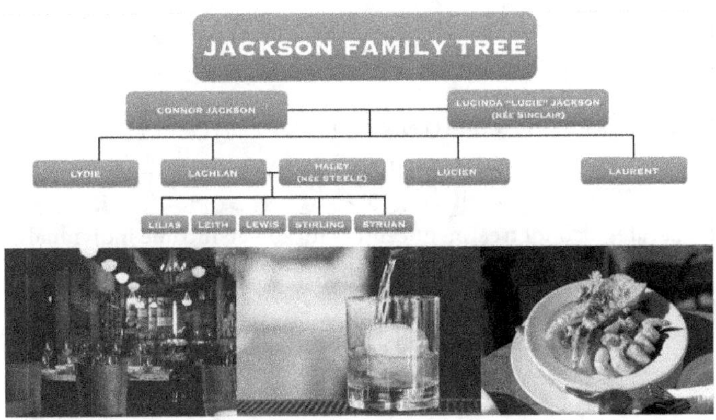

JACKSON CORPORATION

Multigenerational, multibillion-dollar business fine dining,
distilleries, and vineyards corporation

Headquarters:

Jackson Town House, Aberdeen, Scotland

A landmark property built by the founders of Aberdeen granite on
Union Street; the second largest granite building in the world.

Global Offices:

- The United Kingdom (Aberdeen, Scotland;
  London, England)
- The United States of America (New York City,
  New Orleans, Miami, Chicago, Los Angeles,

Napa)
- The Caribbean (Puerto Rico)
- France (Paris, Cannes)
- Monaco (Monte Carlo)
- Australia (Sydney)
- The United Arab Emirates (Abu Dhabi, Dubai)

JACKSON FOUNDATION: ENJOY LIFE
RESPONSIBLY

Operates alcohol treatment centers for lower-income individuals
and support for their family members

Available for download at **bit.ly/JacksonFamilyTree**

Author's Note

Thank you for reading the Trilogy of Harris and Kat's sexy, steamy romance! I hope you enjoyed the Happy For Now conclusion of their sizzling, The One billionaire romance. If so, I'd love to hear your thoughts, please share a review at **amzn.to/3LBINHZ** and tell your friends.

Wait! What's up next in the STEELE World? Follow me on social media including my CLBooks Coterie Fan Club or on your favorite channels below and subscribe to my newsletter **bit.ly/CLBooksSubscribe** for a **Free Book**.

In the meantime, did you catch on to the dynamism of Sebastian and Lola? Well, you'll have your answers! **Visit books2read.com/u/4DPzLg**

A Trilogy of Desires Sebastian & Lola Parts I-III

At **CharmaineLouise.com** take the *Four types of lovers. Which are you?* **Quiz** to match your Sexy Fantasy: sub, Voyeur, Dominatrix, or Dominatrix sub Switch.

Fulfill Your Desires.
xoxo
Charmaine Louise

bookbub.com/authors/charmaine-louise-shelton

facebook.com/CharmaineLouiseBooks

instagram.com/charmainelouisebooks

tiktok.com/@charmainelouisebooks?

goodreads.com/charmainelouisebooks

PREVIEW: A TRILOGY OF DESIRES SEBASTIAN & LOLA PARTS I-III

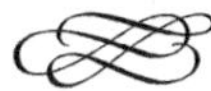

*S*ebastian

"Good evening, Mr. Steele," one of the two stunning greeters purrs as I step into the lobby for LEVELS New York.

This is the flagship location of the global, luxury, members-only BDSM/dance clubs in Manhattan's Meatpacking District. They chose the historic location as a play on the area's name. Put a club where men pack their meat into willing women and willing men allow women to pack them with their toys. The theme for the lobby is minimal and industrial. The fixtures and furniture that appear well worn are high-end, modern replicas used to add authenticity without the grime of old pieces. The two sides have coordinating greeter stations that allow access to the separate Dine & Dance levels and the BDSM levels. The other greeter turns her head in my direction and briefly smiles at me before she returns her attention to a couple entering the BDSM side.

My cousin Lucien Jackson cooked up the idea and roped

my younger brother Malcolm into it. Lucien literally cooked it up since he thought of it as he finished his hospitality and culinary training at Le Cordon Bleu in Paris.

Who the hell goes through that prestigious training to come up with a titty bar? Well, five years later his idea proves it's bigger than that and has a high profit margin with more locations in Paris and London. That's all that concerns me: will it add to STEELE International's bottom line? Yes, well, it's a go. No, then no go.

LEVELS is one of many business partnerships that STEELE has with Jackson Corporation. World-renown for their award-winning eateries, choice cigars, and distinguished liquors and wines, their products pair well within STEELE's casinos, hotels, resorts, and residential and retail properties.

On the personal side, my mother is best friends with the Jackson matriarch. They spent most of their adult lives together forming a closer bond than they have with their blood siblings and relatives. Not sharing DNA doesn't keep our families from being a close-knit group.

"Good evening," I respond as I make my way to the D&D elevator.

Once inside, I place my keycard against the panel to select the third floor for the Level 4 Restaurant. I'm a Global All Access member. I can choose from any of the seven levels: 7th Sky Lounge that offers a stunning, 360-degree view of Manhattan and across the Hudson River to New Jersey's shoreline, a bar, restaurant by day dance club by night, a coverable pool that's open during the warmer months, and a glass-retractable roof; 6th and 5th multilevel dance club with two bars and a lounge for food and drinks; 4th Level 4 Restaurant and bar open for breakfast, lunch, and dinner; 3rd has twelve private suites for members to continue their pleasure apart from the BDSM levels; 2nd Peepshow for BDSM with seating alcoves, primary stage, mini-stages, performance rooms, and a bar that serves non-alcoholic mocktails; below ground the Cellar a BDSM dungeon with mocktails bar. The Dine/Dance members only have access to the party levels—Sky Lounge, Dance Club, and Level 4 Restaurant.

Tonight, I need to eat and fuck hard in that order. I'm bound to find a female at the restaurant or bar who's willing to be my pet for the evening. One night only, maybe two if she's not clingy or a gold digger, but two fucks is my maximum. I'm not looking for a relationship and damn sure not marriage, just enough time to satisfy my Dom needs and my physical release for the moment. A short-term encounter to balance out my business-focused life.

As president of the Retail Properties Division of STEELE, I bust my ass fourteen hours a day to make it super profitable and to prove that I deserve my future role as CEO of the entire luxury real estate development and management company when my father retires next year. It's not just my last name getting me into the head position. I'm damn capable since I've worked my way up the ranks to learn our multigenerational, multibillion dollar business combined with my Harvard undergrad and MBA degrees.

My father, Morgan, trusts me to carry the legacy into the future and my younger brothers and sister respect me and accept my leadership. Each sibling works at STEELE: Malcolm president of the Entertainment Properties Division; Roger, president of the Residential Properties Division; Harris and Haley, fraternal twins, co-founders of the subsidiary STEELE Technology and Cyber Security. At 35, I take my role as the eldest seriously, so I don't have time for nor care to get involved in a relationship. Thanks to

Lucien and Malcolm, LEVELS provides exactly what I need.

As I step off of the elevator, I take in my surroundings. The bar is bustling as usual with the crème de la crème of society. They hobnob with top-shelf drinks. Seating ranges from the leather and black metal stools at the long, reclaimed-wood covered bar to the dozen high-top tables styled to match. The bar along the right wall features a floor-to-ceiling mirrored wall of shelves of only the best spirits and wines—most are from the Jackson labels. The bartenders serve signature cocktails. Tables on the left complete the layout of the open-plan room. A path between the two areas leads to the LEVEL 4 Restaurant's maître d' station. There, the patrons eat delicious meals prepared by chefs trained by Lucien. My destination awaits.

As I stride towards the maître d', my gaze alights on several recognizable faces enjoying nightcaps at the bar area's high-top tables. Tonight, the U.S. Attorney for the Southern District of New York, the former governor of California, and a high-powered female CFO of a Wall Street investment bank are present. The club caters to the most wealthy and influential in society. They prefer the relative safety that one can expect from the ironclad nondisclosure agreement that LEVELS requires every member and their guests to sign.

I smile and nod in greeting—every Steele is instantly recognizable—but keep it moving as I'm not here tonight for small talk. As I approach the hostess at the dining area's maître d' podium, I also notice several pairs of lust-filled eyes including those of a few men track my movement as I walk past them. Sadly for the men, I'm strictly a female to a male individual. As I approach the station, the maître d' on duty tonight looks up with an alluring smile on her pretty face.

"Good evening, Mr. Steele," says Susan, as her name tag denotes. She angles her chin down to allow her to peek up at me from beneath her long eyelashes without direct eye contact.

"Your usual table, Sir?"

I don't miss her emphasis on Sir as a sub innuendo. Susan is one of many LEVELS employees who want to have my marks on them and my dick in every one of their holes. Disappointingly for the staff though, I don't mix business with pleasure. That can only end in a messy situation and unnecessarily complicate matters—doesn't fit with my trajectory.

"Good evening, Susan. That's good, thank you," I reply.

Susan's full lips curl up into a dazzling smile as she visibly preens. Her reaction as though I petted her head for a job well done after I fucked her throat and she didn't spill a single drop of my copious amount of cum. Susan seductively sways her hips, long legs stressed by stilettos and her form-fitted, black mini dress molded to her curvy body. She leads me to my table in the center of the room with an unobstructed view of the large dining area and of the bar. A spot from which I can easily observe all the patrons to cherry-pick my companion for tonight. However, the sight before me has me second-guessing my no business/pleasure rule. Susan deliberately bends over the table to straighten the napkin, giving me a visual of her cuffed to my pommel horse and a cane in my hand. Damn if my cock didn't just twitch from looking at her plump bottom and grip-worthy hips. Fortunately, I hadn't unbuttoned my suit jacket, or my piqued dick would be on full display.

I give the heads, on my neck and at my groin, firm,

shakes to clear the vision. Then, without making eye contact, I thank Susan, take my seat, and pick up the menu discouraging further attention.

With an audible sigh, Susan bids me, "Enjoy your dinner, Mr. Steele," and walks away. Then on second thought she turns and offers, "Should you need anything at all, please let me know."

Keeping my gaze on the menu, I nod, and Susan dejectedly walks away with less sway to her hips, albeit still an eye-catching vision. Sorry, sweetheart.

If I'm not entertaining business associates or attending social gatherings like charity functions, I frequently dine at Level 4. I prefer that then eating takeout at home or hiring a personal chef to cook for only one person. Both are extravagances that I can afford, but why waste resources with my mutable schedule that changes as often as I change boxers.

Dinner out at whatever time is convenient in a city with thousands of excellent restaurants suits my lifestyle. Level 4 is one of them with a menu that offers the expected fare typical of Continental cuisine of pastas, meat, and steaks with favorable sauces. Lucien complements the usual dishes with appealing specials that change daily to keep the choices fresh and habitual guests like me from getting bored.

The client care is impeccable. So, I don't flinch when the server quietly appears at my side and places a napkin-covered basket with an assortment of warm, fresh-baked breads on the table. I glance up to see a youthful man who is model-perfect and well-groomed with a clean-shaven jaw, slicked-back ebony hair, and intelligent brown eyes. His all-black uniform of a long-sleeved shirt, pants, butcher apron, and shiny Oxford shoes is spotless—the de rigueur fashion for LEVELS employees.

"Welcome to Level 4, sir. My name is Andrew and I'll be your server this evening. May I take your drink order?"

"Thank you, Andrew. I'll have a bottle of Pellegrino," I respond with a pleasant smile.

"Very good, sir. We have some lovely specials tonight. May I share them with you?"

Since I plan to play tonight, I select a light meal comprising the tossed salad to start and the grilled langoustines with white wine sauce entrée. A clear head is best for my evening plan of play.

As Andrew heads to the kitchen to submit my order, my gaze wanders around the room admiring the décor. Just as with the lobby and the bar, Lucien and Malcolm stayed true to the original use of the warehouse. Clean lines and antique pieces for the decor: floor-to-ceiling mullion windows allow natural light to filter through to the room during the day, now dimly lit for dinner; light fixtures hang from the ceiling where the dark metal duct work and copper pipes are visible; exposed brick walls; the floor poured concrete; the well-heeled patrons sit on antique leather chairs at wooden tables. The guys really did a hell of a job with their enterprise. Few can pull off and maintain a high-end, respectable establishment, especially one that's a combo BDSM/dance club with a restaurant.

Perfectly situated for visibility by those at the bar and within the dining room, sit two lovely beauties laughing and tossing their long, glossy hair over their shoulders. Their eyes roam the vicinity hoping to connect with potential partners. The duo is more focused on attracting company for the evening, then on eating the salads that they absent-mindedly move around on their plates.

The blonde spots me watching them, and a grin appears on her face lighting up her baby blues. As she nods her head to show her friend she's spotted a potential hookup, her little pink tongue pokes out to dampen her glossy, lush lips.

I wonder if her pussy is as shiny and wet as that mouth.

Her friend shifts slightly in her seat to adjust her position casually. As she runs her red-manicured hand through her sable-colored, shoulder-length hair, she spies me. The green darkens with lust when I wink at her. With a smirk, I turn my attention to Andrew as he places my salad in front of me. Now that I have the attention of both women, I nod and eat. I know they're interested, so no need to rush my meal. They'll be a double order of tonight's dessert special.

I spend the next thirty-five minutes purposely ignoring them. I only allow my gaze to shift occasionally in their direction, never direct eye contact. That dominant behavior —and who I am—will keep them intrigued. As they cross and uncross their legs, the movement affords me a better view higher up their toned thighs. Green Eyes has on a clingy, silk wrap dress that showcases her ample cleavage, the red color complementing her bronze skin. The blue of Luscious' eyes, enhanced by the cobalt color of her strapless, stretch-jersey dress, make them as prominent as her pebbled nipples. Delightful.

First item on tonight's agenda is complete—dinner eaten, now it's time to fuck.

They automatically place the bill on my membership account, so no need to waste time signing the check. I stand and take my time to button my suit jacket, drawing the attention of my pets. Once our eyes lock, I walk past their table to head to one of the high-tops at the bar.

Susan gives me a wistful stare and bids me, "Good night, Mr. Steele. We look forward to seeing you again soon."

"It was a pleasure as always, Susan. Good night," I offer her in consolation.

Moments after I settle at the closest available table, I feel one hand caress my back and another hand lands on my forearm.

I glance to my left and am greeted with a sultry, "Hello." Green eyes glitter in the candlelight like vivid emeralds.

A squeeze to my forearm draws my attention to my right to see freshly glossed lips beaming, "Hello. There aren't any other tables available, would you mind it if my friend and I share with you?"

"Would your friend and you mind sharing me for a fuck?"

Without missing a beat, Green Eyes responds breathlessly, "Absolutely."

***

Click the Link Below or Visit books2read.com/u/4DPzLg For Your Copy

A Trilogy of Desires Sebastian & Lola Parts I-III

WELCOME TO CHARMAINELOUISE — THE SENSUAL LIFESTYLE

GLITZY. GLAMOROUS. STEAMY.

CharmaineLouise New York, Inc. invites you to indulge in *The Sensual Lifestyle* through **CharmaineLouise Books** and **CharmaineLouise Intimates**. CLBrands immerse you in *Sexy Fantasies* with CLBooks contemporary romance novels and give you *Sexy Under Things & Loungewear* with CLIntimates.

Charmaine Louise Shelton the Founder, CEO & Author of CLNY loves all things classic, elegant, feminine, and of course with an erotic edge! Favorite outfit of choice is a cashmere cardigan, leather pencil skirt, and seamed silk stockings with stiletto heels. Sexy Fantasy Type: sub with a dash of Voyeur. When not writing and designing, Charmaine Louise travels and spends time with her Maltese buddies, ZIGGY and Jynger.

CharmaineLouise — *The Sensual Lifestyle*

~ Visit online at **CharmaineLouise.com**

~ Subscribe to **CharmaineLouise Newsletter**

~ Find us on Facebook **@CharmaineLouiseNewYork**

~ Instagram **@CharLouNY**

CharmaineLouise Books *Sexy Fantasies* launched summer 2020. Sizzling, contemporary romance with your soon-to-be favorite Alpha Doms, Powerful Billionaires, and the women they lust after and love for second chances, insta-love, enemies-to-lovers, and more.

Want to chat it up and share your thoughts with other CLBooks Lovers? Read our blog, join our CharmaineLouise Books Coterie Fan Club and follow us on my author pages and social media to be in the know about the book release dates, exclusive content, giveaways, contests, and more!

~ **Purchase your eBook and paperback novels from my Author Page by clicking here!**

~ Read and subscribe to our blog *The World of Sex*

~ Connect on **Amazon Author Page**

~ **Goodreads Author Profile**

~ **BookBub Author Profile**

CharmaineLouise Intimates *Sexy Under Things & Loungewear* debuted in 2003. Inspired by the sensuous sirens and sylph swans of the past and present, the hand crochet cashmere and silk collections are for the sexy: hence, the line names Ginger — Bombshell; Diana — Show-stopper; Jackie — Timeless; Lena — Classic. Also known as The Movie-Star from Gilligan's Island; Ms. Ross The Boss; Mrs. Kennedy Onassis; Ms. Horne.

Do you thrive on seduction and being sexy lounging at home? Read our blog and follow us on social media to receive the tips, the latest additions to the collections, private sales, and more!

~ Read and subscribe to our blog *The Art of Seduction*

~ Find us on Facebook **@CharmaineLousieIntimates**

~ Instagram **@CharmaineLouiseIntimates**

Fulfill Your Desires.